The Routledge Research Companion to Popular Romance Fiction

Popular romance fiction constitutes the largest segment of the global book market. Bringing together an international group of scholars, *The Routledge Research Companion to Popular Romance Fiction* offers a ground-breaking exploration of this global genre and its remarkable readership. In recognition of the diversity of the form, the Companion provides a history of the genre, an overview of disciplinary approaches to studying romance fiction, and critical analyses of important subgenres, themes, and topics. It also highlights new and understudied avenues of inquiry for future research in this vibrant and still-emerging field. The first systematic, comprehensive resource on romance fiction, this Companion will be invaluable to students and scholars, and accessible to romance readers.

Jayashree Kamblé is an Associate Professor of English at LaGuardia Community College in the City University of New York. She is the author of *Making Meaning in Popular Romance Fiction: An Epistemology* (2014) and a Vice-President of the International Association of the Study of Popular Romance.

Eric Murphy Selinger is a Professor of English at DePaul University, Executive Editor of the *Journal of Popular Romance Studies*, and President of the International Association for the Study of Popular Romance. He is the author of *What Is It Then Between Us? Traditions of Love in American Poetry* (1998) and co-editor of *New Approaches to Popular Romance Fiction* (2012) and *Romance Fiction and American Culture* (2016).

Hsu-Ming Teo is a novelist and cultural historian at Macquarie University, Australia, where she is an Associate Professor of literature and creative writing. Her academic publications include her monograph *Desert Passions: Orientalism and Romance Novels* (2012), and the edited books *The Popular Culture of Romantic Love in Australia* (2017) and *Cultural History in Australia* (2003).

The Routledge Research Companion to Popular Romance Fiction

Edited by Jayashree Kamblé, Eric Murphy Selinger, and Hsu-Ming Teo

LONDON AND NEW YORK

First published 2021
by Routledge
2 Park Square, Milton Park, Abingdon, Oxon OX14 4RN

and by Routledge
605 Third Avenue, New York, NY 10017

First issued in paperback 2022

Routledge is an imprint of the Taylor & Francis Group, an informa business

Publisher's Note
The publisher has gone to great lengths to ensure the quality of this reprint but points out that some imperfections in the original copies may be apparent.

British Library Cataloguing-in-Publication Data
A catalogue record for this book is available from the British Library

Library of Congress Cataloging-in-Publication Data
A catalog record has been requested for this book

ISBN: 978-0-367-54320-4 (pbk)
ISBN: 978-1-4724-4330-4 (hbk)
ISBN: 978-1-315-61346-8 (ebk)

DOI: 10.4324/9781315613468

Typeset in Bembo
by Swales & Willis, Exeter, Devon, UK

Contents

Notes on contributors

Kecia Ali is a Professor of Religion and Chair of the Department of Religion at Boston University. In addition to her most recent book, *Human in Death: Morality and Mortality in J. D. Robb's Novels* (2017), she is the author of articles about race, religion, and romance, and several books about Islam. Her work explores the complex intertwining of Muslim and Western norms about gender, sexuality, and marriage. Her current projects include an introductory book on women in Muslim traditions and a study of the gender politics of academic Islamic Studies.

Jonathan A. Allan is Canada Research Chair in Men and Masculinities and Professor in the Department of English and Creative Writing and in the Gender and Women's Studies program at Brandon University. He is the author of *Reading from Behind: A Cultural Analysis of the Anus* and *Men, Masculinities, and Popular Romance*, and he is currently writing a book titled *Men, Masculinities, and the Procreative Realm.*

Amanda K. Allen is an Associate Professor of Children's Literature at Eastern Michigan University. She is currently working on a revised history of twentieth-century young adult literature, in which she argues that the shift between pre-1967 "junior novels" and post-1967 "young adult fiction" was predicated on a conflict between librarians' and academics' differing value systems and institutions. She also publishes on fandom and fan studies.

Rebecca Barrett-Fox is a Professor of Sociology at Arkansas State University. Her research focuses on religion, especially conservative Christianity, sexuality and gender, and hate, politics, and the law. She is the author of multiple articles and book chapters on Christian romance novels.

Amy Burge is a Lecturer in Popular Fiction at the University of Birmingham, U.K. Her work focuses on popular genres, in particular romance, with a focus on intersectional and transhistorical readings and approaches. She is the author of *Representing Difference in the Medieval and Modern Orientalist Romance* (2016), a comparative study of late medieval English romance and twenty-first-century sheik romance novels. She is currently working on a literary history of romantic masculinity and race, and a project on Muslim women's genre fiction.

Kathrina Mohd Daud is an Assistant Professor in Writing and Literature at the Faculty of Arts and Social Sciences, Universiti Brunei Darussalam. Kathrina received a Ph.D. in Creative Writing from the University of Manchester in 2011 and has been published in the *Journal of Commonwealth Literature, World Englishes*, and a number of edited volumes for her work at the intersections of popular fiction, Bruneian literature, and the representation of

Islam in fiction. Kathrina's first novel, *The Fisherman King*, was shortlisted for the Singaporean Epigram Books Fiction Prize and will be published at the end of 2020.

jay Dixon is an independent scholar who has written on various aspects of romance, including Regency-set romances by Georgette Heyer and a book *The Romance Fiction of Mills & Boon 1909–1990s* (1999). In her other life she is a freelance editor of both fiction and non-fiction.

Kristen Donnelly (MSW, M.Div., Ph.D.) is perpetually curious about people—their stories, their lives, their choices, their communities. To that end, she pursued Ph.D. research into the intersections of gender and religion, with particular attention to how Christianity talks about and deals with the female body. She is now the EVP of Abbey Research, a HR consulting firm focusing on emotional intelligence and inclusion. She lives outside Philadelphia with her husband and their overflowing shelves of books and video game consoles, and she reviews for All About Romance.

Sarah H. Ficke is an Associate Professor of Literature at Marymount University in Arlington, VA, U.S.A. Her research and teaching interests focus on nineteenth-century British literature, early African American fiction, and popular culture. Her publications include "Constructing a Post-Victorian Empire: Rupert Gray, a Tale in Black and White" (2015) and "Crafting Social Criticism: Infanticide in 'The Runaway Slave at Pilgrim's Point' and Aurora Leigh" (2013), and she has presented conference papers on steampunk, time travel romance, and the historical romances of Beverly Jenkins and Rose Lerner.

Joanna Gregson is a Professor of Sociology at Pacific Lutheran University in Tacoma, WA. She was appointed Provost and Senior Vice-President for Academic Affairs in 2017. Dr. Gregson has taught and conducted research in the areas of deviance, gender, and qualitative research methods. Throughout her career, she has published on such topics as teenage mothers, incarcerated mothers, and divorced women. Since 2010 she has been conducting participant observation research with the authors of romance novels with collaborator Dr. Jen Lois. Dr. Joanna Gregson earned her Ph.D. in sociology from the University of Colorado at Boulder.

Amira Jarmakani is a Professor of Women's Studies at San Diego State University. She is the author of *An Imperialist Love Story: Desert Romances and the War on Terror* (2015). She also authored *Imagining Arab Womanhood: The Cultural Mythology of Veils, Harems, and Belly Dancers in the U.S.* (2008), which won the NWSA Gloria E. Anzaldúa book prize. She is president of the Arab American Studies Association and a Series Advisor for the Critical Arab American Studies Series with Syracuse University Press. She works in the fields of women's, gender, and sexuality studies, Arab American studies, and cultural studies.

Jayashree Kamblé is an Associate Professor of English at LaGuardia Community College in the City University of New York. She is the author of *Making Meaning in Popular Romance Fiction: An Epistemology* (2014) and a Vice-President of the International Association of the Study of Popular Romance. She has also published articles on mass-market romance novels in journals, popular magazines, and essay collections.

Jennifer Lois, Professor of Sociology at Western Washington University, specializes in the areas of gender, emotions, identity, and ethnography. She has previously studied the gendered culture of mountain-environment search-and-rescue volunteers (*Heroic Efforts* 2003) and the emotional culture of home-schooling mothers (*Home Is Where the School Is* 2012). Her current research project on the gendered culture of romance writers (in collaboration with Dr. Joanna Gregson) has examined the sexual stigma of the genre (*Gender & Society* 2015), and the emotion work aspiring authors do when seeking publication (*Journal of Contemporary Ethnography* 2018).

John Markert is a retired (2019) Associate Professor of Sociology at Cumberland University. He has published widely on issues relating to social dynamics shaping cultural products. Markert is the author of *Publishing Romance* (2016) and has recently completed a book on the music industry, *Making Music in Music City*, that will be published by the University of Tennessee Press in the spring of 2021.

Jodi McAlister is a Lecturer in Writing, Literature, and Culture at Deakin University in Australia. Her research interests include representations of romantic love and the popular fiction and culture industries. She is also an author, and her young adult novels *Valentine* (2017), *Ironheart* (2018), and *Misrule* (2019) are published by Penguin Teen Australia.

Hannah McCann is a Lecturer in Cultural Studies at the University of Melbourne. Her research sits within critical femininity studies, exploring areas such as feminist debates on femininity, affects in beauty culture, and queering the fangirl. Her publications include the monograph *Queering Femininity: Sexuality, Feminism and the Politics of Presentation* (2018), and her co-authored textbook *Queer Theory Now: From Foundations to Futures* (2020).

Julie E. Moody-Freeman is the Director for the Center for Black Diaspora and an Associate Professor in the Department of African and Black Diaspora Studies at DePaul University. She is the co-editor of *The Black Imagination, Science Fiction, and the Speculative* and *The Black Imagination: Science Fiction, Futurism, and the Speculative.* Her scholarly essays on Belizean writer Zee Edgell have been published in *African Identities*, *Macomeré*, *Canadian Women Studies/les cahiers de la femme*, and *Seeking the Self—Encountering the Other: Diasporic Narrative and the Ethics of Representation.* Her work on African American Romance has also appeared in *Romance Fiction and American Culture: Love as the Practice of Freedom?* (2016).

Lauren O'Mahony is a Lecturer in Global Media and Communication at Murdoch University, Western Australia. Much of Lauren's research is focused on the analysis of popular literary and media texts, especially using romance and feminist theoretical frameworks. Her research has been published in *The Australasian Journal of Popular Culture*, *The Journal of Popular Romance Studies*, *Communication Research and Practice*, *Outskirts*, and *TEXT Journal.*

María T. Ramos-García is a Professor of Spanish in the School of American and Global Studies at South Dakota State University. Over the last few years her research has concentrated on paranormal romance and urban fantasy in English, a topic she has developed into an honors colloquium. She is co-editor, with Laura Vivanco, of *Love, Language, Place, and Identity in Popular Culture: Romancing the Other* (2020).

Kristin Ramsdell is a Librarian Emerita at California State University, East Bay. She is the author of the first and second editions of *Romance Fiction: A Guide to the Genre* (1999, 2012) and its predecessor, *Happily Ever After: A Guide to Reading Interests in Romance Fiction* (1987); the editor of the Romance section of the readers' advisory series *What Do I Read Next?* (1990–2016); the editor of *The Encyclopedia of Romance Fiction* (2018); and *Library Journal*'s Romance columnist from 1994 to 2019.

Pamela Regis is a Professor of English at McDaniel College. She has been studying popular romance fiction since the 1980s and is the author of *A Natural History of the Romance Novel.* She has served as both Vice-President and President of the International Association for the

Study of Popular Romance. Her work on romance writer Jane Austen has been published in *Persuasions*.

Catherine M. Roach is a Professor of Gender and Cultural Studies in New College at The University of Alabama, U.S.A. A two-time Fulbright Award winner, she is the author of *Mother/Nature: Popular Culture and Environmental Ethics* (2003) and *Stripping, Sex, and Popular Culture* (2007), along with two historical romance novels published as Catherine LaRoche (2012, 2014). Her most recent academic book, *Happily Ever After: The Romance Story in Popular Culture* (2016), won Silver Medal in the 2017 Independent Publisher Book Awards. She is currently at work on a trade book about America's new gender and sexual revolution.

Eric Murphy Selinger is a Professor of English at DePaul University, Executive Editor of the *Journal of Popular Romance Studies*, and President of the International Association for the Study of Popular Romance. He is the author of *What Is It Then Between Us? Traditions of Love in American Poetry* (1998) and co-editor of several collections, notably *New Approaches to Popular Romance Fiction: Critical Essays* (with Sarah S. G. Frantz 2012) and *Romance Fiction and American Culture: Love as the Practice of Freedom?* (with William Gleason 2016).

Hsu-Ming Teo is an Associate Professor, novelist, and cultural historian based in the Department of English at Macquarie University, Australia, where she teaches literature and creative writing. Her academic publications include her monograph *Desert Passions: Orientalism and Romance Novels* (2012), and the edited books *The Popular Culture of Romantic Love in Australia* (2017) and *Cultural History in Australia* (2003), as well as a wide range of articles on Orientalism, imperialism, fiction, popular culture, romantic love, and popular romance studies. Hsu-Ming is an associate editor of the *Journal of Popular Romance Studies* and an editorial board member of the *Journal of Australian Studies*.

Angela Toscano specializes in the eighteenth-century novel with a particular emphasis on romance and amatory fiction. She has written extensively on genre romance and her article "A Parody of Love: the Narrative Uses of Rape in Popular Romance" was published in the *Journal of Popular Romance Studies*. Currently she teaches at the University of Utah but has previously taught rhetoric, composition, and writing at the University of Iowa.

Laura Vivanco is an independent scholar whose Ph.D. thesis from the University of St Andrews was published in 2004 as *Death in Fifteenth-Century Castile: Ideologies of the Elites*. After changing field from Hispanomedievalism to popular romance studies she has written many articles on a variety of issues relating to romance novels as well as two books: *For Love and Money: The Literary Art of the Harlequin Mills & Boon Romance* (2011) and *Pursuing Happiness: Reading American Romance as Political Fiction* (2016).

Erin S. Young, Ph.D., is an Associate Professor of Literature and Cultural Studies at SUNY Empire State College. She is also the Managing Editor of the peer-reviewed *Journal of Popular Romance Studies*. Her research and teaching interests include popular romance fiction, Asian American fiction, and science fiction.

Acknowledgments

Our heartfelt thanks to all the romance scholars who have pioneered and continue to illuminate and energize this field of research, and to all the romance authors who have actively and generously supported romance scholarship. We are grateful to Ann Donahue, our first editor at Ashgate Publishing, and especially to An Goris, the first managing editor of the *Journal of Popular Romance Studies*, for her time and effort facilitating the growth of popular romance scholarship, and for the part she played in bringing this volume to life

Every effort has been made to trace or contact all copyright holders. The editors would be pleased to rectify any omissions brought to their notice at the earliest opportunity.

Introduction

Jayashree Kamblé, Eric Murphy Selinger, and Hsu-Ming Teo

The romance novel is the most popular and bestselling genre of fiction produced and consumed in the world today. In North America alone, the romance industry generates more than 1 billion dollars of sales each year ("About the Romance Genre"), and this figure does not include the second-hand market, or romance novels borrowed from libraries or other readers. The biggest global imprint of romance novels, Harlequin, publishes more than 110 romance titles a month in print and digital format, in over 30 countries and 150 languages, drawing from a stable of over 200 authors in the U.K. and more than 1300 worldwide, including the U.S.A., Australia, and New Zealand ("About Harlequin"). But the romance genre is important for more than its impressive sales. Although the readers and writers of romance fiction have diversified significantly since the twenty-first century, with a male readership of around 18 percent ("About the Romance Genre"), it is still the most woman-centered form of popular culture in the western world today. Written and read by women globally, the romance novel provides a public platform for women not only to voice ideals about gender and family relationships, but also to articulate opinions about contemporary social, cultural, environmental, economic, and political issues. The romance novel puts women's needs and desires at the center of contemporary life and accounts of the past —and perhaps this accounts for the myths that have multiplied about this complex and colossal genre. Increasingly, in the twenty-first century, the genre also acts as a forum for authors from very diverse backgrounds to explore and express ideas about their intersectional experiences of sexual, gender, racial, ethnic, and cultural identities, and to do so in a narrative that does not give way to despair but to a utopian hope that a happily ever after ending is possible for everyone.

Popular misconceptions

Although many forms of popular culture meet with ridicule and skepticism—comics, games, fan fiction, heroic "sword and sorcery" fantasy—no genre receives as much sustained and widespread disapprobation as mass-market romance fiction. In the popular imagination, romance novels are narratives of sexual encounters meant to titillate the reader. They are (when thought of at all) considered lacking in intellectual merit, stylistic rigor, or innovation, and indistinguishable from each other. Non-readers often use the phrases "a Harlequin" or "bodice-ripper" or "trashy novels" as a catch-all that conflates the thousands of romance novels written over many decades of changing tides involving different trends and thematic preoccupations—novels of various lengths, which span dozens of sub-genres, and contain a variety of literary styles and modes. Similarly, romance publishing, which has a global history and has experienced changes in the primary nationalities and ethnicities of its writers, and in its editorial hubs and distribution modes and mechanisms, remains largely invisible outside academic research (and under-theorized within it). Unsurprisingly then, romance readers are targets of ridicule and condescension, as are romance writers. Both groups are stereotyped in misogynistic, heteronormative, and often ageist terms.

Romance fiction, traditionally a straight cis-woman-centered form (though it has become more inclusive) is thus treated the same as a woman in public often is—as an "open person," a body that heterosexual patriarchy considers open to anyone's approach/acquisition/assault/definition (Gardner 333). The wide acceptance that this reductive ideology enjoys is further visible in the fact that romance fiction is rarely recognized as having a history, or of being shaped by historical forces, or of being created and read by people of varying socio-political and economic communities, sexualities, and gender identities. As a result, romance is constantly misrecognized, conflated with non-romance narratives based on minimal similarities, and equated with descriptions of sexual activity completely divorced from the concerns that "real literature" allegedly examines with care. The truth is far more complex.

Defining the genre

The largest professional organization of romance fiction, the Romance Writers of America, defines a romance novel as containing "a central love story and an emotionally satisfying and optimistic ending" ("About the Romance Genre"). Critic Pamela Regis speaks of a romance novel as "a work of prose fiction that tells the story of the courtship and betrothal of one or more heroines" (14; since 2009 she has revised this to "one or more protagonists") and she lists eight structural elements that must be present for a work to be recognizable as a romance novel:

> [1] the initial state of society in which heroine and hero must court, [2] the meeting between heroine and hero, [3] the barrier to the union of heroine and hero, [4] the attraction between the heroine and hero, [5] the declaration of love between heroine and hero, [6] the point of ritual death, [7] the recognition by heroine and hero of the means to overcome the barrier, and [8] the betrothal. (30)

For the purposes of this collection, the romance genre refers to English-language novels that are written in various parts of the world, aim at a broad (mass-market) readership, and center around a love plot that holds the promise of a future with a unified emotional life for two or more protagonists. Romance novels may involve a plot set in the writer's own time (termed "a contemporary") or be a period piece (termed "historical romance"), be set in our familiar world, or one that includes elements of science fiction/fantasy/paranormal, may or may not include detailed scenes of sexual activity (vanilla or kink), and might foreground straight and/or queer partnerships. A romance novel may be 180 pages long or over 500, the former usually published under a numbered series or imprint (such as Harlequin Mills & Boon's many "lines") and termed a "category romance" and the latter referred to as a "stand-alone" or "single-title" with more room for the narrative to unfold and the author name being given more prominence in the marketing and branding of the work. While the action in a romance novel may range from fighting in a war to solving a mystery, from raising a family to running a small business, and from saving a civilization to coping with trauma, the genre's primary drive is to imagine ways that romantic love and desire (erotic or asexual) might serve as a path to self-fulfillment and, increasingly, socio-political equality.

By and large, the contributors to this volume address the research on twentieth and twenty-first-century romance novels, since it is only in the twentieth century that the romance novel emerges as a distinct category of publishing and readership, marked both by textual features (the necessity of a "happy ending" of successful relationship formation) and by the array of paratextual features (cover art, gendered marketing practices, distinctive networks of distribution and reception) that distinguish it both in the public eye and in the eyes of potential readers. That said, inasmuch as the romance novel is a story of successful courtship, the genre has an old and complex history, and several of our chapters provide a historical genealogy of the genre going back into the eighteenth century or farther.

A brief history of romance

Romance novels have long and tangled roots. As a literary mode, romance can be traced as far back as the first century CE, when Greek prose romances began to be written, recounting stories of young men and women who meet, fall in love, are separated by numerous obstacles, undergo a series of journeys and adventures, and are eventually reunited by the gods to live happily ever after (Reardon 5). These conventions of love, adventure, journeys, and obstacles to the union of the lovers continued during the Middle Ages in chivalric romances such as the fourteenth-century *Bevis of Hampton* or the early fifteenth-century *Sir Degrevant*, but the plot emphasis in such quest romances was on the hero's life of adventure, rather than on courtship or the marriage plot. Pamela Regis suggests that the late sixteenth- and early-seventeenth-century comedies of Shakespeare, including *As You Like It*, bring us closer to the modern incarnation of the romance novel because these plots work toward the freedom of the lovers to choose union with each other, thus creating the happy ending of the romance story (28, 56).

However, it was only with the publication of Samuel Richardson's *Pamela* (1740) in Britain that the romance novel as we recognize it today began to emerge. As jay Dixon observes in Chapter 1, Richardson built on the work of early eighteenth-century English women writers such as Elizabeth Rowe, Susannah Dobson, and Eliza Haywood, who pioneered epistolary novels about the complications of love and courtship. However, Regis argues that *Pamela* was the first prototype of the romance novel because of its focus on courtship and seduction, and the obstacles to be overcome in order for the hero, Mr. B, to marry the virtuous servant heroine Pamela (Chapter 7). As Regis shows in Chapter 2 of this volume, *Pamela* had a significant impact on the development of love and courtship stories in the United States after its publication there in 1742–3. It inaugurated the sentimental novel which, in the hands of women authors such as Sukey Vickery, Catherine Maria Sedgwick, Lydia Maria Child, and Louise May Alcott, gave rise to the romance novel in America.

In Britain, however, the influence of Richardson's novel on the romance genre was eclipsed by Jane Austen's *Pride and Prejudice* (1813) and Charlotte Brontë's *Jane Eyre*

(1847)—two classic novels that would become ur-texts for romance plots even if, in their own time, they were not originally read as romance novels and did not enjoy the status and popularity they would garner in the twentieth century. Both were variations of the broader British domestic novel of manners that was popular in the nineteenth century, and it was from this genre that British romantic fiction would develop from the mid-nineteenth century onwards, after the publication of Charlotte M. Yonge's bestselling *The Heir of Redclyffe* (1853) spawned a host of similar works by writers such as Rhoda Broughton and Mary Elizabeth Braddon. The novels of these writers are certainly concerned with love and the obstacles to courtship and marriage, but while they are romantic fiction, they are not modern romance novels as the term is commonly understood today because the plots often ended tragically, with the lovers parted by death. As Rachel Anderson comments, for the Victorians, "the truest, purest romantic love is a fatal love" (26). It was not until the twentieth century that the happy ending, with the romantic protagonists united at the end of the love story, became a more regular feature of the British romantic novel. Even so, the ambivalence toward the Happily Ever After (HEA) ending can be seen in the British Romantic Novelists' Association broad ranging definition of romantic fiction that, until 2017, included tragic stories such as Tolstoy's *Anna Karenina* or Pasternak's *Doctor Zhivago* as romantic fiction. Even today, the RNA (which is the equivalent of the American Romance Writers Association or the Romance Writers of Australia) keeps its remit broad, talking about "romantic fiction" that "explores and celebrates love in all its messy, unexpected, improbable, imperfection" (RNA website), rather than the narrower American and Australian definition of the "romance novel" that focuses on the development of a love relationship between two (or more) protagonists that ends optimistically in their union. Readers who seek a guaranteed happy ending in British romantic fiction associate this with the Mills & Boon "category romance" novel, rather than with romantic fiction as a genre in its own right.

Many British publishing houses produced romantic fiction in the early twentieth century but by the 1930s romance novel publishing had come to be dominated by Mills & Boon, which increasingly standardized the length and structure of their books during the 1950s, excised extraneous subplots to focus on the developing love relationship between the romantic protagonists, and invariably featured the HEA ending (McAleer 85). Mills and Boon drew their authors from all corners of the British Empire and Commonwealth, so it had a global reach from its inception, while also influencing the style of romance fiction that would be produced in these countries even though specifically national characteristics are still evident (Flesch *From Australia*; Teo "Imperial Affairs"). The nascent North American romance market began to be influenced by Mills & Boon too, after Canadian publishing firm Harlequin signed a deal in 1957 to distribute selected novels as paperback editions. But the influence went both ways, especially after Harlequin bought the British firm in 1971 to form the publishing powerhouse, Harlequin Mills & Boon. Although Harlequin dominated the global Anglophone romance market in the 1970s, it was challenged by New York-based American companies—such as the historical romance publisher Avon in the 1970s, and Silhouette and Dell in the 1980s—which saw a gap in the hitherto British-dominated market and began producing American-centered romances. It should be noted, however, that the United States had its own home-grown traditions of romance fiction, as Pamela Regis shows in Chapter 2 of this volume. Regis points out that this history of the American romance is only starting to be excavated and constructed, but already the underlying associations of love and freedom in the American romance are evident (see also Gleason and Selinger).

Although Harlequin eventually absorbed Silhouette and Dell by the mid-1980s, the end of the twentieth century and the rise of digital publishing in the twenty-first century saw the romance genre diversifying with regard to the representation of gender and gender relations, race and ethnicity, sexuality, and different cultural traditions, as well as the emergence of new subgenres such as the paranormal and erotic, joining existing subgenres such as medical, historical, crime/thriller, and inspirational romances. Today, the romance industry is dominated by the "big five" transnational trade publishers—HarperCollins (which now owns Harlequin), Hachette, Macmillan, Penguin Random House, and Simon & Schuster—alongside a host of independent publishers and self-publishing authors at the forefront of new developments within the romance genre.

It is impossible to cover the various, complex trends within the romance genre throughout the twentieth and twenty-first centuries in this introduction. Generally speaking, the genre has always placed value on the happiness of women and the opportunities for freedom and fulfillment offered them in terms of work and social inclusion, as well as through romantic love. Over time, the intense religiosity of the nineteenth- and early-twentieth-century novels has waned and formed its own subgenre (the inspirational romance), giving way instead to a secularization and, from the 1970s onwards, a sexualization of romantic love. Ideals of femininity, masculinity, and gender relations have changed noticeably over the course of the twentieth century, as jay Dixon shows. By the 1980s, second-wave feminism had a notable impact on the portrayal of women's needs in social, economic, and romantic relationships, while the expansion of civil liberties to address the disadvantages of hitherto marginalized citizens began to impact the genre from the 1990s onwards. The advent of digital publishing and inexpensive e-book readers from 2007–8 onwards has allowed new subgenres to proliferate. A wider range of representation has thus entered the genre, not least because authors of color and LGBTQIA authors (among others) can now bypass the gatekeeping practices of mainstream publishing houses and the limited distribution practices of chain bookstores in order to reach interested readers.

The mass-market romance in the twenty-first century, then, is a genre whose ostensible sameness from book to book—every story centrally a love story; every central love story ending with some promise of romantic futurity—reveals, on inspection, a surprising variety of characters, desires, relationship structures, themes, and areas of ideological (and often immediate, practical) concern to its global writer and reader community. The genre includes progressive texts dedicated to expanding the universe of persons represented as worthy of romantic happiness, whether in terms of race, ethnicity, disability (mental, physical, and emotional), religion, age, size, or sexual and gender identity, but it also includes texts that are conservative and even unabashedly reactionary on all of these topics, and it is easy to find romance novels whose politics and representational practices are a hodgepodge of diverging or contradictory impulses. The same can be said of the genre's treatment of sexual consent, which runs the gamut from an explicit insistence on "exuberant consent" as the sine qua non of sexual activity to romance novels which not only contain scenes of "dubcon" (dubious consent) or nonconsensual sex between protagonists, but are tagged and marketed, mostly online, on this basis. This dynamic tension between convention/familiarity and variation/novelty may be found within all forms of genre fiction (see Roberts 162–72) but only in the twenty-first century has scholarship on popular romance turned, by and large, from claims about the genre as a whole to the disaggregated analysis of texts, subgenres, local traditions, reader communities, and other sites of multiplicity.

Introducing popular romance scholarship

Scholarship on popular romance fiction begins considerably later than the serious consideration of other forms of genre fiction. Thoughtful essays on detective fiction, for example, can be found as early as the mid-1920s, with the first critical history of that genre, Howard Haycraft's *Murder for Pleasure*, published in 1941. By the end of the 1940s, a comparable history of science fiction had been published (Evans 48), and the first scholarly journal dedicated to SF/Fantasy, *Extrapolation*, made its debut in 1959.[1] By the mid-1970s there were monographs and essay collections on important texts and authors from these and other genres, and although prejudice against taking popular fiction seriously certainly still existed, both in print and in university classrooms scholars defended such fiction both on intellectual grounds—as they argued, significant socio-political and philosophical material might well be addressed in genre fiction—and on aesthetic grounds, as when John Cawelti calls Dashiell Hammett and Raymond Chandler "significant artists" (4) and insists that what he calls "formula literature" is, first and foremost, "a kind of literary art" (8).

In principle, popular romance might have received the same sorts of attention and advocacy. In practice, it did not: a gap that is particularly vivid in Cawelti's groundbreaking study, *Adventure, Mystery, and Romance: Formula Stories as Art and Popular Culture* (1976), which despite its title, as Cawelti himself would note a few years later, contains "almost nothing about romance" and indeed discusses not one female author ("Masculine Myths and Feminist Revisions" 123). The first critical history of popular romance did not appear until 30 years after the first such books on detective fiction and SF, and far from defending the genre or singling out authors for their unrecognized merit, Rachel Anderson's *The Purple Heart Throbs: The Subliterature of Love* (1974) describes its subject matter as a "branch of fiction consisting of lightweight, but full-length, novels of no great literary qualities" (14). Five years later, Ann Barr Snitow's "Mass Market Romance: Pornography for Women is Different" likewise insists that "to analyze Harlequin romances is not to make any literary claims for them" (142); indeed, Snitow pauses to reassure her readers that she is "not concerned here with developing an admiration for their buried poetics" (143). Their interest lies elsewhere: for Anderson, in the genre's curious "vitality" (a term she borrows from Q. D. Leavis 14); for Snitow, in the way these novels illuminate—precisely *because* of their artlessness—the "pathological experience of sex difference" created by heteropatriarchy and the "particular nature of the satisfactions we are all led to seek by the conditions of our culture" (143).[2]

As Snitow's analysis suggests, the impulse to take romance seriously from was born out of second-wave feminism, both in its focus on recovering heretofore unexamined or trivialized aspects of women's history and culture (high art or popular) and in its terms of critical engagement, which often quite explicitly set aside the approaches favored by earlier scholars of other genres. In her foundational study *Loving with a Vengeance: Mass-Produced Fantasies for Women* (1982), for example, Tania Modleski begins by mocking the "aggrandized titles of certain classic studies of popular male genres ('The Gangster as Tragic Hero')" and the "inflated claims made for, say, the detective novel which fill the pages of the *Journal of Popular Culture*" (1), and she dismisses as both silly and intellectually incoherent the idea of simply adapting such frameworks for female-focused texts (e.g., "The Scheming Little Adventuress as Tragic Hero" 2). Kay Mussell's *Fantasy and Reconciliation: Contemporary Formulas of Women's Romance Fiction*, published two years later, opens by acknowledging the impact of "the contemporary women's movement" on her project (xi) and by framing its analyses of authors, texts, and genre "formulas" in the context of a discord between second-wave feminism and the enduring, indeed *increasing* popularity of popular romance fiction across the 1970s and early 1980s. "How can such apparently conservative and traditional stories be especially popular today, when we see many women casting off old roles and values and choosing to live more instrumental lives in the world? This book addresses that paradox" (xii).

Although second-wave feminist thought provided the crucial context for taking romance seriously in the academy, a range of critical models and methodologies were deployed in the foundational works of romance scholarship. Modleski's study and Janice Radway's epochal *Reading the Romance: Women, Patriarchy, and Popular Literature* (1984) drew on post-Freudian psychoanalysis, Frankfurt School cultural theory, structuralist and poststructuralist theoretical models, and, in Radway, the emerging disciplines of reader ethnography and publishing studies, what we would now think of as History of the Book. The more theoretical of these moves were not uncommon in studies of popular literature in the 1970s and 1980s. Most and Stowe's anthology *The Poetics of Murder: Detective Fiction and Literary Theory*, published in 1983 (just between Modleski's and Radway's studies) gathered nearly two dozen examples of such investigation by an impressive, international crew including Umberto Eco, F. R. Jameson, Frank Kermode, and Geoffrey Hartman; likewise, as the editor of *Science-Fiction Studies*, Darko Suvin had made the use of Marxist and Russian Formalist theory a staple of scholarship on this genre. The deployment of a sophisticated critical/theoretical apparatus to study popular romance, however, served not as a means to illuminate the complexity of subtly crafted artifacts, attributable to the compositional decisions of romance authors (as, often, in *The Poetics of Murder*), nor to demonstrate the cognitive processes instilled by the genre in its readers (the detective and reader as hermeneutic partners or rivals; the cognitive estrangement central to worldbuilding in SF), but rather to identify unconscious, otherwise invisible tensions, complexities, and ambivalences in popular romance novels and in readers' interactions with them.[3] As Radway memorably announces, romance reading is "a profoundly conflicted activity centered on a profoundly conflicted form" (14).

In their introduction to *New Approaches to Popular Romance Fiction: Critical Essays* (2012), Eric Murphy Selinger and Sarah S. G. Frantz note the personal contexts and professional exigencies behind the recurring tropes of "duality, conflict, ambivalence" that they observe in what they call the "first wave" of popular romance scholarship (4; for more on the difference in critical rhetoric between first wave and later "Millennial" scholarship, see Regis, "What Do Critics Owe the Romance?"). Running from 1979 (Snitow) through the end of the 1980s or perhaps the early 1990s (Jan Cohn's *Romance and the Erotics of Property* appears in 1988; Scottish sociologist Bridget Fowler's *The Alienated Reader: Women and Popular Romantic Literature in the Twentieth Century* in 1991), this first wave of romance scholarship is marked by a twofold effort to identify the appeal of romance to its readers and to *unmask* how this ostensibly optimistic and idealistic genre—and the pleasurable, sustaining act of reading it—in fact encodes any number of real-world angers, anxieties, protests, and conflicts, often through the use of sophisticated critical theory. As the chapters of this Research Companion document, other, less visible modes of romance scholarship were seeded during this first wave and would blossom in the years after it, including structuralist and other formalist accounts of romance topoi (Barbara Bowman's "Victoria Holt's Gothic Romances: A Structuralist Inquiry" is an early instance), archivally-documented publishing history (Carol Thurston's *The Romance Revolution: Erotic Novels for Women and the Quest for a New Sexual Identity*), and the first stirrings of author-focused scholarship (A.S. Byatt's and Kathleen Bells' essays on Georgette Heyer [1991, 1995]), as well as work on the nineteenth- and early twentieth-century history of African American love stories which would be crucial to the study of African American popular romance in the decades to come (see Chapter 10 of this volume).

In the Selinger/Frantz account, a second wave of scholarship begins when popular romance novelists begin to publish as theorists and advocates of their own genre in the 1990s: first in the essays commissioned by Jayne Ann Krentz for the anthology *Dangerous Men, Adventurous Women* (1992), then in a special issue of the journal *Paradoxa* (1997) and a pair of conferences at Bowling Green State University (1997 and 2000), each of which presented romance authors and scholars as equal partners in the investigation of the genre (see Selinger and Gleason 11–13). As Selinger and Gleason document in their introduction to *Romance Fiction and American Culture*(2016), this "second-wave" emergence of romance authors as contributors to scholarship on the genre was part of a concerted effort led by romance novelist Jayne Ann Krentz to push back against what she and others saw as a condescending attitude toward romance authors and readers among first-wave scholars. The feedback loops are worth noting. Just as the ideas of Modleski, Radway, and other first-wave scholars prompted discussion in the romance community (see Selinger and Gleason 11–12), authors' political and aesthetic claims on behalf of the genre drew reaction from scholars. These range from Modleski's sometimes-scathing skepticism ("My Life as a Romance Reader") to Radway's frank curiosity ("Romance and the Work of Fantasy") to the matter-of-fact integration of authorial claims as a resource for further discussion by George Paizis, a British scholar of French literature working at a safe remove from the American fray (see *Love and the Novel: the Poetics and Politics of Romantic Fiction*).

The rhetoric and substance of this contretemps warrants future exploration, whether as an instance of fraught dialog between waves of white American feminism—none of the participants was a woman of color—or as a "ritual matricide" (Goris "Matricide in Romance Scholarship?"). That said, much of the most important scholarship on popular romance during the late 1990s and early 2000s played out in a separate, parallel universe where new topics of interest were introduced, including the first significant work on race and popular romance (Wardrop; Burley "Shadows and Silhouettes"; Caton; Dandridge; Foster), on queer romance and the curiously insistent construction of heterosexuality in the genre (Burley "What's a Nice Girl"; Fletcher *Historical Romance Fiction*); on romance publishing history and the genre's production and readership in diverse national contexts (McAleer; Dixon; Flesch; Puri; Parameswaran, "Reading Fictions"); on individual romance authors and novels (Westman; Hinnant; Fletcher, "Mere Costumery"); and on the relationships between popular romance fiction and fan fiction (Driscoll) and a range of resolutely canonical texts (Osborne "Romancing the Bard", "Sweet, Savage Shakespeare", and "Harlequin Presents"; Regis). In retrospect, this diversity is exciting; at the time, however, there was little critical dialog among the various participants and approaches, as though many were unaware of what the others were up to. Popular romance lacked the academic infrastructure—a dedicated journal, a scholarly association, a regular conference meeting, a comprehensive bibliography, or research guide—that scholars at work on other popular genres had established decades before.

The establishment of this infrastructure marks the start of the current wave of popular romance scholarship and the emergence of "popular romance studies" as a field. The story is easy to trace. In 2005 the Romance Writers of America inaugurated an Academic Research Grant program designed to "develop and support academic research devoted to genre romance novels, writers, and readers" ("Academic Research Grant"). Jayashree Kamblé was the first recipient, using the grant to support her dissertation on romance at the University of Minnesota; the following year Eric Murphy Selinger received the grant and used it to support a series of infrastructure-building efforts, including a listserv (RomanceScholar), a collaborative academic blog on romance (Teach Me Tonight, now written by Laura Vivanco), a review-essay on the past decade in romance scholarship, published in *Contemporary Literature*, and a reboot of the Popular Culture Association's then-dormant PCA Romance Area. Each of these efforts, in turn, bore fruit. The listserv gave rise to a live-linked, steadily growing Wiki bibliography of essays, chapters, books, and dissertations on popular romance compiled by Kassia Krozier, Vivanco, and many others; through it and through Teach Me Tonight, Selinger and Darcy Martin recruited an array of presenters for the 2007 and 2008 PCA national conference, including emerging figures from Australia (Toni Johnson-Woods; Hsu-Ming Teo; Glen Thomas), the U.K. (Amy Burge) and the E.U. (An Goris), as well as established figures whose work he had encountered while writing the *Contemporary Literature* essay-review, notably Kamblé, Pamela Regis, Hsu-Ming Teo, and Sarah S. G. Frantz. With Frantz, Selinger founded the International Association for the Study of Popular Romance (IASPR) and the peer-reviewed *Journal of Popular Romance Studies* (*JPRS*); as Selinger collaborated with William Gleason on a major conference at Princeton (April, 2009) Frantz worked with Australian colleagues to organize the first IASPR conference in Brisbane (June, 2009); the following year Goris received a Fulbright fellowship to work on romance with Selinger in Chicago while she organized a second IASPR conference (Brussels 2010), during which the first issue of *JPRS* was published, with Goris soon joining as Managing Editor and Burge, a bit later, as Book Review editor. Almost all the contributors to this volume have presented at IASPR conferences; several have organized these or other IASPR-affiliated conferences at their home institutions in the E.U., U.K., and Australia; and more than a few have served or currently serve as masthead editors of *JPRS* or on its editorial board.

Although other romance conferences and research projects have emerged in the United States in the 2010s, notably at Bowling Green State University (home of an archive of popular romance texts and of the papers of the RWA), IASPR and the PCA Romance Area remain major hubs for romance scholarship in the United States, along with the ongoing RWA grant program. These have also served as incubators for scholars elsewhere. In the early 2010s, for example, Amy Burge and An Goris (a 2013 RWA grant recipient) led efforts to build a romance cohort at the European Popular Culture Association (EPCA), and Australian scholar Jodi McAlister (RWA 2019) has done the same for the Popular Culture Association of Australia and New Zealand (PopCAANZ). That said, it is important to note that Selinger attributes the creation of IASPR and JPRS to his encounters, in 2007, with the global perspective on romance found in Australian scholarship, and that popular romance studies in the U. K., E.U., and Australia has its own set of institutional frameworks, including university courses and dissertations on the genre, affiliations between scholars and romance writer organizations (the Romance Writers of Australia and, in the U.K., the Romantic Novelists Association), a variety of national and international conferences, and, recently, a range of ambitious and well-staffed research projects, the likes of which have yet to appear in the U.S.A.

In the U.K., early British explorations of the romance genre took place in an ad hoc fashion by writers recounting the history of the British romance in the late nineteenth and early twentieth centuries, such as Rachel Anderson's *The Purple Heart Throbs: The Sub-Literature of Love* (1974), or engaged in research related to Mills and Boon because of its dominance in the British romance industry. From the late 1960s to the early 1980s, sociologist Peter H. Mann carried out a number of surveys on British Mills and Boon readers, publishing his findings in 1969, 1981, and 1985. In 1999, two books outlining the publishing history of Mills and Boon appeared: jay Dixon's *The Romance Fiction of Mills and Boon, 1909–1990s*, and Joseph McAleer's *Passion's Fortune: The Story of Mills and Boon*. More systematic studies on romance was largely carried out in the fields of Women's Studies and feminist literary studies. In 1991 Bridget Fowler published *The Alienated Reader: Women and Romantic Literature in the Twentieth Century*: a Marxist analysis of British romance novels grounding the rise of the genre in the transition to capitalism, Protestantism, and patriarchy, highlighting the agency of working-class readers in their critical responses to certain authors, and the limits of the genre in relation to female-centered fantasies. Stevi Jackson's work in cultural studies emerged in the early 1990s ("Even Sociologists Fall in Love") and in the same year a conference entitled "Romance Revisited" was hosted by the Centre for Women's Studies at Lancaster University with an aim to "put romance back on the feminist agenda": a collection of essays edited by Lynne Pearce and Jackie Stacey emerged from the event in 1995.

This interdisciplinary approach to the study of romance and love has been extended with the creation of the Love Research Network, founded by Michael Gratzke in 2011 (in 2017 Gratzke and Burge co-edited a special issue of the *Journal of Popular Romance Studies* on critical love studies and popular romance scholarship). A number of U.K.-based scholars have undertaken funded research projects on romance topics: Ruth Deller and Clarissa Smith's 2012 survey examined the complex responses of "romance" and "casual" readers to E. L. James' *Fifty Shades of Grey* series; Mary Harrod's British Academy-funded project on romance and social bonding produced research events in 2019 and a forthcoming edited book; and Ria Cheyne won an RWA grant in 2017 to support the *DisRom* project on romance and disability. Significant monographs include Lynne Pearce's *Romance Writing* (2007), Laura Vivanco's *For Love and Money: The Literary Art of the Harlequin Mills & Boon Romance* (2011), Joseph Crawford's *The Twilight of the Gothic?: Vampire Fiction and the Rise of the Paranormal Romance* (2014), Amy Burge's *Representing Difference in the Medieval and Modern Orientalist Romance* (2016), and Ria Cheyne's *Disability, Literature, Genre: Representation and Affect in Contemporary Fiction* (2019).

A steady stream of research and networking events have demonstrated the strength of popular romance scholarship in the U.K., burgeoning connections between the academic community and the industry, and the developing expertise of postgraduate and postdoctoral researchers. A number of these events have signaled the specific U. K. context and history of romantic fiction for romance research; a conference on Regency romance author Georgette Heyer took place at the University of Cambridge in 2009, followed by a further conference on Heyer and contemporary women's historical fiction at the University of London in 2018, while a symposium at the University of Birmingham in 2019 marked 100 years since E. M. Hull's *The Sheik* was published in Britain. Public engagement activities have included an Edinburgh Festival Fringe show on romance devised by Amy Burge, an editor-scholar panel at Sheffield Festival of the Mind in 2016 organized by Ph.D. student Val Derbyshire, and regular romance author events hosted by institutions in collaboration with the U.K.-based Romantic Novelists' Association. There is a growing institutional interest in teaching popular fiction and, correspondingly, romance; a number of institutions offer both undergraduate and postgraduate courses in popular fiction with a few offering romance-specific courses. A significant number of recent and ongoing Ph.D.s are working on romance-related topics in the U.K. (including twenty-first-century LGBTQIA romance, early twentieth-century Orientalist romance, recent romantic subgenres, and feminism and romance).

Romance scholarship in Europe has also expanded southwards to Spain. This is largely due to the efforts of two groups of scholars: the first organized by Maria-Isabel Gonzalez-Cruz from the University of Las Palmas de Gran Canaria; and the second led by Paloma Fresno-Calleja at the University of the Balearic Islands. Both groups focus on representations of exoticism in the romance genre, with *Love, Language, Place, and Identity in Popular Culture: Romancing the Other* (2020), edited by Maria Ramos-Garcia and Laura Vivanco, emerging from the first group. Meanwhile, Fresno-Calleja's group, which includes scholars from the universities of Oviedo and Granada, have embarked on a project exploring "The politics, aesthetics and marketing of literary formulae in popular women's fiction: History, Exoticism and Romance." This research, funded by the Spanish Ministry of Economy, Industry and Competitiveness (MINECO), the Agencia Estatal de Investigación (AEI) and the European Regional Development Funds (ERDF) (see HER website), adopts postcolonial and gender approaches to analyzing Anglophone romances set in the past—especially the British Empire and war-torn Europe in the first half of the twentieth century—or in locations considered "exotic" by romance writers and readers. The aim is to engage critically with the patriarchal legacies in these texts, the use and misuse of historical material, including its neo-colonial and neo-orientalist implications, and to consider how these strategies frame the marketing and reception of the novels, whether deliberately or inadvertently. The novels examined come from western metropolitan centers as well as the Anglophone postcolonial world, and they constitute works that simultaneously appropriate and subvert some of the narrative formulae of historical fiction and popular romance, thereby de-exoticizing their settings and re-politicizing their content. Publications thus far range widely, examining related genres such as women's historical fiction, contemporary romance and chick lit, while topics explored include gender and national identities, and marketing strategies—among many other themes (see HER website).

Government funding has been important for spurring popular romance research in the twenty-first century. This is evident in the case of the Spanish HER research group, but also in the American National Endowment for the Humanities' support for Emmy Award-winning filmmaker Laurie Kahn's documentary *Love Between the Covers*

(2015) about the American romance community. Meanwhile, government funding through the Australia Research Council has supported Hsu-Ming Teo's research into the popular culture of romantic love in Australia, Glen Thomas's industry-based collaboration with Harlequin Mills and Boon Australia, researching romance as a creative industry (see Thomas; Thomas and James), and Lisa Fletcher, Beth Driscoll, and Kim Wilkins' exploration of the romance industry as a "genre world" that "recognises the multiple dimensionality of popular genres: as bodies of texts, collections of social formations that gather around and produce those texts, and sets of industrial practices with various national and transnational orientations."

In Australia, the scholarship of romantic fiction began as an offshoot of the second-wave feminist project to recover marginalized or forgotten Australian women writers in the nineteenth and twentieth centuries. Alison Alexander was among the first to focus on women romance writers in her monograph *A Mortal Flame: Marie Bjelke Petersen. Australian Romance Writer* (1994). Fiona Giles soon followed with *Too Far Everywhere: The Romantic Heroine in Nineteenth-Century Australia* (1998): her exploration of the Australian tradition of romantic literary fiction. This focus on nineteenth century women writers who produced romantic fiction among their literary output continued with author studies such as Patricia Clark's *Rosa! Rosa! A Life of Rosa Praed, Novelist and Spiritualist* (1999).

However, the focus on Australian women writers' romance novels as a specific genre undoubtedly begins with Juliet Flesch's pioneering work in the 1990s identifying and recovering Australian romance novels. Flesch's *Love Brought to Book: A Bio-Bibliography of Australian Romance Novels* (1995), together with Ken Gelder and Rachael Weaver's *Anthology of Colonial Australian Romance Fiction* (2010), have been invaluable references for twenty-first-century romance scholars, for they did the work of digging through the archives and locating the often ephemeral Australian primary sources on romance fiction that Pamela Regis has just started to do for the American romance novel. Because of its origins in feminist interventions in the Australian literary tradition, the specifically Australian focus of Flesch's and Gelder and Weaver's works, and government support for Australian-focused research projects, the Australian scholarship on the romance genre is strongly characterized by the contextualization of this genre within the broader Australian literary tradition, and the desire to distinguish what is particularly "Australian" about the love stories produced by this nation's authors—something Lauren O'Mahony discusses at length in Chapter 3. Nevertheless, Australian romance scholars such as Lisa Fletcher, Jodi McAlister, and Hsu-Ming Teo have also engaged in broader, transnational studies of historical fiction, sexuality and virginity, and Orientalism, imperialism and postcolonialism in romance novels, respectively.

Introducing this volume

Given the 40-year history and twenty-first-century proliferation of popular romance scholarship, the need has emerged for a systematic, comprehensive resource for scholars and graduate students researching the genre, as well as for undergraduate teaching purposes. A course on popular romance fiction whose scholarly framework comes from the 1980s would be as misleading as a course on television centered on scholarship that predates cable and digital streaming; likewise, new research on the texts, reception, distribution, publishing, and readership of popular romance cannot constantly return to the same few foundational studies—Modleski's *Loving with a Vengeance* (1982); Radway's *Reading the Romance* (1984); Regis's *A Natural History of the Romance Novel* (2003)—as definitive descriptions of the genre. This volume presents the first overview of popular romance fiction studies as it has evolved and currently stands. It is designed to provide a history of the genre, an overview of various disciplinary approaches to studying popular romance fiction, and an analysis and critical evaluation of important subgenres and themes or topics. Each chapter also highlights new and still-needed avenues of inquiry for future research.

The first part of this volume offers an introduction to the history of popular romance fiction and some of its most enduring subgenres. Jay Dixon's "History of English Romance Novels 1621–1975" (Chapter 1 in this volume) traces the emergence of modern popular romance fiction—first for contemporary romance novels (that is, works set in the time when they were written) and then for historical romances—from a matrix of other, related genres, such as amatory fiction, the domestic novel of manners, and sensation fiction, and it documents the contested reception of romance by critics, literary historians, and novelists from other, competing traditions. In "The Evolution of the American Romance Novel" (Chapter 2 in this volume) Pamela Regis explores the conceptual and archival challenges of identifying American romance novels before the middle of the twentieth century, offers an outline of American romance from the start of the nineteenth century to just after the Second World War, and presents an overview of major critical works which either aid or, in some cases, actively *impede* the recognition and understanding of these texts. Our third chapter, "Australian Romance Fiction," overlaps chronologically with the first two, as it covers writings from the mid-nineteenth century to the early twenty-first, but unlike Dixon and Regis, contributor Lauren O'Mahony is able to draw on the substantial body of scholarship devoted to the national specificities of Australian romance—the "beetroot in the burger," in Juliet Flesch's memorable metaphor—which have distinguished it from other Anglophone romance traditions and which have enabled it, in the past and now, to serve an "outward facing ambassadorial function" (O'Mahony, 73) in presenting Australia and Australianness to readers elsewhere. (Scholarship devoted to other global Anglophone and non-Anglophone popular romance traditions, with particular attention to India, Malaysia, Japan, and Nigeria, can be found in Chapter 24 of this volume.)

Having introduced the general histories of English, American, and Australian romance, the next part turns to more focused investigations of scholarship on seven enduring subgenres of popular romance fiction and on African American romance, a category whose publishing history is defined by its authorship and characters rather than by setting or other plot conventions. Angela Toscano's chapter (Chapter 4) on Gothic romance explores what was, in the 1960s, the most popular version of the romance novel. Drawing on important early work on the Gothic popular romance by Joanna Russ, Toscano details the conventions of this subgenre, documents the history of Gothic romance criticism during its heyday and after, and makes the case that scholars of the Gothic tradition in literature can benefit from the study of this now-neglected corpus, even as popular romance scholarship can learn from the robust and theoretically-sophisticated world of scholarship on Gothic. A comparable case is made by Sarah Ficke in her chapter (Chapter 5) on historical romance fiction. As she moves chronologically from the foundational Regency and Georgian-set works of Georgette Heyer and Barbara Cartland to the more highly sexualized American historical romances of the 1970s and 1980s to the diverse innovations found in twenty-first-century historical romance, Ficke outlines recurring and emerging themes in scholarship on this work: its treatment of sexualities and desires; its function as a form of alternative (queer, feminist, etc.) historiography; its history of othering Black, Asian, Arab, and Native characters and corresponding efforts by authors of color to resist this practice; and its confrontations with the question of whether some historical periods and contexts cannot or should not feature in the happy-ending context of the romance novel.

In the late twentieth and early twenty-first centuries four romance subgenres experienced significant growth, transforming both the romance marketplace and public perceptions of the genre. Chapter 6, on Paranormal Romance, details the emergence of paranormal romance (and its affiliate genre, urban fantasy), its critical reception, and its contributions to a change in popular romance aesthetics from the centrality of a stand-alone volume which ends with a decisive HEA for its protagonists to a series aesthetic in which what An Goris calls the "post-HEA" life of romance protagonists—sometimes contented, often vexed—appears as a secondary or even central feature of subsequent novels. As Maria Ramos-Garcia shows in this chapter, the popularity of paranormal romance in the 2000s has been linked by many critics to the aftermath of the 9/11 attacks on the United States and the subsequent Global War on Terror; likewise the racial and gender politics of paranormal romance have drawn substantial attention, whether focused on particular texts (the *Twilight* novels; the *Black Dagger Brotherhood* books; *Nalini Singh's Psy-Changeling* series) or on distinct paranormal creatures (werewolves, vampires, shape-shifters, etc.).

Although the popularity of the *Twilight* franchise in the early twenty-first century brought Young Adult (YA) Romance to public attention, Amanda Allen's chapter (Chapter 7) on this subgenre demonstrates that critical debates over fiction written for young readers—especially young women—have existed for many decades. Allen divides her history into three periods: work from the 1940s–60s, when it focused on the socialization of young women through what were called "junior novels" (tales of young love set mostly in American high schools); scholarship from the 1980s, which often including feminist critiques of the same socialization practices lauded some decades before; and scholarship since 2000, which addresses paranormal YA romance, queer and otherwise diverse YA romance, and non-traditional forms of YA romance publishing, including fan fiction and romance in visual media (e.g., graphic novels and manga).

The question of whether YA romances are, to put it crudely, good or bad for their readers has also marked critical debates about Christian Inspirational Romance, the topic of Chapter 8, but this has not been the only question addressed in scholarship on this subgenre. As Rebecca Barrett-Fox and Kristen Donnelly demonstrate, the unabashed sentimentality, religiosity, and cultural conservatism of Christian romance fiction has long made it the target of both aesthetic and political critique, but it has also been investigated and defended, often with considerable nuance, by scholars interested in its deployment of Biblical allusion, its perhaps-unexpectedly complicated construction of romantic masculinity, and its place in the devotional and communal lives of its readers. Although most of this scholarship has focused on white Evangelical romances in the United States, this chapter also surveys important work on non-Protestant Christian romances, Black and Hispanic Christian romances, Amish romances (a popular sub-sub-genre in the United States), and the emerging genre worlds of

Muslim and Jewish romance, both of which are also discussed in Chapter 22 ("Romance and/as religion").

Jodi McAlister's chapter on erotic romance (Chapter 9) begins by framing it in an "industrial context": that is, by looking at how the term is defined and deployed by authors, editors, and publishers, as well as in guides for aspiring authors. She documents the modern publishing history of erotic romance, which long predates its twenty-first-century global visibility, and she clarifies its relationship to fanfiction, with particular attention to the writing, distribution, and impact of E. L. James's *Fifty Shades* trilogy, the erotic romance series that has, to date, received the most sustained and widespread scholarly attention.

A similar attention to publishing history marks Chapter 10, Julie Moody-Freeman's survey of African American romance and its reception, both in academic contexts and in the often-overlooked journalism, much of it from Black publications, which documents its history. Although this history is deeply intertwined with the story of American romance publishing more generally—for example, the author and editor who founded the Romance Writers of America, Vivian Stephens, was a Black woman—it cannot be reduced to a subset of that story, not least because of the long, ongoing, racially-specific struggle to have Black love and marriage recognized, let alone considered "romantic," by white Americans. The scholarship Moody-Freeman surveys thus begins with work on love stories and marriage plots in the first decades of Black fiction after Emancipation—work whose negotiations with the politics of middle-class respectability sets the stage for comparable concerns in twentieth and twenty-first-century Black romance novels—and continues through modern intersectional analyses of race, gender, class, and disability not only in Black romance novels. This chapter also addresses work that has been done to document racism and anti-racist resistance in American romance institutions, in particular the RWA and its RITA awards program.

Few romance subgenres have drawn as much sustained critical attention—including attention to race—as the "desert" romance: books which, as Amira Jarmakani explains, "feature a sheik, sultan, or desert prince as their hero" and which deploy a desert setting as the framework for narratives featuring "gender fluidity, racial anxiety, and the realities of war and terrorism" filtered through "masculine/feminine, black/white, and fantasy/reality dichotomies" (252). Scholarship on this subgenre begins with work on E. M. Hull's epochal bestseller *The Sheik* (1919) and continues with studies of the contemporary desert romance, which surged in popularity in the United States after the 9/11 terrorist attacks. Analyses of the racial status of the desert romance hero feature prominently in this critical corpus—at times, like Hull's Sheikh Ahmed ben Hassan, he is a racially ambiguous figure; at times he is unambiguously Arab—along with studies of how these texts represent gender and sexuality and of the relationship between all of these topics to the artistic and narrative traditions of orientalism. Like McAlister's account of erotic romance, Jarmakani's chapter (Chapter 11) attends to the place of desert romances in the romance industry, and it discusses scholarship on the explanations that desert romance authors give for their attraction to this subgenre and for why, in their view, readers continue to purchase and enjoy them.

The methodologies that critics (academic and popular) of romance novels have used span the humanities and the social sciences. In the second part of this volume, some authors have provided a model of how new scholars could engage with the genre (such as through historicizing mass media criticism in Jayashree Kamblé's chapter

(Chapter 12), literary approaches in Eric Murphy Selinger's chapter, and author studies in Kecia Ali's) while others have surveyed existing methodological practices, outlined their strengths and suggested new lines of inquiry within them. Kamblé's chapter performs a metacriticism of the popular pillorying of romance through a survey of articles on the genre in popular print and other media. It documents how these fluff pieces create an image of the genre as lacking substance, focused on thoughtless sex, and written and read by silly women. She terms this journalism phenomenon a genre in itself, one that endlessly produces the "media romance." Selinger's chapter (Chapter 13) reviews critiques of romance fiction that find it lacking in artistry and identifies the instances within the field that do the opposite, often by challenging the notion that working within genre conventions necessarily limits (or dumbs-down) a novel. He includes cases of the application of techniques from the literature classroom that identify and critique formal elements of a romance novel or an individual romance author's corpus. The chapter thus models how romance novels may be analyzed using the same tools as used in the analysis of canonical works, and it highlights scholarship on the playful, critically self-aware metafictional gestures often found in the novels themselves.

Kecia Ali's chapter (Chapter 14) defines author studies, including both traditional studies of a literary oeuvre by a named individual and studies of the "author function" which emphasize collective elements of production and reception. It explores gendered reasons for the relative scarcity of author studies for popular romance and surveys the extant literature (monographs, journal special issues, as well as dissertations), using Nora Roberts as the primary example. It concludes with a discussion of promising avenues for future research which, by taking account of popular romance writing, could help reimagine the field of author studies.

Sociologists Joanna Gregson and Jen Lois review the existing social scientific research on romance novels, readers, and authors from the last four decades (Chapter 15). They tap into the significant contributions made by social scientists and social science methodology to romance criticism while noting lacunae and calling attention to the need for research that is more attentive to the specificities of the genre. They observe that while content analyses of romance novels reveal conformity to traditional gender roles and sexual scripts, studies of romance readers show that these books serve important functions in women's lives, that they are read critically, and that their takeaway messages are both positive and progressive. The chapter also notes that research with authors reveals how and why they became romance authors, how they experience the stigma of writing in a disparaged genre, and how they forge community with other authors.

Chapter 16, John Markert's survey of international romance publishing history (twentieth and twenty-first century), provides a bird's eye view of the production forces that power the genre's development. Markert calls attention to the role of upper management as "gatekeepers" in the field and the rise and fall of different romance "lines" while he recounts previous studies of the industry-side of the genre. He shows how different publishing houses launched or altered their romance offerings in response to each other's successes, focusing mainly on print but with a brief look at the digital/e-book landscape. It is a concrete narrative that is a needed corrective to the often-abstract understanding of romance as a mass commodity.

Apart from readers, authors, and publishers, another key component of the romance matrix is libraries and librarians. In Chapter 17, Kristin Ramsdell discusses the scholarship on the role played by libraries in disseminating the genre, with the three main foci being public libraries, university libraries, and K-12 libraries, mainly in the United States and Australia. She touches on the varied methodologies and objects of analysis (including readership) in these studies and summarizes their findings on the structural and ideological factors that affect romance collections development, particularly in academic libraries, as well as the potential impact of these factors on the study and long-term preservation of romance novels. The chapter also mentions some studies that reference libraries with relation to Gothic and romance-adjacent works in previous centuries. It ends with a list of several lines of inquiry that remain to be pursued and would broaden this sub-field of romance research.,

The final part of this volume focuses on thematic issues that characterize romance novels or frequently arise in discussions of the genre: class, wealth, materialism, gender, sexuality, romantic love, romance as it overlaps with and articulates a new form of religion, and race and ethnicity. The overwhelming majority of romance novels and the scholarship on it originates from the Anglophone world. However, variations of the genre are emerging in non-Anglophone and non-western markets, and this book concludes with a consideration of this emerging market.

The thematic part opens with Amy Burge's consideration of the scholarship on class, wealth, and materialism in romance novels—a body of work that spans over 30 years, largely emerging from Britain and America (Chapter 18). Burge begins by considering what "class" means in relation to the romance novel, whether it is defined in terms of a materialist relation to property, or a culturalist performance of class identity. After providing a brief overview of portrayals of wealth, class, and social mobility in romance novels since the nineteenth century, in both contemporary and historical modes of the genre, Burge turns her attention to the frameworks scholars employ to analyze class, arguing persuasively that all investigations into class and romance novels are necessarily intersectional, for it is impossible to consider class without simultaneously considering gender and race—specifically, whiteness and white privilege. The chapter ends with a critical discussion of whether feminist scholars' characterization of the genre as middle-class propaganda that generates stultifying and crippling escapist fantasies for working-class women can be sustained.

Chapters 19 and 20 then examine representations of sex, gender, and sexuality in contemporary romance novels. Focusing primarily on heterosexuality in the genre, Hannah McCann and Catherine M. Roach argue that popular romance novels center on fulfilling women's sexual desires and pleasures in sex-positive ways, creating a fantasy space in which to explore the conundrum of women's sexuality and sexual experiences in a male-dominated world (Chapter 19). Romance novels, they suggest, offer women a "reparative reading" of sexuality that allows them to reformulate sexual and gender ideas, consider the principles and limits of sexual consent, and to celebrate sexual and sensuous pleasures, yet the genre is only beginning to embrace representations of more diverse, non-binary, non-heterosexual identities, and more scholarly analysis of these LGBTQIA novels is needed. This call is answered by Jonathan A. Allan in his incisive investigation of the complex social construction and performance of gender and sexuality in romance novels (Chapter 20). Allan begins with a discussion of how foundational works of popular romance scholarship by Snitow, Modleski, and Radway theorized and critiqued gender and sexuality in ways that essentialized gender. He argues that Snitow's "Mass Market Romance: Pornography for Women is Different" marked out the terms in which gender and sexuality in romance novels is discussed by establishing the language of critique, creating a binary between romance and pornography that dominated subsequent discussions and defenses of gender and sexuality in romance. However, the twenty-first century has seen a move toward more diversified methods of analyzing romance novels, influenced by queer approaches, as well as more scholarly interest in gender and sexuality in LGBTQIA novels. His chapter ends with the observation that scholars are only beginning to study constructions of men and masculinities, not only in the genre but also in the romance industry, and that much more work is needed in this emerging field.

The third wave of romance scholarship in the twenty-first century has seen innovations, not only with regard to gender and sexuality, but also in relation to the representation and meaning of love and romance itself—themes that are explored in Chapters 21 and 22. Melding romance scholarship to the historical, sociological and literary scholarship about romantic love in Europe and America, Hsu-Ming Teo's chapter (Chapter 21) begins with a description of how ideas about romantic love developed and changed from the nineteenth to twenty-first centuries, and how these ideas have influenced the portrayal of love in romance novels—particularly who is worthy of being loved and, consequently, who can enjoy the role of romantic protagonist. Teo argues that by the mid-twentieth century, the markers of love had become secularized and sexualized, but that love in late twentieth- and twenty-first-century romance novels began to emphasize the importance of developing and maintaining intimacy—a problematic concept in itself, as the work of David Shumway shows. The chapter then reviews the extant scholarship on the romance novel, charting changing approaches from the early feminist writings arguing that love was precisely the problem for romantic heroines, for it disempowered them individually, economically, and politically, and made them submissive to or accepting of the patriarchal order of society. However, more recent third-wave scholarship on love moves away from the "empowerment versus oppression" (Goade) binary to ask instead how love functions in individual novels, and how these representations of love develop over time and across different cultures.

Eric Murphy Selinger and Laura Vivanco's chapter (Chapter 22) then extends the exploration of love and romance to consider how these representations of these entities overlap with religion and are themselves invested with the structure, purpose, and practice of religion. Chapter 22 begins with a consideration of how religion—especially Protestant Christianity—can be read as a discourse of romance: a redemptive and ennobling relational experience that ends in a happily ever after. Rather than a secularization of the romance novel occurring throughout the twentieth century, Selinger and Vivanco argue that the romance itself took on religious qualities, representing romantic love as unconditional, omnipotent, and eternal, and therefore redemptive or salvific. It is an act of faith. Love as religion is something that romantic characters must learn to "believe in," so that lasting happiness may be achieved. The chapter ends with a call for the connections between romance novels and other forms of religion—such as Islam or Buddhism—to be explored, especially in light of the diversification of the genre with regard to gender, sexuality, race, ethnicity, and cultural diversity in the twenty-first century.

Where Chapters 19 and 20 examine diversity in gender and sexuality, the last two chapters of this volume explore the diversification of the romance genre in relation to the latter themes. Erin S. Young's chapter on "Race, ethnicity, and whiteness" (Chapter 23) begins with a review of the romance scholarship analyzing and critiquing representations of race, blackness, and whiteness in romance fiction. Young observes that extant studies emphasize the role of romance in shoring up white privilege and supremacy, before navigating her way through the fraught problem of how non-white characters and cultures have often been caricatured and (mis)represented in the genre. Romance, she notes, has a race problem. However, this is not only a problem of misrepresentation, but a problem of racial politics as well, evident in the debates over Black authors who feature the "taboo" of Black/White interracial romance. Young's chapter ends with a summary of current concerns among academics working in this field, as well as an optimistic hope that representations of racial, ethnic, and cultural diversity in romance novels are improving because readers are demanding change, as shown in the conversations taking place among the romance community in online venues.

This volume by necessity focuses overwhelmingly on Anglophone romance novels coming out of Britain, the United States, and Australia, simply because these are the countries that have developed the genre and the scholarship. It is with great pleasure, therefore, that we can end with a snapshot of what is happening to the genre globally in the twenty-first century. Kathrina Mohd Daud concludes this volume with a chapter (Chapter 24) considering how romance novels—especially category romances—translate into non-western cultures, focusing specifically on India, Japan, Nigeria, and Malaysia. Daud describes local romance publishing initiatives responding to the success of Harlequin in these markets, with the emergence of local romance lines such as the francophone *Adoras* series (known as the "African Harlequin") in Cote d'Ivoire in 1998, the romance genre called *Littattafan Soyayya* (books of love) in Nigeria, the *Sanrio New Romance* series of Japanese-authored romances, and a more variegated Malay-language romance market in Malaysia. However, Daud notes that local initiatives to imitate the success of Harlequin have not always been successful, as evidenced in the failure of Rupa & Co.'s line of local romances in India because part of the appeal of Harlequin romances was the foreignness of the romantic protagonists. Clearly, much more work needs to be done on non-western traditions of romance but, as Daud argues, a foreign form of fiction that was introduced through the global dominance of Harlequin does not remain a homogenized product when it becomes indigenized. Rather, local variations of the popular romance draw on the authors' own culture and traditions to produce new forms of the genre that can reflect resistance to cultural colonization.

Scholarship on romance novels has been around for more than half a century now. Yet in many ways we are still just beginning to develop new approaches to understand and analyze this complex, heterogeneous and endlessly diversifying genre. It is our hope that this volume, Janus-faced, casts a backward look to what has been written, as well as a forward look to the work still to come.

Notes

1 For these and other relevant details about the history of Science Fiction studies see Latham, 1–6.

2 Two essays on Gothic romance predate Snitow's influential study of (non-Gothic) Harlequin romance novels: Joanna Russ's "Somebody's Trying to Kill Me And I Think It's My Husband", and "Beautiful and Damned: The Sexual Woman in Gothic Fiction" by Kay Mussell. Although Angela Toscano's chapter for this volume says that Russ "engages with romance as

literature, naming titles and describing plots" (108), neither she nor Mussell makes any stronger claim on the texts' behalf than we find in Anderson or Snitow.

3 Exceptions to this general rule are discussed in Chapter 13, "Literary approaches."

Works cited

"About Harlequin." *Harlequin* website, https://corporate.harlequin.com/. Accessed 1 August 2018.

"About the Romance Genre." *Romance Writers of America* website, www.rwa.org/Online/Resources/About_Romance_Fiction/Online/Romance_Genre/About_Romance_Genre.aspx?hkey=dc7b967d-d1eb-4101-bb3f-a6cc936b5219. Accessed 26 September 2019.

"Academic Research Grant." *Romance Writers of America* website, www.rwa.org/Online/Awards/Other_RWA_Awards/Academic_Research_Grant/Online/Awards/Academic_Grant.aspx?hkey=be7fd849-eec0-4e48-90c5-21cdb3c20ed9. Accessed 3 January 2020.

Alexander, Alison. *A Mortal Flame: Marie Bjelke Petersen. Australian Romance Writer.* Blubber Head Press, 1994.

Anderson, Rachel. *The Purple Heart Throbs: The Subliterature of Love.* Hodder and Stoughton, 1974.

Bell, Kathleen. "Cross-dressing in Wartime: Georgette Heyer's *The Corinthian* in its 1940 Context." *War Culture: Social Change and Changing Experience in World War Two Britain*, edited by Pat Kirkham and David Thoms. Lawrence and Wishart, 1995, pp. 151–160. Reprinted in *Georgette Heyer: A Critical Retrospective*, edited by Mary Fahnestock-Thomas, Prinny World Press, 2001, pp. 461–472.

Bowman, Barbara., "Victoria Holt's Gothic Romances: A Structuralist Inquiry." *The Female Gothic*, edited by Julian E. Fleenor. Eden Press, 1983, pp. 69–81.

Burge, Amy. *Representing Difference in the Medieval and Modern Orientalist Romance.* Palgrave Macmillan, 2016.

Burley, Stephanie. "Shadows and Silhouettes: The Racial Politics of Category Romance." *Paradoxa: Studies in World Literary Genres*, vol. 5, no. 13–14, 2000, pp. 324–343.

———. "What's a Nice Girl Like You Doing in a Book Like This? Homoerotic Reading and Popular Romance." *Doubled Plots: Romance and History*, edited by Susan Strehle and Mary Paniccia Carden. University Press of Mississippi, 2003, pp. 127–146.

Byatt, A.S. "An Honourable Escape: Georgette Heyer." *Passions of the Mind: Selected Writings.* Vintage International, 1993, pp. 233–240.

Caton, Steven C., "*The Sheik*: Instabilities of Race and Gender in Transatlantic Popular Culture of the Early 1920s." *Noble Dreams, Wicked Pleasures: Orientalism in America, 1870–1930*, edited by Holly Edwards. Princeton University Press, 2000, pp. 99–117.

Cawelti, John G. *Adventure, Mystery, and Romance: Formula Stories as Art and Popular Culture.* University of Chicago Press, 1976.

———. "Masculine Myths and Feminist Revisions: Some Thoughts on the Future of Popular Genres." *Eye on the Future: Popular Culture Scholarship into the Twenty-First Century in Honor of Ray B. Browne*, edited by. Marilyn F. Motz et al. Bowling Green State University Press, 1994, pp. 121–132.

Cheyne, Ria. *Disability, Literature, Genre: Representation and Affect in Contemporary Fiction.* Liverpool University Press, 2019.

Clarke, Patricia. *Rosa! Rosa! A life of Rosa Praed, Novelist and Spiritualist.* Melbourne University Press, 1999.

Cohn, Jan. *Romance and the Erotics of Property.* Duke University Press, 1988.

Crawford, Joseph. *The Twilight of the Gothic? VampireFiction and the Rise of the Paranormal Romance.* University of Wales Press, 2014.

Dandridge, Rita. *Black Women's Activism: Reading African American Women's Historical Romances.* Peter Lang, 2004.

Deller, Ruth A. and Clarissa Smith. "Reading the BDSM romance: Reader responses to Fifty Shades." *Sexualities*, vol. 16, no. 8, 2013, pp. 932–950.

Dixon, jay. *The Romance Fiction of Mills & Boon, 1909–1990s*. University College London Press, 1999.

Driscoll, Catherine., "One True Pairing: The Romance of Pornography and the Pornography of Romance." *Fan Fiction and Fan Communities in the Age of the Internet: New Essays*, edited by Karen Hellekson and Kristina Busse. McFarland, 2006, pp. 79–96.

Evans, Arthur. "Histories." *The Oxford Handbook of Science Fiction*, edited by Rob Latham and Oxford University Press. 2014, 47–58.

Flesch, Juliet. *Love Brought to Book: A Bio-bibliography of 20th-century Australian Romance Novels*. National Centre for Australian Studies, 1995.

———. *From Australia with Love: A History of Modern Australian Popular Romance Novels*. Curtin University Press, 2004.

Fletcher, Lisa. "Historical Romance, Gender and Heterosexuality: John Fowles's *The French Lieutenant's Woman* and A.S. Byatt's *Possession*." *Journal of Interdisciplinary Gender Studies*, vol. 7, no. 1–2, 2003, pp. 26–42.

———. "'Mere Costumery'? Georgette Heyer's Cross-Dressing Novels." *Masquerades: Disguise in English Literature from the Middle Ages to the Present*, edited by Pilar Sánchez Calle and Casellas. Jesús López-Paláez. Gdansk: University of Gdansk Press, 2004, pp. 196–212.

———. *Historical Romance Fiction: Heterosexuality and Performativity*. Aldershot, U.K. Ashgate, 2008.

Foster, Guy Mark, "How Dare a Black Woman Make Love to a White Man! Black Women Romance Novelists and the Taboo of Interracial Desire." *Empowerment versus Oppression: Twenty First Century Views of Popular Romance Novels*, edited by Sally Goade. Cambridge Scholars Publishing, 2007, pp. 103–128.

Fowler, Bridget. *The Alienated Reader: Women and Popular Romantic Literature in the Twentieth Century*. Prentice-Hall, 1991.

Frantz, Sarah S. G. and Eric Murphy Selinger editors. *New Approaches to Popular Romance Fiction: Critical Essays*. McFarland, 2012.

Gardner, Carol Brooks. "Passing By: Street Remarks, Address Rights, and the Urban Female." *Sociological Inquiry*, vol. 50, no. 3–4, 1980, pp. 328–356.

Gelder, Ken and Rachael Weaver. *The Anthology of Colonial Australian Romance Fiction*. Melbourne University Publishing, 2010.

Giles, Fiona. *Too Far Everywhere: The Romantic Heroine in Nineteenth-Century Australia*. University of Queensland Press, 1998.

Gleason, William A. and Eric Murphy Selinger editors. *Romance Fiction and American Culture: Love as the Practice of Freedom?* Ashgate, 2016.

Goris, An. "Matricide in Romance Scholarship? Response to Pamela Regis' Keynote Address at the Second Annual Conference of the International Association for the Study of Popular Romance." *Journal of Popular Romance Studies*, vol. 2, no. 1, 2011, http://jprstudies.org/wp-content/uploads/2011/10/JPRS2.1_Goris_MatricideRomScholarship.pdf.

———. "Happily Ever After... And After: Serialization and the Popular Romance Novel." *Americana: The Journal of American Popular Culture (1900–present)*, vol. 12, no. 1, 2013. http://www.americanpopularculture.com/journal/articles/spring_2013/goris.htm

Haycraft, Howard. *Murder for Pleasure: The Life and Times of the Detective Story*. D. Appleton-Century, 1941.

Hinnant, Charles H., "Desire and the Marketplace: A Reading of Kathleen Woodiwiss's The Flame and the Flower." *Doubled Plots: Romance and History*, edited by Susan Strehle and Mary Paniccia Carden. University Press of Mississippi, 2003, pp. 147–164.

Jackson, Stevi. "Even Sociologists Fall in Love: An Exploration in the Sociology of Emotions." *Sociology*, vol. 27, no. 2, 1993, pp. 201–220.

Krentz, Jayne Ann editors. *Dangerous Men and Adventurous Women: Romance Writers on the Appeal of the Romance*. HarperPaperbacks, 1996.
Latham, Rob., "Introduction." *The Oxford Handbook of Science Fiction*, edited by Rob Latham. Oxford University Press, 2014, pp. 1–18.
Love Between the Covers. Directed by Laurie Kahn. Blueberry Hill Productions, 2015.
Mann, Peter H. *The Romantic Novel: A Survey of Reading Habits*. Mills & Boon, 1969.
———. "The Romantic Novel and Its Readers." *Journal of Popular Culture*, vol. 15, no. 1, 1981, pp. 9–18.
———. "Romantic Fiction and Its Readership." *Poetics*, vol. 14, no. 1–2, 1985, pp. 95–105.
McAleer, Joseph. *Passion's Fortune: The Story of Mills & Boon*. Oxford University Press, 1999.
McAlister, Jodi. "'That Complete Fusion of Spirit as Well as Body': Heroines, Heroes, Desire and Compulsory Demisexuality in the Harlequin Mills & Boon Romance Novel." *Australasian Journal of Popular Culture*, vol. 3, no. 3, 2014, pp. 299–310.
———. "'You and I are Humans, and there is Something Complicated between Us': *Untamed* and Queering the Heterosexual Historical Romance." *Journal of Popular Romance Studies*, vol. 5, no. 2, 2016, http://jprstudies.org/wp-content/uploads/2016/07/YAIAH.07.2016.pdf.
Modleski, Tania. *Loving with a Vengeance: Mass-Produced Fantasies for Women*. Archon, 1982.
———. "My Life as a Romance Reader." *Paradoxa: Studies in World Literary Genres*, vol. 3, no. 1–2, 1997, pp. 15–28.Reprinted in *Old Wives' Tales and Other Women's Stories*. New York University Press, 1998, pp. 47–65.
Most, Glenn W. and William W. Stowe editors. *The Poetics of Murder: Detective Fiction and Literary Theory*. Harcourt Brace Jovanovich, 1983.
Mussell, Kay J. "Beautiful and Damned: The Sexual Woman in Gothic Fiction." *Journal of Popular Culture*, vol. 9, no. 1, 1975, pp. 84–89.
———. *Fantasy and Reconciliation: Contemporary Formulas of Women's Romance Fiction*. Praeger, 1984.
Osborne, Laurie E. "Romancing the Bard." *Shakespeare and Appropriation*, edited by Christy Desmet and Robert Sawyer. Routledge, 1999, pp. 47–64.
———. "Sweet, Savage Shakespeare." *Shakespeare without Class: Misappropriations of Cultural Capital*, edited by Donald Hedrick and Bryan Reynolds. Palgrave, 2000, pp. 135–151.
———. "Harlequin Presents: That '70s Shakespeare and Beyond." *Shakespeare after Mass Media*, edited by Richard Burt. Palgrave, 2002, pp. 127–149.
Paizis, George.*Love and the Novel: The Poetics and Politics of Romantic Fiction*. Basingstoke, Hampshire. Macmillan, 1998.
Parameswaran, Radhika. "Western Romance Fiction as English Language Media in Postcolonial India." *Journal of Communication*, vol. 49, no. 3, 1999, pp. 84–105.
———. "Reading Fictions of Romance: Gender, Sexuality, and Nationalism in Postcolonial India." *Journal of Communication*, vol. 52, no. 4, 2002, pp. 832–851.
Pearce, Lynne. *Romance Writing*. Polity, 2007.
Pearce, Lynne and Jackie Stacey editors. *Romance revisited*. NYU Press, 1995.
Puri, Jyoti. "Reading Romance Novels in Postcolonial India." *Gender and Society*, vol. 11, no. 4, 1997, pp. 434–452.
Radway, Janice. *Reading the Romance: Women, Patriarchy, and Popular Literature*. University of North Carolina Press, 1984.
———. "Romance and the Work of Fantasy: Struggles over Feminine Sexuality and Subjectivity at Century's End." *Viewing, Reading, Listening: Audiences and Cultural Reception*, edited by Jon Cruz and Justin Lewis. Westview Press, 1994, 213–231.
Ramos-Garcia, Maria and Laura Vivanco editors. *Love, Language, Place, and Identity in Popular Culture: Romancing the Other*. Rowman, 2020.
Reardon, B.P. *The Form of the Greek Romance*. Princeton University Press, 1991.
Regis, Pamela. *A Natural History of the Romance Novel*. University of Pennsylvania Press, 2003.

———. "What Do Critics Owe the Romance? Keynote Address at the Second Annual Conference of the International Association for the Study of Popular Romance." *Journal of Popular Romance Studies*, vol. 2, no. 1, 2011, http://jprstudies.org/wp-content/uploads/2011/10/JPRS2.1_Regis_Keynote.pdf.

Roberts, Thomas J. *An Aesthetics of Junk Fiction*. University of Georgia Press, 1990.

Romantic Novelists Association. "About Romantic Fiction." *Romantic Novelists Association Website*. https://romanticnovelistsassociation.org/about-romantic-fiction/. Accessed 18 September 2019.

Russ, Joanna. "Somebody's Trying to Kill Me and I Think It's My Husband: The Modern Gothic." *The Journal of Popular Culture*, vol. 6, no. 4, 1973, pp. 666–691.

Shumway, David R. *Modern Love: Romance, Intimacy, and the Marriage Crisis*. New York University Press, 2003.

Snitow, Ann Barr. "Mass Market Romance: Pornography for Women is Different." *Radical History Review*, no. 20, 1979, pp. 141–161.

Teo, Hsu-Ming. *Desert Passions: Orientalism and Romance Novels*. University of Texas Press, 2012.

———. "Imperial Affairs: Colonialism, Race and the Early Twentieth-Century Romance Novel." *New Directions in Popular Fiction: Genre, Distribution, Reproduction*, edited by Ken Gelder. Palgrave Macmillan, 2016, pp. 87–110.

Thomas, Glen J., "Romance: The Perfect Creative Industry? A Case Study of Harlequin-Mills and Boon Australia." *Empowerment versus Oppression: Twenty-First Century Views of Popular Romance Novels*, edited by Sally Goade. Cambridge Scholars Publishing, 2007, pp. 20–29.

Thomas, Glen J. and Bridie James, "The Romance Industry: A Study of Reading and Writing Romance." *The reinvention of everyday life: Culture in the twenty-first century*, edited by Howard McNaughton and Adam Lam. Canterbury University Press, 2006, pp. 164–174.

Thurston, Carol. *The Romance Revolution: Erotic Novels for Women and the Quest for a New Sexual Identity*. University of Illinois Press, 1987.

Vivanco, Laura. *For Love and Money: The Literary Art of the Harlequin Mills & Boon Romance*. Humanities E-books, 2011.

Wardrop, Stephanie. "Last of the Red Hot Mohicans: Miscegenation in the Popular American Romance." *Melus*, vol. 22, no. 2, 1997, pp. 61–74.

"Welcome to HER." *History, Exoticism, Romance website*. http://her.uib.es/. Accessed 20 September 2019.

Westman, Karin E., "A Story of Her Weaving: The Self-Authoring Heroines of Georgette Heyer's Regency Romance." *Doubled Plots: Romance and History. Doubled Plots: Romance and History*, edited by Susan Strehle and Mary Paniccia Carden. University Press of Mississippi, 2003, pp. 165–184.

Wilkins, Kim, Beth Driscoll and Lisa Fletcher. "What is Australian Popular Fiction?" *Australian Literary Studies*, special issue on *Genre Worlds: Popular Fiction in the Twenty-First Century*, vol. 33, no. 4, 2018, www-australianliterarystudies-com-au.simsrad.net.ocs.mq.edu.au/articles/what-is-australian-popular-fiction. Accessed 20 September 2019.

Part I

National traditions

1 History of English romance novels, 1621–1975

jay Dixon

Romance is one of the oldest and most enduring literary modes (Radford 8). As Hall says, "The history of the romance novel might begin as early as the first century CE, with Chariton of Aphrodisias's prose romance, *Chaereas and Callirhoe*, the earliest surviving ancient Greek novel." That said, the romance novel is notoriously difficult to define (Saunders 1–2; see also Fuchs) because "romance" means different things to different readers in different periods. In the early years of fiction writing "romance" was used interchangeably with "novel." However, Clara Reeve, herself the author of romances, and the first Englishwoman to write a history of romances, argues in *The Progress of Romance* (1785) that there is a distinction between the "novel," which depicts everyday life, and "romance," which is a more elevated form concerned with high emotion, and past times. A century later, "romance" became linked with male adventure novels. As Judith Wilt says romance can be a story foregrounding inventiveness, fabulation, and "the marvelous"; or a story about the quest for the ideal or heroic; or a story of lovers (vi; see also Beer; Radford).[1]

In the mid-nineteenth century, after Charlotte M. Yonge's bestselling novel *The Heir of Redclyffe* (1853) inspired other writers such as Rhoda Broughton and Mary Elizabeth Braddon to write novels about English heroes and heroines who fall in love and experience internal and external opposition to the consummation of their love, romances were just as likely to end in a tragic parting of the lovers through death as in their marriage. A happy ending was not always assured, nor did readers in the nineteenth and early twentieth century require one.

However, between the ending of the First World War and the start of the Second, the meanings of "romance" and "romantic" as "terms of literary description became more narrowly specialised and signified only those love stories which … end happily in marriage" (Light 160).

In this chapter, I use the term "romance(s)" as a general term for any novel whose foremost concern is a love relationship between the main protagonists: fiction in which the relationship between hero and heroine is paramount, and other types of plot—crime, science fiction—are subordinate to the main relationship. Those stories with a happy ending I refer to as "romance novel" and I use the term "romance fiction" for those that, in today's terms, do not. I concentrate on that fiction written mainly by women, for women, and from the woman's point of view.

This chapter is about both contemporary and historical English (not British) romances. That is, it talks about only those romances set in England, and it ignores those set in the other countries of the United Kingdom and, with one or two exceptions, those written by non-English authors, as Ireland, Scotland, and Wales have a different history and thus, in many respects, a different set of concerns and attitudes. The introduction is followed by a history of contemporary romances (that is, those romances written during the period they are set in) from the beginnings in the seventeenth century to 1975. This also includes positive criticisms of romances. Next comes a history of negative criticism of romance fiction during roughly the same period. The subsequent section is a history of the English historical novel (that is, those romances written at least 50 years after the period they are set in), again followed by a history of criticism. Each section has sub-sections describing the sub-genres prevalent in a certain period.

Contemporary romance before the nineteenth century: the beginnings

When Lady Mary Wroth published a prose romance, *The Countess of Montgomerie's Urania*, in 1621 she was criticized, not so much for writing it, but because she published it. This was in an era when women were meant to be "seen but not heard," and by publishing her novel Wroth brought public attention to herself, and was excoriated for it (Hannay).

Urania is generally acknowledged as the first romance novel in English (Hannay; Lamb; Miller and Waller). It is a radical work, in that it argues against patriarchal rules for women and marriage, by depicting love and marriage from the woman's point of view.

Wroth wrote *Urania* to try and get herself out of debt. She was influenced by her aunt, Mary Sidney, Countess of Pembroke, who was one of the first women to publish her own literary works. The niece of Sir Philip Sidney, Wroth used his *Arcadia* as one of the sources for her own novel. It tells the story of Queen Pamphilia and Emperor Amphilanthus, who are cousins, intertwined with hundreds of sub-plots concerning their siblings and others. None end happily, including the love story of the main characters, as Amphilanthus is constantly unfaithful.

Wroth had to withdraw her book due to the scandal it caused, as it was widely thought to reference her own life, in particular her love for, and her adulterous affair with, her cousin William Herbert, Pembroke's son. Although this first English romance contains few of the tropes to be found in later romances, it has two major similarities to later romance novels: its author was following in the footsteps of another woman's publications, and it is the first literary endeavor to tell its story from a woman's point of view.

Unlike Wroth, an aristocrat, Aphra Behn (1640?–89) was born in obscurity but became the first Englishwoman to earn her living by her pen, becoming a literary model for later female writers (Todd 2017).[2] She wrote poetry, plays, and novels, the best-known of which is *Oroonoko* (1688). Written from the point of view of an unnamed female narrator, it is the story of a captured slave (Oroonoko), whom the narrator claims to have met, and his love for fellow captive Imoinda. Both Oroonoko and Imoinda are dead by the end of the novel. This is hardly the "happy ever after" (HEA) ending we expect from romances these days. But many English romances up to the later nineteenth century were to end with the death of the hero for, as Anderson says, a tragic ending which parted the lovers could be satisfying for readers because "traditionally, the truest, purest romantic love is a fatal love" (26).

Behn's earlier epistolary novel, *Love Letters Between a Nobleman and His Sister*, originally published in three separate volumes between 1684 and 1687, is of more interest for the history of romances. This is because it has many of the tropes that later romances used, although at this time the romance genre did not adhere necessarily to the conventions that we, in the twenty-first century, expect from a romance. Famously, Janice Radway in her *Reading the Romance* (1984) set out 13 points of narrative structure necessary for an "ideal romance" (134). It starts with (point 1) the destruction of the heroine's social identity, and (point 2) the heroine reacting antagonistically to an aristocratic male, who (point 3) responds ambiguously to the heroine. In point 4 "the heroine interprets the hero's behavior as evidence of a purely sexual interest in her" (i.e., he does not love her), to which she responds (point 5) with coldness and anger. The hero reacts to this by punishing her (point 6). In point 7 the protagonists are separated, either physically or emotionally. Then the hero treats the heroine tenderly (point 8), and she responds warmly (point 9), leading her to "reinterpret the hero's ambiguous behavior as the product of previous hurt" (point 10), so when he "openly declares his love for [and] unwavering commitment to" her (point 11), she can respond "sexually and emotionally" (point 12). In point 13 the heroine's identity is restored.[3]

Although she was analyzing twentieth-century mass-market historical romances, this 13-part summary of an ideal romance applies to many English romances, and certain aspects of it can be seen in the first two parts of Behn's romance. The first part is the story of the seduction of Silvia by her brother-in-law Philander. As this was considered to be incest at this time, Behn here is being courageous on two fronts—not condemning the lovers for their illegal affair, and not blaming her immoral hero for seducing the heroine. Instead she celebrates the passion of the lovers and the courage of Silvia in standing up to her father, to convention and to society.[4]

In the second part Silvia disguises herself as a young man and she, her husband, and her lover flee to Holland. Silvia develops a fever, her true sex is discovered, and Philander is forced to leave her to avoid being arrested. Unknown to Silvia, Philander and his two male friends agree that Silvia will join him once she has recovered. But the friends play him false, and Silvia thinks Philander no longer loves her. She attempts suicide. Having been saved from death, Silvia decides to exact revenge on Philander by marrying his best friend, Octavio, despite the fact that she is already married. This part ends with her setting off to her wedding with Octavio. The third part becomes very complicated, and rather loses sight of the love relationships. But, as is evident from the above outline, the second part contains many of the features that Radway outlines: the destruction of the heroine's identity (both through an adulterous and illegal seduction and by her male attire) at the start; then the separation of the lovers and Silvia deciding Philander no longer loves her (points 4 and 7); her attempted suicide (another form of separation); followed by her resolution to take revenge on Philander (point 5). The ending of marriage restores her social identity (point 13). However, this marriage is not to the hero, who has proved unworthy of the heroine as he is not faithful to her (hence his name), which is contrary to our twenty-first-century expectations.

These days it is unusual for the hero and heroine not to come together at the end of a romance, but in earlier periods the convention had not been established. Pamela Regis, however, in *A Natural History of the Romance Novel* (2003) upholds the convention, arguing that there are eight narrative elements of a romance all of which must be present but which can appear in any order:

(i) the initial state of society in which the hero and heroine must court
(ii) the meeting
(iii) the barrier to their love
(iv) an account of the protagonists' attraction
(v) the recognition that fells the barrier
(vi) a point of ritual death
(vii) the declaration of love
(viii) and the betrothal

(30)

Again, most of these can be seen in *Love Letters*. Behn's novel also contains some plot points which are common to romances of the twentieth century, in particular the heroine dressing as a male (or being taken for a boy), and a marriage of convenience.[5]

Behn herself was attacked for lewdness in her writings, and in her plays *The Dutch Lover* (1673) and *Sir Patient Fancy* (1678), and she protested against the double standards for male and female playwrights and defended her right to write as freely as any man. Even so, until the twentieth century her reputation was one of scandal and her writings seen as indecent. But Virginia Woolf, in *A Room of One's Own*, pointed out that she paved the way for other female writers, who could claim that they also would be able to earn a living by their pen (see also Roach).

It was not until the late eighteenth century that the English novel, and the literary romance, really started, when the size of the reading public started to grow and, due to increased literacy, moved down the classes and across the gender divide, and romances emerged as a genre of popular fiction for women readers.

It used to be generally acknowledged that Samuel Richardson was the first English author to write a romance: *Pamela, Or Virtue Rewarded*, published in 1740. Richardson does seem to have set the structural style for later romances, by concentrating on the courtship plot. However, it is now agreed that, although he was the first bestseller (Regis 63), he was standing on the shoulders of many previous women authors. Indeed, the eighteenth century saw an influx of women readers and writers, which caused some men to use female pseudonyms in order to get published (MacCarthy 289). As Dale Spender argues,

> women did not imitate men; it was quite the reverse; many women seized upon women's novels as an entry to a new dimension of understanding ... for so many women these novels meant access to the world of ideas, to self-analysis and social issues.
>
> (5)

Two of the authors were Elizabeth Rowe and Susannah Dobson. Elizabeth Rowe (1674–1737) was a poet, essayist, and novelist. She published two epistolary novels—*Friendship in Death, in Twenty Letters from the Dead to the Living* (in 1728) and *Letters Moral and Entertaining* (in three parts between 1729 and 1732) (Backscheider). Not romances, these novels provided Richardson with the epistolary idea he uses in *Pamela* (1740). Susannah Dobson, who died in 1795, published translations of French works, including Sainte-Palaye's *Memoirs of Ancient Chivalry* (1784) for which she wrote a preface that defends romance writers and stresses medieval chivalry toward women. Her translations made significant contributions to the revival and rehabilitation of romance (Berg; Blain, Clements, and Grundy).

Eliza Haywood (1693–1756) wrote amatory fiction: an "explicitly amorous, politically engaged, and fantasy-oriented" genre of British fiction popular during the late seventeenth and early eighteenth centuries which is generally acknowledged as the precursor of today's romance fiction (Ballaster 10; see also Baldus; Benedict; Bowers; Hultquist; Lutz; Vivanco). These romances were popular from roughly 1660 to 1730 and are narrated from the woman's point of view. Heywood published over 70 works during her lifetime, including fiction, drama, translations, poetry, conduct literature, and periodicals. Her first novel, *Love in Excess; Or, the Fatal Enquiry*, published 1719–20, is in three parts, and set in France and Italy. It is the story of Count D'Elmont, a rake, who is eventually reformed through loving a woman. Many of Haywood's subsequent novels end either with the death of the heroine, or her incarceration in a nunnery. But in the working out of the plot, Haywood depicts heroines who act on their own desire for a man, and she shows in the endings how women are silenced by society. Her later novels, for instance *Betsy Thoughtless*, where the heroine learns that women can find happiness in marriage, moved toward what became the popular domestic novel of the nineteenth century.

Amatory fiction, however, had brought to prominence the romance novel's themes of the conflict for women between public behavior and individual yearning, and the role they are forced to take on by society, irrespective of their own needs and desire. This is particularly evident in Frances Burney's novel, *Evelina* (1778), where a sensitive, young, middle-class heroine, with a sharp eye for the mores of society, eventually, through various courtship trials, is able to marry the man she loves, having rejected the man who romantically harasses her. This "other man" conforms to the conventional romantic suitor, but Evelina sees that the "passionate, romantic man is dangerous in that he physically and sexually violates the autonomy of woman" (Forbes 299; Doody; Rogers). Instead, she marries the man whom she loves as a brother.

This theme of a brother-protector being the ideal man is repeated in Charlotte Smith's *Emmeline* (1788), where the heroine marries the brother of her closest female friend. I have argued elsewhere that the hero-as-brother is also a trope of twentieth-century romances (Dixon) but as the earlier romances were written during the period of "the cult of sensibility," when it was believed that people were innately good and approval was given to a hero who exhibited "almost" a feminine sensibility (Tompkins, qtd. in Modleski 17), it can be argued that the hero as brother can also be seen as the feminization of the hero, a theme which is also prevalent in some twentieth-century romances, particularly in those published by Mills & Boon (Harlequin),where the hero eventually succumbs to the heroine, leaving her triumphant.[6]

These novels strike a new note in romances, as they combine a love relationship with a novel of manners, but at the same time there were other sub-genres being written, in particular the Gothic romance and the domestic novel.[7]

Contemporary romance in the nineteenth century: the Gothic, domestic novels of manners, and novels of sensation

From the 1790s to about the 1820s the Gothic romance was a mainstream of English fiction, read by both men and women. Its plot centered round a virginal heroine who has to fight for her virtue against the man who should have her best interests at heart (generally her guardian) before she can find and marry the man who will protect her. Gothic novels are set in an "unreal world of fantastic happenings" (Terry 50), generally abroad, in turreted castles where eerie events take place. In 1938 Daphne du Maurier published *Rebecca*, which helped to revive the popularity of the Gothic novel after the Second World War (for an extended discussion of the Gothic and its influence on modern popular romance fiction see Chapter 4 of this volume).

For romance readers the towering author of the early nineteenth century is Jane Austen, whose early novel *Northanger Abbey* (completed in 1803, although not published until 1817) satirizes the Gothic while offering an ardent defense of the novel as a genre.[8] Austen's novels portray the main protagonists' growth in self-knowledge through their developing love relationship. Her novels were not bestsellers at the time, but Sir Walter Scott praised their realism, an assessment followed by other nineteenth-century literary critics, including George Lewes (George Eliot's partner) and Henry James. It was not until the twentieth century that she became a world-wide phenomenon.

Jane Austen was part of the rise of the domestic novel of manners (Spacks), which idealized the domestic sphere. This genre was influenced by Maria Edgeworth, who wrote about family life and women's search for equality in marriage. Her novels *Belinda* (1801) and *Patronage* (1814) are about women's search for a compatible marriage, extolling love over duty and reason, a theme also present in Austen's best-loved novel, *Pride and Prejudice* (1813), though handled rather differently.

The domestic novel of manners can be divided into three subgenres: governess novels, the prime example of which is Charlotte Bronte's *Jane Eyre*, 1847 (see Wadső-Lecaros), which are often seen as the precursors of today's category romances;[9] social problem novels, the best example being Elizabeth Gaskell's *North and South*, 1854–5 (Kestner; Vargo; Williams); and religious novels, exemplified by Charlotte Yonge's *The Heir of Redclyffe* (Anderson). These religion-based romances all ended, to today's mind, unhappily, with the hero dying, but at the time the emphasis was on the struggle between faith and doubt, and when the hero dies *as a Christian* it is seen in the novel as a triumph, not a defeat.[10]

Many romances of the mid-Victorian period follow this religious tradition. *Robert Elsmere* (1888) by the popular author Mrs. Humphrey Ward (niece of Matthew Arnold), is about a clergyman who loses his faith when confronted with scientific evidence but recovers it under the influence of his wife before he dies from overwork. Ward portrayed men as intellectually superior to women, but the "emotional register resides within the heroine, Catherine, and her sister, Rose" (Hipsky 32; see also Daly; Terry; Waller). In Rhoda Broughton's *Not Wisely But Too Well* (1867), which has an adulterous relationship at its core, both the villain and the hero die at the end, and the heroine continues doing good works in the slums of London.

In a twist on this ending, in *Under Two Flags* (1867) by Ouida (Maria Louise Ramé), it is the heroine who dies, saving the hero from a firing squad, and he returns to his first love. However, this is not a religiously themed romance, and is more of a male adventure story, despite being written by a woman. Ouida's later 1880 novel, *Moths*, is another adulterous romance, but this time, although the hero is shot, he survives and he and the heroine are able to marry, and the novel is less focused on adventure than on an indictment of contemporary society "for its artificiality, hypocrisy, cruelty, and immorality" (Schroeder 21). Similar plot elements, that is to say, were repurposed to serve quite different ends, evincing the flexibility and variety of the romance during this period.

Many romances published during the nineteenth century can be regarded as domestic novels, particularly those by Margaret Oliphant and Elizabeth Gaskell. These romances sentimentalize the duties of the good wife and faithful daughter while, Modleski argues, revealing a covert longing for power and revenge (24). Issues of power are sometimes quite explicitly on display in the contrasting sub-genre of sensation novels, which started with Wilkie Collins' *The Woman in White* (1860), Ellen Wood's *East Lynne* (1861), and Mary Elizabeth Braddon's *Lady Audley's Secret* (1862), a novel which, Jenny Uglow argues, "uncovered horrors in the very heart of Victorian society, in the sacred institution of marriage itself" (qtd. in Callil 5).

Sensation novels reveled in accounts of insanity, illness, identity-theft, and long-held family secrets, exposing the uncertainties rife in the nineteenth century. The heroine of *The Woman in White*, for example, is forced to marry a man she does not love and then incarcerated in a lunatic asylum under someone else's name. Eventually her husband dies in a fire of his own making and her true identity is restored, enabling her to marry the man she loves. In Ellen Wood's *East Lynne*, the heroine commits adultery, is thrown out of the family home and is disfigured in a railway crash, enabling her to return to the family home in disguise to care for her children. She eventually dies, confessing all to her husband on her death bed. *Lady Audley's Secret* centers on an adulterous relationship, entered into unwittingly by Sir Michael Audley when he marries Lucy Graham. Good ultimately triumphs, with Lucy (the villainess of the title) dying in an institution for the insane and thus enabling the other main characters to marry. "Hinting at shaky moral foundations beneath rock-like respectability, and at undercurrents of violence, greed, or sexual betrayal in every home sweet home," Braddon's novels "threatened the values the reviewers held most dear" (Uglow qtd. in Callil 5). One of the tropes Braddon uses is the beautiful temptress threatening the happiness of the heroine, the good woman, a trope that became a staple of later romances; likewise, her use of "domestic circumstances as the setting for intrigue, secrets, violence and death" makes her work a precursor of modern gothic romances such as du Maurier's *Rebecca* and *My Cousin Rachel* (Callil and Tóibín).

The end of the nineteenth century saw the rise of the New Woman, and a different type of heroine. New Woman novels built on the anxiety about the home that sensation novels had displayed by openly critiquing domesticity and marriage, recasting the home as corrupt, not pure and spiritual as earlier domestic novels had idealized it (Katz 44). These novels upset the domestic ideal of women, portraying women walking alone on the street, reading what they wanted, and refusing to marry. Authors included Sarah Grand, Mona Caird, George Egerton (Mary Bright), and Ella D'Arcy, whose novels emphasized women's freedom and right to live life as they wished to: themes which endure in modern popular romance.

Contemporary romance in the twentieth century

According to R. C. Terry, Victorian authors and artists from a wide range of genres and movements generally agreed that "a visionary world of action, heroism, spiritual revelation and fulfilment made more tolerable a world of sordid gain, intractable social problems and the widespread malaise of religious schism or, worse, no religion at all"

(21). This *zeitgeist* may have been shaken by the end of the nineteenth century, but it endured in popular romance. Marie Corelli's many bestselling novels, for example, "mingled romantic love with Christian spirituality, featured all manner of celestial voyaging, and hummed with affective intensities" even as her protagonists offered "streams of opinion on the urgent social issues of the moment" (Hipsky 65). Corelli often combined mysticism with science to make sweeping pronouncements about the meaning of life, and as a rule her plots and characters are secondary to her opinions on whatever she is inveighing against in the novel—the Press and sexual novels (*The Sorrows of Satan* 1895), drunken fathers (*Boy* 1900), religious hypocrisy (*The Master Christian* 1900), and the dangers of secular humanism (*Innocent: Her Fancy and His Fact* 1914).[11]

Another bestselling author who combined romance with religion—and, unlike Corelli, combined the two with a gripping plot—was Florence Barclay. Barclay's *The Rosary*, published in 1909, presents earthly love as a manifestation of divine love: a connection of the earthly and the sacred which has to be acknowledged by both lovers for the plot to be resolved (Waller). Bloom argues that Barclay's novels are "Christianized" morality tales which are "contemporary in theme (in attitude) and *consolatory* in times of confusion or trouble" (88), and that we see in them the roots of "a thousand Mills and Boon romances" (88). For more on Barclay, see Chapter 21 of this collection.

The novels of Ethel M. Dell combine a semi-religious background with Ouida's imperial adventure romances.[12] Her first novel, *The Way of an Eagle* (1911) is set in India, with a feminine heroine and an alpha male who, like many of Dell's heroes, is ugly-looking but a protector, rescuing the heroine from native uprisings and loving her from afar until she eventually realizes his worth and falls in love with him.

Alongside this new wave of religious romantic fiction, the domestic novel remained popular in the early twentieth century. In 1914 Berta Ruck, who wrote domestic novels aimed at the young working-class woman, published her first novel *His Official Fiancée*, which had first been serialized in the magazine *Home Chat*. The story of a girl who marries her employer, this novel was a hit with the public, and was the forerunner of the Cinderella plot which many later romances were to follow. By the time of her death in 1978, Ruck had written over 100 novels, most about the quest for love by a young girl (Anderson; Blain, Clements, and Grundy).[13]

One hallmark of contemporary romance in the twentieth century is the emergence of more explicitly sexual romances, where love is based on a sexual attraction which is described, rather than implied.[14] In Elinor Glyn's *Three Weeks* (1907), which Martin Hipsky reads as a "further development of the 'New Woman' novel" (16), the hero has a three-week sexual encounter with the queen of an Eastern European country which results in his son being crowned king.

Perhaps the most well-known romance of the early twentieth century is *The Sheik* (1919), by E. M. Hull, which is a prime example of the dangerous lover novel of the twentieth century: "the one whose eroticism lies in his dark past, his restless inquietude, his remorseful and rebellious exile from comfortable everyday living" (Lutz ix, 89). *The Sheik* recounts the story of an upper-class Englishwoman who, while traveling in the Sahara Desert, is abducted by a handsome Bedouin sheik with whom she falls in love, despite being repeatedly raped by him. The brutish hero eventually learns to love her self-sacrificially, while she in turn discovers at the end of the novel that he is not Arab after all but, rather, the half-Spanish son of a Scottish earl. In a reversal of Radway's point 13 regarding the restoration of the heroine's identity by the hero, here it is the heroine who returns the hero to his real racial identity (Hipsky 190). Pamela Regis notes that "*The Sheik* is the ur-twentieth-century popular romance novel" (120) for several reasons. It was the first romance to tell the story almost entirely from the heroine's viewpoint, and to cut away extraneous subplots to focus on the emotional relationship between the hero and heroine. It was also a precursor of romance novels that would explore women's sexual experiences of romantic love and interracial relationships (see Teo). For these reasons, *The Sheik* has generated a wealth of scholarship examining these and other aspects of the novel, including its medieval antecedents and contemporary manifestations in the form of late twentieth- and twenty-first-century "sheik romances" (see Ardis; Bach; Blake; Burge; Chow; Gargano; Holden; Jarmakani; Melman; Raub; Taylor; Teo *Desert Passions* 2012b).

In *Women and the Popular Imagination in the Twenties* Billie Melman describes the rise of the "sex novel" in the 1920s, which she argues presents realistic descriptions of women's sexual experience (42). Beauman also discusses the rise of the sexual novel in the 1920s in her chapter on romance. Melman points out that many of the novels of this period were sadomasochistic (45), even though written by women (Dell, Glyn, Hull) for women. This was a period of sexual liberation for women, and sadomasochism arose again in the novels of the 1970s, when women's sexual freedom was again to the fore (Dixon).

Mills & Boon

The 1930s saw the rise of the mass-market formula romance, when Mills & Boon became a romance-only publisher (see Dixon; Jensen; McAleer; Modleski). Mills & Boon had already published widely in the genre in previous decades, and their pre-1930s romances can be divided into four subgenres—those with city backgrounds, those with country backgrounds, those set abroad and those set among the upper-crust of English society (Dixon 43–63). The city and country novels are in the tradition of the domestic romance, but the other two are more sexual, and these more sexual novels continued into the 1920s, echoing the popularity of sex novels in the mainstream.[15]

Many authors got their start with Mills & Boon (although not Barbara Cartland as is sometimes alleged). Denise Robins, who was the first President of the Romantic Novelists' Association, joined them in 1927, after ten years of successfully publishing elsewhere, but left in 1935. While at Mills & Boon she wrote rather provocative novels, with sexual themes which included adultery. But the most popular author of the 1930s, Mary Burchell, wrote more domestic-set romances, although she tackled some controversial subjects—the heroine having a baby out of wedlock (*Such is Love* 1939), married women working (*After Office Hours* 1939)—which were to become themes of later Mills & Boon romances (Dixon).

At first the Second World War was not mentioned in Mills & Boon romances, but as the war continued, both Mills & Boon authors and other authors of romances took one of two approaches to the conflict—they either ignored it altogether (e.g., Ruby M. Ayres) or used soldiers as heroes, and put their heroines in uniform, though they did not describe the real horrors of war (e.g., Ursula Bloom). The latter novels were set overseas or the home front, with the more independent heroine saving the day for Britain (McAleer 174).[16] According to Anderson, however, by the end of the 1940s,

> war had finally killed off any of the last remaining traces of the reckless spirit of E M Hull and E M Dell, or Elinor Glyn. Heroines were never again to know the wild sweet joy of mad, passionate love. Such experiences began to be classed out of romantic fiction and into pornography. From this point on, the aim of popular romantic novelists was to make their fiction respectable, in both the literary and the moral sense. In the attempt it began to lose much of its earlier vigour.
>
> (223)

To Anderson, the post-war history of Mills & Boon romance is one of decline. "By the end of the 1950s the romantic hero and heroine were becoming increasingly stereotyped," she writes (237), reflecting post-war attitudes, and despite the glamour provided by setting romances abroad in the 1960s, a set of strict taboos ruled Mills & Boon romances throughout the decade: no mixed marriages, no drunkenness, no disability, as romance championed domestic and bourgeois values in the face of the emerging counterculture (Anderson 267, 270). "Today's romantic novelists," she writes in 1974, "have come to see themselves as a restraining, conservative element in society, upholders of proper standards of public morality. No longer pioneers, they have become the curators of a tradition" (276–7). Indeed, she predicts the end of romantic novels, since romantic fiction "will only continue to be an interesting genre if its authors can rediscover a passionate belief in their convictions, the total commitment to dotty ideals which once gave to that inimitable prose style its power, emotional drive and luxuriant vitality" (277) which she thought would not happen.

More recent historians have read this period differently. Even during the 1950s there were some Mills & Boon authors who were beginning to blow away the cobwebs and write about more adventurous and intelligent heroines (Dixon 124ff), and a variety of new hero types emerged as well, as the "boy next door" hero popular in the mid-to-late 1940s (Dixon 70) was supplemented, then largely replaced by "rough and rugged, aggressively masculine" men from the colonies and former colonies (e.g., Australia) and by Spanish, French, Greek, Italian, or other "Latin lover" figures (Teo *Desert Passions* 204–5). (These are also the years, Teo points out, when the Sheik hero is revived in Mills & Boon fiction, [204].) After the 1950s women started to be depicted as being in command of their lives, with many heroines in the 1960s portrayed as "economically independent and emotionally no longer tied to home, with a job she does competently and confidently" (Dixon 90). In these novels the focus is more on the emotional elements of the hero's and heroine's relationship, and the "mingling of sex, work and female equality in the name of 'freedom' that was a hallmark of the emerging counterculture" was increasingly evident (Dixon 127). Far from bringing the story of contemporary romance to a close, then, the 1970s brought about a resurgence of the genre, fueled by new, younger, authors and by feminism. The 1970s was a period of rapid change which, Beer (78) argues, is when romances flourish. Indeed, the following chapters in this volume discussing subgenres and thematic innovations focus on developments within the romance genre from the 1970s onwards—including the Americanization of the romance novel.

Serious novelists on "silly novels"

From the beginning, the romance novel has been criticized as well as defended, not only by literary reviewers, critics, and scholars, but also by novelists. One of the earliest books to satirize the romance genre was Charlotte Lennox's *The Female Quixote* of

1752, which also "inaugurates within the English novel tradition the inherent relationship between heroines and romance" (Langbauer 62). A re-writing of Miguel de Cervantes' *Don Quixote* (1605 and 1615) it tells the story of Arabella, who expects life to be like the French romances she has been brought up on, but who eventually accepts the reality of life and marries the man who has loved her all along. Lennox explores the clash between the romance genre and realism, a theme of romance criticism from the beginning, and one which has often been interwoven with issues of gender. (As Crawford observes, "the eighteenth-century novel tradition ... often went to some lengths to demonstrate that an overly 'romantic' view of the world, and of love, could lead young people—especially young women—very dangerously astray" [14].) Although *The Female Quixote* has often been read along these lines as endorsing the emerging, more realistic discourse of the novel as preferable to the misleading extravagance of romance, recent scholarship has sometimes seen Lennox as "reversing the contemporary opinion that romances teach nothing" in order to critique the limitations imposed by realism (Watson 32). "More than a late attack on romance," Watson writes, *The Female Quixote* "is an early landmark in thinking about how realistic discourse represents reality and interprets desire" (32).

In 1785, some 30 years after Lennox's *The Female Quixote*, novelist Clara Reeve published *The Progress of Romance*, a history of romance and its reputation. "Nearly a novel in itself" (Maxwell 8), this literary history is presented as a debate between Euphrasia and her male antagonist Hortensius, with Sophronia as judge; across the text Euphrasia's knowledge is set against Hortensius' eloquence. Reeve argues, through Euphrasia, that male critics are prejudiced against not only the genre of romance—here defined as a "wild, extravagant, Fabulous story" (vol. 1, 6)—but also its female authors and readers. Praising by name a number of authors discussed in this chapter, including Behn and Heywood, the book is thus "not only concerned with the status and history of romance, it also touches upon attitudes towards literature and upon gender questions" (Omdal 2013). Ros Ballaster argues that *The Progress of Romance* is signally important for its early effort to describe and contest an "association between the 'literary' and the masculine, and the 'popular' and the feminine" (191). As Euphrasia ably refutes Hortensius's charge that romance is simply "trash" (vol. 1, 6), Reeve presents romance as a "formidable, praiseworthy body of writing" (Maxwell 9) and she implicitly defends her own decision to write in the genre, for example in her Gothic novel *The Old English Baron* (1777).

A hundred years later, the reputation of romance remained in dispute. George Eliot belittled popular romantic fiction by women in her 1856 article "Silly Novels by Lady Novelists," where she argued that many female authors are writing such an idealized version of the world that the romances become "silly." Ignoring the critiquing of domesticity and marriage in these stories she concentrates on other aspects of the novels. She particularly decries the perfect heroines these novels describe:

> her eyes and her wit are both dazzling; her nose and her morals alike free from any tendency to irregularity; she has a superb *contralto* and a superb intellect; she is perfectly well-dressed and perfectly religious; she dances like a sylph.
>
> (140; see Roberts' *Silly Lady Novelists?* for a modern reply to this argument)

Instead she praises the realism of literary novels (such as her own).

Four years after Eliot's essay, David Manon published "Three Vices of Current Literature" in *Macmillan's Magazine* in May 1860. In it he criticized the awkward syntax, mixed metaphor, slipshod expression, and triteness in fact, doctrine and thought to be found in popular novels, which, according to him, were full of "extravagant scene-painting, grandiose character description and elaborate effects" (qtd. in Terry 53).

In 1922 Rebecca West attacked romances, echoing the critiques of their style and substance of Eliot and Manon but slightly altering the underlying criticism by concentrating on the lack of *thought* that was purportedly needed to write them. Using Dell's novels as representative she says of one of Dell's heroes:

> And in every line that is written about him one hears the thudding, thundering hooves of a certain steed at full gallop; of the true Tosh-horse ... one cannot reach the goal of best selling by earnest pedestrianism, but must ride thither on the Tosh-horse. No one can write a best-seller by taking thought.
>
> ("The Tosh Horse")

West, a feminist herself, was articulating feminist writers' disapproval of romances, which they believed belonged to childhood and the teenage years and which they thought perpetuated gender stereotypes (Trodd 120).

In *Fiction and the Reading Public* (1932), Q. D. Leavis wanted to explore why serious fiction and the bestseller had been split apart with, for example, Henry James and Marie Corelli having radically different readerships. Like her early mentor, Leslie Stephen, she believed that literature was "the product of the interplay between writer and reader." So, it was always important to Q. D. Leavis to analyze even the best novels with a full awareness of their socio-historical context (Ferns). Like her predecessors Leavis argues that authors of romances seem to lack education, but unlike them, she admires the energy of popular writing, in which "bad writing, false sentiment, sheer silliness, and a preposterous narrative are all carried along with magnificent vitality" (qtd. in Anderson 15).[17]

Leavis was not a novelist, and her engagement with popular fiction coincides with the emergence of a new, professionalized mode of academic literary criticism. The sometimes contentious relationship between such criticism and the genre of popular romance is described, from a variety of angles, in many other chapters in this collection. The treatment of popular romance by post-war English novelists in other genres, both literary and popular, is in need of further study, both in terms of the contemporary romances I have discussed thus far and in terms of historical romance fiction, a genre which pre-exists and often blurs the distinction between literary, middlebrow, and popular forms.

English historical romances[18]

The English historical romance has several sub-genres, including what is now called fictional biography, which is generally about the love lives of royalty, or well-known figures from the past, and family sagas, where the protagonists are generally fictional, and the story chronicles the lives of one or more families over a period of time. Margaret Irwin and Jean Plaidy (Eleanor Hibbert) are two of the best-known authors of fictional biography. Eleanor Hibbert was one of the authors who revived the Gothic in the 1960s, writing as Victoria Holt, and also wrote family sagas as Philippa Carr. The family saga sub-genre includes Storm Jameson's *The Triumph of Time* (1927–30) about a nineteenth-century shipbuilding family based on her own family, Clemence Dane's (Winifred Ashton) *Broome Stages* (1931), which follows a family from strolling players in the eighteenth century to film stars of the 1920s; and Phyllis Bentley's *Inheritance* (1932 about a family of self-made mill owners from Luddites in the nineteenth century to the Depression of the 1930s.

This chapter, however, concentrates on the main genre, which allies a love story between the two protagonists with a historical background. It is often cross-fertilized with fantasy, Gothic, adventure, and detective fiction (Wallace, 3).

According to Diane Wallace the first English historical romance was Sophia Lee's (1750–1824) *The Recess or a Tale of Other Times*, published in 1783, and which was the first female gothic (Wallace 16). (See Chapter 4 on the Gothic for the history of the genre.) In the story of the (mythical) twin daughters (Elinor and Matilda) of Mary, Queen of Scots, and the Duke of Norfolk, Wallace argues, "it is (sexual) desire that shapes the world" (17)—for instance, the failure of the Earl of Essex's campaign in Ireland is blamed on his depression when Ellinor, his lover, is captured by the Earl of Tyrone. The novel was criticized for its lack of historical truth, not adhering to the facts of history, and reducing all motives to romantic emotion (Wallace 17). However, the feminist critic Jane Spencer argues that *The Recess* transforms history into romance in order to reinstate women and the arena of private emotion into history (in Wallace 17). Lee's handling of the female consciousness from the sidelines of history is her most important bequest to her successors (Wallace 18).

Thus, a direct line of descent can be traced from the Gothics of Lee and Ann Radcliffe to present-day women authors of historical romances (Wallace 16), as they write women back into history, reinstating women's matrilineal genealogy (De Groot 69), which has been erased by patriarchal culture (Wallace 16).[19]

The Minerva Press kept the Gothic genre popular, but soon after its demise in 1814 (Wilson 17), the silver fork novel, set in the Regency period, rose to prominence. It flourished from the mid-1820s to the mid-1840s, by which time, of course, the genre had become historical. One of the better-known novels of the genre is *Pelham; or Adventures of a Gentleman* by Edward Bulwer-Lytton, published in 1828 (Sadoff).

Both Bulwer-Lytton and Benjamin Disraeli were prominent silver fork novelists in their early careers, although they were writing more in the dandy-hero subgenre of the silver fork novel. Both Bulwer's *Pelham* (1828) and Disraeli's *Vivian Grey* (1826) feature dandy heroes. These novels were frequently modeled after scandals and events that could be found in gossip columns of newspapers. The genre had mostly gone out of fashion by the 1850s. Of the many female authors of this genre, Catherine Gore is perhaps the most well-known today. Her best-known novel is *Cecil, or Adventures of a Coxcomb*, which purports to be the autobiography of a companion of Lord Byron. Published in 1841, it has a hero, Cecil Danby, who is a dandy. It sheds a witty and revealing light on the Regency and, most significantly, how the Victorians thought of that period. According to Andrew Elfenbein Victorian silver fork novels "bring women to the centre of their plots to suggest that carefree Regency men, including Byron, cause considerable suffering to the women with whom they are associated" (78).

Edward Copeland traces in silver fork fiction many borrowings from Jane Austen, including her characters, dialog, story events (such as *Mansfield Park*'s amateur theatricals), inscription of female subjectivity, and, most importantly, the narrative negotiation of rank and class necessary for individual and social improvement during the age of reform. Later silver fork novels, written by, about, and for women, are not without moral or political critique, ruthlessly satirizing the social system of an earlier generation. Heroines in this sub-genre earn their happy endings, rewarded with a newly intimate marital life.

By the Victorian period, silver fork novels had lost their popularity, and other historical periods rose to prominence, in particular medieval, which led to a revival of the Gothic (see Chapter 4).

The historical novels of the 1890s and 1900s were adventure novels that centered around a mission of public importance. One of the main authors of this genre and period was Baroness Orczy, author of the *Scarlet Pimpernel* series of novels, the first one being published in 1905. In this series the hero rescues French aristocrats from the guillotine, while he and his estranged wife eventually overcome their misunderstandings and declare their love for each other.

Rafael Sabatini's *Scaramouche* (1921) is also set during this period with a hero who is a French lawyer. He has to frequently change sides in order to survive. He saves his cousin from the guillotine and eventually marries her.

Jeffery Farnol wrote swashbuckling novels set in the Georgian and Regency periods. *The Amateur Gentleman* (1913) is about Barnabas Barty who determines to become a gentleman, goes to London, and falls in love with Cleone Meredith.

It was the female authors of the 1920s who gave new life to the historical novel, as the swashbuckling romances of the pre-War period fell out of favor (Wallace 29). Authors such as Sheila Kaye-Smith, Constance Holmes and Mary Webb started the vogue for rural novels, set in the past of a lost rural England. Webb's *Precious Bane* (1924) is today perhaps the most well-known. Set during the Napoleonic Wars, it is the story of Prue Sam, who has a hare lip, and her love for Kester Woodseaves, a weaver, who sees beyond the surface to the beauty of her character.

The other sub-genre of the historical novel of this period was the romance, and in particular the Regency. Partly due to Georgette Heyer who, along with Farnol was the initiator of the twentieth-century Regency romance, the primary readership of these novels changed from male to female (Hughes 38).

These Regency novels of the twentieth century use some of the tropes found in silver fork novels, including brides keen to impress the women who command the social elite at Almack's, the club to which those hoping to rise in social class needed to seek entry. However, silver fork novels rarely recount courtships, but preach fashionable society's dangers for the newly married young woman, unlike the later Regencies, which concentrate on the courtship plot.

Heyer published her first novel, *The Black Moth*, set in the Georgian period, in 1921. Her first Regency was *Regency Buck* (1935), which Germaine Greer tore to shreds in *The Female Eunuch* (1970), calling the hero "a fine example of a stereotype … with such *world-weary lids*! With … patrician features and aristocratic contempt … and the titillating threat of *unexpected strength*! Principally, we might notice, he exists through his immaculate dressing" (175, original emphasis), while she says of the heroine "her intelligence and resolution remain happily confined to her eyes and the curve of her mouth" (176), epitomizing feminist thought on romances of the time. However, Heyer wrote 28 Regencies before her death in 1974, all of which were bestsellers and continue to sell well today.[20] Her novels gradually moved away from the adventure type to the comedy of manners type, with older, independent heroines and sophisticated heroes, as in *Frederica* (1965).

She also subverted the genre with, for example, a young and not particularly clever hero, as Sherry in *Friday's Child* (1944) and shy, retiring heroines, as Lady Hester in *Sprig Muslin* (1956).

In the 1930s and 1940s Heyer wrote three Regencies with cross-dressing heroines, a not unusual occurrence in this period (e.g., Daphne du Maurier's heroines), when the suitability of women for war work was being publicly debated (Bell 152). According to Wallace female cross-dressing was also related to an understanding that femininity is a masquerade, and a desire by women to escape from the confines of it (23), as dressing as a man allowed the heroine to enter into male spaces and encounter the hero without a chaperone. There are, however, some historical romances with cross-dressing heroines which pre-date the Second World War—in Heyer's *These Old Shades*, for instance, the heroine for the first half of the novel is the hero's page, which again draws attention to the constructed nature of femininity (Wallace 39; see also Fletcher 58–63).

These cross-dressing heroines were a part of the transgressive women depicted in the 1940s historical romances, showing heroines as highwaywomen or "wicked ladies" (Wallace 80). Gillian Spraggs argues that these transgressive heroines are important for what they tell us about the fantasies of female autonomy of the women of the 1940s (264). These transgressive heroines were also a way of exploring the new possibilities that were opened for women during the Second World War, and a rebellion against the expectation that after the war women would return tamely to the home and their traditional role as wife and mother.

By the 1970s the Regency had lost its mass-market appeal in England (though not America). However, Mills & Boon (now Harlequin Mills & Boon) kept the genre going with their historical line, which generally included a Regency-set romance each month.

Throughout the twentieth century other authors took different periods as their background.

Barbara Cartland started her writing career with contemporaries, but in 1946 published her first historical, *The Hidden Heart*, set in 1903. She went on to write novels set in the Regency period as well as the Victorian and Edwardian periods, all of them featuring a virginal heroine and a rake for a hero. The remarkably prolific nature of Cartland's output has drawn some attention from scholars. Gwen Robyns and John Pearson have written biographical studies of Cartland, while Rosalind Brunt and Marsha Vanderford Doyle have explored the romantic and fantasy aspects of her confected historical world.

Norah Lofts wrote both stand-alone novels and novels based on a single house and its occupants through the ages. Her most famous series is the *Suffolk* trilogy (1959–63), which starts in the fourteenth century and ends in the twentieth.

Elizabeth Goudge wrote many historicals, including the Victorian-set *Green Dolphin Country* (1944), published in the U.S. as *Green Dolphin Street*. Her novels do have a romantic sub-plot, but most of them concentrate on the themes of redemption and growth through suffering.

Catherine Cookson set her novels in north-east England, publishing both contemporaries and historical romances about overcoming the adversities of life, generally with a poor heroine who has to fight for her place in society, finding love on the way. The combination of "realism and utopia" in her work has been studied in some depth by Fowler (73–98), who finds that it "records … working-class experience while simultaneously offering refuges for conservative myths" (97); a collection of essays on her work and its reception (including television adaptations and Cookson-related tourism) situates "Catherine Cookson Country" in a figurative space at "the intersection of the romantic novel, the historical novel, and social realism" (Taddeo xv).

Daphne du Maurier is also known for both historical and contemporary novels. Her historicals, however, are not strictly romances, as I have defined the term, as most of them do not end with a happily-ever-after for the heroine. She covers various periods, including the English Civil War in *The King's General* (1946) *Jamaica Inn* (1936) set in 1820 on Bodmin Moor, and *Frenchman's Creek* (1941) set during the reign of Charles II, though she is perhaps most famous for her novel *Rebecca* (1938), which is a contemporary.

A motif of historical novels from the 1960s and 1970s was the captive heroine, mainly based on historical figures, such as Sophia Dorothea in Jean Plaidy's *The Princess of Celle* (1976), and this was, of course, echoed in the Gothic romances by the same author writing as Victoria Holt. The trope of captivity in popular romance has so far primarily been explored in the context of American romance novels and American captivity narratives before them (Harders); scholarship is needed on this motif in other national traditions, including English romances. As Wallace says this was a period in which the historical romance exposed women's victimization, but also was used by women to encompass their own desires, re-writing history to show maternal influence and power (149).

Criticism of historical romances

All these authors were accomplished writers, but from the start of the genre critics were dismissive of historical romances, as of contemporary romances. Much of the criticism leveled against contemporary romances is also leveled against historical romances, but historicals have an extra layer of criticism.

Both Thomas Carlyle, in his essay "Sartor Resartus" and Hazlitt in his 1827 essay "The Dandy School" criticized the silver fork novel (Wilson 55), as formulaic, arguing that such books privilege form over feeling, depicting the outward show of the characters' lives rather than their emotions and moral struggles (Wilson 56). This was the start of 200 years of critical dismissal, with few critics even acknowledging the genre.

One of the first English critics to do so was Herbert Butterfield, who sympathetically argued that the historical novel is a "'form' of history—a way of treating the past" and is therefore "linked with legend, and the traditions of localities, and popular ballads" in that it, like these, goes "beyond the authenticated data of history . . . in order to tell its story; and like these it often subordinates fidelity to the recovered facts of history, and strict accuracy of detail, to some other kind of effectiveness" (3). While being a form of fiction it also "claims to be true to the life of the past" (4), and thus the historical novel itself becomes a maker of history (42). A good historical should not be mere picturesqueness, satisfied with mere externals (32) but has to have what he calls historical "atmosphere" (97), without which it can appear to be a modern story in fancy dress. Jerome De Groot argues that to achieve this authentic atmosphere, the author needs what Butterfield calls "historical empathy" (49).

The historical novel "emphasises the influence of personal things in history" (Butterfield 73). This is particularly true of romances, where it is the personal that matters more than the political background.

According to the major Marxist scholar György (Georg) Lukács, Sir Walter Scott was the first (European) author of historical fiction, but neither Lukács nor, indeed, Scott himself, acknowledged his female progenitors, who included Jane Porter, author of *The Scottish Chiefs* (1810). Lukács argues that the period of the Napoleonic Wars was a unique historical moment, which led to an acknowledgment of historicity by individuals for the first time—that is, individuals realized they were living in a historical period, and this awareness of history enabled Scott to seek to understand individuals historically, expressing history through character, and with a nationalistic bent.

Although Lukács was writing about the historical novel, much of what he says is relevant to the historical romance. Thus, nationalism is very evident in the authors of the English historical romance, where English society is shown as essentially harmonious and sound (Hughes 67), and where England is associated with freedom and democracy (Hughes 74). An obvious example of this is Baroness Orczy's *Scarlet Pimpernel* series (1905–40), where England is portrayed as a sound and healthy society, in contrast to revolutionary France (Hughes 76) and where Englishness is tied up with a male aristocratic code of generosity, loyalty, bravery, and love of the land (Hughes 86).

As Wallace (7) says, the historical novel enables female writers to examine masculinity as a social and cultural construct. This is evident in Catherine Cookson's social history romances of the 1970s with her working-class heroes, although Cartland's novels of the same period accept the traditional patriarchal view of the male as all-powerful, without interrogating it further. However, there are differences in political outlook presented by different novelists. Jerome De Groot argues that where Cartland's novels generally affirmed the status quo of a glamorized, hierarchical class society, Cookson's novels presented the past as a place of deprivation and oppression for women: "It is a place of poverty, fear, drunkenness, neglect, illegitimacy and dirt"; a place that women could escape through individual determination, relationships with other women, and romantic relationships with men (55–6).

In Heyer's early novels English masculinity is blended with French style (*The Black Moth*), *Powder and Patch*, first published as *The Transformation of Philip Jettan* (1923), giving masculinity an element of femininity, but in later novels, for instance in her non-Regency *Beauvallet* where the Tudor hero travels into Spain to abduct the willing heroine, there is no element of femininity in him, and this is also the case in the heroes of her Regencies. But for Heyer, as with other historical romance authors, masculinity is a masquerade, with the hero's outward appearance masking his sterling qualities, for example, in *Cotillion* (1953) and *The Unknown Ajax* (1959) (Wallace 104, 107).

By the 1950s masculinity was seen to be lacking. The old warrior trope for men had proved inadequate in the aftermath of both World Wars (Dixon 70; Maslen 18), and other types of masculinity were being explored in historical romances. Thus Heyer's *Cotillion* (1953) has a not particularly clever hero, with not a violent bone in his body. Many heroes of this period are physically damaged, for example, Marcus, in Rosemary Sutcliff's *The Eagle of the Ninth* (1954).

The Marxist critic Fredric Jameson argues that "we live in a world of surface and echo, unable to properly remember or create anything new" which according to Jerome De Groot leads to the acknowledgment that all historical fiction imitates a past which never existed (115). So novelists and historians "use tropes, metaphors, prose, narrative style to interpret and render a version of something which is innately other and unknown" (De Groot 113). This gives women a space into which they can insert a female-centered re-writing of accepted (male) versions of history.

As Linda Hutcheon argues, postmodern imitative techniques have been particularly effective for those excluded by dominant cultural ideology (22–36), allowing "marginalised people to emerge as equal historical subjects and narrators" (De Groot 116). Hutcheon coined the term "historiographical metafiction," referring to postmodern fiction which is highly self-reflective (Tuite 247), which can be seen in those romances which refer to well-known novels of a previous age—e.g., *Pride and Prejudice* is often referred to in Regencies.

One of the first critiques of the genre to concentrate on the historical romance *per se* was Hughes, where she argues that historical fiction can be seen as myth, defined by Barthes as a semiological system which gives a "natural" image of a "reality" that has actually been fabricated within a historical past, and is an ideologically charged construct (8). So that women's historical romances use the past setting and stock motifs of romance as symbolic expressions of female concerns (107).

This is a point picked up by many feminist critics of the genre, including Alison Light, who argues that for women the genre has a subversive potential, creating a dissonant space in which various issues of legitimacy, authority and identity might be considered and depicting a fantasy of female power and agency not found elsewhere (see De Groot 68), and Diana Wallace, who finds that women's historical fiction puts women at the forefront of events, thus imaginatively returning "the girl child to her place within a maternal genealogy, and thus a re-union with the mother" (Wallace x). The historical romance form allows women a freedom and license not granted in other genres, Wallace writes, which women have used to express multiple complex identities and as sites of possibilities and potential (67).

Admittedly, some critics have been skeptical. Anthea Trodd, for example, criticizes historical romance authors who focus on female royal protagonists for implicitly endorsing a view of history as male property, since this focus perpetuates class division and casts "female characters in domestic and sexual roles only" (Trodd 113). De Groot, however, argues that historical romance fiction can be used to challenge the mainstream (140) precisely by putting love at the center of the story, and Teo points out that the focus in historical romance novels on amatory, domestic, and sexual aspects of well-known historical settings (e.g., the Ottoman court of Selim I and his son Suleiman the Magnificent in Bertrice Small's *The Kadin*) presages developments in feminist historiography since the 1980s ("Bertrice Teaches You"). As Wallace points out, authors have also used the form in order to explore taboo subjects, such as sex, or critique the present (Wallace 2). As Naomi Mitchison said when one of her contemporary novels was censored by her publishers in the 1930s, "in some stories in *The Delicate Fires* (1933) there is, I would have thought, far more sex than in *We Have Been Warned* (1935), but apparently it's all right when people wear wolfskins and togas" (qtd. in Beauman 141). Conversely, in the more sexually liberal world of the later twentieth century Barbara Cartland turned to historicals in order to more easily represent the frisson resulting from sexual restrictions and restraint. As she explained to Deborah Philips in a 1986 interview, it was "very difficult to have virgins and all the excitement in the present day."

Conclusion and suggestions for further study

Romantic fiction is a genre of fiction that has long antecedents. It reflects both women's position in society, and the events and ethics of the society it is written in.

For instance, the twentieth century saw a diversity of romantic fiction, with subgenres featuring the New Woman, foreign heroes, more sexual heroines and plots, as well as the continuation of the domestic novel. And from the mid-century on it saw an appreciation of this genre, in particular from female critics. But there are still areas of study to explore. These include investigating the early literary roots of the genre, before the split into the current categories of "literary" and "popular" and the historical antecedents of the romance genre, along with such topics as how death is handled in these apparently upbeat novels, the differences nationality makes to the genre, the effect of feminism (from the first wave to the latest manifestation) have on the novels, how each generation of authors have been affected by the previous generation, how external events impact on what authors wrote about and why they are written mainly by women, not men.

Notes

1 The scholarly bibliography on Romance, broadly construed, is vast and potentially daunting. Foundational studies include Frye (86–205), Jameson, and Mikhail Bakhtin. For a useful history of how medieval Romance evolves into more modern versions, see Crawford (11–59); for discussion of how classical "Greek romances" influenced Renaissance fiction and drama and the subsequent history of the novel, see Doody; for a helpful discussion of the term in its broadest sense, with application to global literatures, see Goyal (1–24).

2 For Behn as a model and resource for modern popular romance, see the encomium by Roach (142–3); Lutz, citing Ballaster 1998, refers to Behn's "amatory fiction" as "the early modern equivalent of the contemporary [that is, 20th-twenty-first century] mass-market romance" (2): a connection elaborated upon by Baldus in her essay on American romance author Jennifer Crusie, "Gossip, Liminality, and Erotic Display: Jennifer Crusie's Links to Eighteenth-Century Amatory Fiction." See also Toscano.

3 Radway's is the first of several attempts to codify the essential structure or defining elements of the romance novel. For others, see Regis (30–9), discussed below, and Roach (21–7).

4 For an extended, historicist analysis of Philander's "Whiggish and libertine antinomianism" (McKeon, 508) and Silvia's measured, undeceived response, see McKeon (506–13).

5 For an extended discussion of cross-dressing by heroines in popular romance (albeit historical romance rather than contemporary-set novels) see Fletcher, 49–92.

6 For a partial list of twentieth-century romances featuring the "hero-as-brother" motif, from a variety of decades, see Dixon, 79; for more on the feminization of the hero, see Beauman; Light; Miller; Showalter. Talia Schaffer's *Romance's Rival: Familiar Marriage in Victorian Fiction* does not focus on feminization—her categories include "neighbour marriage," "cousin marriage," "disability marriage," and "vocational marriage"—but she offers a useful, historically detailed discussion of marriage plots in which the male suitor who offers "security, kindness, safety, care" is preferable to a more erotically compelling rival (x).

7 For a discussion of Jane West's domestic novel *A Gossip's Story* as an inspiration for Jane Austen's *Sense and Sensibility*—with attention in both texts to the phenomenon of gossip, a topic of ongoing interest in popular romance scholarship (e.g., Baldus)—see Goss.

8 Austen's place as a romance pioneer has not always been so assured. As many literary historians have noted, Charlotte Brontë believed that Austen was either unwilling or unable to write about women's passions and desires ("what throbs fast and full, though hidden, what the blood rushes through" as Brontë calls it in a letter [qtd. in Armstrong, 53]; see Weisser, 35–8).

9 Both Heathcliff, from Emily Brontë's *Wuthering Heights*, and Rochester, from Charlotte Brontë's *Jane Eyre*, have been described as the precursor of many twentieth-century heroes (Jensen; Modleski).

10 For an extended discussion of religion and popular romance fiction, including nineteenth-century works, see Chapter 21 of this volume.
11 After many years of derision, Corelli began to receive serious scholarly attention in the late 1970s, and the pace of publication on her work has quickened in the twenty-first century. For useful discussions, see Federico, Hipsky, Masters, Ransom, and Waller.
12 Both Ouida's novels and Dell's romances can be read as part of a subgenre of romantic imperial or colonial fiction that flourished in the late nineteenth and early twentieth century. For an account of this subgenre, especially in terms of its treatments of colonialism and race, see Teo.
13 Although Berta Ruck lived in London for much of her life and wrote romance novels set in England, the author herself was born in the town of Murree in what is now Pakistan and was raised in her paternal grandparents' home in Wales, leaving her with "a strong sense of Welsh identity" (Lloyd-Morgan).
14 The modern "sexualization of love" is discussed at length in Chapter 21 of this collection ("Love and Romance Novels"); it is a staple of today's contemporary romances.
15 In *The Romance Fiction of Mills & Boon, 1909–1990s* I cover this period in chapters on the evolution of the Mills & Boon romance hero (Chapter 4), the Mills & Boon heroine (Chapter 5), and the representations of sex and desire (Chapter 8).
16 For an extended discussion of "War and Aftermath" in Mills & Boon romances, including both the First and Second World Wars, see Dixon (97–112).
17 For an extended discussion of Leavis and popular romance, see Chapter 13 of this volume, "Literary Approaches."
18 See Chapter 5 for a sustained discussion of the post-1970s historical romance.
19 For more on popular historical romance as revisionist historiography, see Teo, "Bertrice Teaches You History."
20 Heyer has been the subject of considerably more scholarship than most popular romance authors. See Chapter 5 for an extended discussion of her historical romances, Chapter 13 for a discussion of her status as a more "literary" author of popular romance, Chapter 14 for consideration of single-author studies devoted to her work, and Chapter 21 for analysis of her treatment of romantic love

Works cited

Anderson, Rachel. *The Purple Heart Throbs: The Sub-Literature of Love.* Hodder and Stoughton, 1974.

Ardis, Ann. "E.M. Hull, Mass Market Romance and the New Woman Novel in the Early Twentieth Century." *Women's Writing*, vol. 3, no. 3, 1996, pp. 287–296.

Armstrong, Nancy. *Desire and Domestic Fiction: A Political History of the Novel.* Oxford University Press, 1987.

Austen, Jane. *Pride and Prejudice.* T. Egerton, 1813.

———. *Northanger Abbey.* John Murray, 1817.

Bach, Evelyn. "Sheik Fantasies: Orientalism and Feminine Desire." *Hecate*, vol. 23, 1997, pp. 9–40.

Backscheider, Paula. *Elizabeth Singer Rowe and the Development of the English Novel.* Johns Hopkins University Press, 2013.

Bakhtin, M.M. *The Dialogic Imagination: Four Essays.* Edited by Michael Holquist, translated by Caryl Emerson and Michael Holquist, University of Texas Press, 1981.

Baldus, Kimberly. "Gossip, Liminality, and Erotic Display: Jennifer Crusie's Links to Eighteenth-Century Amatory Fiction." *Journal of Popular Romance Studies*, vol. 2, no. 2, 2012, n.p.

Ballaster, Ros. *Seductive Forms: Women's Amatory Fiction from 1684 to 1740.* Oxford University Press, 1988.

———. "Romancing the Novel: Gender and Genre in Early Theories of Narrative." *Living by the Pen: Early British Women Writers*, edited by Dale Spender, Teachers College Press, 1992, pp. 188–200.

Beauman, Nicola. *A Very Great Profession: The Woman's Novel 1914–39.* Virago, 1983.

Beer, Gillian. *The Romance.* Methuen, 1970.

Bell, Kathleen. "Cross-Dressing in Wartime: Georgette Heyer's *the Corinthian* in Its 1940 Context." *War Culture: Social Change and Changing Experience in World War Two Britain*, edited by Pat Kirkham, and David Thoms, Lawrence & Wishart, 1995, p. 151.

Benedict, Barbara M. "The Curious Genre: Female Inquiry in Amatory Fiction." *Studies in the Novel*, Johns Hopkins University Press, 1998, pp. 194–210.

Berg, Temma. *The Lives and Letters of an Eighteenth-Century Circle of Acquaintances.* Ashgate, 2006.

Blain, Virginia, Patricia Clements and Isobel Grundy, eds. *The Feminist Companion to Literature in English: Women Writers from the Middle Ages to the Present.* B. T. Batsford Ltd, 1990.

Blake, Susan L. "What 'Race' Is the Sheik? Rereading a Desert Romance." *Doubled Plots: Romance and History*, edited by Susan Strehle, and Mary Paniccia Carden. 1996. University Press of Mississippi, 2003, pp. 67–85.

Bloom, Clive. *Bestsellers: Popular Fiction Since 1900.* Palgrave Macmillan, 2002.

Bowers, Toni O'Shaughnessy. "Sex, Lies, and Invisibility: Amatory Fiction from the Restoration to Mid-century." *The Columbia History of the British Novel*, edited by John Richetti, et al. Columbia University Press, 1994, pp. 50–72.

Broughton, Rhoda. *Not Wisely But Too Well.* Tinsley Brothers, 1867.

Brunt, Rosalind. "A Career in Love: The Romantic World of Barbara Cartland." *Popular Fiction and Social Change*, edited by Christopher Pawling, Palgrave, 1984, pp. 127–156.

Burge, Amy. *Representing Difference in the Medieval and Modern Orientalist Romance.* Palgrave Macmillan, 2016.

Burney, Fanny. *Evelina.* Thomas Lowndes, 1778.

Butterfield, Herbert. *The Historical Novel.* Cambridge University Press, 1924.

Callil, Camilla. *Subversive Sybils: Women's Popular Fiction this Century.* The British Library, 1996.

Callil, Carmen and Colm Tóibín, eds. *The Modern Library: The 200 Best Novels in English Since 1950.* Robinson, 2011.

Chow, Karen. "Popular Sexual Knowledges and Women's Agency in 1920s England: Marie Stopes's 'Married Love' and E.M. Hull's 'The Sheik'." *Feminist Review*, vol. 63, no. 1, 1999, pp. 64–87.

Copeland, Edward. *The Silver Fork Novel: Fashionable Fiction in the Age of Reform.* Cambridge University Press, 2012.

Crawford, Joseph. *The Twilight of the Gothic? Vampire Fiction and the Rise of the Paranormal Romance.* University of Wales Press, 2014.

Daly, Nicholas. *Modernism, Romance and the Fin de Siècle: Popular Fiction and British Culture, 1880–1914.* Cambridge University Press, 1999.

De Groot, Jerome. *The Historical Novel.* Routledge, 2010.

Dixon, jay. *The Romance Fiction of Mills & Boon, 1909-1990s.* University College London Press, 1999.

Doody, Margaret Anne. *Frances Burney: The Life in the Works.* Rutgers University Press, 1988.

Doyle, Marsha Vanderford. "The Rhetoric of Romance: A Fantasy Theme Analysis of Barbara Cartland Novels." *Southern Speech Communication Journal*, vol. 51, no. 1, 1985, pp. 24–48.

Du Maurier, Daphne. *Rebecca.* Victor Gollancz, 1938.

Edgeworth, Maria. *Belinda.* Joseph Johnson, 1801.

———. *Patronage.* Joseph Johnson, 1814.

Elfenbein, Andrew. "Silver-Fork Byron and the Image of Regency England." *Byromania: Portraits of the Artist in Nineteenth-and Twentieth-Century Culture*, edited by Frances Wilson, Springer, 1999, pp. 77–92.

Eliot, George. "Silly Novels by Lady Novelists." *Westminster Review*, Oct. 1856.

Federico, Annette R. *Idol of Suburbia: Marie Corelli and Late-Victorian Literary Culture.* University Press of Virginia, 2000.

Ferns, John. "Q. D. Leavis's Criticism: The Human Core." *Modern Age*, vol. 45, no. 2, 2003. www.firstprinciplesjournal.com/print.aspx?article=764.

Fletcher, Lisa. *Historical Romance Fiction: Heterosexuality and Performativity.* Ashgate, 2008.

Forbes, Joan. "Anti-Romantic Discourse as Resistance: Women's Fiction 1775-1820." *Romance Revisited*, edited by Lynne Pearce, and Jackie Stacey, Lawrence & Wishart, 1995, pp. 293–305.
Fowler, Bridget. *The Alienated Reader: Women and Popular Romantic Literature in the Twentieth Century*. Harvester Wheatsheaf, 1991.
Frye, Northrop. *The Secular Scripture*. Harvard University Press, 1976.
Fuchs, Barbara. *Romance*. Routledge, 2004.
Gargano, Elizabeth. "'English Sheiks' and Arab Stereotypes: E.M. Hull, T.E. Lawrence, and the Imperial Masquerade." *Texas Studies in Literature and Language*, vol. 48, no. 2, 2006, pp. 171–186.
Goss, Erin. "Homespun Gossip: Jane West, Jane Austen, and the Task of Literary Criticism." *The Eighteenth Century*, vol. 56, no. 2, Summer 2015, pp. 165–177.
Goyal, Yogita. *Romance, Diaspora, and Black Atlantic Literature*. Cambridge University Press, 2010.
Greer, Germaine. *The Female Eunuch*. MacGibbon and Kee, 1970.
Hall, Cailey. "The Consolation of Genre: On Reading Romance Novels." *Los Angeles Review of Books*, 27 Aug 2018. https://lareviewofbooks.org/article/consolation-genre-reading-romance-novels/
Hannay, Margaret P. *Mary Sidney, Lady Wroth*. Routledge, 2010.
Harders, Robin Lyn. *Blood Brothers: Indian Captivity and the Fiction of Race*. 1995. University of California, Irvine, Ph.D. dissertation.
Hipsky, Martin. *Modernism and the Women's Popular Romance in Britain, 1885–1925*. Ohio University Press, 2011.
Holden, Stacy. "Love in the Desert." *Journal of Popular Romance Studies* vol. 5, no. 1, 2015, n.p.
Hughes, Helen. *The Historical Romance*. Routledge, 1993.
Hultquist, Aleksondra. *Equal Ardor: Female Desire, Amatory Fiction, and the Recasting of the Novel, 1680–1760*. 2008. University of Illinois at Urbana-Champaign, Ph.D. dissertation.
Hutcheon, Linda. *A Poetics of Postmodernism*. Routledge, 1988.
Jameson, Fredric. "Postmodernism and Consumer Society." *Movies and Mass Culture*, edited by John Belton, Athlone, 1996, pp. 185–202.
Jarmakani, Amira. *Imagining Arab Womanhood: The Cultural Mythology of Veils, Harems, and Belly Dancers in the US*. NYU Press, 2008.
Jensen, Margaret Ann. *Love's Sweet Return: The Harlequin Story*. Women's Educational Press, 1984.
Katz, Tamar. *Impressionist Subjects: Gender, Interiority, and Modernist Fiction in England*. University of Illinois Press, 2000.
Kestner, Joseph A. *Protest and Reform: The British Social Narrative by Women 1827–1867*. Blackwell Publishing, 1985.
Lamb, Mary Ellen. *Gender and Authorship in the Sidney Circle*. University of Wisconsin Press, 1990.
Langbauer, Laurie. *Women and Romance: The Consolations of Gender in the English Novel*. Cornell University Press, 1990.
Leavis, Q.D. *Fiction and the Reading Public*. Chatto & Windus, 1932.
Light, Alison. *Forever England: Femininity, Literature and Conservatism Between the Wars*. Routledge, 1991.
Lloyd-Morgan, Ceridwen. "Ruck, Amy Roberta ('Berta Ruck') (1878–1978)." Dictionary of Welsh Biography. https://biography.wales/article/s10-RUCK-ROB-1878. Accessed February 11, 2020.
Lukács, Georg. *The Historical Novel*. 1937. Translated from the German by Hannah and Stanley Mitchell. Merlin Press, 1962.
Lutz, Deborah. *The Dangerous Lover: Gothic villains, Byronism, and the Nineteenth-Century Seduction Narrative*. Ohio State University Press, 2006.
McAleer, Joseph. *Passion's Fortune: The Story of Mills & Boon*. Oxford University Press, 1999.

MacCarthy, B. G. *The Female Pen: Women Writers and Novelists 1621–1818*. Originally published in two volumes, 1944 and 1947. Cork University Press, 1994.
McKeon, Michael. *The Secret History of Domesticity: Public, Private, and the Division of Knowledge*. Johns Hopkins University Press, 2005.
Maslen, Elizabeth. *Political and Social Issues in British Women's Fiction 1928–1968*. Palgrave Macmillan, 2001.
Masters, Brian. *Now Barabbas was a Rotter: The Extraordinary Life of Marie Corelli*. H. Hamilton, 1978.
Maxwell, Richard. "The Historiography of Fiction in the Romantic Period." *The Cambridge Companion to Fiction in the Romantic Period*, edited by Richard Maxwell, Katie Trumpener, Cambridge University Press, 2008, pp. 7–22.
Melman, Billie. *Women and the Popular Imagination in the Twenties: Flappers and Nymphs*. Macmillan, 1988.
Miller, Jane. *Women Writing About Men*. Virago Press, 1986.
Miller, Naomi J. and Gary Waller, eds. *Reading Mary Worth: Representing Alternatives in Early Modern England*. University of Tennessee Press, 1991.
Modleski, Tania. *Loving with a Vengeance: Mass-produced Fantasies for Women*. Methuen, 1982.
Omdal, Gerd Karin. "Clara Reeve's *Progress of Romance* and the Female Critic in the 18th Century." *Literature Compass*, vol. 10, no. 9, 2013, pp. 688–695.
"Ouida" (Mary Louise Ramé). *Under Two Flags*. Chapman and Hall, 1867.
———. *Moths*. 1880. Edited by Natalie Schroeder, Broadview, 2005.
Pearson, John. *Barbara Cartland: Crusader in Pink*. A&C Black, 2011.
Philips, Deborah. "True Romance: An Interview with Barbara Cartland." *Women's Review*, vol. 13, 1986, pp. 28–29.
Radford, Jean, ed. *The Progress of Romance: The Politics of Popular Fiction*. Routledge, 1986.
Radway, Janice. *Reading the Romance: Women, Patriarchy, and Popular Literature*. University of North Carolina Press, 1984.
Ransom, Teresa. *The Mysterious Miss Marie Corelli: Queen of Victorian Bestsellers*. Sutton Publishing, 1999.
Raub, Patricia. "Issues of Passion and Power in E.M. Hull's *The Sheik*." *Women's Studies*, vol. 21, no. 1, 1992, pp. 119–128.
Reeve, Clara. *The Progress of Romance*. 1785. Facsimile Text Society, 1930.
Regis, Pamela. *A Natural History of the Romance Novel*. University of Pennsylvania Press, 2003.
Roach, Catherine M. *Happily Ever After: The Romance Story in Popular Culture*. Indiana University Press, 2016.
Roberts, Michelle. *Silly Lady Novelists?* Rack Press Editions, 2016.
Robyns, Gwen. *Barbara Cartland*. Doubleday, 1985.
Rogers, Katherine M. *Frances Burney: The World of "Female Difficulties."* Harvester-Wheatsheaf, 1991.
Sadoff, Dianne F. "The Silver Fork Novel, 1824-41." *BRANCH: Britain, Representation and Nineteenth-Century History*, edited by Dino Franco Felluga, Extension of *Romanticism and Victorianism on the Net*, 2014 www.branchcollective.org/?ps_articles=dianne-f-sadoff-the-silver-fork-novel-1824-41. Accessed March 20, 2019.
Saunders, Corinne, ed. *A Companion to Romance from Classical to Contemporary*. Blackwell, 2004.
Schaffer, Talia. *Romance's Rival: Familiar Marriage in Victorian Fiction*. Oxford University Press, 2016.
Schroeder, Natalie. "Introduction." "Ouida" (Mary Louise Ramé). *Moths*. 1880, edited by Natalie Schroeder, Broadview, 2005, pp. 9–36.
Showalter, Elaine. *The Female Malady: Women, Madness and English Culture 1830–1980*. Virago Press, 1985.
Spacks, Patricia Meyer. *Novel Beginnings: Experiment in Eighteenth-Century English Fiction*. Yale University Press, 2006.

Spender, Dale. *Mothers of the Novel.* Pandora, 1986.

Spraggs, Gillian. *Outlaws and Highwaymen: The Cult of the Robber in England from the Middle Ages to the Nineteenth Century.* Vintage, 2001.

Taddeo, Julie, ed *Catherine Cookson Country: On the Borders of Legitimacy, Fiction, and History.* Ashgate, 2012.

Taylor, Jessica. "And You Can Be My Sheikh: Gender, Race, and Orientalism in Contemporary Romance Novels." *Journal of Popular Culture*, vol. 40, no. 6, 2007, pp. 1032–1051.

Teo, Hsu-Ming. "'Bertrice Teaches You about History, and You Don't Even Mind!': History and Revisionist Historiography in Bertrice Small's *the Kadin.*" *New Approaches to Popular Romance Fiction: Critical Essays*, edited by Sarah S. G. Frantz, and Eric Murphy Selinger, McFarland, 2012a, pp. 21–32.

———. *Desert Passions: Orientalism and Romance Novels.* University of Texas Press, 2012b.

———. "Imperial Affairs: Colonialism, Race and the Early Twentieth-century Romance Novel." *New Directions in Popular Fiction: Genre, Distribution, Reproduction*, edited by Ken Gelder, Palgrave Macmillan, 2016, pp. 87–11.

———. "The Romance Genre in the Anglo-Cultural Tradition." *Oxford Research Encyclopedia of Literature*, August 2018. DOI: 10.1093/acrefore/9780190201098.013.415. http://literature.oxfordre.com/view/10.1093/acrefore/9780190201098.001.0001/acrefore-9780190201098-e-415

Terry, R. C. *Victorian Popular Fiction 1860-80.* Macmillan Press, 1983.

Todd, Janet. *Aphra Benn: A Secret Life.* Bloomsbury Reader, 2017.

Tompkins, Joyce M.S. *The Popular Novel in England 1770-1800.* University of Nebraska Press, 1961.

Toscano, Angela. *Resemblances: On the Re-use of Romance in Three 18th-Century Novels.* 2018. University of Iowa, Ph.D. dissertation. https://doi.org/10.17077/etd.5s8fbf8g

Trodd, Anthea. *Women's Writing in English: Britain 1900–1945.* Longman, 1998.

Tuite, Clara. "Historical Fiction." *Companion to Women's Historical Writing*, edited by Mary Spongberg, Barbara Caine, Ann Curthoys, Palgrave Macmillan, 2005, pp. 240–248.

Vargo, Gregory. *An Underground History of Early Victorian Fiction: Chartism, Radical Print Culture and the Social Problem Novel.* Cambridge University Press, 2018.

Vivanco, Laura. *For Love and Money: The Literary Art of the Harlequin Mills & Boon Romance.* Humanities E-Books, 2011.

Wadső-Lecaros, Cecilia. *The Victorian Governess Novel.* Lund University Publications, 2001.

Wallace, Diana. *The Woman's Historical Novel: British Women Writers, 1900–2000.* Palgrave Macmillan, 2005.

Waller, Philip. *Writers, Readers & Reputations: Literary Life in Britain 1870–1918.* Oxford University Press, 2006.

Ward, Mrs. Humphrey. *Robert Elsmere.* Smith, Elder, 1888.

Watson, Daphne. *Their Own Worst Enemies: Women Writers of Women's Fiction.* Pluto Press, 1995.

Watson, Zak. "Desire and Genre in *the Female Quixote.*" *Novel: A Forum on Fiction*, vol. 44, no. 1, Spring 2011, pp. 31–46.

Weisser, Susan Ostrov. *The Glass Slipper: Women and Love Stories.* Rutgers University Press, 2013.

West, Rebecca. "The Tosh Horse." 1922. *The Strange Necessity: Essays and Reviews*, Jonathan Cape, 1928.

Williams, Raymond. *Culture and Society 1780–1950.* Columbia University Press, 1958.

Wilson, Cheryl A. *Fashioning the Silver Fork Novel.* Pickering & Chatto, 2012.

Wilt, Judith. *Women Writers and the Hero of Romance.* Palgrave Macmillan, 2014.

Woolf, Virginia. *A Room of One's Own.* Hogarth Press, 1929.

Yonge, Charlotte M. *The Heir of Redclyffe.* John W. Parker, 1853.

2 The evolution of the American romance novel

Pamela Regis

The "evolution" metaphor in this chapter's title is apt. Those of us writing the American romance novel's literary history must do what paleontologists do when they write the history of life on the planet: we must unearth and identify old, buried, and forgotten objects, i.e., our study texts, the novels we choose to describe and analyze. After exhuming a novel that might be a romance, we must determine that it belongs to the genre we are studying before we can enter it in the literary history of that genre. Put simply, we have to find romances. Our problem is that most romances other than America's twentieth-century brand-name novels—think Silhouette—have not been recognized as romance novels. I will have more to say about how to proceed with this exhumation and identification, but for a preliminary gauge of the difficulty involved, consider that cataloging librarians down the years have often not used the subject heading "romance novel" when they entered even obvious romances such as Silhouettes or Harlequins into their catalogs, that is when they bothered to catalog romances at all. The Library of Congress catalog listing for *Irish Thoroughbred* (1981), Nora Roberts's first published romance novel, offers the following subject headings: "Horse trainers—Fiction," "Maryland—Fiction," and "Form/Genre: Love stories". Older American romance novels are similarly unidentified, and, indeed, the effort to identify older American romance novels is very recent.

Because there are very few works of scholarship that make a direct contribution to the history of the American romance novel, this chapter will be unlike others in this volume whose authors survey the existing scholarship on the topic announced in the chapter's title. Instead, in this chapter I will provide you with an explanation of how to unearth—literally, how to *find* and *identify*—American romances to serve as study texts. I will also offer an outline of the history of the American romance novel from 1803 to just after World War II consisting of a brief analysis of a dozen romance novels published between 1740 and 1952: the first romance novel in America, a British import, Samuel Richardson's *Pamela*, and 11 American novels, written by Americans, and, with one exception, set in America.

Along the way, I will briefly describe works of criticism that contribute to our understanding of these texts *as* romance novels as well as other secondary works whose authors do not read their study texts *as* romance novels, but who nonetheless contribute to our understanding of the American romance novel. In addition, to alert you to the hostile critical view of romances endemic in the foundational texts of American literary history, I will describe works that have actually *impeded* the writing of the history of the American romance novel. Regard this chapter, then, more as a guide to contributing to the history of the American romance novel than as a complete account of the evolution of the romance novel in America.

How to find unknown American romance novels

To excavate forgotten romance novels, you first must know what you are looking for, what exactly you mean by "romance novel." I rely on my own definition, first offered in *A Natural History of the Romance Novel,* which has gained considerable acceptance in the field of popular romance scholarship: "A romance novel is a work of prose fiction that tells the story of the courtship and betrothal of one or more heroines" (19), with "heroines" amended to "protagonists" in my "Female Genre Fiction in the Twentieth Century" (849). For other scholarly definitions of the romance novel, see Lisa Fletcher's argument that the statement "I love you," which she classifies as a speech act, defines the genre "historical romance fiction" (*Historical Romance Fiction: Heterosexuality and Performativity* 25); or see Jayashree Kamblé's identification and description of the "double helix" of the romance novel form, in which characteristics of "romance" and "novel" are intertwined (*Making Meaning in Popular Romance Fiction: An Epistemology* 2); or see Catherine M. Roach's claim that the defining statement of "the romance story" is "Find your own true love and live happily ever after" (*Happily Ever After: The Romance Story in Popular Culture* 2). See also the definition offered by the Romance Writers of America, the professional organization for American romance writers: "a central love story . . . with an emotionally satisfying and optimistic ending" ("About the Genre," www.rwa.org). Of these definitions, mine is the most narrow, in that it draws a bright line between the romance novel and more amorphous designations—such as the "love story."

Love stories are ubiquitous. When I apply my definition, I require that at least half of the novel be devoted to the telling of the courtship tale in order to qualify as a romance novel. Otherwise, the novel has a courtship subplot, but resides more fully in some other genre. The romance novel form, although once largely confined to a heterosexual heroine-centered courtship story, includes among the courting characters protagonists who are anywhere on the LGBTQIA spectrum and betrothals not just between two protagonists, but also among polyamorous courting characters. The undead, individuals of non-earth origin, shape-shifters, ghosts, and other paranormal protagonists also appear.

My approach to analyzing romance novels is structural, an outgrowth of my definition which I expand by identifying the eight essential elements each romance novel contains: the flawed society that the successful courtship will renovate, the meeting between or among the parties to the courtship, their attraction to each other, the barrier to the betrothal, the courting characters' declaration of love, the point of ritual death, the recognition of new information that will overcome the barrier, and the betrothal. For most of the genre's history, the betrothal led to marriage. More recently, marriage is not always the outcome. The parties to the courtship, however, must promise to go forward together (*Natural History* 30). These eight elements can happen in any order, can appear multiple times in the same courtship or be echoed or ironically mirrored in multiple courtships, and they can be reported rather than dramatized. The romance plot's most basic movement is from separation by a barrier to a betrothal and union that restores at least partial order to the flawed society present at the novel's outset.

In addition to understanding what you are looking for, you must also understand what you are *not* looking for. You must disambiguate "romance" from "romance novel." This disambiguation is needed in general because "romance" is such a slippery term, and it is particularly urgent for students of the American romance novel than it is for scholars of other national traditions because of the long-standing prominence of "romance" in histories of the American novel. You will encounter the term "romance" in subject headings in bibliographies and as you read classic works of criticism such as Joel Porte's *The Romance in America: Studies in Cooper, Poe, Hawthorne, Melville, and James* (1969). "Romance" in this sense has been used by an entire school of critics, including Lionel Trilling (1950), Richard Chase (1957), and Leslie Fiedler (1960). In his preface to *The House of the Seven Gables* (1851), Nathaniel Hawthorne offered an early description of this kind of American romance. He explains: "When a writer calls his work a Romance ... he wishes to claim a certain latitude, which he would not have felt entitled to assume, had he professed to be writing a Novel." A novel, he continues, adheres to "a very minute fidelity, not merely to the possible, but to the probable and ordinary course of man's experience" (1). He goes on to describe "the atmospherical medium" that the romance entitles him to use, "to mingle the Marvellous" with the other "flavors" of the work (1). In a second preface, this one to *The Blithedale Romance* (1852), Hawthorne further distinguishes realistic narratives from the "romance," which he calls "a little removed from the highway of ordinary travel, where the creatures of his [the author's] brain may play their phantasmagorical antics, without exposing them to too close a comparison with the actual events of real lives" (1–2). This idea of a departure from the ordinary to embrace the extraordinary threads its way through the histories of American romance. Literary historians addressing the work of James Fennimore Cooper, Edgar Allan Poe, Nathaniel Hawthorne, Herman Melville, Henry James, Saul Bellow, and others have designated novels that employ this sense of "romance" as those novels that occupy the mainstream of the American novel. Privileging this version of "romance" has relegated to a muddy backwater the works that we as students of romance novels call "romance"—i.e., novels of courtship and betrothal usually written using the conventions of nineteenth-century realism. Awareness of the widespread application of the term "romance" to American novels unconcerned with representations of courtships —the central concern of the romance novel—is essential in navigating histories of the American novel and in conducting database searches.

Another issue in the excavation process is setting the temporal boundaries of the search. For many users of the term, "romance novel" designates a modern-day, mass-market phenomenon, especially a text with paratextual branding, which includes covers with a standard design that prominently feature the publisher's name, such as "Harlequin" or "Silhouette." My definition of "romance novel" does, indeed, include these twentieth- and twenty-first-century brand-name novels; however, the assumption that the genre itself emerged in the twentieth-century yields a blinkered, impoverished view of the genre. In *The Mind and Its Stories: Narrative Universals and Human Emotion* (2003), Patrick Colm Hogan has shown that the narrative of lovers separated and reunited is ubiquitous throughout history and across linguistic boundaries. It occurs in literature from every era, culture, and language, and in oral as well as written traditions (101). Perhaps because of its ubiquity literary critics and historians have overlooked, read around, disregarded, and otherwise devalued the romance novel, every one of which includes lovers separated by the barrier and reunited through the element of betrothal. Older romance novels, when they have been included in literary histories at all, have not been recognized or read *as* romance novels.

Given the temporal ubiquity of the romance novel we can expect to find romances among the earliest American novels. Applying the genre designation "romance novel" to texts published before the twentieth century, when the term came into widespread use, means identifying, one by one, the romance novels in the veritable sea of American novels published since colonial times. Of course, because romance novels are still being written, published, and read in large numbers, the temporal endpoint of any excavation is today. And, of course, this endpoint moves every 24 hours, to include works published overnight in our current 24/7-publication cycle enabled by access to online digital self-publication that circumvents traditional print publishers. Scholars must therefore define the temporal slice of the long history of the romance that they will analyze, and be aware that the genre in America is contemporaneous with American literature itself. Examining a decade or even a century's worth of American romance novels will necessarily exclude a significant body of relevant works.

In this chapter I will provide an account of romance novels published in America during the period from the appearance of the first American novels to just after the Second World War. Although such an account is necessarily incomplete, it will serve as a partial corrective to the fragmentary accounts of "the" romance novel that have plagued the field since the publication of the work of the establishing generation of romance critics, the most famous of whom is Janice A. Radway. In her *Reading the Romance: Women, Patriarchy, and Popular Literature* (1984) she analyzes 45 long, sensual historical romances published between 1971 and 1981, a corpus large enough to yield reliable conclusions about this subgenre of romance during this time period, but her conclusions about the entire genre—about "the romance novel"—overstep the evidence in the corpus she has elected to study. The account I offer here will emphasize the importance of suitably qualified conclusions. Given the limitations of my corpus, my account will raise as many questions as it answers, pointing the way to further research. Although men have written romance novels, my account will focus on women writers because women writers have disproportionately been overlooked by literary history, and because women have written far more romances than men. I do not know the answer to the question that this choice raises: What could an examination of novels written by male American romance writers add to our knowledge of the genre's history?

The critics who established the canon of the American novel ignore or dismiss the work of women generally and more specifically novels, like the romance novel, that make central the value of love, the core value of the American romance novel. Herbert Ross Brown in *The Sentimental Novel in America 1789–1860* (1940) claimed that such novels "deserve to appear on any list of the world's worst fiction" (vii). F.O. Matthiessen in *American Renaissance: Art and Expression in the Age of Emerson and Whitman* (1941) ignored female novelists of the early republic entirely (200). Leslie A. Fiedler in *Love and Death in the American Novel* (1960) dismissed wholesale works by nineteenth-century romance novelists, disdaining the "sentimental love religion" of their novels (329). These critics canonized the now-iconic figures of American fiction, installing Cooper, Poe, Hawthorne, Melville, and others into anthologies, syllabi, and the research agendas of many generations of literature scholars.

By the 1980s, as part of the recovery of women's literature led by second-wave feminists, critics began to unearth, read, and analyze writing by American women, including the huge output of nineteenth-century women writers. Jane Tomkins in *Sensational Designs: The Cultural Work of American Fiction, 1790–1860* (1985) observed that works of American sentimental literature "written by, about, and for women," had not traditionally been "considered legitimate objects of literary study" (119–20). Since then, literary scholars have unearthed and analyzed once-forgotten works of American sentimental authors. For a review of the recovery efforts and of the division in critical opinion regarding sentimental literature, see Joanne Dobson's "Reclaiming Sentimental Literature" (1997). This recovery, welcome as it is, has been in spite of rather than in the service of the courtship plots that such novels typically contain. When Cindy Weinstein describes the "low tolerance for sentimental plots that did not end in marriage" shown by antebellum readers ("Sentimentalism" 210), this is a typical dismissal of the HEA, and, by extension, of the events of the courtship plot that the HEA concludes. To navigate their discomfort with the romance novel critics often read against the grain, reading around the events of the courtship rather than with or through them. Despite this disregard for the events and meaning of the courtship plot, the critics who have contributed to the recovery of the sentimental tradition have also contributed, unwittingly, to the excavation of the romance novel tradition. In search of other significances, they unearth and discuss many works in which courtship is the engine of the plot, and the ending in betrothal, and usually, in marriage, is a happy one. Weinstein grudgingly reads with the grain as she analyzes betrothal and marriage in several E.D.E.N. Southworth novels, finding for women in plots "circumscribed by marriage and the demands of convention . . . a degree of agency and freedom within an institutional framework that legally allows neither" ("What Did" 279). Work on best-selling nineteenth-century women writers is likely to touch briefly on the courtship plot in their works, while the analysis that is offered is often a reading against the grain of that plot. The novel in question is worth investigating to find out if it is a romance. Disregard the dismissal. Read with the grain, and the resulting analysis can contribute to the history of the romance novel. A synoptic account of the contribution of the scribbling women to the romance novel's evolution will likely return to the centrality of the sentimental values that inform it.

The romance novel's history has begun to be sketched, albeit in fragmentary, passing glimpses, and for the most part considered not as American texts, but as part of the wider English-language romance tradition, emanating from North America, the UK, and Australia. In their "Introduction: New Approaches to Popular Romance Fiction," Eric Murphy Selinger and Sarah S. G. Frantz conduct a comprehensive overview of romance scholarship in which they identify just two literary histories: Juliet Flesch's *From Australia with Love: A History of Modern Australian Popular Romance Novels* (2004) and jay Dixon's *The Romance Fiction of Mills & Boon, 1909–1990s* (1999). Obviously, neither of these works includes American romances, nor does either reach back beyond the twentieth century. Indeed, the only work that attempts a sustained link between the earliest romance novels and the present is *A Natural History of the Romance Novel* (2003), in which I read the works of ten romance novelists beginning with Samuel Richardson's *Pamela* (1740) followed by Jane Austen's *Pride and Prejudice* (1813), Charlotte Bronte's *Jane Eyre* (1847), Anthony Trollope's *Framley Parsonage* (1861), and E. M. Forster's *Room with a View* (1908). I then analyze a handful of novels by each of the following twentieth-century U.K. and American romance writers: Georgette Heyer (U.K.), Mary Stewart (U.K.), Janet Dailey (U.S.), Jayne Ann Krentz (U.S.), and Nora Roberts

(U.S.). Finally, in "Female Genre Fiction in the Twentieth Century" I offer a fragmentary account of the genre in America, identifying what I take to be the characteristic Americanness of the American romance novel: freedom as experienced and exercised by the parties to the courtship.[1] Literary historians of the romance novel, then, will find in existing scholarship both frequent censure of the genre and an incomplete account of its history. There is much to be done.

To contribute to the writing of the genre's literary history scholars must engage in their own version of fieldwork. As I mentioned earlier, library subject headings and bibliographies do not, for the most part, identify romance novels of the past. Older works of fiction in the Library of Congress (LOC) catalog often have no subject labels of any kind. Click the hot-linked LOC subject heading "romance fiction, American" and your results list will have just 1056 entries. Romance novels, must, therefore, be unearthed by the researcher wishing to understand the decades and decades of novels —thousands of titles—that preceded the advent of the term "romance novel" in the lexicon of literary scholars and librarians. There are tools to hand, even if they have not often been put to use for the purpose of unearthing the romance novels that preceded the twentieth-century mass-market works that we usually associate with the term. One such tool is Kent P. Ljungquist's *Facts on File Bibliography of American Fiction: Through 1865* (1994), which lists titles of fiction, including novels, by just over 100 authors, both canonical and forgotten, concluding with a year-by-year chronology of selected texts beginning in 1741. Another tool is the *Dictionary of Literary Biography* (DLB) consisting of more than 300 volumes organized by author, each compiled and overseen by scrupulous editors. DLB authors distrust, dismiss, read around, and otherwise discount the love story and the ending-in-marriage that many of these novels contain. Volumes in this series nonetheless useful to the romance scholar include *American Women Prose Writers to 1820* (1999), edited by Mulford et al.; *American Women Prose Writers, 1820–1870* (2001), edited by Hudock and Rodier; and *American Women Prose Writers, 1870–1920* (2001) edited by Harris et. al. Each author has her own entry, and reading a title in a list can suggest that a work might be a heretofore unrecognized romance novel. In most of these accounts you will find a distrust of the sentimental and often, inflected through second-wave feminism, a rejection of romance.

Consider, for example, Amy E. Hudock's entry on E.D.E.N. Southworth (1819–99) in the DLB volume *American Women Prose Writers, 1820–1870.* In the lists she provides of the 50 or so novels written by Southworth one finds such titles as *The Island Princess: Or, the Double Marriage* (1858), *Sweet Love's Atonement: A Novel* (1904), and the Southworth novel I discuss in some detail below, *Vivia: Or, the Secret of Power* (1857). These titles *sound* like romances: they mention marriage, or love, or they are named, like *Pamela*, after the heroine herself. I chose *Vivia* for this reason, and because its subtitle intrigued me. My first step was to locate a copy. Sometimes older novels are available in full-text versions online—and a popular writer's novels (Southworth was a bestselling author for decades) are likely to be available for purchase from used book vendors. I paid less than $15 for my copy of *Vivia.* The first thing I read was the ending. If the novel ends in betrothal (romance novels this old are not likely to end with a union other than a marriage proposal or the marriage itself), then courtship is at the very least a substantial subplot. To find out how substantial, I read the entire work. I apply my one-half rule: If representation of the events of the courtship comprises half of the narrative, then in my view, this text is a romance novel.

At this point, I ask what this novel might contribute to the history of the genre. Given the tens of thousands of unidentified romance novels, why include *this* title? To counter what Deborah Kaye Chappel has called critics' "dogged insistence on containment and reduction" of the romance novel, which we have seen in the dismissal of romance by both critics of canonical American literature and by critics of romance itself, I choose to study texts that demonstrate the range of the romance novel (qtd. in Regis *A Natural History* 3). The idea of "range" encompasses answers to questions such as: Is the deployment of formal features—the eight elements—noteworthy? Does the novel deploy tropes that contemporary readers have identified in twentieth-century romance, and if so how does their presence in the earlier work expand our understanding of the genre? Is the novel an early instance of a subgenre? Is the choice of protagonist noteworthy? In the author's choice of protagonists are issues of diversity addressed—do class, race, religion, sexual orientation, disability, or gender factor in the courtship or subplots of the novel? Does it contribute to our understanding of an important individual author, to the work of a given publisher or imprint, or does it demonstrate the genre's diversity, still so dramatically underestimated by critics? Answers to these questions provide a rationale for studying this novel.

Yes, this is a lot of spadework, which helps to explain the lack of comprehensive literary histories of the romance novel, American or otherwise. Yet, as I have argued at length in "What Do Critics Owe the Romance?" I believe that we owe it to the romance novel to do this work, and that it is better to avoid generalizing beyond our evidence as we state our conclusions.

Because the work of unearthing the study texts has just begun, the literary history of the American romance novels that I lay out in the following section must be viewed as a starting place for further exploration. I have chosen the study texts discussed below to illustrate the genre's range between the beginning of the novel in America and 1952, prefaced by an analysis of the first ten Silhouette romances.[2] Despite the radically ahistorial, anachronistic nature of this comparison, I will begin by discussing the first ten Silhouettes, published in 1980, to demonstrate the features of romance novels that non-readers of romance have in mind when they accuse the romance novel of sameness, of being formulaic—of having, in other words, a lack of what I am calling "range." A survey of the formal features, and of the ethnicity, socio-economic status, religion, and sexual orientation of the heroines and heroes in these novels provides a snapshot of some of the authorial and editorial decisions in play as an American publisher—Simon & Schuster—creates the Silhouette brand and enters the short contemporary market to capitalize on Harlequin's unwillingness to publish American authors (Regis *Natural History* 156). Short, brand-name contemporaries are typically the most modest romance novels, although it is always useful to remember that very accomplished romance writers such as Jennifer Crusie, Susan Elizabeth Phillips, and Nora Roberts got their start writing them.

The paratextual elements of these novels—the front covers with their insistent branding features (the words "Silhouette Romance" appear six times on each cover), the blurbs on the back covers, the advertising, marketing, the standard size—all of these suggest similarity from novel to novel. Authorial and editorial decisions about the formal features of the narratives create novels with shared features: Every novel is a contemporary. In each the meeting takes place within the first 25 pages, and in most of the novels within the first ten. The betrothal closes out each book, taking place within the final ten pages. The novels are all 187 to 190 pages long. The writers of the first ten Silhouettes, all of the heroines, and all but one of the heroes are Caucasian. The exception is Karim Singh, the hero of Leslie Caine's *Bridge of Love*, who is Kashmiri. In all ten novels the hero's socio-economic status is higher than that of the heroines. They are rich: the owner of a Greek island, the inheritor of a French chateau, a wealthy business owner, a successful playwright, an industrialist, an attorney, the lord of a Swedish manor, a second wealthy businessman, a mine owner, and a Kashmiri prince. The heroines, by contrast, are middle class: a real estate agent, two professional photographers, a secretary pretending to be a housekeeper, an administrative assistant, a legal secretary, a medical secretary, a private pilot, a journalist, and a buyer for a women's clothing store. All of the heroes and heroines are heterosexual, and, except in the case of the prince, cultural and religious issues do not factor in the barriers. The benchmarks against which to measure diversity, then, are: written by a white author about white people, with a high-status hero, a heroine whose status is lower than the hero's, and barriers that range from dynastic betrothals (numbers 2, and 7), other women, other men, and at least one big misunderstanding.[3] So, the authorial and editorial decisions, whether conscious or otherwise, result in novels depicting heteronormative, ethnically homogeneous characters. Class conflicts are depicted, but they are between middle-class heroines and upper-class heroes. Political engagement, and, for the most part, religion are completely absent. In listing these shared characteristics of short contemporaries that lead casual readers of romances to conclude, usually on scant evidence, that romances follow a formula, I am deliberately engaging in a form of literary stereotyping. Do not mistake these romances for all romances, and do not assume that the characteristics enumerated above account for most of the reading experience produced by these romances, modest though these novels may be.

In contrast, the novels I discuss below have a much greater range: in their formal features, particularly the barrier; in their deployment of major tropes often associated with twentieth-century romance novels; and in their depiction of the protagonist's ethnicity, socio-economic status, religion, and sexual orientation. In addition, many of them belong to the sentimental tradition and realism, mainstream literary movements that include romance novels. Using "range" as a selection criterion permits a wide-lens view of the genre, serves as a caution against generalizing beyond one's evidence, and contributes data points toward an accurate account of the romance's scope. The range of the novels discussed below should alert us as researchers to be on the lookout for characteristics in our study texts not usually associated with romance novels. I will show that the American romance novel begins in novels that are part of the sentimental tradition of American letters, establishes American realism decades before the usual date that literary historians assign to its advent, and confronts and overcomes the danger to heroines' HEAs posed not by a big misunderstanding, but by rakes, dynastic unions, chattel slavery, race, class, unhappy first marriages, pregnancy, and legally mandated heterosexuality.

The American romance novel in the eighteenth and nineteenth centuries

Samuel Richardson and Benjamin Franklin, both printers, are the fathers of the romance novel in America. In London, in 1740, Richardson published *Pamela; or, Virtue Rewarded*, "widely regarded as the first popular romance novel in English"

(Regis "Female" 850). He was also *Pamela*'s author. This act of self-publication predated by more than two and a half centuries the current explosion of this practice enabled by rapid advances in e-publication. Richardson's novel was a huge success, one of the first novels that can be called a bestseller. In Philadelphia, in 1742–3, Franklin reprinted the first edition of *Pamela*, making it not only the first novel, but also the first *romance* novel printed in America. Although Franklin's edition was not a commercial success, I have argued in "*Pamela* Crosses the Atlantic; or, Pamela Andrews's Story Inaugurates the American Romance Novel" that the story of the courtship and betrothal of the novel's heroine was well known to eighteenth- and nineteenth-century American readers through the abridgments of *Pamela*, which were published in volumes whose size and length resemble the short contemporary romances of the current age—such as Silhouettes (26). I conclude, "Beginning with Richardson, American romance novelists . . . will place their heroines—and heroes—in that most American of locales: the state of freedom. American readers will respond enthusiastically" (38).

In Pamela's courtship tale issues of class are prominent—the narrative traces the eponymous heroine's ascent from lady's maid to lady of the manor. The hero, the lord of the manor, is a rake, a character type that has endured in the genre. Pamela tames him by converting him from would-be seducer to honorable suitor. She ends the novel admired by her loving husband, wealthy enough to provide for her indigent parents, and no longer a member of the servant class. Although Richardson's *Clarissa* (1748), whose heroine is seduced and dies, is widely cited as the British novel that most influenced the early American novel by providing a model for Susanna Rowson's *Charlotte Temple* (1794) and Hannah Webster Foster's *The Coquette* (1797), *Pamela*'s literary heirs, whose authors chose Pamela as their model, are indeed legion. They formed part of the "damned mob of scribbling women" who outsold Hawthorne, who, in turn, so famously scorned them.

The American women authors of the sentimental novel discussed below, include Vickery, Sedgwick, Child, Southworth, and Alcott. Sentimental works were by far the most popular form of fiction in nineteenth-century America. Scores of authors wrote, collectively, thousands of novels, which survived in reprinted editions well into the twentieth century. Thus in addition to inaugurating the romance novel in America, Richardson also stands at the head of a long line of sentimental authors. In "Sentimentalism," Cindy Weinstein identifies the "general features" of American sentimental novels as "a focus on day-to-day activities in the domestic sphere, a concentration on relationships, and a profound interest in the emotional lives of women" (209).

With Pamela's story as a starting point, I looked for romance novels written by Americans in the late eighteenth and early nineteenth centuries. An anecdote from that search offers additional insight into the method for unearthing these novels and the decisions that then face the literary historian. At one point in my effort to locate the earliest American romance novels, I sent to a group of Americanists an email inquiry in which I asked if I was missing the obvious—if someone could name an early American romance novel. No one could suggest titles that might qualify. I felt reassured. Sometime later, reading Ljungquist's list, I found two little-known novels by none other than Charles Brockden Brown: *Clara Howard* and *Jane Talbot* (both 1801). Alerted by their titles—they *sound* like romance novels named after their heroines—I located copies. These novels were hidden in plain sight, in the fifth volume of the MLA-sanctioned collected works of one of the most studied American authors. They are both courtship tales, and like Richardson's and Franklin's *Pamela*, they are both epistolary, i.e., told in letters. Brockden Brown, then, at least formally, was a Richardsonian. I found that both *Clara Howard* and *Jane Talbot* hinge, in part, on weak, coincidental plot devices: misplaced or forged letters. In addition, although the novels are named after their heroines, they focus on their heroes. Confronted by this sort of evidence, the literary historian must decide between including these novels in a history of the American romance novel or devoting time and effort to other, more worthy titles. Because analysis of these novels would displace in a developing history of the romance the time and effort that could be devoted to analysis of a novel that focuses on the heroine, one of the romance's important contributions to fiction, a novel that, moreover, is a stronger novel, I moved on. With tens of thousands of romance novels undiscovered, spending time on lesser works, however canonical their authors, perpetuates the idea that there are no other, worthier works to include.

More directly the heir of Richardson's *Pamela*, and a better book than either of Brown's overwrought narratives, is *Emily Hamilton, A Novel: Founded on Incidents in Real Life* (1803), the only novel of Sukey Vickery (1779–1820). In Vickery we recognize another Richardsonian. *Emily Hamilton*, like the full-length *Pamela*, is epistolary, establishing as Pamela's heirs American female characters who write the letters that comprise this novel, and at the same time establishing *Emily Hamilton* as an early example of an alternate choice of point of view (letters are first person) and of narrative voice(s): letters comprise the whole of the narrative in contrast to the Silhouettes, and, indeed, most romance novels, in which the conventions of nineteenth-century realism, including third-person narration, are dominant. *Emily Hamilton* thus contributes to our developing sense of the genre's range. The novel tells in full detail the story of the courtship and betrothal of Emily, as well as, in broader strokes, the courtships of two additional heroines—Mary Carter and Eliza Anderson. These women are, unlike Pamela, the daughters of well-off families. Like Jane Austen's *Sense and Sensibility*, published eight years later with "By a Lady" substituting for the author's name on the title page, the corresponding page of Vickery's novel does not name her. Instead, we read "By a YOUNG LADY of WORCESTER COUNTY." Literary scholars of contemporary romance take for granted the idea of women writing romance novels. It is worth remembering that for Vickery, like Austen, public authorship was viewed as unladylike.

Although unhappy unions and two courtships cut short by death are depicted as well, the emphasis is on navigation to successful unions. The barriers to Emily's marriage to Belmont, the hero, are particularly daunting. They include the attentions paid to her by a rake, a standard feature of the romance novel to this day. The rakes in *Emily Hamilton*, and, as we shall see, other romance novels of this time, are not phantasmagorical creatures, or even exaggerations. The novel belongs to a sub-genre of the romance that the romance community recognizes as a "contemporary," which is to say a realistic novel set in the author's own time. This novel, as the subtitle has it, is "Founded on Incidents in Real Life." The rise of realism in the American novel is usually assigned to the post-Civil War era. Here we see the first of a series of realistic romances, decades in advance of Mark Twain et al. Lambert, Vickery's fictional rake, is realistically dissolute, self-indulgent, and promiscuous. Historian Nancy F. Cott, studying eighteenth-century American relationships, finds ample evidence in Massachusetts court records of rakes whose appetite for seduction was hearty, and whose regret was nonexistent ("Eighteenth-Century" 34). Lambert, while engaged to Emily, has seduced, impregnated, and abandoned Betsey Winslow. Anna Mae Duane notes that this sequence of events is typical in seduction novels, a genre recovered in the twentieth century, now a part of the "origin tale literary historians have spun about American literature" (37). Because of this origin tale, scholars have disregarded happy endings in marriage to fit novels with a seduction subplot into the "seduction novels" genre. Duane follows Cathy N. Davidson's observation that the "unstated premise of sentimental fiction is that the woman must take greater control of her life and must make shrewd judgments of the men who come into her life" (189).

Another constituent of the barrier is Belmont's dynastic, arranged marriage to a woman who is actually in love with another man. Dynastic arrangements still feature in romance novels—both historicals and contemporaries. Although class, race, socioeconomic issues, and sexual orientation do not factor, the danger of rakes and the barrier of an unhappy marriage are present in this early American romance novel.

Catharine Maria Sedgwick (1789–1867), best known for *Hope Leslie* (1827), an early instance of the sympathetic portrayal of the courtship of a Native American woman (albeit without a happy ending), writes *A New-England Tale; or, Sketches of New-England Character and Manners* (1822), a bildungsroman/courtship tale about an orphan who is courted by and marries an older man, an early instance of this common trope. The barriers to Robert Lloyd and Jane Elton's union are religion—he is Quaker, she is not—and, again, the threat to the courtship of the heroine by a wealthy rake. The heroine is a poor relation housed—and abused—by her aunt. Heroines who are orphan or, like Pamela, whose parents are absent or ineffective (Pamela's are both) appear frequently in romance novels. There is a continuum of dissolute men in this novel: David Wilson is the stereotypical rake, who seduces Mary Oakley when she falls "victim to his libertinism," bears his child, and, denounced by her seducer, dies. Edward Erskine, an immoral attorney, but not quite a rake, courts Jane and holds her in "thralldom" (158). His offenses against morality are less serious than Wilson's, but his bad character poses just as serious a risk to Jane as a truly dissolute seducer. We have, then, a novel of manners, a realistic text, an orphan heroine, and a rake successfully evaded and thoroughly discredited—all characteristics that will recur across the history of the American romance.

Lydia Maria Child (1802–80), best known today as the writer of the Thanksgiving song popularly known as "Over the river and through the woods," was a renowned woman of letters in her day whose writing career spanned six decades. Child addressed a series of nineteenth-century issues for a national audience, including interracial marriage, abolition of slavery, sexual rights for women, and tolerance for religions other than Christianity (Karcher 2). Her more than 30 books include novels, biographies, anti-slavery tracts, history, household advice, and, in the multi-volume *Letters from New-York*, moral philosophy. *The Rebels; or, Boston Before the Revolution* (1825) begins, "There was hurrying to and fro through the principal streets of Boston on the night of the 14th of August, 1765" (7). Written in the 1820s, but set in the 1760s, *The Rebels* was a pioneer of the historical romance novel in America. Although in the novel's preface Child seems to demur from offering "a faithful picture of the vacillating, yet obstinate course of the British ministry," in fact, in this novel the political and the domestic are linked in overt analogy. The heroine Lucretia leaves the British Colonel Sommerville at the altar, rejecting him to marry instead the American patriot Henry Osborne. Barrier issues include dynastic versus companionate marriage, the perfidy of a rake who is revealed to be none other than Sommerville, and the true identity of the heroine—these barrier elements echo and mirror the political issues confronting the colonies before the Revolution. Although it casts the events of the American Revolution in domestic terms, this historical romance novel, more than many, directly addresses the politics of the day. The novel is sentimental. It takes place in a series of households, including, notably, Hutchinson's, the loyalist governor of Massachusetts, who is Lucretia's guardian. He gives her an ultimatum—marry Sommerville or leave his house forever. She leaves Sommerville at the altar and then Hutchinson's house.

In Vickery, Sedgwick, and Child, then, we find realism decades earlier than American literary history usually locates it; heroines who sidestep rakes to make companionate marriages; and two depictions of contemporary life, with one depiction of past times. Most important, we find female agency and deft manipulation of incident: early American romance novelists are writing sophisticated, serious accounts of contemporary life and historical events, about active heroines, that nonetheless end happily.

Two additional sentimental authors, E.D.E.N. Southworth (1819–99) and Louisa May Alcott (1832–88), represent what I have come to recognize as the mid-nineteenth-century romance boom in America, predating by at least a century the mid-twentieth-century romance boom inaugurated by the 1972 publication of *The Flame and the Flower.*

Southworth's career—her novels appeared between 1847 and 1905—was the sort that we associate with a twentieth- or twenty-first-century best-selling author. It was made possible by the advent of stereotyping in 1829, an augmentation of the letterpress process for book production.[4] This printing method offered a dramatic competitive advantage over letterpress volumes. By 1853, historian of printing John Tebbel notes, T.B. Peterson, Southworth's publisher, was stereotyping "all the most popular foreign and American books he could obtain, and sell[ing] them for the smallest price possible" (I:246). In 1854, Southworth approached Peterson with a novel she had been unable to sell. He published the novel in question (*The Lost Heiress*), and signed her to a long-term contract, eventually buying from her previous publishers the letterpress plates of her backlist. By 1877, he issued a 42-volume edition of her works. "Of her [almost] fifty . . . novels, nearly all sold at least 100,000 copies," affording her, at one point, $6000 annually in royalties . . . (Tebbel 246–7). Of the 873 writers whose works were published in book form between 1837 and 1857, Southworth was on the list of the 20 most prolific novelists (Zboray and Zboray 74). She is thus an instance of what is often supposed to be a twentieth-century phenomenon, the prolific, best-selling romance writer—Nora Roberts's foremother.

The heroine of Southworth's *Vivia: or The Secret of Power* (1857), is Vivia LaGlorieuse, an American orphan courted by Wakefield, the hero, whom she meets when they are both children. The barrier to this union is, finally, Vivia's refusal to marry Wakefield until he loves not only her, but also God, and God above all: "You seek to live not in and from the Lord; but in and from me!" Vivia tells him, and then dismisses him. (491–2) This is an anti-declaration, as well as the point of ritual death: "He was gone—and she remained pale, cold, faint, as one from whom all life had been withdrawn" (494). Sentimental values infuse the novel: a belief in the importance of emotion; the heroine as the seat of morality, in this case, in the form of true religion. Overt Christianity, such as that in *Vivia,* unremarkable in a nineteenth-century American romance, survives in the twenty-first-century inspirational subgenre.

For a history and analysis of the American inspirational romance novel, whose founding author is often identified as Grace Livingston Hill, see Lynn S. Neal's *Romancing God: Evangelical Women and Inspirational Fiction* (2006).[5] The subgenre is still vibrant. In 2001, inspirational romance writer Robin Lee Hatcher won the 2001 Nora Roberts Lifetime Achievement Award from the Romance Writers of America (rwa.org).

In 1867 Thomas Niles of Roberts Brothers publishers asked Louisa May Alcott, already an established, successful author, to write a story for girls, and she agreed to try (Showalter 1073). The result was Louisa May Alcott's beloved March trilogy, consisting of *Little Women, or, Meg, Jo, Beth and Amy* (1868–69), *Little Men: Life at Plumfield* (1871) and *Jo's Boys, and How They Turned Out* (1886). *Little Women* depicts five courtships, Laurie/Jo; John Brooke/Meg; Fred/Amy; Laurie/Amy; Professor Bhaer/Jo, and, writing beyond the HEA, Alcott followed Jo's subsequent career as the matron of a home for orphan boys and a successful writer in *Little Men* and *Jo's Boys*. Jo's courtship is noteworthy—and beloved to this day—for its iconoclasm. Rejecting the well-heeled Laurie she marries instead an older man, Professor Bhaer, and makes good on her determination to help "earn the home" that the Bhaers would make (506). Like Mr. March, Professor Bhaer is an inadequate provider, but this economic challenge is not a barrier to the union. The gender ambiguity of Jo's name signals her status as a tomboy. Michelle Ann Abate identifies her as the literary "paradigm" for such characters (26). In this regard, she is a pre-twentieth-century assertive heroine, like Pamela, Emily, Jane, Lucretia, and Vivia. Unlike them, Jo, true to her gender-ambiguous name, pursues traditionally male occupations. In this way, she is a harbinger for the explosion of occupations—from homicide detective to fire-jumper to CEO—that contemporary romance heroines pursue. Jo anticipates this explosion of occupations even as the novels' values are sentimental: female empowerment, centered in part on the home, emotion, affection, and love.

The heroines of two additional works unrecognized as romance novels serve to mark ethnic diversification of the genre. In both, the romance form is marshaled to challenge dominant cultural narratives. In *Iola Leroy, or, Shadows Uplifted* (1892), one of the first novels written by an African-American, Frances E.W. Harper (1825–1911) asks readers, through the barriers facing the courting young people, to consider some of the most serious issues that America has ever confronted: the hypocrisy of chattel slavery, including the rape of enslaved women by their masters; the nature of race, including, in nascent form, the identification of race as a legal and societal construct rather than as essential to any individual; and a women's right, and in Harper's view, her obligation, to do meaningful work. The novel, like *The Rebels*, is a historical romance. Published during Reconstruction, Harper set it in the period from the end of the Civil War extending to the war's immediate aftermath. The heroine, Iola, a blue-eyed blonde, was born a slave. Her white father married her mother, his own slave, and together they raised her ignorant of her legal status as a chattel slave. Iola was kidnapped into slavery, then rescued by Union forces from her slave master's threat of rape, and finally freed to make a choice between two suitors—one white, the other African-American. She chooses the African-American. In presenting Iola with this choice, and in having her choose the African-American suitor, Harper offers a narrative other than that of white male sexual violence against female slaves described in slave narratives such as Harriet Ann Jacobs's *Incidents in the Life of a Slave Girl* (1861), and points the way to an improved society. Scholars of the African-American novel recognize the power of the courtship narrative in the hands of authors like LeRoy. Claudia Tate in *Domestic Allegories of Political Desire: The Black Heroine's Text at the Turn of the Century* (1993) claims that "because Iola's story closes with marriage," for present-day readers the heroine's "entire enterprise probably appears as a part of the sentimental discourse of romance." She cautions against this reading of the text, noting that "from Harper's historical perspective, the domestic did not exist apart from the political" (171). Ann duCille in *The Coupling Convention: Sex, Text, and Tradition in Black Women's Fiction* (1993) identifies the "racially charged appropriations of the marriage plot" (4). See also Rita B. Dandridge's *Black Women's Activism: Reading African American Women's Historical Romances* (2004) for analysis of more recent historical novels by and about African-American women that feature heroines who encounter, and prevail over, issues of race, gender, and class.

With Iola LeRoy, we see the beginnings of the African-American romance, whose best-known current practitioner, Beverly Jenkins, was given the 2017 Nora Roberts Lifetime Achievement Award (rwa.org).[6]

"Onoto Watanna" is the pen name of Winnifred Eaton, the child of a British father and a Chinese mother. Eve Oishi, Watanna's modern editor, describes her as "a Eurasian writer of Chinese and Anglo descent who assumed a Japanese identity and a Japanese-sounding pseudonym ... in order to write romance novels about Japanese and Eurasian women" (xi). In *Miss Numè of Japan: A Japanese-American Romance* (1899), recognized as the first novel written by an Asian-American author, Watanna rewrites the typical American narrative of a mixed-race courtship between a white man and an Asian woman, a narrative that survives to this day in Puccini's *Madame Butterfly* (1904). Based on an American short story, Puccini's opera is still performed by opera companies worldwide. In it, U.S. Navy Lt. Benjamin Pinkerton, stationed in Japan, arranges a sham marriage with Butterfly (Cio-Cio San), impregnates her, and leaves her to go home to America. A few years later he returns to Japan with his American wife to claim the child. Butterfly, grief-stricken, commits suicide. Watanna turns to the romance novel form to rewrite this dominant narrative in which the Japanese heroine's response to an American man's duplicity is suicide. In *Miss Numè of Japan*, she constructs a complicated set of overlapping courtships—the Japanese heroine, *Numè*, is courted by Sinclair, an American; Sinclair is engaged to Cleo, also an American; Cleo is in love with Orito, who is Japanese; Orito, to complete the circle, is betrothed to Numè in a dynastic match. The point of ritual death is ritual suicide in this narrative, but, unlike the death of Butterfly in the dominant narrative, the dead are all men: the matchmakers of Numè's dynastic betrothal, Numè's father and Orito's father; and Orito. These three suicides free Numè to marry Sinclair, and with him to establish a home not in America but in Japan—that is, in her home culture, not his. The barriers to this union are the chain of betrothals among the parties to the courtships, including the dynastic betrothal of Numè and Orito; racism, which dooms the Cleo/Orito union but which Sinclair overcomes, and Sinclair's self-deception, which motivates him for a time to remain betrothed to Cleo despite doubting that he loves her.

For both Harper and Watanna, the romance novel form provides the means to personalize the racial issues that the parties to the courtships must face. The societal context of racial prejudice is overcome by love in both novels, with Iola out of a sense of duty and love refusing to "pass" in order to marry a white man, and with Numè refusing to place duty to her father above her love for Sinclair. By its very nature, the romance requires an HEA. Put a marginalized, out-of-the-ordinary heroine/

protagonist in a romance, and she—or he or they—are granted the HEA that racism, gender discrimination, etc. may have denied her, him, or them.

The American romance novel in the first half of the twentieth century

In his account of the publishing landscape for romance at the turn of the twentieth century, William A. Gleason notes "[t]he mid to late 1870s marks a distinct phase in the circulation of popular romance fiction in the US, as story paper and dime novel publishers began experimenting with all-romance titles marketed primarily to women readers" (58). He notes the occurrence during this time of "gender-specific marketing of popular genres by publishers of cheap fiction" (58). He concludes, "recognizing the expansiveness and unpredictability of the genre in the postbellum era . . . can usefully complicate the literary histories of American courtship narratives we are still working to produce" (69). For the romance historian engaging in paleontological excavation, Gleason points us to recently digitized historical American newspapers, where we will find a trove of romance stories, unexplored. Gleason warns that he has found this era to be "marked by diversity and multiplicity that we too commonly think of as an exclusively contemporary phenomenon" citing "multiple points of view, proliferating subgenres, and diverse publishing venues" as features of the romance narratives in the late nineteenth-century and early twentieth-century story papers he studied (57). His work underscores yet again the danger to literary historians of the romance: proceed with caution in ascribing "firsts" to phenomena in relatively recent texts.

Four novels from this period, none of them recognized as romance novels, will further expand our notion of the range of romance. *Daddy-Long-Legs* (1912) by Jean Webster (1876–1916) is epistolary, consisting of the wholly one-sided correspondence written by the heroine to the hero. Elaine Showalter in her introduction to the novel, notes:

> Webster was among the most highly paid women writers in the United States. As the author of five best sellers in addition to *Daddy-Long-Legs*, she earned book royalties averaging more than $10,000 a year. Royalties from the productions of [the stage play] *Daddy-Long-Legs*, averaging almost $2,000 per week, vaulted her into a whole different league of earnings.
>
> (xv)

Daddy-Long-Legs has proven to have an enduring, international appeal: At least four U.S. films have been made based on the novel, along with Japanese, Indian, Korean, and Hong Kongese adaptations for both TV and film (IMDb.com). Judy, the heroine, is an orphan who has been sent to college to become a writer funded by one of the trustees of the orphanage where she was raised. The hero is the trustee himself. Showalter has identified Judy as an "unconventional New Woman" and the work as a *Künstlerroman*, the account of an artist's development (viii). In contrast to the domestic, home-centered heroines of the sentimental tradition—even *The Rebels* takes place largely in domestic settings—the setting for *Daddy-Long-Legs* is "Wilson College" (a stand-in for Vassar, which Webster attended), and the *Künstlerroman* plot is co-equal with the romance plot. Academic themes contribute to Judy's development far more than the hero's direct influence. As an orphan, Judy is an instance of a romance trope that is as least as old as *Pamela* (whose parents are not dead, but absent and powerless; Jane in *A New-England Tale* is another). Judy is also a ward, of sorts, of the hero, another common romance trope, although in this case, she does not know the identity of her benefactor. Having seen only his elongated shadow during a visit he made to the orphanage she gives him the name "Daddy-Long-Legs." It is not until the end, when she has been courted by two men, including, unbeknownst to her, her benefactor, that she identifies him *as* her benefactor. The barrier to the union is class. Judy is forthright about her "lack of antecedents" in contrast to "a family like his [the hero's]" (127). By the time of his proposal, she is independent: she has won a scholarship that replaces his financial support for her education, and rejected his first proposal of marriage. According to Gail Finney, the New Woman "pursues self-fulfillment and independence … tends to be well-educated and to read a great deal … is likely to be more interested in politics than the conventional woman … [and] is physically vigorous and energetic" (195–6). The New Woman, here, is not really as new as one might think: self-determination, at least in one's choice of husband, has been the hallmark of romance heroines throughout the history of the genre, and the description of the New Woman could apply to any number of romance heroines through the ages.

Kathleen Thompson Norris (1880–1966), "between 1910 and 1950, was the equivalent of Nora Roberts or Stephen King" writing 82 novels, "many of them best-sellers and many more serialized in the period's most popular publications" (Carter 197). Many of them are romance novels as well, although this has gone unrecognized. One such is *Rose of the World* (1924). In it the heroine, Rosamund, and hero, Jack, court and become engaged, but are separated by a variety of barriers. Rose is poor, weighed down by her work to support her mother, sister, and grandfather, while Jack is the son of a wealthy owner of an iron mill. His mother objects to his marrying beneath his status. Rose, she points out, "hasn't had a fair education … no languages, no travel, no literary classes or music" and may not be able to "keep step" with Jack (47). She chooses a different wife for her son, a woman who is also wealthy, making it a dynastic union. At the novel's beginning, Jack is immature, "a wasteful, idle, indifferent boy" easily distracted by the woman his mother chooses as his wife (298). He and Rose break off their engagement, and each of them marries someone else, which imposes the barrier of two marriages to their eventual union. The work of the book is to reunite the hero and heroine, both unhappily married to other people. Norris's romances are unusual in the detailed depictions they offer of unhappy marriages. Rose describes her life with her "passionately ambitious," controlling, disapproving husband as "so empty and so hard, and so lonely" (272). She remains in the marriage because she fears that her husband will separate her from their daughter. Jack remains in his marriage out of duty. Deaths of both spouses—Jack's wife in childbirth and Rose's husband by a fall over a cliff—bring Rose and Jack back together again. Rose is no longer an ingénue, Jack no longer idle. Second chances are frequent in romance. Between 1981 and 1989, Berkley published more than 400 titles in their "Second Chance at Love" line (Romance wiki).

Another unrecognized romance novel is *Bad Girl* (1928) by Viña Delmar. It presents us with another sort of heroine—Dot Haley, a working-class girl, with a working-class hero, Eddie Collins. The novel was "one of the Literary Guild's first selections" (Gilette 62). *Bad Girl* was, the *New York Post* reported, "the book everybody read, whether he admitted it or not" (quoted in Gilette 62). Both a Broadway play (1930) and an award-winning film (1931) followed (Gilette 62). Heroine and hero are both "flat- dwellers of New York," employed as a typist and a radio repairman (12). A contemporary set in the Bronx, in this novel betrothal and marriage occur about a third of the way through, and the barrier that threatens this union and the establishment of a new society is not pre-marital sex, although readers were scandalized and fascinated by the couple's consummation of their relationship before marriage. Nor is the barrier financial issues, although Dot stops work after marriage; nor is it family disapproval, although Dot is kicked out of the home that her brother had been providing her with when she begins a relationship with Eddie. The barrier is her pregnancy and the question of whether to abort the child. Dot believes that Eddie does not want a child; Eddie believes that Dot does not want a child. Dot investigates getting an abortion, but decides not to go through with it. They do not resolve this issue until the last page of the book, when they are taking their son home from the sanitarium where Dot has given birth, and Eddie takes the baby from Dot, uncomplaining when he becomes "wet through" (288). The abortion barrier was controversial at the time—so much so that it was omitted from the film altogether—and an early instance of a romance that confronts an incendiary issue.

Patricia Highsmith, author of *Strangers on a Train, The Talented Mr. Ripley*, and other celebrated novels of suspense, wrote what is widely regarded as the first American lesbian romance novel—The *Price of Salt* (1952), published in the U.K. as *Carol* under the pseudonym "Claire Morgan." Highsmith's romance is an example of the romantic suspense subgenre, whose founding author is usually cited as British author Mary Stewart, although Stewart did not publish her first romance until 1955, three years after Highsmith's novel (Regis *Natural History* 143–54). Highsmith's heroines, young Therese Belivet (she turns 21 at the novel's end) and somewhat older Carol Aird, wife of Harge and mother of a young daughter, Rindy, fall in love. Barriers include Therese's boyfriend, who voices the culture's rejection of lesbian union:

> [T]he uppermost emotion I feel towards you is one that was present from the first—disgust. It is your hanging on to this woman to the exclusion of everyone else, this relationship which I am sure has become sordid and pathological by now, that disgusts me.
>
> (222)

Carol's marriage is also part of the barrier, as is her husband Harge's determination to deny her post-divorce visitation rights with their daughter should Carol continue to see Therese. The suspense plot is part of the barrier as well, as Harge hires a private detective to gather evidence of Carol and Therese's relationship. The detective stalks them and bugs the hotel room of the heroines when they flee cross-country, by car, from New York City. The HEA for the two heroines comes at the expense of Carol's access to Rindy. She recants a promise she had made to Harge never to see Therese again, and instead invites her to live with her.

In a 1990 afterword to *The Price of Salt*, Highsmith describes the novel's outcome, despite Carol's loss of her relationship with her daughter, as a

> happy ending for [the] two main characters ... Prior to this book, homosexuals male and female in American novels had had to pay for their deviation by cutting their wrists, drowning themselves in a swimming pool, or by switching to heterosexuality (so it was stated), or by collapsing—alone and miserable and shunned—into a depression equal to hell.
>
> (261)

At least as early as 1952, the largely heterosexual relationships depicted in the American romance novel were joined by courting protagonists who identify as LGBTQIA. In *Lesbian Romance Novels: A History and Critical Analysis*, Phyllis M. Betz explores this subgenre at length, analyzing novels issued by American presses whose founders wished to provide a publishing outlet for lesbian romance, such Naiad Press, founded in 1973, publisher, in 1983 of Katherine V. Forrest's very popular *Curious Wine*, and Bold Strokes Books, founded in 2004 by writer of lesbian romances Len Barot (who writes as Radclyffe). See Barot's "Queer Romance in Twentieth- and Twenty-First-Century America: Snapshots of a Revolution" for an account of the emergence of the lesbian romance novel, which she claims does not occur "until the latter decades of the twentieth century" (387).

Like the paleontologists who piece together the past from long-buried fragments, literary historians must assemble the history of the romance genre from works that have, in many cases, been long forgotten, and in most cases, never identified as romance novels. Although, for instance, finding an early American romance novel permits us to begin the work of rewriting the literary history of that period, it also reminds us of the likelihood that there are other romance novels yet undiscovered, from the long history of the American novel. This reminder is also a caution—there is much we do not know about the history of the American romance novel, and sweeping statements about *the* history of that genre, or, indeed, about *the romance novel* as a genre, require us to carefully qualify our claims. There is much we do not know.

Notes

1 There are other views of freedom in the romance. In the Introduction to *Romance and American Culture: Love as the Practice of Freedom*, editors William A. Gleason and Eric Murphy Selinger assert that in assembling the volume they "maintain an inquisitive posture toward the matter of love's relationship to freedom" (10).

2 Silhouette Romance #1 *Payment in Full* by Anne Hampson, #2 *Shadow and Sun* by Mary Carroll, #3 *Affairs of the Heart* by Nora Powers, #4 *Stormy Masquerade* by Anne Hampson, #5 *Path of Desire* by Ellen Goforth, #6 *Golden Tide* by Sheila Stanford, #7 *Midsummer Bride* by Mary Lewis, #8 *Captive Heart* by Patti Beckman, #9 *Where Mountains Wait* by Fran Wilson, #10 *Bridge of Love* by Leslie Caine.

3 Defined at the blog "All About Romance" (https://allaboutromance.com/can-you-hear-me-now-an-open-letter-to-romance-authors): "The hero or heroine witnesses something or overhears something or is told something that leads him or her to a wrong conclusion about his/her love interest. Rather than confront the potentially wayward lover as soon as possible to ask her/him to explain the situation, the discussion never happens and the romance grinds to a complete halt."

4 A "stereotype" is a solid plate of type, created by molding a letterpress galley using paper mâché or plaster, and then casting from that mold a plate that can be used for printing. A single letterpress galley, then, could be stereotyped as many times as needed. The painstaking letter-by-letter sliding of type onto a composing stick need be done only once for each page. Mass production was thus made possible.

5 Chapters 8 and 21 of this Companion also discuss religion and romance.

6 For more on African American romance see Chapter 10.

Works cited

Abate, Michelle Ann. *Tomboys: A Literary and Cultural History*. Temple University Press, 2008.

Alcott, Louisa. *May. Little Women, Little Men, Jo's Boys*. Edited by Elaine Showalter, Library of America, 2005.

Austen, Jane. *Sense and Sensibility*. Thomas Egerton, 1811.

Barot, Len. "Queer Romance in Twentieth- and Twenty-First-Century America: Snapshots of a Revolution." *Romance Fiction and American Culture: Love as the Practice of Freedom?*, edited by William A. Gleason, and Eric Murphy Selinger, Ashgate, 2016, pp. 390–404.

Betz, Phyllis M. *Lesbian Romance Novels: A History and Critical Analysis*. McFarland, 2009.

Brown, Charles Brockden. *Clara Howard: In a Series of Letters; Jane Talbot: A novel*. Edited by Donald A. Ringe, Kent State University Press, 1986. Vol 5 of *The Novels and Related Works of Charles Brockden Brown*. 6 vols. Edited by Sydney J. Krause.

Brown, Herbert Ross. *The Sentimental Novel in America 1789–1860*. Duke University Press, 1940.

Caine, Leslie. *Bridge of Love*. Silhouette, 1981.

Carter, Catherine. "Poverty, Payment, Power: Kathleen Thompson Norris and Popular Romance." *Studies in American Fiction*, vol. 36, no. 2, Autumn 2008, pp. 197–220. *Project Muse*, doi: 10.1353/saf.2008.0002.

Cassuto, Leonard, *et al.*, editors *The Cambridge History of the American Novel*. Cambridge University Press, 2011.

Chase, Richard. *The American Novel and Its Tradition*. Doubleday, 1957.

Child, Lydia Maria. *The Rebels, or, Boston Before the Revolution*, Cummings, Hilliard, 1825. Google Books, http://books.google.com/. Accessed 15 Nov. 2013.

Cott, Nancy F. "Eighteenth-Century Family And Social Life Revealed In Massachusetts Divorce Records." *Journal of Social History*, vol. 10, no. 1, 1976, pp. 20–43.

Dandridge, Rita B. *Black Women's Activism: Reading African-American American Women's Historical Romances*. Peter Lang, 2004.

Davidson, Cathy N. *Revolution and the Word*. Oxford University Press, 2004.

Delmar, Viña. *Bad Girl*. Harcourt Brace & Co., 1928.

Dixon, jay. *The Romance Fiction of Mills & Boon, 1909-1990s*. University College London Press, 1999.

Dobson, Joanne. "Reclaiming Sentimental Literature." *American Literature*, vol. 69, no. 2, 1997, pp. 263–288. *JSTOR*: 10.2307/2928271.

Duane, Anna Mae. "Susanna Rowson, Hannah Webster Foster, and the Seduction Novel in the Early US." *The Cambridge History of the American Novel*, edited by Leonard Cassuto, et. al., Cambridge University Press, 2011, pp. 37–50.

duCille, Ann. *The Coupling Convention: Sex, Text, and Tradition in Black Women's Fiction*. Oxford University Press, 1993.

Fiedler, Leslie A. *Love and Death in the American Novel*. Criterion Books, 1960.

Finney, Gail. *Women in Modern Drama: Freud, Feminism, and European Theater at the turn of the Century*. Cornell University Press, 1989.

Flesch, Juliet. *From Australia with Love: A History of Modern Romance Novels*. Fremantle Press, 2004.

Fletcher, Lisa. *Historical Romance Fiction: Heterosexuality and Performativity*. Ashgate, 2008.

Forrest, Katherine V. *Curious Wine*. Niaid, 1983.

Gilette, Meg. "Making Modern Parents in Ernest Hemingway's 'Hills like White Elephants' and Viña Demar's *Bad Girl*." *Modern Fiction Studies*, vol. 53, no. 1, Spring 2007, pp. 50–69. *Project Muse*, doi: 10.1353/mfs.2007.0023.

Gleason, William A. "Postbellum, Pre-Harlequin: American Romance Publishing in the Late Nineteenth and Early Twentieth Century." *Romance Fiction and American Culture: Love as the Practice of Freedom?* edited by William A. Gleason, and Eric Murphy Selinger, Ashgate, 2016, pp. 57–70.

Gleason, William A. and Eric Murphy Selinger, editors. *Romance Fiction and American Culture: Love as the Practice of Freedom?* Ashgate, 2016.

Harper, Frances E.W. *Iola Leroy, or, Shadows Uplifted*. Dover, 2010.

Harris, Sharon M., et al., editors. *American Women Prose Writers, 1870-1920. Dictionary of Literary Biography 221*. Gale, 2001.

Hawthorne, Nathaniel. *The Blithedale Romance*. Oxford, 1998.

———. *The House of the Seven Gables*. Oxford, 1998.

Highsmith, Patricia. *The Price of Salt.* W.W. Norton, 2004.
Hogan, Patrick Colm. *The Mind and Its Stories: Narrative Universals and Human Emotion.* Cambridge University Press, 2003.
Homestead, Melissa J. and Vicki L. Martin. "A Chronological Bibliography of E.D.E.N. Southworth's Works Privileging Periodical Publication." Homestead and Washington, pp. 285–306.
Homestead, Melissa J. and Pamela T. Washington, editors. *E.D.E.N. Southworth: Recovering a Nineteenth-Century Popular Novelist.* University of Tennessee Press, 2012.
Hudock, Amy E. *E.D.E.N. Southworth.* Huddock and Rodier, 285–292.
Hudock, Amy E. and Katharine Rodier, editors. *American Women Prose Writers, 1820-1870.* Gale, 2001. Dictionary of Literary Biography 239.
Jacobs, Harriet Ann. *Incidents in the Life of a Slave Girl.* Thayer and Eldredge, 1861.
Kamblé, Jayashree. *Making Meaning in Popular Romance Fiction: An Epistemology.* Palgrave Macmillan, 2014.
Karcher, Carolyn L. *The First Woman in the Republic: A Cultural Biography of Lydia Maria Child.* Durham: Duke University Press, 1994.
Ljungquist, Kent P. editor *Facts on File Bibliography of American Fiction: Through 1865.* Facts on File, 1994.
Matthiessen, F. O. *American Renaissance: Art and Expression in the Age of Emerson and Whitman.* Oxford University Press, 1941.
Mulford, Carla, et al., editors *American Women Prose Writers to 1820.* Gale, 1999. Dictionary of Literary Biography 200.
Neal, Lynn S. *Romancing God: Evangelical Women and Inspirational Fiction.* University of North Carolina Press, 2006.
Norris, Kathleen. *Thompson. Rose of the World.* Doubleday, Page, 1924.
Oishi, Eve. See Watanna.
Porte, Joel. *The Romance in America: Studies in Cooper, Poe, Hawthorne, Melville, and James.* Wesleyan University Press, 1969.
Radway, Janice A. *Reading the Romance: Women, Patriarchy, and Popular Literature.* 1984. University of North Carolina Press, 1991.
Regis, Pamela. *A Natural History of the Romance Novel.* University of Pennsylvania Press, 2003.
———. "Female Genre Fiction in the Twentieth Century." *The Cambridge History of the American Novel,* edited by Leonard Cassuto, et. al., Cambridge University Press, 2011, pp. 847–860.
———. "What Do Critics Owe the Romance?" *Journal of Popular Romance Studies,* vol. 2, no. 1, 2011, n.p. jprstudies.org.
———. "Pamela Crosses the Atlantic; or, Pamela Andrews's Story Inaugurates the American Romance Novel". *Romance Fiction and American Culture: Love as the Practice of Freedom?,* edited by William A. Gleason, and Eric Murphy Selinger, Ashgate, 2016, pp. 25–40.
Roach, Catherine M. *Happily Ever After: The Romance Story in Popular Culture.* Indiana University Press, 2016.
Roberts, Nora. *Irish Thoroughbred.* Silhouette, 1981.
Romance Writers of America. "About the Genre." www.rwa.org/p/cm/ld/fid=582. Accessed 4 July 2017.
———. "Reader Statistics." www.rwa.org/p/cm/ld/fid=582. Accessed 4 July 2017.
Sedgwick, Catharine Maria. *Hope Leslie, or, Early Times in Massachusetts.* 1827.
———. *A New-England Tale; or, Sketches of New-England Character and Manners.* Oxford University Press, 1995.
Selinger, Eric Murphy, and Sarah S. G. Frantz, editors. *New Approaches to Popular Romance Fiction: Critical Essays.* McFarland, 2012.
Showalter, Elaine. "Introduction." *Daddy-Long-Legs and Dear Enemy,* by Jean Webster, edited by Elaine Showalter, Penguin, 2004, pp. vii–xviii.
———. "Chronology." *Little Women, Little Men, Jo's Boys,* by Louisa May Alcott, edited by Elaine Showalter, Library of America, 2005, pp. 1067–1077.

Southworth, E.D.E.N. *Vivia; or, The Secret of Power*. 1857. Federal Book, 1875.
Tate, Claudia. *Domestic Allegories of Political Desire: The Black Heroine's Text at the Turn of the Century*. Oxford University Press, 1993.
Tebbel, John. *A History of Book Publishing in the United States. Vol I: The Creation of an Industry 1630–1865*. R.R. Bowker, 1972.
Tompkins, Jane. *Sensational Designs: The Cultural Work of American Fiction, 1790-1860*. Oxford University Press, 1986.
Trilling, Lionel. *The Liberal Imagination: Essays on Literature and Society*. Viking, 1950.
Vickery, Sukey. *Emily Hamilton and Other Writings*. Edited by Scott Slawinski, University of Nebraska Press, 2009.
Watanna, Onoto. *Miss Numè of Japan*. Edited by Eve Oishi, Johns Hopkins University Press, 1999.
Webster, Jean. *Daddy-Long-Legs* and *Dear Enemy*. Edited by Elaine Showalter. Penguin, 2004.
Weinstein, Cindy. "Sentimentalism." *The Cambridge History of the American Novel*, edited by Leonard Cassuto, et. al., Cambridge University Press, 2011, pp. 209–235.
———. "'What Did You Mean?' the Language of Marriage in *the Fatal Marriage* and *Family Doom*." *E.D.E.N. Southworth: Recovering a Nineteenth-Century Popular Novelist*, edited by Melissa J. Homestead, and Pamela T. Washington, University of Tennessee Press, 2012, pp. 265–283.
Woodiwiss, Kathleen E. *The Flame and the Flower*. Avon, 1972.
Zboray, Ronald J. and Mary Saracino Zboray. "The Novel in the Antebellum Book Market." *The Cambridge History of the American Novel*, edited by Leonard Cassuto, et. al., Cambridge University Press, 2011, pp. 67–87.

3 Australian romance fiction

Lauren O'Mahony

Since it was first published in the mid-1850s, Australian romance fiction has offered readers insights into the nation's changing social and cultural conditions. Many early romance stories explored the fortunes and burdens associated with colonial life. Several post-Federation stories (those published after 1901) ruminated on what it meant to be an Australian, particularly an Australian "girl" or "woman." Today's contemporary romances represent the journey to love with complex interplays between women's rights and responsibilities in daily life. This chapter explores how Australian romance fiction offers glimpses into life in Australia as well as women's "place" within the nation's social, cultural, and environmental fabric. As Juliet Flesch remarks, change is a feature of Australian romance fiction: the genre's readers, writers, and industries have changed and so too have the representations of women. As this chapter argues, Australia's rich history of romance writing has evolved from humble beginnings into the successful industry and community it is today.

Definitions of Australian romance fiction are bound up with the changes that have occurred to the genre and its context since the early colonial romance stories of the 1850s. As Jodi McAlister and Hsu-Ming Teo have observed, Australian romance fiction has been molded by social and cultural conditions as well as industrial forces directly from publishers. Initially, Australian romance fiction was published primarily in journals, magazines, and newspapers; these stories reached a large audience in Australia and abroad. Shorter works of romance and love were complemented by the novels of authors including "Tasma" (a pseudonym for Jesse Couvreur), Rosa Praed, and Catherine Martin. Described as colonial and settler romances, these works depicted love and romantic relationships entangled with life in colonial Australia. Authors frequently tapped into the difficulties of colonial life such as death, remote living, and forced migration to or from Australia; unlike most of today's romances, early Australian colonial stories did not always end happily (Teo; Giles). The twentieth century saw the demise of numerous small Australian publishers and the dominance of larger publishing houses. Subsequently, by the mid-twentieth century, remaining publishers of romance fiction, especially specialists in category texts such as Harlequin Mills & Boon, could exert a greater influence over the content of romance fiction. Since the 1980s, an increasing number of category and trade fiction novels have been published and by the end of the twentieth century, romances increasingly dominated Australian and global book sales. As this chapter shows, the success of Australia's romance novel industry today is attributable to the high quality of works published, the ever-evolving marketing strategies of publishers, the successful adoption of e-book formats by publishers and consumers, and a highly engaged readership whose loyalty to the genre is evidenced by their voracious reading habits.

The success of Australian romance fiction is partly related to ways in which novels exude a sense of "Australianness" or what Juliet Flesch describes as "the beetroot in the burger."[1] The "beetroot" in this case refers to the ingredient that distinguishes Australian romances from their overseas counterparts. Flesch's beetroot analogy acknowledges that Australian romances use the wider genre's familiar romantic ingredients while exhibiting unique cultural qualities that mark such works as distinctly Australian. The degree of Australianness varies between novels and writers; generally, as McAlister and Teo have suggested, such novels may be "written by an Australian," "involve Australian characters or Australian topics" though need "not always [be] set in Australia" (196).[2] Australian authorship certainly applies where an author's identification or nationality as Australian can be confirmed. "Australian characters and topics" may see novels include some Australian characters, ideally the hero, heroine or both alongside an array of supporting characters. These characters may embody unique, sometimes stereotypical, Australian dialects and linguistic traits. Such novels may also engage with cultural and social issues as well as uniquely "Australian topics." Most Australian romances utilize local settings though how each author utilizes place and space depends largely on their own interests, knowledge or the story being told. Given the large number of Australian romances exported overseas (*From Australia* 94–5; "Wide Brown Land" 82; "Love Under" 283), arguably, part of what makes Australian romances successful is the "beetroot" that distinguishes them from novels published elsewhere. How that "beetroot" is constituted in Australian romance fiction varies significantly depending on the texts being considered.

This chapter examines the evolution of Australia's popular romance fiction from the mid-eighteenth century through to today's mass-market publishing phenomenon. The chapter begins by exploring what defines Australian popular romance fiction and how the genre has changed since its inception. The chapter then turns to the production and consumption of Australian romance novels, specifically key publishers and writers in the industry. Having provided contextual information about Australian romance fiction, key themes in the scholarship on this subgenre are discussed. The role of libraries in the genre's development in Australia is considered, especially the status of library collections as a means of preserving the works of authors and publishers. Key developments in the genre since the year 2000 are then explained to argue that Australia's romance fiction industry is currently vibrant and highly successful. The chapter concludes with a brief overview of key areas for future research. Overall, this chapter argues that Australian romances have represented stories of love set against the nation's changing social and cultural context. Such novels may encourage reflection for local readers on what it means to be an "Australian" and women's changing place within the nation's culture. For non-Australian readers, Australian romance fiction may perform an outward-facing ambassadorial function in representing love stories contextualized within the nation's unique culture, society, and environment.

Defining Australian romance fiction

Australian romance fiction reproduces the staples of the wider romance genre with a sense of Australian life, culture, and people. As this section discusses, what constitutes Australian romance fiction has changed over time to reflect contextual changes, including the constraints placed upon authors by publishers. The two main organizations associated with romance novels in Australia, Romance Writers Australia and the Australian Romance Readers Association state that romance novels contain "a central love story" and "an emotionally satisfying and optimistic ending" (Australian Romance Readers (ARRA) "About ARRA" and Romance Writers of Australia (RWA) "About the Romance").[3] ARRA extends these basic elements to describe the breadth of texts under the romance banner:

> Romance fiction is a literary genre that covers a broad range of sub-genres—from historical, paranormal and suspense to comedy, urban fantasy and contemporary. Romance fiction caters to a variety of personal tastes. Romance fiction is written with any tone or style, can be set in any place and time, with any level of sensuality, from sweet to piping hot!
>
> ("About ARRA")

While the two basic romantic elements are shared by the RWA (Australia) and ARRA, setting and context clearly influences a story in various ways. For instance, as RWA (America) state, "distinctions of plot" such as tone, style, and sensuality and importantly the "setting," will "create specific subgenres within romance fiction" (RWA "About the Romance Genre"). Thus, these distinctions create some of the "beetroot" that distinguishes Australian romance fiction from its overseas counterparts. Indeed, as Driscoll et al. argue, Australian romance is not "a subset or satellite of American romance" (68); rather, Australian romance fiction exudes unique characteristics that separate it from novels originating elsewhere.

The unique characteristics of Australian romance fiction trace back to Australia's early romance stories published in the mid-1850s. According to Gelder and Weaver's *Anthology of Colonial Australian Romance Fiction*, many early Australian romance stories were published in the day's periodicals such as the *Australasian* newspaper (1864–2002) and *Bulletin* magazine (1880–2008). Gelder and Weaver's collection samples a small portion of Australian colonial romance fiction. Interestingly, the collection attributes 5 of its 16 stories to male authors thereby showing that romance writing had a good number of male authors before it became known as a "women's genre" in the twentieth century (1). The collection includes shorter works from authors who later became known for their novels including "Tasma" who later published seven novels, Mabel Forrest who published 6 novels, approximately 70 short stories, and nearly 800 poems and Rosa Praed who published 40 novels. As Gelder and Weaver suggest, colonial writers, such as Jesse Couvreur had a "transnational reach" that saw their writing published in Australia, Europe, and North America, sometimes simultaneously (274). Many early romance writers were prolific in their output, successful in Australia and abroad and used romance to reflect on life in early settler Australia.

Early colonial love and romance fiction explored settler life and the emerging sense of what constituted Australian nationalism, especially as it related to women (Gelder and Weaver; Dalziell; Giles). Significant novels published during the second half of the nineteenth century included Catherine Helen Spence's *Clara Morison: A Tale of South Australia During the Gold Fever* (1854), Caroline Leakey's *The Broad Arrow: Being Passages from the History of Maida Gwynnham, a Lifer* (1859), Rosa Praed's *An Australian Heroine* (1880) and Tasma's *The Penance of Portia James* (1891). These stories demonstrate the benefits and disadvantages of romance and settler life, the successful relationships alongside trauma, loss, isolation, separation, and discomfort. As Gelder and Weaver argue, such stories offer "a space in which various kinds of Australian femininity vie for recognition, some more overtly than others" (8). Such stories frequently offered prototypes of a nationally representative woman, often referred to as the "Australian Girl." Gelder and Weaver note two main types of Australian girl, one typified by "social restraint and maturity," the other offering "more romantic incarnations of colonial femininity that emphasized freedom and possibility in the New World" (4). Novels would frequently compare daily life in England and Australia, pitting the "fresher" Australian girl against her "less adventurous" English counterpart.

The twentieth century saw the golden age of romance novel publishing in Australia and changes to the texts available for readers. Juliet Flesch's 43-page *Love Brought to Book: A Bio-Bibliography of Twentieth Century Australian Romance Novels* (1995) provides an overview of many popular and highly successful Australian category romance authors published between 1904 and 1994 including Emma Darcy, Helen Bianchin, Marie Bjelke-Petersen, Joyce Dingwell, Maysie Greig, Marion Lennox, Valerie Parv, Dorothy Lucie Sanders, and Margaret Way. The bio-bibliography provides a short biographical note on each author and a list of their known works. Flesch explained that her bio-bibliography was compiled around texts where the relationship between two central characters was at the center "to the virtual exclusion of everything else" ("A Labour of Love" 172). For Flesch, the focus on the love relationship "must be paramount, if not absolute, and this kind of concentration on a single relationship is rarely, if ever, achieved in a long novel" (*Love Brought to Book* xi). Her discussion acknowledged the importance of short stories and serials but focused on "novels" specifically. Short stories were excluded because of their brevity and the difficulty in tracing their publication in periodicals. Flesch excluded authors who wrote much longer and expansive narratives such as the so-called "sweeping sagas" exemplified by Colleen McCullough's *The Thorn Birds* (1977).[4] In terms of what constituted "Australian," Flesch's bio-bibliography included authors who self-identified as Australian, including those born, living or naturalized as residents or citizens. In *Love Brought to Book*, Flesch decided not to include novels written by non-Australians even if they were set in Australia (xii). She reasoned that "I could hope to identify only an unfairly small proportion of them" (xii). As well, Flesch reasoned that adult and teen categories of romance often overlap whereby adults may read novels aimed at teenagers and vice versa. Flesch therefore included teenage romance novels published under the *Dolly Fiction* series though she noted that their authors were often more difficult to locate in comparison to novels aimed at adult readers.[5] The majority of novels in the bio-bibliography were written by women though at least two male authors were listed.[6] In her longer qualitative study, *From Australia With Love*, Flesch provides a compelling defense of Australian romance writers, publishers, readers and novels drawing upon mostly category romances while excluding "historical romances and longer contemporary novels" (*From Australia* 43).

Flesch's definition and concentration on shorter romance novels is suitable for her tasks: to list the works of key Australian romance authors and use category romances to defend the genre in her follow-up study. However, a wider survey of definitions shows that what constitutes Australian romance fiction is much wider than the works listed and discussed in Flesch's two main publications, thereby demonstrating more openness and inclusivity which matches the composition of the genre today. Much of Flesch's work focuses on the category romance and shorter works of romance fiction. Yet, many romance fiction works have been and continue to be published as trade fiction. With fewer boundaries in terms of length and themes than the category romance, trade fiction texts have repositioned contemporary romances under the more general definitions of the genre cited by the RWA and ARRA at the start of this section.

Australian romance fiction has distinct qualities that differentiate it from its overseas counterparts. In her landmark study of Australian romance novels, *From Australia With Love* (2004), Juliet Flesch asks "do Australian romance novels form a distinct subgroup within the global phenomenon?" (249). Flesch's text, the first in-depth analysis of Australian post-war romances, examines the industry including publishers, writers, readers, the representation of Australian romance heroines, and the representation of violence and race/ethnicity. Flesch shows that Australian romance fiction uniquely represents local places and locations, language and vernacular, characters, issues, and a somewhat progressive approach to the representation of sex, relationships, and cultural diversity. Australian romance fiction especially utilizes local settings, inclusive of the iconic and idiosyncratic aspects of the Australian continent. Representations of setting and "place" appeal to Australian and non-Australian readers alike. Flesch remarked in the Introduction of *Love Brought to Book* that Australian romance novels are "for the most part, firmly rooted in place" (x). There are "descriptions of towns and landscapes, and of the way communities operate, which make them inescapably and unmistakably Australian" (x). Given the huge diversity in Australian landscapes and regions, the continent provides a rich canvas for romance writers to situate their stories and a broad choice for readers who may select their next novel based on where the story is set. As Amit Sarwal has noted:

> And when one speaks of Australia, one is often reminded of the exotic locations, outback, the bush, the desert, the beaches and wide open spaces—the stuff that romances are made of!
>
> (xi)

Flesch emphasizes that most Australian romance novels are "reasonably accurate" in depicting Australian settings and scenes ("Wide" 93–4). Australian readers may see in Australian romances "the way Australians like to see themselves—egalitarian, optimistic, resilient, welcoming, etc." ("Wide" 93). Overseas, where many Australian novels achieve great success, readers may relish the immersive experience of alighting in an Australian setting. In *From Australia With Love*, Flesch explains that Australian romance novels often seek to "portray Australian scenery accurately, but also to show the reader a distinctively Australian society" "egalitarian and welcoming" and show "[the] unacceptability of bullying and violence and privileging a humorous and resilient attitude to hardship and adversity" (*From Australia* 42). Flesch argues that the inclusion of natural disasters in some novels facilitates the representation of two qualities often associated with Australians: "mateship and a refusal to accept defeat" ("The Wide" 89). Flesch identifies the ways in which Australian romance novels appeal to readers: Australian readers may be positioned to reflect on the nation's culture and society while international readers may enjoy the immersive feeling of being swept into a love story set within Australia.

Producing Australian romance fiction

This section discusses some of the key publishers and writers who have contributed to building Australia's romance fiction industry. Much has changed in the writing and production of romance fiction in Australia since colonial and settler romances. The publishing of Australian romance fiction in the twentieth century reflects wider boom and bust changes to the wider publishing industry. The range of publishers listed indicates an interplay with the content of the novels published. Pre-World War Two there were many publishers of Australian romance fiction and indeed there seemed to be more freedom in terms of the content. As McAlister and Teo have highlighted, World War Two marked a thematic shift in Australian romance fiction: authors had much less freedom in terms of the themes they incorporated into their stories. McAlister and Teo note a conservative turn in romance fiction from the 1950s to the 1980s with publishers careful that texts did not offend readers, especially in relation to the representation of love and sex. One reason for this shift may be the reduction in the number of Australian romance publishers and the increasing dominance of Harlequin Mills & Boon.

Juliet Flesch's *Love Brought to Book* provides insight into the evolution of romance fiction publishing in Australia during the twentieth century, particularly the industry's consolidation away from many smaller publishers to the dominance of several large publishing houses. Although Flesch acknowledges that the bio-bibliography does not capture all works published between 1904 and 1994, it indicates the range of works published, when they were published and by whom. The earliest listing is author Mabel Forrest's *The Rose of Forgiveness and Other Stories* (1904) published by Brisbane based company W. Brooks. Her novels were later published by London based publishers Hutchinson and Cassell. Flesch's bio-bibliography lists works published by more than 20 Australian publishers, 20 British publishers, and less than ten North American publishers. Between the early 1920s and 1960s, Australian romance fiction was published predominantly by Australian publishers including Dymocks, Greenhouse, Pan, Horitz, National Press, Angus and Robertson, and Access Press. English publishers included Hale, Collins, Hodder and Stoughton, Futura, Long and Anglo-Eastern Publications with a small number of publishers from the United States, mostly based in New York including New American Library, Doubleday, and Silhouette. North American publishers produced novels by authors including Maysie Greig, Caroline Farr, Lucy Walker, Francis Lloyd, and Dorothy Cork. Maysie Greig was one of the most prolific writers from the mid-1920s to 1970, publishing up to six novels a year, many with exotic locations. Though she was born in Australia, few of Greig's novels had Australian settings. Greig's entry in the bio-bibliography is interesting in its length with more than 90 novels listed as well as the range of publishers she worked with. Noticeably absent from the publishers in Greig's entry are Mills & Boon and Harlequin. Just as Greig was approaching the publication of her last novel, Harlequin was setting itself up to be a major force in Australian publishing. The story that the bio-bibliography tells is one of declining small publishers and the emergence of one dominant publisher: Mills & Boon/Harlequin.

In the early to mid-twentieth century, many Australian romance novels were published by Harlequin and Mills & Boon. Author Alice Grant Rosman had at least five novels published by Mills & Boon between 1928 and 1931, Elizabeth Milton had novels published by Mills & Boon London between 1929 and 1933, while

Queensland writer Joyce Dingwell had novels published by Mills & Boon from 1955 and Harlequin from 1967 (see Flesch *Love*). Although Harlequin and Mills & Boon published a number of novels before 1970, the bio-bibliography shows a huge increase in the production of Australian romance fiction by Harlequin Mills & Boon from the early 1970s. In 1971, when Harlequin acquired Mills & Boon, they armed themselves with a new and somewhat aggressive growth and innovation strategy. They opened an office in Sydney in 1974, and as McWilliam observes, it was one of the first offices established outside of Canada and England. Part of the remit of the Sydney office was to formulate context specific marketing strategies to "vigorously distribute 'Mills & Boon' romance fiction throughout the continent" (142). Toni Johnson-Woods notes that Harlequin or Mills & Boon category romances of the 1970s "reintroduced fiction factory conditions" ("Introduction" 12) whereby authors such as Valerie Parv and Margaret Way "found steady work and a faithful readership in both Australia and overseas" ("Introduction" 12). McWilliam cites a number of innovations spearheaded by the Sydney office: it was the first branch to have its own website in 1998 (later redeveloped and relaunched in 2000) and the first to introduce e-book novels. As McWilliam states, "these innovations, among the largest developed by the Sydney office, are all focused on improving the publisher's targeting and capture of the national market" (142). In 2006, the branch hired their first local commissioning editor. As McWilliam argues, "this was a shift in the branch's approach to content specifically, and its approach to targeting the national market generally" (143). The recruitment of a local commissioning editor means that authors are signed primarily to suit the context and local market. At the same time, authors may benefit from the global reach of a publisher such as Harlequin. As Tapper has noted, Harlequin's global presence, including publishing in 31 languages and locating branch offices in eighteen countries, means that Australian romance authors can potentially reach readers across "national boundaries" (252). This includes Australian author Sarah Mayberry who has had success in Australia and North America (McWilliam 252).[7] Harlequin Enterprises is regarded as the dominant publisher of romance fiction in Australia and globally, bucking a worldwide trend of falling revenues in the publishing industry. In 2007, Harlequin commanded a 20 percent market share of paperback sales in Australia and a 90 percent share of the lucrative women's fiction market (McWilliam 142). Despite Harlequin's dominance, other publishers such as Penguin/Random House, Allen and Unwin, and Pan Macmillan currently publish romance novels under trade fiction and category titles. Several independent and small publishers also produce romance fiction in Australia, particularly in e-book format.

Australian romance writers have found huge success at home and abroad. Yet, as Laura Vivanco has remarked not unlike their counterparts overseas, "[u]nfortunately, despite the international success of Australian romance authors, their novels have not tended to be treated with a great deal of respect." Academic inquiries have focused on writers including Marie Bjelke-Petersen, Emma Darcy, Rosa Praed, Lucy Walker, and Edwina Shore.[8] Meanwhile two authors, Emma Darcy and Valerie Parv, have published romance writing guides to assist aspiring writers. Together, the academic investigations and the two romance writing guides, challenge any suggestion that romance novels are easy to write, that they are written to formula and that writers are motivated primarily by money-making. Rather these investigations illustrate that Australia's prominent romance writers take great pride in their work, are receptive to social and cultural issues alongside changes to reader tastes and above all, have a deep respect for their readership base.

One of Australia's earliest successful romance authors was Rosa Praed (1851–1935). Between 1880 and 1916, she wrote more than 40 novels, many reprinted multiple times (Giles 139). Not all of her novels can be regarded as romances, nor were they all focused or set in Australia. Nevertheless, her novels *An Australian Heroine* (1880), *The Romance of a Station* (1889), and *Lady Bridget in the Never-Never Land* (1915) are regarded as colonial romances that offer telling insights into Australian life and culture. *Lady Bridget in the Never-Never Land*, for example, explores the fraught romantic relationship between Lady Bridget O'Hara, an Irish aristocrat, and a Queensland station owner, Colin McKeith. Set against fluctuating climatic conditions, Bridget and Colin attempt to navigate married life while making a living in remote Australia. As Pam Gilbert has explained, the novel explores the aspirations for equality in marriage, especially for Bridget, and asks questions about the treatment of indigenous Australians. In the Introduction to Praed's biography, Patricia Clarke explains the success of her novels in conjunction with the discomfort they created in some parts of colonial society. Clarke specifically refers to the novels Praed set in colonial Queensland that "touched a raw nerve with Australian readers and reviewers" (2). As Clarke explains,

> They expected one of their own to be a propagandist for a pure, almost childlike colonial way of life. Instead her portrayal of colonial social and political life was too close to the bone, her love scenes were too graphic and her moral sense was worse. (2)

As Clarke notes, "Even as late as 1995 ... she was described disparagingly as 'the writer of nineteenth century bodice rippers with outback settings'" (qtd. in Clarke 2). Chris Tiffin has remarked that some of Praed's novels exhort an almost anti-romantic sense in that they offer an "analysis of the debilitating choices women are called upon to make in the course of their courtship and marriage." Dale Spender has argued that Praed's novels included Aboriginal characters and explored issues relevant to indigenous Australians including a defense of their human rights (202). Praed's novels therefore engaged with some of the uncomfortable aspects of colonial life and the difficult choices to be made by women at the time.

Another author who offered a sizeable contribution to Australian romance fiction was Marie Bjelke-Petersen (1874–1969). The representation of Australian natural environments and landscapes is central to her works. Bjelke-Petersen's novels including *The Captive Singer* (1917) and *Jewelled Nights* (1924) tell romantic stories against the backdrop of the Australian landscape, defying any categorization of Australia as "terra nullius" (Haynes "Romanticism"). The basic interpretation of "terra nullius" is a land belonging to nobody or an empty land, a notion that had stark implications for the colonization of Australia. Importantly, "terra nullius" does not deny that there are inhabitants; rather, it does not recognize the existing people's sovereign rights so that their "culture, customs and custodianship of the land was denied" (Ogelby). Haynes argues that this resulted in a notion of early colonial Australian "emptiness"; a country deficient in culture, history, and beauty. Petersen's novels glorified the Australian environment, especially her native Tasmania and, later on, Queensland while demonstrating cultural richness in music and theater (Haynes "Marie Bjelke-Bjelke" 43). Petersen's works required extensive research, including touring places to obtain detail about specific settings such as the mining industry in *Jewelled Nights* and the logging of native forests in *Jungle Nights* (1937). Her novels represented causes that interested her including religion, sobriety, conservation, and championing nature. Bjelke-Petersen exemplifies the way that Australian romance authors inflect their novels with social issues of the day. *The Captive Singer* sees the developing relationship between English heroine Iris Dearn and the driver with gentlemanly ways, Justin Rees, hindered by his apparent poverty and his confession that he is a "drunkard." Yet, the scenic Tasmanian setting, Iris's unflinching love and religious salvation contribute toward Justin's reformation in time to discover his true ancestry and wealth. Authors such as Praed and Bjelke-Petersen exemplify two successful Australian romance authors writing in the early twentieth century. They were followed by many others who were published during the twentieth century and achieved great success, such as Maysie Greig, Lucy Walker, Margaret Way, Joyce Dingwell, and Dorothy Cork.

From the late twentieth century, writers such as Emma Darcy and Rachael Treasure have found huge success within Australia and abroad. Glen Thomas goes so far as to claim Darcy as the "Best Australian Romance Novelist" ("The Best"). For Thomas, Darcy's superiority is evident in the quality and quantity of her writing. Darcy is a prolific producer of romances, averaging four per year and totaling more than 90 novels up to 2008. This impressive output is backed by equally impressive sales figures which, according to Thomas, "exceed those of other Australian authors" ("The Best" 65). Many Emma Darcy novels have been republished in 26 languages with her total sales amounting to more than 60 million copies ("The Best" 65). Moreover, Thomas argues that the novels attract readers because of their high quality, the originality of her plots, the representation of sex, and her ability to engage with topical cultural and social issues ("The Best" and "And I"). Furthermore, Thomas emphasizes the way that Darcy's novels exude a sense of sustained "Australianness" comprising a "strong sense of place" inclusive of "exotic" Australian settings as well as "more real" characters ("The Best" 66–7). Emma Darcy has also shared her knowledge of romance writing in a guide to the genre. The text combines personal insight from her writing career with practical tips for aspiring writers. The guide demonstrates a keen insight into what appeals to romance readers and how writers should orient their work to maintain reader interest. Darcy emphasizes the effort involved in keeping her writing and plots fresh for readers, acknowledging that her success results largely from persistence, and constantly seeking feedback on her writing to improve. For Darcy, the "rules" of the romance form are not determined by a "formula" dictated by publishers. Rather, readers, and readers alone, make the rules as to what is successful. Reader tastes and interests change; the successful romance writer must too, as Darcy asserts, move with the times and constantly evolve. For Darcy, her ultimate aim in writing is: "to write books that leave the readers satisfied, and with a keen desire to read Emma Darcy's next book" (Darcy 180). Her guide to romance writing evidences her desire to share her knowledge for the benefit of budding romance writers.

Australian romance writers across a variety of genres have seen success at home and abroad in recent years: they have won international awards, sold millions of copies, and are published in a variety of languages. Marion Lennox, author of more than 110 romance novels, has twice won the Romance Writers of America RITA Award in recognition of the best in romance publishing.[9] Author Barbara Hannay won a RITA in 2007 in the category of Traditional Romance novel. Also in 2007, Bronwyn Parry (under the pen-name Bronwyn Clarke) received the prestigious Romance Writers of America Golden Heart Award for a romance manuscript in the suspense subgenre. Authors such as urban fantasy writer Erica Hayes and teenage and adult writer Maggie Gilbert have found success outside Australia. As Gilbert has explained, "Although my stories are set in Australia, I have readers in the US, Europe and Asia who are interested in the Australian experience and culture, but a romance story is universal" (qtd. in Thorpe). Having had more than 29 million novels published globally, Valerie Parv was the first Australian writer to receive the Pioneer Award from the now-defunct *Romantic Times Book Reviews*, New York. Parv has also received recognition as part of the 2015 Queen's Birthday Honours List by being made a Member of the Order of Australia (AM) for "significant service to the arts as a prolific author and as a role model and mentor to young emerging writers" (Parv "Bio"). This is a small overview of the achievements of Australian romance writers who have found success at home and abroad alongside recognition within and outside the romance industry.

Scholarship

Since the mid-1990s, a growing number of researchers have analyzed Australian romance fiction, inclusive of its readers, publishing industry, writers, and the novels. Until the mid-1990s, while many novels had been published, there was little in the way of bibliographic listings of Australian popular romance writers and novels beyond publisher title lists and library catalogues. The ephemeral nature of romance novel publishing has therefore made some scholarly investigations, especially historical studies, more difficult. As this section discusses, key scholarly works in the field, especially those by Juliet Flesch, have sought to map Australian romance fiction and describe what makes the genre unique including changes in the content represented, publishing innovations, and reading habits.

Two of the most important scholarly works focused on Australian romance fiction were published by Juliet Flesch: her 43-page *Love Brought to Book: A Bio-Bibliography of Twentieth Century Australian Romance Novels* (1995) and her longer qualitative investigation into post-war romances, *From Australia With Love* (2004). *Love Brought to Book* lists the known works of 213 popular Australian romance authors published between 1904 and 1994 and provides a short biography of each author including Emma Darcy, Helen Bianchin, Marie Bjelke-Petersen, Joyce Dingwell, Maysie Greig, Marion Lennox, Valerie Parv, Dorothy Lucie Sanders, and Margaret Way. These authors published a wide array of novels from the medical romances of Joyce Dingwell, Marion Lennox, and Shane Douglas, to the tales of English heroines being swept off their feet by farming magnates by Dorothy Sanders, to the royal romances of Valerie Parv and the outback romances of Dorothy Cork. Flesch's bio-bibliography sought to acknowledge and value Australian popular romance authors, publishers, and readers. Without the bio-bibliography, the romance authors listed and their creative works would have likely remained unrecognized or obscure; others may have simply been "allowed to fade from our cultural history" (*Love* ix). The bio-bibliography foregrounded the existence of a large body of romance novels and with it, a large community of authors, publishers, and readers. In *From Australia With Love*, as Flesch reveals, Australian romance authors showcase some of the most enjoyable aspects of Australian life and society. This often occurs through the out-of-doors adventures of protagonists in an array of settings, some of which are "exotic" (*From Australia* 257) from city to beach to rainforest to farm and accompanied by unique flora and fauna. Moreover, Australian romance novels engage with current social and cultural issues including those associated with intercultural relations (racism and social inclusion), sexual relationships (including sexual abuse and violence), and gender roles (especially the work, family, and personal lives of heroines and other female characters). As Flesch argues, examples of Australian romance fiction can be used as evidentiary support to defend the genre against a range of criticisms historically leveled at romances, their writers, and readers.

This initial work by Flesch has been complemented by Fiona Giles's analysis of romantic heroines in colonial novels, Tanya Dalziell's investigation into class, race, and gender in early Australian romance novels, and *The Anthology of Colonial Australian Romance Fiction*, a collection of 18 short stories published between 1866 and 1909 by numerous authors. Dalziell and Giles investigate the emerging sense of Australian nationalism after the country's federation and women's place within Australia's culture and society. Australian romance fiction has also engaged with cultural relations, specifically how Aboriginal people and their culture has been included or excluded within the pages of Australian romance fiction (see *From Australia*; Levy; Platt and Taylor; McAlister and Teo). Another aspect of cultural relations represented in Australian romance fiction is related to sex and gender (see *From Australia*; Delamoir; Taylor; Haynes "Marie Bjelke"; O'Mahony "In Search"; O'Mahony and Murphy; McAlister and Teo). Scholarly investigations have also focused on the representation of place in romance fiction, including concerns about the environment and conservation (see "In Search," "Death," and "Rural Romance"; Mirmohamadi; *From Australia*; Haynes "Romanticism").

The readers of Australian romance fiction have also been the focus of academic investigations of this genre. Since Janice Radway's groundbreaking research into the culture around romance novel reading in the mid-1980s, many researchers have sought to understand what draws readers to romance fiction, the context of reading, the meanings that readers derive from their textual encounters, and the possible effects of romance reading. Researchers have employed various methodologies including surveys (Crane; Bonomi et al.; Owen), content analysis (Alberts), interviews (Crane), participant observation/ethnography (for example Christian-Smith *Becoming*; Christian-Smith "Voices" and Weaver-Zercher), focus groups (Parameswaran; Alberts), and experiments (Harris et al.), often in conjunction with researcher-led approaches through content and textual analysis.[10] Research into Australian romance readers falls into two broad categories: those studies undertaken by academic researchers and those undertaken by publishing or industry bodies, such as the Romance Writers of Australia (RWA) and Australian Romance Readers Association (ARRA).

Academic research into Australian romance readers is largely confined to a handful of studies, the most recent being Juliet Flesch's chapter in *From Australia With Love* (2004), as well as Gilbert and Taylor's research (2002) and Glen Thomas's focus group study of Australian romance readers (2007). Flesch canvasses the field of scholarly investigations into romance readers as a way to orient her own observations.[11] Flesch discusses two Masters dissertations that have investigated adolescent readers in Australia. Maylyn Lam (1986) surveyed 42 high school girls finding that the girls "saw clear differences between the world they lived in and the world of the teen romance novel" (qtd. in Flesch *From Australia* 123). This finding suggests that the teenage readers rejected the fictional world as different to the "real" world and in doing so illustrated their awareness of idealized representations of reality in romance novels. Like Lam, Margaret Somerville's Masters research utilized a survey, this time with 78 students (both male and female) from a Victorian high school (as discussed in Flesch *From Australia* 122). Somerville found a high level of critical awareness in the reading practices of these students including questioning the heroine's "physical perfection" (Somerville qtd. in *From Australia* 122). As Flesch notes, these two inquiries illustrate that for the young readers, "enjoyment of the fantasy presented in these novels does not imply acceptance of it" (*From Australia* 123).

This high level of reader engagement is evidenced in two other Australian reader studies. The first by Gilbert and Taylor involved three girls aged 11 to 13 who read a selection of 18 Dolly Fiction novels over a two-week period. All three girls were from middle-class families, had university-educated parents, had a history of regular reading, and were regarded as "successful" at school. The girls kept reflective notes on their textual encounters and spoke to one of the researchers after completing their reading. Generally, the girls were "resistant" readers of the Dolly romances. As Gilbert and Taylor noted, their parents may have exerted an influence so that "[n]one of them really wanted to like romance fiction" (250). The girls expressed critical awareness of the narrative structures, the degree (or lack) of verisimilitude, the construction of key characters, and the language and written expression (Gilbert and Taylor 251–3). Gilbert and Taylor interpreted the critical reading position taken by the three girls as echoing authority figures around them including their parents and teachers. Together with the studies by Lam and Somerville, Gilbert and Taylor illustrate the resistant reading practices of teenage Australian readers. Gilbert and Taylor question why "some women reject the subject positions formula romance fiction offers, and why are other women apparently seduced by them?" (255). Gilbert and Taylor critique a "romance ideology" that provides limiting and denigrating discourses that box women in and warn of the consumerist and patriarchal motives behind the production of romance novels.

Glen Thomas's study ("Romance") offers insight into Australian romance readers and the romance novel industry. Thomas conducted focus groups with female readers aged between 20 and 60 years. He found a high level of dialogue between the producers and consumers within the romance industry; this dialogue drove future developments in publishing and marketing. The participants explained that they were motivated to read believable narratives where they could empathize with the heroine. Ultimately, this believability was associated with the idea that regardless of the difficulties or problems faced by the heroine, the novel would resolve them and offer a satisfying conclusion. Readers in this study noted the importance of novel length, particularly criticizing the brevity of category romances where, as one research participant stated, "you just get into it and it's over" (Thomas "Romance" 24). Some participants avoided category romances specifically for this reason. The comments about novel length illustrated a key challenge faced by romance publishers in that the average age of romance readers is increasing; in Thomas's study, the average age was 46 ("Romance" 25), but Thomas also found that focus group participants commented that category romances and their readers were "a bit old-fashioned." As such, focus group participants were reluctant to "be seen" holding a category romance. As Thomas remarks, romance publishers face the competing demands of retaining their established readers while attracting new (ideally younger) readers. Therefore, publishers must retain some of the traditional brand associations such as those of Mills & Boon for established readers while developing new lines, modes of marketing and text delivery for newer and/or younger readers. Thomas's study reveals a dynamism in the industry: readers are astute and critically aware of the texts they are buying and reading; publishers are keen to innovate and evolve to suit the changing tastes and needs of those same readers. This impetus to innovate and evolve is reflected in in-house studies conducted by Harlequin Mills & Boon Australia into Australian romance readers.[12]

Studies conducted by the ARRA (Australian Romance Readers Association) provide further insight into Australian romance readers. The ARRA is a special interest group that aims to publicize the romance form and provide opportunities for readers to network and discuss the genre. Since 2009, ARRA has undertaken an annual survey of romance readers, usually attracting between 250 and 340 respondents, the majority of which are women.[13] The survey results between 2009 and 2018 tell an interesting story about the changing culture of romance reading habits in Australia, especially in terms of the preferred modes of reading, purchasing habits, and book formats. The digitalization of the romance industry is a central theme developed across the surveys, especially the introduction and adoption of e-books and the popularity of social networking as a source for information about romance novels.[14] While "home" is where the majority of reading occurs, a proportion of readers like the ability to access, purchase, and read while on the move, affordances offered predominantly by e-books. Moreover, e-books offer readers privacy: a reader will appear to be viewing a tablet, kindle reader or smart phone but not necessarily a romance novel.[15]

Linked to this digitalization of reading is the finding from the ARRA surveys about how readers learn about romance novels. In 2018, readers were asked which social media platforms they used; interestingly this question was not asked in the 2009 survey. Of 287 respondents to the question in 2018, only five people chose the option, "I don't use social media." This result is important in conjunction with the responses to another question asking "Where do you most often find out about upcoming romance releases"; 67 percent of respondents chose "social networking" while 42 percent chose author websites. While the online habits of Australian romance readers were not investigated in 2009's ARRA survey, the 2018 survey results show most respondents are digitally literate and social media savvy; they learn about, communicate, and purchase romance novels via the internet and through mobile media devices. This insight is useful for romance publishers and writers wishing to connect with their readers. Moreover, the ARRA surveys show that as romance novels are increasingly obtained online, there has been a steep decline in purchases from independent and chain bookstores.[16] The ARRA surveys, though drawing upon a relatively small voluntary sample, capture key changes for Australian romance readers that reflect wider market, technological and industry forces.

Leisure readers and academic researchers share a need to access Australian romance fiction texts. Texts need to be available and readers need to be able to search for them, especially in Australian libraries. Flesch sums up some of the issues associated with access to romance novels:

> "Novels" in public libraries are generally controlled differently and retained longer in the collections than "romances." Novels are individually listed in the catalogue and loan records are maintained for them. Romances may not be catalogued or individually classified and records of how often they are borrowed may not be kept.
>
> (*From Australia* 76)

Vassiliki Veros argues that libraries have misunderstood romance as a category and this misunderstanding has led to the "marginalization" of readers, authors, and texts ("Scholarship in Practice" 299–300). Veros even suggests that historical library practices may result in a censoring of romance novels in Australia. Veros ("Scholarship in Practice") examines the interaction between romance novels, libraries, and readers in her investigation into library approaches to romance novels. As Veros argues, while libraries carefully catalog and collect other genres and types of fiction, many libraries failed to enter romance novels into their search catalogues. In "A Matter of Meta," Veros argued that Australian libraries frequently assign individual romance novels with catalog titles such as "romance" or "Mills & Boon" (2) rather than designations by "author" and "title" (7). For Veros, genre or publisher designation "creates an absence of metadata which in turn prevents the interplay between cultural capital and economic capital" ("A Matter" 2). Of particular concern is the inability of some library catalogues to record the author's name; as Veros explains, this prevents readers from searching for other publications by that author. Authors, meanwhile, have a diminished visibility in the library catalog ("A Matter"). Consequently, readers cannot search the catalog for specific books and must rely on physically searching library shelves for new titles. High-volume readers may experience difficultly in tracking new books against those previously read. With impediments to tracking the loaning of romance novels, authors have found themselves ineligible for payments under the Public Lending Right Act 1985. As Veros asserts, how libraries approach and manage Australian romance fiction clearly affects the entire romance industry.

Arguably, as Veros ("Scholarship in Practice," "A Matter") pointed out, the attitude of libraries historically toward romance fiction translates into a lack of romance fiction collections in Australia's state and national libraries. As Toni Johnson-Woods has remarked, "few libraries in Australia have complete runs of our most popular authors ... romance and western are virtually ignored" ("Introduction" 13). Without full collections of author works, a significant proportion of Australian romance fiction has been lost forever or remains hidden in private collections. A significant issue with romance fiction, not just in Australia but globally, is its ephemerality. A large number of texts are printed per month and few are reprinted. Publishers then pulp unsold copies. As well, libraries rarely have enough space to house a large volume of texts without having to discard a proportion sequentially.

Despite these issues, a number of university libraries have small collections of Australian romance novels. The National Library of Australia, The University of Melbourne, The University of Queensland, and Murdoch University now house collections of various sizes.[17] In 1994, the state library of New South Wales started a collection of Valerie Parv's work, correspondence, and manuscripts ("Bio"). The National Library of Australia has nearly 20,000 romance novels published and distributed by Mills & Boon, Harlequin, and Silhouette before 1990. As Veros has noted, publishers have donated many novels to the National Library collection due to legal deposit requirements.[18] The University of Melbourne romance novel collection includes the works of Australian and New Zealand authors published from the 1960s onwards. In 1997, Juliet Flesch described Melbourne as "the only research library in Australia to collect romance novels" ("Not Just"). She explains, the initial impetus to establish the collection was bound by restrictions in terms of "money, space and time," an acknowledgment of the volume of works produced and the difficulty in purchasing and accommodating every text.[19] Flesch notes that the collection contains more contemporary than historical novels ("Not Just").[20] Researchers wishing to access the collection may only do so within the library. Melbourne's collection is also not extensively catalogued because texts are constantly added and removed to maintain the collection. Juliet Flesch compiled much of the romance collection at Melbourne University library before collecting romances published from the 1990s onwards. Flesch later donated more than 1500 Australian romance novels to the University of Queensland's Fryer Library.[21] The majority of novels in Fryer library's holding were published in the twentieth century. Murdoch University, Western Australia, holds a Mills & Boon collection, donated in 2008 by former Film Australia archivist, Judy Adamson. The collection of 3700 books contains many novels published between 1942 and 2003. Although titled the "Mills & Boon" collection by the library, a proportion of the novels were published by Harlequin, Silhouette and Masquerade.[22] It should be noted that researchers must request the exact texts they wish to access in Murdoch's collection and may only view that text or texts within the confines of the library. These collections show that Australian romance fiction has been preserved to an extent and is accessible, even if only in a restricted way, to the public and researchers.

In recent years, there has been a renewed scholarly interest in Australian romance fiction. This has been thanks in part to the hosting of romance-focused conferences in Australia, including the International Association for the Study of Popular Romance (IASPR) "Popular Romance Studies" conference in Brisbane in 2009, the "Elizabeth Jolley Conference: Reading and Writing Romance in the twenty-first Century" in 2013, and the IASPR "Think Globally, Love Locally" conference in Sydney in 2018. Such conferences indicate the key interests and research foci of scholars working in the field. As this chapter has shown, the Australian romance industry is frequently changing to accommodate evolving technological, reader, and publishing developments. The following section therefore appraises romance fiction in Australia since the year 2000.

Australian romance fiction after 2000

Since the year 2000, the romance genre in Australia has further evolved with cultural, technological, and social conditions, alongside reader tastes. Romance fiction, as described above, encompasses a diverse range of texts from the category romance made famous by Harlequin/Mills & Boon to single title texts published by mainstream publishers. Within both category and single title releases Australian romance fiction may fall into one of many subgenres. MIRA books editor Valerie Gray, explains:

> The interesting thing about romance fiction is that the number of sub-genres is growing by leaps and bounds. Chick lit, kick-ass women, inspiration, romantic fantasy, paranormal are some examples of the kinds of interests our readers have—and we are responding to that.
>
> (qtd. in Parv *The Art* 7–8)

One reason for the continued success of Australian romance writers is their ability to innovate and change to complement reader preferences, including to write about current social issues. Since the year 2000, there has been a diversification in the romance industry: the definition of what constitutes romance has widened and become more inclusive and as such, new subgenres have emerged. The remainder of this section discusses three recent developments in Australian romance fiction: chick lit, Aboriginal romance/chick lit and rural romance.

Like the wider romance genre, chick lit contains many formulations and sub-genres. Caroline J. Smith argues that chick lit is a dynamic and evolving genre that has expanded from the initial novels about "young, single, White, heterosexual, British and American women in their late twenties and early thirties, living in metropolitan areas" (2) and typified by Helen Fielding's satirical romance *Bridget Jones's Diary* and Candace Bushnell's novella *Sex and the City*. Australian chick lit began to be published in 2000 and featured Australian settings and heroines. Initially, these novels reproduced the definitional traits of their English, Irish, and North American chick lit counterparts. While Australian chick lit published in the early 2000s overwhelmingly featured city-based seemingly "White" women, the genre has since evolved distinctively to include a range of heroines and settings including suburban novels, Aboriginal chick lit, rural romances, and red dirt romances (O'Mahony *In Search*). Two sub-genres of chick lit, Aboriginal chick lit and rural romance, are discussed in more detail below.

Pioneered by Aboriginal author and academic Anita Heiss, Aboriginal chick lit is one contemporary version of popular Australian romance fiction. In 2004, Juliet Flesch stated that, "there are no Aboriginal writers of popular romance in Australia, so all romance writing about Aboriginal people and life is from the outside in" (*From Australia* 226). Further, Australian romance fiction has largely omitted Aboriginal heroines and heroes as well as intercultural relationships between Aboriginal and non-Aboriginal protagonists (McAlister and Teo).[23] Anita Heiss decided to publish chick lit with Aboriginal heroines, as she has explained, "I've published a textbook and maybe 500 people have bought it but I've published commercial women's fiction and 15,000 people buy it" (Valentine). Heiss's novels utilize the distinctive elements of romance, however, as Mathew ("Educating the Reader") and O'Mahony ("More than") have argued, her novels serve a didactic function in examining a range of issues relating to Aboriginal people. Thus, Heiss's novels use romance as a narrative structure to situate issues or topics associated with Aboriginal people and their culture. As such, readers of her work become educated about the issues represented. Heiss dubs her novels "Koori lit" rather than chick lit to indicate the focus on Koori heroines. The term "Koori" refers to the Indigenous peoples from New South Wales and Victoria. Her first four novels, *Not Meeting Mr. Right*, *Avoiding Mr. Right*, *Manhattan Dreaming*, and *Paris Dreaming* feature successful and well-educated Aboriginal heroines working in the public sector, education, or the arts. These novels fulfill readers' expectations of romance to explore the developing relationship between a hero and heroine and to end happily. They differ from chick lit in which the "White girl in the big city searches for Prince Charming" (Merrick vii).

As Mathew and Ommundsen have argued, Heiss's chick lit challenges the boundaries of the genre chiefly through the inclusion of Aboriginal heroines. Her novels explore the romantic lives of her heroines and their progression from single to coupled; however, Heiss often leaves the resolution of romance in these novels to the final chapters or pages. In doing so, her novels focus predominantly on the professional, personal, and travel adventures of her heroines, and examine a range of social and cultural issues. These issues include Aboriginal deaths in custody; Aboriginal-police relations; racism in Australia; the contested date for Australia Day which is celebrated on January 26—the date when the first White British settlement of Australia occurred in 1778 and a date that is hotly contested by some indigenous Australians as "Invasion Day"; the forcible removal of Aboriginal children from their families between 1910 and 1970 (known as "the Stolen Generation"); the nation's history and Aboriginal rights to vote. Heiss's novels demonstrate the potential of romance novels to serve a pedagogical function. As Mathew argues, Heiss's five Koori lit novels can be read as "advice manuals" in that they "expose readers to the correct norms and behaviours for interacting with Australia's First Peoples" ("Educating" 334). *Tiddas*, Heiss's fifth Koori lit novel, is particularly adept at performing this educative function. In *Tiddas*, five female friends (three of whom are Aboriginal) meet regularly to discuss works of Australian Aboriginal and Torres Strait Islander fiction as a reading group. The life situations of the women vary markedly from Izzy, an Aboriginal woman about to have her own television show, Xanthe, a married woman trying to fall pregnant, and Nadine, a successful writer with an alcohol addiction. Heiss weaves together the lives of the five women through multiple plotlines. As I have argued (2018), *Tiddas* is a romance and a metafictional text; the novel reflects on the process of writing and publishing alongside the process of reading and interpreting. The Tiddas group reads nine novels; each book acting as a touchtone for the women to reflect on their own lives and issues affecting Aboriginal Australians. Likewise, the reader is positioned to reflect on issues relevant to Aboriginal Australians as well as the novels read by the women. Like *Tiddas*, Heiss's sixth novel *Barbed Wire and Cherry Blossoms* (2016) employs a romance narrative to explore issues relevant to Aboriginal Australians. This novel utilizes a historical romance format to tell the story of an Aboriginal woman and an escaped Japanese prisoner during World War Two. Mathew explains that *Barbed Wire and Cherry Blossoms*, like Heiss's previous Koori lit novels, "aims to instruct the reader in Aboriginal culture, history and politics" and "captur(e) the day-to-day life of Aboriginal women" ("Love"). Mathew describes the novel as a romance where the "growing attraction [between the protagonists] is one of the novel's chief pleasures" ("Love"). In Heiss's fiction, readers discover romantic stories that have a political and educational function. Mathew asserts that many readers will be challenged by Heiss's fiction and that being challenged has the potential to lead to education and as Mathew emphasizes, "education can create change" ("Educating").

Australian chick lit has provided a platform for new authors to be published, has challenged the mores of the genre and in a way has returned Australian romance fiction to a focused engagement with women's place in the nation's culture. One highly successful sub-genre is a clutch of suburban-set novels including Catherine Jinks's *Spinning Around* (2004), Rebecca Sparrow's *The Girl Most Likely* (2003) and Pip Karmel's *Me, Myself and I* (2000). In these novels, previously successful urban career woman protagonists find themselves transformed into suburban wives, mothers, or divorcees. These sometimes-painful transformations invite reflection and introspection on the part of the heroine and reader. "Red dirt romances" such as Loretta Hill's *The Girl in Steel-Capped Boots* and *The Girl in the Hard Hat* depict inexperienced heroines inserted into remote work locations, usually in male dominated industries such as building, mining and construction in the north of Western Australia or Queensland (see O'Mahony and Murphy). Red dirt romances prompt thinking about women's place in those industries generally as well as those remote locations.

The most successful romance and chick lit subgenre to emerge in recent years has been the Australian rural romance novel (variously dubbed "chook lit," "farm lit," or "ru-ro"). The use of "rural" in the sub-genre's name is an almost demographic designation where "rural" spaces sit between outer urban areas inclusive of the suburbs and the "bush," remote areas of wilderness or the desert, or "outback." The origin of rural romance can be pinpointed to the novels of farmer-cum-author Rachael Treasure. Her first novel *Jillaroo* (2002) inverted the perceived traditional role of women in rural contexts from garrisoned homemaker to active participant and matriarch. Treasure's first three novels reportedly tapped into what was then an unknown market of readers, selling more than 260,000 copies (Darby).[24] Treasure continues to write rural romances and, as of 2019, has published seven rural focused novels and two short story collections. While Treasure alone has successfully innovated the romance genre through rural focused novels, her success has inspired many writers to develop similar novels and publishers to print them. Major Australian publishers including Penguin, Random House, and Harlequin Rural publish rural romances mainly as single titles. Penguin Australia's website currently dedicates a page to rural fiction texts, both new and recommended, as well as three rural subgenres: "Dirty Boots" distinguished by its "can-do country women," "Country Escapes" that will "sweep you away on an outback adventure," and "Best in the West" with "unforgettable rural stories set on Australia's western fringe" ("Rural Fiction"). Harlequin's rural romance webpage shows book cover images for "must read" texts with options for hard copy and electronic purchase. Harlequin's use of symbols in book cover design to indicate the content of the stories and the word choices in the book titles indicate the narrative focus and explicitness of sexual content.[25] Such book cover design practices follow wider conventions in the romance genre to indicate to readers what type of romance they have encountered (see Owen; Johnson-Woods "Introduction"; Mirmohamadi). Authors of Australian rural romance united in 2014 to form the Australian Rural Romance website, an online location for information about new releases and events from new and established authors. Writers also contribute guest blog posts and include book giveaways (Australian Rural Romance).

Academic interest in the rural romance genre has grown in recent years (see O'Mahony "Teaching"; O'Mahony "Australian"; O'Mahony "In Search"; Mirmohamadi; O'Mahony "Death"). Mirmohamadi, in her analysis of rural romance fiction set in the "Mallee lands" argues that such novels "rewor[k] conventional forms to address current socio-historical conditions in rural Australia" (204). "Place" and setting are a vital ingredient in this type of romance fiction, where, as Mirmohamadi argues, often the narrative progression is about a heroine's "transition towards full belonging and participation in a local community and romantic fulfillment" (205). Building on the observation that rural romances engage with women's "place" in rural life, O'Mahony ("Australian") examines how such novels contemplate gender inequality to revisit what constitutes women's "place" within a contemporary context. Heroines such as *Jillaroo*'s Rebecca Saunders contest the gendering of space by entering locations such as stockyards and sale yards usually dominated by men and deemed masculine. Once there, heroines including *Jillaroo's* Rebecca perform roles usually assigned to men, sometimes outperforming them. Rural romance heroines often work to "fit-in" and find success in owning or, in some cases, running farm and station properties. Such themes suggest that contemporary rural romances return to the preoccupations with women's "place" found in the narratives of settler and colonial romances. While some colonial and settler romance stories explored the differences between life in Australia and England, it seems that the rural romance dichotomizes to varying degrees the urban heroines of contemporary romance (such as city-set chick lit) with heroines in rural, remote, or outback locations (See O'Mahony *In Search*; Whelehan and Pini). Rural romances, specifically because of their setting, seem to emphasize the redemptive and purifying qualities of life beyond the city, something lacking in city-based romances.

Conclusion

This chapter has examined popular romance fiction from Australia as a subgenre of the wider romance genre. Australian romance fiction shares the recognizable hallmarks of romance fiction while utilizing Australian landscapes, the nation's language, character, and social and cultural concerns. Since colonial times, Australian romance fiction has represented life in a developing nation and engaged with what it means to be an Australian. Significantly, the analysis of representations of Australian masculinity remains an under-explored topic in the scholarship on Australian romance fiction, despite the work of Melissa Bellanta on C.J. Dennis's verse narrative, *The Songs of a Sentimental Bloke* (1915). Yet Australian men have often functioned as symbols of "Australianness," from representations of the iconic Bushman in the literature of the 1890s to the Australian Tourism Commission's international campaign in the 1980s ("Paul Hogan Ad"), in which Paul Hogan (of *Crocodile Dundee* fame) promises to "slip an extra shrimp on the barbie" for visitors. Further research on representations of masculinities in Australian romance fiction is much needed to supplement the existing scholarly focus on Australian women. Because romance fiction often focuses on the heroine's journey, Australian novels have explored women's identity in various ways, particularly the "place" of women within the nation and its culture. This exploration of place has occurred in a range of settings from colonial settlements of early Australia to the cities, suburbs, farms, and outback of modern Australia. What is clear is that Australian romance novels have engaged with the status of women since the nation was settled. Alongside changes in representation have been changes in the production, consumption, and reception of Australian romances, especially the digital production of novels. Despite its relatively small population of 25 million people, Australia produces some of the most successful and innovative romance writers in the world.

The Australian romance publishing industry is dynamic and constantly evolving to move with readers' tastes. Further research is needed into Australian romance readers, as well as non-Australian readers of Australian romance novels, especially using qualitative methodologies. This includes further investigation into the digital reading and networking habits associated with romance reading as indicated by the ARRA readers' surveys discussed above. Investigations into the processes and creative drivers of contemporary Australian romance fiction writers is still an under-researched area. As studies of novelists such as Marie Bjelke-Petersen and Emma Darcy have demonstrated, the process of producing romance novels is of equal importance to the texts themselves and their reception. New insights into the life of authors will likely assist those wishing to write their own romances. Current publishing and marketing practices is another rich area for future research. This includes the editorial processes involved in selecting and marketing individual works as well as decision-making about cover-art. Fandom and fan cultures around romance fiction is another under-researched area, with little investigation to date into the kinds of fan texts created in response to Australian romance fiction.

Notes

1 Flesch draws her "beetroot in the burger" analogy from an Australian inspired hamburger, the McOz Burger, previously found at the McDonald's burger chain. The McOz Burger included a slice of cooked beetroot. The burger has since been discontinued and replaced

with a range of Angus Beef burgers, only one of which (the "Gourmet homestyle Angus" burger) contains beetroot.

2 It must also be remembered that the term "Australia" is, as Tanya Dalziell explains, "caught up in the vocabularies of colonial discourse" (16). To use the term "Australia" implies a straightforward application to describe a place, however as Dalziell draws attention to, the term is one deployed to serve a colonial purpose. It does not necessarily speak to all the peoples that call Australia the continent as a place home.

3 ARRA draws their basic definition of a romance novel from the Romance Writers of America (RWA).

4 *The Thorn Birds* is reportedly the highest selling novel from Australia with 30 million copies sold globally.

5 Flesch discovered that teen romance writers of Dolly fiction seemed reluctant to identify themselves as writers of teenage romances, more so than adult romance writers (*Love Brought to Book* xii). The *Dolly Fiction* series has a detailed listing in the *Australian Children's Books* bibliography inclusive of more than 100 novels. Dolly fiction novels were mainly published between 1988 and 1993 by Greenhouse Publications and in association with Dolly Magazine Australian Consolidated Press (White).

6 Flesch argues that between the 1930s and 1950s male writers were more common in Australian romance publishing ("Women Talk" 420). One male author, Frank Brennan, wrote novels with his wife Wendy under the pseudonym "Emma Darcy." Frank Brennan died in 1995; however, his wife Wendy still writes under the "Emma Darcy" pen-name. Shane Douglas (real name Richard Wilkes Hunter) is another male romance author listed in the bio-bibliography (15). Flesch also mentions Gordon Aalborg in "Feminists Talk" as a male writer of Australian romance fiction under the pseudonym "Victoria Gordon" (420). It is unclear how many other male romance writers may use a feminine pseudonym; it seems less likely that a female author would employ a male pseudonym to write romance fiction.

7 Sarah Mayberry is an Australian author published by Harlequin. She writes across imprints including "Blaze" and "Super romance." She has also been recognized by the Romance Writers of Australia in the RUBY Awards.

8 For academic inquiries focused on Marie Bjelke Peterson see Alexander; Taylor; Haynes "Marie"; Haynes "Romanticism" and Delamoir. For discussions of Emma Darcy see Thomas "And I Deliver"; Thomas "The Best Australian" and Moran. Analyses of Rosa Praed include those by Platt and Clarke. Lucy Walker has been examined by Flesch in "Blushing Bride" while author Edwina Shore has been discussed by Curthoys and Docker.

9 Lennox won the RITA Award in 2004 and 2006 for two of her traditional romance novels.

10 The selection of a research methodology is often tied to how the researcher may view romance readers. Some may assume a passive reader and direct media effects. Such an approach may reflect the approach taken by some feminist scholars who, as Bronwyn Levy notes, "saw romance readers as like empty signifiers, waiting to be filled with stories of love." Other researchers may alternatively assume readers play a more active role in romance reading whereby the act of reading may be subversive or that readers will interpret texts through negotiated or privileged subject positions.

11 Flesch noted a large readership of rural women, this fact gleaned from the large numbers of romance novels for sale in country second-hand bookshops (*From Australia* 111). Flesch also found that translated Australian romance novels are popular with Japanese readers (*From Australia* 114).

12 Juliet Flesch outlines quantitative and qualitative studies undertaken by Harlequin Enterprises in 1998. The survey involved 1800 respondents and asked demographic questions as well as the frequency of romance novel buying (*From Australia* 59). This was followed up by qualitative focus groups of romance novel buyers aged between 14 and 65 in October of the same year to investigate book selection, reading processes and the evaluation of texts (Flesch *From Australia* 60). As Flesch emphasizes, the commissioning of these studies demonstrates a keen interest in the views and opinions of readers (*From Australia* 61).

13 Surveys between 2009 to the present are listed and available separately on the ARRA's "About" webpage.

14 In the ARRA 2009 survey, 42.5 percent of respondents always carried a romance novel with them. In 2018, the survey asked if readers always carried a romance novel with them and offered an answer option that incorporated the mobility of e-books. In the 2018 survey, 73 percent of respondents always carried a romance novel, 43 percent of those usually carried e-books. Despite this portability of romance texts, between 2009 and 2018 there has only been a slight decline in where reading occurs with 89 percent choosing "at home" in 2009 compared to 83 percent in 2018. "Travelling and commuting" as the site where most reading occurred remained stable at about 10 percent between 2009 and 2018.

15 See Brackett for "facework strategies" of romance readers. She noted that concealment of reading material was a "first line" defense to avoid judgement or disapproval.

16 Purchases from discount stores remain stable. These changes may relate to changes in the formats available; mass market paperback purchases have fallen from 69 to 20 percent between 2009 and 2018 while e-books have increased from 10 percent in 2009 to 60 percent in 2018. The popularity of e-book purchases may explain the falling interest in library borrowing for respondents with 33 percent in 2009 stating they never borrow romances from the library rising to 54 percent of respondents in the 2018 survey.

17 Veros notes that Sydney University Library is a legal deposit library similar to the National Library of Australia. However, Veros found that the Sydney Library appears to have only a small proportion of novels that should be collected under legal deposit (303).

18 Legal deposit is defined in Veros as "a statutory provision which obliges publishers to deposit copies of their publications in libraries in the region in which they are published" (National Library of Australia as cited in "Romance Reader" 302).

19 The library decided that the collection would focus primarily on Australian and New Zealand authors or texts set in Australia or New Zealand (Flesch "Not Just Housewives").

20 A number of novels translated into Japanese can also be found in the collection; Flesch notes that Japanese language students frequently borrow them (*From Australia with Love* 120).

21 The novels were collected as part of her doctoral research and later publication of *From Australia With Love* (2004).

22 The library provides a very useful Excel spreadsheet of the novels in the collection so that researchers can reorganize the list by author, year, or title according to their interests ("Mills and Boon Collection").

23 McAlister and Teo in their review of Aboriginal protagonists in romance fiction explain that only one Harlequin Mills & Boon novel featured an Aboriginal heroine (216) though a small number of novels had an Aboriginal hero. Beyond Harlequin Mills & Boon novels, McAlister and Teo find a small number of Aboriginal heroes though as they emphasize, they are "extremely rare" (217).

24 Treasure's publisher Penguin gambled on this innovative debut novel. There was no established market for rural romance fiction. To sell more than 260,000 copies of her first three novels represents success in many ways. Valerie Parv, a bestselling category romance author, refers to a romance editor who claims that "an Australian paperback novel can expect to sell between 3000 and 5000 copies" (*The Art* 3).

25 Harlequin's Rural Romance webpage shows the cover image and purchase options. The 20 covers previewed in August 2017 predominantly show an image of a woman, usually her face with varying expressions from serious to contemplative to smiling. Some novels showed a woman's back from the waist up against a rural landscape. A small number of the novels displayed a man's face, presumably the hero. One novel stood out for the chiseled naked upper body of a man against green rolling hills.

Works cited

Alberts, J. K. "The Role of Couples' Conversations in Relationship Development: A Content Analysis of Courtship Talk in Harlequin Romance Novels." *Communication Quarterly*, vol. 34, 1986, pp. 127–142.

Alexander, Alison. *A Mortal Flame: Marie Bjelke Petersen, Australian Romance Writer 1874–1969.* Blubber Head Press, 1994.

ARRA (Australian Romance Readers). "About." (including links to reader surveys) available at: australianromancereaders.com.au/about/ Accessed 21 May 2017.

Australian Rural Romance. "Media." 2017, australianruralromance.com/media Accessed June 20 2017.

Bellanta, Melissa. "A Masculine Romance: The Sentimental Bloke and Australian Culture in the War and Early Interwar Years." *Journal of Popular Romance Studies*, vol. 4, no. 2. jprstudies.org /2014/10/a-masculine-romance-the-sentimental-bloke-and-australian-culture-in-the-war-and -early-interwar-yearsby-melissa-bellanta/

Bonomi, Amy E., Lauren E. Alternburger and Nicole L. Walton. "'Double Crap!' Abuse and Harmed Identity in *Fifty Shades of Grey*." *Journal of Women's Health*, vol. 22, no. 9, 2013, pp. 733–744.

Brackett, Kim Pettigrew. "Facework Strategies Among Romance Fiction Readers." *The Social Science Journal*, vol. 37, no. 3, 2000, pp. 347–360.

Bushnell, Candace. *Sex and the City*. Abacus, 1996.

Christian-Smith, Linda K. *Becoming a Woman Through Romance*. Routledge, 1990.

———. "Voices of Resistance: Young Women Readers of Romance Fiction." *Beyond Silenced Voices: Class, Race and Gender in United States Schools*, edited by Lois Weis, and Michelle Fine, State University of New York Press, 1993, pp. 169–189.

Clarke, Patricia. *Rosa! Rosa! A Life of Rosa Praed, Novelist and Spiritualist*. Melbourne University Press, 1999.

Crane, Lynda L. "Romance Novel Readers: In Search of Feminist Change?" *Women's Studies*, vol. 23, no. 3, 1994, pp. 257–269.

Curthoys, Ann and John Docker. "Popular Romance in the Postmodern Age. And an Unknown Australian Author." *Continuum*, vol. 4, no. 1, 1990, pp. 22–36.

Dalziell, Tanya. *Settler Romances and the Australian Girl*. University of Western Australia Press, 2004.

Darby, Andrew. "Bush Bard Laments Loss of Sixth Sense of Fire." *The Age*, September 26 2009.

Darcy, Emma. *The Secrets of Successful Romance Writing*. Arrow/Random House, 1995.

Delamoir, Jeannette. "Marie Bjelke Petersen's 'Virile Story': *Jewelled Nights*, Gender Instability, and the Bush." *Hecate*, vol. 29, no. 1, 2003, pp. 115–131.

Driscoll, Beth, Lisa Fletcher and Kim Wilkins. "Women, Akubras and E-readers: Romance Fiction and Australian Publishing." *The Return of Print? Contemporary Australian Publishing*, edited by Aaron Mannion, and Emmett Stinson, Monash University Publishing, 2016, pp. 67–88.

Fielding, Helen. *Bridget Jones's Diary*. Picador, 1996.

Flesch, Juliet.. *Love Brought to Book: A Bio-bibliography of 20th-century Australian Romance Novels*. National Centre for Australian Studies, 1995.

———. "A Labour of Love? Compiling A Bibliography of Twentieth Century Australian Romance Novels." *Aplis*, vol. 9, no. 3/4 September/December, 1996, pp. 170–178.

———. "Not Just Housewives and Old Maids." *Collection Building*, vol. 16, no. 3, 1997, pp. 119–124.

———. *From Australia with Love: A History of Modern Australian Popular Romance Novels*. Fremantle Arts Centre Press, 2004.

———. "Blushing Bride to Bush Matriarch: Women in the Fiction of Lucy Walker." *Journal of Publishing*, vol. 1, 2005, pp. 37–52.

———. "Love under the Coolabah: Australian Romance Publishing since 1990." *Making Books: Contemporary Australian Publishing*, edited by David Carter, and Anne Galligan, University of Queensland Press, 2007, pp. 279–285.

———. "'Feminists Talk about Sisterhood; I Do Not Know How Deeply They Feel It': Australian Mass Market Romance Novels and Their Critics." *Reading Down Under: Australian Literary Studies Reader*, edited by Amit Sarwal, and Reema Sarwal, Sports and Spiritual Science Publications, 2009, pp. 419–428.

———. "The Wide Brown Land and the Big Smoke: The Setting of Australian Popular Romance." *Sold by the Millions: Australia's Bestsellers*, edited by Toni Johnson-Woods, and Amit Sarwal, Cambridge Scholars Publishing, 2012, pp. 82–95.

Gelder, Ken and Rachael Weaver. "Colonial Australian Romance Fiction." *The Anthology of Colonial Australian Romance Fiction*, edited by Ken Gelder, and Rachael Weaver, Melbourne University Press, 2010, pp. 1–11.

Gilbert, Pam. "Introduction." In Rosa Praed, *Lady Bridget in the Never-Never Land*, Pandora Press, 1987, pp. vii–xiii.

Gilbert, Pam and Sandra Taylor. "Reading the Romance." *Nation, Culture, Text: Australian Cultural and Media Studies*, edited by Graeme Turner, Routledge, 1993, pp. 246–256.

Giles, Fiona. *Too Far From Everywhere: The Romantic Heroine in Nineteenth-Century Australia*. University of Queensland Press, 1998.

Harris, Emily Ann, Michael Thai and Fiona Kate Barlow. "Fifty Shades Flipped: Effects of Reading Erotica Depicting a Sexually Dominant Woman Compared to a Sexually Dominant Man." *The Journal of Sex Research*, vol. 54, no. 3, 2017, pp. 386–397.

Haynes, Roslynn. "Romanticism and Environmentalism: The Tasmanian Novels of Marie Bjelke-Petersen." *Australian Literary Studies*, vol. 20, no. 1, 2001, pp. 62–75.

———. "Marie Bjelke Petersen's Romances: Fulfilling the Contract, Subverting the Spirit." *Southerly*, vol. 7, no. 2, 2010, pp. 41–63.

Heiss, Anita. *Not Meeting Mr. Right*. Bantam, 2007.

———. *Avoiding Mr. Right*. Bantam, 2009.

———. *Manhattan Dreaming*. Bantam, 2010.

———. *Paris Dreaming*. Bantam, 2011.

———. *Tiddas*. Simon & Schuster and Cammeray, 2014.

———. *Barbed Wire and Cherry Blossoms*. Simon & Schuster and Cammeray, 2016.

Hill, Loretta. *The Girl in Steel-Capped Boots*. Bantam, 2013a.

———. *The Girl in the Hard Hat*. Bantam, 2013b.

Jinks, Catherine. *Spinning Around*. Allen & Unwin, 2004.

Johnson-Woods, Toni. "Crikey It's Bromance: A History of Australian Pulp Westerns." *Sold By the Millions: Australia's Bestsellers*, edited by Toni Johnson-Woods, and Amit Sarwal, Cambridge Scholars Publishing, 2012a, pp. 141–161.

———. "Introduction: Two Centuries of Popular Australian Fiction." *Sold by the Millions: Australia's Bestsellers*, edited by Toni Johnson-Woods, and Amit Sarwal, Cambridge Scholars Publishing, 2012b, pp. 1–21.

Karmel, Pip. *Me, Myself and I*. Allen & Unwin, 2000.

Lam, Maylyn. "Reading the Sweet Dream: Adolescent Girls and Romance Fiction." M.Ed Thesis, Melbourne, 1986.

Leakey, Caroline. *The Broad Arrow: Being Passages from the History of Maida Gwynnham, A Lifer*. Richard Bentley, 1859.

Levy, Bronwen. "Up from Under, or on Not Marrying the Racist Aussie Boss: Strategies for Reading Romantic Fiction." *Hecate*, vol. 13, no. 1, 1987, pp. 7–20.

Mathew, Imogen. "'The Pretty and the Political Didn't Seem to Blend Well': Anita Heiss's Chick Lit and the Destabilisation of a Genre." *JASAL: Journal of the Association for the Study of Australian Literature*, vol. 15, no. 3, 2015, pp. 1–11.

———. "Educating the Reader in Anita Heiss's Chick Lit." *Contemporary Women's Writing*, vol. 10, no. 3, 2016, pp. 334–353.

———. "Love in the Time of Racism: 'Barbed Wire and Cherry Blossoms' Explores the Politics of Romance." *The Conversation*, September 7 2016, theconversation.com/love-in-the-time-of-racism-barbed-wire-and-cherry-blossoms-explores-the-politics-of-romance-64126. Accessed March 18 2017.

McAlister, Jodi and Hsu-Ming Teo. "Love in Australian Romance Novels." *The Popular Culture of Romantic Love in Australia*, edited by Hsu-Ming Teo, Australian Scholarly Publishing, 2017, pp. 194–222.

McWilliam, Kelly. "Romance in Foreign Accents: Harlequin-Mills & Boon in Australia." *Continuum: Journal of Media & Cultural Studies*, vol. 23, no. 2, 2009, pp. 137–145.

Merrick, Elizabeth. "Introduction: Why Chick Lit Matters." *This is Not Chick Lit*, edited by Elizabeth Merrick, Random House, 2006, pp. vii–xi.

Mirmohamadi, Kylie. "Love on the Land: Australian Rural Romance in Place." *English Studies*, vol. 96, no. 2, 2015, pp. 204–224.

Moran, Albert. "'No More Virgins': Writing Romance—An Interview with Emma Darcy." *Continuum*, vol. 4, no. 1, 1990, wwwmcc.murdoch.edu.au./ReadingRoom/4.1/Darcy.html

Murdoch University Library. "Mills & Boon Collection," library.murdoch.edu.au/Researchers/Special-Collections/Mills-and-Boon-Collection/ Accessed January 24, 2017.

O'Mahony, Lauren. "Australian Rural Romance as Feminist Romance?" *Australasian Journal of Popular Culture*, vol. 3, no. 3, 2014a, pp. 285–298.

———. "Teaching an Old Dog New Tricks? Romance, Ethics and Human-Dog Relationships in a Rural Australian Novel." *Journal of Popular Romance Studies*, vol. 4, no. 2, 2014b. jprstudies.org/2014/10/teaching-an-old-dog-new-tricks-romance-ethics-and-human-dog-relationships-in-a-rural-australian-novelby-lauren-omahony/ Accessed November 29, 2014.

———. *In Search of Feminist Romance in Australian Romance*. Ph.D. Dissertation, Murdoch University, 2015.

———. "Death and the Rural Romance Novel." *Text Journal*, vol. 23, 2 no. 45, 2017, pp. 1–14.

———. "'More than Sex, Shopping and Shoes': Cosmopolitan Indigeneity and Cultural Politics in Anita Heiss's Koori Lit." *Theorizing Ethnicity and Nationality in Chick Lit*, edited by Erin Hurt, Routledge, 2018, pp. 41–68.

O'Mahony, Lauren and Olivia Murphy. "From Polite Society to the Pilbara: The Ingénue Abroad in *Evelina* and *the Girl in Steel-Capped Boots*." *Outskirts*, vol. 38, 2018, pp. 1–23.

Ogelby, Cliff. "*Terra Nullius*, the High Court and Surveyors." *Australian Surveyor*, vol. 38, no. 3, 1993, pp. 171–189.

Ommundsen, Wenche. "Sex and the Global City: Chick Lit with a Difference." *Contemporary Women's Writing*, vol. 5, no. 2, 2011, pp. 107–124.

Owen, Mairead. "Re-Inventing Romance: Reading Popular Romantic Fiction." *Pergamon*, vol. 20, no. 4, 1997, pp. 537–554.

Parameswaran, Radhika. "Reading Fiction of Romance: Gender, Sexuality and Nationalism in Postcolonial India." *Journal of Communication*, vol. 52, no. 4, 2002, pp. 832–851.

Parv, Valerie. *The Art of Romance Writing*. 1993. Allen and Unwin, 2004.

———. "Bio." Valerie Parv Website, www.valerieparv.com/bio.html Accessed April 19, 2017.

"Paul Hogan Ad 1984." YouTube, March 28 2009, www.youtube.com/watch?v=Xn_CPrCS8gs

Platt, Len. "'Altogether Better-bred Looking': Race and Romance in the Australian Novels of Rosa Praed." *Journal of the Association for the Study of Australian Literature*, vol. 8, 2008, pp. 31–44.

Praed, Rosa. *An Australian Heroine*. Chapman and Hall, 1890.

———. *Lady Bridget in the Never-Never Land*. 1984. Pandora Press, 1987.

Radway, Janice. *Reading the Romance*. University of North Carolina Press, 1984.

"Rural Fiction." Penguin Books Australia, 2017, www.penguin.com.au/browse/rural-fiction Accessed July 19, 2017.

RWA (Romance Writers of America). "About the Romance Genre," 2019 www.rwa.org/Online/Romance_Genre/About_Romance_Genre.aspx

Sarwal, Amit. "Foreword." *Sold By the Millions: Australia's Bestsellers*, edited by Toni Johnson-Woods, and Amit Sarwal, Cambridge Scholars Publishing, 2012, pp. viii–xv.

Smith, Caroline J. *Cosmopolitan Culture and Consumerism in Chick Lit*. Routledge, 2007.

Sparrow, Rebecca. *The Girl Most Likely*. University of Queensland Press, 2003.
Spence, Catherine Helen. *Clara Morison: A Tale of South Australia During the Gold Fever*. John W. Parker and Son, 1854.
Spender, Dale. "Rosa Praed: Original Australian Writer." *A Bright and Fiery Troop*, edited by Debra Adelaide, Penguin, 1988, pp. 199216.
Tapper, Olivia. "Romance and Innovation in Twenty-First Century Publishing." *Publishing Research Quarterly*, vol. 30, 2014, pp. 249–259.
Tasma. (Jessie Couvreur). *The Penance of Portia James*. William Heinemann, 1891.
Taylor, Cheryl. "Tropical Flowers: Romancing North Queensland in Early Female Fiction and Poetry." *LiNQ (Literature in North Queensland)*, vol. 36, 2009, pp. 135–160.
Teo, Hsu-Ming. "'We Have to Learn to Love Imperially': Love in Late Colonial and Federation Australian Romance Novels." *Journal of Popular Romance Studies*, vol. 4, no. 2, 2014, jprstudies.org/2014/10/we-have-to-learn-to-love-imperially-love-in-late-colonial-and-federation-australian-romance-novelsby-hsu-ming-teo/
Thomas, Glen. "Romance: The Perfect Creative Industry? A Case Study of Harlequin-Mills & Boon Australia." *Empowerment versus Oppression: Twenty First Century Views of Popular Romance Novels*, edited by Sally Goade, Cambridge Scholars Publishing, 2007, pp. 20–29.
———. "'And I Deliver': An Interview with Emma Darcy." *Continuum: Journal of Media and Cultural Studies*, vol. 22, no. 1, 2008a, pp. 113–126.
———. "The Best Australian Romance Novelist: Emma Darcy." *Beautiful Things in Popular Culture*, edited by Alan McKee, Blackwell, 2008b.
Thorpe, Clarissa. "Australian Romance Writers Find 'Happily Ever Afters' with Overseas Sales of Novels." ABC News Australia, March 7, 2015, www.abc.net.au/news/2015-03-07/australian-romance-writers-build-strong-sales-overseas/6287704
Tiffin, Chris. "Rosa Praed." *Victorian Fiction Research Guides*, December 1988, victorianfictionresearchguides.org/rosa-praed/
Treasure, Rachael. *Jillaroo*. Penguin, 2002.
University of Melbourne Library. "Australian and New Zealand Romantic Fiction Collection." library.unimelb.edu.au/__data/assets/pdf_file/0009/2198313/romance2016.pdf Accessed May 15, 2017.
Valentine, James. "Interview with Anita Heiss." *ABC Australia Radio*, 2011, blogs.abc.net.au/files/anita-heiss-1.mp3
Veros, Vassiliki. "Scholarship in Practice: The Romance Reader and the Public Library." *The Australian Library Journal*, vol. 61, no. 4, 2012, pp. 298–306.
———. "A Matter of Meta: Category Romance Fiction and the Interplay of Paratext and Library Metadata." *Journal of Popular Romance Studies*, vol. 5, no. 1, 2015. jprstudies.org/2015/08/a-matter-of-meta-category-romance-fiction-and-the-interplay-of-paratext-and-library-metadataby-vassiliki-veros/ Accessed January 19, 2017.
Vivanco, Laura. "Australian Romance Writing—What's There to Take Seriously?" 2012 australianwomenwriters.com/2012/02/australian-romance-writing-whats-there-to-take-seriously/
Weaver-Zercher, Valerie. *Thrill of the Chaste: The Allure of Amish Romance Novels*. Johns Hopkins University Press, 2013.
Whelehan, Imelda and Barbara Pini. "Farm Lit: Reading Narratives of Love on the Land." *Cultural Sustainability in Rural Communities*, edited by Catherine Driscoll, Kate Darian-Smith, and David Nichols, Routledge, 2017, pp. 68–83.
White, Kerry. *Australian Children's Books, A Bibliography*, Vol. 3. The Miegunyah Press, 2004.

Part II

Sub-genres

4 Gothic romance

Angela Toscano

Before the blockbuster romances of the 1970s, there was the modern popular Gothic romance. Structurally, its plots, settings, and characters are equivalent to the classic Gothic novel of the eighteenth and nineteenth centuries in which a young woman finds herself in mysterious and perilous circumstances, but for the fact that the modern version puts its emphasis on the love story. Most identifiable by its covers featuring women clad in diaphanous nightgowns fleeing crumbling, ancient houses, the Gothic romance dominated popular women's reading for two decades between the late 1950s and the early 1980s. As such, the first forays of scholarly criticism on the popular romance focused not on the sweeping historicals that Kathleen Woodiwiss and Rosemary Rogers would make popular, but on the paperback Gothic novel. Joanna Russ' article "Somebody's Trying to Kill Me And I Think It's My Husband" (1973) as well as Kay Mussell's "Beautiful and Damned: the Sexual Woman in Gothic Fiction" (1975) critiqued the modern Gothic romance, but in so doing established the terms and methods for approaching popular romance that would later be utilized by Janice Radway and Tania Modleski.

Despite these early forays by scholars, the modern popular Gothic romance has been mostly neglected as a subject of critical inquiry by both those scholars looking at the Gothic and by those looking at popular romance. The reasons for this neglect, however, varies from field to field. Like much traditional academic scholarship, Gothic studies has predominantly looked at literary fiction, film, and those pieces of genre fiction that have achieved cultural capital or large-scale notoriety. The modern popular Gothic romance rarely falls into any of these categories, and thus has often been left out of critical discussions of the Gothic. However, I contend that mid-twentieth-century popular Gothic romances fall under the same rubric as other texts ascribed to this category and, therefore, may be categorized similarly without causing confusion. The circumstance that has led to the modern Gothic romance being left out of Gothic studies, though, hardly holds true for popular romance studies, which has made a concentrated effort to illuminate texts that have often been overlooked by more canonical approaches to literature. Yet popular romance studies, too, has made sparse critical inquiries into the Gothic romance since the early 1980s. The current omission of the Gothic in romance studies is due partly to the sheer volume of scholarly work still needed to be done in the field, but also to the peculiar absence of the Gothic in the current landscape of popular romance. While historicals, contemporaries, paranormals, inspirationals, and erotic romances have maintained, and even grown their markets, the Gothic has all but disappeared as a publishing category. Consequently, this has produced its corresponding absence from popular romance studies.

Absences, then, mark the Gothic romance—its absence from the critical discourse, its absence from the catalogs of publishers, booksellers, and libraries; its absence even as a material object of another decade. This absence is rather ironic since the Gothic is a genre in which absence—or rather, the presence that is an absence—drives the plot and delineates the space of the story. It defines itself in the spectral and the spectacular, the phantom and the phantasmic. Through apparitions and hauntings, in vanishings and losses, the Gothic depicts an uncanny space that is neither wholly realistic nor wholly fantastic. It narrates at the threshold of opposing worlds, ideas, and bodies. It is a genre that wrestles with the not-quite-there, the secret, the hidden, the unmarked, and the transgressive. In this chapter I will survey this absence. First, by recounting the history of the Gothic form, its attendant critical conversations, and its relation to the modern Gothic romance. I will then define the modern popular Gothic romance as well as differentiate it from its daughter genres: romantic suspense and the paranormal romance. Third, I will examine the contemporary scholarship on the Gothic romance, and finally, I will conclude by offering some avenues for further research.

The origins of the Gothic: the eighteenth-century Gothic and its critics

It is generally agreed upon that the first Gothic novel was *The Castle of Otranto: A Gothic Story*, written in 1764 by Horace Walpole. While earlier fictions may bear a narrative resemblance to it, this novel was certainly the first text to attach the word "gothic" to its form. However, the origins of the Gothic as a genre and a mode are less easily identifiable. Later critics of the novel would see the Gothic as curiously out of place within the cultural and historical context of the Enlightenment. As Carol Margaret Davison puts it, "At first glance, the Gothic novel seems to be an anachronistic and paradoxical cultural production of the era" (25). The sense that the Gothic is anachronistic is principally due to the notion that the novel as a form breaks with the prose traditions of previous centuries, i.e., the epic and the chivalric romance. This break can be summarized as the rise of realism. The novel's realism was a critical construction during the eighteenth century as demonstrated by such figures as William Congreve and Samuel Johnson,[1] all of whom focused on the novel's verisimilitude as its defining distinction from the romance. Moreover, this is a critical attitude that continues to dominate histories of the novel. As Anne Williams remarks in *Art of Darkness: A Poetics of the Gothic*, "Realism has provided an explicit definition and an implicit standard of value even in those leisurely histories of 'the novel' with no self-conscious theoretical bias" (2). This bias has largely informed the most critical views of the novel's realism, which functions as sign of its rupture with previous prose fictions. This is most notably evident in Ian Watt's *The Rise of the Novel*, in which he argues that,

> If the novel were realistic merely because it saw life from the seamy side, it would only be an inverted romance; . . . the novel's realism does not reside in the kind of life it presents, but in the way it presents it.
>
> (11)

Watt sees the novel as reflecting not just life as it is, but the turn that occurred in eighteenth-century philosophy and epistemology toward the perspective of the individual subject. Thus, the English novel is positioned as being manifestly different than either the epic or the French heroic romance because it enacts through narrative the shift from a truth conceived via tradition to a truth conceived via individual observation. Rather than focusing on the aristocratic and the fantastic, the novel as a realist form attempts to represent the world as it is for particular persons in particular places. Thus, realism is a product of the age, expressing the dominant sensibility of reason through literary mimesis. The emergence of the Gothic in the mid-eighteenth century appears to be a peculiar phenomenon, incongruous with the contemporary culture. Like the "misty, diffuse, intuitive romance," the Gothic "seems 'feminine' in contrast to the Realistic novel's focus on manners, morals, society, and consciousness" (Williams 3). Thus in its origin and expression, the Gothic deviates from later critical scripts surrounding the century in which realism reigns supreme.

Yet, the Gothic was neither so incongruous nor as peculiar as narratives about the realist novel would suggest. As David Punter argues in *Literature of Terror*, the emphasis in the Enlightenment on positivism, or the idea that everything can be known, means that "Nothing can remain outside" knowledge "because the mere idea of outsideness is the very source of fear." Thus, "fear is both the root and product of the attempt to bring all things under rational control" (26–7). In effect, the Gothic as a literary form represents this contradiction at the heart of the Age of Reason. It narrates stories about pasts, persons, and places that seem to escape the rational, secular world of the Enlightenment. In many ways, the Gothic anticipates and enacts notions of the sublime we often associate with the Romantics. In *The Rise of Supernatural Fiction 1762–1800*, E.J. Clery suggests that the same historical conditions surrounding ideas of reason and education that first caused the exclusion of the supernatural from fiction, eventually led to its return. She argues that this exclusion is tied to ideas of the imagination as "a passive medium for the imprint of external impressions, liable to be permanently disordered by the excessive input of improbabilities" (3). The susceptible nature of the imagination, then, suggests that "it would be best if ghost stories could be withdrawn from circulation altogether" (3), thus not risking corrupting impressionable minds. However, the supernatural as popular fiction does not remain long gone from the market. Indeed, Clery's argument centers on the idea that the rise of supernatural fiction is linked to the rise of consumerism: "the expansion of the reading public, and the devising of new methods for distributing and marketing books" (6–7). While the influence of reason may have first suppressed supernatural fiction, rational exploitation of the market enabled its return to popular forms.

As such, the Gothic emerged from a contradictory cultural moment in which economic shifts in the way books were circulated coincided with philosophical discussions about reason, the real, and the place of the individual. As Walpole puts it in his preface to the second edition of *The Castle of Otranto*, the intention of the novel was "to blend the two kinds of romance,[2] the ancient and the modern. In the former all was imagination and improbability: in the latter, nature is always intended to be, and sometimes has been, copied with success" (65). Andrew Smith notes in his book *Gothic Literature* that Walpole's two prefaces, one for each edition, established the terms of how the Gothic would be read later, i.e., as both ancient romance and realist novel (19). Smith further notes that Walpole's positioning, as well as the convoluted plot of *The Castle of Otranto*, "captures one of the key terms of the Gothic: ambivalence" (23). From the outset, the Gothic genre is defined by intersecting, and often opposing, elements, i.e., an ambivalence. This ambivalence gets reproduced in various ways as the form develops. Narratives toggle between the conservative and the radical, presenting simultaneously contradictory notions of gender, race, and religion. In short, the emergence of the Gothic as a popular form in the mid- to late-eighteenth-century mirrors and recasts the ideological changes taking place in the larger culture, exploring the space between reason and feeling, natural and supernatural, past and present, men and women, Catholic and Protestant, and so forth, without settling into any fixed subject position or perspective.

Therefore, what distinguishes the Gothic genre across variations and adaptations is its hybridity. Like Mary Shelley's monster in *Frankenstein* (1818), it is a narrative amalgamation of variant parts that create a new whole. As Jerrold E. Hogle puts it in his introduction to *The Cambridge Companion to Gothic Fiction*,

> No other form of writing is as insistent as the Gothic on juxtaposing potential revolution and possible reactions… leaving both extremes sharply before us and far less resolved than the conventional endings in most of these works claim them to be.
>
> (13)

Hogle's argument here is particularly useful when we apply a similar rubric of juxtaposition to read iterations of the Gothic in popular romance, especially since most of the criticism on the Gothic romance erases this ambivalence. Rather, contemporary critics have censured the Gothic romance, noting its conservative bent without acknowledging its radical aspects, seeing it as a means of indoctrinating women into accepting patriarchal mores without seeing them as equally capable of opposing them. This censure, though, is not new. The association of the Gothic with women readers, particularly during the 1780s when the Gothic was at its apex of popularity, raised concerns about the effect this would have on individuals and society.[3] As Maggie Kilgour notes in *The Rise of the Gothic Novel*,

> The spread of literacy, the growth of a largely female and middle-class readership and the power of the press increased fears that literature could be a socially subversive influence. Prose fiction was particularly suspect: romances, for giving readers unrealistic expectations of an idealized life, novels for exposing them to the sordidness of an unidealized reality.
>
> (6)

What is important to note here is that although the specifics have changed over the centuries as new content and contexts have emerged, the thrust of the critique has not. Gothic romance, indeed, all popular romance, still finds itself subject to this suspicion. The sense of the Gothic as something women read, as a feminized genre, expresses eighteenth-century anxieties about the place of women in the literary and cultural landscape. Moreover, it is an anxiety that attaches itself to terms of especial interest to popular romance scholars: fancy, fantasy, romance, emotion, sensibility, sentimentality, affect, the body, popular, consumerism. These terms and their connotations in the critical discourse signal an aesthetic bias against those forms of literature which interest women most. The often pejorative interrogation of these terms and the genres attached to them demonstrates the continuing need to re-frame and revisit discussions of the Gothic. Diana Wallace expresses this most succinctly in her monograph, *Female Gothic Histories*, asserting that scholars must work "to uncover what has been repressed within history—the maternal and matrilineal genealogies" that influence women's literary endeavors, and their concurrent attempt to represent the often hidden and erased experiences of women (24).

Gothic adaptations: moving from genre to mode in the nineteenth century

Eighteenth-century Gothics established the narrative patterns and devices that structured the genre. However, when these elements were then re-used in their nineteenth-century progeny, the Gothic began to lose its status as a distinct generic category. Instead, it was retained as a mode of literary expression. Over the subsequent centuries, the Gothic's constitutive parts were adapted and modified to new mediums, such as periodicals and film. However, during the nineteenth century, the Gothic as a mode was expressed less in the rise of new mediums as it was in the development of more familiar literary genres within a more familiar literary marketplace. This shift from genre to mode allows the Gothic to be altered in order to accommodate different cultural and socio-historical contexts. In his chapters on nineteenth-century and post-romantic iterations of the Gothic, Andrew Smith highlights the way the Gothic mutated from its earlier novelistic form: "the Gothic does not disappear but subversively infiltrates other forms of writing, including poetry, and the realist Victorian novel" (53). Jerrold E. Hogle makes a similar observation, saying, "This highly unstable genre then scattered its ingredients into various modes" not only the more realist Victorian novel but "in flamboyant plays and scattered operas, short stories or fantastic tales for magazines and newspapers, 'sensation' novels for women and the literate working class, portions of poetry or painting, and substantial resurgences of full-fledged Gothic novels" (1). Furthermore, these other forms of writing begin to take on their own distinct generic categories as the century passed: sensation fiction, the detective story, and horror. The principal difference between these genres and the Gothic proper is that the Gothic is pre-occupied with the past in a way that, as Diana Wallace argues, anticipates, and inverts the historical novel (5–19). Instead of focusing on the past, these categories of narrative move the now-familiar Gothic elements into new settings and scenes, i.e., into the contemporary world of the middle class, the future, other societies, planets, and fantasy worlds. The Gothic, then, in the nineteenth century, becomes a mode where each form that adapts and modifies it does so in order to address particular anxieties about empire, gender, sexuality, and race. As these anxieties found new expression in new generic forms, they in turn offered new ways of managing the fear at the root of the Gothic.

While the Gothic was principally a genre confined to the medium of the novel, by the beginning of the twentieth century it had adapted itself to new forms, the most significant of which was film. Cinematic adaptations of nineteenth- and twentieth-century novels, in turn, contributed to the development of the modern Gothic romance by familiarizing a broader audience with its tropes and conventions. This is evidenced first, by Hitchcock's direction of *Rebecca* (1940), based on the Du Maurier novel of the same name (published 1938). Du Maurier's novel revived the Female Gothic, exemplified by Ann Radcliffe's late-eighteenth-century novels, as well as those of the Brontë sisters.[4] In so doing, Du Maurier establishes a model for Gothic romances that would dominate the paperback market during the mid-twentieth century. Immensely popular, *Rebecca* was serialized in newspapers as well as adapted to the radio and the stage as well as the screen. It also influenced other similar movies, most notably *Suspicion* (1941) and *Gaslight* (1940), both of which developed parallel plots and structures to *Rebecca*. For example, *Suspicion* is about an heiress who marries a handsome playboy and begins to suspect that he is trying to murder her for her money. Similarly, *Gaslight*, based on the 1938 stage play of the same name by Patrick Hamilton, is set in fin de siècle London. It follows a heroine whose husband attempts to drive her insane through a series of manipulations, one of which is tampering with the gas lamps in their home (it is from this move that we get the term gaslighting, which is to manipulate a person into questioning their sanity, much in the manner of the film's villain). These texts, like the eighteenth-century Gothic, deal with the terrors of a familial and familiar space. They wrestle with contemporary fears, specifically women's fears regarding sex, love, marriage, and men's violence.

The Gothic, as a novelistic genre, re-emerges in the mid-twentieth century. The twin successes of film noir and Du Maurier's novels lead to various imitators throughout the 1950s. However, it was Victoria Holt's *Mistress of Mellyn*, published in 1960, that truly entrenched the Gothic romance as mass-market publishing mainstay. *Mistress of Mellyn*, though, was hardly the first of the modern Gothic romances. Throughout the 1950s, paperback publishers like Ace and Dell experimented with the genre. According to Lori A. Paige in her recent monograph, *The Gothic Romance Wave: A Critical History of the Mass Market Novels, 1960–1993*, Dell books was responsible for "pioneering the design that eventually became known as 'woman running from the house,'" the first instance of which was artist Robert Stanley's cover for Lucille Emericks' *Web of Evil* in 1951 (18). Yet, it was not Dell, but Ace Books that claimed to be "First in Gothics." As Janice Radway notes in *Reading the Romance*, this claim originates with Ace editor Gerald Gross who, noticing the ongoing popularity of *Rebecca*, published Phyllis Whitney's *Thunderheights* under the term "Gothic" in 1960. Similar origin stories for the Gothic category are recounted by both Kay Mussell in *Women's Gothic and Romantic Fiction* and in Joanna Russ in "Somebody's Trying to Kill Me and I Think It's My Husband."

Defining the modern Gothic romance

The defining feature of the Gothic as a genre is its ambivalence or hybridity. This is as true for the twentieth-century Gothic romance as much as it was for the eighteenth-century Gothic. In the Gothic novel, a sustained, contradictory expression of opposing ideologies and ideas is articulated in the structure, the characters, the plot, and the atmosphere of the novel. The supernatural is both real and imagined, there and not there. So, too, is the past similarly ephemeral. Due to this hybridity, the secret at the heart of the novel's mystery is not uncovered by rational methods, but through supernatural and fated interventions. Justice is served not by legal apparatuses or evidences producible in court, but by divine right and the reassertion of a natural order. For example, in *The Castle of Otranto*, the mystery is resolved chiefly through the supernatural intervention of Alfred, the ghost of the usurped lord, the timely and coincidental appearance of the true heir, Theodore, and the spontaneous confession and contrition of the principal villain, Manfred, at the end of the novel; a confession that re-establishes the rightful and natural heir as the true lord of the castle.

As the genre developed, these contradictions and vacillations between different ideological perceptions so intrinsic to the form in the eighteenth century, were erased in the nineteenth century's use of the Gothic as a mode. Genres like sensation fiction, detective stories, and horror would borrow and play with the form, but ultimately abandon the ambivalence that is its hallmark. Indeed, what constitutes a Gothic is often disputed in part because the genre itself is inherently amorphous due to this suspension of contradictions. Its boundaries and borders are porous and invisible, making it hard to distinguish between a proper Gothic and its daughter forms. Yet, these generic distinctions are important to understanding the development of the Gothic genre and its re-emergence within the twentieth-century romance market. Moreover, these distinctions enable us to mark the lines between the Gothic romance and other subgenres, like the paranormal romance and the romantic suspense novel.

The paratextual devices are the most easily distinguishable features of the modern popular Gothic romance, as they were meant to be. The cover is nearly always in tones of blues, grays, browns, and blacks. Occasionally, there will be one in reds and oranges, but this is more indicative of horror. The painting—as all covers were illustrated between the 1950s and the 1980s[5]—features a house or castle in the background. There is always the figure of a woman in the foreground. Sometimes she is running toward you. Sometimes she is standing still with her head turned back to look at the building's edifice. Rarely is there a man, and when there is, something in the rendering of his features and face make it clear that he is brooding. The textual devices, however, are less easily identifiable. Joanna Russ's "Somebody's Trying to Kill Me and I Think It's My Husband: The Modern Gothic" (1973) developed a shorthand for the Gothic romance's structural features—a shorthand which is useful for understanding the basic form of these texts. Moreover, Russ's structural shorthand is useful in connecting the twentieth-century Gothic romance to its antecedents in the eighteenth and nineteenth centuries. The principal difference is in how these different texts, in their respective historical periods, play out the conventions of the Gothic. I will, therefore, employ her shorthand to define and distinguish the modern Gothic romance. Russ italicized and capitalized these terms in her article (Russ, "Somebody's Trying to Kill Me," 667–9). As such, I will reproduce this same technique of hers along with her original terms in the same style. I will add my own terms for these elements in bold to aid easier distinction.

The events of the Gothic romance plot occur in a single locale, or dominant location. Usually this is a *House* or castle; a domestic scene, in which the central conflict revolves around a *Buried Ominous Secret*. Moreover, the secret is often itself a secret, as there is an uncertainty about whether a secret actually exists. The *Heroine*'s position in the novel is defined by this secret: she does not know what it is, but she also does not realize what it is she does not know. Therefore, the secret is invisible to both the reader and the heroine. The Gothic is thus a genre whose plot works through nested uncertainties, resulting in an epistemological ambiguity: that is, a sense that knowledge itself can never be enough to resolve the tension between opposites; the recognition that there is no clear, objective, or single truth to be discovered in answer to the central mystery of the text. This explains why the roles of hero and villain are not clearly delineated within the modern popular Gothic romance as they were in previous centuries' iterations of the form. Whether the *Super-Male* is villain or hero remains mutable and indistinct until the end of the story, at least to the *Heroine* if not the reader. This is done in order to maintain the central ambivalence at work in the text. Thus, the heroine not only does not know who the antagonist is, but does not know why they are doing what they are doing, or even if they are doing anything at all. In response to these unknowable unknowns, the heroine ventures into the recesses of the secret. These are often manifested in the space and dimensions of the house itself. She makes ventures not to deduce or reveal the secret, but rather to understand what is hidden. Thus, it is the heroine's curiosity that engenders the *Threat.* And like the secret, the threat is ephemeral and unnamed, so that there is even a question about whether or not a threat exists at all.

This is in contrast to the detective novel in which the threat is real. Romantic suspense is the popular romance form of the detective novel and the rules are very similar. Both rely on clues and deduction to drive the plot forward. Threats in these texts manifest as crimes. Therefore, as in detective fiction, a crime has usually already been committed in a romantic suspense. Sometimes, it is committed within the first act of the story. Sometimes in texts where there is a serial killer, the crime is ongoing. In short, while there is a mystery, there is not a mystery about whether or not there is a mystery. The mystery is a puzzle to be solved, not a secret to be exposed. Paranormals, too, nearly always have a mystery, often ongoing across a series. In both romantic suspense and paranormals, then, the detective works to accumulate knowledge until the mystery is solved. Whereas in the Gothic the *Secret is Revealed*, often through a sudden confession or telling statement made by the villain. Critics from Russ to Tania Modleski have noted the Gothic heroine's passivity. Russ says, "Unconscious foci of intrigue, passion, and crime, these young women (none of whom is over thirty) wander through all sorts of threatening forces of which they are intuitively, but never intellectually, aware" ("Somebody's Trying to Kill Me," 678). Though the Gothic heroine performs the work of a detective, her detective work does little to solve the mystery, precisely because she is not interested in solutions but rather relationships. What her work does is to make the secret more visible. She doesn't gain knowledge so much as she gains access to the *House* and the *Super-Male*—moving further into the literal and figurative space of the secret without necessarily breaching it.

The ambivalence that characterizes the dramatis personae and the secret likewise characterizes the presence of the supernatural. In the paranormal romance there is no question that the supernatural exists. In fact, it is often a main character in the novel. This, too, marks one of the distinctions Gothic has with the horror novel, which is one of the parent genres of the paranormal romance along with science fiction and fantasy. There, the threat is supernatural and manifested. It is visible both to the characters and to the reader. This is because horror is interested in the ways that the external, public body is violated, corrupted, and mutilated. Horror is about seeing and showing social violence: in flayed bodies, in torture porn, and satanic rituals. Our disgust and fear come in being witnesses to these extremes. As such, horror is more interested in the threats posed to the public body in the public space, by institutions and practices, by religions and governments.[6] This is distinct from the modern Gothic romance, whose terror is predicated on the unseen and unknown. It is interested in intimate, private, and psychological violence in the relationships between individual persons, whereas horror is interested in how collective and public violence marks the body. Gothic violence works through gaslighting and the uncertainty of the senses rather than on torment and torture. Consequently, the resolution of the Gothic romance often depends on the heroine's ability to develop intimate relationships. She acts by instinct and affect, rather than on reason, law, or analysis. This accounts for her passivity in the face of the *Buried Ominous Secret* as well as the *Super-Male*'s brutishness.

By mixing the real and the fantastic, the spectral and the material, the modern Gothic romance creates a genre of the uncanny. It narrates, as much as it did in previous centuries, at the threshold of male and female, known and unknown, natural and supernatural, feeling and reason. However, in the modern Gothic romance, what distinguishes it from its prior instantiations is how the uncanny space produced in these texts works to highlight the central, nebulous anxiety of women's heterosexual experience; anxiety that is itself uncanny and contradictory as it oscillates between a desire for the *Super-Male* and a fear of him; a longing for home and yet, the wish to escape home; the fear of losing your identity and yet, the simultaneous fear that you are insufficient, i.e., orphaned from your own identity; the deep, yearning for love and yet, the fear that you are unlovable precisely because you are lacking an identity and a home. For example, in Mary Stewart's *Nine Coaches Waiting*, the heroine, Linda, takes a job with the de Valmy family as a governess to the young count. Her reasons for taking the job are, in part, due to a desire to return to France. Though English by nationality, her childhood was spent in that country before she was orphaned, and her one desire has been to return to that space as a way to regain a lost identity and a lost family. Her time at the Chateau de Valmy is, of course, not a homecoming. Typically for governesses in novels, her position is one that is neither servant nor family member. When she meets her young charge's dashing and dangerous cousin, Raoul, she is both attracted to him and afraid of him. Similarly, she is also attracted to and afraid of Raoul's father, Leon de Valmy—a charming, egotistical man driven by family honor. The *Threat* that these men pose to Linda is not just physical or psychological, but sexual. Her vulnerability to them is precisely because she is heterosexual, and thus desires a reciprocity of feeling—feeling that might reclaim the domestic space into the safe and secure space she recollects from her childhood.

Thus, the Gothic romance's representation of the uncanny space of femininity arises from anxieties born out of the contradictory demands of traditional womanhood. For example, in *Nine Coaches Waiting*, Linda's role as surrogate mother to her young charge puts her in opposition to her own desired role as a romantic heroine. Moreover, as a figure in a Gothic novel, she must be both smart, yet ignorant; curious, yet innocent; sexually appealing, yet not seductive. These contradictory demands are precisely why the Gothic romance seems to uncritically express conservative values and ideologies, such as anti-Jacobin sentiments in the eighteenth century and heteronormative conceptions of gender in the twentieth. And yet, these same anxieties produce a simultaneous subversion of those demands by narrating those moments and periods when women are most likely to experience the uncanny—moments when intimate and private spaces are both inaccessible and yet in threat of exposure by a stranger who is also a close relation. This is certainly the template set by the *Castle of Otranto*, in which Manfred determines to marry his ward after the death of his son—despite the fact his wife is still living. And of course, in Anne Radcliffe's *The Mysteries of Udolpho* (1794), in which Emily's uncle—the villainous Montoni—is constantly attempting to force her to marry in order to gain her inheritance. In many mid-twentieth century Gothic romances—such as Du Maurier's *Rebecca* (1938), Victoria Holt's *Menfreya in the Morning* (1966), or Dorothy Eden's *Crow Hollow* (1950)—the heroine is newly married at the beginning the novel, with the husband acting as an intimate stranger, that close relation whose secrets, family history, and silence threaten the heroine.

Furthermore, this experience of the uncanny, the mysterious, and the secret is structured as an embodied one in the Gothic romance: it is emotional, mental, and physical all at once. It is also an experience that transpires between bodies, so that knowledge is gained through relationships and intimacy, not through reason. This relational approach to the secret is manifested in the uncanny double of *Another Woman* and the *Shadow-Male*. As such, the double becomes the guiding device for the ambiguity and ambivalence of the genre. Doubles structure the plot, appearing as characters as well as events. Sometimes characters operate as their own opposites, their own shadows and doppelgangers. And in doing so, the Gothic romance depicts an anxiety at the threshold of epistemology and identity—i.e., how we know what we know, and how we know who we are. Moreover, this anxiety is conceptualized as a particularly feminine one, even though it is one experienced by all persons. This anxiety revolves around the fear of being porous, of being open, of being penetrable, of being accessible to others and the world, and yet, simultaneously, of feeling that the world itself is inaccessible, closed, buffered, cordoned off from those we love most, and that our love itself is unreasonable, unreciprocated, and grotesque. Thus, the heroine's mutability and the hero's cruelty are motifs that speak to us of some of our most intimate fears. It is in this liminal space that the Gothic romance most deftly narrates the love story. And it is this space that has defined the Gothic as a mode and a genre since its inception in the eighteenth century. Yet, the liminal and uncanny form of the Gothic is also what has led to scholars to see these novels as insidious purveyors of conservative sexual politics. Because the modern Gothic romance depicts the domestic space as being broken, and yet fails to fully reject that space in favor of a more progressive feminist ideology, most critics working on the genre assert that these texts work to reintegrate women into the patriarchal order by satisfying their desires through repetitive forms of fiction. In the section that follows, I will outline these various critical positions.

Gothic romance scholarship

This fear and its manifestation as a plot device in the Gothic romance is most succinctly expressed in the aforementioned title of Russ's article, "Somebody's Trying To Kill Me and I Think It's My Husband" in *The Journal of Popular Culture*. This article constitutes the first major academic work on popular romance fiction. While Germaine Greer discusses romance reading in *The Female Eunuch*, it is Russ who first engages with romance as literature, naming titles and describing plots in her article.[7] Two years later, Kay Mussell publishes the article, "Beautiful and Damned: The Sexual Woman in Gothic Fiction," also in *The Journal of Popular Culture*. As indicated by the timeline in the following table, scholarly work on the modern popular Gothic romance demonstrates how integral this subgenre of romance was to the formation of popular romance studies. Most of the early major critics attended to the Gothic romance in their monographs. Additionally, the timeline reveals how the little academic scholarship in total there was published on the modern Gothic romance after Russ's article. By 1997, when Sylvia Kelso publishes her essay reflecting back on the genre and its critics, it certainly had tapered off to a near standstill. This further confirms that the disappearance of the modern popular Gothic romance from the literary marketplace was mirrored in its disappearance from critical treatments.

Russ' article establishes some of the principal beats familiar to scholars of popular romance. In her essay, she maps the form of the modern popular Gothic romance by

Table 4.1[8] Criticism since 1970

Year of publication	*Gothic romance criticism*
1973	Russ, Joanna. "Somebody's Trying to Kill Me and I Think It's My Husband: The Modern Gothic."
1975	Mussell, Kay, "Beautiful and Damned: The Sexual Woman in Gothic Fiction."
1977	Ruggiero and Weston, "Sex-Role Characterization of Women in 'Modern Gothic' Novels."
1978	Weston and Ruggiero, "Male-Female Relationships in Best-Selling 'Modern Gothic' Novels."
1979	Abartis, Caesarea, "The Ugly-Pretty, Dull-Bright, Weak-Strong Girl In the Gothic Mansion."
1981	Radway, Janice. "The Utopian Impulse in Popular Literature: Gothic Romances and 'Feminist' Protest."
1981	Mussell, Kay, *Women's Gothic and Romantic Fiction: A Reference Guide.*
1982	Modleski, Tania, *Loving with a Vengeance: Mass Produced Fantasies for Women.*
1982	Radway, Janice, "The Aesthetic in Mass Culture: Reading and the 'Popular' Literary Text."
1983	Fleenor, Juliann E., *The Female Gothic* (edited collection).
1983	Ruggiero and Weston, "Conflicting Images Of Women in Romance Novels."
1984	Radway, Janice, *Reading the Romance.*
1984	Mussell, Kay, *Fantasy and Reconciliation.*
1990	Massé, Michelle, "Gothic Repetition: Husbands, Horrors, and Things That Go Bump in the Night."
1992	Massé, Michelle, *In the Name of Love: Women, Masochism, and the Gothic.*
1997	Kelso, Sylvia, "Stitching Time: Feminism(s) and Thirty Years of Gothic Romance."

identifying its structural features. Her argument centers on the ways in which women use the Gothic romance to deflect and dissipate anxieties surrounding their position and role in the culture. However, she does not provide a close-reading, so much as she provides a list of various features and attendant commentary. And though she quotes heavily from various Gothic romances, these examples are used as evidence of how the Gothic romance is "directly expressing the traditional feminine situation" (Russ 671) rather than their individual narrative shapes. She sees these texts as reflections of the problems and demands of ordinary women's lives; problems second-wave feminists like Greer had already begun to excavate and explicate. Thus, though Russ's argument looks at the structure of the genre, she does so in order to argue that these novels are "an accurate reflection of the feminine mystique and a glamorized version of the lives many women do live ... it is a means of enabling a conventionally feminine heroine to have adventures at all" (686). Russ sees the Gothic romance as a way of avoiding the awakening necessary to feminist work. She ends the article with a list in which she voices reader reactions to the Gothic through the first person, as though they were now her own, concluding, "I will go and read another Gothic novel" (668). This self-implicating conclusion implies that the proliferation, repetition, and cyclicality of romance reading traps women into complacency, preventing them from critiquing the circularity of the culture, and their own logic and desires.

This reading of the modern Gothic romance is extended and carried on by the scholars that came in Russ' wake. For example, Kay Mussell's article, "Beautiful and Damned: The Sexual Woman in Gothic Fiction," compares the role of the other woman in the Gothic romance to that of the heroine, pointing to the way female sexuality and desire are marked as transgressive when openly expressed. She argues:

> The formula "proves" that if women fulfill traditional roles, then the family can be a viable institution. If, however, they do not, then the family is in trouble because women who are interested in sex rather than motherhood cannot hold it together.
>
> (89)

Like Russ, Mussell's central argument focuses on the way in which the texts reflect and distort women's lived experience; how these texts do the work of reinforcing traditional gender norms in heterosexual patriarchy. But unlike Russ, Mussell would continue to study the Gothic romance over the next decade, establishing herself as one of the foremost critics on the genre. This same argument is re-asserted in her 1984 monograph, *Fantasy and Reconciliation: Contemporary Formulas of Women's Romantic Fiction*. She says in the preface that "Romances rarely challenge the social order, and they do not urge women to recognize oppression or revolt" (xii). Yet, Mussell's argument does attempt to treat romances with respect by making structural distinctions between what the subgenres do and how they execute certain narrative elements, chiefly through a trope she calls "The Domestic Test" and which she explores in a chapter of the same name. She argues that Gothic romances tell the courtship narrative in "a more confined, claustrophobic, and domestic context" (46), one in which the attainment of the "traditional roles and possessions of a successful woman" are more significant or important because their receipt is dependent on "solving a mystery ... and running risks that would not be asked of most women" (97). Mussell recognizes romance's possibilities as a narrative for women. That said, the Gothic romance is mainly treated as an example of the larger argument she makes about the narrative and ideological aspects of romance's structures generally rather than as its own object of study.

A more in-depth treatment of the Gothic romance is evident in Mussell's 1981 book, *Women's Gothic and Romantic Fiction*. She called this work a reference guide, and, indeed, it remains one of the most useful texts on the modern Gothic romance. She provides a history of the genre, connecting it to earlier works. This is followed by a formidable bibliography of references and sources for study, before she goes on to explore related genres. The final chapters outline different methodological approaches to the Gothic, before covering popular commentary in newspapers, magazines, etc. Although Mussell again critiques the genre for its conservatism, the depth and breadth with which she approaches the Gothic romance not only offers a valuable resource for scholars of popular romance, but also provides an excellent model of a comprehensive, archival methodology.

By the time Janice Radway publishes *Reading the Romance* in 1984, the Gothic romance had already begun to dwindle in popularity. However, Radway's work builds on a decade of scholarship, much of which dealt with the Gothic romance in one shape or another. This was also true of Tania Modleski, who examined the Gothic romance as part of her larger project on popular romance, *Loving with a Vengeance: Mass Produced Fantasies for Women* in 1981. Where Mussell might be said to be using a cultural studies and structuralist approach, Modleski primarily employs a psychoanalytic reading of these Gothic romances. In the relevant chapter, she argues that whereas the Harlequin heroine has her fear transformed into love, the reverse is true for the Gothic heroine (60). Though she examines the formal elements of these texts, Modleski reads them as reflections of women's actual lives. She sees these texts not so much as literature, but more as self-help books which "probe the deepest layers of the feminine unconscious, providing a way for women to work through profound psychic conflicts, especially their ambivalence toward the significant people in their lives" (83), namely their husbands and mothers. While critics of the literary Gothic read ambivalence as a narrative technique employed to explore contradictions and paradoxes, Modleski presents its ambivalence as a symptom of women's cultural and collective neuroses. Thus, the effect of the psychoanalytic reading is to interpellate the Gothic romance into a kind of mass-produced dream that can only be read and understood by the critic.

One of the major gaps in these critical examinations is that they make few distinctions and differentiations among Gothic romances, focusing instead on how they are perceived to affect readers. As a result, this early scholarship has often ignored variations in plot and character. For instance, Radway's 1981 article, "The Utopian Impulse in Popular Literature: Gothic Romances and 'Feminist' Protest," provides a rich structural and formal examination of the elements of the genre, mapping its plots, devices, and its "conceptual oppositions" (151). But in so doing, it collapses the idiosyncratic aspects of individual texts, confirming the Gothic romance's conservative bent without accounting for discrepancies. She concludes that

> The gothic carefully re-establishes the basic structure of patriarchy ... by demonstrating to the reader that in the heroine's world, sexual submission wins a woman both the protective care of another *and* an opportunity to realize her truest self. (160)

The structural elements reinforce the idea of the Gothic romance as an interchangeable category with an interchangeable and fixed ideological position. Thus, Radway posits, like Modleski and Russ, that any contradictions and ambivalences in these Gothic romances are effectively erased by the happily ever after.

Two points can be made at this juncture about early criticism of the Gothic romance. The first is that these scholars see the romance in conversation with second-wave feminism whether they state this explicitly or not. The second is that because they do not see popular texts as having the distinction and originality of literary texts, they rarely employ sustained close-readings of any single novel. At best, they will provide structural and generic analysis, while still flattening differences and variations. Thus, lack of close-reading relegates the Gothic romance to the status of product rather than literary endeavor. In short, there is an aesthetic bias at work that sees these texts not so much as well-wrought urns as it does cheaply-made tchotchkes. The effect of this is that the Gothic romance has rarely been put into conversation with its eighteenth- and nineteenth-century progenitors. One exception to this is Juliann E. Fleenor's edited collection, *The Female Gothic* (1983). This collection brings together articles and essays that run the gamut from Mary Shelly to Victoria Holt. Russ's article is reproduced here as is one by Kay Mussell. Still, this collection does not dispute the principal critical assertions made about the modern Gothic romance. Of the early critical works on this subject, the only authors to attempt to make distinctions among texts were sociologists Josephine Ruggiero and Louise Weston.

Between 1978 and 1983, they published three articles, ("Sex-Role Characterization," "Male-Female Relationships," and "Conflicting Images") examining the depiction of sex roles in Gothic romance novels. Ruggiero and Weston attend to the distinctions in representations of the hero and heroine, as well as the secondary characters. They claim their research "has shown that, contrary to the critics' portrayal of the novel, the Gothic heroine is frequently depicted as rather nontraditional in her attitudes and behavior" ("Male-Female Relationships" 648). In both "Sex-Role Characterization of Women in 'Modern Gothic' Novels" and "Male-Female Relationships in Best-Selling 'Modern Gothic' Novels," they define traditional and nontraditional gender roles on a spectrum. This approach rejects the binary that defines most of the other criticism of this period, seeing the role of the heroine as dynamic rather than fixed. Thus, any single heroine or hero might simultaneously demonstrate both traditional and nontraditional sexual characteristics. What Ruggiero and Weston highlight in their study is that the Gothic romance remains a genre of ambivalence working less through stable meanings and denotations than it does through fluid positions and connotations based on specific contexts.

In summation, early popular romance criticism and the modern popular Gothic romance are defined and delineated by second-wave feminism. In many ways, they function as doubles, mirroring and distorting each other much in the same way doppelgangers in the Gothic do. Sylvia Kelso's 1997 article, "Stitching Time: Feminism(s) and Thirty Years of Gothic Romance" explores this connection to the "events, initiatives, and cultural image of second-wave American feminism(s)" (165). In it, she argues that shifts in the structures and plots of the Gothic romance are concurrent with shifts in American second-wave feminism(s). She looks specifically at the texts of Barbara Michaels, noting how she draws on "feminist intellectual initiatives and newly-developed feminist sensibilities in a way that destabilized the Gothic formula itself" (167), and suggesting that the Gothic romance is a form that parallels the political and philosophical discourses expressed in second-wave feminism. Thus, her article both reflects back on feminist criticism of the genre, as well as reiterating some of the same fundamental critiques that have threaded their way through contemporary scholarship on the form. Separated by 30 years, Kelso's argument still presents a similar claim as Russ's originary essay, thus book-ending a century's worth of scholarship on the popular Gothic romance. Though Kelso focuses on the productive relationship between second-wave feminism and the Gothic romance, she, too, concludes with the idea that "Female Gothic texts almost always retreat into ideologically acceptable happy endings" (176), replicating the most oft-expressed criticism of genre romance. Russ and Kelso, then, exemplify the major trend in twentieth-century criticism on the popular Gothic romance. Sparse as this criticism is, it overwhelmingly sees the Gothic romance as a conservative genre, re-inscribing patriarchal norms for a female reading audience.

Between the mid-1980s and the latter part of the 1990s, very little was published on the modern popular Gothic romance novel. However, beginning in the earlier 2000s and concurrent with the revival of popular romance studies, critical work on the Gothic romance began to appear again. Most notable among these is Deborah Lutz's work. In her illuminating 2007 article "The Haunted Space of the Mind," she re-asserts the ambivalent as the constitutive attribute of the Gothic: "At the heart of the Gothic we thus find ourselves, following shadows, trying to make absence present, trying to draw out the darkness from the light" (82). She argues that there was a revival of the Gothic in romance at the turn of the twenty-first century and that this revival speaks to "a post-feminist openness to a wide range of representations of women's erotic desire" (82), suggesting that a renewed interest in reading and writing the Gothic romance indicates that women are once again interested in exploring the uncanny space of women's heterosexual desire. However, Lutz's analysis focuses less on the Gothic as a genre, than it does on the Gothic as a mode. I note this because the texts that she reads belong to other popular romance subgenres, not just the Gothic proper. Still, Lutz's argument offers a clear-sighted examination of the formal elements of the Gothic romance and the way in which they are used to explore thresholds and transgressions. This is a motif she had earlier employed in her 2006 monograph, *The Dangerous Lover: Gothic Villains, Byronism, and the Nineteenth-Century Seduction Narrative*. There, Lutz argues that the figure of the dangerous lover embodies a series of subjectivities, often in opposition to each other. I began this section with the idea that what the twentieth-century modern Gothic romance returns to is, precisely, this dangerous lover; the one whom Joanna Russ refers to as the *Super-Male*; the one of whom the heroine is so uncertain.

The uncertain attraction which both readers and heroines are meant to feel toward the hero demonstrates the central ambivalence at work in the Gothic romance. This ambivalence is expressed not only in the uncertain position the hero holds, but also in the heroine's attitude toward sexuality, family, gender and gender roles, and the domestic. It is these elements that most strongly tie the modern popular Gothic romance back to the eighteenth-century form. The twentieth-century Gothic romance restores the genre, departing from the mode that dominated nineteenth-century iterations of the Gothic. While Lutz's argument focuses on the hero, I would argue that part of this restoration is dependent upon the reinstatement of the heroine as the undisputed, central protagonist. In so doing, they also return the Gothic to the uncanny and often violent space of a feminine heterosexual experience.

Furthermore, because the Gothic romance centers on ambivalence and ambiguity, as well as on a heroine who is herself ambiguous ("ugly-pretty, dull-bright, weak-strong," as Caesarea Abartis puts it in the title of her 1979 article), it narrates the experience of uncertainty almost exclusively in feminine terms: i.e., in relationships and through embodiments. As such, the modern popular Gothic romance predominantly defines itself through the representation of an ambivalent female experience within an ambiguous domestic space. These aspects demonstrate how the Gothic differs from other kinds of popular romance, but also establishes how they connect to their literary foremothers.

Conclusion with suggestions for further research

The modern popular Gothic romance is one of the foundational subgenres of the field. Moreover, its decline in popularity among romance readers and romance scholars has left many opportunities for further research to students and scholars of the genre. Like much popular romance, the modern Gothic has suffered from being approached in the collective, rather than through the examination of individual texts and authors. While no longer a fashionable or trending methodology, the Gothic romance would benefit from New Critical style close-readings—readings that would undercut the assumption long held that romances are interchangeable and indistinct. Questions that might prove fruitful to ask in such a formalist approach might be:

How does this individual Gothic arrange the tropes and conventions of the genre? Where does it deviate from generic norms? In what ways? And why is this significant?

Similarly, scholars might embark upon a single author study of writers like Mary Stewart, Victoria Holt, Dorothy Eden, Virginia Coffman, and Barbara Michaels. Such single-author studies not only add a great deal to our understanding of popular romance, its history and context, but provide excellent resources for teachers who might wish to include such texts on their syllabi (and perhaps need to justify that inclusion by pointing to relevant scholarship). Moreover, both close-readings and single-author studies provide a foundation for other methodologies—like comparing the Gothic to romantic suspense and paranormal romance, generating literary and cultural histories,[9] inquiries into the connections and ramifications upon feminism and gender, and exploring why the modern popular Gothic romance is no longer the publishing phenomenon from the reader response perspective.

Finally, since the modern popular Gothic romance finds its origins in the literary Gothic, there are many potential avenues for connecting, examining, and including this much-derided genre into the larger conversations about the rise and return of the Gothic. For scholars, the Gothic is one of those areas that has been over-mined, especially texts from the eighteenth and nineteenth centuries, and the amount of already existing work exploring the Gothic in its more literary instantiations can be intimidating to those entering the field. By contrast, the mid-twentieth-century Gothic romance remains under-represented, not only in popular romance studies but in Gothic studies as well. Attending to these texts as inheritors of the eighteenth-century Gothic might prove a fruitful way to intervene in these ongoing conversations around the Gothic, as a genre, form, and historical phenomenon.

Notes

1 For examples of contemporary distinctions between the romance and the novel can be found in Ioan Williams, ed., *Novel and Romance 1700–1800: A Documentary Record.*

2 Walpole uses the word "romance" to refer to an older form of the novel as well as previous long, prose forms of Chivalric and adventurous fiction. He uses it more broadly than the modern usage. Significantly, his use of romance points to the ongoing conflation in the eighteenth century among romances, novels, and histories, which were terms often used interchangeably by publishers and authors.

3 It is interesting to note that what engenders this suspicion of the literary feminine is connected to the availability and abundance of such texts in the marketplace. Indeed, the Gothic dominated the book market during late eighteenth and early nineteenth century. This is most readily exemplified by Montague Summer's massive *Gothic Bibliography*, which lists works by European as well as English authors. A more succinct version of this can be found in Frederick S. Frank's *The First Gothics: A Critical Guide to the English Gothic Novel,* which lists just over 500 works published between 1764 and 1820.

4 Anne Radcliffe and Matthew Lewis are the most famous of the eighteenth-century Gothic novelists. Their works are often cited as expressing connected, but opposing versions of the Gothic. Radcliffe was the first to distinguish herself from Lewis, calling her stories gothics of terror, and the other, gothics of horror in her essay "On the Supernatural in Poetry." She writes, "Terror and horror are so far opposite, that the first expands the soul, and awakens the faculties to a high degree of life; the other contracts, freezes, and nearly annihilates them" (149). Twentieth-century critics have made similar distinctions between Radcliffe and Lewis. For example, Eileen Moers identifies Radcliffe as originating the tradition "in which the central figure is a young woman who is simultaneously persecuted victim and courageous heroine." She defines the Female Gothic simply as "the work that women writers have done in the literary mode that, since the eighteenth century, we have called the Gothic"

(123–4). Later critics would trouble and tweak this definition. As Andrew Smith and Diana Wallace noted in their introduction to a 2004 special issue of *Gothic Studies*, "partly as a result of poststructuralism's destabilizing of the categories of gender, the term was increasingly being qualified and there has been an ongoing debate as to whether the Female Gothic constitutes a separate literary genre." However, as the collected essays in the issue indicate, it is "still a flexible and recognizable term for an area which is if anything gaining in vigor and complexity" (1, 6). I would add that both the term and its description of devices, figures, themes, and contexts on which the Gothic converges is particularly useful for understanding the relationship of twentieth-century Gothic romances to the history of the Gothic largely. As such, it is a term worth retaining as the field expands to include these texts.

5 For general information on romance novel cover art see Jennifer McKnight-Trontz's *The Look of Love: the Art of the Romance Novel*, as well as Joanna Bowring and Margaret O'Brien's book *The Art of Romance: Mills & Boon and Harlequin Cover Designs*. Additionally, the article from Washington University Libraries archivist, Andrea Degener, "An Eerie Sense of Deja-Vu: 1960s Gothic Romance Paperback Covers" details the work of Louis Marchetti, who created many Gothic romance covers.

6 For further information on horror as a genre, see Noël Carroll's *Philosophy of Horror or Paradoxes of the Heart.*

7 While some may argue Germaine Greer's *The Female Eunuch* is the first piece of scholarly criticism on the popular romance, I would contend that she paints it with such broad strokes in addressing larger feminist cultural and political concerns as to render the genre invisible in its universal application to these issues.

8 This table lists most of the major criticism on the modern popular Gothic romance published to 1997 when, as Selinger and Frantz argue in their introduction to *New Approaches to Popular Romance Fiction*, a third-wave of popular romance begins with the publication of the 1997 special issue of *Para*doxa* (McFarland 8). Kelso's article appears in that issue, and her argument both reaffirms previous scholarly interventions in the genre as well as anticipates the changes occurring in romance criticism generally. I would further argue that after the year 2001, approaches to modern popular Gothic romance novels also shift. As such, I have chosen not to include those titles in this chart. However, this table represents almost all of the criticism that addresses the modern popular Gothic romance previous to the twenty-first century, with only a few exceptions. I have also chosen not to list all of the titles in Fleenor's edited collection separately.

9 During the final proofing of this chapter, one such example of this kind of scholarship was published. In Lori A. Paige's *The Gothic Romance Wave: A Critical History of the Mass Market Novels, 1960–1993,* she argues that these texts present the heroine as an agent of liberation, while also presenting a history of the genre.

Works cited

Abartis, Caesarea. "The Ugly-Pretty, Dull-Bright, Weak-Strong Girl in the Gothic Mansion." *The Journal of Popular Culture*, vol. 13, no. 2, 1979, pp. 257–263.

Bakhtin, Mikhail. *The Dialogical Imagination: Essays.* edited by Michael Holquist, trans. Caryl Emerson and Michael Holquist, University of Texas Press, 2010.

Birkhead, Edith. *The Tale of Terror: A Study of the Gothic Romance.* Constable, 1921.

Botting, Fred. *Gothic.* Routledge, 2013.

Botting, Fred and Dale Townshend. *Gothic: Eighteenth-century Gothic: Radcliffe, Reader, Writer, Romancer*, Vol. 2. Taylor & Francis, 2004.

Bowring, Joanna and Margaret O'Brien. *The Art of Romance: Mills & Boon and Harlequin Cover Designs.* Prestel, 2008.

Carroll, Noël. *Philosophy of Horror or Paradoxes of the Heart.* Routledge, 1990.

Castle, Terry. *The Female Thermometer: Eighteenth-Century Culture and the Invention of the Uncanny.* Oxford University Press, 1995.

Clery, E. J. *The Rise of Supernatural Fiction, 1762-1800.* no. 12. Cambridge University Press, 1995.

———. *Women's Gothic: From Clara Reeve to Mary Shelley*. Northcote, 2000.
Copeland, Edward. *Women Writing About Money: Women's Fiction in England, 1790–1820*, Vol. 9. Cambridge University Press, 2004.
Davison, Carol Margaret. *Gothic Literature 1764-1824*. University of Wales Press, 2009.
Degener, Andrea. "An Eerie Sense of Deja-Vu: 1960s Gothic Romance Paperback Covers." *Dowd Modern Graphic History Library*, last modified October 23, 2014, http://library.wustl.edu/10203-2.
DeLamotte, Eugenia C. *Perils of the Night: A Feminist Study of Nineteenth-Century Gothic*. Oxford University Press, 1990.
Doody, Margaret Anne. "Deserts, Ruins, and Troubled Waters: Female Dreams in Fiction and the Development of the Gothic Novel." *Genre*, vol. 10, 1977, pp. 527–572.
Du Maurier, Daphne. *Rebecca*. Victor Gollancz, 1938.
Eden, Dorothy. *Crow Hollow*. 1950. Ace, 1978.
Ellis, Kate Ferguson. *The Contested Castle: Gothic Novels and the Subversion of Domestic Ideology*. University of Illinois Press, 1989.
Fleenor, Juliann E. *The Female Gothic*. Eden Press, 1983.
Frank, Frederick S. *The First Gothics: A Critical Guide to the English Gothic Novel*, Vol. 710. Routledge, 1987.
Frantz, Sarah S. G. and Eric Murphy Selinger eds. *New Approaches to Popular Romance Fiction: Critical Essays*. McFarland, 2012.
Greer, Germaine. *The Female Eunuch*. MacGibbon and Kee, 1970.
Haggerty, George E. "Fact and Fancy in the Gothic Novel." *Nineteenth-Century Fiction*, vol. 39, no. 4, 1985, pp. 379–391.
Hogle, Jerrold E ed. *The Cambridge Companion to Gothic Fiction*. Cambridge University Press, 2002.
Holland, Norman N. and Leona F. Sherman. "Gothic Possibilities." *New Literary History*, vol. 8, no. 2, 1977, pp. 279–294.
Holt, Victoria. *Menfreya in the Morning*. 1966. Fawcett Books, 1982.
Johnson, Samuel. "*The Rambler*, no. 4 [The New Realistic Novel] (1750)". *Samuel Johnson: The Major Works*, edited by Donald Greene, Oxford University Press, 2009, pp. 175–178.
Kelly, Gary. *Varieties of Female Gothic*. Pickering & Chatto, 2002.
Kelso, Sylvia. "Stitching Time: Feminism(s) and Thirty Years of Gothic Romance." *Para*doxa: Studies in World Literary Genres*, vol. 3, no. 1–2, 1997, pp. 164–179.
Kilgour, Maggie. *The Rise of the Gothic Novel*. Routledge, 2013.
Kramer, Kyra. "Raising Veils and Other Bold Acts: The Heroine's Agency in Female Gothic Novels." *Studies in Gothic Fiction*, vol. 1, no. 2, 2011, pp. 24–37.
Lutz, Deborah. "The Erotics of Ontology: Failed Presence in Heidegger and the Mass-Market Romance." *Comparative Literature and Culture*, vol. 5, no. 3, 2003, pp. 1–14.
———. *The Dangerous Lover: Gothic Villains, Byronism, and the Nineteenth-Century Seduction Narrative*. Ohio State University Press, 2006.
———. "The Haunted Space of the Mind: The Revival of the Gothic Romance in the Twenty-First Century." *Empowerment versus Oppression: Twenty First Century Views of Popular Romance Novels*, edited by Sally Goade, Cambridge Scholars Publishing, 2007, pp. 81–92.
Massé, Michelle A. "Gothic Repetition: Husbands, Horrors, and Things that Go Bump in the Night." *Signs: Journal of Women in Culture and Society*, vol. 15, no. 4, 1990, pp. 679–709.
———. *In the Name of love: Women, Masochism, and the Gothic*. Cornell University Press, 1992.
McKnight-Trontz, Jennifer. *The Look of Love: The Art of the Romance Novel*. Princeton Architectural Press, 2002.
Miles, Robert. *Gothic Writing, 1750–1820: A Genealogy*. Manchester University Press, 2002.
Modleski, Tania. *Loving with a Vengeance: Mass-Produced Fantasies for Women*. Routledge, 1982.
Moers, Eileen. "Female Gothic." *Gothic: Critical Concepts in Literary and Cultural Studies*, edited by Fred Botting, and Dale Townshend, Routledge, 2004, pp. 123–144.

Mussell, Kay. *Women's Gothic and Romantic Fiction: A Reference Guide*. Greenwood Press, 1981.

———. *Fantasy and Reconciliation: Contemporary Formulas of Women's Romance Fiction*. Greenwood Press, 1984.

———. "Beautiful and Damned: The Sexual Woman in Gothic Fiction." *Journal of Popular Culture*, vol. 9, no. 1, 1975, pp. 84–89.

Paige, Lori A. *The Gothic Romance Wave: A Critical History of the Mass Market Novels, 1960–1993*. McFarland, 2018.

Punter, David. *The Literature of Terror: A History of Gothic Fictions from 1765 to the Present Day*. Longman, 1980.

Radcliffe, Ann. *The Mysteries of Udolpho*. 1794. Penguin Classic, 2001.

———. "On the Supernatural in Poetry." *New Monthly Magazine*, vol. 16, no. 1, 1826, pp. 145–152.

Radway, Janice A. "The Utopian Impulse in Popular Literature: Gothic Romances and 'Feminist" Protest.'" *American Quarterly*, vol. 33, no. 2, 1981, pp. 140–162.

———. *Reading the Romance: Women, Patriarchy, and Popular Literature*. University of North Carolina Press, 2009.

Ruggiero, Josephine A. and Louise C. Weston. "Sex-Role Characterization of Women in 'Modern Gothic' Novels." *The Pacific Sociological Review*, vol. 20, no. 2, 1977, pp. 279–300.

———. "Conflicting Images of Women in Romance Novels." *International Journal of Women's Studies*, vol. 6, no. 1, 1983, pp. 18–25.

Russ, Joanna. "Somebody's Trying to Kill Me and I Think It's My Husband: The Modern Gothic." *The Journal of Popular Culture*, vol. 6, no. 4, 1973, pp. 666–691.

Sedgwick, Eve Kosofsky. "The Character in the Veil: Imagery of the Surface in the Gothic Novel." *PMLA*, vol. 96, no. 2, 1981, pp. 255–270.

Smith, Andrew. *Gothic Literature*. Edinburgh University Press, 2013.

Smith, Andrew and Diana Wallace. "Female Gothic." *Gothic Studies*, vol. 6, no. 1, 2004, pp. 1–130.

Stewart, Mary. *Nine Coaches Waiting*. Hodder & Stoughton, 1958.

Summers, Montague. *A Gothic Bibliography*. Russell & Russell Publishers, 1964.

Vinson, James ed *Twentieth-Century Romance and Gothic Writers*. Macmillan Education, 1982.

Waldman, Diane. "'At Last I Can Tell It to Someone!': Feminine Point of View and Subjectivity in the Gothic Romance Film of the 1940s." *Cinema Journal*, vol. 23, no. 2, 1984, pp. 29–40.

Wallace, Diana. *Female Gothic Histories: Gender, History and the Gothic*. University of Wales Press, 2013.

Walpole, Horace. *The Castle of Otranto and The Mysterious Mother*. edited by Frederick S. Frank, Broadview, 2003.

Watt, Ian P. *The Rise of the Novel: Studies in Defoe, Richardson and Fielding*. 1957. University of California Press, 2001.

Weston, Louise C. and Josephine A. Ruggiero. "Male-Female Relationships in Best-Selling 'Modern Gothic' Novels." *Sex Roles*, vol. 4, no. 5, 1978, pp. 647–655.

Williams, Anne. *Art of Darkness: A Poetics of Gothic*. University of Chicago Press, 1995.

Williams, Ioan ed. *Novel and Romance 1700-1800: A Documentary Record*. Routledge, 1970.

Wright, Angela. *Gothic Fiction: A Reader's Guide to Essential Criticism*. Palgrave, 2007.

5 The historical romance

Sarah H. Ficke

Historical romance is one of the oldest subgenres of popular romance fiction. Romantic love stories set in historical periods can be traced back to antiquity through the Greek story *Chaireas and Kallirrhoé*, which was written sometime between 50 B.C.E. and 140 C.E. and set around 400 B.C.E. (Doody xv, 36). Similar ancient Greek novels, translated and transmitted across the centuries, inspired epic-length historical adventure-romances by European authors like Madeleine de Scudéry (1607–1701) (Doody 257). After that period, tales set in the past incorporating romantic plots can be traced through Gothic fiction, the action-adventures of Sir Walter Scott (1771–1832) and Baroness Orczy (1865–1947), and other, less adventure-oriented, eighteenth- and nineteenth-century European authors. Scott's historical novels dramatize specific moments of cultural and national conflict, and his substantial influence on the genre can be seen in the prevalence of historical novels where "the centerpiece is the battle or struggle between two opposing political forces over unresolved sociopolitical issues" (Dandridge *Black Women's Activism* 3). The generic elements from these historical tales—adventure, love, secrets, drama, political struggles, epic journeys—provide what can be seen as the genetic material for the popular historical romance genre as we know it today.

Popular historical romances are most simply defined as "love stories with historical settings" (Ramsdell 185). They are novels where the author is consciously setting their plot during a period that feels historically distant from the one in which it is published. Kristin Ramsdell observes in *Romance Fiction: A Guide to the Genre* (2012) that "Most people are not likely to consider as 'historical' a time period they can actually remember, nor are they likely to remember the difficult realities of those times as 'romantic'" (186). Generally speaking, historical romances tend to take place at least 45–50 years before their date of publication. Ramsdell notes that historical romances written in the early twenty-first century tend to be set before the end of World War II. In the second decade of the twenty-first century, books set in the 1960s are starting to emerge, such as *Star Dust by* Emma Barry and Genevieve Turner and *Let It Shine* by Alyssa Cole. However, there are no hard and fast rules about how historical a historical romance must be. Because of its broad definition, popular historical romance is often approached not as a subgenre of romance fiction so much as it is an overarching category that includes popular subgenres like medieval romance, Regency romance, Viking romance, and the American Western romance, and that also overlaps with other subgenres like inspirational, gothic, LGBTQIA, Young Adult, and paranormal (as reflected in other chapters in this collection).

Historical romance flourished in the mid-twentieth century thanks to authors like Georgette Heyer and Barbara Cartland, and the subgenre later drove the dramatic shift toward single-title "blockbusters" in American romance publishing in the 1970s. It remains one of the most well-loved types of romance in the marketplace. Historical romance is unquestionably visible. However, from a scholarly perspective, historical romance can be oddly hard to pin down. Many studies of popular romance fiction don't identify historical romance as a separate category warranting special study or a historically-informed approach. The "historical" element of the novels often gets lost in assessments of their characters, plot structures, and socio-cultural messages. Historical romances are pervasive, yet paradoxically invisible in many overarching studies of romance. It is impossible in one essay to discuss—or even touch on—every aspect of this massive category within popular romance fiction. Instead, this essay is meant to function as an overview and map to a romance landscape that needs more exploration.

The modern story of the popular historical romance begins with Georgette Heyer and her novel *The Black Moth*, which is set during the Georgian period (the mid-late 1700s) in England. *The Black Moth* was published in 1921, just two years after E.M. Hull's *The Sheik*, which is often described as the first modern romance novel. As scholars Diana Wallace and Helen Hughes observe, Heyer's style emerged from an existing tradition of historical fiction that was romantic in the sense that it contained elements of improbable adventure in a stylized, rather than completely realistic, historical setting (Wallace 14). *The Black Moth* and Heyer's other early novels more closely resemble swashbuckling adventures by authors like Baroness Orczy (famous for *The Scarlet Pimpernel*) and Jeffrey Farnol than the romance formula we think of today (Hughes 3). However, she quickly evolved her own style largely driven by her interest in witty dialogue and female points of view (Hughes 38–9). Her most famous novels, set during the British Regency period, are often compared to those by Jane Austen.[1] However, Heyer is intensely conscious that she is writing fiction set in a historically distant time, which Austen was not. As Pamela Regis observes in *A Natural History of the Romance Novel*, "In historical romance novels the society is carefully drawn and its unfamiliar principles explained" (31). This expectation can be traced back to Heyer's meticulous research into the details of upper-class Regency life, which she used to "make the past appear vivid and intelligible to her readers" (Joannou 76). While Heyer was careful to create a realistic-seeming Regency world in her novels, her characters are fundamentally modern: Regis describes Judith from *Regency Buck* as "a twentieth-century romance heroine in a nineteenth-century setting" (129). Heyer's ability to create the "impression of verisimilitude" in her settings while crafting characters and plots that resonated with contemporary issues (Hughes 2) is perhaps one reason why, as Regis states, "Her influence is felt in every historical romance novel written since 1921, particularly in the Regency romance novel" (125).[2]

Heyer also pioneered several plot motifs that have become standards in historical romance, particularly cross-dressing, which has been the subject of much scholarly attention. Studies of cross-dressing in Heyer's work highlight the many, potentially complex, relationships that exist between a book's historical setting and its period of publication. Kathleen Bell, writing about *The Corinthian* (1940), explicitly connects the novel's cross-dressing heroine and Napoleonic war setting to British anxieties about women entering the workforce in the early years of World War II. Drawing on articles and speeches from 1940, Bell argues that the novel's model of femininity, which is enterprising but ultimately limited, reflects conservative impulses to view women's wartime work as a temporary and unwelcome detour from their domestic duties.

Sallie McNamara's article on cross-dressing in *These Old Shades* (1926) and *The Masqueraders* (1928) is focused less on concrete historical events. Instead, she explores how Heyer's depiction of Georgian-period clothing and gender roles relates to 1920s and 1930s ideas about gender and sexuality. Employing an approach grounded in cultural studies, and combining written sources and oral histories, McNamara suggests that Heyer's novels offer a "space for private consumption" that may be "transgressive" in moral and sensual terms (94). Diana Wallace also examines Heyer's representation of gender roles in the context of the 1920s, noting her attention to gender as a masked performance wherein the successful heroes and heroines strategically combine masculine and feminine traits. Karin Westman draws a similar conclusion by analyzing speech acts in Heyer's novels to demonstrate that Heyer's most successful heroines adopt "masculine" speech and knowledge (166). Employing theories on gender performativity (primarily Judith Butler), queer theory, and J.L. Austin's speech act theory in *How To Do Things With Words* (1962), Lisa Fletcher argues that despite Heyer's insistent re-inscription of conventional heterosexual love, these novels exhibit a "continual narrative of anxiety" about gender and sexuality that can be traced into modern novels using the cross-dressing trope (71).

As jay Dixon and John Markert observe in their books on the romance novel industry, the popularity of Heyer's Regency-set novels inspired many other authors to write historical (particularly Regency) romance fiction that was distributed by paperback publishers like Mills & Boon, either as individual titles or as part of a line. Although there were numerous authors writing in the genre during the second half of the twentieth century, the most dominant—in terms of numbers—was Barbara Cartland, who published 723 books, most of them historical romances (Barbaracartland.com).[3] Cartland's earliest historical romances were heavily modeled on Heyer's, to the point that Heyer sent her solicitor a letter accusing Cartland of plagiarism (Kloester 281–5). Heyer's statements show that it was not just the copying that offended her, but Cartland's "palpable ignorance of the period and her apparent lack of historical integrity" along with her unsophisticated writing style (Kloester 284). As Rosalind Brunt notes, Cartland's writing is comparatively simplistic, and her plots are made up of repetitive motifs (146). In a 1981 essay published in *Spare Rib*, Janet Batsleer writes that "The conflicts of Cartland's fiction are the conflicts which have produced feminism: conflicts *between* the private world of marriage, family and home and the world of public decision making and conflicts *within* the private world of marriage and patriarchal sexuality"; conflicts that, Batsleer argues, Cartland perpetuates rather than resolves (55). Cartland's work is much more conventional than Heyer's. While Heyer's novels have been read as interrogating traditional definitions of gender and identity, Cartland's exaggerate and reinforce those definitions. Rosalind Brunt writes in her 1999 examination of Cartland's career and work that in Cartland's novels "a notion of 'gender,' which would point to the differences between men and women as having social and cultural origins, is simply denied or collapsed into the eternal verities of 'the sexes'" (140). Marriage, in Cartland's novels, is a union between two disparate beings in which, according to Brunt, the man's "baser sexuality" is "redeemed by the heroine's virginity" (142). Cartland's commitment to female virginity as a plot point is what led her to historical fiction, since she said "it's very difficult to have virgins and all the excitement in the present day" (qtd. in Wallace 7). While Cartland is not credited with the same impact on the historical romance subgenre as Heyer, virgin heroines, and the idea that sex with a virgin is transformative for the hero became common motifs in historical romances, even as the romances themselves became more openly erotic.

Roughly 50 years after Georgette Heyer started writing, the historical romance—and indeed the romance genre as a whole—underwent a significant shift with the publication of the blockbuster novel from Avon Publishing *The Flame and The Flower* (1972) by Kathleen Woodiwiss. Set at the turn of the nineteenth century, the novel focuses on Heather, a beautiful young English orphan who is mistaken for a prostitute on the London docks and raped by Brandon, an American ship captain. The story that follows includes an arranged marriage, a transatlantic voyage, several mysterious murders, and slowly-growing love between the two protagonists. Compared to the Georgette Heyer and Barbara Cartland-style historical romances that preceded it, *The Flame and the Flower* appeared epic in its transatlantic scope, its length (over 500 pages) and its detailed portrayal of Heather and Brandon's stormy sex life. The novel's popularity (according to Avon's "Kathleen E. Woodiwiss" webpage, its sales topped 2.3 million copies within four years) followed up by the success of another sexually-explicit Avon epic historical romance, *Sweet Savage Love* (1974) by Rosemary Rogers, started what has been often termed a revolution in romance novel publishing. However, that revolution was not created out of thin air.

Read in the context of "sweet" historical romances by authors like Heyer and Cartland, the erotic content of novels like *The Flame and the Flower* and *Sweet Savage Love* seems to appear out of nowhere, but they are less surprising viewed in the context of women's historical fiction.[4] According to Diana Wallace,

> as a genre, the historical novel has allowed women writers a license which they have not been allowed in other forms. This is most obviously true of sexuality where it has allowed coverage of normally taboo subjects, not just active female sexuality but also contraception, abortion, childbirth and homosexuality.
>
> (6)

Though not genre romances, earlier historical novels that explore female sexuality and desire, like Kathleen Winsor's *Forever Amber* (1944), suggest the potential historical fiction offered to women that was acted upon by the original "Avon Ladies" (Rosemary Rogers, Kathleen Woodiwiss, Bertrice Small, Johanna Lindsey, Joyce Verrette, Laurie McBain, and Shirlee Busbee) and other romance authors writing during the sexual revolution of the 1970s and 1980s. This period also saw the first sustained scholarly criticism of romance fiction from feminist authors like Germaine Greer, Tania Modleski, Kay Mussell, Carol Thurston, and Janice Radway. Often this early criticism focuses on romance as a monolithic genre, using both historical and contemporary novels as examples to make generalized points about the genre and its readers.[5] However, some of this first-wave criticism did examine the historical romance as a specific subgenre with its own appeals.

In her book *Fantasy and Reconciliation: Contemporary Formulas of Women's Romance Fiction* (1984), Kay Mussell devotes specific sections of her chapters on romance formulas and settings to historical romance. According to her, "The imaginative historical setting often locates impediments to love in the power relationships of a patriarchal society that devalues women's emotions and desires" (69). Mussell argues that these romances reimagine history to place female domestic concerns at the center of the story and characterize successful love as a rebellion against societal constraints, while the whole story takes place at a convenient "psychic distance" from the reader (64). That same year, Radway observes in *Reading the Romance* that historical romance is one of the most popular subgenres among the readers in her study. While she doesn't discuss historical novels extensively, Radway makes two important points about the historical romance. One is that "Romances do not begin by placing their characters in the timeless, mythical space of the fairy tale" but instead locate their stories in a concrete time and place (204). The other, related point is that the readers care about the historical accuracy of the books they're reading. As she writes, "All of the Smithton women cited the educational value of romances in discussion" although they did not consistently indicate that on the anonymous survey that she administered (108, 107). Radway's hypothesis is that the educational dimension of historical romance is more often a "justification" when speaking to non-romance readers rather than a primary motivation for readers (107). That said, Dorothy Evans, a bookstore clerk interviewed by Radway, commented that "You don't feel like you've got a history lesson, but somewhere in there you have," which echoes more contemporary readers and authors of historical romance who extol the genre for what Beverly Jenkins calls "edutainment," education and entertainment folded together in one story (White).[6] Nevertheless, scholars focused on romance readers' experiences have tended to follow Radway's lead by looking at the social, cultural, and/or political aspects of romance-reading, rather than the educational ones.

Carol Thurston provided the most extensive first-wave examination of the historical romance in her 1987 work *The Romance Revolution: Erotic Novels for Women and the Quest for a New Sexual Identity*. While she briefly touches on Regency and "sweet" historical romance in her discussions of the evolution of the genre and its representations of sexuality, publishing and marketing, etc., she focuses most of her attention, unsurprisingly, on the erotic historical novels of the 1970s and 1980s. While Mussell and Radway tend to view historical romance (and romance fiction in general) as ultimately lacking in feminist potential, Thurston argues that the erotic historical romances "project a powerful sense of shared experience and unity among women, one that transcends both time and place and is often explicitly articulated" (88). Thurston also provides the most detailed early analysis of one of the most controversial aspects of the erotic historical romances, which is the presence of rape and other forms of sexual violence. The insistent association between erotic historical novels and rape, as well as sex scenes where consent is unclear, delayed, or seems forced, may be traced to Brandon's initial rape of Heather in *The Flame and the Flower*, and the numerous rape scenes in Rosemary Rogers' *Sweet Savage Love*, including the hero's repeated rape of the heroine. Thurston finds that the heroine is raped in 54 percent of the erotic historical romances that she surveyed, and notes that the rape is described in "pleasurable" terms "in only 18.5 percent of the stories," thus discounting the idea that a vast majority of the novels perpetuate the idea that women desire to be raped which was a concern raised by other feminist critics (78). That said, the presence of rape and scenes of dubious consent in historical romances are troubling to many readers.[7] A useful contemporary discussion of rape in Avon's early romances can be found in the essay by Sarah Frantz Lyons and Eric Murphy Selinger, "Strange Stirrings, Strange Yearnings: *The Flame and the Flower*, *Sweet Savage Love*, and the Lost Diversities of Blockbuster Historical Romance," in which they argue that "neither

The Flame and the Flower nor *Sweet Savage Love* can be described as a vehicle for 'rape fantasy' without doing violence—in the case of Woodiwiss, considerable violence—to the actual text of the novels" (107). Instead, Lyons and Selinger make a case for viewing these novels as part of the larger cultural conversation about rape in the 1970s, reading their depiction of patriarchy, power, and sexuality in the context of other popular media as well as feminist texts. Lyons and Selinger also suggest that early erotic historical romances could be a fruitful subject to study, not solely for their representation of rape, but to look for the "tonal, structural, and ideological possibilities within the genre" that have been obscured by the focus on rape and by the consolidation of the definition of the "romance novel" during the early 1980s (100–1).

The erotic historical romances did more for the genre than increase its heat level. Historical romances published throughout the rest of the twentieth century continued to explore a wider range of periods, including the Middle Ages, the Restoration and Tudor eras in Britain, and antebellum and postbellum decades in America. The geographical range of historical romance novels also broadened during this time, but their plots tended to follow European and American maps of empire and influence, and their protagonists were almost always white. Ramsdell notes that these books provide "the occasional exotic romantic adventure" but never became as common as British- or American-set historical romances (186). From a historical perspective, such books are open to the accusation of using their setting as a simple exotic backdrop against which the white protagonists play out their idealized love story.[8] There are some books that engage with the society and politics of their historical setting. For example, Maura Seale demonstrates that Mary Jo Putney's 1992 novel *Veils of Silk* explores the Indian tradition of sati through a lens of early 1990s white feminism. However, not much academic work has been done in this area. The twenty-first century has seen a slow uptick in historical romances that feature mixed-race characters and interracial romances. These novels dig more deeply into questions of identity because those questions are implicated in the protagonists' romantic journey. As an example, in her dissertation, completed in 2015, Mallory Jagodzinski argues that American authors Theresa Romain, Meredith Duran, and Courtney Milan, write British-set interracial historical romances featuring Indian or mixed-race heroes that use classic romantic tropes or elements to "challenge the dominance of the contemporary post-racial narrative in the United States." However, she concludes, the authors are not uniformly successful in addressing racial issues in ongoing or systematic ways (178).

English-language historical romances set in diverse locations around the globe written by non-white authors and/or starring non-white characters as the romantic leads have had an even slower growth pattern, especially from traditional outlets. For example, Jeannie Lin published a well-reviewed series of books with Harlequin set during the Tang dynasty in China starring Chinese characters, but faced challenges with print book sales, which caused her to move to electronic publishing.[9] In India, which is a large market for Mills & Boon romances, Random House launched a line of historical romances in 2009 called Kama Kahani written by and about Indian protagonists; however, only five books were ever published in that series.[10] There is no formal statement from the publisher about the line's cessation. Those books were discussed, among others, in Kim T's *Dear Author* post "If You Like … Romances Set in South Asia or featuring South Asian characters." One commenter, Sunita, who identifies herself as Indian, suggests that Kama Kahani and other Indian-set romances might not succeed because "I think that a lot of readers like M&B and other Western romances precisely for the fantasy element (the way U.S. readers like Regency and European-set historicals). Once you locate the books in familiar territory, they're a different reading experience." Jasveen Sahota, another commenter who locates herself in Chandigarh ("near Delhi"), agrees and further suggests that there is a mismatch between Western romance tropes or character types and Indian stories, writing, "If I want to read about people talking and acting like foreign characters [then I'd] much rather read a book set in the western world." These anecdotal comments point to interesting gaps in the scholarship of historical romance vis-à-vis contemporary romance in an international context, particularly in parts of the world where British or American historical romances circulate.

There is some evidence that certain historical settings and situations resist romantic novelization. *Ti Marie*, a novel published in 1988 by Valerie Belgrave portraying a romance between a mixed-race woman and a white English aristocrat set on a plantation in eighteenth-century Trinidad, provides a case in point. In the early- to mid-nineteenth century, British- and American-authored interracial romances where a wealthy white man falls in love with a light-skinned enslaved woman and either frees her or fails and experiences her tragic death were somewhat popular due to public interest in the abolitionist movement, but are viewed with justifiable discomfort by modern authors and audiences.[11] Belgrave was aware of this, but also felt that "the popular reading audience sustains itself on white heroes" ("Thoughts on the Choice of Theme" 325). However, she well knew that the typical coercive or abusive sexual relationship between a white man and black woman during slavery would "neither be truly romantic nor ennobling to black readers; nor would the hero be a positive white role model" (325). In order to meet her own goal of writing a historical romance that would reach a popular audience but "still remain faithful to progressive ideas and reflect black consciousness," Belgrave intentionally constructed her story as a "fairy tale" where the enchantment manifests in the progressive politics of the characters (325, 326). Scholars Jane Bryce and Paula Morgan have both praised Belgrave for stepping forward to write a romance with a Trinidadian heroine that took into account the island's rich and complicated history; however, neither of them found it to be an entirely satisfactory novel. Bryce characterizes the book as a "brave struggle, and ultimate failure" against the more conservative elements of romantic plotting (355), while Morgan concludes that "the marriage between the political, ideological elements and the romantic fairy tale elements remains uneasy" (825).[12] It isn't impossible to write historical romance set during slavery (as is discussed later in this chapter), but Belgrave's example highlights the extent to which traditional historical romance stories rely upon limited, sanitized settings or the erasure of dehumanizing political and economic systems.

A more recent example of this issue is the discussion surrounding Kate Breslin's inspirational historical romance *For Such a Time* (2014), "a riff on the Old Testament's Book of Esther" which describes a romance between a Nazi camp commander at Theresienstadt and a female Jewish prisoner (Flood). This book was nominated for a Romance Writers of America RITA award in 2015, prompting serious questions from the romance-reading and -writing community about the limits of what can, or should be viewed as "romantic." Sarah Wendell, co-founder of the romance review website *Smart Bitches, Trashy Books*, points out that in this novel "the hero is redeemed and forgiven *for his role in a genocide*. The stereotypes, the language, and the attempt at redeeming an SS officer as a hero belittle and demean the atrocities of the Holocaust"

("Letter to the RWA Board," emphasis in original). This type of redemption, Wendell argues, is not just impossible for her to believe based on the power imbalance between the characters, but also "insensitive and offensive" because it is predicated on the heroine's abandonment of her Jewish identity in favor of Christianity. Nevertheless, this book received positive reviews from outlets like *Library Journal* and from readers on Goodreads (Flood, Lerner). The book's ending rewrites history in two significant ways: the Red Cross delegation to Theresienstadt leaves unsatisfied (in reality, they left with a positive impression of the camp), and—more importantly—the hero successfully hijacks one of the trains headed for Auschwitz in order to save Jewish lives and to live happily ever after with the heroine. Altered facts are nothing new to historical romance, but, as reviewer Sunita put it: "It's one thing to alter facts to create a more real-feeling 'truth.' It's another to write a lie to get your main characters to an HEA" (Janine and Sunita). Revising recent history to ameliorate an atrocity and redeem a character responsible for genocide is clearly unacceptable to many readers and authors in the field of historical romance. However, the extent to which historical romance must or should accurately represent the past remains under discussion.

There has been some scholarly work on the complicated relationship between historical romance fiction and actual historical places and people, and particularly how historical periods and settings are often reflected through popular cultural understandings and expectations of those periods. Amy Burge describes how the medieval romances of Mills & Boon rely on "instantly recognizable medieval motifs" inspired by Victorian representations of the medieval (101). Euan Hague similarly notes that Scottish-set romances rely on popularized motifs that are simplified or taken out of their historical context. In both of these cases, as with Georgette Heyer's Regency England, an imagined construction of the period becomes the concrete reality of romantic fictions about it.

One of the most thoroughly-documented examples of historical romance's reliance on shared motifs and stereotypes can be found in the novels set in the Middle East. In her book *Desert Passions*, Hsu-Ming Teo examines the trend of "Orientalist" historical romances, starting with Johanna Lindsey's *Captive Bride*, which came out the same year that Edward Said published his groundbreaking analysis of Orientalism in European culture (144). Teo traces the roots of these romances to eighteenth- and nineteenth-century European representations of the Middle East that mixed adventure (wars and piracy) with sensual or salacious images of harem life. While the historical accuracy of these Orientalist romance novels is often questionable, Teo finds interesting connections between the novels' historical plots and current issues in the 1970s and 1980s when they were so popular. However, these connections are not, she notes, with geopolitical events. Instead, she finds in these books "the sexual liberation movement's transformation of the tried and true titillations of Orientalist pornographic motifs into a new form of female-authored erotica for women" (146). Teo argues that these novels help explore what emotional and sexual success for women looks like in a potentially-hostile world, transforming women from the object of Orientalist pornography into the subject of Orientalist romantic fantasies. In some cases, the novels move beyond women's sexual empowerment to a broader statement about the centrality of women's experience in history. Teo's analysis of *The Kadin*, Bertrice Small's 1978 novel of love and intrigue in the Ottoman Empire during the reigns of Selim I and Suleiman the Magnificent, identifies the ways the novel does or does not correspond with historical facts, either due to weaknesses in the research works available to

Small at that time or to the demands of the romantic narrative. However, as she argues, the novel participates in the larger feminist trend in historical study through its representation of "women's agency" at the Ottoman court, which includes companionate romantic love and maternal care, as well as financial power, political capital, and female friendship (180).

The surge in American-published historical romances at the end of the twentieth century also saw a dramatic expansion in the books set in America, especially on the frontier. As with the Orientalist romances discussed by Teo, American-set historical romances draw as much on earlier fictional portrayals of the frontier as they do historical fact. Adventure novels set in the American West date back to the 1800s. At the time they would have been classed as contemporary fiction, but as the decades went by the genre (in both novel and film) became historical, fixated on the period when white settlers seized land from the indigenous populations and battled with each other over its use. Westerns, as Jane Tompkins argues in *West of Everything*, narrate the victory of masculinized ideals of independence, silence, and emotional repression over feminized qualities of love, forgiveness, and interdependence. Nevertheless, as Laura Vivanco claims "the West has in fact proved to be an eminently suitable locale for romantic love" because of the symbolic connections between fertile land and fertile families, and the potential for women to grow and change through the frontier experience (*Pursuing Happiness* 64, 67). There are romantic plots in many Western novels, including those by the big authors: Owen Wister, Zane Grey, and Louis L'Amour. However, as Tompkins and other scholars have demonstrated, the romance plots are usually in service to larger ideological or thematic aims, and often diminish the women involved. For example, William Handley describes how the marriage at the end of *The Virginian* dramatizes a moment where both the heroine and the reader "must effectively consent to her own inferiority" (69). Similarly, Nancy Cook, in her assessment of romances set in Montana, suggests that "these novels offer their women empowerment in a mythic, rather than actual world" (60). Neither Cook nor Vivanco separate historical-set Western romances from contemporary-set romances, embracing the idea that the American West in these novels is a romanticized space, the important characteristics of which transcend time and historical specificity.

The Western historical romance novel picks up on many of the elements of the older Western adventure: the mysterious stranger who comes to town; the couple is drawn together against the harshness of frontier life; the clash of orderly civilization (often coded as feminine) and (masculine) competitiveness and violence; and the theme of new beginnings in a dynamic and evolving society. However, these novels have been re-centered to focus first and foremost on the romantic journey of a central couple, thereby redefining American success as domestic love and partnership, rather than masculine individuality and emotional restraint. While that may seem like a somewhat conservative challenge to a conservative genre, LGBTQIA Western romances push further, reminding readers that the heterosexuality of the Western genre is both carefully constructed and fragile. In his entry on the Western for the *glbtq Encyclopedia*, Eric Patterson points out that the typical Western hero's "most significant relationships are with other men" and that, in contrast, his relationships with women may contain "considerable ambivalence" (3). By extension, historical Western romances about relationships between men take advantage of that genre convention and explore the potential for homosexual love that is studiously avoided or strictly policed in traditional Westerns. Lesbian Westerns, on the other hand, challenge the narrative that women were a precious commodity for male possession on the frontier, instead suggesting that women may seek and lay claim to a version of the American dream in which men are peripheral. Scholarly sources explicitly addressing heterosexual or queer Western historical romances and their relationship to either the Western genre or popular romance as a whole are scarce. Larger media discussions on the Western genre, particularly film, tend to focus on whether or not it is dying (the jury is out), so scholarship on the still-thriving Western historical romance could be useful and interesting. It is possible that the Western romance novel is adapting to changing public taste more effectively than other forms of the Western.

The Native American romance is another revision to a traditional American genre. In her 1994 article "Palimpsest of Desire: The Re-Emergence of the American Captivity Narrative as Pulp Romance," Kate McCafferty argues that this branch of historical romance, which gained popularity in the 1980s and 1990s, looks back to captivity narratives of the eighteenth and nineteenth centuries. Although their form and function changed over time, the original captivity narratives were female-focused (sometimes female-authored) texts that dramatized a woman's capture by and life with an American Indian tribe. Additionally, the Native American historical romance can be seen as an offshoot of the Western genre, which often dramatized (negative) contact between white settlers and indigenous communities.[13] These romances, as McCafferty and others have observed, transform the relationship between white and indigenous people on the American frontier from adversarial to romantic, though often perpetuating stereotypes about American Indians (particularly men) in the process.

One of the most obvious shifts from early white-authored narratives about American Indians to Native American romances, which are also primarily written by white authors, is in the positive portrayal of the tribes featured in the books. McCafferty notes this in her essay, as does Stephanie Wardrop, who writes that the romances "[place] more emphasis on the Native Americans' culture as representing an alternative spiritual and political community that appeals to contemporary women" (68). Authors of Native American historical romances where a white woman marries an American Indian man present the union as an escape from the patriarchal expectations ingrained in white society as much as they present it as a romance. As Macdonald et al. note in *Shape-Shifting: Images of Native Americans in Recent Popular Fiction*, "twentieth-century ideologies" play a larger role in the novels than the realities of Native American life (137). Throughout their argument, they stress the fundamental whiteness of the Native American romance subgenre as it currently exists and focus on how the romance novels elide or minimize the cultural differences that would have existed between the hero and heroine in real life. While these novels may have been intended to redress the negative portrayals of American Indians in Westerns and other American genres, Macdonald et al. reiterate that "even fervent cheerleading for lusty Native American warriors can be offensive, continuing the centuries-old tradition of refusing to see the Indian whole" (138). The assimilation of American Indian heroines to the white hero's culture may be viewed as equally problematic. Hovering over all of these novels is the specter of white violence against indigenous American people. The imperative of the happy ending means that the romance cannot easily engage with "those periods of history in which Indian populations were decimated" (Macdonald et al. 131), a problem of historical representation similar to that faced by the Caribbean and Nazi romances discussed earlier in this chapter. White-authored Native American historical romances represent a fictionalized and exoticized version of

America made possible by white America's long-standing and persistent attempts to displace and erase indigenous peoples and cultures.[14]

Native American romance is not the only historical subgenre affected by America's racist past. Historical romances set during the antebellum period, set in the American South, or focused on African-American characters are notable for the ways they confront, or evade, the realities of slavery and racism. Evasion is common, especially in earlier novels. For example, in *The Flame and the Flower* Woodiwiss uncritically adopts the stereotypes of kind slave masters and happy slaves developed by pro-slavery authors in the nineteenth century and perpetuated into the twentieth by fictions like *Gone with the Wind* (another fore-runner of historical popular romance). While such romances may well subvert the stereotype of the fragile Southern Belle, as Glinda Fountain Hall argues in her 2008 article, they also highlight the exclusion of non-white women from mainstream romance narratives and their marginalization by mainstream publishers. For that reason, the development of African-American historical romance follows a different path.

The roots of African-American historical popular romance fiction can be traced back to mid-nineteenth-century abolitionist novels like *Clotel* (1853) by William Wells Brown, and late-century romantic dramas like *Iola Leroy, or Shadows Uplifted* (1892) by Frances Ellen Watkins Harper and *Contending Forces: A Romance Illustrative of Negro Life North and South* (1900) by Pauline Hopkins. Those two dramas are notable for including doubled plots: a doomed romance set in the recent past of slavery, and a successful romance set during the present day. Hopkins further developed the historical romance formula in her 1902 serialized novel *Winona*. That story features an English lawyer sent to the wilds of America to discover the long-lost heir to an aristocratic fortune. Instead, he rescues and falls in love with the missing aristocrat's mixed-race daughter as they both join John Brown's Kansas uprising. These novels, as Rita B. Dandridge argues in her 2004 work *Black Women's Activism: Reading African American Women's Historical Romances*, "had as their primary function to address the sociohistorical issues challenging African Americans as a race at specific historical moments" (3). In these cases, the conflict between pro- and anti-slavery characters in the past stands in for the ongoing oppression of Black Americans during and after Reconstruction.

Dandridge notes that there is a significant thematic change between early African-American historical romance novels and the "second wave" of historical romance that started with Anita Richmond Bunkley's publication of *Emily, The Yellow Rose* in 1989 (28).[15] While politics and activism had always been a part of African-American historical romance, "in post-1989 novels, black women activists inveigh against, rather than acquiesce to, black patriarchy in the romance because it challenges their right to self-definition and their endeavors to uplift the race" (8).[16] These developments in the historical romance genre during the late 1980s and 1990s were exciting, but not mainstream. Of the five authors Dandridge examines, only one, Beverly Jenkins, was published as a single-title author by a major publishing house (Avon).[17] Shirley Hailstock's and Francine Craft's novels were both published by Arabesque, Kensington's African-American Romance line. Gay G. Gunn's novel *Nowhere to Run* (1997) was published by the African-American-owned Genesis Press. There are many more historical romances featuring African-American characters available now from authors like Kianna Alexander, Alyssa Cole, Piper Huguley, and Chanta Rand, but small presses and self-published authors are where the growth has largely taken place.[18] Despite the growth, white-authored and white-focused romances still dominate the American romance publishing scene. As of May 2018, "no black author has ever been awarded the RITA, the Romance Writers of America's award for excellence in romantic fiction" (Adewunmi).[19]

While African-American historical romances are first and foremost love stories, a strong thread of discovery and education runs through them, a point visible in the works of Beverly Jenkins who describes her books as "edutainment," education and entertainment packaged together in a genre specifically for women (Dandridge "The African American Historical Romance"). Jenkins's novels range from the Caribbean to California, incorporate Native American and Latinx characters, and narrate the lives of impoverished farmers and outlaws, as well as well-to-do ranchers, pirates, and lawmen. An author's note and bibliography of sources at the end of each book encourages readers to learn more about the history that Jenkins brings to life through her characters. In addition to being open about her research process, Jenkins often discusses the challenges of writing historical romance about African Americans set in the violent climate of the 1800s. One of the most poignant examples is in the Author's Note to *Indigo* (1996), where Jenkins describes finding the story of Wyatt, a free man who voluntarily became enslaved in order to marry a woman named Carrie. Jenkins writes about being moved by the story, but says,

> I knew I could not write a story about Wyatt and his Carrie. Being a woman of color, I feel that the harsh and painful realities of slavery have no place in the feel-good arena of mainstream romance—because there was nothing feel-good about it!
>
> (386)

Instead, Jenkins tells the imagined story of their daughter and her freedom. While she couldn't tell Wyatt and Carrie's love story, Jenkins and other African-American historical romance authors don't shy away from the oppression their characters would have faced, the radical nature of Black love and marriage during the periods they write about, or how the racism in America's past has shaped contemporary America.

The twenty-first century has also seen more diverse sexualities represented in historical romance. Historical romance novels published by mainstream companies in the twentieth century occasionally included gay or lesbian characters, but they were either the villain or a marginal character used, as Kathleen Therrien argues, to more strongly define the boundaries of heterosexuality. The stories primarily about gay and lesbian relationships in historical settings that did appear throughout the twentieth century were notorious for their unhappy, or at least unsatisfying endings. Two notable exceptions are *Patience and Sarah* by Isabel Miller[20] and *Pembroke Park* by Michelle Martin. Miller's novel was inspired by the real-life relationship between the painter Mary Ann Willson and her companion Miss Brundage, who lived together on a farm in Greenville, New York in the first decades of the nineteenth century ("Mary Ann Willson"). Although Miller didn't set out explicitly to write a romance novel, the story's focus on a central love story and optimistic ending fit the genre conventions, as Paulina Palmer demonstrates in her article "Girl Meets Girl: Changing Approaches to the Lesbian Romance." According to an interview with Miller, fans also responded to it as a romance. She mentions one letter from a woman "glad there was something to read about two women in love" (Katz 658).

Michelle Martin's novel, on the other hand, was intentionally written to explore the queer potential of the Regency setting that Georgette Heyer only flirted with. Subtitled by Martin "A bit of a departure: the first lesbian Regency novel," *Pembroke Park* adapts elements from Jane Austen, like the rich new neighbor and a relationship that transforms from prejudice to love (Palmer 197–9). In 2005, Ann Herendeen also pushed the boundaries of the Regency formula by writing what she describes as "a 'homoerotic' novel from the 'third perspective'" (Herendeen 410). Her book *Phyllida and the Brotherhood of Philander* is a ménage à trois Regency romance about a woman, her bisexual husband, and his lover finding happiness together in a committed relationship. Like Miller, Herendeen originally published the novel herself before it was picked up by a major press in 2008.[21] Like Martin's, Herendeen's book explicitly embraces the witty, charming style of Heyer's romances and their grounding in a fantasized Regency world. Georgian and Regency settings have also been popular in male/male (m/m) historical romance, a rapidly-growing subgenre of LGBTQIA historical romance. K.J. Charles, an m/m author, explicitly links her books to Heyer's type of historical romance: "I wanted sexy queer Heyer, so I did my best to write some" (Charles).[22] However, m/m Regency romances are significantly different from Heyer's novels, and not just in the sexuality of their protagonists. Like twenty-first-century authors of heterosexual Regency romance (see Rose Lerner), they tend to include a wider range of classes, occupations, and political views. Authors of m/m Regency romance, and LGBTQIA historical romance more broadly, also work to reconcile the romance genre's need for a happy ending with the social and legal challenges faced by LGBTQIA people in a wide variety of historical periods and settings. Cat Sebastian, who writes m/m Regency romances set in England during a time when sodomy was punishable by death, articulates this as a "balancing act," saying "I want to be respectful of the hardships that queer people faced then and face now, but I want to also make sure that they're as thoroughly happy as they can be" (Sebastian).[23]

The comparatively rapid growth of LGBTQIA romance in the twenty-first century can be linked to the rise of electronic publishing as a business model for independent presses. As Len Barot explains in "Queer Romance in Twentieth- and Twenty-First-Century America," queer romance publishing has happened largely out of the mainstream: "the majority of queer romances between 1970 and 2000 were published by independent queer presses" (397). She goes on to describe how the dramatic expansion in the availability of LGBTQIA romances has gone hand-in-hand with the evolution of digital publishing and online book sales. Many of the most creative historical romances are coming out of small presses that can experiment with settings and characters who have not traditionally been part of the romance landscape, and that effectively use social media and digital marketing to get those books to the readers who want them.[24] That said, more traditional publishing houses are also starting to expand their queer romance offerings. Penguin Random House's digital imprint, Loveswept, has published m/m romances by K. J. Charles, and Avon's Impulse line has released m/m romances by Cat Sebastian as part of a mission to publish "inclusive and diverse romances that reflect our world—all sexualities, races, ethnicities, religions, genders, body types, disabilities, and ages" ("Give in to Your Impulses"). Though the British Regency (and the decades immediately preceding and following it) continue to be a very popular setting for LGBTQIA historical romance, readers looking for more variety can find novels set anywhere from ancient Rome to eighteenth-century Japan, to World War II-era Europe.

Despite its growing popularity, there has not yet been much published scholarship on LGBTQIA historical romance, and what exists focuses on British Regency-set novels. In addition to the articles by Palmer and Herendeen cited above, Catriona Rueda Esquibel published an analysis of *Pembroke Park* in 1992 titled "A Duel of Wits and the Lesbian Romance Novel or Verbal Intercourse in Fictional Regency England," which concludes that the novel mirrors the traditional Regency formula while gender-bending its protagonists. In 2016, Jodi McAlister published "'You and I are humans, and there is something complicated between us': *Untamed* and queering the heterosexual historical romance" which compares Anna Cowan's Regency romance about a bisexual cross-dressing duke to Georgette Heyer's cross-dressing novel *The Masqueraders* in order to examine the potential for queer historical romance to successfully disrupt the conventions of the Regency genre. She concludes that "Overall, the responses to *Untamed* demonstrate that there is an appetite among historical romance readers, for a kind of fluidity that we might call queer, particularly in terms of portrayals of gender"; however, some readers resisted the anachronisms that Cowan incorporates as part of her queering of the Regency romance. These articles suggest that there is much yet to be explored about LGBTQIA historical romance's formal elements, theoretical positions, readership, and authorship.

The many new and exciting directions emerging in historical romance writing demonstrate that while it is one of the oldest subgenres of popular romance fiction, it is far from tired. The arrogant lords and charming misses who populated Georgette Heyer's Regency world may still dominate fictional British ballrooms, but they have been joined in the historical romance genre by vibrant suffragettes, Jewish con artists, gender-queer dukes, formerly enslaved businessmen, disillusioned cowboys, disabled soldiers, gun-running revolutionaries, brilliant inventors, pragmatic courtesans, entrepreneurs, spies, lesbian bootleggers, God-fearing ministers, and many, many other characters that highlight the breadth and depth of human experience. Historical romance has also had a robust impact on other romance subgenres, crossing over with romantic fantasy, science fiction (in the form of steampunk), and mystery-suspense.

Scholarship on historical romance has equally exciting potential for expansion. Studies of historical fiction occasionally incorporate romance novels into their assessments of the genre, but no long-form study solely about popular romance novels as historical fiction exists at this moment. Specific subgroups of historical romance have a strong and growing body of analytical work about them, particularly novels featuring Native American, African-American, or Middle Eastern protagonists. However, many of the types of historical romance mentioned in this essay would reward further study from scholars who could apply historical but also other theoretical lenses to these works. Certainly, romances set in non-Anglo-American settings and/or with non-white or non-Anglo-American protagonists need more attention.[25]

There is also much room for interdisciplinary work on historical romance. Disability Studies scholars, for example, have started to publish perceptive analyses of the representations of disabled protagonists and secondary characters in historical romance. In her 2013 article "Disability Studies Reads the Romance," Ria Cheyne uses Mary Balogh's historical romances to argue that "romances with disabled protagonists offer significant opportunities to challenge negative stereotypes around disability" (37). Emily Baldys and Sandra Schwab, in their works on disability in the romance, identify some of the genre's weaknesses in dealing with disabled characters, though, like Cheyne, they believe it has the potential to shift fictional representations of disability. Alternatively, as Teo's work on Orientalist historical romance shows, there is opportunity for historians of specific periods and places to assess these novels in their supposed historical context. Religious studies scholars could provide valuable insights on historical romances that incorporate religiously-inflected plots or spiritual conflicts, as Lynn S. Neal does in *Romancing God*, her book on evangelical romance (see Chapter 8 in this volume on inspirational romance for more information on the subgenre). Specialists in linguistics or translation studies could follow the work of Mary Ellen Ryder or Bianchi and D'Arcangelo and look at the language of historical romance, librarians and archivists could follow the lead of Caryn Radick and examine the research processes of historical romance authors, while business scholars could assess the market for such fictions.[26]

And, of course, there is a need for even more single-author studies that examine the many innovative and successful historical romance novelists that have built careers in the late twentieth and early twenty-first centuries.[27] Hopefully, the lively and growing community of professors, authors, independent scholars, and graduate students studying the genre today will continue to build our knowledge of historical romance so that we may better understand how the genre's reimagining of the past impacts our perceptions of love now and in years to come.

Notes

1 Anthea Trodd addresses the similarity in her book *Women's Writing in English: Britain 1900–1945* (Trodd). Essays further exploring the connections between Heyer and Austen by A. S. Byatt, Barbara Bywaters, Kay Mussell, and Lillian S. Robinson can be found in Mary Fahnestock-Thomas's compendium of writing by and about Heyer: *Georgette Heyer: A Critical Retrospective*. For Austen's influence on Regency romance more generally, see Susan M. Kroeg.

2 Heyer is also one of the most frequently studied historical romance authors. Readers interested in Heyer's writing in the context of her personal life and literary influences should see essays by Elizabeth Barr, Elizabeth K. Spillman, and Laura Vivanco, and *Georgette Heyer: Biography of a Bestseller* by Jennifer Kloester.

3 There has been less scholarship on Cartland than on Heyer. For an overview of Cartland's career and writing see Rosalind Brunt. See Mary Ellen Ryder for a linguistic analysis of action in Cartland's novels, and Roger Sales for analysis of Byronic hero in Cartland.

4 A note on terminology: these books were collectively known as "erotic historical" "sensual historical" or "sweet savage romance" novels, and later as "bodice rippers." See Lyons and Selinger 92–3.

5 For more information on these critics and major scholarship on romance overall, see the introduction to this book.

6 The readers of evangelical historical romance that Lynn Neal interviewed for her study *Romancing God* also mentioned the educational aspect of the books as a draw (174–5).

7 For more scholarly perspectives on rape in historical romance fiction, see Diane M. Calhoun-French, Dawn Heinecken, and Angela Toscano. An informative, though less scholarly take, can be found in "Chapter Bad Sex" from *Beyond Heaving Bosoms* by Wendell and Tan. For an interesting alternative look at *The Flame and the Flower*, see Charles Hinnant's analysis of gendered economics in the novel.

8 Examples of this type of novel include *Dawn of Fire* by Susannah Leigh (set in French Indochina in the 1840s), *Rangoon* by Christine Monson (set in British colonial Burma), and *Sea Flame* by Katharine Kincaid (set in colonial Macao).

9 Whether these challenges were a result of poor marketing decisions by Harlequin, the increasingly cramped historical romance print market, or readers' reluctance to purchase

a romance with non-white characters was a subject of online commentary, but as yet there has been no formal research on the subject. See Lin's article "Jeannie Lin Tells Us: How My Worst Seller Became a Bestseller and What It Means to Write 'Different'" and Courtney Milan's blog post "A Note on Historical Romance Sales in Print."

10 Laura Vivanco published an article "Links: India, Covers and Romance" addressing these novels on the academic romance blog *Teach Me Tonight* in February of 2010.

11 For examples see "The Quadroons" by Lydia Maria Child, *Clotel* by William Wells Brown, *The Quadroon* by Mayne Reid, *The Octoroon or Life in Louisiana* by Dion Boucicault, and *The Octoroon; or, The Lily of Louisiana* by Mary Elizabeth Braddon. Academic studies addressing this topic include Jules Zanger "The 'Tragic Octoroon' In Pre-Civil War Fiction," Werner Sollors *Neither Black Nor White Yet Both*, and Eve Allegra Raimon *The "Tragic Mulatta" Revisited.*

12 Romance novels of any subgenre written by Caribbean authors for a Caribbean audience are still rare. Bryce and Morgan also examine contemporary Caribbean romance novels and theorize about the challenges of writing more realistic romances set in a location that serves as the exotic Other for so many American and British romance novels.

13 According to the authors of *Shape-Shifting: Images of Native Americans in Recent Popular Fiction*, "The romance genre includes more Native American stories than any other genre except the Western" (114).

14 I am only aware of one indigenous author writing romantic historical fiction, Evangeline Parsons Yazzie, whose series set during the forced removal of the Navajo from their lands begins with the book *Her Land, Her Love.*

15 Bunkley's novel is based on the real story behind the song "The Yellow Rose of Texas" (Harris).

16 For further work on intersection of love and politics, see Dandridge, "Love Prevailed Despite What American History Said: Agape and Eros in Beverly Jenkins's *Night Song* and *Through the Storm*."

17 Vivian Stephens, the agent Jenkins worked with for *Night Song*, was one of the first African American romance editors and a co-founder of the Romance Writers of America (Drew; "RWA's Origin Story").

18 The shifting and somewhat unpredictable publishing scene for romances by and about women of color can be observed by reading Julie Naughton's *Publisher's Weekly* article "In Loving Color: Diversity in Romance Publishing, 2014" and comparing it to the 2017 landscape. Samhain, one of the publishers that she mentions, closed in 2017 (Wendell "GO GET YOUR BOOKS"), and Kimani, Harlequin's African American line, which Naughton discusses at length, is now set to be discontinued (Rea). Among the authors I mentioned, Kianna Alexander published several of her historical romances with Ellora's Cave, which closed in 2016. Piper Huguley initially published with Samhain, but also publishes independently. Alyssa Cole publishes independently through CreateSpace, but her 2017 novel *An Extraordinary Union* was published by Kensington. Blogs can be a useful resource for finding romances by authors of color. See, for example, *Romance Novels in Color* and *WOC in Romance.*

19 There is an ongoing discussion in the American romance industry about diversity in writing and publishing romance. For more information see the RWA's "RWA Report on Diversity and Inclusion" and Bea and Leah Koch's "The State of Racial Diversity in Romance Publishing Report."

20 Isabel Miller (the pen name for Alma Routsong) first self-published the novel in 1969 as *A Place for Us.* It was retitled *Patience and Sarah* and published by McGraw-Hill in 1972.

21 Although *Phyllida and the Brotherhood of Philander* is indisputably a romance, Herendeen explains that HarperCollins picked it up for its "literary" qualities and published it as a trade paperback, not a mass market novel as is typical with romance fiction (406).

22 Not all m/m historical romance looks back to Heyer. For example, *False Colors* by Alex Beecroft, features two British naval officers and the setting and plot has more in common with Victorian adventure novels by authors like Frederick Marryat or W.H.G. Kingston—and with Patrick O'Brian's *Master and Commander*—than with Georgette Heyer's books.

23 Many m/m romance authors, including K.J. Charles and Cat Sebastian, are women, as are their readers, which has led to an ongoing conversation about the appropriation or

fetishization of queer sexuality, particularly gay male sexuality, in the romance genre. The conversation is not limited to historical romance and is too extensive to recap here. Interested readers can see Alimurung, Wilson, Brownworth, Thornton, Fessenden, and Meeker to get a sense of the discussion.

24 For example, in her essay, Barot references ManLoveRomance Press, Dreamspinner Press, and her own company Bold Strokes Books. John Markert includes those publishers as well as Torquere Press and Riptide in his section on GLBTQ publishers (234). Online articles recommending LGBTQIA romances are also a useful way to identify queer romance publishers. See, for example, Christine Grimaldi's 2015 article on *Slate* that references Bold Strokes Books and Riptide Publishing, or Jessica Pryde's 2017 post on *Book Riot* that mentions those two presses, as well as Dreamspinner Press and Bella Books. Like African American romance authors, some LGBTQIA authors had published with now-closed companies like Amber Quill Press, Ellora's Cave, and Samhain.

25 For example, in my reading, I've found few historical romances by or about Latinx people, and no scholarly work on the presence or absence of Latinx characters in the genre (recently published Latinx historical romance authors include Liana De la Rosa, Lydia San Andres, and Mimi Milan).

26 Schiffman and Schnaars published a consumer analysis of historical romance in 1981; a similar study done today would likely provide interesting results.

27 The Spring/Summer 2008 issue of *Teaching American Literature: A Journal of Theory and Practice* featured biographical and bibliographic information on selected American romance authors, including Anita Bunkley, Beverly Jenkins, LaVyrle Spencer, and Rosemary Rogers. Scholars interested in those writers would find it a useful source to build on.

Works cited

Adewunmi, Bim. "Meet The Black Women Upending The Romance Novel Industry." *BuzzFeed*, May 1 2018, www.buzzfeed.com/bimadewunmi/meet-the-black-women-upending-the-romance-novel-industry. Accessed June 1, 2018.

Alimurung, Gendy. "Man on Man: The New Gay Romance." *L.A. Weekly*, 2009, www.laweekly.com/arts/man-on-man-the-new-gay-romance-2162963. Accessed June 5, 2018.

Baldys, Emily M. "Disabled Sexuality, Incorporated: The Compulsions of Popular Romance." *Journal of Literary & Cultural Disability Studies*, vol. 6, no. 2, 2012, pp. 125–141.

"Barbara Cartland - Welcome." *Barbaracartland.com*, www.barbaracartland.com/. Accessed April 24, 2019.

Barot, Len. "Queer Romance in Twentieth- and Twenty-First-Century America." *Romance Fiction and American Culture: Love as the Practice of Freedom?*, edited by William A. Gleason and Eric Murphy Selinger. Routledge, 2016, pp. 389–404.

Barr, Elizabeth. "'Who the Devil Wrote That?': Intertextuality and Authorial Reputation in Georgette Heyer's Venetia." *Journal of Popular Romance Studies*, vol. 3, no. 2, 2013, n.p., http://jprstudies.org/2013/06/who-the-devil-wrote-that-intertextuality-and-authorial-reputation-in-georgette-heyers-venetia-by-elizabeth-barr/.

Barry, Emma and Genevieve Turner. *Star Dust*. Penny Bright Publishing, L.L.C., 2015.

Batsleer, Janet. "Pulp in the Pink." *Spare Rib*, no. 109, August 1981, 52–55.

Belgrave, Valerie. "Thoughts on the Choice of Theme and Approach in Writing *Ti Marie*." *Caribbean Women Writers: Essays from the First International Conference*, edited by Selwyn Reginald Cudjoe. Calaloux Publications, 1990, pp. 325–328.

———. *Ti Marie*. iUniverse, 2014.

Bell, Kathleen. "Cross-Dressing in Wartime: Georgette Heyer's the Corinthian in Its 1940 Context." *War Culture: Social Change and Changing Experience in World War Two*, edited by Pat Kirkham and David Thoms. Lawrence & Wishart, 1995, pp. 151–159.

Bianchi, Diana and Adele D'Arcangelo. "Translating History or Romance? Historical Romantic Fiction and Its Translation in a Globalised Market." *Linguistics and Literature Studies*, vol. 3, no. 5, 2015, pp. 248–253.

Boucicault, Dion. *The Octoroon*. 1859. Mnemosyne Pub. Co., 1969.

Braddon, M. E. *The Octoroon*. 1859. Edited by Jennifer Carnell, Sensation Press, 1999.

Brown, William. *Clotel, Or, the President's Daughter*. 1853. Edited by M. Giulia Fabi, Penguin Books, 2004.

Brownworth, Victoria. "The Fetishizing of Queer Sexuality. A Response." *Lambda Literary*, August 19, 2010, www.lambdaliterary.org/features/oped/08/19/the-fetishizing-of-queer-sexuality-a-response/. Accessed June 5, 2018.

Brunt, Rosalind. "A Career in Love: The Romantic World of Barbara Cartland." *Popular Fiction and Social Change*, edited by Christopher Pawling. Palgrave, 1984, pp. 127–156.

Bryce, Jane. "'A World of Caribbean Romance': Reformulating the Legend of Love (Or: 'Can a Caress Be Culturally Specific?')." *Caribbean Studies*, vol. 27, no. ¾, 1994, pp. 346–366. *JSTOR*, www.jstor.org/stable/25613264.

Bunkley, Anita Richmond. *Emily, The Yellow Rose: A Texas Legend*. Rinard Publishing, 2011.

Burge, Amy. "Do Knights Still Rescue Damsels in Distress? Reimagining the Medieval in Mills & Boon Historical Romance." *The Female Figure in Contemporary Historical Fiction*, edited by Katherine Cooper and Emma Short. Palgrave, 2012, pp. 95–114.

Calhoun-French, Diane M. "Time-Travel and Related Phenomena in Contemporary Popular Romance Fiction." *Romantic Conventions*, edited by Anne K. Kaler. Bowling Green State University Popular Press, 1999, pp. 100–112.

Charles, K.J. "Alexis Hall Interviews K.J. Charles." *All About Romance*, May 20 2016, http://allaboutromance.com/alexis-hall-interviews-k-j-charles/. Accessed June 5, 2018.

Cheyne, Ria. "Disability Studies Reads the Romance." *Journal of Literary & Cultural Disability Studies*, vol. 7, no. 1, 2013, pp. 37–52.

Child, Lydia Maria. "The Quadroons." 1842. *Uncle Tom's Cabin & American Culture*. The University of Virginia, http://utc.iath.virginia.edu/abolitn/abfilmcat.html. Accessed April 24, 2019.

Cole, Alyssa. "Let It Shine." *The Brightest Day: A Juneteenth Historical Romance Anthology*. CreateSpace Independent Publishing Platform, 2015.

Cook, Nancy. "Home on the Range: Montana Romances and Geographies of Hope." *All Our Stories are Here: Critical Perspectives on Montana Literature*, edited by Brady Harrison. University of Nebraska Press, 2009, pp. 55–77.

Cremant, Laurel, et. al. *Romance Novels in Color*. http://romancenovelsincolor.com/. Accessed June 1, 2018.

Dandridge, Rita B. *Black Women's Activism: Reading African American Women's Historical Romances*. Peter Lang, 2004.

———. "The African American Historical Romance: An Interview with Beverly Jenkins." *Journal of Popular Romance Studies*, vol. 1, no. 1, 2010, n.p., http://jprstudies.org/2010/08/interview-beverly-jenkins-by-rita-b-dandridge/.

———. "Love Prevailed despite What American History Said: Agape and Eros in Beverly Jenkins's Night Song and through the Storm." *Romance Fiction and American Culture: Love as the Practice of Freedom?*, edited by William A. Gleason and Eric Murphy Selinger. Routledge, 2016, pp. 151–166.

Dixon, jay. *The Romance Fiction of Mills & Boon, 1909–1990s*. University College London Press, 1999.

Doody, Margaret Anne. *The True Story of the Novel*. Rutgers University Press, 1996.

Drew, Bernard Alger. "Beverly Jenkins." *100 Most Popular African American Authors: Biographical Sketches and Bibliographies*. Libraries Unlimited, 2007, pp. 176–178.

Esquibel, Catriona Rueda. "A Duel of Wits and the Lesbian Romance Novel or Verbal Intercourse in Fictional Regency England." *New Perspectives on Women and Comedy*, edited by Regina Barreca. Gordon and Breach, 1992, pp. 123–134.

Fahnestock-Thomas, Mary. *Georgette Heyer: A Critical Retrospective*. Saraland, AL: Prinnyworld Press, 2001.

Fessenden, Jamie. "My Take on Women Writing MM Romance." *Jamie Fessenden's Blog*, June 28 2014, https://jamiefessenden.com/2014/06/28/my-take-on-women-writing-mm-romance/. Accessed June 5, 2018.

Fletcher, Lisa. *Historical Romance Fiction: Heterosexuality and Performativity*. Ashgate, 2008.

Flood, Alison. "When a Jew Loves a Nazi: Holocaust Romance's Award Listings Cause Outrage." *The Guardian*, August 10 2015, www.theguardian.com/books/2015/aug/10/jew-loves-nazi-holocaust-romance-award-nominations. Accessed October 3, 2017.

"Give in to Your Impulses." *Avon Romance*. www.avonromance.com/impulse/. Accessed October 25, 2017.

Greer, Germaine. *The Female Eunuch*. McGraw-Hill, 1971.

Grimaldi, Christine. "Reader, He Married Him: LGBTQ Romance's Search for Happily-Ever-After." *Slate*, October 8 2015, https://slate.com/human-interest/2015/10/lgbtq-romance-how-the-genre-is-expanding-happily-ever-afters-to-all-queer-people.html. Accessed April 24, 2019.

Gunn, Gay G. *Nowhere to Run*. Genesis Press, 1997.

Hague, Euan. "Mass Market Romance Fiction and the Representation of Scotland in the United States." *The Modern Scottish Diaspora: Contemporary Debates and Perspectives*, edited by Duncan Sim and Murray Stewart Leith. Edinburgh University Press Ltd., 2014, pp. 171–190.

Hall, Glinda Fountain. "Inverting the Southern Belle: Romance Writers Redefine Gender Myths." *The Journal of Popular Culture*, vol. 41, no. 1, 2008, pp. 37–55.

Handley, William R. *Cambridge Studies in American Literature and Culture: Marriage, Violence and the Nation in the American Literary West*. Cambridge University Press, 2002.

Harper, Frances Ellen Watkins. *Iola Leroy; Or, Shadows Uplifted*. 1893. *Making of America*, http://name.umdl.umich.edu/ABX9698.0001.001. Accessed March 3, 2017.

Harris, Trudier. "'The Yellow Rose of Texas': A Different Cultural View." *Callaloo*, vol. 32, no. 2, 2009, pp. 529–539.

Heinecken, Dawn. "Changing Ideologies in Romance Fiction." *Romantic Conventions*, edited by Anne K. Kaler. Bowling Green State University Popular Press, 1999, pp. 149–172.

Herendeen, Ann. *Phyllida and the Brotherhood of Philander: A Novel*. Harper Perennial, 2008.

———. "Having It Both Ways; or Writing from the Third Perspective: The Revolutionary M/M/F Ménage Romance Novel." *Romance Fiction and American Culture: Love as the Practice of Freedom?*, edited by William A. Gleason and Eric Murphy Selinger. Routledge, 2016, pp. 405–419.

Heyer, Georgette. *The Black Moth*. Houghton Mifflin Company, 1921. *A Celebration of Women Writers*, University of Pennsylvania, https://digital.library.upenn.edu/women/heyer/moth/moth.html. Accessed March 3, 2017.

———. *The Masqueraders*. Fawcett, 1976.

———. *These Old Shades*. Arrow, 2004.

Hinnant, Charles H. "Desire and the Marketplace: A Reading of Kathleen Woodiwiss's *the Flame and the Flower*." *Doubled Plots: Romance and History*, edited by Susan Strehle and Mary Paniccia Carden. University Press of Mississippi, 2003, pp. 147–164.

Hopkins, Pauline. "Winona." 1902. *The Magazine Novels of Pauline Hopkins*, edited by Hazel V. Carby. Oxford University Press, 1990, pp. 287–437.

———. *Contending Forces: A Romance Illustrative of Negro Life North and South*. 1900. Oxford University Press, 1991.

Hughes, Helen. *The Historical Romance*. Routledge, 1993.

Hull, E. M. *The Sheik: A Novel*. 1919. University of Pennsylvania Press, 2001.

Jagodzinski, Mallory. *Love Is (Color) Blind: Historical Romance Fiction and Interracial Relationships in the Twenty-First Century*. 2015. Bowling Green State University, Ph.D. dissertation.

Janine and Sunita. "Joint Discussion: For Such a Time by Kate Breslin." *Dear Author*, August 11, 2015, https://dearauthor.com/features/letters-of-opinion/joint-discussion-time-kate-breslin/. Accessed October 3, 2017.

Jasveen, Sahota. Comment on "If You Like ... Romances Set in South Asia or Featuring South Asian Characters." *Dear Author*. Comment posted May 25, 2012, at 2:27 am, https://dearauthor.com/need-a-rec/if-you-like-misc/reading-list-by-jane-for-if-you-likeromances-set-in-south-asia-or-featuring-south-asian-characters/. Accessed October 1, 2017.

Jenkins, Beverly. *Indigo*. iUniverse, Inc., 2000.

Joannou, Maroula. *Women's Writing, Englishness and National and Cultural Identity: The Mobile Woman and the Migrant Voice, 1938–62*. Springer, 2012.

"Kathleen E. Woodiwiss." *Avon Romance*, www.avonromance.com/book-author/kathleen-e-woodiwiss/. Accessed March 2, 2017.

Katz, Jonathan. *Gay American History: Lesbians and Gay Men in the U.S.A.: A Documentary*. Avon Books, 1978.

Kim, T. "If You Like ... Romances Set in South Asia or Featuring South Asian Characters." *Dear Author*, May 21, 2012, https://dearauthor.com/need-a-rec/if-you-like-misc/reading-list-by-jane-for-if-you-likeromances-set-in-south-asia-or-featuring-south-asian-characters/. Accessed February 18, 2017.

Kincaid, Katharine. *Sea Flame*. Kensington Pub. Corp., 1989.

Kloester, Jennifer. *Georgette Heyer: Biography of a Bestseller*. William Heinemann, 2011.

Koch, Bea and Leah Koch. "The State of Racial Diversity in Romance Publishing Report." *The Ripped Bodice*, www.therippedbodicela.com/state-racial-diversity-romance-publishing-report. Accessed June 1, 2018.

Kroeg, Susan M. "'Truly Our Contemporary Jane Austen': Thinking like an Austen Fan about Regency Romances." *Kentucky Philological Review*, vol. 27, 2012, pp. 50–58.

Leigh, Susannah. *Dawn of Fire*. Onyx, 1992.

Lerner, Rose. "5-star Reviews of "For Such a Time"." *Rose Lerner*, 2015, https://roselerner.tumblr.com/post/125853628248/5-star-reviews-of-for-such-a-time. Accessed October 3, 2017.

Lin, Jeannie. "Jeannie Lin Tells Us: How My Worst Seller Became a Bestseller and What It Means to Write 'Different.'" *R.T. Book Reviews*, 2014, www.rtbookreviews.com/rt-daily-blog/jeannie-lin-tells-us-how-my-worst-seller-became-bestseller-and-what-it-means-write-%E2%80%9Cdi. *Internet Archive*, web.archive.org/web/20181008135016/www.rtbookreviews.com/rt-daily-blog/jeannie-lin-tells-us-how-my-worst-seller-became-bestseller-and-what-it-means-write-%E2%80%9Cdi. Accessed April 24, 2019.

Lindsey, Johanna. *Captive Bride*. Avon Books, 1977.

Lyons, Sarah Frantz and Eric Murphy Selinger. "Strange Stirrings, Strange Yearnings: The Flame and the Flower, Sweet Savage Love, and the Lost Diversities of Blockbuster Historical Romance." *Romance Fiction and American Culture: Love as the Practice of Freedom?*, edited by William A. Gleason and Eric Murphy Selinger. Routledge, 2016, pp. 89–110.

Macdonald, Andrew, Gina Macdonald and MaryAnn Sheridan. *Shape-Shifting: Images of Native Americans in Recent Popular Fiction*. Greenwood Press, 2000.

Markert, John. *Publishing Romance: The History of an Industry, 1940s to the Present*. McFarland, 2016.

Martin, Michelle. *Pembroke Park*. Naiad Press, 1986.

"Mary Ann Willson." *National Gallery of Art*. National Gallery of Art Website. N.d.

McAlister, Jodi. "'You and I are Humans, and There Is Something Complicated between Us': *Untamed* and Queering the Heterosexual Historical Romance." *Journal of Popular Romance Studies*, vol. 5, no. 2, 2016, n.p. http://jprstudies.org/2016/07/you-and-i-are-humans-and-there-is-something-complicated-between-us-untamed-and-queering-the-heterosexual-historical-romanceby-jodi-mcalister/.

McCafferty, Kate. "Palimpsest of Desire: The Re-Emergence of the American Captivity Narrative as Pulp Romance." *Journal of Popular Culture*, vol. 27, no. 4, 1994, pp. 43–56.

McNamara, Sallie. "Georgette Heyer: The Historical Romance and the Consumption of the Erotic, 1918–1939." *All the World and Her Husband: Women in Twentieth-Century Consumer Culture*, edited by Maggie Andrews and Mary M. Talbot. Cassell, 2000, pp. 82–96.

Meeker, Lloyd A. "About Who Writes MM Romance." *Lloyd A. Meeker*, July 4 2014, http://lloydmeeker.com/writers-mm-gay-romance/. Accessed June 5, 2018.

Milan, Courtney. "A Note on Historical Romance Sales in Print." *Courtneymilan.com*, 18 January 2014, www.courtneymilan.com/ramblings/2014/01/18/a-note-on-historical-romance-sales-in-print/. Accessed February 15, 2017.

Miller, Isabel. *Patience and Sarah*. McGraw-Hill, 1972.

Milton, Suzanne, ed. *American Romance Authors*. Special issue of *Teaching American Literature: A Journal of Theory and Practice*, vol. 2, no. 2/3, 2008, pp. 1–35.

Modleski, Tania. *Loving with a Vengeance: Mass Produced Fantasies for Women*, 2nd ed. Routledge, 2007.

Monson, Christine. *Rangoon*. Avon, 1985.

Morgan, Paula. "'Like Bush Fire in My Arms': Interrogating the World of Caribbean Romance." *The Journal of Popular Culture*, vol. 36, no. 4, 2003, pp. 804–827.

Mussell, Kay J. *Fantasy and Reconciliation: Contemporary Formulas of Women's Romance Fiction*. Praeger, 1984.

Naughton, Julie. "In Loving Color." *PublishersWeekly.Com*, 2014, www.publishersweekly.com/pw/by-topic/new-titles/adult-announcements/article/64666-in-loving-color-romance-2014.html. Accessed April 24, 2019.

Neal, Lynn S. *Romancing God: Evangelical Women and Inspirational Fiction*. The University of North Carolina Press, 2006.

Pagliassotti, Dru. "Love and the Machine: Technology and Human Relationships in Steampunk Romance and Erotica." *Steaming into a Victorian Future: A Steampunk Anthology*, edited by Julie Anne Taddeo and Cynthia J Miller. The Scarecrow Press, 2013, pp. 65–87.

Palmer, Paulina. "Girl Meets Girl: Changing Approaches to the Lesbian Romance." *Fatal Attractions: Re-Scripting Romance in Contemporary Literature and Film*, edited by Lynn Pearce and Gina Wisker. Pluto Press, 1998, pp. 189–204.

Patterson, Eric. "The Western." *The glbtq Encyclopedia*, 2008, pp. 1–16. *glbtq Archives*, www.glbtqarchive.com/arts/western_arts_A.pdf. Accessed January 22, 2017.

Pinto, Jerry. "India Embraces Mills & Boon." *The National*, 27 February 2010, www.thenational.ae/arts-culture/india-embraces-mills-boon-1.490879. Accessed March 3, 2017.

Pryde, Jessica. "A (Semi) Comprehensive Guide to LGBTQ+ Romance." *BOOK RIOT*, 2017, https://bookriot.com/2017/03/29/a-semi-comprehensive-guide-to-lgbtq-romance/. Accessed April 24, 2019.

Putney, Mary Jo. *Veils of Silk*. Signet, 2002 (reprint edition).

Radick, Caryn. "Romance Writers' Use of Archives." *Archivaria*, vol. 82, no. 0, May 2016, pp. 45–73.

Radway, Janice A. *Reading the Romance: Women, Patriarchy, and Popular Literature*, 2nd ed. The University of North Carolina Press, 1991.

Raimon, Eve Allegra. *The "Tragic Mulatta" Revisited: Race and Nationalism in Nineteenth-Century Antislavery Fiction*. Rutgers University Press, 2004.

Ramsdell, Kristin. *Romance Fiction: A Guide to the Genre*, 2nd ed. Libraries Unlimited, 2012.

Rea, Kay Taylor. "Harlequin Closing Five Lines, Including Kimani Romance." *BOOK RIOT*, May 15 2017, https://bookriot.com/2017/05/15/harlequin-closing-five-lines-including-kimani-romance/. Accessed April 24, 2019.

Regis, Pamela. *A Natural History of the Romance Novel*. University of Pennsylvania Press, 2003.

Reid, Mayne. *The Quadroon*. 1856. G.W. Dillingham, 1897.

Rogers, Rosemary. *Sweet Savage Love*, 4th ed. Avon Books, 1975.

"R.W.A. Report on Diversity and Inclusion." *Romance Writers of America*, May 30 2018, www.rwa.org/p/bl/et/blogid=20&blogaid=2212. Accessed June 14, 2018.

"R.W.A.'s Origin Story." *Romance Writers of America*, www.rwa.org/p/cm/ld/fid=519. Accessed June 1, 2018.

Ryder, Mary Ellen. "Smoke and Mirrors: Event Patterns in the Discourse Structure of a Romance Novel." *Journal of Pragmatics*, vol. 31, no. 8, 1999, pp. 1067–1080. *ScienceDirect*, https://doi.org/10.1016/S0378-2166(99)80001-0.

Sales, Roger. "The Loathsome Lord and the Disdainful Dame: Byron, Cartland and the Regency Romance." *Byromania: Portraits of the Artist in Nineteenth- and Twentieth-Century Culture*, edited by Frances Wilson. Macmillan, 1999, pp. 166–183.

Schiffman, Leon G. and Steven P. Schnaars. "The Consumption of Historical Romance Novels: Consumer Aesthetics in Popular Literature." *S. V. - Symbolic Consumer Behavior*, edited by Elizabeth C. Hirschman and Morris B. Holbrook. Association for Consumer Research, pp. 46–51, http://acrwebsite.org/volumes/12226/volumes/sv04/SV-04. Accessed March 3, 2017.

Schwab, Sandra. "It Is Only with One's Heart that One Can See Clearly." *Journal of Literary & Cultural Disability Studies*, vol. 6, no. 3, 2012, pp. 275–289.

Seale, Maura. "'I Find Some Hindu Practices like Burning Widows, Utterly Bizarre': Representations of Sati and Questions of Choice in Veils of Silk." *Empowerment versus Oppression: Twenty First Century Views of Popular Romance Novels*, edited by Sally Goade. Cambridge Scholars Publishing, 2007, pp. 129–147.

Sebastian, Cat. "A Chat with Cat Sebastian about Writing Queer Characters in Historical Romance." *The Muse*, February 16 2018, *Jezebel*, https://themuse.jezebel.com/a-chat-with-cat-sebastian-about-writing-queer-character-1823034046. Accessed June 5, 2018.

Small, Bertrice. *The Kadin*, Reissue ed. HarperCollins e-books, 2010.

Sollors, Werner. *Neither Black nor White yet Both: Thematic Explorations of Interracial Literature*. Oxford University Press, 1997.

Spillman, Elizabeth. "The 'Managing Female' in the Novels of Georgette Heyer." *New Approaches to Popular Romance Fiction: Critical Essays*, edited by Sarah S. G. Frantz and Eric Murphy Selinger. McFarland, 2012, pp. 84–98.

Sunita. Comment on "If You Like … Romances Set in South Asia or Featuring South Asian Characters." *Dear Author*, Comment posted May 22, 2012 at 12:03 pm, https://dearauthor.com/need-a-rec/if-you-like-misc/reading-list-by-jane-for-if-you-likeromances-set-in-south-asia-or-featuring-south-asian-characters/. Accessed October 1 2017.

Teo, Hsu-Ming. *Desert Passions: Orientalism and Romance Novels*, Reprint ed. University of Texas Press, 2012.

Therrien, Kathleen. "Straight to the Edges: Gay and Lesbian Characters and Cultural Conflict in Popular Romance Fiction." *New Approaches to Popular Romance Fiction: Critical Essays*, edited by Sarah S. G. Frantz and Eric Murphy Selinger. McFarland, 2012, pp. 164–177.

Thornton, Marshall. "M/M Romance and Gay Fiction Duke It Out." *Marshall Thornton*, https://marshallthorntonauthor.com/thoughts-and-ideas/mm-romance-and-gay-fiction-duke-it-out/. Accessed June 5, 2018.

Thurston, Carol. *Romance Revolution: Erotic Novels for Women and the Quest for a New Sexual Identity*. University of Illinois Press, 1987.

Tompkins, Jane. *West of Everything: The Inner Life of Westerns*. Oxford University Press, 1992.

Toscano, Angela. "A Parody of Love: The Narrative Uses of Rape in Popular Romance." *Journal of Popular Romance Studies*, vol. 2, no. 2, 2012, n.p. http://jprstudies.org/2012/04/a-parody-of-love-the-narrative-uses-of-rape-in-popular-romance-by-angela-toscano/.

Trodd, Anthea. *Women's Writing in English: Britain 1900–1945*. Longman Pub Group, 1998.

Vivanco, Laura. "Links: India, Covers and Romance." *Teach Me Tonight*, February 27, 2010, http://teachmetonight.blogspot.com/2010/02/links-india-covers-and-romance.html. Accessed October 1, 2017.

———. "Georgette Heyer: The Nonesuch of Regency Romance." *Journal of Popular Romance Studies*, vol. 3, no. 2, 2013, n.p. http://jprstudies.org/2013/06/georgette-heyer-the-nonesuch-of-regency-romance-by-laura-vivanco/.

———. *Pursuing Happiness: Reading American Romance as Political Fiction*. Humanities-E-book, 2016.

Wallace, Diana. *The Woman's Historical Novel: British Women Writers, 1900–2000.* Palgrave Macmillan, 2005.

Wardrop, Stephanie. "Last of the Red Hot Mohicans: Miscegenation in the Popular American Romance." *MELUS*, vol. 22, no. 2, 1997, pp. 61–74. *JSTOR*, www-jstor-org.proxymu.wrlc.org/stable/468135.

Wendell, Sarah. "Letter to the R.W.A. Board regarding for Such a Time by Kate Breslin." *Braised W.T.F.*, August 4, 2015, https://sarahwendell.tumblr.com/post/125859299894/letter-to-the-rwa-board-regarding-for-such-a-time. Accessed October 3, 2017.

———. "Go Get Your Books." *Smart Bitches, Trashy Books*, February 9 2017, https://smartbitchestrashybooks.com/2017/02/go-get-books-samhain-publishing-will-close-february-28-2017/. Accessed April 24, 2019.

Wendell, Sarah and Candy Tan. *Beyond Heaving Bosoms: The Smart Bitches' Guide to Romance Novels.* Fireside, 2009.

Westman, Karin E. "A Story of Her Weaving: The Self-Authoring Heroines of Georgette Heyer's Regency Romance." *Doubled Plots: Romance and History*, edited by Susan Strehle and Mary Paniccia Carden. University Press of Mississippi, 2003, pp. 165–184.

White, Nicola R. "Edutainment: A Beverly Jenkins Spotlight." *Heroes and Heartbreakers*, Macmillan, 2016, www.heroesandheartbreakers.com/blogs/2016/03/edutainment-a-beverly-jenkins-spotlight. *Internet Archive*, web.archive.org/web/20160331105054/www.heroesandheartbreakers.com/blogs/2016/03/edutainment-a-beverly-jenkins-spotlight. Accessed April 24, 2019.

Wilson, Cintra. "W4M4M?" *Out*, August 17 2010, www.out.com/entertainment/2010/08/17/w4m4m. Accessed June 5, 2018.

Winsor, Kathleen. *Forever Amber.* Macmillan, 1947.

WOC in Romance. WOCIR, www.wocinromance.com/. Accessed June 1, 2018.

Woodiwiss, Kathleen E. *The Flame and the Flower*, Reissue ed. HarperCollins e-books, 2009.

Yazzie, Evangeline Parsons. *Her Land, Her Love.* Salina Bookshelf, 2014.

Zanger, Jules. "The 'Tragic Octoroon' In Pre-Civil War Fiction." *American Quarterly*, vol. 18, no. 1, 1966, pp. 63–70.

6 Paranormal romance and urban fantasy

María T. Ramos-García

Paranormal romance and urban fantasy are two genres with significant commonalities that in the twenty-first century have experienced a rise in popularity and share a significantly overlapping readership. Within the romance community, "paranormal" stands as shorthand for all the subgenres that belong to the larger alternative reality/ speculative fiction group, and may include urban fantasy when the term romance is used in its extended sense (i.e., as a fictional work with romantic elements). Thus, the Romance Writers of America (RWA) defines paranormal romance as "[r]omance novels in which fantasy worlds or paranormal or science fiction elements are an integral part of the plot." Diana Gabaldon provides a more detailed definition of the term:

> *Paranormal* is any romance in which either the setting or one or more of the protagonists is "different." He (it's normally, though not invariably, the hero who gets to be different) might be a vampire, for instance. Or he might be an alien. Or a werewolf. Or a citizen of a future civilization. Or a time traveler. You know, *different*.
>
> (143)

In more recent examples of the genre the "other" can be either the hero or the heroine, or most often both of them. Nevertheless, the assumption that the hero would be the "other" was accurate at the time of Gabaldon's writing. This definition emphasizes an important aspect of what has become a common trait in most examples of the genre as it is known today: the "otherness" of one or both of the protagonists. That is, although technically any supernatural element would qualify a romance as paranormal according to RWA, the large majority of the protagonists of these novels, regardless of other paranormal elements in the plot, are supernatural. Gabaldon also emphasizes another essential element of paranormal romance as a fantasy genre: world-building. "Paranormal stories can be set anywhere, any time. However, whenever and wherever they are, the world of the story must be logical and consistent" (Gabaldon 147).

The world-building process is complex and time-consuming, requiring an investment for both author and reader that may explain why virtually all paranormal romance is sold as a series of connected novels, although each novel has a different couple at its center. In this context, the term series does not refer to publishing lines (also called category romances) but to what Kristin Ramsdell in *Romance Fiction. A Guide to the Genre* has defined as linked novels. Most paranormal romances are sold as single-titles. In fact, paranormal seems to be more successful among single-title readers than among category romance readers, and paranormal romance series may extend over decades, some of them including over 30 books and counting. Although there is a recent tendency toward seriality in the romance genre in general, which has been studied by An Goris in "Happily Ever After … and After: Serialization and the Popular Romance Novel," this publishing method has become the norm in paranormal romance—one of the traits it has in common with urban fantasy.

Urban fantasy is a separate genre that is not constrained by the romance expectation of a happily ever after (HEA) at the end of each novel. In fact, there is no universally accepted definition of urban fantasy or, more accurately, of which authors belong in the genre. The most commonly accepted definition was offered by John Clute and John Grant in *The Encyclopedia of Fantasy* (1997): "Urban fantasies are normally texts where fantasy and the mundane world intersect and interweave throughout a tale which is significantly *about* a real city" (975). While according to this definition—and consequently for most readers, writers, librarians, and publishing companies—many bestsellers written by women in the last two decades belong to this genre, critics often classify them as romances or use other terminologies of their own creation. The reason many critics ignore them or dismiss largely all urban fantasy written by women is that their works often contain a romantic narrative, be it ever so small part of the story. In *The Cambridge Companion to Fantasy Literature* (2012), Alexander C. Irvine shows his contempt for such works:

> [Urban fantasy] has also retroactively extended to include virtually every work of the fantastic that takes place in a city or has a contemporary setting that occasionally incorporates a city, with the result that any particularity the term once had is now diffused in a fog of contradiction (and, it must be added, marketing noise; the writers of 'paranormal romance' have all but co-opted the term for the broad American readership).
>
> (200)

In spite of his vitriol, Irvine does not offer an alternative definition of the genre that would suggest the exclusion of those works. The only characteristic he includes (apart from Clute and Grant's definition) is that the protagonists of urban fantasy are usually intellectuals or artists. However, the main character of Neil Gaiman's *Neverwhere* (1996)—one of his prime examples of urban fantasy—works in banking, specifically in securities. Ironically, one of the early examples Irvine offers for urban fantasy is Emma Bull's *War for the Oaks* (1986), which contains a significant amount of romance and ends with the main character reaching her HEA after mutual declarations of love. Hence, Bull's novel fits the romance model, while more recent urban fantasy novels written by women do not. In fact, Irvine does not offer a reason as to why most urban fantasy written by women in the last 20 years does not fit his definition, unless we consider a possible elitism regarding what kinds of text deserve the critic's attention, or a gendered idea of genre.

Conversely, also in *The Cambridge Companion to Fantasy Literature*, Roz Kaveney's article entitled "Dark Fantasy and Paranormal Romance" rejects the definition of dark fantasy previously offered by Clute and proposes a taxonomy in which dark fantasy is quite similar to what Clute had defined as urban fantasy, but includes only male protagonists. What she defines as paranormal romance are texts that most readers would consider urban fantasy: Laurell K. Hamilton's *Anita Blake* series (1993–onwards) and Charlaine Harris' *Sookie Stackhouse* (2001–13). According to Kaveney:

> What identifies a book as a paranormal romance has to be the extent to which its plot is determined by its erotic dimensions. Charlaine Harris publishes the Sookie Stackhouse novels as paranormal romance, which is right because the mundane world her telepath inhabits is one coping with the existence of vampires and others, and the plots of intrigue take much of their motive force from Sookie's relationships with supernatural beings.
>
> (220)

Aside from the fact that the Sookie Stackhouse novels are published by Ace as Fantasy/Mystery, not paranormal romance, this definition, based solely on the two series mentioned above and Stephenie Meyer's *Twilight* (2005–8), would not apply to many of the urban fantasy series written by women in which their love life and sexuality are only a marginal aspect of the plot. In series such as *Mercy Thompson* by Patricia Briggs and *Kate Daniels* by Ilona Andrews (the writing couple Ilona and Gordon Andrews), the main character, in a story arc that takes place over several books, meets and eventually commits to a relationship with a partner. However, the narrative continues for several more books with no major developments in the love relationship. That is, their romantic relationships are part of what defines these characters, but are only one dimension among many, such as their friendships, family history, and abilities. While they affect the narrative, they do not drive it, and they constitute only one aspect of the characters' identity and evolution. Furthermore, Kaveney's essay does not mention any of the paranormal series that would fit the RWA definition of a romance novel.

This position is quite common when critics address urban fantasy written by women. Leigh McLennon in "Defining Urban Fantasy and Paranormal Romance: Crossing Boundaries of Genre, Media, Self and Other in New Supernatural Worlds" does a great job of tracking criticism, publisher information, and genre theory in a well-informed article on the topic. In fact, she quotes a number of the same sources this chapter does. However her conclusion—paranormal romance and urban fantasy are the same genre—is faulty because all the novels she uses in her analysis are, in fact, urban fantasies (i.e., one usually female protagonist whose point of view is utilized exclusively across the series), and none of them follows the paranormal romance expectation of a series of novels with the HEA of a different couple at the end of each novel. Joseph Crawford, in *The Twilight of the Gothic? Vampire Fiction and the Rise of the Paranormal Romance*, so far the only book-length study on this topic, opts to avoid the distinction by ignoring the RWA definition of romance. In his view, since both genres have paranormal and romantic elements, such distinction is not needed. Paula Guran, editor of the 2006 anthology *Best New Paranormal Romance* also evades the question. Ignoring the term urban fantasy, she makes a distinction between paranormal Romance and paranormal romance. The first category would include those novels that match the RWA definition of romance, while the second would include the urban fantasy written by women that contains varied doses of romance.

In spite of the resistance on the part of literary critics to address these distinctions, the basic differences between paranormal romance and urban fantasy—as the genres are understood by most—create very distinctive kinds of narrative and reader expectations. In paranormal romance, each novel ends with the HEA of one or more couples, therefore the romantic elements consistently play a major role in the narrative; the point of view alternates between the hero and heroine, and occasionally other characters. The covers of these books (at least in this century) tend to depict the male protagonist instead of the couple more typical in other types of romance. That is the case in series such as ones by Larissa Ione or Gena Showalter or the more recent books of *The Black Dagger Brotherhood* by J.R. Ward. On the other hand, urban fantasy is narrated exclusively from the point of view of the same protagonist across all the books in the series (in the case of the texts relevant for this study, a female protagonist). Quite often the story is told in the first person, and the happy ending of each book is based on the resolution of a non-romantic conflict. The love life of the heroine evolves along with the series, but the story line is not HEA-dependent, and even if/when the heroine finds a romantic partner, the series can go on indefinitely. The amount of the narrative space devoted to her love life varies greatly from series to series and sometimes from book to book. The covers usually depict the protagonist alone[1]. Examples of the genre (and the characteristic covers) are Patricia Briggs's *Mercy Thompson* series, Carrie Vaughn's *Kitty Norville*, and Ilona Andrews' *Kate Daniels* among many others.

The distinction between the genres, and the different expectations, are important to the readers. According to Gwenda Bond in "When Love Is Strange," an article that appeared in *Publishers Weekly* in 2009,

> In fact, the terms urban fantasy and paranormal romance are often used interchangeably. But most of the category's major editors work on books that fall into both categories and caution that while the two frequently cross over among audiences, there is a key distinction. Avon executive editor Erika Tsang explains: "In paranormal romance the relationship between the couple is the focus of the main plot. In urban fantasy, the world that the couple exists in is the focus."
>
> Figuring out the best category can sometimes be hard. Tsang remembers the fan reaction when she chose to publish Jeaniene Frost's *Halfway to the Grave* as romance rather than urban fantasy. "Readers were up in arms because the characters didn't end up together. But the relationship was essential to the story, so it's a romance to me," says Tsang.
>
> Choosing the category can be dangerous ground, says Heather Osborn, romance editor at Tor. She employs a simple standard for making the decision. "My number one consideration is if there's a resolution of the romance at the end of the book. If there's no resolution of the romance, and it's in the romance section, readers will let their anger be known."

However expedient the blurring of the distinction may be, there is a significant part of the reading public that is well aware of the conventions of the genres, and feel cheated when a book marketed as a paranormal romance doesn't end with an HEA (as in the urban fantasy series *Night Huntress*, of which *Halfway to the Grave*, the example mentioned by Tsang above, is the first installment). Conversely, if a reader purchases a book as urban fantasy, the reader would be disappointed when the second book in the series barely mentions the main characters of the first one, especially the heroine, whom they assumed would be the protagonist for the entire series.

What both paranormal romance and urban fantasy have in common is the world-building and the combination in different quantities of romance and complex adventure or mystery-type plots. By the same token, there are many readers who are interested in both genres, as a look at any reader recommendations website illustrates. An examination of both genres delivers a global perspective that explains what Crawford has called the "rise of the paranormal romance" in this century.

An even more distinct category is young adult (YA) paranormal, which includes some of the characteristics of both. YA paranormal is usually narrated from the exclusive point of view of a female protagonist, and individual novels are non-HEA-dependent; on the other hand an entire series can be seen as a single romance novel with a well-defined HEA. YA paranormal also tends to put more emphasis on the love relationships of the protagonist than urban fantasy. This is the type of paranormal that benefited most from the success of *Twilight* and—judging by the number of reviews on online sites and the number of film and television adaptations—the one with the largest sales. This subgenre shows the most influence from *Twilight* and much of it can be considered derivative, although the most successful series are highly original and markedly different from the saga in the complexity of the moral issues the protagonist confront and their depiction of teenage sexuality. While YA paranormal tends to be less explicit than its adult counterparts, the sexual awakening and (in most cases) first sexual experiences of the protagonist take place over the course of the series. In addition to L.J. Smith's *Vampire Diaries* of the 1990s, other major hits include *Vampire Academy* (2007–10) by Richelle Mead, *The Mortal Instruments* (2007–14) by Cassandra Clare, *Blue Bloods* (2006–13) by Melissa de la Cruz, *The Morganville Vampires* by Rachel Caine (2006–13), *House of Night* by P.C. and Kristin Cast (2007–14), and *The Immortals* by Alyson Noel (2009–11), just to name a few. The series mentioned have all come to an end, a tendency found also in urban fantasy, but not often in adult paranormal romance. However, most authors have continued publishing spin-offs and new series.

Classification

Although individual novels have received critics' attention, there has not been much effort in the systematic study of the genre, so it should not come as a surprise that most information regarding categories comes from librarians, publishers, and editors. Kristin Ramsdell, in the first edition of *Romance Fiction: A Guide to the Genre* (1999) called all romance novels with any kind of fantastic elements quite accurately "Alternative Reality Fiction," and divided it into the self-explanatory subcategories of fantasy romance, futuristic romance, paranormal romance (paranormal elements in a world similar to ours), and time travel romance. In the second edition of the book in 2012 she added urban fantasy romance as a fifth, separate category. However, she acknowledges the problematic nature of her distinction when she states that many of the novels she categorizes as paranormal romance "could be claimed by this or the Urban Fantasy subgroup" (329). She classifies the work of Kresley Cole and Sherrilyn Kenyon, as well as Stephenie Meyer's *Twilight*, as paranormal romance, but also includes in this group the *Fever* series by Karen Marie Moning, which clearly falls into the urban fantasy genre as defined above. Conversely, she includes authors such as Christine Feehan, Nalini Singh, and J.R. Ward, who write romances, in the urban fantasy category, in which she also includes Briggs's *River Marked* (2011), one of the books in the Mercy Thompson urban fantasy series because it "has more romance than some and may appeal to romance fans, as well as introduce them to a new fantasy genre" (354). Ramsdell acknowledges the existence of urban fantasy as a separate genre from romance, and at the same time acknowledges the connection between urban fantasy and paranormal romance and tries to account for it, however her methodology lacks rigor.

Patricia O'Brien Mathews in *Fang-tastic Fiction: Twenty-first-Century Paranormal Reads* (2011), a publication of the American Library Association, classifies the paranormal according to a number of different criteria. Regarding plot types she includes: soulmate romances (paranormal romance); urban fantasy (following John Clute's definition); chick lit (distinguished by its humor and use of pop culture); cozy mysteries (detective stories that "generally have no profanity and no sexual details" (14)); and historical series. In addition to the plot categories, she also divides the different series according to three different criteria: violence, sensuality, and humor. Since the different plot lines can intersect in different ways according to each of these three criteria, the variation is enormous. Some paranormal romance series, such as the *Love at Stake* series (2005–14) by Kerrelyn Sparks, or the *Broken Heart* series (2006–ongoing) by Michele Bardsley, can be as humorous as the chick-lit series *Undead* by MaryJanice Davidson (2004–16) or Gerry Bartlett's *Glory St. Claire* (2007–ongoing). On the other hand, the comic series can be at times as violent and the worlds portrayed as dangerous and unstable as in the more dramatic paranormals. The main difference lies in the tone, not the content.

So far, this chapter has centered on mainstream, widely read, paranormal romance and urban fantasy. Most of the series mentioned so far appear in the major bestsellers' lists. There are also some other types of paranormal that have become successful among smaller groups of readers. Joey Hill's *Vampire Queen* (2007–ongoing) and Yasmine Galenorn's *Otherworld/Sisters of the Moon* series (2006–ongoing) are major series of erotic paranormal (romance or urban fantasy), characterized by sexual experimentation, BDSM, and/or polyamory. Paranormal has also become a major seller among gay and lesbian romance readers, and gay and lesbian paranormal seems to have taken off about a decade later than mainstream paranormal.[2] The first successful series began publication starting in 2010. Some of the most relevant authors are Tina Folsom, K.J. Charles, and L.L. Raand (a.k.a. Radclyffe). Unfortunately, while those books appear in trade and reader publications, so far they have not been studied in academic circles.

While, as mentioned above, paranormal romance and urban fantasy are distinc genres, hybridity does also occur. One example is the *Women of the Otherworld* series by Kelley Armstrong (2001–13), which has six different heroines in a total of 13 books. All of them achieve their HEA and continue being protagonists of their own stories and telling them in first person narratives. In the *Dark Huntress* series (2007–14), Jeaniene Frost presents an urban fantasy with a spin-off: *Dark Huntress World* which contains two novels *First Drop of Crimson* (2010) and *Eternal Kiss of Darkness* (2010), both romance novels with secondary characters in the main series as protagonists. J.R. Ward presents an interesting case. In *The Black Dagger Brotherhood* (2005–ongoing) she shifted in the 12th book in the series, *The King* (2010) from the predictable pattern of a new pairing per book. In it, the couple of the first novel in the series, *Dark Lover*, go through a crisis, and the fictional world's narrative advances, but there is no new coupling. Some other books in the series have followed this pattern. Many readers expressed their distress over the changes in the genre, so on December 1, 2015, she published the first book of the spin-off *Black Dagger Brotherhood Legacy*, which, while still connected to the characters of the main series, guarantees an HEA in each book. At the same time the novels in the main series remain "big, juicy, epic releases with lots of drama and erotic stuff in them," as the author explained in her blog on Goodreads.

Two other types of hybridization deserve special mention. First, there are series that combine the aesthetics of steampunk with these genres, such as the paranormal romance *Iron Seas* (2010–14) by Meljean Brook and the urban fantasy *Vampire Empire* (2010–12) by Clay and Susan Griffith. It is also worth mentioning Deborah Harkness, a historian of science who wrote the extremely successful *All Souls* trilogy (2011–14) and in 2018 *Times Convert*, a spin-off of the first series. According to the author, she was inspired by the vampire romances she saw in bookstores, and decided to write her own. Her books, full of erudition and complex plots, can be seen as a more "literary" version of the urban fantasy described in this essay. The second volume, *Shadow of Night* (2012) includes time travel and takes place mostly in Shakespeare's time, and has received some critical attention for that reason. Lindsay Ann Reid compares the volume to two other novels both entitled *The School of Night* by Alan Wall and Louis Bayar; and Regina Buccola makes a similar comparison, adding Erin Morgenstern's *The Night Circus* to the mix. Taking a different approach, Ashley Szanter in "Deborah Harknesss's *All Souls Trilogy*, Supernatural Heredity, and 'Creature' Genetics" looks at the trilogy to demonstrate how the genetics of the paranormal beings compare to those applied in the *Harry Potter* novels, and how, at least to a certain extent, they follow Mendel's laws of genetic inheritance. It is significant that none of these critics mentions the corpus of paranormal romance and urban fantasy that Harkness's work is a part of, in spite of the fact that she has been quite open regarding the fact that it was the success of *Twilight* and other texts that inspired her to write her novels in the first place, as she has frequently acknowledged.[3]

History of the genres

Paranormal romance and urban fantasy are both very new genres. In both cases some novels have been traced to the 1980s and the genres as such were consolidated in the 1990s. However, there is a plethora of different genres that have influenced contemporary paranormal: especially romance, fantasy, Gothic, horror, and vampire and werewolf narratives. Many scholars have traced the origins of paranormal through some of these genres, although rarely all of them. Kristin Ramsdell in *Romance Fiction* offers a brief but detailed genealogy of alternative reality genres in general. Clute and later Irvine consider Emma Bull and Charles de Lint the pioneers of urban fantasy in the 1980s, and the genre as we know it today was consolidated in the early 1990s with China Mieville and Neil Gaiman as the archetypical models. Joseph Crawford in his book *The Twilight of the Gothic?* traces the romance tradition through the Middle Ages to the present, and the Gothic from its origins in the eighteenth century to the present, including the transformation of the vampire from monstrous and sub-human into a sympathetic character during the twentieth century. In his view, the paranormal romance is the combination of both traditions in the present. He concludes his pre-history of the genre arguing that:

> By the late 1980s, then, the once firm cultural divide between the desirable and the monstrous had undergone an immense process of attrition. On one side, the heroes of popular romance had been growing steadily darker, increasingly encroaching upon the terrain once reserved for the monsters and villains of Gothic fiction: the road from Darcy to Rochester to Maxim De Winter and Brandon Birmingham had carried the romantic hero from respectability to criminality, and from self-control to physical and sexual aggression. On the other side, the villains, vampires and monsters of the Gothic fiction had been growing increasingly sympathetic: the path from Lord Ruthven to Dracula to Barnabas Collins and Lestat de Lioncourt had transformed them from horrific, inhuman predators into attractive, remorseful anti-heroes, capable of love and aching for redemption.
>
> (58)

As is the case quite often in Crawford's book, his deep knowledge of the Gothic is coupled with a very superficial knowledge of romance, which explains his use of *Rebecca* (1938) and *The Flame and the Flower* (1972) as relevant models for the romance hero in the late 1980s, at a time when that kind of hero was no longer the norm, as Dawn Heinecken pointed out in "Changing Ideologies in Romance Fiction." He considers *The Mummy* (1989), by Anne Rice, the first paranormal romance, pointing out that only two years later "paranormal romance began its steady rise toward the levels of popularity it enjoys today" (61).

Crawford continues with a detailed development of the paranormal romance and urban fantasy written by women during the 1990s. As relevant early examples he includes the *De Morrisey* (1991–3) series by Lori Herter, Linda Lael Miller's *Vampire* series (1993–6) and Maggie Shayne's *Wings in the Night* (1993–2011), a traditional paranormal romance series, which started publication as category romance in the line *Silhouette Shadows*. Simultaneously, as he points out, young adult paranormal (romance) was born with Annette Curtis Klause's novel *The Silver Kiss* (not technically a romance since the vampire hero chooses to die in the end), and L.J. Smith's *The Vampire Diaries* (1991–2)—the basis for the homonymous television series—and later on *Night World* (1996–8) by the same author.

Harlequin introduced its Silhouette Shadows line in 1993. However, this line was not devoted to paranormal romance exclusively. Some of the novels featured vampires and werewolves while others fit better into the Gothic category. Nevertheless, the venture did not last for long, and the Shadows line disappeared in 1996, only to be revived in the early 2000s as Silhouette Dreamscapes, when the same books were reprinted in addition to other new—mostly paranormal—novels.[4] Harlequin Shadows opened the doors for paranormal romance as a category with a readership, albeit a small one. In 1994, Leisure added the LoveSpell line and Topaz Dreamspun, both dedicated to alternative reality romances, but paranormal titles amounted to only 2 per cent of the romances published that year (Ramsdell "The Year in Romance Fiction" 78–9).

Crawford describes the urban fantasy *Blood Books* (1991–4) by Tanya Huff (which was adapted to television as *Blood Ties* for two seasons in 2007–8) as mystery fiction, but emphasizes the role of L.K. Hamilton and her ongoing *Anita Blake* series, which began publication in 1993 as an extremely influential series on the urban fantasy side, a fact also recognized by other scholars, like Angela Ndalianis. Both Huff's and Hamilton's series were originally published as horror. According to Crawford:

> The early *Anita Blake* novels amply deserved their designation as horror fiction: they depict a world of shocking violence and casual sexual predation ... They are characterized by stylized hard-boiled dialogue and noir-style plots, full of corruption, seduction and exploitation, in which vampires and other supernatural creatures play the role of mobsters to Anita's less-hard-boiled-than-she'd like to be PI.
> (113)

However, later on "Anita steadily acquires more and more supernatural powers, along with an ever-greater capacity for violence, finally becoming one of the most powerful and dangerous supernatural beings in the world" (114). Simultaneously, "[h]er romantic and sexual relationships with a variety of supernatural partners are given ever-greater prominence, and from *Narcissus in Chains* (2001) onwards substantial portions of each book are devoted to sex scenes and her growing harem of male lovers" (114–15). Thus, the series evolves, as Crawford puts it, "from noir-themed urban fantasy to paranormal erotica" (115). The same occurs in Hamilton's other series, *Merry Gentry* (2000–14). Crawford points to how Hamilton's evolution led to "a set of assumptions," now taken for granted in the genre, "that sexy monsters can and should be desirable romantic interests, that urban heroines can be violent and sexually experimental without ceasing to be heroic or sympathetic, and that monsters are basically people too" (121).

There is no doubt that *Anita Blake* has been an important influence in more recent paranormal works; however, while the other assumptions are true, Crawford missed one very important aspect of the genres (both paranormal romance and urban fantasy) at least in their mainstream versions: while the heroines are not necessarily virgins, and previous sexual experience is the norm, both genres tend toward monogamy and long-lasting relationships. This is obvious for paranormal romance, but it is also one of the major distinctions between other urban fantasy works and those of the twenty-first -century women writers mentioned in this chapter. Their tendency to establish monogamous, loving, long-lasting relationships is precisely what distinguishes them from other fantasy fiction and the urban fantasy of the 1990s, and what has relegated them (as seen above) to the realm of romance in the eyes of critics. It is not the depiction of sex or lack thereof, but the stable love lives (or the process toward achieving stable love lives) that brings them down in the eyes of many academics and critics (Irvine, Crawford, etc.) On the other hand, as Crawford himself points out, Hamilton's work did not evolve toward urban fantasy, but toward paranormal erotica (115)—a subgenre that also developed in the twenty-first century, but a separate subgenre nonetheless.

While paranormal romances continued to be published during the 1990s, they did not reach the critical mass they would in the next decade. In 1997, Ramsdell noted that time travel romances (not paranormal) accounted for the majority of the titles published in the alternative reality category. While Gabaldon defines the genre in 1997 as "hot stuff," by 2000, Ann Bouricius explains in *The Romance Readers Advisory*:

> Readers of paranormals are usually quite devoted to their subgenre. They will often comment that not enough of them are published. The publishers, on the other hand, usually say that the market for them is not there, that there aren't enough readers.
> (19)

On the other hand, the 1997 centennial of the publication of Bram Stoker's *Dracula* brought a new interest on vampire fiction, and the launching of the television series *Buffy the Vampire Slayer* (1997–2003) had tremendous impact on the development of paranormal romance and urban fantasy, bringing the "revisionist vampire" and the "kick-ass heroine" to a much wider audience. This opinion is shared by many editors, according to Gwenda Bond. *Buffy* was extremely successful. Although in some ways the series provides a traditional view of vampires, in which most of them are evil, the fact that the vampires Angel and Spike become love interests for the protagonist, and the more nuanced view of other supernatural beings through the series are part of the paranormal lore. There is a plethora of research on Buffy, but regarding the romantic aspects of the series it is worth mentioning Jennifer Crusie's article "Dating Death: Essay: Love and Sex in Buffy the Vampire Slayer" in which the romance writer/academic points to the varied and realistic depictions of love across the seven seasons of the series.

It is in the next few years that both paranormal romance and urban fantasy take off, both on the number of titles and sales. At the turn of the century some of the current series made their appearance. In 1999, Christine Feehan, considered for some time the queen of paranormal romance published her first book in the *Carpathian* series, *Dark Prince*. Feehan's *Carpathian* series is still today more similar to the paranormal of the 1990s. Although later on she incorporated more action and long-term external threats, her tone is still more intimate and the content more psychological.[5] On the same year, the PEARL awards (Paranormal Excellence Award for Romantic Literature) were held for the first time, and until 2003 Feehan won at least one of the awards every year (Crawford 138–9). In Crawford's words, "Feehan's popularity marked the point at which the vampire romance transitioned from being a relatively minor romance subgenre (as it had been since 1991) to a much more significant presence within the romance genre" (144).

During the 1990s, and most of the 2000s, urban fantasy was not well defined, so many series that nowadays are included in that genre were classified earlier by editors, librarians, and booksellers as horror or fantasy, or even mystery, and only rarely as romance. Even today, the placement of these books in bookstores is quite haphazard. Two of those series had their debut on 2001: the aforementioned *Sookie Stackhouse* and Kelley Armstrong's *Women of the Otherworld* (2001–13). In both series, the first installment is more psychological with limited external conflict in the form of murders to be solved, and the novels have much in common with the mystery or detective genre. However, as the series evolve, the external conflict escalates and national or global level conspiracies have to be thwarted, a plot type that aligns them with later texts. Because of the success of *True Blood* on HBO the *Sookie Stackhouse Novels* have achieved a level of critical attention reserved only for series that have been adapted to film or TV, including *True Blood and Philosophy: We Wanna Think Bad Things with You* (2010), edited by George A. Dunn and Rebecca Housel.

Paranormal romance and urban fantasy take off and reach a much wider readership in the period 2002–7. While paranormal romance constituted only 2 per cent of the romance titles marketed in the 1990s, the number had grown to 5.7 percent in 2003 and 7.6 percent in 2004. The number of titles published as alternative reality (i.e., not including other romances with paranormal elements that were published under other categories) went from 88 in 2002, to 120 in 2003, and 173 in 2004, as was noted by Kristin Ramsdell in her yearly reports on romance for the yearly reference books

What Do I Read Next? This number increased to 9 percent by 2007, according to Jane Little of the website *Dear Author*. Numbers multiplied in the following years.[6] With the success of the novels also came a number of websites, blogs, and even podcasts on paranormal romance, notably the "Fated Mates" podcast (begun in 2018) by romance author Sarah MacLean and online romance critic Jen Prokop, which discussed Kresley Cole's *Immortals After Dark* series (2006–ongoing) book by book. In the second season they are discussing different authors.

The first *Dark Hunter* novel, *Dark Pleasures* and the prequel *Fantasy Lover*, by Sherrilyn Kenyon were both published in 2002, as well as Holly Black's *Tithe. A Modern Faerie Tale*, the first installment in a YA trilogy. In 2003 Christine Feehan introduced the *Ghost Walkers* series, and Christine Warren *The Others*. *Single White Vampire* (also 2003) is the first novel published (although it is considered the third in the series) in the ongoing *Argeneau Vampires* series by Lynsay Sands, one of the first humoristic paranormal romance series. This same year L.A. Banks (Leslie Esdaile Banks) published the first two novels of the urban fantasy *Vampire Huntress Legend* (2003–9), with an African American heroine, who is also a spoken word artist. John Lennard explains that Banks "deals primarily with vampires, and the strongly religious themes and cosmogony of her 'Vampire Huntress Legend' series tend to make other cast-creatures infernally demonic" (132). The next year Kim Harrison published the first installment of *The Hollows* (2004–14), and from then on the number of new series and new installments continued growing every year.

Twilight, the first novel of the eponymous saga by Stephenie Meyer was published in 2005. This book sold over 100 million copies worldwide, and generated not only hordes of enthusiastic fans, but, in an odd turn of events for a YA novel, organized groups of anti-fans. The unprecedented success of *Twilight*, not just with teenagers but among millions of adult women brought to the saga the attention that paranormal romance had previously lacked with the general public and engendered not only abundant fan, anti-fan, and journalistic material, but also an unprecedented level of scholarly attention, mostly negative.[7] Critics also assumed that *Twilight* was an accurate representative of all paranormal romance, and therefore spread their judgments of the saga to the entire genre, and, in many cases, assumed that all paranormal romance and urban fantasy novels were a by-product of the success of *Twilight*. Although there is no doubt that *Twilight* provided more visibility to the emerging genre and attracted new readers to it, Meyer's novels did not create the genre—which was already well defined by the time *Twilight* became a sales boom. Meyer has often admitted that she had never read a book or watched a film on vampires before, therefore—while to some extent her work was probably inspired by the existing zeitgeist—it was in no way influenced by or connected to the ongoing rise of the genre[8]. Additionally, *Twilight* was published and read first as a YA romance, and its fame did not happen overnight. After its release, it appeared on the corresponding tome of *What to Read Next?* under the category of horror, not romance. By the time it was starting to become a social phenomenon (around 2008 with the release of the final novel, *Breaking Dawn*, and the release of the first film based on the novels) most of the best-selling authors of paranormal romance and urban fantasy had already published at least one or two novels and had defined their fantasy worlds and the tone in their series.

Some of the many authors that initiated successful series of paranormal romance or urban fantasy between 2004 and 2007 are J.R. Ward, Kresley Cole, Kerrelyn Sparks, MaryJanice Davidson, Nalini Singh, Karen Chance, Katie MacAlister, Rachel Caine,

Patricia Briggs, Richelle Mead, Ilona Andrews, Jennifer Rardin, Jeaniene Frost, P. C. and Kristin Cast, Cassandra Clare, Melissa de la Cruz, and Gena Showalter. As mentioned above, the most striking similarity among most of these narratives is the kind of world-building that takes place. They depict unstable worlds, with major threats to the existence of the main characters and even to humanity. The conflict tends to escalate overall even if immediate threats are overcome at the end of individual novels. In some cases, the end of a book may bring some emotional closure and/or a HEA but leave a cliff-hanger or a worsening overall situation. The world is presented as menacing, and although there is a clear sense of a battle between good and evil, sometimes the main characters do not know who the real enemy is. Furthermore, they often act in unethical ways justified by the dire situations they are in; forced to choose between two evils, they opt for the lesser one. In many ways, the worlds represented in these texts, are the heirs of L.K. Hamilton. The setting tends to be urban, but the space/s in which the novels take place—whether a real city or town, or an imaginary one—are always key to the story. The location of the characters and their movements across the narrative space are integral to the world-building and the action.

The paranormal texts of the 1990s tended to portray somehow more benign worlds. The characters in that period had enemies, but they were usually rogue elements that represented a limited threat, and the main barriers to the HEA of the protagonists were psychological. The twenty-first century brought a hostile world of fear, betrayal, and hidden threats. It is no coincidence that the 1990s paranormal was overall in decline by the year 2000, but the numbers of novels published began to multiply exponentially after the events of 9/11 changed the perception of the world globally but especially in the United States of America. The period immediately after brought a new readership interested in dark narratives, and authors writing them. Most of the characteristics described above can be found in individual texts published in the previous decade, but the convergence of a large body of texts that consistently display most or all of them is clearly a post-9/11 phenomenon. Although the influence of 9/11 has been observed on individual texts (Jayashree Kamblé writing about Sherrilyn Kenyon's *Dark Hunter* series, for example, and Mary Bly addressing J.R. Ward's *Black Dagger Brotherhood*, among others) its application to the genre as a whole has not been thoroughly addressed yet. One important reason for this absence is the fact that it is hard to find a single text of the period which even mentions this traumatic event. However, a careful analysis reveals that most paranormal heroes (and many heroines) are warriors in one fashion or another, and the connection of terrorism with heinous threats that would easily overpower conventional law enforcement is hard to miss. In the first few years after the terrorist attack, series after series began with the discovery by one or more characters of the existence of the supernatural and the threat of dangers they could have never imagined before. In paranormal romance, this discovery is repeated in subsequent books, with the addition of new human characters to the series. In urban fantasy the heroine usually has knowledge of the supernatural, and even of her own powers, from the beginning, but her world soon becomes more complex and menacing.

In 1997, Diana Gabaldon was advising paranormal romance writers to make sure that the action in their novels did not detract from the development of the romantic relationship of the protagonists, which should always be at the forefront. While this was sound advice for paranormal romance writers in the 1990s, the 2000s bring about a significant change. The world-building and the external conflict become paramount in the new paranormal. The emphasis on the world-building and the action/adventure is key to its convergence with urban fantasy and explains why many critics, in view of the commonalities, consider them as part of the same genre.

On the other hand, the representation of sexuality and relationships in the new series diverges considerably from Hamilton's.[9] Indeed, Hamilton's Anita Blake, although timid on sexual matters in the first five novels, becomes sexually active later on with multiple partners. In her narrative, sex is connected to pleasure and power, but not to exclusive, long-term relationships. John Lennard points out that the contrast with the reception of later Anita Blake novels by some fans and reviewers is striking. Citing newspaper and Amazon reader reviews, the Wikipedia article on Hamilton reports growing dissatisfaction with the frequency, narrative construction, and extremity of Blake's sexual acts, posited on a condition called "the ardeur," which requires her to have sex with multiple partners and absorb powers from them (141).

What is largely absent in the paranormal romance and urban fantasy of this period is any explicit mention of politics, the war in Iraq or Afghanistan, or any other reference to the conflicts in the Middle East. One exception to this rule was Jennifer Rardin, who even placed the action of some of her Jaz Parks novels (2007–11) in the Middle East. Unfortunately, the premature death of the author in 2010 left the series truncated. For the most part, the novels work at one level as a form of escapism while at a different level addressing the fears and anxieties of the period. However, these commonalities do not lead to any kind of stable allegory across novels and authors. The connections are fluid and changing, and different series embody different attitudes toward power, violence, and gender roles. This fluidity is accentuated by the serial nature of these narratives, which unavoidably evolve over the years.

Hence, by the late 2000s, changes started to emerge. Many new series veered from the contemporary world of urban fantasy to fantastic, futuristic or dystopian settings such as Ilona Andrews's *Kate Daniels* (2007–ongoing) and *The Edge* (2009–12) series, and Nalini Singh's *Psy-Changeling* (2006–ongoing) and *Guild Hunter* (2009–ongoing) series. Examples in YA include *The Mortal Instruments* by Cassandra Clare (2007–14) and *Vampire Academy* (2007–10) by Richelle Mead.[10] Simultaneously, ongoing series tended to focus on the supernatural world, with less human/mundane characters and conflicts, and more relationships between supernatural characters. This tendency is easy to observe in paranormal romance in authors such as Sherrilyn Kenyon, J.R. Ward, Christine Feehan, and many others. Nonetheless, the discovery narrative (a superficially normal woman discovers that supernatural beings are real as she inexorably becomes part of the newly discovered world) is still alive and well.

Current numbers indicate that the paranormal is still selling, and new authors and titles enter the book market every day. One clear tendency is the move from vampires, the most popular monsters in the 1990s and early 2000s, to all sorts of other supernatural beings, such as werewolves and other shifters, fairies, demons, angels, etc.[11] The major authors in the last decade are still publishing and enjoy solid followings. At the same time, e-publishing has created an explosion of new authors geared toward more and more specific niches. In spite of Crawford's statement in 2014 that paranormal was in decline, the sales of the same year contradict his prediction (Ramsdell).

Criticism

Research on paranormal romance—except for *Twilight*, and to a lesser extent, for those texts that have been adapted to film and television—is scarce and the approaches varied, so there are no cohesive lines of inquiry beyond acknowledgment of the varied genres it originates from (fantasy, horror, romance, Gothic, vampire literature, etc.). Additionally, the hybrid nature of the genre, which can be found in such varied sections in bookstores such as romance, horror, science fiction, or fantasy has complicated even the definition of the genre as such. By the same token, critics occasionally study some of the paranormal authors in books and articles addressing overlapping categories, such as vampire literature, horror, or fantasy, where they are not always easy to find. So far, though, the only comprehensive analyses come from librarians, since in their role they are more in tune with reader habits and less concerned about literary prestige, and many insightful observations can also be found on non-academic internet sites.

There were a few very influential articles published at the turn of the century (that is, when paranormal romance was rare and in many ways different from the successful novels of the twenty-first century). Diane Calhoun-French wrote "Time-Travel and Related Phenomena in Contemporary Popular Romance Fiction," in which she analyzes four time-travel novels to conclude that they perpetuate sexist relationships and abuse, including rape. She considers that "it cannot be acceptable for writers to reinforce negative behaviors toward and destructive stereotypes about women, even with the legitimate ends of creating compelling popular escapist literature" (109). In "Paradox in Popular Romances of the 1990s: The Paranormal versus Feminist Humor" Sandra Booth reiterates the same opinion, comparing the paranormal romances of the decade by Maggie Shayne and Mallory Rush with more feminist humorous romances by Jennifer Crusie and Beverly Sommers. She observes that in the former even consensual sex is described using terms we tend to associate with a forcible act, so according to her, "despite its surface daring (more explicit sex scenes etc.) the paranormal, with respect to gender roles appears to be largely a regressive form of romance" (96). Drawing on both these critics, Christian inspirational romance author Lee Tobin-McClain provides a more nuanced interpretation of the paranormal romance of the late 1990s in "Paranormal Romance; Secrets of the Female Fantastic." In her view, the ideological positioning of paranormal romances is mixed. She observes two particular functions for readers. The first one is "believable transport and healing." She explains that while many paranormals start with common problems, the alternative universe creates solutions to those problems that would not be plausible in the real world. The second function is to allow "unspeakable elements of contemporary gender identity and relationships, [such as] gender reversals, anti-feminism and masochism among women, female issues with domesticity versus professionalism, and infantilism" (300). After debating the potential masochism involved in enjoying an overbearing alpha-hero, she points that "the paranormal romance provides a location for those secret pleasures" but adds that not all readers are looking for the same thing: "many women suffering from the supermom syndrome seek not advanced pleasures, but simply relief from their multiple obligations" (302), relief they can find in the escapism of the paranormal romance, an explanation that echoes feminist interpretations of the romance novel since Janice Radway's seminal work *Reading the Romance* (1984). On the other hand, she points out how other fantasies allowed by the paranormal romance, such as the bad girl, allow the reader to "experience the fun of 'bad' behavior without guilt or negative consequences" (303). She concludes that these novels "do not eliminate confusing or disturbing aspects of women's real lives. Instead they not only incorporate such elements but may encourage work around them" and that "these books tell us more than any other branch of the fantastic about the real fears and secret desires of women now" (300). Although Tobin-McClaine's observations are quite insightful, they are nevertheless impressionistic in nature. They are based on a personal reading and intuition, without much textual or theoretical support.

The only full-length book available that purports to examine the genre, Joseph Crawford's *The Twilight of the Gothic?*, analyzes the origins of the paranormal romance from the Gothic and, to a lesser extent, from the romance perspective, and provides a solid overview of the 1990s paranormal romance. However, his work, with almost teleological zeal, seems to be tracing not the history of the genre, but the prehistory of *Twilight*, so once the book reaches the 2000s it glosses over most of the paranormal production. His interest on the topic was awakened, precisely, by the polarization of the reactions to this text—the best-selling novel of its decade—which, in his assessment, "points to its position astride a major fault line in contemporary culture" (3). He believes that this fault line comes from the major social changes of recent times that have identified previously marginalized groups as "just like us," a change represented in the monsters of the Gothic becoming love interests. However, this assimilation of the "other" has been imperfect, so, in his words:

> [t]he triumph of *Twilight* has been to express those contradictions in their purest form, in a kind of dream-work within which all manner of impossibilities are staged and celebrated. For the unsympathetic reader, the result is moral and artistic nonsense, self-evidently absurd; but for the reader who shares the combination of fears and longings that the *Twilight* novels express they perform a rare and valuable service, articulating a range of desires and anxieties that mainstream media generally strives to keep decently out of sight. It is the strangeness of *Twilight*, its oddness and incoherencies, which set it apart from the very many, much more polished, paranormal romances which preceded and followed it.
>
> (7)

Later he points out that vampires such as *Twilight*'s

> may no longer represent the experience of the real social outsider in any meaningful way, but they do still possess three features which make them highly useful to authors of romance: they have a guilty secret they must hide, they have a predatory urge against which they must struggle and they have superhuman powers.
>
> (98)

He links those characteristics to the alpha-hero typical of romances such as *The Sheik* and *Rebecca*, and concludes that "it is the task of the heroine to forgive the first and tame the second, thereby earning the right to profit from and be protected by the third" (98). Furthermore, he considers that vampirism can work as "a stand-in for a whole range of lifestyles and behaviors which would once have been forbidden, but were now permitted as long as they did not interfere with other social duties" (105).

While in some ways this analysis is valid, it is based on a plotline that applies only to paranormal romance and not urban fantasy, and only to some novels, since the narrative of a human woman falling in love with a vampire and eventually becoming a vampire herself, while very frequent in the 1990s and early 2000s, has never been the only possible plot, and since around 2008 it has become less and less common.

According to Crawford, the *Twilight* controversy "proved to be only the first stage in a larger cultural event: the rise of the paranormal romance" (4). While there is no doubt that the success of Meyer's saga provided more visibility and surely helped the number of first time readers of the genre, as the data offered above proves, the rise of the paranormal was already underway by the time *Twilight* became a phenomenon, and even now at the end of the next decade, when its success has faded, the major authors of adult paranormal that came out of the 2000s keep successfully publishing the same or new series.

Chiho Nakagawa had already observed that the otherness of the vampire hero in *Twilight* was only relative in "Safe Sex with Defanged Vampires: New Vampire Heroes in *Twilight* and the *Southern Vampire Mysteries*." According to this critic, Edward Cullen is a safe vampire, which in her opinion "reflect[s] contemporary women's lowered sense of danger concerning sexuality and heightened sense of danger in terms of the boundaries of the self." In the case of Harris' narrative, she observes that while initially this seems to be also the case, the real danger of the vampire is revealed later on, to conclude that "[s]afe vampire heroes … are young women's fantasies, but safe vampires may not stand the test of more mature readers, especially when they are readers of popular romance," a statement that can be applied to Harris, but not to the majority of paranormal romances in the market.

Within the scarcity and variety of approaches to the study of paranormal romance and urban fantasy, certain areas of inquiry are becoming delineated. One of them is the study of the paranormal hero, which Crawford linked directly to the "dark and dangerous" romance hero of Gothic romances. Several authors have paid special attention to the best-seller series *The Black Dagger Brotherhood* (BDB) by J.R. Ward, who, while sharing many characteristics with other twenty-first-century paranormal and urban fantasy series, has definitely developed a very unique voice, with complex plots and multiple narrative points of view. Ward's world is especially dark and her aristocratic heroes display attitudes and tastes similar to those of an inner-city gang (according to Amanda Hobson) or a biker club (in Mary Bly's interpretation). In "Darcy's Vampiric Descendants: Austen's Perfect Romance Hero and J.R. Ward's Black Dagger Brotherhood" Sarah Frantz compares Ward's heroes to Austen's Darcy. She asserts that Ward's hyper-masculine heroes are, in fact "Darcy's ultimate heirs" because they "represent the hyperbolic extreme of Darcy's attractiveness, power, and pride. Their tears of love, acceptance, and despair break through strong taboos of masculinity and represent the inevitable physical embodiment of Darcy's verbal expression of his emotional maturation." Mary Bly takes yet another tack, observing the homosocial and even homosexual undertones of some of the relationships of the heroes with each other:

> Clearly the boundaries between the homosocial and the homoerotic have broken down by Ward's 2007 and 2008 novels, since the symbolic center of the Brotherhood series is not male-female relationships (as is commonly assumed with mass-

> market romance) but rather identification with male-male relationships. We are left with a world in which the most revered relationships are between two men, rather than between a man and a woman. Ward's emphasis on the functional phallus as the key to good and evil leads to a singular focus on the male body—and in return that admiration threatens to swamp the heteronormative drive of the frame, or male-female romance.
>
> (69)

She concludes that "The 'patriarchy' is a queer thing in Ward's novels" (70). Andreea Şerban also observes in "Romancing the Paranormal: A Case Study on J.R. Ward's *The Black Dagger Brotherhood*" that "Ward brings into the popular mainstream the still sensitive issue of homoerotic desire without taking the reader out of her comfort zone" (108), but overall dismisses the series, alleging that "it reinforces the romantic schema of heterosexual courtship and gender stereotypes, according to which women have to patiently wait to be seduced—sometimes forcibly—and show they enjoy it" (108). Already in 2009 Maria Lindgren Leavenworth had written about the contrast between the "staunchly heterosexual relationships" (443) in Ward's novels versus the slash fan fiction on the series, which showed erotic relationships between Vicious and Butch, two of the heroes in the early books of the series. In 2013, Ward published *Lover at Last*, in which the first homosexual pairing is formed, with mating ceremony (i.e., marriage) included, probably the first case of a homosexual couple as protagonists in a paranormal mainstream heterosexual series. An Goris also pointed to the traditional male and female roles in this series in comparison with Nora Roberts. While Roberts's couplings stay together throughout a series, Ward's couples fight, and occasionally break up temporarily. On the other hand, according to Goris, Ward's women, once they achieve their HEA, disappear from the narrative except in relation to their heroes, and they are rarely seen at their jobs. That observation was probably more accurate in the first few books in the series, but the male-centeredness of the series remains.

Since Nina Auerbach's *Our Vampires, Ourselves* (1995) vampires and other monsters are often read as symptomatic of the society in which they are written. The historic-political event that coincides with the rise of the paranormal is the 9/11 terrorist attacks. Mary Bly establishes parallels between the monstrous *lessers* in Ward's series (the undead and—literally—heartless humans who exist only to exterminate the "vampire race") and terrorists, an observation that can be applied widely within the genre. Jayashree Kamblé, within her wider study on the epistemology of the romance novel, *Making Meaning in Popular Romance Fiction. An Epistemology* (2014), analyzes how paranormal romance can address contemporary political problems specifically in its representation of the warrior:

> The genre has also witnessed the development of the warrior hero from official soldier to private devotee of the cause of defending freedom, particularly in the rise of the paranormal romance genre, whose heroes are engaged in epic struggles in supernatural wars.
>
> (79)

However she observes that in the case of Sherrilyn Kenyon,

> [i]nstead of being sure of who their opponents are by lumping them together under labels that never need questioning, Kenyon's heroes are constantly forced to make case-by-case assessments of alleged enemies, partly because they themselves were once seen as the "Enemy." The romance hero trait is primarily manifested in this case as the formerly wronged Other who must be careful not to condemn someone blindly.
>
> (80)

Kamblé discusses the binary impulses of the *Dark Hunter* novels embodied in Acheron, the leader of the group, since "[h]is human appeal positions him in the antiwar narrative project while his destructive skills testify to his alignment with the dogged belief in fighting shadowy enemies" (81). Within the series, she uses examples from *Kiss of the Night* (2004), in which the hero has to abandon his deep-seated hatred for the entire Apolite race (who die at 27 unless they take human souls to stay alive) and accept that only a few of them become the soul vampires he is charged to fight. The parallels with the common association of Muslims with terrorists is hard to miss. This, however, is not an isolated example. Characters in paranormal romance and urban fantasy frequently have to adapt their thinking and accept that appearances can be misleading. While Kenyon is more transparent and insistent on this point than other authors, the revision of formerly held beliefs in the good or evil nature of an entire group are constantly challenged in paranormal romance to an extent that it is difficult to explain just as a plot strategy. Deborah Mutch also points to the effect of globalization and 9/11 in "Coming Out of the Coffin: The Vampire and Transnationalism in the *Twilight* and *Sookie Stackhouse* Series." She comments on the transnational nature of the vampire identity, while at the same time emphasizing the formation of niche identities within the nation-state in both series. She concludes her comparison with:

> Auerbach's argument regarding the shared fears addressed through the literary vampire implies a known group identity, and in the face of increasing globalization it is the uncertainty of this very assumption of homogeneous identity which is the basis for the twenty-first-century vampire. As national boundaries become diminished and previously hidden identities emerge, who "we" are is problematized. A flattened vision of the racial and cultural landscape is associated, on the other hand, with racism and reactionary ideals... Criticism of such reactionary attitudes, the acknowledgement of the problems of integration and a celebration of a multicultural community are the basis of both Meyer's and Harris's work.
>
> (87–8)

Amira Jarmakani addresses the surprising relative success of the sheikh novel after 9/11 in *An Imperialist Love Story*, a subgenre that she connects to paranormal romance in the otherness of the hero. In a complex analysis she convincingly explains how the romance is an expression of desire:

> The story of how the heroine comes to desire the desert sheikh turns out to symbolize how desire functions as an engine for contemporary U.S. imperialism as manifested in the war on terror ... The sheikh-hero represents an oasis of security in a chaotic world of danger and terrorism ... Moreover, their union is meant to be symbolic of the exceptionalist technology of liberal multiculturalism, where

> ethnic and cultural differences are commodified and capitalized into spicy details that give the exceptional-universalist power its flavor.
>
> (19)

Jarmakani argues that "it is because sheikh-heroes exist in a completely different world that they have been compared to vampires, werewolves and other paranormal heroes" (10), and later on, she discusses the "monstrosity" of the sheikh. However, she acknowledges that the sheikh novel is a very small subgenre within the romance novel, and not representative of the whole. There are significant differences between paranormal and sheikh romances, the most obvious one is the sheer number of novels and approaches to characterization in paranormal romance, and also the location. While the sheikh romance takes place in the Middle East (usually in a fictional country), most paranormal romance takes place within the territory of the U.S. However, Jarmakani's framework can be extremely useful to understand the surge of the paranormal romance after 9/11.

Amanda Hobson has addressed race in paranormal romance in "Brothers under Covers: Race and the Paranormal Romance Novel." Hobson point out the scarcity of characters of color in the genre, and centers her analysis on Kerrelyn Sparks and J.R. Ward. She criticizes Sparks' *Love at Stake* (2005–14) for the negative stereotypical portrayal of Phineas, the only African American hero in the series. She also condemns Ward's *Black Dagger Brotherhood* for what she considers appropriation of African American culture by a white author, a questionable conclusion. While Hobson's main premise (the pervasive whiteness of the genre) and many of her observations are accurate, her tendency to look at race as a binary opposition between Black and white weakens her argument. She condemns Nalini Singh's *Psy-Changeling* series (2006–ongoing) because none of the major characters is identified as "African American" or "Black" but she overlooks the racial diversity present in the novels. While Singh never describes her main characters in terms of race, she describes in detail their diversity in physical features and coloring which suggest an array of ethnicities, including characters identified clearly as Black, such as Ashaya Aleine, the heroine of *Hostage to Pleasure* (2008) and her twin sister. In a more nuanced approach, Kamblé also addresses race in paranormal romance through the *Psy-Changeling* series. She notes that Singh, a New Zealander of South Asian origin born in Fiji, started her career as a romance writer with novels that were traditionally white, or with the typical staple of exotic characters such as the sheikh. However, once more established as an author, and taking advantage of what Kamblé calls the carnivalesque in paranormal romance, her characters in this series became increasingly varied in their racial background. Furthermore, according to this critic, Singh's series further destabilizes the category of whiteness through a number of interracial couples which include different permutations of extremely intellectual and controlled "psy" (a race with mental powers that has eschewed emotion) protagonists who are paired with the emotional, sexual "changelings" (shapeshifters in touch with their animal side and their emotions).[12] She also points out how the packs, as extended families, challenge Western notions of family. Although there is much more to be done, Kamblé explains how there is an evolution taking place in the genre regarding racial diversity and inclusion.

As with other romance subgenres, paranormal novels address the social tensions of the period in which they are written, and especially their effects on women. So if race is at times problematized, that is even more the case when it comes to what are often considered women-specific issues. As John Lennard states, "[u]nsurprisingly, given the strongly female authorship of the sub-genre, broadly feminist treatments of problems including rape, domestic abuse, and cultural expectations of female sexual submissiveness to male partners are also apparent" (133). One example of this approach is Erin Young's 2011 article "Flexible Heroines, Flexible Narratives: The Werewolf Romances of Kelly Armstrong and Carry Vaughn" on the heroines of Armstrong's *Women of the Otherworld* and Vaughn's Kitty Norville. Part of her argument was based on the impossibility for Kitty and the refusal of Elena to have a child. However, Elena becomes pregnant later on, and by the end of the series in 2013 she has 5-year-old twins, and she also becomes the alpha of the North American werewolves. Still, her observation of the apparent impossibility for a woman to be an urban fantasy heroine and a mother holds true in many texts, an area of inquiry that deserves further exploration.

Rape is one of the topics that gathers critics' attention when it comes to popular literature read by women. Suanna Davis's "Representation of Rape in Speculative Fiction: From the Survivor Perspective" looks at rape in Briggs, Harris, and two other authors, comparing the reactions of the characters to those of real-life victims. Kristina Deffenbacher in "Rape Myths' Twilight and Women's Paranormal Revenge in Romantic and Urban Fantasy Fiction" deplores the persistence of some problematic scenes that she perceives as rape of the heroine by the hero, but points out that those are rare in the genre. She presents numerous examples of rape-revenge narrative, and concludes that:

> These romantic urban fantasy stories contribute to a new mythology that counters some effects of the rape myths lurking in one strain of paranormal romance fiction. As a broader genre, fiction that incorporates paranormal fantasy and romantic conventions thus reveals both a vision for change and the discourses that keep in place mutually reinforcing constructions of rape, rapability, and gender.
>
> (933)

Taking a different tack, from the point of view of horror, Angela Ndalianis provides one of the best-informed overviews on paranormal, which she identifies as horror-paranormal romance:

> These fictions are about grasping and giving voice to the sensory and emotional expression of female desire. Horror-paranormal romance, in particular, turns to its heritage—classic romance, contemporary romance, gothic horror, contemporary horror—and mashes up its sources. The final result is a new form of romance fiction that explicitly explores questions of desire, eroticism, and love through the lens of horror. In doing so, paranormal romance gives voice not only to the ideal conception of romance and love (union with the soul mate) but also to its darker, more dangerous and, sometimes potentially destructive side.
>
> (85)

Ndalianis' selection of authors, Christine Feehan and L.K. Hamilton, is limited, and the authors are to a certain extent—as seen before—outliers, but she brings important issues to the forefront in a subtle and complex analysis that can be applied to a wide range of texts.

In a 2018 article, Stefan Ekman has opened another area of research, especially in regards to urban fantasy: crime stories. Utilizing three texts of urban fantasy—in one of them, *Dead Witch Walking* (2004), the first book in *The Hollows*, by Kim Harrison—he makes the connection between traditional crime and detective stories and newer urban fantasies, which apply the older tropes into the new texts, adding through them valuable social commentary. In Kim Harrison's case, she follows the tradition of the PI with a pure heart in a corrupt society, who is just trying to survive but accidentally becomes the leader of a group of friends who help her.

Lt. Col. Karalyne Lowery of the Air War College, approaches the figure of the werewolf mostly in the works of Ilona Andrews and Lora Leigh, and notes how it has been associated with the military in "The Militarized Shape-Shifter: Authorized Violence and Military Connections as an Antidote to Monstrosity" (2018). Lowery emphasizes the trust society places in the military and the justification of their actions, no matter how brutal. She concludes her work by asking:

> How does the public, which is trained to see military members acting under official orders as being heroic—no matter the intensity of the violence, no matter what kind of supernatural monster, and no matter if the violence is fictional—realistically evaluate and participate in authorizing violence?
>
> (211)

Lowery poses a question that could be applied to many contemporary fictions, but that is rarely considered when studying romance.

Conclusion

According to the Romance Writers of America statistics, "[m]ost frequent readers [of romance] are younger, with half of frequent and very frequent readers aged 34 and below," and "younger readers read more young adult, erotic, and paranormal romance and less contemporary romance than older readers," so we can anticipate that paranormal romance and urban fantasy are here to stay. Yet, as can be seen, many important areas of inquiry to understand these new genres have not been sufficiently explored if at all. Six of these seem particularly pressing.

First, more scholarship is needed on the historical context to which paranormal romance and urban fantasy appear to respond, changing as socio-political events change, and the complex and varied ways in which the fantasy worlds respond to those realities. Second, within this line of questioning, the power relations and political organization of the worlds represented, something that has been mostly overlooked, show a very disturbing tendency toward autocratic leaders, and democracy is rarely a factor; this needs to be studied. Third, the (non-sexual) violence that is pervasive in paranormal romance, the brutality of its justice, and the lack of concern for the body count of many heroes and heroines has barely raised an eyebrow, and these should also be areas of critical focus. The economic relations in those fictional words also deserve attention beyond the observation that vampires are always rich. For example, there is also an economy of magic, life, blood, and/or immortality that deserves further exploration. Regarding the couples formed in these series, there has been an overwhelming amount of attention devoted to the human heroine with the vampire hero, to the neglect of the varied couplings, heteronormative or not, that take place in these series, including the post-HEA, in Goris' terms, of the female protagonists, and maternity, especially in the case of urban fantasy heroines. More scrutiny of these would be valuable.

Finally, inquiry has scarcely begun on the corpus of paranormal romance and urban fantasy written by and/or with protagonists that belong to a minority, either in terms of ethnicity, race, gender, or sexuality (among others). For example, the fantastic elements of the paranormal acquire new meanings when a rich landowner is offering undocumented immigrants to a fae as food to keep him appeased, because nobody would miss them, as in Maria Lima's urban fantasy *Blood Lines* (2005–11); or when a protagonist who can change gender at will and is, as a woman, in a heterosexual relationship, is forced into a fixed state as a man by their family in L.A. Witt's *Static* (2011).

In short, while the combination of romance and fantasy has placed paranormal romance and urban fantasy among the most despised of genres, this combination has also allowed them to address many pressing issues of contemporary society. As those issues change (and endure), so will these genres, and they deserve sustained and substantial scholarly engagement.

Notes

1 For a humorous but accurate description of both genres and their covers see Regina TV "WTF . . . Is Paranormal Romance?"

2 It is difficult to find a single source to substantiate this claim. The first urban fantasy with strong romantic elements that became a success, judging by the number of ratings and the lists in which it is included in Goodreads, is *PsyCop* (2006–ongoing) by Jordan Castillo Price. However, there seems to have been some gay and lesbian paranormal romance in the mid 2000—the Lambda awards, which include PNR and UF in the category of Horror, Fantasy and SF, not in romance, began to feature a scattering M/M paranormal romances written by women among their finalists in 2006, and the number expands rapidly around 2009. This is also the year that Bold Strokes Books began to publish paranormal romance, adding several new books every year after that. Len Barot, the publisher of Bold Strokes Books, commenced her paranormal *Midnight Hunters* series in 2010, under the pen name L.L. Raand, and most of the internet articles providing lists or reading suggestions of gay and lesbian paranormal romance date from the early 2010s as well, with 2013 being the most prolific year in terms of both books published and internet articles.

3 It is interesting how even the author herself admits her debt to paranormal romance but considers her work as "*Harry Potter* for adults," refusing the acknowledge the undeniable commonalities with PNR and UF, as can be seen in her interview with Peter Haldeman for the *New York Times* when the TV series based on the trilogy went on air, titled precisely "All Souls Trilogy: Harry Potter for Grown-Ups?" www.nytimes.com/2019/01/17/books/deborah-harkness-discovery-of-witches-all-souls-trilogy.html?login=smartlock&auth=login-smartlock

4 Sweet Rocket. "The End of a Very Gothic Week—What Happened to the Gothic Revival?" April 26, 2012 https://sweetrocket.wordpress.com/tag/silhouette-dreamscapes/ Retrieved December 13, 2016. After Dreamscapes, Harlequin published for a few years LUNA, and currently Nocturne. The category paranormal romance does not seem to enjoy the success of the single-title novels. The Super-Walmart in my Upper Midwest town only started to carry Harlequin Nocturne in 2018, and not regularly, although they always have the latest installments of the most popular paranormal romance series.

5 Her relationships tend to be more traditional, especially after the couples are formed, and, in Crawford's words, "for all their obvious earnestness, the repetitive and stylistic naivety of her novels compares poorly to" other paranormal romance and urban fantasy authors (145).

6 It is almost impossible to find reliable information on book sales. The RWA used to include the percentage of romance readers who read a specific subgenre. In 2014, among romance readers paranormal romance was read by 19 per cent of print readers and 30 per cent of ebook readers. The current statistics in the site do not include this information, although they point out that younger readers tend to read more paranormal romance. Numbers for urban fantasy are even more elusive, since the genre is sold under different categories.

7 See Chapter 7 on Young Adult romance for more on the reactions to *Twilight*.

8 Gregory Kirschling, "Interview with Vampire Writer Stephenie Meyer." *Entertainment Weekly* July 5, 2008, https://ew.com/article/2008/07/05/interview-vampire-writer-stephenie-meyer/. Retrieved January 19, 2019

9 Merry Gentry, the heroine of another urban fantasy series by Hamilton (2000–ongoing) does become a mother of triplets, all by different fathers, and she is not in an exclusive relationship. For an analysis of sexuality in this series see: Lennard, John. "Of Sex and Faerie: Meredith Gentry's Improbable Code of Orgasm and Other Paranormal Romance" In *Of Sex and Faerie: Further Essays on Genre Fiction*. To the contrary, in the new urban fantasies the relationship model has a lot more in common with another successful and ongoing series that started in the 1990s, the futuristic/science fiction *In Death* series by Nora Roberts/J.D. Robb (1995–ongoing). Her protagonist, Eve, met her partner in the first novel, and their relationship is an integral part of series since then (43-novel-long and counting). Eve is still the main character and the story is consistently narrated from her exclusive point of view. The mysteries she encounters as a police detective are hers to solve, even if sometimes her husband plays a supportive role. While these novels depict an unstable, menacing, and violent society, they compensate with strong, stable, emotional ties as those in Robb/Robert's series. First of all through coupledom, but also through the social networks that are built throughout the series by the accumulation of interconnected couples and/or the friendship and loyalty ties developed by the heroine. The instability of the world is balanced by the stability of the community created by family and friendship.

10 Although outside of the purview of this chapter, the success of the dystopian worlds of The Hunger Games (2008–10) and Divergent (2011–13) young adult trilogies—among many others—confirms the tendency.

11 This trend was already predicted by Sarah Wendell and Candy Tan in *Beyond Heaving Bosoms* (2009).

12 Kamblé draws on Richard Dyer's argument that whiteness has been constructed as a group of traits, such as intellectual prowess and control over sexual desire, which allegedly are absent in people of color and present more often in men than women.

Works cited

Primary sources

When a series is mentioned, only the first title in the series is included in the bibliography, followed by the title of the series and dates of publication of the series.

Andrews, Ilona. *Magic Bites*. Berkley, 2007. *Kate Daniels* (2007–2018).

Armstrong, Kelley. *Bitten*. Random House Canada, 2001. *Women of the Otherworld* (2001–2012).

Banks, L.A. *Minion*. St. Martin Press, 2003. *Vampire Huntress Legend* (2003–2009).

Bardsley, Michele. *I'm the Vampire, That's Why*. Signet, 2006. *Broken Heart* (2006–2016).

Bartlett, Gerry. *Real Vampires Have Curves*. Berkley, 2007. *Glory St. Claire* (2007–2016).

Bayar, Louis. *The School of Night*. Henry Holt and Co., 2011.

Black, Holly. *Tithe. A Modern Faerie Tale*. Simon and Schuster, 2002. *Modern Faerie Tales* (2002–2007).

Briggs, Patricia. *Moon Called*. Ace Books, 2006. *Mercy Thompson* (ongoing).

———. *River Marked*. Orbit, 2011. *Mercy Thompson*.

Brook, Meljean. *The Iron Duke*. Berkley, 2010. *Iron Seas* (2010–2014).

Bull, Emma. *War for the Oaks*. Tom Doherty Associates Inc., 1986.

Butcher, Jim. *Storm Front*. Penguin ROC, 2000. *The Dresden Files* (ongoing).

Caine, Rachel. *Glass Houses*. NAL Jam, 2006. *The Morganville Vampires* (2006–2013).
Cast, PC and Kristin Cast. *Marked*. St. Martin's, 2007. *House of Night* (2007–2014).
Clare, Cassandra. *City of Bones*. Margaret K. McElderry Books, 2007. *Mortal Instruments* (2007–2014).
Cole, Kresley. *A Hunger Like No Other*. Pocket Star Books, 2006. *Immortals After Dark* (ongoing).
Cruz, Melissa de la. *Blue Bloods*. Hyperion, 2006. *Blue Bloods* (2006–2013).
Davidson, MaryJanice. *Unwed and Undead*. Berkley, 2004. *Undead* (2004–2016).
Feehan, Christine. *Dark Prince*. Love Spell, 1999. *Carpathians* (ongoing).
Frost, Jeaniene. *Shadow Game*. Berkley, 2003. Ghost *Walkers* (ongoing).
———. *Halfway to the Grave*. Avon, 2007. *Night Huntress* (2007-14).
———. *First Drop of Crimson*. Avon, 2010.
———. *Eternal Kiss of Darkness*. Avon, 2010.
Gaiman, Neil. *Neverwhere*. William Morrow, 1996.
Galenorn, Yasmine. *Witchling*. Berkley, 2006. *Otherworld/Sisters of the Moon* (ongoing).
Griffith, Clay, and Susan Griffith. *The Greyfriar*. Pyr, 2010. Vampire *Empire* (2010–2012).
Hamilton, Laurell K. *Guilty Pleasures*. New English Library, 1993. *Anita Blake, Vampire Hunter* (ongoing).
———. *A Kiss of Shadows*. Del Rey, 2000. *Merry Gentry* (2000–2014).
Harkness, Deborah. *A Discovery of Witches*. Viking Penguin, 2011. *All Souls Trilogy* (2011–2014).
———. *Shadow of Night*. Viking Adult, 2012. *All Souls Trilogy*.
———. *Time's Convert*. Headline, 2018.
Harrison, Kim. *Dead Witch Walking*. Harper Voyager, 2004. *The Hollows* (2004–2014).
Harris, Charlaine. *Dead Until Dark*. Ace Books, 2001. *Sookie Stackhouse/Southern Vampires Mysteries* (2001–2013).
Herter, Lori. *Obsession*. Berkley, 1991. *De Morrisey* (1991–1992).
Hill, Joey. *The Vampire Queen's Servant*. Berkley, 2007. *Vampire Queen* (ongoing).
Huff, Tanya. *Blood Price*. DAW Books, 1991. *Blood Books* or *Vicki Nelson* (1991–1997).
Kenyon, Sherrilyn. *Night Pleasures*. St. Martin's Press, 2002. *Dark-Hunter* (ongoing).
———. *Fantasy Lover*. St. Martin's Press, 2002.
Klause, Annette Curtis. *The Silver Kiss*. Delacorte, 1990.
Lima, Maria. *Matters of the Blood*. Quiet Storm Books, 2005. *Blood Lines*(2005–2011).
Mead, Richelle. *Vampire Academy*. Razorbill, 2007. *Vampire Academy* (2007–2010).
Meyer, Stephenie. *Twilight*. Little, Brown and Company, 2005. *Twilight Saga* (2005–2008).
Miller, Linda Lael. *Forever and the Night*. Berkley, 1993. *Vampire* (1993–1996).
Moning, Karen Marie. *Darkfever*. Delacorte Press, 2006. *Fever* (ongoing).
Morgenstern, Erin. *The Night Circus*. Doubleday, 2011.
Noel, Alyson. *Evermore*. Griffin, 2009. *The Immortals* (2009–2011).
Rardin, Jennifer. *Once Bitten Twice Shy*. Orbit, 2007. *Jaz Parks* (2007–2011).
Rice, Anne. *The Mummy or Ramses the Damned*. Turtleback Books, 1989.
Sands, Lynsay. *Single White Vampire*. Dorchester Publishing, 2003. Argeneau Vampires (ongoing).
Shayne, Maggie. *Twilight Phantasies*. Silhouette Books, 1993. *Wings in the Night* (1993–2011).
Singh, Nalini. *Slave to Sensation*. Berkley Sensation, 2006. *Psy-Changeling* (ongoing).
———. *Angels' Blood*. Berkeley Sensation, 2009. Guild Hunter (ongoing).
Smith, L.J. *The Awakening*. Harper Collins, 1991. *Vampire Diaries*.
Sparks, Kerrelyn. *How to Marry a Millionaire Vampire*. Avon, 2005. *Love at Stake* (2005–2014).
Vaughn, Carrie. *Kitty and the Midnight Hour*. Grand Central, 2005. *Kitty Norville* (2005–2015).
Wall, Alan. *The School of Night*. Martin Secker & Warburg Ltd, 2001.
Ward, J.R. *Dark Lover*. Penguin, 2005. *Black Dagger Brotherhood* (ongoing).
Warren, Christine. *One Bite with a Stranger*. St. Martin's Press, 2008. Originally Published as *Fantasy Fix*. Ellora's Cave, 2003. *The Others* (2003–2010).
Whedon, Joss. *Buffy the Vampire Slayer*. WB, Mutant Enemy Productions. 1997–2003.
Witt, L.A. *Static*. Amber Quill Press, 2011.

Secondary sources

Auerbach, Nina. *Our Vampires, Ourselves*. University of Chicago Press, 1995.
Bly, Mary. "On Popular Romance, J. R. Ward, and the Limits of Genre Study." *New Approaches to Popular Romance Fiction: Critical Essays*, edited by Sarah S. G. Frantz and Eric M. Selinger, McFarland, 2012, pp. 60–72.
Bond, Gwenda. "When Love Is Strange." *Publishers Weekly*, vol. 256, no. 21, May 26, 2009, p. 26.
Booth, Sandra. "Paradox in Popular Romances of the 1990s: The Paranormal versus Feminist Humor." *Paradoxa: Studies in World Literary Genres*, vol. 3, no. 1–2, 1997, pp. 94–106.
Bouricius, Ann. *The Romance Reader's Advisory. The Library's Guide to Love in the Stacks*. American Library Association, 2000.
Buccola, Regina. "The School of (The) Night Circus: Performing Shakespeare Arcana in Novel Forms." *Shakespeare and Millennial Fiction*, edited by Andrew James Hartley, Cambridge University Press, 2018, pp. 64–80.
Calhoun-French, Diane M. "Time-Travel and Related Phenomena in Contemporary Popular Romance Fiction." *Romantic Conventions*, edited by Anne K. Kaler and Rosemary E. Johnson-Kurek, Popular, 1999, pp. 100–112.
Carter, Margaret L. "The Vampire." *Icons of Horror and the Supernatural*, edited by S. T. Joshi, Greenwood Publishing Group, 2006, pp. 619–52.
Clute, John and Grant, John. *The Encyclopedia of Fantasy*. St Martin's Press, 1997.
Crawford, Joseph. *The Twilight of the Gothic?: Vampire Fiction and the Rise of the Paranormal Romance*. University of Wales Press, 2014.
Crusie, Jennifer. "Dating Death: Essay: Love and Sex in Buffy the Vampire Slayer." Jennie Crusie.com, http://jennycrusie.com/excerpts/dating-death-love-and-sex-in-buffy-the-vampire-slayer/ Retrieved December 30, 2018.
Davis, Suanna. "Representations of Rape in Speculative Fiction: From the Survivor's Perspective." *FEMSPEC: An Interdisciplinary Feminist Journal Dedicated to Critical and Creative Work in the Realms of Science Fiction, Fantasy, Magical Realism, Surrealism, Myth, Folklore, and Other Supernatural Genres*, vol. 13, no. 2, 2013, pp. 9–23.
Deffenbacher, Kristina. "Rape Myths' Twilight and Women's Paranormal Revenge in Romantic and Urban Fantasy Fiction." *Journal of Popular Culture*, vol. 47, no. 5, 2014, pp. 923–936.
Dunn, George A. and Rebecca Housel Eds. *True Blood and Philosophy: We Wanna Think Bad Things with You*. Blackwell Philosophy and Pop Culture series #19. Wiley, 2010.
Ekman, Stefan. "Crime Stories and Urban Fantasy." *Clues: A Journal of Detection*, vol. 35, no. 2, 2017, pp. 48–57.
Faludi, Susan. *The Terror Dream. Fear and Fantasy in Post-9/11 America*. Henry Holt and Company, 2007.
Frantz, Sarah S. G. "Darcy's Vampiric Descendants: Austen's Perfect Romance Hero and J. R. Ward's Black Dagger Brotherhood." *Persuasions: The Jane Austen Journal On-Line*, vol. 30, no. 1, 2009. http://www.jasna.org/persuasions/on-line/vol30no1/frantz.html (Retrieved February 2, 2020).
Gabaldon, Diana. "Paranormal Romance: Time Travel, Vampires, and Everything Beyond." *Writing Romances. A Handbook by the Romance Writers of America*, edited by Rita Gallagher and Rita Clay Estrada, Writer's Digest Books, 1997. (pp. 143–150).
Goris, An. "Happily Ever After… And After: Serialization and the Popular Romance Novel." *Americana: The Journal of American Popular Culture (1900–present)*, vol. 12, no. 1, 2013. http://www.americanpopularculture.com/journal/articles/spring_2013/goris.htm (Retrieved February 2, 2020).
Guran, Paula Ed. *Best New Paranormal Romance*. Wildside Press, 2006.

Haldeman, Peter. "*All Souls Trilogy*: *Harry Potter* for Grown-Ups?" *New York Times*. January 17, 2019. https://www.nytimes.com/2019/01/17/books/deborah-harkness-discovery-of-witches-all-souls-trilogy.html?login=smartlock&auth=login-smartlock (Retrieved April 7, 2019).

Heinecken, Dawn. "Changing Ideologies in Romance Fiction." *Romantic Conventions*, edited by Anne K. Kaler and Rosemary E. Johnson-Kurek, Popular, 1999, pp. 149–172.

Hobson, Amanda. "Brothers under Covers: Race and the Paranormal Romance Novel." *Race in the Vampire Narrative*. edited by U. Melissa Anyiwo, Sense Publishers, 2015, pp. 21–43.

Irvine, Alexander C. "Urban Fantasy." *The Cambridge Companion to Fantasy Literature*, edited by Edward James and Farah Mendlesohn, Cambridge University Press, 2012, pp. 200–213.

Jarmakani, Amira. *An Imperialist Love Story. Desert Romances and the War on Terror*. New York University Press, 2015.

Kamblé, Jayashree. *Making Meaning in Popular Romance Fiction: An Epistemology*. Palgrave, 2014.

Kaveney, Roz. "Dark Fantasy and Paranormal Romance." *The Cambridge Companion to Fantasy Literature*. Edited by Edward James and Farah Mendlesohn. Cambridge University Press, 2012, pp. 214–223

Lennard, John. "Of Sex and Faerie: Meredith Gentry's Improbable Code of Orgasm and Other Paranormal Romance." *Of Sex and Faerie: Further Essays on Genre Fiction*. Humanities E-books (HEB), 2010.

Leavenworth, Maria Lindgren. "Lover Revamped: Sexualities and Romance in the Black Dagger Brotherhood and Slash Fan Fiction." *Extrapolation: A Journal of Science Fiction and Fantasy*, vol. 50, no. 3, 2009, pp. 442–462.

Litte, Jane. "Romance Books Comprise 21% of the $631 Billion Book Industry." *Dear Author*. November 14, 2007. http://dearauthor.com/features/industry-news/romance-books-comprise-21-of-the-631b-book-industry/. (Retrieved December 31, 2016).

Lowery, Karalyne. "The Militarized Shapeshifter: Authorized Violence and Military Connections as an Antidote to Monstrosity." *University of Toronto Quarterly*, vol. 87, no. 1, 2018, pp. 196–213.

Mathews, Patricia O'Brian. *Fang-tastic Fiction. Twenty-First Century Paranormal Reads*. American Library Association, 2011.

MacLean, Sarah and Jen Prokop. "Fated Mates." *Apple Podcast*. https://itunes.apple.com/us/podcast/fated-mates/id1440190146?mt=2 (Retrieved April 7, 2019).

McLennon, Leigh M. "Defining Urban Fantasy and Paranormal Romance: Crossing Boundaries of Genre, Media, Self and Other in New Supernatural Worlds." *Refractory: A Journal of Entertainment Media*, vol. 23, 2014, p. 2104.

Mutch, Deborah "Coming Out of the Coffin: The Vampire and Transnationalism in the *Twilight* and *Sookie Stackhouse* Series." *Critical Survey* vol. 23, no. 2, 2011, pp. 75–90.

Nakagawa, Chiho. "Safe Sex with Defanged Vampires: New Vampire Heroes in Twilight and the Southern Vampire Mysteries." *Journal of Popular Romance Studies*, vol. 2, no. 1, 2011. https://www.jprstudies.org/2011/10/%e2%80%9csafe-sex-with-defanged-vampires-new-vampire-heroes-in-twilight-and-the-southern-vampire-mysteries%e2%80%9d-by-chiho-nakagawa/. (Retrieved May 17, 2020).

Ndalianis, Angela. *The Horror Sensorium. Media and the Senses*. McFarland, 2012.

Radway, Janice. *Reading the Romance: Women, Patriarchy, and Popular Literature*. University of North Carolina Press, 1984.

Ramsdell, Kristin. "The Year in Romance Fiction." *What Do I Read Next? A Reader's Guide to Current Genre Fiction*. Gale Research Inc., 1994, pp. 77–162.

———. "The Year in Romance Fiction." *What Do I Read Next? A Reader's Guide to Current Genre Fiction*. Gale Research Inc., 1997, pp. 85–172.

———. *Romance Fiction. A Guide to the Genre*. First edition. Libraries Unlimited, 1999.

———. "Romance Fiction in Review." *What Do I Read Next? A Reader's Guide to Current Genre Fiction*. Thomson Gale, 2005, pp. 83–158.

———. "Romance Fiction in Review." *What Do I Read Next? A Reader's Guide to Current Genre Fiction*. Thomson Gale, 2006, pp. 79–151.

———. *Romance Fiction. A Guide to the Genre*. Second edition. Libraries Unlimited, 2012.

———. "Romance Fiction in Review." *What Do I Read Next? A Reader's Guide to Current Genre Fiction*. Gale, Cengage Learning, 2014, pp. 343–430.

Regina TV "WTF... Is Paranormal Romance?" Published February 23, 2015 https://gaming.youtube.com/watch?v=8Nn1Gw0EuiI&list=PLvUl0D9hfyGTeMRZp6X-pkRE-fnHM9mEX. Retrieved January 2, 2017.

Regis, Pamela. *A Natural History of the Romance Novel*. University of Pennsylvania Press, 2007.

Reid, Lindsay Ann. "The Spectre of the School of Night: Former Scholarly Fictions and the Stuff of Academic Fiction." *Early Modern Literary Studies: A Journal of Sixteenth- and Seventeenth-Century English Literature*, vol. 23, 2014, p. 31.

Romance Writers of America. "About the Romance Genre." https://www.rwa.org/Online/Romance_Genre/About_Romance_Genre.aspx#Romance_Reader. Retrieved January 20, 2019.

Șerban, Andreea. "Romancing the Paranormal: A Case Study on J. R. Ward's The Black Dagger Brotherhood." *Romance: The History of a Genre*, edited by Dana Percec, Cambridge Scholars, 2012, pp. 89–110.

Sweet Rocket. "The End of a Very Gothic Week – What Happened to the Gothic Revival?" April 26, 2012 https://sweetrocket.wordpress.com/tag/silhouette-dreamscapes/. Retrieved December 13, 2016.

Szanter, Ashley. "Deborah Harkness's All Souls Trilogy, Supernatural Heredity, and 'Creature' Genetics." *The Supernatural Revamped: From Timeworn Legends to Twenty-First-Century Chic*, edited by Barbara Brodman and James E. Doan, Fairleigh Dickinson UP, 2016, pp. 115–130.

Tobin-McClain, Lee. "Paranormal Romance: Secrets of the Female Fantastic." *Journal of the Fantastic in the Arts*, vol. 11, no. 3 [43], 2000, pp. 294–306.

Ward, J.R. "J.R. Ward's Blog: *Blood Kiss*, BDB Legacy #1" in *Goodreads*. December 1, 2015. https://www.goodreads.com/author/show/20248.J_R_Ward/blog Retrieved January 19, 2019. http://www.jrward.com/meet-the-warden/

Wendell, Sarah and Candy Tan. *Beyond Heaving Bosoms. The Smart Bitches Guide to Romance Novels*. Touchstone, 2009.

Young, Erin S. "Flexible Heroines, Flexible Narratives: The Werewolf Romances of Kelley Armstrong and Carrie Vaughn." *Extrapolation: A Journal of Science Fiction and Fantasy*, vol. 52, no. 2, 2011, pp. 204–226.

7 Young adult romance

Amanda K. Allen

Unlike other types of popular romance, what defines young adult (YA) romance is its audience. This statement is obvious, but it also masks a complicated set of conventions and assumptions that reflect changing ideologies concerning our collective notion of "teenagers," and what constitutes "appropriate" reading material for them. Whether one examines YA romance as a subgenre of adult popular romance, or as a sub-genre of young adult fiction, most critics recognize the power imbalance between adult producer/distributor (author, editor, librarian, teacher, parent, etc.) and reader (assumed young person), which is inherent to these texts. In some ways, then, scholarship on YA literature—of any genre—is always about power, and analyses of YA romance are no exception.

The following is an overview of scholarship on YA romance from the 1940s to now. I have organized this overview chronologically rather than thematically because the changing nature of our socially-constructed concepts of "adolescence" and the "teenager" directly impact how scholars examine the romance literature intended for or read by young people. The scholarship itself has been dominated by three periods, reflecting the rise of romance YA during each period. Thus, the earliest scholarship included in this overview comes from the 1940s through the 1960s, when texts known as "junior novels" dominated the field. Written by authors such as Maureen Daly, Betty Cavanna, Anne Emery, Rosamond du Jardin, Mary Stolz, and Amelia Walden, the "junior novels" were stories of first romance set primarily within the American high school milieu. The second period arose with the establishment of teen romance series lines in the 1980s, particularly Scholastic's *Wildfire*, Dell's *Young Love*, Simon & Schuster's *First Love*, Bantam's *Sweet Dreams*, and, of course, Random House's *Sweet Valley High*. Finally, the third period of scholarship stems from 2000 to now, and demonstrates the most breadth in examining histories of teen romance, standalone or trilogy contemporary young adult literature, the rise of supernatural teen romance such as *Twilight*, queer YA romance, and non-traditional forms of YA romance (including fan fiction, graphic novels, and manga).

The field of young adult literature

The history of scholarship of YA romance is intertwined with the complexities and contradictions that form the field of young adult literature itself. It is therefore important to take a little space at the outset to provide a brief overview of three key aspects that complicate the scholarship of this literature. These aspects are as follows: a) YA literature is both indefinable and paradoxically recognized by everyone; b) both YA texts and scholarship about those texts predate the codification of the field itself; and c) the field is not cohesive, but is split by the differing methodologies and agendas of the three dominant disciplines that form it.

The first aspect (YA literature is both indefinable and paradoxically recognized by everyone) gestures to the fundamental question at the heart of the broader field of children's literature:[1] What *is* children's literature? As Roger Sale puts it, "everyone knows what children's literature is until asked to define it" (1). Most scholars define it as texts *read by* young people (a definition that, of course, could include *Charlotte's Web*, math textbooks, and *Hamlet*); texts *written for* young people (a definition that relies on social constructs of "the child" and "the adolescent" that are historically, culturally, and socioeconomically determined); texts *published for* young people (a definition based on publisher-designated lists that, as Marah Gubar notes, "would exclude titles that appeared before eighteenth-century booksellers such as John Newbery set up shop, including Aesopica, chapbooks, and conduct books" [209]); and texts *distributed to* young people: a definition that focuses on the intermediaries of the texts—parents, teachers, librarians, etc.—whose roles inevitably position them in a place of power over young people, thereby speaking to Jacqueline Rose's famous assertion that the child of children's literature is the construct of *adult* needs and desires (1–11).[2] As a literature defined around a dominated audience, then, young adult literature—and this includes YA romance—is, like children's literature, what Jack Zipes calls "imaginary;" that is, it refers to "what specific groups composed largely of adults construct as their referential system ... There never has been a literature conceived by children for children, a literature that belongs to children, and there never will be" (40).[3]

The problem of defining (or not defining) YA literature impacts scholarship of YA romance for the simple reason that it creates difficulty in determining what encompasses the field. *Sweet Valley High* might be easily recognized as YA romance, but what of Richardson's *Pamela*? Pamela Regis refers to it as the first romance novel, and particularly the first romance novel printed in the United States, yet Tim McLoughlin's historical examination of the text situates it as YA literature. Thus, while Regis suggests that *Pamela* "[marks] the beginning of a history of American romance publication unbroken to this day" (25), I would assume that she is hailing it as specifically American *adult* romance. As McLoughlin points out, however, *Pamela* "had close ties with a projected conduct-book, [Richardson's] *Familiar Letters* (1741) written to 'instruct handsome Girls, who were obliged to go out to Service ... how to avoid the Snares that might be laid against their Virtue'" (93), and the text therefore functions as Richardson's realization that the moral purpose of the conduct-book "might be more pleasantly and extensively served by the novel" (93). The text was both aimed at and read by young women; might it be that *Pamela* is not only the first romance novel, but also the first young adult novel, *and* the first young adult romance? This confusing history points to an important question: how does one provide an overview of the scholarship of a field when the critics writing this scholarship are unable, themselves, to define it?

Most scholars follow what Marah Gubar describes as "cheerfully [carrying] on with their scholarship on specific texts, types, and eras of children's literature as though the lack of an overarching definition constituted no real impediment to their work" (210). With a few notable exceptions, the majority of criticism on YA romance simply assumes that readers recognize their texts as representative of YA literature and, within that, as popular romance. Indeed, perhaps they are right to do so; as Gubar notes, "we should abandon such activity [of defining the field], because insisting that children's literature is a genre characterized by recurrent traits is damaging to the field, obscuring rather than advancing our knowledge of this richly heterogeneous group of texts" (210).

Gubar's point leads to the second aspect that complicates scholarship of children's and YA literature: both YA texts and scholarship about them predate the codification of the field itself. A large majority of academic texts—and textbooks, in particular—suggest "real" YA emerges around 1967 with the publication of S. E. Hinton's *The Outsiders* and the rise of the "New Realism."[4] Both the academy and librarianship shifted during this time, slowly recognizing the emergence of a new literature. It is not a coincidence, for example, that the American Library Association established its Young Adult Services Division in 1966.[5] The problem with this shift, however, is that it has led many critics to ignore YA literature—particularly YA romances—*and* the scholarship that predates the late 1960s. This neglect, in turn, demonstrates Gubar's point: once the field is codified around a specific set of texts/time periods, it obscures our knowledge of outsider texts, of the maligned, of the texts that do not fit neatly into a definition. This outsider space, moreover, is where both twentieth-century YA romance and its scholarship starts: with the junior novels of the 1940s through 1960s.[6]

The final aspect that complicates the field is perhaps the most important to understand when reading the scholarship: the field of YA literature (and children's literature, more generally) is not cohesive, but is split by the differing methodologies and agendas of the three dominant disciplines that form it. These disciplines are English, Education, and Library Science. Although they overlap, their disciplinary boundaries often lead to scholarly isolation. Thus, as Shelby A. Wolf, Karen Coats, Patricia Enciso, and Christine A. Jenkins—critics representing each of the disciplines—collectively explain,

> Scholars in English and literature tend toward a text-oriented approach that historically excluded the reader from view. Scholars in Education focus on the reader, but may well ignore the insights to be gained from the text being read. And scholars in Library and Information Science are often between intellectual worldviews of either end of the text-reader continuum, because their professional work is located precisely in the intersection between texts and young readers. (xi)

The three main periods of scholarship similarly reflect which disciplines tend to be more interested in young adult romance at a given time. Thus, the first period of scholarship, from the 1940s to the 1960s, is situated heavily within Education and Library Science methodologies. In contrast, the latest period, from 2005-onward, has been driven predominantly by textual analysis coming from English. The key aspect to remember is that regardless of which discipline may seem to dominate scholarship of YA romance in a given moment, the field is always a combination of the three disciplines.

First period of scholarship: 1940s–60s

The first period of scholarship accompanied the rise of "junior novels," defined by Arthur Stephenson Dunning in 1959 as "an extended piece of prose fiction written for adolescents which has known adolescent activities or interests as central elements of the plot. It pretends to treat life truthfully" (61).[7] The junior novel, like YA literature now, was an umbrella term for all texts published and marketed toward teenagers. Within this umbrella, however, romance novels quickly became the dominant genre, recounting the dating woes and social successes of pretty, white, middle-class American girls. In essence, although the junior novel incorporated many genres and audiences, it was most often known as a romance novel intended for a teen girl readership.

What is most apparent within scholarship of this era is the space scholars provide to describing characteristics of junior novels. Scholarship in later periods assumes that the reader is already familiar with YA romance. In this earlier period, however, scholars list characteristics in an effort to separate the junior novel from other literature. Texts that pay particular attention to the conventions of the junior novel include Dwight L. Burton's *Literature Study in the High Schools* (1959), Arthur Stephenson Dunning's unpublished dissertation, "A Definition of the Role of the Junior Novel Based on Analyses of Thirty Selected Novels" (1959), and Cecile Magaliff's *The Junior Novel* (1964).

Dunning's unpublished dissertation was one of the most-quoted sources of scholarship on junior novels. In particular, it outlines key characteristics of the texts: "most junior novels reflect the mores and the living of the upper-middle class. Intended as they are for younger adolescents, the books seldom contain either profanity or allusions to any sexual activity other than kissing" (64). Similarly, Dwight Burton, perhaps the best-known critic of junior novels (and Dunning's dissertation director) methodically articulates lists of characteristics within his influential *Literature Study in the High Schools* (1959):

> the dividing line between the junior and adult novel may be tenuous. The junior novel is not merely "easier" or less mature than the adult novel, although in the main it is shorter and easier to read than its adult counterpart. Its uniqueness, for better or worse, however, is born of some rather rigid conventions of form and content.
>
> (61–2)

These conventions include taboos regarding appropriate content: "the 'seamy' side of life is generally avoided; erotic drives are ignored; smoking and drinking are seldom alluded to (adolescents, of course, never drink in the books); swearing and bad grammar are avoided" (62). The junior novel is inherently didactic, which Burton recognizes is "partly because its sale depends largely on the favorable judgments of teachers and librarians who are much interested in the power of fiction to 'teach' and to dramatize values" (63). Still, for all of its taboos and didacticism, Burton carefully acknowledges "the junior novel is realistic, pointing toward adjustment" (63).

In his focus on adjustment rather than romance, Burton uses the heading, "Literature that treats personal problems" to group his examination of "representative junior novelists." This thematic grouping gestures to the dominant thrust of scholarship during the first period. At the outset of his analysis, he articulates three dimensions that he thinks define a full program of literary study for the teen reader:

> the developmental dimension, which concerns the role of literature in providing personal delight and insight into human experience; the humanistic dimension, which concerns the role of literature in bringing youth into contact with a cultural tradition; and the dimension of form, which concerns the understanding of genres and development of skill in reading them.
>
> (3)

The first and third dimensions became the prevailing methods through which most scholars analyzed junior novels during the first period: through socialization, or through "bridge" texts. The second dimension—bringing youth into contact with a cultural tradition—became the dominant site for criticism *against* junior novels.

If it sounds as if scholarship fell within a binary of "the junior novels are good/the junior novels are bad," that characterization is intentional. Margaret A. Edwards, then head of young adult services at the Enoch Pratt Free Library (and a great proponent of junior novels) noted that many critics take "a dim view of this field" (463), asking "on what grounds can we defend it?" (463). Her "oppositional" reasoning is the following:

> (1) to teach the apathetic the love of reading; (2) to satisfy some of the adolescent's emotional and psychological needs; (3) to throw light on the problems of adolescence; (4) to explore the teen-ager's relationship to his community; (5) to lead to adult reading.
>
> (174)

These reasons are very similar to the dimensions suggested by Burton,[8] and both focus on the junior novels' ability to help girls socialize into their gender roles and societies. Richard Sanford Alm provided the context for that focus, combining bibliotherapy—that is, therapy through reading—with psychologist R.J. Havighurst's theory of the developmental task.[9] Ultimately, however, it may be Cecille Magaliff who best summarizes first-period scholars' arguments concerning junior novel use: "The adolescent, basically insecure, inexperienced but observant, searching for answers when unsure of the questions, can and does use books to get experience vicariously, since society says it cannot be had firsthand. Thus, the junior novel" (Magaliff 6).

While helping girls to socialize was one use of junior novels, the other was as a "steppingstone" to "adult" literature. Emma L. Patterson, a librarian who provides the first historical overview of junior novels in "The Junior Novels and How They Grew" (1956), outlines the concept of the texts as a bridge:

> the modern adult novel assumes on the part of the reader a sophistication, a maturity, and a background of experience that the average adolescent does not have. Indiscriminate reading in this field can give him a warped and unhealthy concept of life. Hence the junior novel was introduced to take the place, in some degree, of the adult novel.
>
> (56)

To critics like Patterson, junior novels were transitional texts leading to more sophisticated literature. Margaret Edwards similarly noted in 1957 that when girls read the junior novels, "they also develop a love of genuine reading which remains long after the girl outgrows this interest in stories of first love" (338). The telling aspect of Edwards's statement is the assertion that girls' love of the romance plot itself is temporary—in addition to the temporariness of YA literature—with the added implication that girls will move on to non-romance literature as they mature as readers.

Although she was on the "pro" side of the junior novel debate, Edwards's assertion ties directly into the arguments of junior novel detractors, whose allegations against the texts focused on their status as bad, lowbrow, and ultimately unrealistic literature. Richard Alm equates this lack of realism with a lack of literary quality, noting

> most novelists present a sugar-puff story of what adolescents should do and should believe rather than what adolescents may or will do and believe ... Their stories are superficial, often distorted, sometimes completely false representations of adolescence. Instead of art, they produce artifice.
>
> ("Glitter" 317)[10]

Frank G. Jennings (1956), one of the more expressive detractors, similarly attacks the junior novel romances for their lack of realism, observing, "with the treasure house of our literary heritage ... we deal up confections of the No-Cal stamp" (530). Regarding sex, he states:

> Sex never rears its curly head in these antiseptic volumes. Body chemistry is suspended, and personality friction is lubricated out of existence with the sweet syrup of ersatz "teen-talk" of dates and dances ... And all of this happens only to the clean-limbed, the well-bred, the comfortably-house-and-clothed middle class miss and boyfriend.
>
> (530)

Jennings's frustration is particularly interesting because it is aimed at scholars for their *lack* of criticism:

> if we respect the child as much as we claim to ... then we as teachers should assume a far more active role than we have as critics of contemporary writing for children. The need for a creative, constructive criticism is nowhere so apparent as in the field of books for the teen-ager.
>
> (528)

In his criticism of the scholarship, Jennings was ultimately correct: although first-period critics generated a plethora of scholarship, much of it functioned at the level of "good for readers/bad for readers," refusing to acknowledge that not all readers read in the same way, or for the same reasons.[11] A similar problem would plague second-period criticism. Still, I do not want to deride first-period scholarship; it was, after all, attempting to define a new area of literature before the field itself had become codified and structured.

Second period of scholarship: 1980s and 1990s

"Dangerous" texts

While the second period continued to theorize and examine the impact of romance novels on young readers, its tone changed drastically. Gone was the "good for readers/bad for readers" binary; replacing it was an almost universal disparagement of 1980s teen romance. In particular, the vilification focused on the dangers that the texts posed to female readers. While first-period scholarship often focused on positive aspects, including the texts' role in socializing girls, the second period viewed this same internalization of norms as dangerous. Feminism had obviously (and, perhaps, finally) seeped into scholarship on YA romance, and many critics now used a feminist lens to make apparent the damaging repetition of patriarchal power and gender norms within the texts.

In 1981, the *Interracial Books for Children Bulletin* became the first major publication to take this view, releasing a special double issue dedicated to preteen and teenage romance series novels. In the editorial "About Romance Series," the editors made it clear that the Council on Interracial Books for Children viewed these texts as "trash," and explicitly dangerous. The danger sprang from the texts' presumed status as "brainwashers," defined within the editorial as "the most dangerous players, because they aim to induce a new generation to internalize patriarchal values" (3). The Council thus placed itself—and education generally—in opposition to these texts:

> As concerned educators ... we must challenge patriarchal values and controls whenever and wherever we can. The new romances *are* trivial trash ... we must find ways to give young people alternative messages to patriarchal pap.
>
> ("About Romance Series" 3)

The warning is echoed in "The New Preteen and Teenage Romances—A Report to Educators and Parents Issued in Concert with the National Education Association," on the following page. The introduction to the report refers to "private corporations' use of teachers as agents to promote, sell, and distribute these wretched books" (4), as well as to the assumed justification for reading the texts in schools, namely "that they turn girls onto reading" (4), thereby echoing the "bridge" rationalization of the first period—a justification that is now criticized: "The idea that one book is as good as another, or that it doesn't make any difference what a child reads just as long as he or she reads something is pure sop" (4).

Looking back, the special double issue is fascinating for its unrelenting disparagement. The first articles, Brett Harvey's "Wildfire: Tame But Deadly," Emily Strauss Watson's "Wishing Star: Hiding Trash with a Veneer of 'Reality,'" and Sharon Wigutoff's "First Love: Morality Tales Thinly Veiled" analyze the problematic aspects of the books, paying specific attention to what they may be teaching young readers to internalize in terms of gender, race, and disability. The next articles argue against the "steppingstone" claim, focusing on the problematic values that "the books transmit" (Meyers 18).[12] As Ruth Meyers clearly articulates, "if students are encouraged to read romances in the authoritative context of the classroom, teachers and the education establishment are in effect endorsing them and the destructive messages they convey" (18). Finally, the special double issue ends with articles that suggest helpful alternatives, from Wigutoff's bibliography of recommended books, to a lesson plan written by Wigutoff in conjunction with the Council Staff. Together, the articles within the special issue form a damning view of the newly-emerging literature.

Young adult romance versus adult romance

Writing roughly a year later, Lois Kuznets and Eve Zarin attempt a slightly more sophisticated examination than what the *Bulletin* produced. In "Sweet Dreams for Sleeping Beauties: Pre-Teen Romances" (1982), Kuznets and Zarin examine six of Bantam Books' *Sweet Dreams* Romances—a new line aimed at pre-teen girls—

through the lens of John Cawelti's theories of popular formulaic literature (Cawelti). They focus on Cawelti's statements regarding communal fantasies and the boundaries between the permitted and the forbidden, noting that teen romances provide a site for these two aspects to come together for pre-teen girls. They thus position the romances as a kind of "safe space" against the more famous (and supposedly more realistic) YA literature of the same period—the infamous "problem novels." After comparing the Sweet Dreams Romances to the most famous junior novel, Maureen Daly's *Seventeenth Summer* (1942), Kuznets and Zarin assert that the contemporary romances seem *more* formulaic and less realistic than the junior novels. Still, they acknowledge that the stresses that pre-teen girls undergo may lead them to "seek their retreat in Sweet Dreams—just as realistic adult stresses of other sorts turn housewives to Harlequin Romances" (32). Ultimately, their final statement is one of grudging acceptance coupled with the hope for something better:

> for pre-teens, the uses of romance can be progressive rather than regressive: life and love are really ahead of them. It is simply a pity that young girls do not have more to look forward to than Sweet Dreams, either as reading matter or as visions of life ... We need better romances for pre-teens. The present commercial success of this line clearly identifies a willing and waiting audience.
>
> (32)

In their use of Cawelti's theories and their gestures toward Harlequin, Kuznets and Zarin start a new line of inquiry: the comparison of teen romances to adult romance novels, and how the similarities and differences between those texts define the YA romance. M. Daphne Kutzer employs a similar inquiry in her 1986 article, "'I Won't Grow up'—Yet: Teen Formula Romance," in which she suggests girls' "needs and desires ... must be different from those met by adult romances; otherwise, teen girls would have been snapping up Harlequins and Silhouettes for some time now, and there is no evidence that they have" (90). As support, she provides the tropes of teen romance novels, noting a key difference from adult romance: "teen romances are concerned with the beginnings of the romantic search, not with the final triumph" (91). Ultimately, Kutzer suggests that these novels act as a safe shield for younger readers, in that they provide them with an immature romance plot—one that is specifically *not* adult or long-term: "They offer the illusion that the readers are indulging in adult fare, yet in reality the novels shield readers from the adult world and give them instead simple stories of common teen problems in an idealized world" (94). Most scholarship after these two articles treats YA romance as its own genre, purposely refraining from comparing it to adult romances. Thus, a novel and potentially revealing methodology for future scholars would be to reexamine the two popular romance literatures against each other, rather than treating them as separate audience-divided entities.

Linda K. Christian-Smith

Although the texts I've listed above acted as preliminary investigations into YA romances of the 1980s, it was the prolific analyses by Linda K. Christian-Smith that dominated second-period scholarship. Christian-Smith first articulates her ideas in a 1987 article, in which she uses the codes of "romance," "beautification," and "sexuality," to examine how adolescent femininity is constructed in 34 teen romance novels written from 1942 to 1982, ultimately finding that "Femininity consists of administering to the heart and tending the hearth" (394).

Christian-Smith more fully investigated these ideas in her well-known *Becoming a Woman Through Romance* (1990). As in her earlier article, she positions the YA romance novels into three groups: 1942–59, 1960–79, and 1980–2. In the first period, she finds that protagonists are fixated on attaining beauty, and are generally unassertive: "he leads, she follows" (17). In the second period, "romance itself is now fraught with conflict and disappointment" (17). Protagonists are more assertive, but that assertiveness is derived from having to take a stand against the pressure to engage in genital sexuality. Conversely, period three romance is smooth, paralleling the first period in terms of the harmony of the relationships, in protagonists' focus on making themselves beautiful, and in the chasteness of hugs and kisses.

In addition to the three periods, Christian-Smith also splits her text into three parts: textual analysis, an examination of interviews with girl readers, and an analysis of the political significance of girls' romance reading.[13] With this three-part focus, she became one of the first critics of YA romance to cross-employ multiple methodologies (each traditionally associated with one of the disciplines that forms the field).

Perhaps unfortunately, Christian-Smith's vision is bleak, and her argument boils down to the same thesis found in other scholarly texts of this period: YA romances are bad for girls. She notes that romance "ultimately constructs feminine subjectivity in terms of a significant other, the boyfriend" (28), which secures the protagonists' gender subordination. In turn, that subordination is connected to the assertion that "romance creates young woman as terms in a circuit of exchange where their value is acquired through affiliation with boys" (29). She asserts that the novels control the range of the heroine's sexual pleasure, suggesting that "in the end [the heroines] accommodate themselves to whatever autonomy they can secure" (42), and, in their focus on beautification for their boyfriends, accept "another's version of reality as [their] own" (54). Ultimately, Christian-Smith's textual analysis demonstrates the consistency in gender role indoctrination of YA romances: "Despite the fact that these novels span forty years ... one thing remains constant: women and girls' lives begin and should end at home" (78).[14]

Bleakness aside, Christian-Smith's texts are important for including a new site of analysis: race. She examined Black characters and readers, observing that the type and amount of domestic housework is different for Black and white girls: "girls of color experience the world of work from a young age ... This is not the casual housework and babysitting of white heroines. Rather, it is continuing heavy domestic work" (75). She uses early intersectionality in her analysis, noting, "Race interacts with gender and class to create the economic and social conditions requiring these [Black] girls to be economically contributing members of families" (75). Racial identities other than Black and white are not discussed within the text.

Although Christian-Smith's texts paved the way for more nuanced scholarship, the limitations of her publications include the blending of series and non-series texts, creating a potentially problematic generalization of YA romances, and a heavy focus on American texts.[15] Her next book, *Texts of Desire: Essays on Fiction, Feminism, and Schooling* (1993), an edited collection of essays, rectified these limitations by opening up cross-cultural, transnational analyses of YA romance—albeit still with an overall focus on gender. In the chapter, "Retailing Gender: Adolescent Book Clubs in

Australian Schools," for example, Dianne Cooper analyzed American-owned Ashton Scholastic Corporation's business practices in Australian schools, focusing on the use of book club fliers to turn classrooms into marketplaces and to construct young women as consumers. Meredith Rogers Cherland and Carole Edelsky examined young Canadian women's reading of "improper texts" (such as series and horror novels) as symbols for their feelings of powerlessness regarding school readings. John Willinsky and R. Mark Hunniford paralleled Lacan's theory of the mirror stage to suggest that books provide mirrors for their teen readers, but that the mirrors demonstrate gendered views. Gemma Moss analyzed teen romance stories written by Angelique, a Black girl who uses predominantly white teen characters and "standard" English when she writes at school, and Black teen characters and vernacular when she writes at home. Moss suggests that Angelique's writing establishes a space in which she poses questions of power, emotion, and plural and fragmented subjectivity. Overall, these and other essays establish a much broader scope than had appeared in previous first-period scholarship, creating multiple future pathways for third-period analysis.

Transitional text: Michael Cart and from romance to realism

Finally, an influential transitional text appeared toward the end of the second period: Michael Cart's *From Romance to Realism: 50 Years of Growth and Change in Young Adult Literature*(1996). I call this text "transitional" because the first edition comes to us from the second period, but foregrounds a new interest in the historical contextualization of YA romance (which would become a major area of analysis in the third period). While Cart's focus is on YA literature generally, the large role that romance has played within that literature means that part of Cart's text also acts as a short history of YA romance. Thus his first two chapters include an acknowledgement of the difficulty of defining "young adults" (and their texts), as well as an analysis of YA texts that predate canonical young adult literature, including the often-romance-focused junior novels. Although he singles out some of these texts as worthy for praise, he views most junior novels as escapist and unrealistic, contrasting them against late-1960s "New Realism." In doing so, he participates in a long pattern of excising these earlier romance novels from the YA canon:

> In fact, since there was no "old" realism, I think it is sufficient to say that the real birth of young adult literature came with its embrace of the novel of realism, beginning, as we will see in the next chapter, in the late 1960s.
>
> (39)[16]

Cart again turns his focus to romance in his fourth chapter, "The Rise of the Paperback Romance" (98). While he notes similarities between these 1980s paperbacks and the 1940s and 1950s junior novels, Cart emphasizes that one of the main differences between the two generations of texts is that "the new romances ... had little individual identity, being slick mass-market paperback series appearing at the rate of one new title a month under such saccharine rubrics as 'Wildfire,' 'Caprice' ... and on and on" (99). 1980s romance YA was no longer published for an institutional market; instead, "these series and their runaway commercial success signaled the rise of a new retail market for young adult books" (103)—a success that was also connected to the 1980s rise of the chain bookstores, and to the "emergence of a new type of book: the paperback original" (106).

Cart's text was influential not only because it was one of the first to trace a multi-decade history of YA, but because it examines that history in relation to literary criticism, psychological and educational theories, *and* print and publishing history. Thus, when Cart briefly turns to YA romance again, in Chapter 5, "The Nineties and the Future: A Literature at Risk?" (141), it is to note that "the popularity of genre series is perhaps the most durable phenomenon in the ongoing history of publishing for young readers" (148), and that while horror became the preeminent genre series in the 1990s, romance continued to sell briskly. His key point is that "unlike realistic hardcover novels, which were bought by librarians and teachers—these paperbacks are being bought by the teenagers themselves" (149), which means "it is now the buyers for the chains—not librarians, not educators, and not psychologists—who dictate how we define 'young adult'" (150). Cart was one of the first critics to trace these changes in the field.

Twenty years after its first publication, Cart's text is now in its third edition (2016), having undergone a title change to *Young Adult Literature: From Romance to Realism*. The demotion of the original title to subtitle is paralleled by the downgrading of romance within the text: Part I retains the first four chapters of the 1996 edition (with its focus on romance in the 1940s–50s and 1980s), but the other two-thirds of the text focus on new forms, themes, and controversies, and the focus on romance is noticeably lessened. The current edition therefore remains important within the field of YA generally, but less so for YA romance studies.

Third-period scholarship: 2000s–present

History and the expansion of readership

In some ways, the third period feels less prolific than previous periods, but the seeming lack of scholarship masks a diversification in areas in which critics now study YA romance. Simply put: YA romance is no longer a single area; it has expanded to include multiple sub-genres of its own, including contemporary, historical, romantic suspense, paranormal, Christian, and queer. As Carolyn Carpan states in her bibliographic reference book, *Rocked By Romance: A Guide to Teen Romance Fiction* (2004), "fewer books written for teens are labeled 'romance,' but romance can be found in most literature written for young adults today" (xx).[17] YA romance has also broadened in form, so that in addition to traditional print novels, readers may also consider manga (particularly shōjo), graphic novels, and fanfiction. Critical methodologies and analyses have thus transformed to fit these changes in content and form. As a result, any overview of this period is decidedly limited, and can only gesture to the multiplicity of scholarship now emerging.

One theoretical approach that dominates third-period scholarship is New Historicism, which investigates literature in relation to the social, political, and historical milieu that produced it. This focus may have been influenced by Michael Cart's overview of the YA road "from romance to realism," but I suspect it more likely reflects the codification of YA literature as its own field (with its own history of production and dissemination). There are now multiple histories to consider in relation to YA romance. For example, Carolyn Carpan's *Sisters, Schoolgirls, and Sleuths: Girls' Series Books in America* (2009) investigates the history of girls' series books, with a specific nod to romance as a dominant genre rising in the 1940s and 1950s, and the revival of 1980s teen romance in both standalone and soap opera series formats. She argues against the negative view held by second-period critics, asserting:

> But critics hadn't studied these titles closely, or they would have noted that many teen romances were actually coming-of-age stories.... [they] taught a generation of teenage girls that they could have it all—marriage, children, and careers. Teen romance fiction was training girls to become superwomen.
>
> (123)

Such a statement is almost a direct reversal of much second-period scholarship, demonstrating a shift in how third-period critics examine YA romance within a historical tradition. With its rejection of "victimhood feminism" and focus on individual empowerment, it may also gesture toward a change from second to third wave feminist ideas within the scholarship.[18]

Interestingly, many of these history-focused analyses question and expand assumed readership. My own article, "'Dear Miss Daly': 1940s Fan Letters to Maureen Daly and the Age-Grading and Gendering of *Seventeenth Summer*" (2016) pinpoints the moment when *Seventeenth Summer*—the best-known junior novel, narrating the story of teen Angie Morrow's first love relationship with town heartthrob Jack Duluth—became age-graded and gendered as a "girls'" text (and became the wellspring for the junior novel genre). I investigate how fans uphold and challenge such categorization, ultimately suggesting that men's focus on *Seventeenth Summer* evinces dissatisfaction with wartime masculinity that the critics' categorization of the text as a romantic "girl's junior novel" cannot incorporate. The history of YA romance is anything but straightforward; by relying solely on scholarly criticism as it has been passed down, we lose insight into readerships that complicate our understanding of that literature.

Similarly, Amy Pattee's *Reading the Adolescent Romance: Sweet Valley High and the Popular Young Adult Romance Novel* (2011) provides an excellent overview of the history of the genre, while simultaneously questioning the limits of its readership. In investigating fan bloggers who re-read *Sweet Valley High* as adults, Pattee suggests they

> ask the same questions Anne Booth Thompson asks about her mid-century reading of Janet Lambert: "Why, I wonder now, did I feel so passionately about the characters in the first place? Why did I love these books so much when their weaknesses are so readily apparent to me?"
>
> (127)[19]

Like Christian-Smith's texts, Pattee's book weaves together multiple methodologies to provide an analysis of both content and readership of the *Sweet Valley High* series. The first chapter traces the evolution of YA fiction, while the second provides ideological contextualization of the series vis à vis the "moral panic" of the Reagan era. The remaining chapters collectively support ideas proposed in the first chapters by focusing on textual analysis of the series in relation to its readership, its "new" series, "SVH: Senior Year," and its legacy. These latter chapters articulate a feminist overview of the series' use of romance conventions, while also focusing on the series' initial readers' remembered interpretations and experiences, as well as those of online "anti-fans." What Pattee's analysis does that breaks with previous scholarship is to examine YA romance not only in terms of current readers, but through the eyes of adult readers looking backward. This backward glance is not rosy; instead, as Pattee asserts, "the Sweet Valley bloggers' responses represent an attempt to un-do the messages they argue the texts espouse and that they admit to acknowledging and even accepting as young people" (135). This new lens provides not only an extension of readership, but one that recognizes how time and maturation affect readers' responses to YA romance.

On the other end of the age scale, Sherron Killingsworth Roberts also examines *Sweet Valley High*, but in terms of *Sweet Valley Kids*, which she calls "romance novels for children" (124). Using Jungian and feminist theory to examine 22 chapter books within the series, she notes that their marketing "to impressionable, independent readers from 6 to 8 years of age accentuates the importance of examining relationships among gender roles, the various archetypes, and stereotypic characters" (132–3). Although her findings feel reminiscent of second-period scholarship in her conclusion that "the stereotypic portrayals of Jessica and Elizabeth ... offer little in the way of positive role-models for developing young girls" (133), they are intriguing for recognizing the *Sweet Valley Kids* novels as not only part of a brand, but as part of a life-long marketing strategy:

> Readers can first become acquainted with Jessica and Elizabeth through the innocence of *Sweet Valley Kids* and *Sweet Valley Twins*, and later through *Sweet Valley Junior High*. Then, they can graduate to *Sweet Valley High* and *Sweet Valley University* as a precursor to adult romance novels.
>
> (124)

While first-period scholarship supported the notion of using YA romance with teens as a "steppingstone" to promote eventual adult reading, articles like this one suggest that texts published in the third period era use a similar steppingstone concept to market romance YA by age and to create life-long romance novel brand loyalty.

Twilight: *crossover YA romance and gender violence*

Age-graded YA romance novel marketing and brand loyalty becomes more complicated when it comes to the enormously popular *Twilight Saga*. Like second-period scholarship, most contemporary examinations of *Twilight* focus on gendered readings of the text, and its effect on female readers. In so doing, they make apparent the crossover readership of adult women reading contemporary YA romance. This readership is the focus of Jennifer Stevens Aubrey, Melissa Click and Elizabeth Behm-Morawitz's 2016 examination of "Twilight Moms," who they define as "adult women who have at least one child and identify as fans of Twilight" (61). Their results reveal that Twilight Moms who identify as non-feminist (and who hold traditional beliefs regarding women) seemed more "transported" by the series than feminist-identifying mothers. The authors suggest that this difference may be due to the fact that "readers with pre-existing feminist attitudes could not completely immerse themselves in the text because they were too distracted by the conservative gender roles in the series" (67). While this conclusion is a far cry from the "good/bad" binary of the previous periods, it is not difficult to detect an underlying moral judgment of the series (regardless of the assumed age of its readership)—a judgment that frankly appears present in much scholarship on the series.

It is perhaps safest to suggest that many scholars view *Twilight* as highly problematic —and not only for younger readers. Lydia Kokkola suggests that the *Twilight* series derives its appeal from its conformity to the romance genre and the satisfaction of readers' expectations. In investigating the instances in which the series departs from those norms, however, she asserts that those very departures may be what generate its popularity. Thus, she suggests that Meyer combines the love triangle structure often more prevalent in the adult romance tradition with the repression of carnal desire in teen romances, with the result that

> the combination confounds expectations from adult and teenage romances in a manner which apparently appeals to adult readers jaded by over-exposure to depictions of sexual intimacy and teen readers tired of being shamed for experiencing sexual desire or fantasies of being desired.
>
> (178)

Yet Kokkola also heavily critiques the series' presentation of gender. She notes that Meyer "reverts to the chauvinistic stereotype of the femme fatale" (179) when describing Edward's vampire sisters, as well as newborn vampire Bella, thereby "suggesting that a sexually empowered adolescent girl is a danger to herself and her society" (179), and that "Equally disturbingly, the series as a whole . . . glorifies female submissiveness and valorizes self-abusive behaviour as a consequence of true love" (179).

It is perhaps unsurprising that questions of female agency—and whether or not it exists within the saga—pervade scholarship of the novels. Several recent analyses of *Twilight* focus on romance and gendered violence. Jessica Taylor performs close readings of the texts to examine the physical and emotional violence within the saga. In examining moments of physical violence, she observes the troubling pattern that the (female) "victim is again blamed for the actions of the perpetrator, and the [male] perpetrator appears to be absolved of any responsibility" (391). This victim-blaming is similarly evident in the emotional violence within the texts. Using Evan Stark's theory of coercive control, Taylor observes that "Bella's public silence is paramount within these texts; she is lauded for keeping the presence of the vampires and the werewolves secret, despite great personal risk to herself" (393). The result of Bella's continual assumption of sole responsibility for the danger around her is the emergence of the concept that "any problems or issues that an individual woman faces become her own responsibility to solve" (393).

Taylor admits her point of view is "grounded in my initial unease with the series" (389), but also asserts that "by introducing the concept of a female gaze which positions male bodies as desirable, and the series as pleasurable, a new interpretation of the popularity of the series can be offered" (389). She concludes by noting that while the saga's "almost naïve application of romance conventions and retrograde gender roles, may appear incongruent with the empowerment discourses of a postfeminist society, its popularity suggests that it has resonated strongly with contemporary female audiences" (400). Her conclusion is interesting for its lack of harsh judgment—a far cry from previous periods. While she obviously views aspects related to violence and gender as problematic within the texts, Taylor is more ambiguous in her final points, ultimately arguing that the "way the series caters for an emergent female gaze ... makes it of our time" (400).

The Hunger Games: *gender and dystopian romance*

What may also be "of our time" is the emergence of dystopian novels as one of the most popular YA genres. Scholarship on texts such as *The Hunger Games* trilogy focuses predominantly on the relationship between gender and dystopia, but much of it also acknowledges the romance plots that appear implicit in current incarnations of this genre.[20] This acknowledgement is often negative, demonstrating the role of romance in positioning the female characters of dystopias as passive and docile. In "'The Dandelion in the Spring': Utopia as Romance in Suzanne Collins's *The Hunger Games* Trilogy" (2013), Katherine R. Broad observes that the contradiction between Katniss's "professed disinterest and her nascent desires" (119) functions as a source of tension, so that the "romance plot self-consciously calls attention to itself as a way of manipulating an audience's emotions to ensure its continued engagement" (119). Katniss's sense of revolution is fueled by her desire for a normative family life, to the extent that she assumes the role of the Mockingjay (the face of the rebellion) to protect Peeta, her future husband and father of their children. As Broad states, "romance cements Katniss's cause to the revolution at the same time that it renders her a docile subject manipulated by both sides of the war" (122). Ultimately, Katniss is never allowed to make the choice of suitor (between Peeta and her other potential lover, Gale), and the resolution of the trilogy's love triangle is passive, leading Broad to observe that Katniss is not a feminist icon, but is instead a "flattened" female figure. Thus, Broad calls out the use of romance plots within YA dystopias, stating:

> One important way for YA dystopias to imagine social transformation that does more than reinsert female characters into conservative gender roles is therefore perhaps to start by complicating, subverting, or even downright rejecting the conventions of the romance plot that place women in such positions.
>
> (127)

Queer romance and new forms

While third-period scholars investigate ways in which romance plots associated with YA dystopias appear to reassert traditional norms (particularly as they relate to gender roles or to the primacy of heterosexual and cis-gendered couples), a new scholarly lens is simultaneously emerging that focuses on *multiplicity* of sexualities and genders. This new lens allows scholars to recognize that romance exists within same-gender relationships, and that the readers of these texts are not necessarily female. While that statement may appear obvious to contemporary eyes, one must remember the extent to which first and second-period scholarship was fundamentally based on such aspects as girls' heterosexual socialization (period one), or the dangers of patriarchal portrayals of romance specifically for girls (period two).

Much contemporary scholarship pursues notions of what is "helpful" or "unhelpful" for young readers—particularly those struggling with their own gender or sexual identities—but without the psychological/educational rhetoric of "adjustment" or "developmental tasks" that informed first-period scholarship. In "From Romance to Magical Realism: Limits and Possibilities in Gay Adolescent Fiction" (2009), Thomas Crisp asserts that there are two methods for representing forms of gayness within "acceptance" titles of LGBTQIA adolescent literature. One version uses homophobia as a foil against which a gay couple struggles, while the other "imagines away" homophobia, allowing queer characters to interact in a seemingly discrimination-free world. He notes that both versions are problematic:

> on the surface, these accounts are in some ways "affirmative" and give voice and representation to gay males, but because they so heavily rely on heteronormative constructions of romance, sex, sexuality, and the world more broadly, they often actually work to continue the invisibility of gay males by filtering queer existence and distancing readers (i.e., queer characters are safely viewed through layers of heterosexuality).
>
> (345)

Ultimately, Crisp suggests that both methods assume that the goal of LGBTQIA youth is monogamous coupling, and thus both re-inscribe heteronormativity.

Crisp's gesture to the ambiguity of the texts—to what is affirmative (helpful) but also to what problematically erases certain identities and re-inscribes heteronormativity (unhelpful, damaging)—is representative of much third-period scholarship that examines queer romance YA. In particular, scholars tend to lean heavily toward the "helpful" side of the continuum in their examination of queer YA romance written in non-traditional-novel forms, including fanfiction and manga. Scholarship that focuses on these non-traditional texts often investigates the "helpfulness" of queer representations through lenses of freedom, openness, and celebration. In "Homosexuality at the Online Hogwarts: Harry Potter Slash Fanfiction" (2008), Catherine Tosenberger suggests freedom in the genres of *Harry Potter* fanfiction—buddyslash, enemyslash, powerslash—because there is no typical *Harry Potter* slash story, and thus any tropes that define one are dependent on the character pairing. That freedom creates a "safe space" for young adult readers/writers of fanfiction "not only to improve their writing skills, but also to explore discourses of sexuality, especially queerness, outside of the various culturally official stances marketed to them, and with the support of a community of like-minded readers and writers" (202). Since they are not bound to a "pedagogical imperative," these young readers/writers can access "a space where queer sexuality, whether teen or adult, can be depicted in its full, messy, exuberant glory" (201).

Similarly, Lisa Goldstein and Molly Phelan explore issues of gender and sexuality through the lens of manga. In their humorous "Are you There God? It's Me, Manga: Manga as an Extension of Young Adult Literature" (2009), Goldstein and Phelan suggest that manga's unconventional narratives (often including gender changes and sexual ambiguities) give its female readers agency, allowing their interpretations of the text to be free from conventional sexual and gender role expectations. They assert that the idealized faces and bodies within the art, coupled with the androgynous appearance of the male heroes, allows girls "to assign whatever gender and kind of relationship the reader wants" (34). They further note that the "opportunity to navigate a romance through a male character's perspective gives female readers of boys' love a chance to contemplate relationships outside of the usual gender role dichotomy, with the man as the pursuer and the woman as the pursued" (35). Moreover, in contrast to the frazzled male characters, the female protagonists "are calmly confident in their sexuality and desires" (35). Ultimately, Goldstein and Phelan suggest that the readers of boys' love manga are free to break the man/woman gender binary, allowing them the opportunity "to contemplate privately a break with societal expectations" (37). Unlike Crisp's argument about problematic erasure of gay identity within contemporary LGBTQIA YA romances, both Tosenberger's and Goldstein's and Phelan's arguments about the helpfulness of their texts are inextricably linked to the non-traditional, unregulated format of those texts. Although the majority of these texts still retain a relationship structure of monogamous coupledom, they allow for more identity play through their inclusion of multiple genders and sexual identities. When it comes to queer YA romance, at least, the scholarship suggests that the most helpful texts may be the non-traditional texts.

There are, of course, many more areas of third-period scholarship than I am able to outline in this space. These include a focus on consumerism within YA romance (Johnson); an expansion of the second-period focus on race to include more than only Black and white identities (de Jesús); and "abstinence porn," or the idealization and objectification of girls' bodies through the fetishization of virginity (Seifert). Third-period scholarship is also important for its emerging international focus. YA has traditionally been known as a specifically American genre; as Michael Cart states, "there is a ready and well-nigh universal agreement among experts that something called 'young adult literature' is—like the Broadway musical, jazz, and the foot-long hot dog —an American gift to the world" (*Young Adult* 3). What may have started as American, however, has clearly expanded to the rest of the world (particularly Australia), and this expansion includes YA romance and, mainly in the third period, international scholarship on YA romance.

I suspect the explosion of scholarship in this period (particularly in the last ten years) may be due to the rise of crossover reading of YA romance by young women in their 20s and 30s. This crossover may have placed YA romance on the radar of scholars coming from disciplines outside the traditional three of English, Education, and Library Studies. Indeed, the expansion of scholarship within journals dedicated to communications, women's and gender studies, and fandom studies would seem to support this hypothesis.

Conclusion

The proliferation of scholarship within the third period of YA romance studies suggests that the genre itself is finally expanding past its traditional disciplinary boundaries. It has changed immensely within 80 years, emerging first as good/bad judgments of junior novels, focusing on their use in girls' socialization or as "steppingstones" to mature texts, or deriding them for their lack of realism. In the second period, scholarship turned to repeated disparagement of 1980s romances, emphasizing their damaging portrayals of patriarchal power and gender norms. Still, the criticism also broadened, investigating the intersectionality of Blackness with gender, and opening into cross-cultural, transnational analyses. The third period represents a global flowering of analysis into wide-ranging new territories (including supernatural, dystopian, and queer YA romance) and formats (including fanfiction and manga), as well as an active historicizing of the field itself. What has remained across each of these periods—and, perhaps, what may always remain—are critics' underlying conventions and assumptions regarding our collective notion of "teenagers," and what constitutes "appropriate" reading material for them. Thus, the scholarly focus of each period may have changed, but as long as YA romance is written primarily by adults and aimed at a younger audience, scholarship on these texts will inevitably address some aspect of power.

There persist many avenues of scholarship still to be explored. What is the future of YA romance? Will the emergence of "New Adult" romance—that is, high drama romance novels focusing on characters in their early twenties and aimed at nostalgic adults, older teens, and college students—come to dominate the field, even as most contemporary academic criticism ignores it? How will a focus on age continue to expand definitions of "popular romance," particularly considering that a focus on youth necessarily negates the presupposition of a long-term Happily Ever After? These are only beginning questions; the field of scholarship remains wide open to interested critics. That the overall focus will remain on gender for some time is likely, yet I remain hopeful that the way in which gender will be explored in YA romance will continue to expand, as will intersectional focuses on race/ethnicity, class, sexuality, and age. Scholarship on YA romance has legitimated itself as a viable area of study; it needs only to continue to grow.

Notes

1 Whether or not young adult literature falls under the umbrella term of "children's literature" is an additional site of contestation within the field/s. In this essay, I will use the traditional structure of situating young adult literature as an aspect within the larger field of children's literature.

2 In many ways, Rose's *The Case for Peter Pan* became to children's literature studies what Janice Radway's *Reading the Romance* became to popular romance studies: a seminal text that helped to codify the field around a specific way of thinking about the genre, but which has become, as An Goris notes of Radway's text, "subjected to quite harsh and even unforgiving critiques which seem to create and perpetuate a stereotypical image and too simplistic interpretation of this complex and theoretically sophisticated study" ("Matricide in Romance Scholarship").

3 The ease of access to contemporary fanfiction may provide a possible counterexample to Zipes's claim.

4 For examples of texts about young adult literature that cite Hinton's 1967 novel, *The Outsiders*, as heralding the rise of realistic YA, see Herz and Gallo, 10; Hill, 1; and Short, Tomlinson, Lynch-Brown, and Johnson, 6. The longest-published and best-known textbook on YA, Alleen Pace Nilsen and Kenneth L. Donelson's *Literature for Today's Young Adults*, is more nuanced in providing an excellent historical overview of the socio-cultural elements that impacted earlier YA from 1800–1966, but ultimately still establishes 1967 as the "milestone year" in the turn to realistic YA (11).

5 The Young Adult Services Division was not, however, the first group within the ALA dedicated to teen reading. In 1930 the ALA formed the Young People's Reading Round Table (encompassing both children's and what-would-become young adult literature), and in 1941 that group became part of the ALA Division of Libraries for Children and Young People.

6 Of course, there exist many earlier texts that could be categorized as young adult romance, notably Louisa May Alcott's *Little Women* (1868), Susan Coolidge's *What Katy Did Next*, and various series novels by Lucy Maud Montgomery (1908–39). While young people certainly read these novels, most scholars categorize them as "family stories" (or a similar term) because the texts predate both the construction of adolescence as a psychological "separate

state" (not officially sanctioned until G. Stanley Hall's work in 1904), and the rise of the teenager as a distinct consumer demographic in the 1930s and 1940s.

7 I must note that the junior novels (and their scholarship) were not the first romance novels for a younger audience. Once again I am confronted with the problem of delimiting the field, and thus I claim the 1940s through the 1960s as the "first period" of scholarship on YA romance because it occurs during the rise of the teenager as both a developmental *and* a commodified life stage (thus separating it from the slightly earlier "adolescent," which focused on biological stages). The first period therefore coincides with the rise of the teenager not only as a developmental stage, but as a specific economic demographic of its own—one that directly led to and maintained the junior novel.

8 Similarly, in "The Junior Novel—Pro and Con" Anne Emery and James L. Summers took the "pro" position, noting that:

> Most of these young readers, from 11 to 15 or so, are not ready for the subtleties and intricacies of adult fiction . . . They are trying to find values, firm beliefs and philosophies and understand people and life, beginning with themselves ... Intense experience with immature books, are valuable in themselves, but they also furnish links with more significant literary experiences later. (qtd. in Magaliff 18)

9 Havighurst defines a developmental task as "a task which arises at or about a certain period in the life of the individual, successful achievement of which leads to his happiness and to success with later tasks, while failure leads to unhappiness in the individual, disapproval by the society, and difficulty with later tasks" (qtd. in Alm "Study" 27).

10 Richard Alm's view of the junior novel is not wholly negative; indeed, the majority of his article is actually spent in reviewing junior novels "of real stature" (317). Ultimately, Alm provides a methodology for distinguishing between excellent, mediocre, and inferior junior novels.

11 Burton was one of the few scholars to write against the concept of the single, monolithic adolescent reader:

> when we speak of "adolescent readers" we may feel that we are talking about a very limited audience, but actually the "adolescent" or "the adolescent reader" is something only theoretical and amorphous, for, as every high school teacher knows, the quantitative and qualitative differences in reactions to literature are as great among adolescent readers as among the general reading population. (Burton "Novel" 363)

12 These three articles are Ruth S. Meyer's "Does Reading Pulp Lead to Reading Literature?" Barbara Ann Porte's "In Turning Children on to Reading, Quality Counts," and Wigutoff's "A Short Course on Answering Those Who Defend Romance Series."

13 For the middle section, Christian-Smith administered a reading survey to 75 girls, and performed extensive interviews with 29 girls. Although this approach suggests a methodology derived from Education, that section is dominated by the textual analysis, suggesting an English-disciplinary focus. Obviously, no methodology belongs to a discipline, but it is important to recognize that part of what made Christian-Smith's arguments new and different was that she combined multiple methodologies—traditionally representing different fields—within a single scholarly text. Indeed, this cross-disciplinary methodology would be used in future criticism, most notably in Amy Pattee's 2011 *Reading the Adolescent Romance.*

14 Christian-Smith's analysis of readers' responses proves to be as disheartening. Within a schoolroom setting, the interviewees—categorized as "reluctant readers"—read romances as a site of resistance against such categorization, and against schooling that failed to recognize their interests. Their resistance, however, "perpetuated and reinforced these girls' identities as students that would not finish school or would graduate with skills that would qualify them only for low-skill exploitative jobs" (116). Ultimately, as Christian-Smith suggests:

> Romance fiction's universe of conspicuous consumption meshes with the girls' longing for a life of comfort and affluence. The school identities of these 29 girls as reluctant readers, and the work undertaken to buy commodities, help to consolidate their class identities around low-paying service-sector work (135).

15 This problem may be partially attributed to the time period in which the text was published: although Christian-Smith's book was published in 1990, she stops her analysis with

texts published in 1982, at which point young adult series romance had only be around for two years.

16 Cart himself provides examples of scholars' removal of romance fiction from the canon of young adult literature. He points out, for example, that G. Robert Carlsen's *Books and the Teen-Age Reader* (1967), a highly influential text from the first period of scholarship, divided YA into ten categories, but that "Romance, amazingly, is not on Carlsen's list of categories, although he does append a lengthy list of what he calls 'girls' stories'" (Cart 32).

17 Caplan's text is aimed primarily at librarians working with teenagers. It is organized by type (classic romance, contemporary romance, contemporary romance series, issues romance, alternative reality romance, romantic suspense, historical romance, and Christian romance) which mostly holds today, but may be somewhat dated in its inclusion of "Gay, Lesbian, and Bisexual Romance" as a subtopic of "Issue Romance."

18 Additional scholarship focused on historical contextualization includes the following: Mills; Thompson; Allen, "Charm", "The Cinderella-Makers").

19 Anne B. Thompson similarly calls us to complicate this history. In "Rereading Fifties Teen Romance: Reflections on Janet Lambert," she contextualizes Lambert's junior novels against Francine Pascal's *Sweet Valley* series. In reviewing scholarship on Lambert's texts, she recognizes that "no one ... cites much from the novels themselves, or subjects them to detailed commentary with regard to their content and style" (374). The thesis of her article, then, is to "hold the books up to our gaze to see properly what is there and to explain why I think they need to be discussed with a bit more care and interest" (374).

20 See Day et al. and Basu et al.

Works cited

"About Romance Series." Editorial. *Interracial Books for Children Bulletin*, vol. 12, no. 4/5, 1981, p. 3.

Allen, Amanda. "The Cinderella-Makers: Post-War Adolescent Girl Fiction as Commodity Tales." *The Lion and the Unicorn*, vol. 33, no. 3, 2009, pp. 282–299.

Allen, Amanda. "Charm the Boys, Win the Girls: Power Struggles in Mary Stolz's Cold War Adolescent Girl Romance Novels." *Journal of Popular Romance Studies*, vol. 3, no. 1, Oct, 2012. jprstudies.org/2012/10/charm-the-boys-win-the-girls-power-struggles-in-mary-stolzs-cold-war-adolescent-girl-romance-novels-by-amanda-k-allen/

Allen, Amanda. "'Dear Miss Daly': 1940s Fan Letters to Maureen Daly and the Age-Grading and Gendering of *Seventeenth Summer*." *Children's Literature Association Quarterly*, vol. 41, no. 1, Spring, 2016, pp. 24–40.

Alm, Richard. *A Study of the Assumptions Concerning Human Experience Underlying Certain Works of Fiction Written for and about Adolescents*. 1954. University of Minnesota, Ph.D. dissertation.

Alm, Richard. "The Glitter and the Gold." *The English Journal*, vol. 44, no. 6, Sep, 1955, pp. 315–322, 350.

Aubrey, Jennifer Stevens, Melissa Click and Elizabeth Behm-Morawitz. "The Twilight of Youth: Understanding Feminism and Romance in the Twilight Moms' Connection to the Young-Adult Vampire Series." *Psychology of Popular Media Culture*, vol. 7, no. 1, 2018, pp. 61–71.

Basu, Balaka, Katherine R. Broad and Carrie Hintz. *Contemporary Dystopian Fiction for Young Adults: Brave New Teenagers*. Routledge, 2013.

Broad, Katherine R. "'The Dandelion in the Spring': Utopia as Romance in Suzanne Collins's *the Hunger Games* Trilogy." *Contemporary Dystopian Fiction for Young Adults: Brave New Teenagers*, edited by Balaka Basu, Katherine R. Broad, and Carrie Hintz, Routledge, 2013, pp. 117–130.

Burton, Dwight L. "The Novel for the Adolescent." *The English Journal*, vol. 40, no. 7, Sep, 1951, pp. 363–369.

Burton, Dwight L. *Literature Study in the High Schools*. Holt, Rinehart and Winston, 1959.

Carpan, Carolyn. *Rocked by Romance: A Guide to Young Adult Romance Genre Fiction*. Libraries Unlimited, 2004.

Carpan, Carolyn. *Sisters, Schoolgirls, and Sleuths: Girls Series Books in America.* Scarecrow Press, 2009.

Cart, Michael. *From Romance to Realism: 50 Years of Growth and Change in Young Adult Literature.* HarperCollins, 1996.

Cart, Michael. *Young Adult Literature: From Romance to Literature.* Third ed. American Library Association, 2016.

Cawelti, John. *Adventure, Mystery, and Romance.* University of Chicago Press, 1976.

Cherland, Meredith Rogers and Carole Edelsky. "Girls and Reading: The Desire for Agency and the Horror of Helplessness in Fictional Encounters." *Texts of Desire: Essays on Fiction, Feminism, and Schooling*, The Falmer Press, 1993, pp. 28–44.

Christian-Smith, Linda K. "Gender, Popular Culture, and Curriculum: Adolescent Romance Novels as Gender Text." *Curriculum Inquiry*, vol. 17, no. 4, Winter, 1987, pp. 365–406.

Christian-Smith, Linda K. *Becoming a Woman through Romance.* Routledge, 1990.

Christian-Smith, Linda K. *Texts of Desire: Essays on Fiction, Feminism, and Schooling.* The Falmer Press, 1993.

Collins, Suzanne. *The Hunger Games.* Scholastic, 2008.

Collins, Suzanne. *Catching Fire.* Scholastic, 2009.

Collins, Suzanne. *Mockingjay.* Scholastic, 2010.

Cooper, Dianne. "Retelling Gender: Adolescent Book Clubs in Australian Schools." *Texts of Desire: Essays on Fiction, Feminism, and Schooling*, edited by Linda K. Christian-Smith, The Falmer Press, 1993, pp. 9–27.

Crisp, Thomas. "From Romance to Magical Realism: Limits and Possibilities in Gay Adolescent Fiction." *Children's Literature in Education*, vol. 40, 2009, pp. 333–348.

Day, Sara K., Miranda A. Green-Barteet and Amy L. Montz. *Female Rebellion in Young Adult Dystopian Fiction.* Routledge, 2016.

De Jesús, Melinda L. "'Two's a Company, Three's a Crowd?': Reading Interracial Romance in Contemporary Asian American Young Adult Fiction." *Lit: Literature Interpretation Theory*, vol. 12, no. 3, 2001, pp. 313–334.

Dunning, Arthur Stephenson. *A Definition of the Role of the Junior Novel Based on Analyses of Thirty Selected Novels.* 1959. Florida State University, Ph.D. dissertation.

Edwards, Margaret A. "Let the Lower Lights Be Burning." *The English Journal*, vol. 46, no. 8, Nov, 1957, pp. 461–469, 474.

Goldstein, Lisa and Molly Phelan. "Are You There God? It's Me, Manga: Manga as an Extension of Young Adult Literature." *Young Adult Library Services*, vol. 7, no. 4, 2009, pp. 32–38.

Goris, An. "Matricide in Romance Scholarship? Response to Pamela Regis' Keynote Address at the Second Annual Conference of the International Association for the Study of Popular Romance." *Journal of Popular Romance Studies*, vol. 2, no. 1, October, 2011, jprstudies.org /2011/10/%E2%80%9Cmatricide-in-romance-scholarship-response-to-pamela-regis%E2% 80%99-keynote-address-at-the-second-annual-conference-of-the-international-association-for -the-study-of-popular-romance%E2%80%9D/. Accessed 20 Oct. 2017.

Gubar, Marah. "On Not Defining Children's Literature." *PMLA*, vol. 126, no. .1, 2011, pp. 209–306.

Harvey, Brett. "Wildfire: Tame But Deadly." *Interracial Books for Children Bulletin*, vol. 12, no. 4/ 5, 1981, pp. 8–10.

Herz, Sarah K and Donald R. Gallo. *From Hinton to Hamlet.* 2nd ed. Greenwood, 2005.

Hill, Crag. "Introduction: Young Adult Literature and Scholarship Come of Age." *The Critical Merits of Young Adult Literature*, edited by Crag Hill, Routledge, 2014, pp. 1–24.

Jennings, Frank G. "Literature for Adolescents—Pap or Protein?" *The English Journal*, vol. 45, no. 9, Dec, 1956, pp. 526–531.

Johnson, Naomi R. "Consuming Desires: Consumption, Romance, and Sexuality in Best-Selling Teen Romance Novels." *Women's Studies in Communication*, vol. 33, 2010, pp. 54–73.

Killingsworth Roberts, Sherron. "Twenty-Five Years and Counting of Sweet Valley: Jessica and Elizabeth in Romance Novels for Young Children?" *Journal of Research in Childhood Education*, vol. 24, no. 2, 2010, pp. 123–139.

Kokkola, Lydia. "Virtuous Vampires and Voluptuous Vamps: Romance Conventions Reconsidered in Stephenie Meyer's 'Twilight' Series." *Children's Literature in Education*, vol. 42, no. 2, June, 2011, pp. 165–179.

Kutzer, M. Daphne. "'I Won't Grow up'—Yet: Teen Formula Romance." *Children's Literature Association Quarterly*, vol. 11, no. 2, Summer, 1986, pp. 90–95.

Kuznets, Lois and Eve Zarin. "Sweet Dreams for Sleeping Beauties: Pre-Teen Romances." *Children's Literature Association Quarterly*, vol. 7, no. 1, Spring, 1982, pp. 28–32.

Magaliff, Cecile. *The Junior Novel: Its Relationship to Adolescent Reading*. Kennikat Press, 1964.

McLoughlin, Tim. "Fielding's Essay on Conversation: A Courtesy Guide to Joseph Andrews?" *The Crisis of Courtesy: Studies in the Conduct-Book in Britain, 1600–1900*, edited by E.J. Jacques Carre, Brill, 1994, pp. 93–104.

Meyer, Stephenie. *Twilight*. Little Brown and Co., 2005.

Meyer, Stephenie. *New Moon*. Little, Brown and Co., 2006.

Meyer, Stephenie. *Eclipse*. Little, Brown and Co., 2007.

Meyer, Stephenie. *Breaking Dawn*. Little, Brown and Co., 2008.

Meyers, Ruth S. "Does Reading Pulp Lead to Reading Literature?" *Interracial Books for Children Bulletin*, vol. 12, no. 4/5, 1981, p. 18.

Mills, Claudia. "Redemption through the Rural: The Teen Novels of Rosamond Du Jardin." *Children's Literature Association Quarterly*, vol. 38, no. 1, 2013, pp. 48–65.

Moss, Gemma. "The Place for Romance in Young People's Writing." *Texts of Desire: Essays on Fiction, Feminism, and Schooling*, edited by Linda K. Christian-Smith, The Falmer Press, 1993, pp. 106–125.

Nilsen, Alleen Pace and Kenneth L. Donelson. *Literature for Today's Young Adults*. 6th ed. Longman, 2001.

Pattee, Amy. *Reading the Adolescent Romance: Sweet Valley High and the Popular Young Adult Romance Novel*. Routledge, 2011.

Patterson, Emma L. "The Junior Novels and How They Grew." *The English Journal*, vol. 45, no. 7, Oct, 1956, pp. 381–387, 405.

Regis, Pamela. "Pamela Crosses the Atlantic; Or, Pamela Andrews's Story Inaugurates the American Romance Novel." *Romance Fiction and American Culture: Love as the Practice of Freedom?* edited by Eric Murphy Selinger, and William A Gleason, Ashgate, 2016, pp. 25–40.

Rose, Jacqueline. *The Case of Peter Pan, or the Impossibility of Children's Fiction*. The Macmillan P., 1984.

Sale, Roger. *Fairy Tales and After: From Snow White to E.B. White*. Harvard U.P., 1978.

Seifert, Christine. *Virginity in Young Adult Literature After Twilight*. Rowman & Littlefield, 2015.

Short, Kathy G., Carl M. Tomlinson, Carol Lynch-Brown and Holly Johnson. *Essentials of Young Adult Literature*. 3rd ed. Pearson, 2015.

Taylor, Jessica. "Romance and the Female Gaze Obscuring Gendered Violence in the Twilight Series." *Feminist Media Studies*, vol. 14, no. 3, 2014, pp. 388–402.

"The New Preteen and Teenage Romances—A Report to Educators and Parents Issued in Concert with the National Education Association." *Interracial Books for Children Bulletin*, vol. 12, no. 4/5, 1981, p. 4. http://digicoll.library.wisc.edu/cgi-bin/Literature/Literature-idx?type=turn&entity=Literature.CIBCBulletinv12n0405.p0004&id=Literature.CIBCBulletinv12n0405&isize=M&pview=hide

Thompson, Anne B. "Rereading Fifties Teen Romance: Reflections on Janet Lambert." *The Lion and the Unicorn*, vol. 29, 2005, pp. 373–396.

Tosenberger, Catherine. "Homosexuality at the Online Hogwarts: Harry Potter Slash Fanfiction." *Children's Literature*, vol. 36, 2008, pp. 185–207.

Watson, Emily Strauss. "Wishing Star: Hiding Trash with a Veneer of 'Reality'." *Interracial Books for Children Bulletin*, vol. 12, no. 4/5, 1981, pp. 11–12.
Wigutoff, Sharon. "First Love: Morality Tales Thinly Veiled." *Interracial Books for Children Bulletin*, vol. 12, no. 4/5, 1981a, pp. 15–17.
Wigutoff, Sharon. "An Antidote to Series Romances: Books about Friendship." *Interracial Books for Children Bulletin*, vol. 12, no. 4/5, 1981b, pp. 21–22.
Wigutoff, Sharon the Council Staff. "Examining the Issues: What Teachers Can Do." *Interracial Books for Children Bulletin*, vol. 12, no. 4/5, 1981, pp. 23–25.
Willingsky, John and R. Mark Hunniford. "Reading the Romance Younger: The Mirrors and Fears of a Preparatory Literature." *Texts of Desire: Essays on Fiction, Feminism, and Schooling*, The Falmer Press, 1993, pp. 87–105.
Wolf, Shelby A., Karen Coats, Patricia Enciso and Christine A. Jenkins. "Preface." *Handbook of Research on Children's and Young Adult Literature*, Routledge, 2011, pp. xi–xii.
Zipes, Jack. "Why Children's Literature Does Not Exist." *Sticks and Stones: The Troublesome Success of Children's Literature from Slovenly Peter to Harry Potter*, Routledge, 2002, pp. 39–60.

8 Inspirational romance

Rebecca Barrett-Fox and Kristen Donnelly

The question of whether literacy was good for women has occupied significant space in religious debates, for it centers on whether reading undermines women's abilities to be devoted wives and mothers. Perhaps more surprisingly, it is also a concern for scholars who have questioned whether romance novel reading, and particularly Christian romances, are bad for women precisely because of the books' conservative messages about gender, marriage, and family. Both perspectives are rooted in a history of demeaning women's reading (and writing) choices and doubting women's ability to discern between fiction and nonfiction, between fantasy and reality, as part of a larger cultural project that denies women authority over their own experiences. As a result, women's fiction has often been evaluated by both feminist and anti-feminist critics not according to its own merits but according to its effects on its presumably inordinately impressionable readers. As Eric Murphy Selinger writes in "Rereading the Romance," the question asked of romance novels in particular has long been

> are these novels good or bad for their readers? Put plain, the question is either empirical, and yet to be properly answered, or absurdly moralistic, although in either case it suggests a dandy parlor game.
>
> (319)

This "dandy parlor game" has been played very seriously by conservative Christians who expressed skepticism toward fiction far longer than the general public (Gutjahr 209) as well as by Christian romance novel readers, writers, and critics, who have read (and written) into the books lessons in gender, sex, love, and religious faith that their fans say cannot be found in "secular" romances. Still, such books are often read in the context of a subculture that warns women of the dangers of both "emotional pornography," as Caryn Rivadeneira documents in her defense of the books in the evangelical magazine *Christianity Today*—that is, the idealization of romantic love to the detriment of real-life marriage—and a frivolous distraction from better literature (de Rossett 29). Readers argue in response that they turn to the books not merely because they are "clean" (that is, sex-free) but because they promote a vision of romance that aligns with and reinforces their faith in a way that their secular counterparts do not. As such, the books and the reading experience are not merely a leisure activity but a devotional one—a religious activity that supports religious choices in other domains of life, or, in the words of Lynn S. Neal, who has authored the only scholarly monograph focusing on evangelical romances, the books are "instruments of faith" (Neal *Romancing God* 108).

Today's Christian publishers, writers, and readers stress the distinguishing marks of their faith on these books: 1) romance through each partner's relationship with God, so that God is the center of their relationship, 2) a lack of detail about theology or religious ritual, 3) no sexual contact or, if the couple is married, only monogamous sex that is not described, 4) a focus on faith to restore brokenness of some kind, 5) a happily-ever-after ending that includes marriage or the promise of marriage between heterosexual partners who have not been divorced from other partners, and 6) traditional gender roles but heroes who may be less traditionally masculine than men in secular romances. These conventions remain true across subgenres of Christian romances published by evangelical publishing houses, though non-evangelical presses and self-published authors may not hold to them as tightly.

In order to better understand this burgeoning genre, this chapter will map the history and scope, including subgenres, of Christian romances. It starts with a historical overview of Christian romances. As the demand for such works grew, the genre continued to develop in several different directions, leading to new subgenres that continue to challenge the larger field of romantic fiction. An examination of the interplay between these genres follows, and the chapter concludes with considering the current state of religious romance scholarship and publishing. Although non-Christian religious romances are published (see Chapter 21 of this volume and the "For Further Research" section, below), this chapter focuses on what booksellers in the U.S. term "inspirational" romances: those targeted at conservative, evangelical, Protestants.

History of a genre

Even though the distinct genre of Christian romances began in the 1970s, one can argue all romance novels may be considered religious romances, for "while the romance narrative is 'religious' in its faith in the healing power of love and in the scope of its mythic quest for love, the central religious narrative of western history is also 'romantic,'" as Catherine Roach notes in her insightful "Getting a Good Man to Love: Popular Romance Fiction and the Problem of Patriarchy" (4). Though Roach is not writing narrowly about Christian romances, she notes that "Christianity, that central religious narrative, is easily read as a love story" (4). As Jyoti Raghu notes in her analysis of on-screen kisses in American fiction, the kiss and romantic love "have the capacity not only to bear a theological significance, but to offer an opportunity for divine encounter and transformation, as well as containing the possibility of a religious discourse" (18).

And it is not merely a transcendental ideal of love that informs romances as well as inspires religion. Religion is concerned, in practical terms, with the pairing off of partners, the rituals of domestic life, gender norms, sex, lifelong partnerships, and child-bearing and rearing. Across the eighteenth and nineteenth centuries and in many of its forms, romance fiction did not need a Christian romance genre; to the extent that romance fiction promoted the Christian norms of heteronormative marriage as the result of women's faithfulness, modesty, and chastity and Providence, it was *de facto* Christian (or at least Christian-compatible) romance. Additionally, even romances, both older texts and current ones, that do not address faith frequently, explicitly, or in detail may make passing references to God, faith, fate, destiny, prayer, or other religious themes, including the possibility of love allowing spiritual rebirth, a topic Robert Rix explores in his analysis of Barbara Cartland's work. Though Rix's "'Love in the Clouds': Barbara Cartland's Religious Romances" is unique in its contextualization of Cartland's work—particularly her 1979 novel *Love in the Clouds*—within religious romance, certainly many readers understand romances to be "inspirational" regardless of whether they invoke religion explicitly. As Rix argues, and as countless romance readers know, the line between *secular* and *religious* fiction has not always been clear or deemed necessary, for both can depict characters who transcend the everyday problems of the world (even worlds that are wild, exotic, and thrilling) to an "absolute reality" that is the terrain of the divine.

Early Christian romance novelist Grace Livingston Hill was the first author to successfully and consistently distinguish between explicitly religious and secular romance in her work. The daughter of a Presbyterian pastor and a woman who herself wrote women's fiction, as well as the wife of a church organist, Hill wrote more than 100 novels as well as short stories, mostly romances, aimed at women or girls between 1877, when, as a child, she published her first story, and 1945 with her daughter Ruth completing the novel she was writing at her death. She first achieved significant commercial success with the release of *Marcia Schuyler*, the first novel in her *Miranda* trilogy, in 1908. This was a time of increased public anxiety about Christianity, which, advocates of "muscular Christianity" feared, was becoming too feminized. Hill's novels preserved a "softer" version of Christianity in a form that did not threaten men pushing for rough-and-tumble expressions of their faith.

Hill's writing was both a source of income and a way for her to have a public voice —two unusual accomplishments for a woman at the time—and her success depended in part on writing stories that segregated religious romance from women's fiction. Writing as Grace Livingston Hill, Grace Livingston Hill Lutz (*Lutz* being the name of her second husband, though she dropped it after he abandoned her), and Marcia Macdonald (her own mother's name), Grace Livingston Hill set the parameters for the Christian romance genre: a heterosexual couple thrown together by circumstances, overcoming a barrier that prevents them from acting on their instant attraction to each other, one or both of them Christians at the start and both of them Christians by the end. Because the young woman was often financially poor but spiritually rich, John Mort, the longtime Christian fiction reviewer for *Booklist*, with respect for both Hill's output and her contribution to Christian fiction, has called Hill's books "Horatio Alger, Jr. types of tales for women" (30). Indeed, Hill wrote even more books than Alger, whose popular stories of poor young boys, through enterprise, pluck, and a little luck, ended up as success stories, were nineteenth-century bestsellers.

Not surprisingly, Hill's work was both popular and reviled in its day. Herbert Carroll, in a 1933 essay in *The English Journal*, used Hill's as an example of the worst kind of writing, worrying that "the student who could not differentiate between Sigrid Undset [the winner of the 1928 Nobel Prize for literature] and Grace Livingston Hill Lutz has hardly profited greatly from his study of English" (185). And literary scholars have generally agreed about the relative merit of studying Hill's work: although there is a lively Grace Livingston Hill fan scene and biographies of the Christian romance genre's founder were published in 1948 (Karr), 1986 (Munce), and 1997 (Everett), her work is mostly ignored by scholars. Neal's excellent chapter on the history of evangelical romances in *Romancing God* rightfully puts Hill at the start of this history and remains the only scholarly work on Hill.

Despite Hill's remarkable output and her financial success as a writer, she was not immediately followed by other writers. Instead, Christians eager to read romance were easily able to pick up the sweet romances of the 1950s and 1960s that were published by secular publishing houses such as Harlequin without any fear of offending their religious sensibilities. It was not until the 1970s, with the increase of more sexually explicit novels, that Christian readers faced a dilemma: could they read such novels without moral harm to themselves? Could they in good conscience allow their mothers, daughters, husbands, sons, and neighbors to see them with the books in their hands? Why not, if given the opportunity, support Christian writers and Christian publishing? (Gandolfo 65).

Even as mainstream—that is, secular—romances were introducing more sexually explicit and sexually violent scenes, conservative evangelical Christian culture was developing its own popular culture (and thus consumer markets) and its own brand of politics. Moving into the 1980s, conservative evangelical Christians rejected pop, heavy metal, rap, and hip-hop as too sexualized or overtly evil. The 1989 Christian documentary *Hell's Bells: The Dangers of Rock 'N' Roll* (and its 2004 update, *Hell's Bells 2: The Power and Spirit of Popular Music*) argued against Christians listening to such music, while books like Phil Phillips's *Turmoil in the Toybox* (about children's toys) and *Saturday Morning Mind Control* (about cartoons) guided concerned parents away from Toys "R" Us and toward Christian retailers. (Not surprisingly, men's secular culture, such as professional sports, was less frequently attacked by Christian critics, though pornography, assumed to be the domain of men, remained a concern.) In response to the perceived need for "safe" Christian entertainment, Christian media devoted more airtime to Christian pop, rock, and heavy metal, which had been developing at music festivals since the early 1970s. Christian booksellers still focused heavily on nonfiction, including Bible studies and apocalyptic guides as those by author Hal Lindsey, who observed in the late Cold War world signs of the end of the world, but a model of Christian pop culture distinct from secular culture was being developed.

At the same time, the white conservative Protestants who make up the bulk of the market for evangelical Christian media began to mobilize politically around opposition to policies and cultural shifts that they saw as threatening the "traditional family" and, by extension, American civilization: advances in abortion rights and access to abortion, no-fault divorce, gay rights, and (more covertly) desegregation (Balmer 16). In this context, evangelical leaders and publishers pushed new versions of old teachings about gender, sex, and family that vaunted abstinence until marriage, stay-at-home motherhood, and patriarchal family structures. Books like Tim and Beverly LaHaye's *The Act of Marriage: The Beauty of Sexual Love* (1976), Marable Morgan's *The Total Woman* (1973), and others directed their readers—primarily women—on their role in protecting their individual families as well as the nation by preserving traditional femininity, which was to include being sexually desirable to and desirous of one's husband, and gender roles (Heller). Outfits such as Focus on the Family and the American Family Association, "pro-family" media endeavors that include publishing and radio programming, delivered not just advice to individual families in need of guidance on corporal punishment for children and homeschooling but also pressure on political leaders to listen to "values voters." The resulting vision of America as corrupt but evangelical Christian culture as a separate subculture of citizens who are "in the world but not of the world" has continued to maintain politically-motivating distress for many conservative evangelicals (also often joined by politically conservative Catholics, Latter-Day Saints, and Jews) while also ensuring a continued market for Christian pop culture.

Christian romance novels speak very clearly to the threats to family that conservative Protestants began to sense in the 1970s. As fictive sex got explicit, divorce rates skyrocketed, and gay rights advanced, Canadian author Janette Oke released *Love Comes Softly*, set on the Canadian prairie during westward expansion. The 1979 release has been followed by more than 75 additional books by Oke, some co-authored by her daughter, Laurel Oke Hogan. Soon after the book's release, Christian booksellers found that they had to make more shelf space for Christian romances as, to the chagrin of some male authors, Oke's books, published by the evangelical Bethany House, were selling very well—well enough, in fact, to reshape the Christian market and the fiction market more broadly. With Oke's contribution, Christian romance novels were "back," and she was soon joined by others focusing on inspirational romance.

As the genre took definition in the 1980s, more Christian publishers committed to romance lines, and Harlequin eventually introduced the Steeple Hill and Love Inspired lines, aimed at Christian women. The boom in popularity led to some market difficulties as new lines were launched, merged, and died, as John Markert outlines *in Publishing Romance: The History of an Industry, 1940s to the Present.* An apex of Christian fiction was seen in the 1990s with the publication of Tim LaHaye and Jerry B. Jenkins's *Left Behind* series of books. Focusing on a United States after the Rapture, the series follows two pilots who convert from atheism to Christianity and become leaders in the fight against the Anti-Christ, who is rising to global power. Eventually turned into a series of movies starring Kirk Cameron, then later remade into a film starring Nicholas Cage, the series was incredibly popular. Though the larger Christian fiction market saw a decline, sales in the years after the *Left Behind* series of apocalyptic fiction concluded, Christian romance novels continue to comprise a significant portion of romance sales.

As with popular fiction more broadly, digital and on-demand publishing has allowed more authors to enter the market and more readers to access books. Authors who found success in print publishing have purchased the rights to their early books and re-released them digitally, giving those books longer life spans and making the authors' full works available to fans. Additionally, online publishing has ensured that readers who may not have access to these books through public libraries (either because the library does not maintain a robust collection or because the readers are in rural areas without easy access to a library), church libraries (which may not circulate the books because they promote an "unrealistic" version of romantic love), or secular or Christian bookstores (which may not stock the books) can get them.

Christian romance novels, unlike secular romances, are thus supported by three unlikely allies: 1) secular presses (which provided, through their increasingly explicit books, impetus for Christian romances fiction's rebirth in the 1970s) and secular organizations that recognize the merit of faith-based romances, 2) religious presses and organizations, and 3) entrepreneurial authors who pursue writing as both a paid job (if often a low-paid one) and a religious calling, using traditional presses as well as digital distribution and print-on-demand to reach audiences directly through self-publishing. Given this, they appear in both religious and secular bookstores and both public and church libraries, as well as through online distributors such as Amazon. That expansive shelf space gives them access to audiences that secular books may not be able to tap and provides authors and publishers incentive to innovate to keep very large audiences engaged, and authors have responded by innovating in multiple ways—including by refining and challenging the genre.

The genre of Christian romances

The publication of Janette Oke's *Love Comes Softly* ushered in a permanent space for inspirational romances in the publishing sphere. From there, however, the Christian romance genre has diversified, both in response to cultural shifts and to market movement. Oke's *Love Comes Softly* is the story of Marty, a suddenly widowed (and pregnant) pioneer, who accepts a marriage of convenience to Clark, who is in need of a mother for his young daughter. A 2003 made-for-TV film adaptation starring Katherine Heigl as the protagonist and directed by Michael Landon, Jr., son of the star of *Little House on the Prairie*, was remarkably profitable for the Hallmark Channel. That film's success inspired the production of movies based on *Love Comes Softly*'s seven sequels, which move Marty and Clark's family ahead a few generations, as well as two prequel films not based on books. The setting of the books in bygone days allows for readers dismayed at contemporary culture to turn to a romantic (and rural) past in which they imagine life—including gender roles and ideas about romance, love, and sex—was simpler. That past seems to present a vision of lifelong heterosexual romantic partnership that was arduous—after all, prairie life wasn't easy, and the way of true love never runs smooth—but worthy. A valuable counterpoint to this idea is provided by Nelina Esther Backman in her 1999 dissertation on Christian fiction. In comparing the writing of T. S. Eliot, C. S. Lewis, and contemporary Christian romance novelists, Backman concludes that, for romance novelists, "history, the cultural object most regularly brought into these novels to lend them an air of Christian seriousness, ends up itself being trivialized" (218). Backman's criticism points to the ubiquity of a revisionist history of the founding and westward expansion of America found extensively throughout conservative evangelicalism, not just in romance fiction (Barrett-Fox "Love, Hope, and Toughness" 101). Historical details in these novels are intended as evidence for the authenticity of the story and the expertise of the author but, from a critical, scholarly perspective, are always in service of a plot that advances women's subordination in a literary endeavor that "strives to produce a reading experience that evokes more definitively than it alters the cultural and commercial values of its mainstream counterparts," as Backman notes in a comment that captures much of her derision for both secular and Christian romances (21).

As with secular romances, historical Christian romances are set in a variety of periods and places, including Scottish Highland novels, Regency novels, Manifest Destiny novels set in the U.S. and Canada, Civil War-era novels, and novels set in Europe during World War II that often blend romance and spy or adventure fiction. Some novels occur in "Biblical time," including stories based on Biblical texts and some set during early Christianity, particularly during its persecution, such as Carla Capshaw's *The Gladiator* (2009) and *The Champion* (2011).

Wherever they are set, the novels are marked by a closed-door treatment to sexual activity—meaning the author closes the bedroom door—or by a lack of sex completely, though this still makes them "contingent upon sexuality, restrained or otherwise" (Backman 225). But the novels have another interesting absence: "scant representation of plausible Christian institutions or formal religious practice" (Backman

243). Backman cites the editorial guidelines of Heartsong, once owned by Barbour and later by Harlequin, which ended the imprint in 2015: no references to water baptism, spirit baptism, glossolalia or other "gifts of the Holy Spirit," End Times prophecy, communion, or women's ordination, all of which are too doctrinally contentious among the varied readers of the genre (243). The doctrines presented in Christian romances must be palatable to a wide audience, and that is best accomplished by not addressing theology or doctrine at all. What is left is a generic, sanitized Protestantism recognizable to many, but ambiguous enough to allow readers to insert their specificities onto the characters. Characters rarely appear in church or discuss their religious experiences except in emotional terms. "Christianity," Backman argues, "is described no more elaborately than as the redoubtable 'personal relationship' with Jesus" (248). Backman, who clearly prefers the religious expression of Eliot and Lewis, scoffs at the vacuity of this kind of religion, but it aligns with the other kinds of religious expression familiar to evangelical believers, even if the "hypocognized nature of sentimentality implicitly discourages evangelicals from exploring not only the reason sentimentality should be used in evangelicalism but also the structures of power and authority that are covered by a syrupy, sweet veneer" (Brenneman 152). It may have its theological critics, but this "sentimental aesthetic exhibited in much of evangelical popular culture" (Neal *Romancing God* 194) has found similar expression in visual art, music, and even architecture (Kilde 146)

Romance novel plots occur, according to Pamela Regis in *The Natural History of the Romance Novel*, in the context of a corrupt society that love alone can reform (14). Thus, the story is about more than the couple at its center; it is about the power of love to transform what is corrupt and corruptible, to redeem what is fallen—the very heart of evangelical Christianity's understanding of the salvific death and resurrection of Jesus and the reason for such readers' faith. In a typical evangelical conversion narrative being "born again"—that is, the religious journey of evangelical Christians—the soon-to-be believer is engulfed in a culture that does not love or follow Jesus. This may look like freedom, just as the swinging life of a single woman may look like pleasure, but it is actually spiritual emptiness. Then, Jesus calls. There may be moments when it appears that the will-be believer will not respond to that call. As in a romance novel, some barrier—addiction, sexual shame, the busyness that keeps women's days full of meaningless activity—may arise that causes hesitation. But then the believer is overcome by God's love, which closes that gap between the believer's own sinful nature and God's love and wipes away the new believer's individual sins. God promises salvation for eternity and peace now, a love that is not deserved and cannot be lost and which establishes a new identity (Griffin 160; Hardin 173).

The power of love to reform is present in every romance but is key to Christian romances, even as those novels have to tread lightly in presenting the problems that heroes and heroines face. For example, editorial standards across the major publishing houses require that the novels not mention alcohol, drugs, gambling, magic, profanity, or illicit sex. Tension instead often comes from internal battles, particularly characters learning to rest in God's overwhelming love as they doubt whether they are worthy of it—a tension that sometimes appears between the hero and heroine in secular novels.

No Christian romance better captures this tension than Francine Rivers' *Redeeming Love*, a favorite of many readers (published by Bantam in 1991, republished by Multnomah in 1997). Rivers was a popular secular writer prior to the publication of *Redeeming Love*, which she based on the book of Hosea, a minor prophet from the

Hebrew Bible. While there are other elements of the book, the part that Rivers lifts for her purpose is story of Hosea's marriage, demanded by God, to the prostitute Gomer, a marriage that is a metaphor for God's relationship to Israel, a people who continually stray from him just as Gomer is sexually unfaithful to Hosea. Still, Hosea follows God's call to be faithful to his wife, going so far as to rescue her when she sells herself into sexual slavery. Similarly, through Hosea's prophetic voice in other parts of the Biblical book, God continues in his steadfast love for Israel, despite the people's wanton disregard for him.

Set in California during the Gold Rush era, *Redeeming Love* tells the story of a similarly faithful love, this one between Angel, a prostitute since childhood, and Michael Hosea, a patient farmer called by God to marry her. Written during Rivers' development as an evangelical Christian after her conversion in adulthood and first published by Bantam, the original novel included some language and descriptions of sex that would not meet Christian publishers' standards and did not include the baptism that would follow Angel's eventual conversion. When the rights to the novel became available, Rivers republished it with Multnomah, a Christian publishing house. Rivers shares about writing her favorite of her own novels in an interview with C.J. Darlington:

> The impact of the book Hosea is what cracked me wide open. [In a Bible study on Hosea], I thought I'd been so much like Gomer, turning to all kinds of other things to find fulfillment and happiness. God kept taking me back, and I thought about how we're all so much like that. We always look in every other place but the Lord. And when we finally do look to Him, that's what we've been looking for all our lives . . .
>
> I could just hear God saying, "This is the love story I want you to write." That whole year I felt like HE was sitting right with me saying, "Do you see how much I love you?"
>
> (Darlington 2016)

Throughout *Redeeming Love*, God tells Angel, too, that he loves her, in the form of Michael's care for her. At the start of their relationship, Michael pays Angel's pimp to have access to her in order to speak to her and convince her to leave the brothel and marry him. She repeatedly refuses, but when he returns to find her severely beaten, she finally capitulates and moves to his farm. There, though they are married, Michael never moves to have sex with Angel. Instead, he physically cares for her and nurtures her spirit so that, over time, she begins to trust her new husband after a lifetime of abuse at men's hands. Just as it appears that Angel may be responding to Michael's love, feelings of worthlessness overcome her, and, fearing that she is a burden to Michael, whose purity of heart deserves a better reward than her as a wife, she flees back to San Francisco. Her dignity restored by Michael's love, she does not return to sex work, but, after a conversion experience, runs a boarding house that helps women leave prostitution, fully in love with Michael but unwilling to destroy his chance of happiness with a more worthy woman and a chance at happiness and a family with a woman who has never been a sex-worker and is presumably able to bear many children, neither of which is true for Angel. Eventually, the barriers between them fall, as Angel learns that Michael continues to wait for her alone, and she returns to beg his forgiveness for her fearful running away and start a new life together.

The story follows not just the story of Hosea but the conversion narrative of a God who will pursue every lost sheep (Matthew 18:12–14), search for every lost coin (Luke 15:8–10), and to whom every single soul—including women who doubt their value—matters; most importantly, though men may be transformative figures in their lives, God takes priority and until a woman is secure in God's love for her, she cannot be a truly loving partner. While Christian readers often admit that *Redeeming Love* is more sexually fraught than other novels (and publishers, to their credit, did not publish *Redeeming Love* knockoffs that kept stories of sex slavery circulating), it remains one of the highest-selling Christian romances. It is also, not surprisingly, one that, along with Janette Oke's *Love Comes Softly* series and Beverly Lewis' romances set in Amish country and featuring characters who present themselves as Amish (though their theology is decidedly evangelical), has received the most scholarly attention. Lisa M. Gordis's insightful close reading of excerpts from the novel demonstrate Rivers' nuanced use of language that demand readers' careful attention in order to explore the full theological ramifications of the story (332–6). Indeed, the strength of Gordis's chapter, which considers the triangular relationship between husband, wife, and God in both Puritan narratives and Christian romances, is in its close reading of the novel and, by extension, her argument that such novels can be read as literary texts, not just studied as interchangeable social artifacts. Gordis's analysis could easily be used in either a classroom or a Bible study discussion of *Redeeming Love*, a book that may be purchased with its own study guide.

Though it violates some norms regarding generic conventions, *Redeeming Love* also captured what readers wanted in their novels: a story deeply rooted in God's enduring love, love that could, indeed, change not only the characters and their relationship to each other but also the larger world—just as it inspired Angel to start a halfway house for women. The hero is a man of faith, a "tender warrior" who is a spiritual leader and protector, as the title of Stu Weber's mid-1990s gender manual declares. While secular romances were often delivering heroes whose stony exterior was breached by emotionally vulnerable women, novels such as *Redeeming Love* and *Love Comes Softly* depicted men as emotionally available spiritual caretakers reaching out to women hurting in a world that exploits them. Both books follow the model that Laura Clawson identified in her content analysis of 120 Christian romances: heroes who are "never hyper-masculine" but whose "masculine authority is ultimately more stable, vulnerable to taming only by God" (431). Because the heroine must love God before she can love the hero, the larger story is of women finding rest, safety, and care in the promise of God to love them forever—a promise that even the most romantic secular novel cannot deliver. Couples who have recognized their attraction must put it aside, sometimes even sacrificing it, to focus on obedience to and their identity in God; indeed, God may be the obstacle that threatens to prevent their hoped-for union (Regis 14). Though a Christian romance always eventually "takes the dyad of the hero/heroine relationship and makes it a triad" (Neal "Evangelical Love Stories" 4), the threat that a duty to God may require the sacrifice of the romance is often present. Eventually, the individual's and couple's devotion to God is prioritized above—but also makes possible—their love for each other, an idea that runs through Christian gender and marriage manuals as well, as I argue in "Hope, Faith, and Toughness: An Analysis of the Christian Hero," which examines Christian marriage and gender self-help books alongside Christian romances to identify how Christian gender and marriage is constructed differently in fiction and nonfiction targeted to evangelical audiences (94). Drawing from Ecclesiastes 4:12, Christian romance author Gail Gaymer Martin reminds aspiring writers that "the romance is based on a three-fold cord" of hero, heroine, and God (92). This ideal of romantic love is infused throughout evangelical Christian culture, though critics have often lamented the "feminization" of the faith and the worship experience (See, for example, Leon D. Podles's *The Church Impotent: The Feminization of Christianity* or David Munrow's *Why Men Hate Going to Church.*). These critics have not, though, been able to curtail the popularity of Christian romances, which for decades have comprised a healthy minority of romance novels published and books checked out of public libraries, especially in regions of the U.S. with high concentrations of evangelical Christians (Dilevko and Atkinson 393).

The insertion of God between the characters, as a potential threat that could thwart their emerging love, or as the engine behind their unity, is the most important difference between Christian and secular sweet romances. It signals a fundamentally different understanding of the place of romantic love, which for Christian romances, is not the ultimate love. Instead, the novels must address (though it may not comprise the main plot) "confidence in God's care" that reflects an "intimate sense of divine providence" (Gordis 330). The endings of such novels are frequently presented as a more fulfilling ending than a secular romance could provide, for the novels end with the realization that the heroine's "responsibility is to love two bridegrooms, heavenly and earthly, both of whom love her" (Gordis 343). This fulfillment in God's love, as well as her husband's love, is the most important distinction for inspirational romance; it cannot be achieved in a secular romance.

Additionally, though secular romances traditionally end with the unification of the protagonists in a satisfying happily-ever-after, Christian romances present singleness as an option, albeit one that is never realized in the books, in the main characters' commitment to God above marriage. It could be that you love someone—and even that they love you—but God does not allow that relationship to take priority. The possibilities that this opens, particularly for single readers or those in unhappy or dysfunctional marriages, have not yet been explored by scholars but warrant study by those focusing on readers' experiences.

A final generic convention that has received attention from scholars focusing on the books themselves concerns gender roles. In "Cowboys and Schoolteachers: Gender in Romance Novels, Secular and Christian," Laura Clawson concluded that Christian heroines are more likely than their secular counterparts to hold up traditional family structures, evidence also found in Neal Christopherson's earlier analysis of secular and religious teen fiction, which is not limited to romance (Clawson 475; Christopherson 453). Clawson's work, which appeared in *Sociological Perspectives*, adopts a social scientific orientation toward the books, and her literature review is rooted not in studies of fiction but in sociological texts on religion and gender. She identifies several differences between secular and religious romances: Christian characters are more likely to have relationships with supporting characters such as family members or friends prior to the start of the romance, and references to non-traditional family structures were always negative, with divorce and previous spousal abuse to be largely absent in Christian romances (Clawson 468). On an array of measures, she finds that Christian novels are more likely than secular ones to show a couple following traditional gender roles, with Christian heroines more likely than other characters to clean, cook, and care for children or others (Clawson 472).

Clawson identifies the hero to be the most interesting figure in both secular or Christian romances, but in very different ways: Christian heroes are far less likely to be highly individualistic or stunningly handsome or to give visible displays of wealth or power; they are, she says bluntly, "by the standards of secular romance, weak" (Clawson 472). Clawson theorizes that evangelical doctrine does the work of reinforcing male superiority. "The Christian hero," she argues, "occupies the categorically dominant position of maleness, so he does not need to be a drop-dead, gorgeous, multimillionaire cowboy doctor" (469). In fact, one can argue that he actually cannot be. A typical "alpha" hero would not be able to coexist in the necessitated triad of God, spouse, and spouse. At the same time, his effectiveness as a hero is measured not by his money or muscles but by his "ability to lead—not the world, but a family" (Clawson 473). Though Clawson sees this "weak" hero as evidence of the strength of patriarchal gender norms within evangelical Christianity, he may also be an inspiration for women, even those comfortable with the ideal of patriarchy, to demand more companionate, egalitarian marriages, a key finding from my own interviews with readers responding to conservative Christian criticism of the genre as dangerous or damaging to their marriages (Barrett-Fox "Christian Romance Novels" 365). For example, if a woman is in an unsatisfactory marriage with a domineering husband, reading stories of inspirational heroes may assist her in articulating her disaffection and allow her language to dialogue with her husband about improving their particular triad. Indeed, conservative Christian critics of the genre fear exactly this: that the novels will reshape women's understanding of gender in such a way as to undermine traditional ideas of male dominance (Barrett-Fox "Higher Love").

Non-protestant Christian romances

Some non-Protestant Christian romances, such as books written specifically for Catholic and Mormon readers, incorporate beliefs particular to people of a religious subgroup. Catholic books may, for example, involve priests and nuns, while Latter-Day Saint (LDS) books may reference wards (LDS congregations) and stakes (groups of at least five wards, provided that they are able to supply the minimum number of men at the level of the higher order of priesthood with the LDS faith) as well as Mormon-specific organizations such as Young Women's and Young Men's, church auxiliary organizations for unmarried young people. Doctrines about sex and reproduction, such as Catholicism's focus on natural family planning, a theme of Pope John Paul II's Theology of the Body teachings, or LDS teaching on eternal marriage (in which a couple is "sealed" in a ceremony in an LDS temple, ensuring that their marriage will continue in the afterlife) inform the plot and the characters' spiritual development. As previously noted, these books do not dominate the market and are not frequently published by the larger houses. A robust Catholic market has yet to develop, pushing Catholic writers to independent presses and digital self-publication, as Kathryn Lively notes in the faith-based magazine *Catholic Exchange*. The unique structure of LDS publishing—the Church of Jesus Christ of Latter-Day Saints publishes books through Deseret Books and sells them through Deseret and Seagull bookstores—provides easier access to a market for LDS authors, who produce both "proper" (that is, sweet historicals that are not explicitly religious) and contemporary LDS-themed romances.

African American Christian romances

Likewise, authors writing about characters of color, including those in interracial relationships, have found easier access to audiences through publishers prioritizing books about non-white characters and through self-publication. Harlequin's Love Inspired line, for example, includes few novels by or about people of color, despite the fact that black women, in particular, express higher levels of religiosity than other groups (Brown, Taylor, and Chatters 453). Instead, with the exception of contributions to Love Inspired by Cecelia Dowdy and Felicia Mason, books focusing on the romantic experiences of people of color or interracial couples are often published by imprints focusing on racial and ethnic minorities, such as Kensington's Urban Christian, or by presses focusing on women of color, such as Brown Girl Books, which maintains an inspirational line led by Christian romance writer Rhonda McKnight. Kimani, Harlequin's imprint focusing on characters of color, launched New Spirit in the mid-2000s after purchasing the imprint from BET Books, but New Spirit failed to produce the African American Christian fiction it promised, and larger presses have since avoided developing an entire imprint devoted to the subgenre of African American Christian romances, leaving authors to publish with smaller presses, such as the charismatic Whitaker Press, or on their own. Indeed, Kimani released its final books in May 2019.

Writers of color may find better publishing success if they are willing to work across genres and markets. For example, Beverly Jenkin's *Blessings* series, set in a Kansas town founded by freed slaves, includes romance but also appeals to readers of Christian women's fictions more broadly, in part because of plot lines that address issues other than romance and the inclusion of protagonists older than the typical romance novel hero and heroine. Others of her books, though, include scenes that violate Christian romances' rules of sexual propriety, even as concepts of community-based loved (agape love), "with its power to change systems of domination," are central to both Jenkins' novels and Africa American expressions of Christianity (Dandridge 151). Such flexibility may increase the market for books featuring and written by women of color. Likewise, Angela Benson, who has won or been a finalist for a RITA Award from Romance Writers of America, a Christy Award for Christian fiction from the Evangelical Christian Publishers Association, and an Emma Award for inspirational fiction from Romance Slam Jam, which serves black romance writers, moves between secular and religious presses such Tyndale House, which serves a large evangelical population, and Walk Worthy, an African American-focused imprint of the Christian publisher Harrison House. Market savvy authors help keep books about African American women on bookshelves, but for readers seeking depictions of Latinx or Asian American characters, the choices are relatively few.

However, one of the major stories in the romance novel industry since the 1980s has been the explosion of affordable romance novels written by and for Philippine readers. Written in Tagalog, these novels have been wildly successful, with companies such as Precious Hearts Romances publishing 50 titles a month. Among the bestselling books in the Philippines, Tagalog-language romances travel the world with the migrant workers who read them and should be considered an international phenomenon (Encanto 27). Some of the books reject explicit messages of sex and promote a vision of femininity, marriage, and sexuality that aligns with traditional Catholic (the dominant religion in the Philippines) teachings on these topics, but no U.S. publishers have capitalized on the market to produce faith-based romances for Pinoy readers, and no scholarly work has been done in English on the religious aspects of such books.

Still, digital publishing has brought far more Christian romances by or about people of color to market and has allowed for them to develop in ways that may not address the editorial standards of romances targeted to white evangelicals. Books featuring black characters, for example, often focus on life in charismatic churches organized around a strong pastor and his wife, the "first lady" of the church, or love interest, such as in Brigette Manie's *Pioneers in the Pulpit* series (2014). Significant attention is given to the aesthetics of the worship experience, including church music. In contrast, romances focusing on white characters, in an effort to be as religiously generic as possible, rarely include such level of detail.

Romance novels focusing on black and Latino/a Christians diverge from the standards set by Love Inspired and white-focused evangelical publishers in other ways, too. In novels about African American characters, characters are often sexually experienced prior to the start of the novel. Recovering from sexual shame is sometimes a part of the plot. In Rhonda McKnight's *The Winter Reunion* (2016), for example, Tamar Johnson is "YouTube famous" for losing her virginity in a viral video. In *A Virtuous Ruby* (2015) by Piper Huguley and *Awakening Mercy* (for which she was a RITA finalist for inspirational fiction) by Angela Benson (2011), the heroines both have children prior to meeting the hero. In Tia McCollors' *Sunday Morning Song* (2014), the hero is married to an abusive man, now behind bars, and romantically pursued by the officer who helped in his arrest. Redemption during time spent in prison is occasionally a theme, as in Pat Simmons' *Crowning Glory* (2014) (an Emma Award Winner for inspirational romance) or Brigette Manie's *Convict to Christianity* series (2016). While *Redeeming Love* includes a woman who has been sexually abused, it is the exception, as few Christian romances marketed to white women include characters who have suffered victimization or divorce or characters who have committed crimes. Additionally, novels depicting interracial relationships are generally not part of Christian romances published by major houses. In a smaller market, reached heavily through digital publishing, where access is not mediated by editors and there is no press to fear backlash or boycott, authors focusing on the love lives of Christians of color may have more flexibility to address the real-life concerns, needs, and experiences of people of color–concerns often shared by white readers but not generally addressed by books marketed to them.

Amish romances

The most significant subgenre within Christian romances is the Amish romance. Almost always written by evangelical Christians—Linda Byler is the only Amish author of the subgenre—books about the Amish and other Plain People (Mennonites, Quakers, as well historical groups such as the Puritans) are so profitable that one Bethany House marketing executive noted that "You slap a bonnet on the cover and double the sales" (Miller). The exoticization of the Amish in the so-called "bonnet rippers" reveals the books to be evangelical stories, "the main themes, characterizations, and plot points of the stories ... often in direct conflict with traditional Anabaptist ideals of simplicity and nonviolence" and instead indicative of evangelical thinking about femininity, gender, and, most importantly, religious belief, which includes, for the Amish, an anti-missionary stance that makes little sense in American evangelicalism (Barrett-Fox, Review of *When Mercy Rains*).

Indeed, in their "didactic" function, the novels "instruct readers in evangelical doctrines of what faith and salvation are—and aren't" by assigning the "unappealing Amish attributes" to unlikable characters (Weaver-Zercher *The Thrill of the Chaste* 126). In the end, the books are, in some ways, anti-Amish, for they teach that "the antidote to Amish rigidity is evangelicalism," as Sigrid Cordell argues in "Loving in Plain Sight: Amish Romance Novels as Evangelical Gothic" (2). Literature scholar Cordell reads Beverly Lewis' earliest Amish romances, which, in the mid-1990s "established the commercial viability of the genre and inspired other authors to follow" (13) with attention to the Gothic details on the books. The novels, she argues, "draw on Gothic motifs to emphasize an image of the Amish as 'fallen' because of their rigid adherence to rules" what evangelical Christians call "legalism" (14). "[T]he protagonist always ends up, well, an evangelical"—even if still Amish, a key to their tremendous success among evangelical readers (Weaver-Zercher "Tracing the Backstory of Amish Romance Novels" 120). The complexity of the union of evangelical pop culture and Amish culture—"two parties that, depending on your perspective, either make the strangest of bedfellows or the perfect couple" (Weaver-Zercher *The Thrill of the Chaste* xii)—has inspired some of the most insightful scholarship on Christian romances: Valerie Weaver-Zercher's sensitive and sophisticated *Thrill of the Chaste: The Allure of Amish Romances*. Weaver-Zercher adopts a cultural studies approach, using interviews as well as scholarship on the Amish faith and culture and religion and popular culture and analyses of books and media coverage, to examine the novels in their context. While those studying Christian romances from a gender perspective, like Backman and Clawson, often express negative or frustrated views of readers, those coming from a religious studies point-of-view, like Weaver-Zercher and Neal, are more nuanced in their attempt to understand why people read. Yes, Weaver-Zercher recognizes, readers may have a "penchant for commodified escapism or regressive nostalgia," but they also may be "rehearsing a fictional alternative to supercharged contemporary life," following a "desire for a sane, coherent, and communal future" (*The Thrill of the Chaste* 250). Maja Štekovič sees this desire as the reason why non-Amish are attracted to media representations of Amish, arguing, "It might be paradoxical but it is precisely because of the Amish's wish to remain separated from modern society that they keep attracting media attention and have appeared as leading characters in . . . fiction" (20).

In this way, the novels are not just as escape *from* but an escape *to*. Not surprisingly, even authors and readers who are not religious are drawn to hybrid Amish romances, which combine Amish characters and pastoral settings with elements of supernatural thrillers, such as vampires or other shapeshifters, as well as erotic and queer Amish novels. (See, for example, Leanna Ellis, *Plain Fear: Forsaken*, Kiera Andrews *A Forbidden Romance*, or Yolanda Wallace's *Rum Spring: A Love Story*.) Though these novels are not Christian romances in the sense that they promote traditional Christian teachings about sexuality, romance, or love, they draw on purity/rigidity of Amish culture in the same ways that evangelical books do.

For further research

The relatively little scholarship published on Christian romance novels has emerged from a diversity of disciplines: literature, American studies, sociology, religious studies, and theology. The research that has been published is dispersed across journals that serve different fields—the *Journal of Popular Romance Studies*, for example, has yet to publish any scholarship focusing on it. The benefit of this is that scholars have thought about the topic in terms of reading and writing practices; publishing, marketing, and library collections; gender; family and marriage; and religious belief and practices. The potential for rich conversations across disciplines has not been fulfilled yet, though, as only two books—Lynn S. Neal's *Romancing God: Evangelical Women and Inspirational Fiction* and Valerie Weaver-Zercher's more narrowly focused *The Thrill of the Chaste: The Allure of Amish Romance Novels*—three book chapters, and fewer than a dozen articles have been devoted to the topic. Notably, only a few of the scholars who have contributed to academic understandings of the subgenre have published more than one scholarly manuscript on the topic, suggesting that research on Christian romance novels is a side project, one that scholars approach through their work on popular romance or their work on popular religion.

Perhaps because the scholars who work on the subgenre are not located in English departments, except in the case of Juliette Wells' essay on Christian adaptations of Jane Austen's work, Lisa Gordis' reading of *Redeeming Love*, Nelina Esther Backman's dissertation, and Sigrid Cordell's reading of Beverly Lewis's Amish trilogy, *The Heritage of Lancaster County* (1996–8) in "Loving in Plain Sight," scholarship on Christian romances does not maintain extended concentration on the texts narrowly. Instead, it tends to focus on the genre's messages about gender, as Clawson does in "Cowboys and Schoolteachers," Neal Christopherson does in "Accommodation and Resistance in Religious Fiction," Peter Darbyshire does in "The Politics of Love," and I do in "Faith, Hope, and Toughness: An Analysis of the Christian Hero," and "Christian Romance Novels: Inspiring Convention and Challenge," and how those messages resonate with broader evangelical teachings, or on the relationship between readers and their texts, as in Neal's *Romancing God*, Weaver-Zercher's *The Thrill of the Chaste*, and I do in "Higher Love: What Women Gain from Christian Romance Novels," an ethnographic study of fans and authors of the genre that appeared in *The Journal of Religion and Popular Culture*, and "Christian Romance Novels." While Backman is hostile to the genre as literature, the careful treatment of these texts by Wells, Gordis, and Cordell suggest that readers can rend more from their reading experience than simple affirmation of traditional notions about gender, something that women affirmed in my own research. Even though, as Clawson and Christopherson document from a social science perspective, the messages about gender tend toward the conservative, only Peter Darbyshire, writing about books from Harlequin's Love Inspired line in the 1990s, goes so far as to call these messages Religious Right propaganda.

Instead, as the stories that readers tell about their own reading experiences suggest, Christian romances and the experience of reading them and sharing them in a community of readers are viewed by readers as aids in personal piety, a key finding in Neal, Weaver-Zercher, and my own work. While this does not, of course, preclude the books from being used to bolster traditional understandings of gender, it does not appear that readers select the books for this purpose, and any book with a heavy-handed political message would likely be treated with the same kind of disdain that readers feel for Christian romances that are "too preachy." Interestingly, the focus on human subjects—readers and writers—has not been in literature but in religious studies, by scholars who have rejected the idea that readers simply accept, absorb, and then reproduce secular romance's ideas about gender roles. Instead, they believe readers when they say that they engage in reading strategies that give them more control over the process and results of meaning-making. In my own work, readers share intimate stories of how the books speak to their needs, providing them with encouragement and hope, often through passages that they are sure that God put in the book just for them. In interviews and correspondence, readers and writers alike shared with me that they are spiritually edified by what they read and by the practice of reading. As I share in "Higher Love," readers deliberately seek out such novels to ensure that their reading has a positive effect on their faith lives. In "Christian Romance Novels: Inspiring Convention and Challenge," published as a chapter in *Romance Fiction and American Culture: Love as the Practice of Freedom?*, edited by William A. Gleason and Eric Murphy Selinger (and in which Gordis' work also appears), readers shared in interviews and surveys that the books are "romance and ministry all in one" (353).

Given the small number of scholars working in this area, it may be too much to conclude that scholars with training in religion are more open to interpretations that give credence to individuals' religious experiences, but the pattern holds so far in the literature. Such a perspective is one of the blessings, so to speak, of having scholars from different fields working on the topic, and it is particularly important since evangelical Christianity itself is a subculture changing so fast as to produce "no one view on or definition of the evangelical romance novel" (Neal "Evangelical Love Stories" 17). Simply put, the field needs scholars with eyes on religion and on romance novels.

Changes in publishing, in particular, have opened up new opportunities for non-evangelical Christians such as Catholics and Mormons as well as African American and Hispanic evangelicals to develop their own books, and the relationships among "inspirational" books that speak to various forms of Christianity are worth studying, especially as white evangelicals may share political visions of gender and marriage with Mormons, Catholics, and evangelicals of color. John Market's "God is Love: The Christian Romance Market" tells the history of this market and looks forward to changes in the industry, but the project of tracking market changes is an ongoing one, not merely because of changes in how books are sold but because of changes in the evangelical population and changes that might emerge as new writers push the boundaries of the definition of "Christian," the "romance," and the "novel." Any study of the books must address the diverse subculture of evangelical Christianity, a subculture changing so fast as to produce "no one view on or definition of the evangelical romance novel" (Neal "Evangelical Love Stories" 17). While "Inspirational romance" is synonymous, in terms of marketing in bookstores, with "Christian romances," writers seeking to address other religions' takes on romance should also be included in scholarship on "inspirational romance." The popularity of books such as *When Dimple Met Rishi* by Sandhya Menon, Na'ima B. Robert's *She Wore Red Trainers: A Muslim Love Story*, Ayisha Malik's *Sofia Khan is Not Obliged*, or the novels of Falguni Kothari, Chaya T. Hirsch, and Paula Marantz Cohen, which feature Hindu, Muslim, and Jewish protagonists respectively, demands study of these texts on their own as well as in the larger context of religious fiction. As it has done for Christian romance novels, online publication provides new opportunities for writers of other faiths to find new markets. Additionally, the anonymity of online writing has allowed for some Muslim women, for example, to write short stories and novels that include graphic scenes of "halal sex," and independent publishing has provided Muslim authors with opportunities that traditional Muslim publishing houses, which often focus on non-fiction, do not offer. Scholars such as Hsu-Ming Teo, Maimuna Huq, and Zariat Abdul Rani Mohd, who have studied Muslim romances, and Emily Robins Sharpe, Michael Galchinsky, and Sarah Irving, who have studied Jewish romances, can expect more colleagues to join them as markets for these books continue to expand.

While scholarship on Christian romance novels has focused on books written specifically for a Christian market, need remains for scholarship on the ways that secular romances address religion. Some work has been done on Scarlett O'Hara's Catholicism in *Gone with the Wind* (Giemza 242) and much more on LDS themes in Stephenie Meyer's *The Twilight Saga* (Lampert-Weissig; Ledvinka 195; Toscano 21). But overall, scholars of popular literature have not effectively addressed religion in the literature they study or the religion of the readers of secular romances.

Readers' religion is important not just in the details of belief but of practice and religiosity—a measure of the intensity of one's religious commitments. Among evangelicals, there is diversity not merely in religious affiliation, doctrine, and devotional practices but also in the emphasis that these are given in a reader's life. The sociology of religion can assist scholars in understanding, for example, whether the content of individual teachings about, say, abstinence before marriage is more salient in understanding readers' experiences than the intensity of support for that belief. Likewise, library science scholars will find their work enriched if they understand theological arguments about reading, arguments that erupt with some frequency in meetings of churches' library committees, and scholars of literacy should examine how readers organize themselves into online reading groups, such as Glory Girls, an African American group boasting thousands of members, church-based reading groups, and intergenerational reading relationships between older and younger women (and writing, in the cases of both Grace Livingston Hill and her daughter and Janette Oke and her daughter). For scholars of race and ethnicity, work at the intersection of race, religion, and romance could yield deeper understandings of the reading and writing experiences of women of color and faith. Finally, media scholars should consider the ways that Christian romance is told across film, television, fiction, and nonfiction. For example, Kendrick and Kendrick's bestselling *The Love Dare*, a self-help book for couples, inspired *Fireproof*, an evangelical film about a firefighter attempting to save his imploding marriage. The film explicitly references the book, as viewers see the protagonist implementing its strategies. Readers can write their own testimonials, post daily updates in forums devoted to each of the 40 days of the dare, and upload their own video testimonials to the book's website, joining a community of those "taking the dare" as writers as well as readers, while FireProofYourMarriage.com, associated with the film, provides links to a novelization of the film, *Fireproof Your Life* by Southern Baptist pastor Michael Catt (an additional self-help book), a *Fireproof* small group curriculum, and romantic greeting cards for spouses. None of these can be understood, though, apart from evangelical religion.

Christian romance reading is part of "the complicated piety of ordinary people" their lived experience of a faith in a God who transforms the chaos of history "from a series of random events into a carefully ordered design that demonstrates [his] romance with humanity" (Neal, *Romancing God* 10, 184). As evangelical Christianity and the romance novel industry change, how readers live out their faith in reading and writing will also change, inviting scholars to continue to examine the dynamic genre of Christian romance.

Works cited

Andrews, Kiera. *A Forbidden Romance.* Amazon Digital Services, 2014.

Backman, Nelina Esther. *Evangelicalism Embarrassed: Christian Literature in a Post-Christian Culture.* 1999. Brown University, Ph.D. dissertation.

Balmer, Randall. *Thy Kingdom Come: How the Religious Right Distorts Faith and Threatens America.* Perseus, 2006.

Barrett, Rebecca Kaye. "Higher Love: What Women Gain from Christian Romance Novels." *Journal of Religion and Popular Culture,* vol. 4, no. 1, 2003.

Barrett-Fox, Rebecca. "Hope, Faith, and Toughness: An Analysis of the Christian Hero." *Empowerment v. Oppression: Twenty-First Century Views of Popular Romance Novels,* edited by Sally Goade, Cambridge Scholars Press, 2007, pp. 93–102.

———. Review of *When Mercy Rains,* by Kim Vogel Sawyer. *Mennonite Life,* vol. 69, 2015. ml .bethelks.edu/issue/vol-69/article/review-when-mercy-rains/. Accessed February 1, 2019.

———. "Christian Romance Novels: Inspiring Convention and Challenge." *Romance Fiction and American Culture: Love as the Practice of Freedom?,* edited by William A. Gleason, and Eric Murphy Selinger, Ashgate, 2016, pp. 347–368.

Brenneman, Todd M. *Homespun Gospel: The Triumph of Sentimentality in Contemporary American Evangelicalism.* Oxford University Press, 2013.

Capshaw, Carla. *The Gladiator.* Steeple Hill, 2009.

———. *The Champion.* Steeple Hill, 2011.

Carroll, Herbert A. "A Method of Measuring Prose Appreciation." *The English Journal,* vol. 22, no. 3, 1933, pp. 184–189.

Catt, Michael. *Fireproof Your Life: Building a Life that Survives the Flames.* Christian Literature Crusade, 2008.

"Christian Romance Novels: Edifying Entertainment or Emotional Pornography?" *Up for Debate.* Moody Bible Radio, Chicago, February 8, 2014. moodyaudio.com/products/christian-romance-novels-edifying-entertainment-or-emotional-pornography.

Christopherson, Neal. "Accommodation and Resistance in Religious Fiction: Family Structures and Gender Roles." *Sociology of Religion,* vol. 60, no. 4, 1999, pp. 439–455.

Clawson, Laura. "Cowboys and Schoolteachers: Gender in Romance Novels, Secular and Christian." *Sociological Imagination,* vol. 48, no. 4, 2005, pp. 461–479.

Cordell, Sigrid. "Loving in Plain Sight: Amish Romance Novels as Evangelical Gothic." *Journal of Amish and Plain Anabaptist Studies,* vol. 1, no. 2, 2013, pp. 1–16.

Dandridge, Rita B. "Love Prevailed despite What History Said: Agape and Eros in Beverly Jenkins' *Night Song* and *Through the Storm.*" *Romance Fiction and American Culture: Love as the Practice of Freedom?* edited by William Gleason, and Eric Murphy Selinger, Ashgate, 2016, pp. 151–166.

Darbyshire, Peter. "The Politics of Love: Harlequin Romances and the Christian Right." *The Journal of Popular Culture,* vol. 35, no. 4, 2004, pp. 75–87.

Darlington, C. J. "Francine Rivers Interview." *TitleTrakk,* no date, titletrakk.com/author-interviews/francine-rivers-interview.htm. Accessed November 2, 2016.

de Rossett, Rosalie. *Unseduced and Unshaken: The Place of Dignity in a Young Woman's Choices.* Moody, 2012.

Dilevko, Juris and Esther Atkinson, "Myth or Reality: The Absence of Evangelical Christian Fiction Titles in the Public Libraries of the United States." *Library & Information Science Research,* vol. 24, no. 4, 2002, pp. 373–396.

Ellis, Leanna. *Plain Fear: Forsaken.* Sourcebooks Landmark, 2011.

Encanto, Georgina R. "Savoring Romance Pinoy Style in Foreign Climes: Why Women Migrants Love Reading Tagalog Romance Novels." *Review of Women's Studies,* vol. 18, no. 1, 2008, pp. 27–52.

Everett, Betty Steele. *Grace Livingston Hill: Gracious Writer for God*. Christian Literature Crusade, 1998.

Fireproof. Directed by Alex Kendrick, performances by Kirk Cameron and Erin Bethea, Sony Home Pictures, 2008.

Galchinsky, Michael. *The Origin of the Modern Jewish Woman Writer: Romance and Reform in Victorian England*. Wayne State University Press, 1996.

Gandolfo, Anita. *Faith and Fiction: Christian Literature in America Today*. Praeger, 2007.

Giemza, Bryan. *Irish Catholic Writers and the Invention of the American South*. Louisiana State University Press, 2013.

Gleason, William A. and Eric Murphy Selinger editors. *Romance Fiction and American Culture: Love as the Practice of Freedom?* Ashgate, 2016.

Gordis, Lisa M. "'Jesus Loves Your Girl More than You Do': Marriage as Triangle in Evangelical Romance and Puritan Narratives." *Romance Fiction and American Culture: Love as the Practice of Freedom?*, edited by William Gleason, and Eric Murphy Selinger, Ashgate, 2016, pp. 332–336.

Griffin, Charles J. G. "The Rhetoric of Form in Conversion Narratives." *Quarterly Journal of Speech*, vol. 76, no. 2, 1990, pp. 152–163.

Gutjahr, Paul C. "No Longer Left Behind: Amazon.com, Reader Response, and the Changing Fortunes of the Christian Novel in America." *Book History*, vol. 5, 2002, pp. 209–236.

Hardin, Susan F. "Convicted by the Holy Spirit: The Rhetoric of Fundamental Baptist Conversion." *American Ethnologist*, vol. 14, no. 1, 1987, pp. 167–181.

Hell's Bells: The Dangers of Rock 'N' Roll. Directed by Eric Holmberg, American Portrait Films, 1989.

Heller, Jennifer. "Marriage, Womanhood, and the Search for 'Something More': American Evangelical Women's Best-Selling 'Self-help Books, 1972-1979." *The Journal of Religion and Popular Culture*, vol. 2, no. 1, 2002.

Huq, Maimuna. "From Piety to Romance: Islam-Oriented Texts in Bangladesh." *New Media in the Muslim World: The Emerging Public Sphere*, 2nd ed., edited by Dale F. Eickelman, and Jon W. Anderson, Indiana University Press, 2003, pp. 129–157.

Irving, Sarah. "Gender, Conflict, and Muslim-Jewish Romance: Reading ʿAli Al-Muqri's *the Handsome Jew* and Mahmoud Saeed's *the World through the Eyes of Angel*." *Journal of Middle East Women's Studies*, vol. 12, no. 3, 2016, pp. 343–362.

Karr, Jean. *Grace Livingston Hill: Her Story and Her Writings*. Grosset and Dunlap, 1948.

Kendrick, Stephen and Alex Kendrick. *The Love Dare*. B & H Publishing, 2008.

Khari, Brown, R., Robert Joseph Taylor and Linda M. Chatters. "Religious Non-involvement among African Americans, Black Caribbeans and Non-Hispanic Whites: Findings from the National Survey of American Life." *Review of Religious Research*, vol. 55, no. 3, 2013, pp. 435–457.

Kilde, Jeanne Halgen. *When Church Became Theatre: The Transformation of Evangelical Architecture and Worship in Nineteenth-Century America*. Oxford University Press, 2002.

LaHaye, Tim and LaHaye. Beverly. *The Act of Marriage: The Beauty of Sexual Love*. Zondervan, 1976.

LaHaye, Tim and Jerry B. Jenkins. *Left Behind: A Novel of the Earth's Last Days (Book 1 of 16 book series)*. Tyndale House, 1995.

Lampert-Weissig, Lisa. "A Latter Day Eve: Reading *Twilight* through *Paradise Lost*." *Journal of Religion and Popular Culture*, vol. 23, no. 3, 2011.

Ledvinka, Georgina. "Vampires and Werewolves: Rewriting Religious and Racial Stereotyping in Stephenie Meyer's *Twilight* Series." *International Research in Children's Literature*, vol. 5, no. 2, 2012, pp. 195–211.

Lively, Kathryn. "Catholic Authors Weave the Fabric of Faith and Romance." *Catholic Exchange*. March 16, 2004. catholicexchange.com/catholic-authors-weave-the-fabric-of-faith-and-romance. Accessed February 3, 2019.

Malik, Ayisha. *Sofia Khan is Not Obliged*. twenty7, 2015.

Manie, Brigette. *The Man Beside Her* (Book 1 of the Pioneers in the Pulpit series), edited by Shaakirah Medford, self-published by Brigette Manie, 1014.

Markert, John. *Publishing Romance: The History of an Industry, 1940s to the Present*. McFarland, 2016.

Martin, Gail Gaymer. *Writing the Christian Romance*. Writer's Digest Books, 2007.

Menon, Sandhya. *When Dimple Met Rishi*. Simon Pulse, 2017.

Miller, Lisa. "Amish Romance Novels." *Newsweek*, December 2, 2010, www.newsweek.com/books-amish-romance-novels-69049. Accessed February 4, 2019.

Mohd, Zariat and Abdul Rani. "Islam, Romance and Popular Taste in Indonesia: A Textual Analysis of *Ayat Ayat Cinta* by Habiburrahman El-Shirazy and *Syahadat Cinta* by Taufiqurrahman Al-Azizy." *Indonesia and the Malay World*, vol. 40, no. 116, 2012, pp. 59–73.

Morgan, Marabel. *The Total Woman*. Fleming H. Revell, 1970.

Mort, John. *Christian Fiction: A Guide to the Genre*. Libraries Unlimited, 2002.

Munce, Robert L. *Grace Livingston Hill: The Biography*. Tyndale House, 1986.

Munrow, David. *Why Men Hate Going to Church*. Thomas Nelson, 2011.

Neal, Lynn S. *Romancing God: Evangelical Women and Inspirational Fiction*. University of North Carolina, 2006.

———. "Evangelical Love Stories: The Triumphs and Temptations of Romantic Fiction." *Evangelical Christians and Popular Culture: Pop Goes the Gospel*, Vol. 1, edited by Robert H. Wood, Praeger, 2013, pp. 1–20.

Oke, Janette. *Love Comes Softly*. Bethany House, 1979.

Phillips, Phil. *Turmoil in the Toybox*. Starburst, 1986.

———. *Saturday Morning Mind Control*. Thomas Nelson, 1991.

Podles, Leon D. *The Church Impotent: The Feminization of Christianity*. Spence Publishing, 1999.

Raghu, Jyoti. "True Love's Kiss and Happily Ever After: The Religion of Love in American Film." *Journal of Popular Romance Studies*, vol. 5, no. 1, 2015. http://jprstudies.org/2015/08/true-loves-kiss-and-happily-ever-after-the-religion-of-love-in-american-filmby-jyoti-raghu/ Accessed January 20, 2020.

Regis, Pamela. *The Natural History of the Romance Novel*. University of Pennsylvania Press, 2007.

Rivadeneira, Caryn. "Why Romance Novels Aren't Emotional Porn." *Christianity Today*, June 7 2011, www.christianitytoday.com/women/2011/june/why-romance-novels-arent-emotional-porn.html. Accessed February 5, 2019.

Rivers, Francine. *Redeeming Love*. Multnomah, 1997.

Rix, Robert W. "'Love in the Clouds': Barbara Cartland's Religious Romances." *The Journal of Religion and Popular Culture*, vol. 21, no. 2, 2009. web.archive.org/web/20091119103047/www.usask.ca/relst/jrpc/art21%282%29-LoveClouds.html Accessed January 20, 2020.

Roach, Catherine. "Getting a Good Man to Love: Popular Romance Fiction and the Problem of Patriarchy." *Journal of Popular Romance Studies*, vol. 1, no. 1, 2010. http://jprstudies.org/2010/08/getting-a-good-man-to-love-popular-romance-fiction-and-the-problem-of-patriarchy-by-catherine-roach Accessed January 22, 2020. Unpaginated.

Robert, Na'ima B. *She Wore Red Trainers: A Muslim Love Story*. Kube, 2014.

Selinger, Eric Murphy. "Rereading the Romance." *Contemporary Literature*, vol. 48, no. 2, 2007, pp. 307–324.

Sharpe, Emily Robins. "Traitors in Love: The Spanish Civil War Romance Novel in Jewish North America." *Studies in American Jewish Literature*, vol. 35, no. 2, 2016, pp. 147–167.

Štekovič, Maja. "Crossing Cultural Frontiers: Representations of the Amish in American Culture." *Acta Neophilologica*, vol. 45, nos. 1–2, 2012, pp. 19–31.

Teo, Hsu-Ming. *Desert Passions: Orientalism and Romance Novels*. University of Texas Press, 2012.

Toscano, Margaret. "Mormon Mortality and Immortality in Stephenie Meyer's Twilight Series." *Bitten by Twilight: Youth Culture, Media, & the Vampire Franchise*, edited by Melissa A. Click, Jennifer Stevens Aubrey, and Elizabeth Behm-Morawitz, Peter Lang, 2010, pp. 21–36.

Wallace, Yolanda. *Rum Spring: A Love Story*. Bold Strokes, 2010.

Weaver-Zercher, Valerie. "Tracing the Backstory of Amish Romance Novels." *Mennonite Quarterly Review*, vol. 86, no. 4, 2012, pp. 409–435.

———. *The Thrill of the Chaste: The Allure of Amish Romance Novels*. Johns Hopkins University Press, 2013.

Weber, Stu. *The Tender Warrior: God's Intention for a Man*. Multnomah, 1993.

Wells, Juliette. "True Love Waits: Austen and the Christian Romance in the Contemporary U.S." *Persuasions Online*, vol. 28, no. 2, 2008.

9 Erotic romance

Jodi McAlister

Erotic romance has become one of the most recognizable forms of the romance novel in contemporary Western publishing. While the subgenre has a history spanning decades, if not longer, it exploded into mainstream consciousness with the runaway success of E.L. James' *Fifty Shades* trilogy (2012) and has enjoyed continued popularity via the works of authors like Sylvia Day, Maya Banks, Lisa Renee Jones, Tiffany Reisz, Jenny Trout, and Alisha Rai, among many more.

However, what "erotic romance" actually constitutes seems to be a question of some confusion. While romance writers and readers have some strong working definitions of the subgenre, confusion still exists between the relationship between erotic romance and neighboring categories, such as erotica, erotic fiction, sexy/spicy/steamy romance, and Romantica. This is particularly true in the post-*Fifty Shades* erotic romance landscape, as new readers with varying degrees of "genre competence" encounter the subgenre (Fletcher, Driscoll, and Wilkins 11). This also appears to be true in much of the scholarship on *Fifty Shades*, which often describes it as "erotic romance" without description or interrogation of what that term means, and rarely takes into account the position of the text within the existing erotic romance corpus: one piece on *Fifty Shades*, for example, cavalierly describes erotic romance as "a fairly new subgenre on the market" (Gosa 73).

While erotic romance is indeed a subgenre which has a history longer than ten years, the incredible popularity of *Fifty Shades*—as well as texts like Sylvia Day's *Crossfire* series, the first installment of which was also published in 2012—makes it easy to understand why this erroneous impression lingers. The market for erotic romance has changed. Whereas once it was a market we might describe as covert—it is not accidental, I think, that some of the earliest innovations in digital publishing were strongly tied to the publication of erotic romance novels—the impact of *Fifty Shades* means that erotic romance is now a highly visible subgenre. This chapter will seek to better and understand and define the erotic romance subgenre by positioning it in its industrial context. If we can understand where erotic romance has been, I contend, we can better understand it as a contemporary phenomenon, and perhaps predict its trajectories in the future.

What is erotic romance?

"Erotic romance" encompasses two key and distinct terms: "erotic" and "romance."

"Romance" here refers to the romance novel, the form which the Romance Writers of America (RWA) contends must encompass two key elements: a central love story and an emotionally satisfying ending. Both these elements remain key to the erotic romance novel, with the added requirement that sex—the "erotic" element of "erotic romance"—must be centered in the love story. This is reinforced in the definition of the genre given by Passionate Ink, the erotic romance special interest chapter of RWA. This definition draws on the same language as the RWA definition of romance, stating that erotic romance is:

> Romance in which erotic elements are integral to the plot and take the book beyond traditional romance boundaries. The erotic elements (in the context of any traditional or non-traditional romantic relationship) play a major part in plot and/or character development, and the end of the book is emotionally satisfying and optimistic.
>
> (Passionate Ink)

Perhaps the most interesting phrase in this definition is "beyond traditional romance boundaries." Kristen Phillips writes in her introduction to *Women and Erotic Fiction* that "[o]ne significant sense in which erotic fiction departs from romance fiction is its apparent intention to transgress" (10). She is writing here about erotic *fiction*, not erotic *romance*, and so we should be cautious in applying this principle of transgression directly to erotic romance. However, erotic romance is a space in which plot elements which might be considered less traditional do appear with more frequency than they would in other forms of the genre. For example, while most iterations of the romance novel feature a focus on a couple, erotic romances which focus on a ménage a trois are not uncommon: see, for instance, Shayla Black and Lexi Blake's *Master of Ménage* seven-book series, which utilizes Harlequin-style keyword titles in the plural (*Their Virgin Captive*, *Their Virgin's Secret*, etc.). However—as, perhaps, neatly highlighted by the Harlequin-esque titles of Black and Blake's erotic romance series, with that implicit reference to the mainstream category romance—in the erotic romance this transgression must be embedded within the recognizable framework of the romance novel, which requires an emotionally satisfying ending: that is, the protagonists must live happily ever after. We might think of the "erotic" as an additional project of the erotic romance novel. It must meet the generic needs of the romance novel, but it must also be driven by sex (often, sex which is "beyond traditional romance boundaries" in that it troubles key assumptions, such as the assumption of monogamy). It is not enough that sex in the erotic romance be frequent, although it generally is. Sex must drive the erotic romance narrative: the story would not make sense without the presence of sex. This is summed up neatly in the definition of the genre offered by Kristin Ramsdell in her guide to the romance genre: erotic romances are, she contends, "romance novels—complete with happy endings—in which the love relationship between the protagonists develops through and is inextricably linked to sexual interaction which is explicitly described" (533).

This is supported in other definitions of the genre offered by writers, readers, and industry figures, which offer further elaboration on the relationship between sex and love (or, perhaps, "the erotic" and "the romance") in the genre. Kate Duffy was an iconic romance editor who pioneered the Brava line at Kensington Books in 2001, a line which was one of the first to be dedicated to erotic romance. In her editorial note on this line, Duffy wrote that, "[e]rotic romance is sexual love and desire combined with deep emotional commitment. It is not erotica. It is, first and foremost, romance, exemplified by its sexual expression" ("Note from Editorial Director"). She elaborated on this some years later in a guest post on Michelle Buonfiglio's blog "Romance: B(u)y the Book," contending that:

> I think it's that commitment that separates some of the erotic romance from some of the erotica. In other words, the hero and heroine may think it's lust, the reader knows it's love. The hero and heroine may think it's temporary, the reader knows it's forever.
>
> ("Love, Not Lust")

In the erotic romance, then, desire and love always exist or come to exist simultaneously, and the simultaneity of their existence must ultimately be recognized by the protagonists, even if they do not realize this at first. In this way, the erotic romance must largely follow the trajectory of the romance novel, which includes as one of its central elements, as Pamela Regis argues, a declaration of love (30). Indeed, as Sarah Frantz argues, sexual interactions between the protagonists supply most of Regis' elements, including this one (47–8). However, the fact that desire and love ultimately come to be collapsed together in the erotic romance also draws attention to the tension between these two, and often, the assertion by one or more protagonists that sexual desire and romantic love are independent creates conflict that drives the plot forward. This is exemplified, for instance, in *Fifty Shades*, where Christian's belief that he is incapable of romantic love and initial insistence on maintaining a purely physical relationship with Anastasia is the source of considerable conflict, particularly in the trilogy's first installment.

It is this collapsing together of sexual desire and romantic love, along with the fact that sex must be central to the plot of the erotic romance, which are the genre's defining features: quite literally, as they are the features used to differentiate it from other forms of both erotic fiction and the romance novel. For instance, erotic romance author Sylvia Day differentiates erotic romance from the genres of pornography, erotica, and sexy romance in the following way:

- Porn: stories written for the express purpose of causing sexual titillation. Plot, character development, and romance are NOT primary to these stories. They are designed to sexually arouse the reader and nothing else.
- Erotica: stories written about the sexual journey of the characters and how this impacts them as individuals. Emotion and character growth are important facets of a true erotic story. However, erotica is NOT designed to show the development of a romantic relationship, although it's not prohibited if the author chooses to explore romance. Happily Ever Afters are NOT an intrinsic part of erotica, though they can be included.
- Erotic Romance: stories written about the development of a romantic relationship through sexual interaction. The sex is an inherent part of the story, character growth, and relationship development, and couldn't be removed without damaging the storyline. Happily Ever After is a REQUIREMENT to be an erotic romance.
- Sexy Romance: stories written about the development of a romantic relationship that just happen to have more explicit sex. The sex is not an inherent part of the story, character growth, or relationship development, and it could easily be

> removed or "toned down" without damaging the storyline. Happily Ever After is a REQUIREMENT as this is basically a standard romance with hotter sex.
>
> ("What is Erotic Romance?", emphasis in original)

Another genre term that must be understood when discussing erotic romance is Romantica, because this is a space with which much erotic romance overlaps. However, it should be understood that Romantica is a publisher-specific term: it was used exclusively by the recently-closed Ellora's Cave. It was used to describe works which

> follow most of the conventions of the romance genre, focusing on the development of a central love story culminating in with [sic] an emotionally satisfying, happy ending. The difference lies in the erotic component of Romantica stories. Romantica books contain frequent sex scenes, described explicitly using frank language rather than flowery euphemisms. Because of our astounding success, many people erroneously use the term Romantica to describe any erotic romance, but it is accurately used to describe only erotic romance published by Ellora's Cave.
>
> ("New to EC?")

At the time of its closure, Ellora's Cave listed 14 different Romantica lines on its website, including Branded (erotic romance featuring married couples), Fusion (multicultural/interracial), Sophisticate (older woman/younger man), and Taboo (BDSM). Interestingly, it also included two lines—Kink (fetish) and Shivers (horror)—which it listed as "HEA optional." While the closure of Ellora's Cave means that the term Romantica will likely fall gradually out of use and I will not consider it at any further length, this is both an important term to understand when examining the historical context of erotic romance and an excellent example of how erotic romance pushes "traditional genre boundaries." Many of the Romantica lines listed above revolved specifically around the boundary being pushed: the pairing of an older woman and a younger man, for instance, is by no means unheard of in more "mainstream" romance, but it is certainly not the most common pairing.

The "HEA optional" Romantica lines listed above also point to another way in which erotic romance pushes traditional genre boundaries. The happy ending, wherein the couple (or other configuration) are concretely committed to each other for the future, while not optional in erotic romances the way that it might have been in these specific Romantica lines, is often delayed and/or positioned at a different place in the narrative arc. This is particularly true of erotic romances in the post-*Fifty Shades* landscape, and is something we can perhaps attribute to the success of that trilogy. Many of what we might think of as "mainstream" romance novels focus on courtship—so much so that Pamela Regis defines the romance genre as "a work of prose fiction that tells the story of the courtship and betrothal of one or more heroines" (19). However, the nature of erotic romance means that this is not always necessarily the case. These are narratives which focus on sex, and so the key characters at the center of the novel must be—in some senses, at least—together for the narrative to continue. If the characters are not having sex, then the erotic romance novel is not fulfilling its mandate.

This does not necessarily mean that the couple/ménage/other configuration need to be together in *all* senses: the most cursory look at *Fifty Shades* proves this to be incorrect. Anastasia and Christian continue to have sex even while they are in different emotional spaces and while they have different romantic priorities, particularly in the first installment of the trilogy. Likewise, in Sylvia Day's *Crossfire* series, hero and heroine Eva and Gideon continue to have sex while other aspects of their relationship seem to be non-functional, as can be seen in the following excerpt from *Reflected in You*, the second of the *Crossfire* books, in which Eva and Gideon are attending couples' therapy:

> Dr Petersen sat back. "Eva has brought up concerns of infidelity and lack of communication in your relationship. How often is sex used to resolve disagreements?"
>
> . . .
>
> "Most interactions between us lead to sex," I conceded, "including fights."
>
> "Before or after the conflict is considered resolved by both of you?"
>
> I sighed. "Before."
>
> . . .
>
> "Your relationship has been highly sexualised from the beginning?" he asked.
>
> I nodded, even though he wasn't looking. "We're very attracted to each other."
>
> "Obviously." He glanced up and offered a kind smile. "However, I'd like to discuss the possibility of abstinence while we—"
>
> "There is no possibility," Gideon interjected. "That's a nonstarter. I suggest we focus on what's *not* working without eliminating one of the few things that is."
>
> (50, emphasis in original)

We might read Gideon's adamant refusal to stop having sex with Eva as a meta-commentary on the genre: a reassurance to the reader that no matter what happens in the narrative, Eva and Gideon's sexual exploits will continue to drive the novel forward.

However, while the characters at the center of the erotic romance do not necessarily need to be in a committed, concrete, and functional relationship, as seen above, often they do make a commitment to each other a considerable time before their narrative ends. Christian and Anastasia get married between the second and third books of their trilogy, but despite what we might consider a "bedrock" (pun intended) commitment, their story continues—and continues to be driven by sex. Likewise, Eva and Gideon get married in *Entwined with You*, but this is only the third of the five *Crossfire* books. Increasingly, erotic romance has begun to explore what An Goris calls the "post-HEA." Goris writes that:

> [G]enerally the romance novel spends remarkably little time narratively depicting the romantic love and happiness that is teleologically pursued throughout its courtship plot. Traditionally, the HEA then functions more as a narrative promise than a narrative actuality. It implies romantic love, stability, and happiness for its protagonists, but it does not include extensive actual representations of this happiness.
>
> (n.p.)

Goris' article is about serialization, and it focuses on the way the serialized romance novel explores this hitherto largely unexplored post-HEA space, where the commitment has been made and the promise of the happy ending is actually extensively represented in texts, including exploration beyond a cursory epilogue. However, this is a space that, arguably, the erotic romance was exploring even before it became a popularly serialized form. The nature of the erotic romance novel means that the characters *being* together, rather than the characters *getting* together, is necessarily one of its narrative focuses. This means that, while the erotic romance still has the markers of a "mainstream" romance, with a central love story and an ending to that love story which is emotionally satisfying and optimistic, the structure of the erotic romance is often somewhat different, encompassing the post-HEA. Elsewhere, I have argued that the erotic romance fuses together the generic structures of the romance novel and pornography. The former builds toward an emotional climax, while the latter is based on the repetition of sexual climaxes. The erotic romance combines these apparently incompatible forms: in erotic romance, "pleasure is infinite and infinitely repeatable," and the texts offer "instant and delayed gratification, sexual and emotional pleasure, [and] titillation in a 'safe' discursive space" for women (McAlister 23–33). The erotic romance fuses together the structures of romance and pornography as well as some of their ideological properties, combining titillation with emotional satisfaction.[1] In *Fifty Shades of Grey*, Anastasia and Christian have the following exchange, which offers a neat description of the nature of erotic romance:

> "I thought you didn't make love. I thought you fucked hard." I swallow, my mouth suddenly dry.
> He gives me a wicked grin, the effects of which travel all the way down *there*.
> "I can make an exception, or maybe combine the two, we'll see."
> (110)

While it is certainly the most famous, *Fifty Shades* is by no means the only text to combine "making love" and "fucking hard." This is the space in which erotic romance exists: a space which pushes the boundaries of the romance genre, both structurally and in terms of content.

The history of erotic romance

Contrary to popular opinion (some of which, as mentioned earlier, has been perpetuated in scholarship), erotic romance is not a new genre. We can see its roots in some of the earliest novels in the English language: John Cleland's *Memoirs of a Woman of Pleasure* (1749), for example, might be considered one of the ancestors of the genre. In this pornographic novel, protagonist Fanny Hill, whose name is often substituted as the book's title, details her erotic exploits as a prostitute in England. While this is primarily a book about lust, and not love, it is framed by a love story. Fanny loses her virginity to Charles, a young nobleman with whom she falls in love. Although he disappears after their initial love affair, and Fanny continues her career as a prostitute for many years, he does eventually return at the end of the novel and he and Fanny get married.

We should be wary of drawing too direct a line between *Memoirs of a Woman of Pleasure* and modern erotic romance—the fact that Fanny and Charles' love story is not exactly central to the narrative is one of the key reasons why. In addition, Cleland is a man writing for a presumably male audience, whereas erotic romance is, like other forms of romance, female-dominated. However, if Bradford K. Mudge is correct when he asserts that "the pornographic novel of the mid- to late eighteenth century grew directly out of women's fiction" (29),[2] it is unsurprising that a feminized version of this narrative later appeared. If not a grandmother of the modern erotic romance, *Memoirs of a Woman of Pleasure* is perhaps a great aunt: we can see here the emergence of the narrative model that would eventually be co-opted by writers of love stories and adapted to form the modern erotic romance novel.

Many histories of erotic fiction would now embark upon a discussion of literary figures such as the Marquis de Sade and Anaïs Nin and texts like *Venus in Furs* and *The Story of O*. However, I have deliberately chosen to omit them here. This is not to say that they have not had an influence on the formation of the erotic romance subgenre, as this would be a rather sweeping claim to make. However, their influence is, I think, overstated, particularly in the discussion of texts like *Fifty Shades*. When discussing erotic romance, we cannot privilege the erotic over the romance. The texts above are certainly erotic fiction, but because they do not include these romantic elements and the frame narrative of the love story, to talk about them in the same breath as today's erotic romance novel is to misunderstand some of the modern genre's appeal.

More productive texts to discuss as ancestors are texts like E.M Hull's novel *The Sheik* (1919), which, despite the fact that it did not explicitly represent sex, certainly implied it—in a way that, like many erotic romances, went "beyond traditional romance boundaries"—and whose explosive and incredible popularity makes it a logical text to read against *Fifty Shades*, as I have done elsewhere (McAlister). Similarly, we cannot ignore the influence of the erotic historical romance novel. Kathleen Woodiwiss' *The Flame and the Flower* (1972) is generally said to be the first novel in this genre; however, more direct ancestors of the modern genre can be found in the works of authors like Bertrice Small, Thea Devine, Susan Johnson, and Robin Schone in the late 1970s,[3] a period referred to by Hsu-Ming Teo as the "burgeoning of the erotic romance novel" (156), where texts like these, according to Carol Thurston, "served as models for much of what follows" (51). As noted in a comprehensive post on erotic romance on the romance blog *The Misadventures of Super Librarian*, these authors were marketed as historical, rather than erotic, romance authors, but their brand was constructed as such that "[y]ou read one book by Small, Devine, Johnson or Schone and *you knew* the next book you pick up by them is more than likely going to singe your eyebrows off" (Wendy).

As Katherine E. Morrissey claims, the romance market in the late 1970s "was organised around two poles: steamy historicals and sweet contemporaries" (45). This meant that most of what we would describe as erotic romance was historical fiction. Although works by authors like Schone and Johnson continued to be bestsellers well into the 1990s (Frantz 58), the polarization of the market began to change in the 1980s, where one of the most distinct shifts was the emergence of erotic and romantic narratives set in contemporary as well as historical settings. In Britain, Jilly Cooper's *Riders* (1985) and Jackie Collins' *Rock Star* (1988) were both very popular, and while they might not exactly fit the mandate of the modern erotic romance, are commonly referents in the same "bonkbuster" discussion as *Fifty Shades* (Goldhill). Less famously, but still importantly, British author Anne Weale's novel *Antigua Kiss* (1983) was an early example of a contemporary romance featuring an oral sex scene and a scene where the heroine initiated sex, pushing generic norms in the way that erotic romance so often does. In category romance publishing, the 1980s saw the emergence of lines like Dell Candlelight Ecstasy (1980), Silhouette Desire (1982) and Harlequin Temptation (1984), as the competition between publishers in what is often referred to as the "Romance Wars" drove the growth in erotic content (Thurston 53). Books in these lines were not exactly what we would now describe as erotic romance—sex was not fundamental to the narrative in the same way that it is in the modern genre. However, sex did become much more important than it had hitherto been in contemporary category romance, as can be seen in this excerpt from the "Emphasis" section of the Silhouette Desire guidelines:

> realistic and detailed love scenes will be possible, providing they are tastefully handled. Sexual encounters—which may include nudity and lovemaking even when the protagonists are not married—should concentrate on the highly erotic sensations aroused by the hero's kisses and caresses rather than the mechanics of sex. A celebration of the physical pleasures of love, as well as its emotional side, should be an important part of these books.
>
> ("Silhouette Desire Guidelines Circa 1982")

Similarly, the Dell Candlelight Ecstasy guidelines specified that, while they did not want sex scenes in the books to be "pornographic, or overly explicit," they did "feel that sexual chemistry and emotional involvement do bring men and women together in the most wonderful ways" ("Candlelight Ecstasy Guideline Circa 1980"). We can see in these series the emergence of the ideological, if not the structural, framework that would come to govern the erotic romance novel: the one that positions good sex as an indicator of true love, and ties the two inextricably together.

The market continued to diversify in the 1990s. In 1993, Black Lace, an imprint of Virgin Books, was founded in the United Kingdom, with the mission statement to publish erotic fiction "written by women, for women" (Ebury). These books did not necessarily have a happy ending, although many did, and were, if not necessarily romance, romance-adjacent. In the United States, Red Sage Publishing was founded in 1994. As Katherine Morrissey notes, Red Sage clearly advertises its position as a progenitor of the modern erotic romance novel (49), writing on its website:

> Readers love sophisticated, fun, adventurous romances with a wide-open bedroom door, something that Red Sage has provided right from the beginning. Before there were e-books, before there was something labelled "erotic romance," there was Red Sage.
>
> (Red Sage)

Red Sage was particularly well-known for its *Secrets* anthologies, which draws our attention to one of the more interesting points about erotic romance. This is, as I have already discussed, a subgenre in which generic boundaries are regularly pushed. These are not just boundaries of content, but boundaries of form. There is clearly a considerable difference between the anthologized short story form and the now-more common serialized form of erotic romance; however, the fact that one of the texts pointed to as a progenitor of the erotic romance novel is not, in fact, a novel is telling when we consider the apparent desire of the subgenre to push the boundaries of the broader romance genre.

In 1999, Kensington also published an erotic anthology, *Captivated*. This included works by Small, Devine, Johnson, and Schone. Arguably, this marks the moment when "the erotic" and "the romance" collided: when the erotica market, led by houses like Black Lace and Red Sage, was colonized by romance. Although, as Morrissey notes, the marketing for authors like Schone during the 1990s was already drifting toward the erotic (50), these were authors who were known as romance authors. By positioning them explicitly (pun intended) as *erotic* romance authors, both via *Captivated* and, in 2001, through the launch of Kensington's Brava line, which promised "the best in erotic romance fiction" (Ramsdell 536), Kate Duffy, the editor behind both initiatives, had a considerable hand in shaping the trajectory of what would eventually become the modern erotic romance novel.

Kensington was not alone: the emergence of Brava was part of a definite market shift. Other publishing houses were also testing their own erotically-inclined material. In 1997, Harlequin started publishing Blaze books as part of their Temptation line, signaling their increased erotic content paratextually to the reader via, among other things, images of flames on the covers. Blaze proved so popular that in 2001 Harlequin separated it from Temptation and made it its own distinct line. Temptation closed in 2005, but Blaze survived: something which suggests a distinct growth in the demand for erotic romance. (Harlequin closed Blaze in 2016; however, in 2018, it pioneered a new line, Dare, which effectively took its place.)

There are many reasons we could suggest for this demand. Chief among these reasons is the fact that, with the emergence and expansion of the erotic romance market, readers were now becoming more comfortable in this sub-genre. There were words and genre labels for the kind of stories they were looking for: readers could connect with books more easily, and so the demand for these books grew. But this is by no means the only reason: demand was also being driven because a new market—the e-book market—was beginning to open up.

It is important to understand that the emergence of the e-book market was by no means sudden, nor was there an instant uptake. The first Amazon Kindle was launched in 2007, and while there was certainly an e-book market before this point, it was hardly what could be called mainstream. However, this market did exist, and many of the first interventions in this space were to do with erotic romance. The online publisher Ellora's Cave was launched in 2000, primarily to give founder Tina Engler a way to publish "sexually explicit romantic fiction" ("About Ellora's Cave"), which was consistently rejected by publishers because of its erotic content. According to the Ellora's Cave website:

> Engler was not one to give up on what she believed was an untapped market in romance literature: erotic romance, which she called Romantica®. She believed that women would enthusiastically embrace these sexually charged romance stories, where the love scenes are explicit and leave nothing to the imagination. She decided that if she couldn't persuade anyone else to publish her work, she'd find a way to do it herself.
>
> ("About Ellora's Cave")

Engler did indeed do it herself, publishing her own work under the name Jaid Black, as well as going on to acquire and publish the work of other writers—including Joey W. Hill, whose *Nature of Desire* series were well-known BDSM romances years before

E.L. James appeared—and Ellora's Cave fairly swiftly became a highly successful company (Frantz 47). While, as I mentioned, we should not assume that uptake of e-reading was instant among readers, a number of small digital romance presses emerged, which suggests a natural kind of affinity between the two forms. Not all of these were erotic romance presses, but many did publish erotic romance lines—such as Mundania Press' (est. 2002) Phaze line (which commenced in 2004) as well as the erotic romance published by Samhain (est. 2005) (Frantz 58–9).

According to the blog *The Misadventures of Super Librarian*, the interventions made in erotic romance by Ellora's Cave are often overstated: while they were important in the emergence of the genre, they certainly did not invent it. Similarly, the fact that they were a digital-only press in a period where e-reading was a fairly marginal practice means that it is also difficult to argue that they mainstreamed the genre:

> stumbling across a digital-only publisher like EC back in the very early days of digital reading? Not an easy thing unless word of mouth hit their ears. But walk into any bookstore and chances were pretty good that you'd find a Brava title, or for that matter—a Harlequin Blaze.
>
> (Wendy)

However, what Ellora's Cave did do, especially at their inception in 2000, when the major erotic romance texts being published were anthologies of short stories and/or novellas such as Red Sage's *Secrets* or Kensington's *Captivated*, was publish stand-alone novels. They also "really helped ramp it all up": their books contained much more intense and transgressive sexual content than those being published by the more mainstream presses (Wendy). We should be careful ascribing too much responsibility for the modern erotic romance genre to Ellora's Cave; however, we should note, as Sarah Frantz does, the way in which their success and the success of erotic romance as a niche digital market both reflected and contributed to a growing eroticization of the more mainstream print market in the early twenty-first century (47).

One of the oft-cited reasons for the success of erotic romance in digital form is paratextual: when you read on an e-reader, paratext is flattened out, and no one can tell what you are reading. It is easy to see why this might improve the appeal of erotic romance for its female readership, many of whom, given the dominant cultural codes around female behavior, might have been too ashamed to access it otherwise. But paratext is not the whole of the thing here—other innovations in the digital space also contributed to the explosive success of erotic romance in the 2010s. Chief among these is the emergence of fanfiction: in particular, erotic fanfiction.

Fanfiction and *Fifty Shades*

Fanfiction is, of course, a form with its own detailed literary history, which I do not have time to trace here (for a fuller history, see Jamison). Like erotic romance, fanfiction did not suddenly spring into existence in the early twenty-first century. However, what this period did offer is a new accessibility for the form, as fanfiction communities began to grow online.

The emergence of the online space as a forum for writing led to a collision between erotic romance and fanfiction that was, perhaps, inevitable, as there are certain similarities in the impetuses behind each form. As outlined above, one of the characteristics of erotic romance is its tendency to push boundaries. Fanfiction has a similar mandate —in this case, pushing at the boundaries of the canonical texts in which it is rooted. As Lev Grossman writes in his foreword to Anne Jamison's *Fic*:

> [Fanfiction is] not about simply churning out more and more iterations of existing characters and worlds that their creators couldn't or wouldn't do. It's about boldly going where no man or woman has gone before, because oh my God, who would even have thought of that?
>
> (xii)

Grossman goes on to say that fanfiction is "subversive and perverse and boundary-breaking" (xii), something which distinctly echoes the language used around erotic romance. It is unsurprising, then, that, while certainly not all fanfiction is erotic, much is, as fic writers push the boundaries and limits of their canonical texts, just as erotic romance writers push the boundaries and limits of the romance genre.

There is much that can be said about the ways in which fanfiction and erotic romance are intertwined; however, for the sake of this chapter, I will focus specifically on the ways in which fanfiction gave rise to erotic romance's most (in)famous text: *Fifty Shades*.

As has been well-documented, *Fifty Shades* began life as *Master of the Universe*, erotic fanfiction of Stephenie Meyer's young adult romantic saga *Twilight*, in which corporate success and BDSM stand in for Edward's vampirism, and in which the interludes of erotic abstinence in *Twilight* are replaced by actual erotic interludes. Anne Jamison offers a comprehensive history of *Master of the Universe*'s history, where she makes the interesting argument that, as the *Twilight* fandom developed, the focus of the fandom and the fanfiction moved away from the canonical texts and eventually became more about "romance writing in a mix of subgenres" (181). Jamison contends that:

> Aspiring writers began repurposing their original work as Twilight fanfiction, changing the names *to* Edward, Bella, Rosalie, Jacob. Writers with little if any connection to Twilight began writing stories about its characters because they could get attention and feedback and *so many readers* if they played along.
>
> (181, emphasis in original)

The fandom's most popular fics, including *Master of the Universe*, enjoyed "readership that dwarfed most *New York Times* bestsellers" (Jamison 181). For the fandom charity auction Fandom Gives Back in 2010, E.L. James (then writing under the moniker Snowqueens Icedragon) donated a chapter of *Master of the Universe* from Edward's perspective—*Master of the Universe* being written in the first-person from Bella's perspective, as *Fifty Shades* is from Anastasia's—which sold for U.S.$30,000 (Jamison 220). There is no evidence to suggest that James intended for *Master of the Universe* to be a commercial enterprise—she claimed that she had "done it as a sort of exercise" (Jamison 249): however, the enormity of the readership of *Master of the Universe* and the fact that a single alternative-point-of-view chapter could raise so much money pointed distinctly to the commercial potential of the work. As Jamison writes, "[h]er [James'] readers had proven her own marketability—the Twilight fandom had become, in effect, a test market" (249).

James' move to commercially repackage her fic—in a move that came to be known as "pull to publish" or P2P—was not the first of its kind. In 2009, the fanfiction hosting site Twilighted launched its own publishing house, Omnific. Its first title, published in early 2010, was *Boycotts and Barflies*, a Twilight fic of the same name that had been minimally edited and repackaged, and it later went on to repackage the erotic fic *The University of Edward Masen* as *Gabriel's Inferno*. While Omnific is not specifically an erotic romance publisher, the language it uses does highlight the common ground between fanfiction and erotic romance: its tagline is "romance ... without rules" (Omnific). James eventually published with a similar nascent small press: The Writer's Coffee Shop (TWCS), which grew out of a fanfic site of the same name. Although, unlike Omnific, TWCS "was not started as a place to publish popular fanfic" (Beaty 257), they did acquire some, including *Master of the Universe*. According to Tish Beaty, who was James' editor at TWCS, "[t]he decision to publish *Fifty* was an easy one" (257), because the popularity and immense existing readership would effectively put TWCS on the map.

This decision proved to be a fruitful one. Within a year of publication, TWCS sold a combined 100,000 print and e-book copies of what was now the *Fifty Shades* trilogy. As Andrew Shaffer prosaically writes, "the books *blow up*. Not just explode: they actually *blow the fuck up*" (268, emphasis in original). In March 2012, the series was acquired from TWCS by Vintage (an imprint of Random House) in a seven-figure deal. With the strength of a Big Five publishing house—in particular, its distribution capabilities—behind it, the popularity of *Fifty Shades* became even more explosive. Other enormous publishing deals for P2P fics-cum-erotic-romance-series followed: for instance, Sylvain Reynard's *Gabriel's Inferno* was acquired by Berkley (an imprint of Penguin) from Omnific for a seven-figure deal in August 2012 (Lewis, "Mysterious Author"); *Beautiful Bastard*, a reworking of the Twilight fic *The Office*, was acquired by Gallery Books (an imprint of Simon & Schuster) in November 2012 in a deal described as "substantial" (Lewis, "'Twilight' Fanfiction Hit"); and *The Submissive*, a reworking of the BDSM Twilight fic of the same name by Tara Sue Me, was acquired by New American Library (an imprint of Penguin) in February 2013 (Fleming).

The rise of P2P fic changed not just the face of erotic romance publishing, but of publishing more broadly. No longer the province of category romance lines or small, dedicated publishing houses like Ellora's Cave (or, indeed, of fanfiction sites),[4] erotic romance suddenly became a publishing sensation, with the weight of Big Five publishers thrown behind it. While the acquisition of P2P fics by major publishing houses seems to have slowed somewhat—particularly in the wake of the P2P acquisition by Simon & Schuster of Anna Todd's One Direction fic *After* (originally published on Wattpad, where it had over one billion reads), which does not seem to have done particularly well in the mainstream market—the acquisition and publication of erotic romance more generally does not seem to have slowed. The career of Sylvia Day, author of the erotic romance *Crossfire* series, for instance, has flourished, as even the most cursory glance at the industry news section of her website reveals (Day "All the Industry News"). (It is worth noting that, in the immediate wake of *Fifty Shades*, Day signed an eight-figure contract with Penguin U.S. and a seven-figure contract with Penguin U.K. for the fourth and fifth *Crossfire* titles). Several erotic romance series, including *Crossfire* and Lisa Renee Jones' *Inside Out*, have been optioned for television: a space into which more "mainstream" romance has been unable to penetrate, with the possible exception of Diana Gabaldon's *Outlander* series.

Erotic romance has also succeeded in the self-publishing arena. Alisha Rai's *Serving Pleasure* was the first self-published title ever to appear in a *Washington Post* best-of-the-year book lists (Maclean). Rai's work is emblematic of a gradual but perceptible move toward a diversification in the forms of post-*Fifty Shades* erotic romance, especially in self-publishing: her protagonists are not white, nor is the setting corporate. And perhaps the most interesting case of success following the publication of *Fifty Shades* is the success of the self-published erotic romance series *The Boss* by Abigail Barnette. Out of frustration with the *Fifty Shades* series, Barnette—one of several pseudonyms of the author Jenny Trout—wrote chapter-by-chapter recaps on her blog. These proved highly popular. She decided to write and self-publish her own erotic romance series in which to better model BDSM and consent practices, and the resultant series—*The Boss*—proved considerably successful, and re-energized what had hitherto been her flagging career.

The success of *Fifty Shades* and the erotic romance boom that followed in its wake points to two interesting areas for further future developments and scholarly analysis. First, while it is incorrect to say that *Fifty Shades* originated a new form of erotic romance, it made erotic romance uniquely visible. With the emergence of *Fifty Shades*, erotic romance went from being arguably the least to the most visible subgenre in popular romance fiction. With that visibility comes a level of influence and power. As scholarship on erotic romance develops, interrogating the influence and power of the subgenre may prove to be a fruitful area of study. To what extent has it shaped, grown, or planted the seeds for other subgenres of romance? The launch of the new Harlequin Dare sign seems to suggest that this continues to be a fruitful space, even six years after the explosive popularity of *Fifty Shades*. The submission guidelines for Dare solicit stories which "push the boundaries of sexual explicitness while keeping the focus on the developing romantic relationship," but which are "sexy contemporary romances ... we're not accepting erotica or erotic romance" (Harlequin). This distinction between the "sexy contemporary" and the "erotic romance" is a fascinating one, and one which may prove fascinating for popular romance scholars: even despite its explosive mainstream popularity, does erotic romance remain tightly associated with transgression?

This leads neatly to the second area for future development and scholarly analysis. As I have outlined above, erotic romance is a form to which pushing boundaries is fundamental. This is evident not just in terms of content, but also in terms of genre: the move toward serialization, for instance, raises questions about the generic structure of the romance narrative. If and how the explosive popularity of erotic romance reshapes the romance novel more broadly remains to be seen. This should be a subject for further scholarly inquiry, as it is hard to think that there will not be a marked and noticeable effect, given the sudden and extraordinary visibility of these novels in which sexual episodes drive the romantic narrative—novels in which, as Gideon says in *Reflected in You*, abstinence is not a possibility.

Notes

1 It is also worth noting that erotic romances often incorporate other plot structures to support the erotic/romantic narrative, perhaps to keep the narrative moving after the work of the romance narrative has been resolved and the text has moved into the post-HEA space. Lisa Renee Jones' *Inside Out* series, for instance, includes a suspense plot that

drives the novels even after the romantic relationship between protagonists Sara and Chris is solidified.

2 Specifically, Mudge is referring to the work of female authors like Aphra Behn, Eliza Haywood, and Delarivier Manley.

3 These four writers were identified by Kate Duffy as "four of the great writers of erotic romance of all time," and she went on to recruit all four to write for Kensington Brava. (Duffy "Note from Editorial Director.")

4 While this shift in publishing mode for erotic romance is certainly not the only reason for the recent closure of Ellora's Cave, it should not be discounted as a factor.

Works cited

Barnette, Abigail. *The Boss*. Self-published, 2013.

Barnette, Abigail. *The Girlfriend*. Self-published, 2013.

Barnette, Abigail. *The Bride*. Self-published, 2014.

Barnette, Abigail. *The Ex*. Self-published, 2014.

Barnette, Abigail. *The Baby*. Self-published, 2015.

Beaty, Tish. "Bittersweet." *Fic: Why Fanfiction is Taking Over the World*, edited by Anne Jamison. BenBella Books, 2013, pp. 253–258.

Black, Shayla and Lexi Blake. *Their Virgin Captive*. Self-published, 2011.

Black, Shayla and Lexi Blake. *Their Virgin's Secret*. Self-published, 2011.

Black, Shayla and Lexi Blake. *Their Virgin Concubine*. Self-published, 2012.

Black, Shayla and Lexi Blake. *Their Virgin Hostage*. Self-published, 2013.

Black, Shayla and Lexi Blake. *Their Virgin Princess*. Self-published, 2013.

Black, Shayla and Lexi Blake. *Their Virgin Secretary*. Self-published, 2014.

Black, Shayla and Lexi Blake. *Their Virgin Mistress*. Self-published, 2015.

Cleland, John. *Memoirs of a Woman of Pleasure*. 1749. Wordsworth Editions, 1993.

Collins, Jackie. *Rock Star*. Heinemann, 1988.

Cooper, Jilly. *Riders*. Corgi Books, 1985.

Day, Sylvia. "What is Erotic Romance?" *SylviaDay.com*, 2005, www.sylviaday.com/extras/erotic-romance/. Accessed November 8, 2016.

Day, Sylvia. *Bared to You*. Penguin, 2012.

Day, Sylvia. *Captivated by You*. Penguin, 2012.

Day, Sylvia. *Reflected in You*. Penguin, 2012.

Day, Sylvia. *Entwined in You*. Penguin, 2013.

Day, Sylvia. *One with You*. Penguin, 2016.

Day, Sylvia. "All the Industry News." *SylviaDay.com*, n.d., www.sylviaday.com/media-kit/industry/. Accessed November 8, 2016.

Dell. "Candlelight Ecstasy Romance Guidelines Circa 1980." *RomanceWiki*, n.d., web.archive.org/web/20170304151848/www.romancewiki.com/Candlelight_Ecstasy_Romance_Guidelines_Circa_1980. Accessed January 20, 2020.

Duffy, Kate. "Love, Not Lust." *Michelle Buonfiglio's Romance: B(u)y the Book*, December 4, 2006, http://romancebytheblog.blogspot.com.au/2006/12/kate-duffy-guestblog-love-not-lust.html. Accessed January 20, 2020.

Duffy, Kate. "Note from Editorial Director, Kate Duffy." *RomanceWiki*, n.d., www.romancewiki.com/Brava. Accessed November 8, 2016.

Ebury. "Black Lace." *Penguin Random House U.K*, n.d., www.penguinrandomhouse.co.uk/publishers/ebury/black-lace/. Accessed November 8, 2016.

Ellora's Cave. "About Ellora's Cave." *Ellora's Cave*, n.d.a, www.ellorascave.com/about-elloras-cave/. Accessed November 8, 2016.

Ellora's Cave. "New to EC?" *Ellora's Cave*, n.d.b, www.ellorascave.com/about-elloras-cave/new-to-ec/. Accessed November 8 2016.

Fleming, Mike, Jr. "NAL Hopes for *Fifty Shades* Audience, Acquires Steamy Fan Fiction Trilogy *The Submissive*." *Deadline*, February 14, 2013, http://deadline.com/2013/02/nal-hopes-for-fifty-shades-audience-acquires-steamy-fan-fiction-trilogy-the-submissive-430489/. Accessed November 8, 2016.

Fletcher, Lisa, Beth Driscoll and Kim Wilkins. "Genre Worlds and Popular Fiction: The Case of Twenty-First-Century Australian Romance." *Journal of Popular Culture*, vol. 51, no. 4, 2018, pp. 997–1015.

Frantz, Sarah S. G. "How we love *is* our soul: Joey W. Hill's BDSM Romance *Holding the Cards*." *New Approaches to Popular Romance Fiction: Critical Essays*, edited by Eric Murphy Selinger and S. G. Frantz. Jefferson, McFarland, 2012, pp. 47–59.

Gains, Alice, Bonnie Hamre, Ivy Landon and Jeanie Legendre. *Secrets*. Red Sage Publishing, 1995.

Goldhill, Olivia. "The History of Erotic Fiction." *The Telegraph*, March 6, 2015, www.telegraph.co.uk/women/sex/11455231/The-history-of-erotic-fiction.html. Accessed November 8, 2016.

Goris, An. "Happily Ever After . . . And After: Serialization and the Popular Romance Novel." *Americana: The Journal of American Popular Culture (1900–present)*, vol. 12, no. 1, 2013. www.americanpopularculture.com/journal/articles/spring_2013/goris.htm. Accessed November 8, 2016.

Gosa, Codruta. "From Fantastic *Twilight* to *Fifty Shades* Fanfiction: Not Another Cinderella Story." *Reading the Fantastic Imagination: The Avatars of a Literary Genre*, edited by Dana Percec. Cambridge Scholars Publishing, 2014, pp. 57–76.

Grossman, Lev. "Foreword." *Fic: Why Fanfiction is Taking Over the World*, edited by Anne Jamison. BenBella Books, 2013, iii–xiv.

Harlequin. "Dare Submission Guidelines." *Submittable*, n.d., https://harlequin.submittable.com/submit/62305/harlequin-dare-50-000-words. Accessed August 10, 2018.

Hill, Joey W. *Holding the Cards*. Ellora's Cave, 2003.

Hill, Joey W. *Natural Law*. Ellora's Cave, 2004.

Hill, Joey W. *Ice Queen*. Ellora's Cave, 2006.

Hill, Joey W. *Mirror of My Soul*. Ellora's Cave, 2006.

Hill, Joey W. *Mistress of Redemption*. Ellora's Cave, 2006.

Hill, Joey W. *Rough Canvas*. Ellora's Cave, 2007.

Hill, Joey W. *Branded Sanctuary*. Ellora's Cave, 2010.

Hull, E.M. *The Sheik*. 1919. ReadHowYouWant, 2008.

James, E.L. *Fifty Shades Darker*. Vintage, 2012.

James, E.L. *Fifty Shades Freed*. Vintage, 2012.

James, E.L. *Fifty Shades of Grey*. Vintage, 2012.

Jamison, Anne. *Fic: Why Fanfiction is Taking Over the World*. BenBella Books, 2013.

Jones, Lisa Renee. *If I Were You*. Pocket Books, 2012.

Jones, Lisa Renee. *Being Me*. Pocket Books, 2013.

Jones, Lisa Renee. *Revealing Us*. Pocket Books, 2013.

Jones, Lisa Renee. *I Belong To You*. Pocket Books, 2014.

Jones, Lisa Renee. *No In Between*. Pocket Books, 2014.

Jones, Lisa Renee. *All Of Me*. Pocket Books, 2015.

Lauren, Christina. *Beautiful Bastard*. Gallery Books, 2013.

Lauren, Christina. *Beautiful Player*. Gallery Books, 2013.

Lauren, Christina. *Beautiful Stranger*. Gallery Books, 2013.

Lauren, Christina. *Beautiful Secret*. Gallery Books, 2015.

Lauren, Christina. *Beautiful*. Gallery Books, 2016.

Lewis, Andy. "Mysterious Author Scores Seven-Figure Deal for *Fifty Shades*-esque Novel." *Hollywood Reporter*, August 1 2012. www.hollywoodreporter.com/heat-vision/gabriel's-inferno-sylvain-reynard-book-deal-356544. Accessed November 8, 2016.

Lewis, Andy. "'Twilight' Fanfiction Hit 'The Office' Scores Two-Book Deal." *Hollywood Reporter*, November 8 2012. www.hollywoodreporter.com/news/twilight-fanfiction-hit-office-gets-387539. Accessed November 8, 2016.

Maclean, Sarah. "Best Romance Novels of 2015." *Washington Post*, November 18, 2015. www.washingtonpost.com/entertainment/books/the-best-romance-novels-of-2015/2015/11/18/5d661010-7902-11e5-b9c1-f03c48c96ac2_story.html?tid=a_inl. Accessed November 18, 2016.

McAlister, Jodi. "Breaking the Hard Limits: Romance, Pornography and the Question of Genre in the *Fifty Shades* Trilogy." *Analyses/Rereadings/Theories*, vol. 5, 2015, pp. 23–33.

Meyer, Stephenie. *Twilight*. Little, Brown, 2005.

Meyer, Stephenie. *New Moon*. Little, Brown, 2006.

Meyer, Stephenie. *Eclipse*. Little, Brown, 2007.

Meyer, Stephenie. *Breaking Dawn*. Little, Brown, 2008.

Michaels, Victoria. *Boycotts and Barflies*. Omnific Publishing, 2010.

Morrissey, Katherine E. "Steamy, Spicy, Sensual: Tracing the Cycles of Erotic Romance." *Women and Erotic Fiction: Critical Essays on Genres, Markets and Readers*, edited by Kristen Phillips. McFarland, 2015, pp. 42–58.

Mudge, Bradford K. *Women, Pornography, and the British Novel, 1684–1830*. Oxford University Press, 2000.

Omnific. "About Omnific." *Omnific Publishing*, n.d., http://omnificpublishing.com. Accessed November 8, 2016.

Passionate Ink. "FAQ: 1) What is Erotic Romance?" *Passionate Ink*, n.d. www.passionateink.org/faq/. Accessed November 8, 2016.

Phillips, Kristen. "Introduction: Shattering Releases." *Women and Erotic Fiction: Critical Essays on Genres, Markets and Readers*, edited by Kristen Phillips. McFarland, 2015, pp. 1–21.

Rai, Alisha. *Serving Pleasure*. Self-published, 2015.

Ramsdell, Kristin. *Romance Fiction: A Guide to the Genre*. Libraries Unlimited, 2012.

Réage, Pauline. *The Story of O*. translated by John Paul Hand, 1954. Blue Moon Books, 1993.

Regis, Pamela. *A Natural History of the Romance Novel*. University of Pennsylvania Press, 2003.

Reynard, Sylvain. *Gabriel's Inferno*. Berkley, 2012.

Reynard, Sylvain. *Gabriel's Rapture*. Berkley, 2012.

Reynard, Sylvain. *Gabriel's Redemption*. Berkley, 2013.

Romance Writers of America. "About the Romance Genre." *Romance Writers of America*, n.d., www.rwa.org/p/cm/ld/fid=578. Accessed November 8 2016.

Sage, Red. "About Red Sage." *Red Sage Publishing*, n.d., http://redsage.securesites.net/store/ABOUT_RED_SAGE.HTML. Accessed November 8, 2016.

Shaffer, Andrew. "Fifty Shades of Gold." *Fic: Why Fanfiction is Taking Over the World*, edited by Anne Jamison. BenBella Books, 2013, pp. 268–273.

Silhouette. "Silhouette Desire Guidelines Circa 1982." *RomanceWiki*, n.d., www.romancewiki.com/Silhouette_Desire_Guidelines_Circa_1982. Accessed November 8, 2016.

Small, Bertrice, Susan Johnson, Thea Devine and Robin Schone. *Captivated*. Kensington, 1999.

Sue Me, Tara. *The Dominant*. New American Library, 2013.

Sue Me, Tara. *The Submissive*. New American Library, 2013.

Sue Me, Tara. *The Training*. New American Library, 2013.

Teo, Hsu-Ming. *Desert Passions: Orientalism and Romance Novels*. University of Texas Press, 2012.

Thurston, Carol. *The Romance Revolution: Erotics Novels for Women and the Quest for a New Sexual Identity*. University of Illinois Press, 1987.

Todd, Anna. *After We Collided*. Gallery Books, 2014.

Todd, Anna. *After We Fell*. Gallery Books, 2014.

Todd, Anna. *After*. Gallery Books, 2014.

Todd, Anna. *After Ever Happy*. Gallery Books, 2015.

Todd, Anna. *Before*. Gallery Books, 2015.

Trout, Jenny. "Jealous Hater Book Club." *JennyTrout.com*, n.d., http://jennytrout.com/?page_id=5720. Accessed November 8 2016.

Von Sacher-Masoch, Leopold. *Venus in Furs*. 1870. Project Gutenberg, n.d..

Wendy. "The Quick and Dirty History of Erotic Romance." *The Misadventures of Super Librarian*, October 2 2014. http://wendythesuperlibrarian.blogspot.com.au/2014/10/the-quick-and-dirty-history-of-erotic.html. Accessed November 8, 2016.

Woodiwiss, Kathleen. *The Flame and the Flower*. Avon, 1972.

10 African American romance

Julie E. Moody-Freeman

This chapter examines scholarly literature and contemporary journalism about African American romance fiction. Romance fiction by African American authors and featuring African American protagonists, like other popular romance, follows the Romance Writers of America's (RWA) required elements: "a central love story" and "an emotionally satisfying and optimistic ending" ("About the Romance Genre").[1] Sub-genres of African American romance include contemporary, historical, paranormal, erotic, suspense, and religious/spiritual ("Romance Sub-Genres"). While popular African American Romance fiction fits the construction that RWA prescribes, scholars agree that Black writers have included elements of the romance convention in literary fiction since the 1800s. Therefore, this chapter begins by studying scholarly discussions that emerge between 1987 and 1993 which examine how late nineteenth- and early twentieth-century Black women writers imbued their literary fiction with messages about love, marriage, and social uplift. Next, I examine scholarly publications from the early 2000s that highlight the intergenerational links and departures between contemporary African American romance writers and writers from the 1800s. Scholars conclude that while both generations integrate agape love into their romantic narratives—that is, love for community through racial uplift—Black writers publishing after the 1980s incorporate both agape and erotic love. The study of scholarship on African American romance fiction, however, is not limited to just engaging with the intergenerational links between contemporary romance writers and writers from the 1800s. I examine how both scholarly and journalistic publications document a history of African American romance publishing by highlighting the contributions of publishers, editors, and writers to developing and diversifying the romance industry. Finally, I examine scholarship that employs a variety of theoretical and methodological approaches to studying interracial romance as well as publications that examine sexuality, health, and disability in African American romance novels.

Studies on romance and racial uplift in literary fiction

Scholarly discussions from 1987 and 1993 highlight how love, marriage, and social uplift intersect in Black women writers' novels published in the 1800s. Hazel Carby's 1987 publication *Reconstructing Womanhood: The Emergence of the Afro-American Woman Novelist* notes the use of romance in Frances Harper's 1892 novel *Iola Leroy*. Carby argues that Harper "initially utilize[s] romantic convention and then discard[s] the romance" (79). On the one hand Dr. Latimer was represented as the "ideal of a high, heroic manhood" (Carby 79). However, Carby concludes that the "partnership" between Iola and Latimer served Harper's didactic purpose to illustrate that "the life of the two young intellectuals would be based on a mutual sharing of intellectual interest and a common commitment to the 'folk' and the 'race'" (80). In her analysis, Carby notes: "It was through Dr. Latimer's and Iola's 'desire to help the race [that] their hearts beat in loving unison'" (80). This analysis of *Iola Leroy* is useful in highlighting how Harper uses the lexicon of romance (hearts, loving, unison ...) to serve the political goals of Black social uplift during the Reconstruction era.

While Carby's discussion in *Reconstructing Womanhood* highlights how Harper utilizes "romance convention" to further an uplift agenda, Claudia Tate's 1992 publication *Domestic Allegories of Political Desire: The Black Heroine's Text at the Turn of the Century* uncovers additional novels written in the late 1890s in which love, romance, marriage, and uplift intersect. Tate argues that

> The post-reconstruction domestic novels of Black women, most of which cluster in the 1890's, constitute a specific category of African American fiction in which the virtuous heroine generally undergoes a series of adventures en route to marriage, family happiness, and prosperity.
>
> (5)

Tate studies 11 "domestic novels," including Harper's *Iola Leroy* and Katherine D. Tillman's *Beryl Weston's Ambition: The Story of an Afro-American Girl's Life* (1893). Published one year apart, the novels are shaped by "the mid-nineteenth century ideology of love as duty" (Tate 98), yet the novels also reflect varying ideologies about women's roles in public spaces after marriage. Tate argues that in *Iola Leroy*, the heroine Iola is engaged in education but within the more domestic boundaries of the church in "Sunday School" (98) with her husband as a "helpmate" (187). In contrast, Iola's sister-in-law, Lucille Delaney, who serves as a secondary character, is committed to her role as educator in the "public sphere" (Tate 98, 187). In contrast to Harper's heroine who seemingly doesn't breach the conventions governing "feminine roles" during the 1800s, Katherine D. Tillman's heroine Beryl in *Beryl Weston's Ambition* is a married woman, with two children and a "rewarding career" teaching at a college (Tate 187, 188). Tate notes that the novel clearly distinguishes and even rewards "love as duty" (98) over "passionate love" (186). It does this by juxtaposing Beryl and Norman, who "express their devotion to one another as tender pronouncements of their desire to work together for the advancement of the race," with Cora and Reverend Griswold, who perceive relationships through "superficial romance sentiment and the frivolity of the moment and not from steadfast mutual respect, admiration, and compassion" (Tate 186). For Tate, Tillman's novel does not use marriage as the goalpost for Beryl since the novel "does not end on Beryl's wedding day or shortly thereafter" (186). Tillman's goal is to represent a heroine who has successfully achieved her "professional" "ambitions" (187). As Tate notes: "These realized ambitions are personally rewarding for Beryl, and they are also important to racial progress" (187). The novel leaves no doubt that Beryl has "an ideal compassionate husband" in Norman Warren, who is supportive of his wife. However, Tate concludes, the novel transgresses conventional ideas that women, once married, should withdraw from the public sphere to attend to husband, children, and home.

According to Tate, to challenge society's belief about the hypersexuality of Black women and men, in novels like *Iola Leroy* "There is love ... however, it is not passionate ardor but rather compassionate duty, spiritualized affection, and sentimental attachment" (167). In the 1993 publication, *The Coupling Convention: Sex, Text, and Tradition in Black Women's Fiction*, Ann duCille agreed that late nineteenth-century literary texts challenged "racist imaging of sexuality" by representing married couples serving and uplifting the race. However, she challenges Hazel Carby's argument that *Iola Leroy* "is displaced by a joint desire, not for each other, but to uplift the race" (qtd. in duCille 45). duCille closely reads one scene in which Dr. Latimer's proposes to Iola, and she concludes that "The love scene ... moves metaphorically from the foreplay of verbal lovemaking to the afterglow of orgasmic release" (46). For duCille, while the narrative language is not "explicitly sexual," the "language and imagery" are "sensual" (46).

duCille's *The Coupling Convention* is useful to examine how literary representations of marriage, sexuality, and Black womanhood changes during different time periods. duCille explains that the African American novel itself "has developed around the marriage plot or what I call—because of the freedom it gives me to move outside the traditional legal and social meanings of marriage—the 'coupling convention'" (13). For example, she illustrates how a novel like William Wells Brown's *Clotel; or, the President's Daughter* (1853) "destabilize[s] the customary dyadic relation between love and marriage" and "reflect[s] the problematic nature of the institution of marriage for a people long denied the right to marry legally" (duCille 14). For duCille, nineteenth- and early twentieth-century Black writers subversively utilized "marriage conventions" "to explore ... questions of race, racism, and racial identity but [also] complex questions of sexuality and female subjectivity" (duCille 3–4). duCille separates novels by Black writers into two distinct periods to illustrate how representations and meanings derived from representations of "marriage, sexuality, and Black womanhood" transform during different time periods. During a period spanning 1853, when *Clotel; or, the President's Daughter* was published, to 1900, when *Contending Forces: A Romance Illustrative of Negro Life North and South* was published, duCille notes a "celebration of marriage" but a desexualization of Black womanhood and "a seemingly sexless meeting of like minds and sociopolitical ambitions" (10). duCille argues that Pauline E. Hopkins' novel *Contending Forces: A Romance Illustrative of Negro Life North and South* (1900) "is a novel self-consciously aware of the dictates of its romantic form" (13). In the novel there is a "happily-ever-after ending" for the heroine Sappho with the hero Will Smith after a protracted time during which Sappho runs away to escape the Blackmailing efforts of Langley, Will's friend and prospective brother-in-law (39–40).

In *Contending Forces*, duCille also argues that a "resexualization of Black womanhood" can be evidenced between 1924 and 1948 when Zora Neale Hurston published *Their Eyes Were Watching God* (10), a novel which celebrates the early sexual awakening and mature sexual happiness of its heroine, Janie. However, in her chapter "Passion, Patriarchy, and the Modern Marriage Plot," duCille goes against the grain of some scholars who read *Their Eyes Were Watching God* as a romance. She argues:

> I cannot read *Their Eyes Were Watching God* as an "expression of female power," any more than I can read it as a celebration of heterosexual love. Indeed, *Their Eyes Were Watching God* critiques, challenges, and subverts male authority,

> ultimately eliminating the male oppressors, but female subjectivity does not win out over patriarchal ideology.
>
> (duCille 121)

Indeed, scholars who do use the term romance to describe this novel often use this term in its more expansive literary sense, rather than as the name for narrative of "individuals falling in love and struggling to make the relationship work" ("About the Romance Genre"). When Janice Daniel argues that "the pattern of Janie's experiences closely parallels that of the traditional literary romance" (66), for example, she does so in order to map Janie's progress onto elements outlined in Northrop Frye's *The Secular Scripture*—"ascent, descent, 'and then' episodes, doppelganger, allies and enemies, Beulah state, *froda*, and *forza*" (66)—and thereby to make the case that this novel's realism encodes a fundamentally mythic quest for identity. The conclusion of this novel also complicates its relationship with the romance understood as a love story with an "emotionally satisfying and optimistic ending" ("About the Romance Genre"). As Kim Gallon observes, although it has become "something of a touchstone for Black love stories," *Their Eyes Were Watching God* "does not give us a HEA ending for the couple [Janie and her third husband, Virgible 'Tea Cake' Woods]," but only for its heroine, since "before the novel is through, Janie must shoot Tea Cake, who has become rabid and crazed from a dog bite, in order to save her own life" ("The Black Feminist Love Story").

Studies on first and second wave African American romance writers

A second set of scholarly discussions emerged between 2004 and 2016 which highlight the intergenerational links and departures between contemporary romance writers and writers from the 1800s. Scholars Rita Dandridge and Belinda Edmondson examine how African American popular romance builds upon an earlier African American thematic tradition that weds love and social uplift. They illustrate how contemporary writers (in both historical and contemporary romance fiction as well as film) expand 1800s writers' predominant focus on agape love to a focus on the reconciliation of agape and eros. Both writers argue that writers in the 1990s emphasize eros, but heroines remain connected to racial uplift.

In her 2004 book, *Black Women's Activism: Reading African American Women's Historical Romances*, a 2010 article "The African American Historical Romance: An Interview with Beverly Jenkins," and a 2016 book chapter "Love Prevailed Despite What American History Said…," Rita Dandridge categorizes Black romance writers into two waves. She classifies African American women's historical romance published between 1892 and 1920 as the first wave and argues that these works were instrumental in developing in nineteenth-century novels the "romance element center[ed] in courtship and marriage that usually develop from the couple's mutual involvement in racial uplift missions to advance the status of the colored community" ("The African American Historical Romance: An Interview with Beverly Jenkins"). Frances Harper's 1892 novel *Iola Leroy, or Shadows Uplifted* begins Dandridge's first wave. This novel is followed by Pauline Hopkins' *Contending Forces: A Romance Illustrative of Negro Life North and South* (1900) as well as Zara Wright's *Black and White Tangled Threads*

(1920) and *Kenneth* (1920) ("The African American Historical Romance: An Interview with Beverly Jenkins"). According to Dandridge in *Black Women's Activism*:

> These early historical romances had as their primary function to address the socio-historical issues challenging African Americans as a race at specific historical moments. This specific function coincided with the broader sociopolitical intention of modern historical romances, which called attention to the struggle of various cultures and ethnic groups throughout history.
>
> (3)

For Dandridge, the "modern historical romance" dates back to the early nineteenth century, notably to the Waverly Novels of Sir Walter Scott; Harper and Hopkins utilized this version of the genre to center Black characters who challenge various forms of "disenfranchisement" in America (*Black Women's Activism* 3). The second wave historical romance, Dandridge argues, is the popular genre-fiction version that begins with Anita Buckley's *Emily, the Yellow Rose* (1989) and Beverly Jenkins' 1994 novel *Night Song* ("The African American Historical Romance: An Interview with Beverly Jenkins" and *Black Women's Activism* 4). This wave also includes Shirley Hailstock (*Clara's Promise* 1995), Francine Craft (*The Black Pearl* 1996), Gay G. Gunn (*Nowhere to Run* 1997) (see Dandridge, *Black Women's Activism*; "The African American Historical Romance"; and "Love Prevailed").

Currently, Rita Dandridge's *Black Women's Activism: Reading African American Women's Historical Romances* (2004) remains one of the only full length books on popular romance fiction by Black writers, and she is the only scholar to pair the discussion of popular romance novels and racial uplift or what she calls the "helping tradition" (*Black Women's Activism* 12–13). Her publications study historical romance novels set during slavery and Reconstruction. In these settings, writers depict how free Black populations participated in abolition movements during slavery and in post emancipation established Black enclaves that had their own businesses, educational institutions, and health care providers. According to Dandridge in "The African American Historical Romance: An Interview with Beverly Jenkins," these historical romance novels "dramatize" and "document" the history of slavery, Reconstruction, and Post-Reconstruction, and they also center Black women's activism "in the nineteenth century public sphere." One distinguishing characteristic between the two waves of writers, Dandridge argues, is that second wave writers like Jenkins depict "darker-hued" heroines which revises the first wave writers' tendency to depict "mulatta" heroines ("The African American Historical Romance: An Interview with Beverly Jenkins"). Another characteristic is that Jenkins' heroines challenge the Black heroes' sexism. Finally, in contrast to the first wave novels, second wave writers like Beverly Jenkins blend agape and eros by focusing on "sex in romantic relationship" ("The African American Historical Romance: An Interview with Beverly Jenkins"). In "Love Prevailed Despite What American History Said . . .," Dandridge argues that in *Night Song* and *Through the Storm*, the heroines Cara and Sable are able to find a synthesis between agape and eros to "convert the eros hero into a more selfless and empathetic character" (164).

Like Rita Dandridge, Belinda Edmondson's 2007 article "The Black Romance" bridges our understanding of "Black romance" from the 1800s and 1900s. Edmondson echoes Dandridge's writings by arguing that "Black romance" connects "the romantic/erotic and the collective, social responsibility," but, unlike Dandridge, her article studies literature and "popular Black romantic films" (195, 202). She argues that contemporary representations of romance "in which the Black hero and heroine couple marry for the good of the community" had its origins in early African American narrative" (Edmondson 193). This accounts for Edmondson's characterization of *Iola Leroy* as a romance but one that "contains very little erotic or romantic material, even by the chaste standards of the Victorian romance" (196). Instead, Harper's novel centers "on social upliftment over eroticism" Edmondson argues (195). In contrast, twentieth-century "Black romance" "allows. . .a privileged, kind of connection to love that is both erotic and yet romantic, that does not deny collective identity yet allows Black people to see themselves as individuals" (Edmondson 206). Future scholarship on popular romance fiction might well employ Edmondson's method of putting into conversation a variety of genres, including love in film, music, visual art, and other forms of media by Black writers, filmmakers, and artists.

Studies on African American romance publishing

A third set of publications center on documenting a history of African American romance publishing. I examine how both scholarly and journalistic publications document a history of African American romance publishing by highlighting the contributions of publishers, editors, and writers in developing and diversifying the romance industry.

Scholarship

Ann Yvonne White's dissertation *Genesis Press: Cultural Representation and the Production of African American Romance Novels* employs a Cultural Studies lens to examine the production of African American novels at Genesis Press, a Black owned publisher established in 1993 by two African American lawyers, Wilbur and Dorothy Colom (1; 53). The Coloms, White argues, intended their books to "include characters and themes that negotiate, conflict with, and even oppose some of the problematic mainstream messages contained in current dominant forms of African American media" (White 4). The husband and wife were attorneys who housed the offices for the press in the same building as the Colom Law Firm in Columbus, Mississippi (White 58). The Colom's daughter Niani Colom was eventually brought into the company as an Associate Publisher, but since the company was small, she played several roles as "acquisitions editor, production manager," marketer and salesperson (White 51–2). In 1995, Genesis Press released its first publications under the Indigo Romance imprint (White 49). The publishers went on to establish several other imprints, including Indigo After Dark (Erotica) and Indigo Love Spectrum (53). Some of their earliest writers were Rochelle Alers, Gwen Forester, and Donna Hill who "were already writing romances" (White 55). White noted that the first printing of novels was usually 2500 (White 56). Once this amount sold out, a second printing was made (White 56). In 2004, a little under ten years after Genesis published its first books, a distribution deal was struck with Kensington so that "Genesis ... produce[d] the books and Kensington ... warehouse[d] and [sold] them" (White 56).

White's study of Genesis Press illuminates the relationship between a philosophy of racial uplift explicitly advocated by editors and publishing houses and the philosophy which pervades the plots of romance novels they choose to publish. For example, White argues that her study of Genesis Press reveals that from its inception the founders brought "activism" to the industry by challenging negative images about African Americans as "more than mainstream stereotypes such as those from the underside of the life in America's urban ghettos" (66–7). Therefore, editors put submission guidelines in place for "ethnicity, cultural distinction, and positive heroes and heroines" (White 77). White notes that African American individuals work at all levels of its press. African Americans are responsible for the "selection, processing, marketing, and distribution" of books at Genesis Press (108). She cites Deborah Schumacher, an executive editor, for example, and argues that Schumacher, who decides whether manuscripts will be published, looks for novels that are "uplifting and show African American women in positive situations" (White 111). Heroines in books published by Genesis Press are therefore usually "professional women who are looking for lasting relationships and a stable family life" (White 111). According to White, African Americans write the books, and the books are marketed to African American readers, but both the "African American authors who write the books and the readers who buy them also help shape the romances produced by the company" (White 108). Writers and publishers "negotiate" what goes into the books, White notes, so that Dyanne Davis, one romance writer, rather than focus on challenging stereotypes, argues that she focuses on characterizing heroines as "strong and powerful" (qtd. in White 78).

In John Markert's *Publishing Romance: The History of an Industry, 1940–the Present* (2016) a subsection of Chapter 9, "Love Across the Color Spectrum: African American and Multicultural Romances," outlines a publication history of African American romance since 1980 and identifies key writers, editors, presses and e-book publishers that publish African American line of romance novels (location 4895). Markert opens "Love Across the Color Spectrum" by discussing how the first published African American popular romance novel, *Entwined Destinies* by Rosalind Welles (pen name for Elsie B. Washington), came to be published in 1980. According to him, Vivian Stephens, a 46 year old African American editor at Dell Publishing was responsible for this novel's publication (Markert location 1672).[2] The novel, as well as detailed information about it, is challenging to acquire, so a quick summary of it useful here before highlighting Markert's accounts about its historical significance. *Entwined Destinies*' setting is London, and the novel's heroine Kathy Goodwin is a journalist for *Upbeat Magazine* while Lloyd Craig, the hero, is a division manager with TransGlobal Supply and Transportation Department. The novel's conflict centers around Lloyd's reticence to partner with career minded Kathy. His fear of abandonment stems from his childhood experience after his parents divorced due to conflicts that arose from his mother's abandonment of her family for her job as a radio journalist. While Lloyd is unsure that Kathy can work and remain devoted to a husband and family, Kathy feels that she can have both. Readers are not privy to Lloyd's thoughts or to his daily and professional activities. Instead, Rosalind Welles, the writer, centers the plot around Kathy's experiences as a career journalist. An attempt at exploring intimacy results in Lloyd's attempted rape of Kathy. Lloyd apologizes profusely, but Kathy rejects his apology. However, the novel's HEA ending is promised after Lloyd reunites with Kathy at the site of the *Upbeat Magazine* office after it has been bombed in retaliation of a news story that Kathy published. While book sales were "modest," Markert observes that "The book did open the door for other Black authors by challenging the prevalent view by white mainstream publishers that publishing executives were reputed to have said: 'Black women don't read'" (location 4738). Vivian Stephens continued to publish romance novels by and for African American readers even after she was "wooed ... away from Dell" Markert notes (location 4738).

According to Markert, at Harlequin, Stephens became the "launch editor for Harlequin's American Romance Line" (location 4738). She published Jackie Weger's 1983 novel *A Strong and Tender Thread* as the fifth book under the American line (Markert 4742). Weger, a white writer, centered her romance on a Black couple, Gabrielle Hensley, a Black ballet dancer who, while recovering from a car accident, moonlights as a translator for the hero Micah Davidson, a corporate executive who lives in Panama. In 1984, Stephens published *Adam and Eva*, another romance novel featuring Black characters, but this time the writer was Sandra Kitt, an African American (Markert 4751).

In addition to highlighting the first contemporary African American romance novels to be published, Markert writes that Terry McMillan's wildly successful novels *Waiting to Exhale* (1992) and *How Stella Got Her Groove Back* (1996) demonstrated a Black woman writer's ability to draw audiences and the purchasing power of Black women readers. He argues that McMillan's *How Stella Got Her Groove Back* "is basically a romance novel" (location 4758). Furthermore, he credits this novel as "more directly related to the surge in romance novels with African American women as the central character" (Markert 4758). He links the success of McMillan's novels and films to some of the writers whose "careers ... were launched during this period," including Brenda Jackson, Zane (Kristina Laferne Roberts), and Beverly Jenkins (Markert 4758–67). For Markert, the success of McMillan's novels and films spearheaded the increase in publication of Black romance writers who released novels during mid to late 1990s (location 4762).

Markert's chapter also points to e-book publishing of interracial romance featuring "Black/white romance" (location 4890) since mainstream publishers like Harlequin advertised writing guidelines that "likely dissuaded [writers] from submitting a multicultural romance since the guidelines specified African American characters" (location 4887). According to him, the four e-book publishers who publish interracial romance are Beautiful Trouble, Sugar and Spice, Changeling, and Amira, all based in the United States, and UK based Totally Bound (location 4895). Of the four, Markert reports, Beautiful Trouble and Sugar and Spice no longer accept manuscripts but the publishers, who are themselves writers, continue to publish their own works (location 4926–30).

A great deal of work remains to be done on African American romance publishing. Markert's chapter in *Publishing Romance: The History of an Industry, 1940–the Present* and Yvonne White's work on Genesis Press are invaluable contributions. However, a more expansive and inclusive book-length history of African American romance publishing is sorely needed so that scholars of African romance would have a more accurate and consistent record. As it stands, scholars have to scour articles, chapters, and essays to piece together timelines and double check discrepancies in dates of publications. Nevertheless, in lieu of a thorough history of publishing, in the following section, I'll highlight how journalism has contributed to our understanding of African American romance.

Journalism

So far I have focused my discussion solely on what scholars have written about African American romance. In this section, I continue this trend by examining Kim Gallon's study of an African American newspaper that published stories, real-life features, letters, and photographs of interracial love and relationships during segregation. However, I also expand my focus to how journalists have contributed to this genre by documenting the development of African American romance publishing and by publishing feature articles on key publishers, editors, and writers.

Kim Gallon's scholarship offers important insight into how early twentieth-century journalism engaged with the topic of interracial romance. In "'How Much Can You Read About Interracial Love and Sex Without Getting Sore?': Readers Debate Over Interracial Relationships in the Baltimore *Afro-American*," Gallon studies the *Afro-American* newspaper's features on interracial romance stories as well as readers' letters to the editors responding to the paper's query on whether it should "change its policy of 'turning down fiction stories dealing with love affairs between the races' and 'rake up the snappiest Black and tan tales' the paper could find" (104). Debate ensued on the pages of the *Afro-American* between April and July 1934. Readers voted to include them with 55 percent responding yes, 40 percent saying no, and 5 percent having "no preference" (Gallon 101). As a lens to analyze the *Afro-American*, Gallon uses David Nord's argument that "journalism is always political" and "how readers respond to newspapers hold great value for an understanding of a particular readership" (105). Her study illustrates that editors' use of interracial fiction contributed to U.S. Civil Rights struggle (107). In turn, Gallon argues, "readers' debates over intermarriage and interracial romance were also a deliberation over definitions of African American progress" (105). This is crucial to note because during this period, discussing the topic of interracial love in public could expose African Americans, particularly those living in the South, "to bodily injury and death" (Gallon 108). In fact, leading scholars, like W.E.B. Dubois, at the time argued that there were more important social issues than interracial relationships facing Blacks. Nevertheless, the readers voted, and the newspapers published letters that fostered debates about whether the editors should be discussing this topic. In turn, editors also featured several interracial stories and photographs of interracial couples. One story was titled "Empress: A True Love Story of the Love of an Ofay Lad for a Brown Girl" was published on April 28, 1934 (Gallon 112). The newspaper also illustrated that interracial love expanded beyond the Black and white dyad when it published the stories "Chinese Love: The story of an Interracial Love That Was Slightly Hampered by an Old Chinese Custom" and "Dusky Flower: A Girl Who Deserted Harlem for Her Oriental Husband" (Gallon 112).

Rosemary L. Bray's article "Love for Sale" published in the 1982 edition of *Black Enterprise* magazine is a great complement to read alongside Markert's "Love Across the Color Spectrum" because it features the story of how Vivian Stephens came to publish *Entwined Destinies* and provides sale figures for the novel. She documents that the novel sold "40,000 copies of the 60,000" first print copies (Bray 72). Bray's article also supplements Markert by discussing an additional Black writer published by Stephens who he does not mention. According to Bray, two years after *Entwined Destinies*, Stephens published Lia Sanders, pen name for Angela Jackson and Sandra Jackson-Opoku (Bray 72). Bray does not provide insight into the novel's plot, so I'll provide a summary here. Sanders' novel *The Tender Mending* (1982) tells the story of a Black couple, Dee Woods, a writer and producer of educational filmstrips, and Dr. Paul Douglas, a pediatrician. Dee's brother Jessie and his wife dies leaving her to care for her orphaned niece Abenaa (Beanie) Wood. Dee and Paul first meet in a children's hospital emergency room when Beanie checks herself into the hospital after falling off a tree and breaking her wrist. Paul believes that Dee is either an abusive or neglectful parent, so he prescribes parenting classes for her. Through a series of contrivances, Beanie facilitates bringing Dee and Paul together.

Bray's feature on African American publishing reveals that in some instances African American publishers and editors explicitly sought out Black writers whose novels countered stereotypes about Black women and relationships. Bray featured four editors who were actively requesting submissions for ethnic/Black writers writing about Black people (74). Valerie Flournoy was requesting synopsis of "stories that portray black women as 'lovely, lovable and loved by Black men'" for her Second Chance at Love series at Jove Publications (Bray 74). Vivian Stephens was marketing her Harlequin American Romance Line and "recruiting ethnic writers" (Bray 74). Cheryl Woodruff at Ballantine Books was "looking for Black authors who can write about the problem facing women in contemporary relationships in a meaningful and positive manner." However, Woodruff preferred romance as "an element but not the central theme" (Bray 74). Finally, Veronica Mixon wanted "stories about Black people in all areas of life" for Doubleday's Starlight Romances which produced hardcover romance fiction, but she preferred that "people [not] write anything that teenagers shouldn't read" (Bray 74).

Bray's article points to how Black editors at established presses were attempting to diversify the Romance industry by calling for submissions and by beginning to publish romance fiction with African American characters. These larger publishers had yet to devote an entire line to African American romance. However, Vincent Young's 1991 article features an independent publisher who set out to do this very thing. According to Young, Leticia Peoples launched Odyssey Press after noting publishers' lack of interest in publishing African American romance fiction in a market where Black readers like herself were increasingly wanting to see themselves reflected in the novels. Vincent Young reports that Peoples developed her submission guidelines because she argued that "it would be very difficult to express myself as a Black woman within the confines of the guidelines ... from mainstream publishers." According to Young, Peoples "used more than 10,000 from her federal government retirement fund to set up shop." Armed with "one year" of research about the "publishing industry" itself as well as her guidelines and personal financial investment in the business, she opened her publishing company Odyssey Books in Silver Spring, Maryland (Young). Rochelle Alers' *My Love's Keeper* was published by Odyssey Books in 1991. During the 1990s Donna Hill's *Rooms of the Heart* and Mildred Riley's *Yamilla* were also published with Odyssey Books (Young).

Throughout the early 2000s, Gwendolyn Osborne's articles contributed to documenting the evolution of the African American romance publishing industry. Osborne's articles about the production aspect of the romance industry provide foundational information about the industry which scholars like Markert have referenced in publications. Her articles "How Black Romance Novels, That Is—Came to Be" and "Love in Color" document the development of the industry. "How Black Romance Novels, That Is—Came to Be (romance)" documents the evolution of African American romance between the 1960s and 1990s by pointing out the contributions Frank Yerby's novels, *True Confessions* magazine, *Bronze Thrills*, and *Black Romance and Jive* have made to the genre through their publication of established romance writers Donna Hill and Francis Ray. "Love in Color," a 2006 publication in

Black Issues Book Review, discusses the acquisition of BET books by Harlequin in November 2005. Osborne's feature on Harlequin's acquisition reports that Kensington Publishing, an established Company with Pinnacle Books, entered the business of publishing African American Romance in the 1990s. Walter Zacharius, CEO at Kensington Publishing Company, established the Arabesque line in 1994. Gwendolyn Osborne reports that it cost Kensington $400,000 to launch the line, but when they sold it to BET, they netted "$11 million" ("The Color of Love" 14).

Journalists continue to provide some of the most current insights into the production of African American romance. In her May 2018 article, "Meet the Black Women Upending The Romance Industry," Bim Adewunmi accomplishes this in her feature about Alyssa Cole's *Loyal League* miniseries. She attributes *An Extraordinary Union*, Cole's first novel in the series, to how: "The company [Kensington] has forged a chain uncommon in mainstream publishing: an unbroken line of Black women, from the novel's protagonist, via the author, to the editor, to the art director who created the cover art (featuring a black woman)." In this article, Adewunmi highlights the two influential Black women at Kensington Publishing Company who contribute to diversifying the romance industry and, in turn, to the successful publication of Cole's historical novel miniseries. Her feature reveals that Esi Sogah, a senior editor, discovered *An Extraordinary Union*, Cole's first book from The Loyal League book series, when it "crossed her desk." Kris Noble, another Black woman and art director at Kensington, directed the design of Cole's novel.

Lois Beckett's 2019 article, "Fifty Shades Of White: The Long Fight Against Racism in Romance Novels," discusses the controversial exclusion of Alyssa Cole's *An Extraordinary Union* from the Rita awards in 2018 and the debates regarding charges of racism and bias in the RWA selection of Rita award finalists in 2018 and 2019, which reflects a larger problem of prejudice in the romance industry. When the Rita awards were announced in March 2018, Cole's critically acclaimed historical novel *An Extraordinary Union* had been excluded as a finalist. Historical romance by white writers won this category, as well as other categories, which, Beckett reports, led to the "outpouring of grief and frustration from Black authors and other authors of color, describing the racism they had faced again and again in the romance industry" on Twitter (Beckett). RWA followed up these accusations of discrimination with research which confirmed that "less than 0.5% of the total number of Rita finalists" over an 18-year period had been Black writers and no Black writer had ever won a Rita award (Beckett). Beckett notes that Black writers were again excluded for the 2019 Rita awards when only three writers of color were nominated out of a total of 80 writers. Alyssa Cole was again excluded, even though she had a book on the *New York Times* "100 notable books of the year" list. Twitter response to the snub of Black writers again in 2019 led to a furor over the legitimacy of an award "in their current form" (Beckett).

In "Fifty Shades of White ..." Beckett contextualizes her report of racism and bias in Rita awards with a discussion of the romance publishing practices in general. Beckett writes that Black writers feel that bookstores and superstore chains' shelving practices segregate their romance to African American sections only, and she highlights the practice of segregating romance series based on race, which leaves Black writers conflicted. While some Black writers feel that Harlequin's dedicated Black line, Kimani books, which features Black heroines, is helpful for readers to "locate what they wanted to read," other Black writers feel this does not provide them with marketing opportunities for their books. In 2017, Harlequin announced that it would be "gradually phasing out" Kimani, which left Black writers' future publishing with Harlequin uncertain.

In the history of publishing, publishers and editors have been reluctant to publish Black writers who wrote romance with Black characters for fear they would not sell. Suzanne Brockmann, a white writer who wanted to include a Black hero in one of her Navy Seals novels, was told by Harlequin that "You will make half the money … We cannot send it to our subscription list" (qtd. in Beckett). Publishers feared getting "angry letters" from white readers (qtd. in Beckett). Black writers also report white readers' reluctance to read romance with Black heroes and heroines for fear they are not relatable. Other white readers who have read romance by Black writers express their surprise that "Black folks fall in love like white folks" (qtd. in Beckett).

Studies on approaches to reading race, gender, sexuality, and disability in popular romance

In this final section, I examine scholarship that employs reader response as well and qualitative textual analysis for studying African American romance. I begin by examining the writings of Gwendolyn Osborne, Hsu-Ming Teo, and Susan Weisser. Together their writings provide complex interpretations that attend to how race, gender, and class intersect in romance fiction. These scholars also highlight how writers navigate social and cultural stereotypes and assumptions when they adapt romance conventions that are themselves imbued with the problems of race, racism, and sexism that affect our society. This section concludes by studying scholars—from fields that include Cultural Studies, Women's and Gender Studies, Queer Studies, Disability Studies, and Love Studies—who examine race, gender, sexuality, and love in romance fiction.

As I have noted above, Gwendolyn Osborne' publications have contributed to understanding the production of African American romance in the early 1990s and 2000s. However, her publications also focus on readers' responses to romance fiction. In a 2004 book chapter "'Women Who Look Like Me': Cultural Identity and Reader Responses to African American Romance Novels," Osborne reports her findings based on a study of romance readers to answer "what it is about Black romance that draws so many African American book buyers to the romance sections of the nation's bookstores" (61). Osborne classifies the readers she studied into two groups: 1) first generation readers who had purchased romance novels written by white authors and 2) second generation readers who started reading romance after African American romance novels were published (61). The readers' ages were between 20 and 50 years old. They were "college-educated" and "worked outside the home" (Osborne 61). Readers reported that they read "one to twenty-five romances a month" and had attended an official romance industry event "within 12 months of the interview" (Osborne 61). Among the conclusions drawn, Osborne observed that the research group saw themselves as "feminist" or "womanist" (62). They read romance because of their "positive" representations of romantic love between Black couples (Osborne 62). Most important, the women researched told Osborne that they enjoyed romance because they had "stories about 'women who look like me'" (62). According to Osborne, readers preferred romance that featured "middle-class" couples and articulated their preference for romance fiction over "sister-girl fiction" (64). One reader noted that "African-American heroines are more in charge of their futures" (Dalton qtd. in Osborne 64). She notes that readers challenge perceived ideas of romance as "porn," by citing one reader's argument that "In romance novels, a man puts a woman's pleasure first. This is not the case in pornography" (Caldwell qtd. in Osborne 64). Black women can see reflected in these books women like themselves who represent various body shapes, sizes, skin tones, hair textures, and ages. Therefore, Osborne concludes, Black women state that their reasons for reading African American romance have to do with how they reflect their racial, ethnic, "cultural or social identities" as well as their desires to read about Black women who end up in positive, loving relationships with men who respect and desire them (67).

Osborne's article "It's All About Love: Romance Readers Speak Out," written for the AALBC two years prior to her book chapter, also uses reader response to discuss African American romance, but in this article, Osborne interviews readers as well as writers and editors to understand romance novels' appeal to Black readers. Osborne argues that African American writers are expanding their novels with portrayal of heroines who are young as well as mature, slender as well as full-figured. She quotes Renee A. Redd, a psychologist, who argues that "romance fiction provides an escape from the social realities many African American women face." On the other hand, romance novels appeal to readers because they offer empowering messages that teach how to deal with social issues that affect Black communities, including racism, intraracial conflicts, homelessness, cancer, and substance abuse, among others. For Osborne, because "African American romance readers are not a monolithic group," the novels require the genre's happily ever after; however, storylines must also include some of the following qualities: they should include African American culture and history, must "dispel stereotypes" about African Americans as well as "provide an escape and are devoid of racial conflict, gratuitous sex and profanity" ("It's All About Love: Romance Readers Speak Out").

Hsu-Ming Teo also uses reader response to study African American romance. In Chapter 9 of her book *Desert Passions: Orientalism and Romance Novels*, Teo examines readers' response to Brenda Jackson's novel *Delaney's Desert Sheikh*. Teo argues that even though African American romance featuring Black protagonists have been published since the 1980s, it wasn't until 2002 that a sheik novel was published by an African American writer. This chapter analyzes readers' comments from Amazon.com reviews and from Gwyneth Bolton's online blog from June 12, 2007 (Teo 290, 291). Amazon.com reviews had several responses to *Delaney's Desert Sheikh*. Some reviewers loved the book because they enjoyed Jackson's sensually intense depiction of the sexual relationship between Jamal and Delaney. On the other hand, a second group of readers felt that *Delaney's Desert Sheikh* was devoid of "references to Black culture," and that they couldn't relate to Jamal, a Middle Eastern sheikh (Teo 290). A third group of readers were grateful that the writer did not focus on racism faced by characters in this interracial novel (Teo 291).

In addition to examining the Amazon.com reviews, Teo also studied comments from Gwyneth Bolton's blog. Readers here responded to Bolton's questions regarding the novel's representation of race, particularly in regard to white readers' preference of the sheikh romance over the romance featuring a Black hero (291). Teo notes that some readers surmised that African American men are not seen as desirable, as wealthy, or as exotic as the sheik hero (293). Some readers attribute the dearth of

Black heroes in romance to them being too "Black" (Teo 293). She argues, however, that this debate circled around a more pressing issue. Rather than debating about the need for increased presence of Black men in romance, Teo argues that readers might want to consider what that representation might look like if there is an increase in Black heroes (293). She pushes us to consider whether that increase would correspondingly result in reader satisfaction with Black heroes who are "exotic," or who reflect the sociocultural, political, and economic dominance over others as some white mainstream romance fiction (293). She reveals that readers' comments at times exhibited stereotypical assumptions about "Muslims and Middle Easterners" as exhibited by one reader who stated that: "a sheik is simply 'a white man wearing a turban ... You have the fantasy of the rich exotic sheik, without dealing with the reality of how a real Middle Eastern man would behave with a female'" (Teo 292). Furthermore, she asserts that Jackson's novel uses a stereotypical frame which represents Jamal as an "authoritarian desert sheik who is tamed and transformed into good husband material by the strong, independent American heroine" (Teo 293). Teo concludes that readers' comments seem locked in a binary that "non-white" characters should either be "invisible" in romance fiction or represented as "stereotypes" (293–4).

In 2013, Susan Weisser published *The Glass Slipper: Women and Love Stories*, one chapter of which tries to understand the appeal of African American romance to Black readers, to examine how race was represented, to examine whether African American romance resembled or was distinct from white mainstream romance, and also to examine whether tensions emerge from African American "appropriation" of traditional romance conventions (166). In this chapter, "A Genre of One's Own: African American Romance Imprints and the 'Universality' of Love," Weisser studies ten romance novels written by white writers and ten written by Black writers. One of her findings is that there were "almost no Caucasians in African American romance" and "almost no women of color—or *people* of color—in white mainstream romances" (Weisser 155). That said, she argues that the novels were similar in the use of the "set of core plot and standardized vocabulary" (Weisser 156). For example, both draw from a lexicon that identifies the hero as an "alpha" (156) who can be "sensitive and tamable" (157) because he is "mysteriously drawn" (157) to "something special about the heroine" (Weisser 156–7). Weisser argues that both use a "third person indirect style" which allows the reader (not the heroine) to experience the hero's thoughts and feelings about the heroine (159). According to Weisser, "This device is especially popular for making mild fun of or explaining the hero's chauvinism or misogyny" (159). They also both depict sexual encounters in which the heroine's stimulation and pleasure are of primary importance (160).

Weisser asserts that the difference between Black and white writers has to do with the personal and professional stability of the hero and heroine, the representation of physiognomy, and the representation of conservative sexual politics. For Weisser, in contrast to white heroines, Black heroines tend to be more "educated, professional, and intelligent" (162). Novels by white and Black writers follow "a standard formula" in which heroes who are "emotionally distant, difficult, and noncommittal" are eventually transformed into marriage material by their love for the heroine (Weisser 162). However, in African American romance, writers represent Black males as "successful and stable" to counteract negative media images (162). Black writers also make clear references to "texture of hair and color of skin," unlike white writers who almost never do this, observes Weisser (163). Another difference Weisser observes is the "sexual conservatism" of African American romance imprints (165). She notes that Harlequin guidelines for Kimani Arabesque, for example, are stricter than those for Harlequin Teen and Christian Love (Weisser 165). This is reflected in novels which depict the heroine's "virginity before marriage" (165).

There are a few tensions that emerge as a result of Black writers' "appropriation" of "the traditional marriage plot" argues Weisser (166). One main tension results from the depiction of an "entirely Black ... world" (166). Weisser argues that the representation of a world devoid of white characters is an understandable response to the absence of Black characters in "mainstream romances" (166). However, she argues: "the doubling of segregation hardly seems to push the issue of racial alienation to a better place. For example, without a representation of the white world, no critique of race or racism in America seems possible" (166). Another tension that emerges is tied to the representation of class. For Weisser this "is especially poignant ... where the social situation of many Black women's lives and the crisis-level correlation of African American unemployment, housing, education, and male incarceration are simply excluded from its imagined world" (166). She feels that these types of novels that represent one privileged class result in novels where the only "princess" who is able to win a man is one who has the financial means.

Weisser's claims stand in sharp contrast to the analysis offered by Osborne, especially when it comes to reading the representations of class and of socioeconomic disenfranchisement of Black communities in romance fiction. In "It's All About Love," for example, Osborne quotes novelist Gwynne Forster who argues:

> What makes characters uniquely African American is their perspective of the world around them: their optimism and tenacious pursuit of dreams and goals in the presence of towering social impediments; and their ability to laugh at awesome obstacles, or to ignore them and, often, climb over them.

From this perspective, the depiction of prosperous Black professionals is evidence of success "in the presence of towering social impediments": impediments which do, in fact, appear in the novels (Osborne "It's All About Love"). (Osborne cites *Rendezvous* by Bridget Anderson, which deals with homelessness, and *Slow Burn* by Leslie Esdaile and *One Love* by Lynn Emery, both of which focus on substance abuse.) A number of writers—including Beverly Jenkins, Brenda Jackson, Gwyneth Bolton, Felicia Mason, among others—write novels that feature heroines and heroes whose lives are shaped by social ills like slavery, racism, and class disenfranchisement. For instance, Felicia Mason's *For the Love of You* (1999) centers around the heroine Kendra, a middle-class professional who works for a law firm. The novel focuses on how Kendra, a young unwed mother of twins, has emerged from poverty and subsistence on welfare to become successful. Given a larger sample size than the ten examined in Weisser, scholars can begin to watch a pattern unfold wherein African American writers use their representations of middle-class characters to illustrate how Blacks have uplifted themselves in spite of a society that has disenfranchised them. In total, Osborne, Teo, and Weisser's essays are all important readings whose varying approaches to reading romance fiction allows us to see different dimensions of how writers imagine relationships so that love might flourish in spite of social ills and to see how readers/writers/scholars from different races/cultural background respond to what they read.

While Weisser sees tensions in romance novels that adapt romance conventions, Consuela Francis highlights how Zane's stories can actually be considered romance fiction. In "Flipping the Script: Romancing Zane's Urban Erotica," Consuela Francis uses the Romance Writers of America's and Jennifer Cruise's definitions of romance fiction to argue that Zane's novel *Addicted* be read "as romance rather than erotica" (169). A brief summary of *Addicted* will assist in understanding the importance of Frances' argument. In *Addicted*, Zoe Reynard, a self-made businesswoman who deals in reproducing artwork into prints, has requested an emergency meeting with Dr. Marcella Sanders. She requests counseling because she and her husband, Jason, are having marital problems. We discover through the course of her conversation with her therapists that Zoe has a sexual addiction and has been juggling three lovers because her husband is not sexually satisfying her. The novel moves us from childhood to adulthood, examining Zoe and Jason's turbulent first encounter, relationship, and marriage. It depicts Zoe's dissatisfaction with the marriage as a result of her husband's refusal to discuss their sexual problems. Jason is a perfect provider and father, but according to Zoe, selfish in bed. Zoe seeks satisfaction outside the marriage, but during therapy, decides to end her illicit relationships. This ends in violent confrontation between her, her lovers, and Jason. In order to save their marriage, Zoe and Jason agree to further counseling whereupon both Zoe and Jason discover that their sexual problems resulted from childhood sexual trauma. Interestingly, we do not discover this until the novel's conclusion.

The market for Black Erotica is dominated by Zane, a pseudonym for Kristina Laferne Roberts. According to Francis, Zane entered the romance publishing market with her self-published postings online in 1997 and self-published novels. Sales for her publications went over 250,000 copies. When Simon and Schuster noted this, the publisher reissued her 1998 self-published novel *Addicted*, in 2003 (Francis 168). It is this novel which is the primary focus of "Flipping the Script: Romancing Zane's Urban Erotica." In it, she advocates reading this novel as a romance instead of just "a story about Zoe's sexual escapades" (Francis 190). First, Francis argues that because Cruise defines romance novels as those which "demonstrate women's abilities and strengths by showing their heroines taking active, intelligent control of their lives," *Addicted* fits this definition since Zoe, the novel's heroine, "seeks help" through therapy when she realizes that her "actions" can "irrevocably ruin her marriage" (170). Second, using Cruise's argument that "romance fiction 'reinforces the validity of women's preoccupations,'" Francis argues that the novel's development fosters both for Zoe and readers "a cultural space for new conversations about representations of Black female pleasure and desire" (170). More specifically, readers are taken along on "Zoe's sexual journey" in her extramarital affairs with Quinton and Tyson and rather than seeing this as "transgressive," readers "are rooting for Zoe as we would any romance heroine" (Francis 174). Francis reminds us that the novel presents Zoe's choices as "wrong" (174–5). However, it's Zoe's "sexual journey" that leads to knowledge about her own sexual desires and about the flawed sexual relationship with Tyson.

Francis also uses Cruise's argument that "romance fiction puts women at the center of their stories, reinforcing their instincts about the meanings of the events in their lives" to argue for *Addicted* to be read as a romance (170). Since the story is told from Zoe's first person point of view, she explains, the reader is privy to several important things about Zoe: "they experience her pleasure" (175); they "question ... the insufficient narrative frames Zoe has been offered" (175); and they experience her sexual experiences of "oral sex, anal sex, public sex, and bondage" as "pleasure" rather than "perversions" (176). In so doing, Zane challenges a "politics of respectability" that governs the standards of behavior Black women are supposed to adhere to, which, Francis argues, "sacrifice[s] ... personal pleasure and desire" (179). Finally, using RWA's assertion that romance novels should have "an emotionally satisfying and optimistic ending" (169, 176), Francis argues that *Addicted* satisfies this definition since Zoe saves her marriage and she and her husband Jason "learn to enjoy each other again" outside the boundaries of Black middle-class respectability politics and within a relationship that values Black women's "pleasure and desire" (177, 180). While scholarship on African American erotic/kink romance have yet to address this topic, the Women of Color in Romance website (www.wocinromance.com/themes/bdsm/) is a resource for writers and readers interested in African American authored material.

Francis' work expands how the romance scholar as well as the scholar "who specializes in Black women's and contemporary African American literature" can approach the study of Zane's writings by "draw[ing] on the definition of the popular romance genre used by the Romance Writers of America" (168, 169). On the other hand, Sami Schalk engages with the tensions that result in fiction that utilize romance genre conventions. In "Happily Ever After for Whom? Blackness and Disability in Romance Narratives," Schalk uses Eric Selinger and Sarah S. G. Frantz's approach to reading romance novels "'at once within and against the traditions and possibilities' of their genre" to examine "how texts work both within and against the figurations of race, (dis)ability, gender, and sexuality" (1242). According to Schalk, writers negotiate (some more than others) how to challenge stereotypical representations of race, gender, sexuality, and disability using romance genre conventions that themselves are based on "social norms" which prescribe stereotypes. Her study highlights how "texts work with and against conventions of the romantic narrative, which have traditionally excluded Black and disabled subjects" (Schalk 1256).

Schalk examines two novels that represent Black disability. The first, Gwynne Forster's *Forbidden Temptation*, published by Kimani Press, is explicitly a romance novel. Schalk argues that while *Forbidden Temptation* challenges the stereotype of "Black men's sexuality as hyperactive, uncontrolled or animalistic" by depicting Luther as a disabled Black veteran who lost a leg due to war (Frances 1247), it doesn't "critique ableism" (1249). For instance, Forster juxtaposes other disabled double-amputee veterans with Luther to emphasize his "desireab[ility]" as a hero who is more able than others and therefore more deserving of love and marriage (Schalk 1250). In addition, Schalk considers the successful happily ever after ending between Ruby and the disabled veteran Luther to be predicated on "normaliz[ing]" an ableist script that "disabled veterans continue to fit into the heteronormative capitalist soldier-hero trope by working, marrying, and having children" (1249). The second novel, N.K. Jemisin's *The Broken Kingdom*, which features a disabled heroine, is categorized as fantasy but "has a prominent romance plot line" (Schalk 1250). The novel's heroine Oree is depicted as a "disabled Black woman making active and self-aware choices about her sexual and romantic life rather than just settling for just any relationship or changing to attract a partner" (Schalk 1253). During the course of the novel, Oree eventually loses two partners. Because this novel is not a romance novel, it doesn't require a happily ever after ending, so, the heroine is, at the novel's conclusion "Poor, unwed, disabled, Black, and pregnant" (Schalk 1255). Schalk argues, "This ending is . . . not presented as tragic or negative, but rather fairly neutral, with an undercurrent of hope" (1255). Schalk's chapter, which employs an approach that reads narratives with and against the grain of romantic conventions, is intended to help us "understand more about the limits and potential of this genre not only as a representational medium, but also as a lens into contemporary sociopolitical structures" (1257). Her analysis of romantic narratives that work at the intersections of Blackness and disability challenge genre prescriptions of who can love and who is deserving of love (Schalk 1257).

Love and pleasure in romance fiction are examined from a Black feminist perspective in "Scripting Black Love in the 1990's: Pleasure, Respectability, and Responsibility in an Era of HIV/Aids." In this 2016 anthology chapter, I examine the intersection of "pleasure, responsibility, and respectability" in Brenda Jackson's 1995 debut novel *Tonight and Forever.* I use a Black feminist lens to discuss the history of the sexual politics constructing negative perceptions and images about Black women's and men's race and sexuality as well as how Black women writers have historically challenged these images, laying bare white supremacy that undergirds historical representations of, for example, Black men as rapists and Black women as Jezebels. I analyze Jackson's depiction of condom use between the Black protagonists, Justin and Lorren. First, I argue that in this depiction, the writer models for readers how Black couples can enjoy pleasurable intercourse using condoms while comporting themselves with a respectability that challenges historically pervasive stereotypes that paint Blacks as hypersexual. Second, I closely read Jackson's depiction of Justin' responsible act of protecting Lorren and argue that the novel is an activist text that teaches readers about the pleasure and responsible act of using condoms, particularly during the 1990s when the numbers of cases of Black women contracting HIV/AIDS was increasing. Furthermore, I cite Jackson's novel as ground-breaking for its depiction of condom use at a time when research shows that romance novels written between 1981 and 1999 were not including representations of condom use. Using Patricia Hill Collins's call for us to consider what a more transformative body politics might look like, I conclude that Jackson's *Tonight and Forever* models this by transforming HIV/AIDS prevention lexicon centered on the "restriction of pleasure" to one where "readers not only experience pleasure . . . but can also envision it through safe sex practices" (125).

In "Love as the Practice of Bondage: Popular Romance Narratives and the Conundrum of Erotic Love," Catherine Roach examines Beverly Jenkins' 1996 novel *Indigo* through the framework of bell hooks' notion of "love as the practice of freedom" (Roach 369; see hooks, 289). As the object of study, Roach examines Beverly Jenkins' appropriation of a story from the 1930s Federal Writers' Project which recounted how a free Black man gave himself into slavery to be with an enslaved woman (372). Roach's analysis focuses on Jenkins' adoption of this story that Hester, the novel's heroine, tells of her father David, a freeman, who becomes a slave in order to be with her mother Frances with whom he is in love. Roach draws on hooks' specific definition of love as "the will to extend one's self for the purpose of nurturing one's own or another's spiritual growth" (Roach 376). She also traces the derivation of *freedom* in Old English, German, and Sanskrit showing how it's linked etymologically to love (Roach 371).

Using these definitions, Roach argues that romantic love is a "conundrum" and "a paradox" because "true love equals freedom equals good bondage" (377–8). This can be evidenced in the case of David, Roach argues, for "The one freedom whose exercise he refuses to give up, the freedom he staked his life upon and declared most precious to him ... was the freedom to love" (377). In *Indigo*, David and Frances are predictably separated when Frances' owner dies, and she is sold down South by the master's son. David dies after an illness, and David and Frances' young daughter is sold to a slaver who produces indigo on the islands off the Carolinas. In the novel, Hester, working for the Underground Railroad, receives her happy ending with Galen Vachon and is reunited with her mom, yet Roach observes that her marriage by the novel's conclusion does not mean that Hester is totally happy. Hester cannot completely be contented until slavery has ended and enslaved Blacks are free of the institution of slavery (Roach 386). Roach's analysis uncovers the paradox of romance that the story of David rehearses. Therefore, Roach concludes that we learn that while loving someone, like David does Frances, can bring suffering and a cessation of love, love and the happy ending in romance novels also offer succor which allows one to "hide from this knowledge and work it through" (386).

Popular African American romance fiction tends to be overwhelmingly heterosexual. For this reason, Marlon B. Ross' article in the Summer 2013 issue of *Callaloo* does the important work of documenting Black gay romance published in the mid-1980s and early 1990s. In "'What's Love But a Second Hand Emotion?': Man-on-Man Passion in the Contemporary Black Gay Romance Novel," Ross studies "how gay romance novelists adapt rather rigid formulae—including the homonormal formula of gay love ..." (676). His essay contextualizes the analysis by discussing the challenges faced by Larry Duplechan, James Earl Hardy, and E. Lynn Harris writing in the 1980s and 1990s to represent Black men's love and desire for each other without inscribing the pathologies society attribute to Black people, Black masculinity (straight and gay), and Black love. For example, Ross points to ideologies of race in which "Black masculinity is being prescribed as hypermasculine," which intersects with ideologies about sexuality in the 1980s that attributed sexuality to "prison rape" (675). That is, people believed that Black men became gay in prison as a result of rape. These works by Duplechan, Lynn, and Hardy challenge this belief. Instead, in these works, "Black erotic attractions inhabit the same romance formulae as straight white love and white gay love while also insisting that romantic love is conditioned by the difference that race makes" (Ross 676).

Ross argues that while Duplechan's romance is centered in primarily white gay spaces, Hardy and Lynn, on other hand, use these spaces peripherally or not all. For instance, Duplechann's 1985 novel *Eight Days a Week* depicts a younger Black male romance with an older white male. Ross credits this novel with depicting an interracial romance during a period "when there was a resounding silence about these relationships in the white gay discourse" (679). Hardy's novel *B-Boy Blues* was set primarily in Black communities and featured a romantic relationship between two Black men from different classes. According to Ross, white characters in the novel serve peripherally as "predatory interlopers" (681). On the other hand, in Harris's novels, white gay culture is "totally erased as irrelevant" (Ross 681). Harris' characters are middle-class befitting the "uplift ideology ... of the post-Civil Rights generation" (Ross 681). In addition, Ross argues that Harris does not present his bisexual protagonist Ray on the "down low" (682). Instead, "Ray's bisexuality is authentic" (682). Ray's sexual preference for men is also not presented in binary opposition to Nicole because the novelist sets both characters on a path to healthy self-discovery about insecurities due to colorism and about "sex and sexuality" (682). This leads to "consolidating their commitment to, and love for, Black family and community" (Ross 683).

In a 2007 chapter, "How Dare a Black Women Make Love to A White Man . . .," Guy Mark Foster affirms the important cultural work African American interracial romance fiction engages in, not least by dealing with the fraught issue of "interracial sex" (125). Examining three novels, Lizzette Carter's *The Color Line* (2005), Monica White's *Shades of Desire*, and Dyanne Davis's *The Color of Trouble*, Foster discovers "some of the same anxieties and fears that are often associated with Black-white intimacy among contemporary Blacks and whites who exist in the world *outside* the text" (105). He adds, however, that the "formulaic structure of romance novels" allows interracial romance writers to push back at societal "stigmas" about Black women's relationship with white men (115). More than any other "literary form," Foster asserts, these interracial romance fiction have taken on "the subject of contemporary Black women's sexual relationship to white men" (125), and he concludes that such fiction, with its commitment to exploring anxieties surrounding Black women's sexualities, ought to serve as examples that can encourage scholars to think beyond certain "binary oppositions" that limit Black women's lives (124).

Because Foster's primary texts date from the mid-1990s and early 2000s, and all of them are contemporary-set romances, his study cannot be taken as the final, or even current, word on Black/white interracial romance fiction in the United States (or elsewhere). More scholarship is needed on this pairing, on other interracial Black romance (e.g., Black/Asian romance novels), and on how the dynamics Foster outlines might differ in other subgenres (historical romance, paranormal romance, etc.) and in novels about LGBTQIA protagonists. Likewise, the (de)construction of whiteness in interracial Black romance novels has yet to receive the scholarly attention it deserves.

As the critical scholarship about African American romance develops, there is need for studies about African American Christian romance and African American Muslim romance. Layla Abdullah-Poulos has begun scholarly work on the latter with her recent publication "The Stable Muslim Love Triangle—Triangular Desire in African American Muslim Romance Fiction." Abdullah-Poulos argues that romantic unions between characters in this fiction are mediated through "Islamic teachings" which structure a plot "with the constant presence of a Stable Muslim Love Triangle (SMLT)" (Abdullah-Poulos). That is, African American Muslim writers structure triangular romantic relationships where "at least one of the protagonists' commitment to Allah (swt), as opposed to attraction to the object of desire, serves as a lynchpin to the union" (Abdullah-Poulos).

Further study is also needed about representations of popular African American queer romance. It's understandable that the literature about this is sparse since the romance novels written by Black writers are overwhelming heterosexual. African American queer romance does indeed exist, however. For example, Rebekah Weatherspoon's 2014 novella *Treasure* features a lesbian couple, Alexis and Trisha/Treasure. Alyssa Cole has published two novellas titled *That Could Be Enough* (2018) and *Once Ghosted Twice Shy* (2019) also featuring Black lesbian couples. Future scholars of Black queer romance can draw on resources provided by Weatherspoon who runs the Women of Color in Romance, a website and social media presence (Twitter, Instagram, Facebook, and Tumblr) which is "trans inclusive and open to non-binary and gender fluid folks as well" (Weatherspoon qtd. in "Women of Color in Romance . . .").

Since the 1980s, journalistic and scholarly publications about African American Romance have documented a rich history of literary and popular fiction imbued with didactic messages about love, marriage, and social uplift. These publications which I have discussed point to a tradition of Black literary writers writing about love since the 1800s as well as to popular romance fiction writers who continue this tradition well into the twentieth and twenty-first century. While this chapter focuses more on the writings about African American romance writers than on the writers and their actual publications—i.e., the primary sources—I must note that romance novels and novellas continue to proliferate through online, self-published, and traditional mainstream publishers. There is a lively market for these writers as readers purchase and engage with their favorite writers. It will be up us as scholars to continue the work of documenting this rich tradition of representing love in African American romance fiction.

Notes

1 The research and writing of this chapter were supported by the following grants: a DePaul University Academic Initiative Grant and a Faculty Research and Development Summer Research Grant from the College of Liberal Arts and Social Sciences at DePaul University.

2 For more on Vivian Stephens's contributions see Chapter 16.

Works cited

Abdullah-Poulos, Layla. "The Stable Muslim Love Triangle – Triangular Desire in African American Muslim Romance Fiction." *Journal of Popular Romance Studies*, vol. 8, 2018. n.p. http://jprstudies.org/2018/11/the-stable-muslim-love-triangle-triangular-desire-in-african-american-muslim-romance-fictionby-layla-abdullah-poulos/. Accessed March 30, 2019.

"About the Romance Genre." Romance Writers of America. December 2017, www.rwa.org/Online/Resources/About_Romance_Fiction/Online/Romance_Genre/About_Romance_Genre.aspx?hkey=dc7b967d-d1eb-4101-bb3f-a6cc936b5219. Accessed March 27, 2019.

Adewunmi, Bim. "Meet The Black Women Upending The Romance Novel Industry." *BuzzFeed* News, May 1 2018. www.buzzfeednews.com/article/bimadewunmi/meet-the-Black-women-upending-the-romance-novel-industry. Accessed January 20, 2020.

Beckett, Lois. "Fifty Shades of White: The Long Fight against Racism in Romance Novels." *The Guardian*, April 4, 2019, www.theguardian.com/books/2019/apr/04/fifty-shades-of-white-romance-novels-racism-ritas-rwa. Accessed June 17, 2019.

Bray, Rosemary L. "Love For Sale." *Black Enterprise*, December 1982, pp. 71–76.

Campbell, Jane. *Mythic Black Fiction: The transformation of history*. University of Tennessee Press, 1986.

Dandridge, Rita B. *Black Women's Activism: Reading African American Women's Historical Romances*. Peter Lang, 2004.

———. "The African American Historical Romance: An Interview with Beverly Jenkins." *Journal of Popular Romance Studies*, vol. 1, no. 1, August 2010, n.p. http://jprstudies.org/2010/08/interview-beverly-jenkins-by-rita-b-dandridge/. Accessed July 19, 2018.

———. "Love Prevailed despite What American History Said: Agape and Eros in Beverly Jenkins's *Night Song* and *through the Storm*." *Romance Fiction and American Culture: Love as the Practice of Freedom?*, edited by William A. Gleason, and Eric Murphy Selinger, Ashgate Publishing Ltd., 2016, pp. 151–166.

Daniel, Janice. "De Understandin' to Go 'Long Wid It": Realism and Romance in *Their Eyes Were Watching God*." *The Southern Literary Journal*, vol. 24, no. 1, Fall 1991, pp. 66–76.

duCille, Ann. *The Coupling Convention: Sex. Text, and Tradition in Black Women's Fiction*. Oxford UP, 1993.

Edmondson, Belinda. "The Black Romance." *Women's Studies Quarterly*, vol. 35, no. 1/2, 2007, pp. 191–211.

Foster, Guy Mark. "How Dare a Black Woman Make Love to a White Man! Black Women Romance Novelists and the Taboo of Interracial Desire." *Empowerment Versus Oppression: Twenty-First Century Views of Popular Romance Novels*, edited by Sally Goade, Cambridge Scholars Press, 2007, pp. 102–128.

Francis, Consuela. *Flipping the Script: Romancing Zane's Urban Erotica*, edited by William A. Gleason, and Eric Murphy Selinger, Ashgate Publishing Ltd., 2016, pp. 167–180.

Gallon, Kim. "'How Much Can You Read about Interracial Love and Sex without Getting Sore?': Readers' Debate Over Interracial Relationships in the *Baltimore Afro-American*." *Journalism History*, vol. 39, no. 2, Summer 2013, pp. 104–114.

———. "The Black Feminist Love Story." *The Popular Romance Project: Rethinking Love and Romance*, July 1 2014, https://web.archive.org/web/20170506083910/http:/popularromanceproject.org/Black-feminist-love-story/.

Gleason, William A. and Eric Murphy Selinger, editors. *Romance Fiction and American Culture: Love as the Practice of Freedom?* Ashgate Publishing Ltd., 2016.

Goade, Sally. *Empowerment Versus Oppression: Twenty-First Century Views of Popular Romance Novels*. Cambridge Scholars Press, 2007.

hooks, bell. "Love as the Practice of Freedom." In *Outlaw Culture: Resisting Representations*, Routledge, 1994, pp. 289–298.

Lind, Rebecca Ann, editor. *Race, gender, media: Considering diversity across audiences, content, and producers*. Pearson/Allyn and Bacon, 2004.

Markert, John. *Publishing Romance: The History of an Industry, 1940- the Present*. McFarland & Company, Inc., 2016.

Moody-Freeman, Julie. *Scripting Black Love in the 1990's: Pleasure, Respectability, and Responsibility in an Era of HIV/Aids*, edited by William A. Gleason, and Eric Murphy Selinger, Ashgate, 2016, pp. 111–127.

Osborne, Gwendolyn. "How Black Romance–novels that Is Came to Be. (Romance)." *The Free Library*, 2002, www.thefreelibrary.com/How+Black+romance–novels%2C+that+is–came+to + be.+(romance).-a082511066. Accessed August 4, 2017.

———. "'Women Who Look like Me': Cultural Identity and Reader Responses to African American Romance Novels." *Race, gender, media: Considering diversity across audiences, content, and producers*, edited by Rebecca Ann Lind, Pearson/Allyn and Bacon, 2004, pp. 61–68.

———. "Love For Sale." *Black Issues Book Review*, January–February 2006, pp. 14–15.

———. "It's All About Love: Romance Readers Speak Out." *African American Literature Book Club*, February 1 2002, aalbc.com/authors/article.php?id=1907. Accessed October 3, 2015.

Ramsdell, Kristin. *Romance Fiction: A Guide to the Genre*. Second edition. Libraries Unlimited, 2012.

Roach, Catherine. "Love as the Practice of Bondage: Popular Romance Narratives and the Conundrum of Erotic Love." *Romance Fiction and American Culture: Love as the Practice of Freedom?* edited by William A. Gleason, and Eric Murphy Selinger, Ashgate Publishing Ltd., 2016, pp. 368–387.

"Romance Sub-Genres." Romance Writers of America. December 2017, www.rwa.org/Online/Resources/About_Romance_Fiction/Online/Romance_Genre/About_Romance_Genre.aspx?hkey=dc7b967d-d1eb-4101-bb3f-a6cc936b5219. Accessed March 27, 2019.

Ross, Marlon. "'What's Love but a Second Hand Emotion?': Man-on-Man Passion in the Contemporary Black Gay Romance Novel." *Callaloo*, vol. 36, no. 3, Summer 2013, pp. 669–687.

"RWA's Origin Story." Romance Writers of America. www.rwa.org/Online/About/History.aspx. Accessed July 19, 2018.

Schalk, Sami. "Happily Ever after for Whom? Blackness and Disability in Romance Narratives." *The Journal of Popular Culture*, vol. 49, no. 6, 2016, pp. 1241–1259.

Tate, Claudia. *Domestic Allegories of Political Desire: The Black Heroine's Text at the Turn of the Century*. Oxford UP, 1992.

Teo, Hsu-Ming. *Desert Passions: Orientalism and Romance Novels*. University of Texas Press, 2012.

Vivian, Angela. *Final Summer*. Doubleday, 1988.

Weisser, Susan Ostrov. *The Glass Slipper: Women and Love Stories*. Rutgers UP, 2013.

White, Yvonne Ann. *Genesis Press: Cultural Representation and the Production of African American Romance Novels*. University of Iowa Dissertation, 2008.

"Women of Color in Romance with Rebekah Weatherspoon." August 26 2015. Sarahhallanauthor.blogspot.com/2015/08/women-of-color-in-romance-with-rebekah.html?m=1. Accessed March 30, 2019.

Young, Vincent. "Focus." *Washington Post*, 22 April 1991, www.washingtonpost.com/archive/lifestyle/1991/04/22/focus/3a42d590-d2b5-4e09-9b95-452dff2629c4/?noredirect=on&utm_term=.b503cafe3d30. Accessed July 25, 2018.

11 Explorations of the "desert passion industry"

Amira Jarmakani

Desert romances, which feature a sheikh, sultan, or desert prince as their hero, are so named because of the primacy of the desert in the narrative. If the sheikh plays the prototypical role of the alpha-male hero through his portrayal as a virile, aggressive, fierce man of the desert (who nevertheless has his cultured, sensitive side), the desert provides some of the quintessential elements of the romantic plot: it is at once a wide-open space of exploration for the independent heroine and an unpredictable dangerous terrain in which she can be held captive (either by the sheikh himself or by an evil character from whom the sheikh must save the heroine). The duality of the desert—simultaneously as a space of possibility and of danger—structures the larger set of dichotomies that echo throughout desert romances. As the scholarship focused on desert romances demonstrates, they take up the themes of gender fluidity, racial anxiety, and the realities of war and terrorism through their explorations of the masculine/feminine, black/white, and fantasy/reality dichotomies.

As metaphor, the desert illustrates the two main frames through which desert romances have been interpreted; they can be understood both as orientalist escapist fantasies and as feminist explorations of female sexual desire. Each of these characterizations is equally reductive and simplistic. Accordingly, the most interesting research on the subgenre combines these two broad interpretations to look at how an ostensibly feminist framework can both contribute to orientalism (through what Joyce Zonana has called "feminist orientalism") and intervene in a monolithic understanding of orientalism (by providing a perspective of the romanticized, yet masculine, East) (Zonana 594).

Given the success of what Billie Melman calls the "desert passion industry" (104), contemporary desert romances inevitably invoke the legacy of *The Sheik*, and even sometimes closely mirror the plot and details of Hull's influential novel. Indeed, *The Sheik* itself both builds on the popularity of earlier novels, like Hichens's *The Garden of Allah*, and gives way to a subsequent spate of desert-themed romances penned to capitalize on the success of *The Sheik*.

The Sheik therefore undoubtedly holds a supremely influential position in relation to the subgenre of desert romances. Early scholarship on the impact of Hull's novel focuses on two broad themes: 1) recuperating Hull's importance in the literary canon, despite the fact that her work had long been relegated to a denigrated status of "low culture" (Melman; Ardis). The important work of re-valuing Hull and, by extension, the genre of romance, sets up the second major theme: 2) arguing that *The Sheik* participated in the "cultural work of legitimizing female sexual desire" (Ardis 294) and, in so doing, articulated with contemporary debates about modernism and the New Woman.

If early scholarship takes up the themes of female independence, liberty, and sexual desire and the erosion of traditional patriarchal notions of femininity vis-a-vis *The Sheik*, the success of the major motion film starring Rudolph Valentino invited scholarship that built on these themes. Film Studies scholars Gaylyn Studlar and Ella Shohat explore the contemporaneous social anxieties both about effete masculinity embodied by Valentino as well as the racial anxieties provoked by the miscegenation plot.

Though technically part of the body of scholarship covering Hull's novel, Patricia Raub's article "Issues of Passion and Power in E. M. Hull's *The Sheik*" provides a bridge to subsequent desert romance scholarship. In framing *The Sheik* as the "progenitor of the modern romance" (119), Raub prefigures the turn to a focus on mass-market romances (especially category romances like Harlequin) in desert romance scholarship. Among this set of scholars is Evelyn Bach, perhaps the first to write about mass-market desert romances, as well as Susan Blake and Jessica Taylor, who analyze the hybridity of the sheikh-hero, as well as Hsu-Ming Teo ("Orientalism"), who takes up the relationship of desert romances to orientalism (discussed further below). In particular, these scholars take up questions about the sheikh's relative racialization (Blake, though she is focused largely on Hull) and complicate the orientalist critique by emphasizing both the sheikh's masculinity (in contrast to the feminized East of classic orientalism) at the same time that they pay attention to a female perspective on the Middle East (Taylor; Teo "Orientalism").

The most recent set of scholarship analyzes the popularity and impact of desert romances in an era (following the events of 9/11) in which they are concurrent with mainstream predominant notions of Arab masculinity as violent and dangerous. Notably, this group of scholarship includes three monographs (Teo; Jarmakani; Burge). I will discuss these, among other more recent scholarship (Haddad; Holden) in greater detail later in the essay.

Given the importance of *The Sheik* to the overall romance industry, desert romances hold a privileged position in the romance genre even if the sheikh-hero is a relatively derided figure among readers contemporarily (Jarmakani viii, 13–14). While desert romances have certainly increased in popularity over the last decade, they still represent a relatively small proportion of overall romance novel sales, coming in at about 1.2 percent of the market share in the most generous of estimates (see Jarmakani x, for more on these statistics).

If the sheikh grew in popularity concurrently with the war on terror, this relationship also posed a new problem for desert romance authors. Indeed, one key feature distinguishing contemporary desert romances from their predecessors (even mass-market novels from as late as the 1990s) is the fact that the vast majority of them are set in a fictionalized Middle Eastern country. Because successful romance novels are often those that faithfully and realistically represent far-flung geographical locations (Radway 107), it is significant that desert romance authors would choose to fabricate the setting of their novels. When asked, many desert romance authors confirm that they steer clear of actual Middle Eastern countries because of the overwhelmingly negative popular associations with them in the current political context (Jarmakani 10–11; Holden 6–8). Building on the significance of fictionalized Arabia in contemporary desert romances, this chapter uses the metaphor of cartography to explore the contemporary landscape of scholarship on desert romances. How do sheikhs help to map the field of romance?

Imagined cartographies

The back cover of the early editions of Edith Maude Hull's *The Sheik* displays a stylized map of "Arabia," presumably meant to highlight the sense of adventure and exploration that would take the heroine, Diana Mayo, to the North African desert where she would meet her captor and then-lover Sheik Ahmed. This romantic representation of a map points to several important aspects of romance novels, including and perhaps even highlighted in desert romances: it gestures to the importance of distant, faraway lands for the development of erotic fantasy stories; it invokes the desire among romance readers to learn about geography and history; and it demonstrates the important metaphorical role of the topography of the Middle East (i.e., deserts and isolation) in romance novels.

Considering desert romance from the perspective of cartography reveals that they are indisputably orientalist. Orientalism, a term coined by Edward Said, refers to the idea that scholars from Western (and usually colonizing) countries produced knowledge about the "Orient" (West, Central, South, and East Asia in addition to North Africa), creating one accepted and monolithic understanding of the "East," which was more grounded in a Western perspective than on the realities of the region they wrote about. Because this body of knowledge consistently reproduces itself while simultaneously rendering unintelligible anything that falls outside of its rubric, it also functions to create uneven power dynamics between the dominant "West" and the subjugated "East." Regarding the Middle East, in particular, the orientalist framework casts it as a lascivious, feminized, and eroticized space (e.g., through the trope of the harem) while simultaneously portraying it as barbaric and hyperviolent (e.g., the cruel sultan).

Since Said's publication of *Orientalism* in 1978, multiple scholars have built on and complicated his argument, which tends to reify the East/West binary, thereby oversimplifying it. Several desert romance scholars participate in such critical expansions on Said's argument, noting that the focus on a female perspective, and female desire for a romanticized Arab male, disrupts, or at least expands, the usual orientalist binary of either lascivious and feminized or hyper-violent and brutal Arab men (Teo, "Orientalism," *Desert Passions*; Taylor).

One of the principal ways that orientalism works is by discursively formulating the geopolitical region of the "Orient." Maps are nothing if not a frame of colonialism; they literally chart the division and usurping or annexation of land. In the Middle East, this process is graphically demonstrated by the Sykes-Picot agreement of 1916, through which colonialist powers Britain and France literally carved up the remnants of the Ottoman Empire and inscribed the modern national borders of most contemporary Middle Eastern nations. The science of drawing maps—known as cartography—therefore participates in legitimating colonialist and imperialist projects of military intervention and occupation by rationalizing and naturalizing the redrawing of borders, particularly by presenting itself as a neutral or objective scientific endeavor.

Transnational feminist scholars Jacqui Alexander and Chandra Talpade Mohanty claim that "'stories' are simultaneously 'maps' in that they mobilize both histories and geographies of power" (31). Though they are not talking about mass-market romances (and, indeed, may be surprised to find their words applied to them), desert romances could equally be understood as stories that simultaneously map the histories and geographies of power in relation to those regions of the world associated with the Middle East.

Edward Said's notion of "imagined geographies" provides a framework for understanding how the West shaped hegemonic understandings of the Orient, or the East, through its internally coherent discursive formations. Even if "West" and "East" have fallen out of popular use, the longstanding construct of the "Middle" (not to mention "Far" and "Near") East themselves demonstrate the way that language works to shape popular perceptions—or imaginative understandings—of vast regions of the world (see Said 54). Extending analysis of "imagined geographies" to the contemporary context of the war on terror, Derek Gregory demonstrates how orientalist discursive formations still impact contemporary neocolonial military practices on the ground. For example, Raphael Patai's orientalist thesis in *The Arab Mind* that the tribal nature of Arab culture breeds terrorism has reportedly been used as a U.S. military training manual as recently as 2002, when it was reprinted with an introduction from U.S. army colonel Norvell De Atkine. Though Said and Gregory do not necessarily use the word "imagine" as synonymous with fictional—in fact, most applications of their theory are careful to specify that "imaginative" geographies are nonetheless real —the term itself still invites an exploration of the "unnatural boundary" (Anzaldúa 3) between the two terms. In other words, reality and fiction are often opposed to one another in a simple binary despite the much more complicated and nuanced relationship between the two.

Romance novels navigate the interrelationship between fantasy and reality in interesting ways, particularly since successful romance writers are often those who convincingly incorporate accurate historical and geographical details into their fantasy narratives. Yet this characteristic of romance novels also opens up a set of questions about the relationship of what is understood to be "real" to that which is understood to be "imagined" and/or "fantasy." Contemporary desert romances are self-consciously fictional in a way that many other forms of global or internationally-based romances are not—they purposely create fictionalized settings in order to avoid subjects and settings that their readers may find uncomfortable or difficult to fantasize about. My research into authors' reasons for creating fictionalized Arabia indicates that their reasons are—wittingly or not—parallel to the logic of orientalism. Many explained that they sought to draw on the longstanding erotically charged figure of the sheikh—as associated with many tropes and themes within the discourse of orientalism, such as Lawrence of Arabia, *Arabian Nights*, and the idea of the East as sexually lascivious – without invoking the figure of the violent terrorist or oppressive and hyper-masculine Arab man. In other words, romance authors choose one pole of the classic orientalist binary—that of the erotic and sensual Middle East—to craft their sheikh-heroes, while reserving the other pole—that of the irrationally violent terrorist —to graphically represent the obstacle that the sheikh-hero and his heroine must overcome.

In her recent book, Amy Burge points out that "the romance East, in both sheikh romance and Middle English romance, is an amalgam of fantasy and reality that deliberately and, sometimes, explicitly draws on contemporary geopolitical reality" (68), thereby extending this observation beyond the contemporary context. Taking into consideration Hsu-Ming Teo's body of work on desert romances as well (see, in particular, "Orientalism and Mass-Market Romance Novels"), it becomes clear that while all romance novels must navigate the boundaries between fantasy and reality in their narratives, desert romances' engagements with the realities of the Middle East are significantly mediated by the geopolitical and colonialist contexts and histories, whether they are invoking colonialist narratives of the East or using the associations of war and terrorism as plot points to drive the romantic trajectory.

Particularly given reports about the rise in popularity of desert romances after the events of 9/11,[1] recent scholarship on the sub-genre has especially had to grapple with the question of the extent to which these novels reflect and perhaps even help shape contemporary realities like the war on terror. Perhaps most importantly, recent scholarship on desert romances demonstrates that romance novels participate in the discursive construction of what can be known about the Middle East. Through their own imaginative renderings of a sometimes fictionalized Eastern setting, desert romances certainly reinforce classic orientalist themes, but they also push back on popular stereotypes about violent, irredeemable Arab masculinities (Teo, *Desert Passions*; Holden) and sometimes even set the gendered historical record straight even before academic sources reach the same conclusions, as Hsu-Ming Teo argues about Bertrice Small's *The Kadin* ("Bertrice Teaches You History").

The legacy of *The Sheik*

As mentioned earlier, the most direct link between the sheikh sub-genre and the wider field of mass-market romance novels is the 1919 novel *The Sheik* (later made into a major motion picture starring Rudolph Valentino), which is heralded as the progenitor of the modern romance in some of the defining scholarly books in the field of romance studies (Flesch; Dixon 138; Regis 166–17). Even as new research on desert romances expands the horizons of its reach, the sub-field remains inexorably and closely tied to *The Sheik* and all that it invokes, including sexual exoticism and masculine virility to the extent of naming a brand of condoms Melman 91; Teo "Bertrice Teaches You History" 1); anxieties about race and fears of miscegenation; and clear yet sometimes disavowed links to colonialism, war and militarism.

Contemporary research is still exploring Hull and the importance of *The Sheik* both to the overall industry and to the sub-genre of desert romances. Sarah Garland notes that in the U.S. *The Sheik* was the "first book to be a top ten bestseller two years in a row" (198), and in exploring the question of how *The Sheik* came to be a bestseller and maintained its popular status, she suggests that it reflected a contemporaneous intersection of the rise in consumerism and mass consumption with expansionist policies that would lead toward U.S. imperialist policies and status. Arguing that *The Sheik*'s bestseller status could be attributed to a "preexisting middle-brow taste for Orientalism" (198), she relates the rise of consumerism to the idea of "ornamentalism" as proposed by David Cannadine. Here, the lure of opulence described in the lavish decorations, details, and settings of desert romances help to emphasize the sheikh's civilized and refined status, even as the ornamentalism thesis elides the simultaneous importance of race and ethnicity both for the exoticization and the general derision of the sheikh-hero.

Returning to the question of the stature of desert romances in larger conversations about the romance industry despite their relative unpopularity, ongoing scholarship on *The Sheik* reminds us of the way that orientalism and imaginative associations with the Middle East may impact U.S. popular culture in ways that reach beyond desert romances themselves to echo in larger themes of the romance industry. Taking up Garland's framework of "ornamentalism," it is important to avoid conceptualizing it as "mere adornment." Indeed, in his book about the impact of Arabs and Islam on the nineteenth-century U.S. imagination, Jacob Berman asserts that

> to dismiss the presence of referents such as Sherezade [sic], Mecca, Alhambra, and the Sahara in contemporary America as kitsch or as mere adornment is to ignore the deep influence Arab culture has had and continues to have on the American imaginary.
>
> (Berman xi)

Such influence is evident in the longevity of desert romances, and in the fact that they remain a consistent sub-genre even if their popularity waxes and wanes. Moreover, the romanticized East may reach beyond the confines of the desert romance sub-genre to impact the larger romance industry in uncharted or unmapped ways.

In my interview with U.S.-based romance author Linda Conrad, for example, she revealed that as a little girl, she was most compelled by the classic *Arabian Nights* stories, and named Ali Baba as an example. She further intimated that "As a teenager, her first dreams of being with a man were of the dark, mysterious guy who rides in on a horse from exotic lands and carries you off" (Conrad). While quick to assert that she has since moved on to other types of heroes that mostly capture her imagination, Conrad avers that the sheikh is nevertheless "way buried in [her] psyche." Though admittedly anecdotal, Conrad's observations here illustrate the prominent role that sheikhs and the Middle East play in the imaginative construction of the overall romantic landscape. The seemingly endless well of research on Hull's *The Sheik* and desert romances more generally perhaps testifies to the way that the figure of the sheikh is buried in the romantic psyche of the genre as a whole.

Gender and sexuality in *The Sheik* and beyond

Hull's novel foregrounded at least two major themes, which continue to inform contemporary research on the topic: These two themes can be roughly aligned with the two main characters in the novel. There is the feisty, independent heroine, who raises questions about female liberation, and the fierce yet ultimately sensitive alpha-male, who raises questions about gender fluidity and the social anxieties it provokes. Ellen Turner has recently returned to the overall topic of female liberation in Hull's work. Noting that Hull was disparaged by her literary contemporaries, Turner wishes to recuperate Hull through her subsequent works. Focusing on the two romances that Hull wrote in between *The Sheik* and its sequel *Sons of the Sheik*—*The Shadow of the East* (1921) and *The Desert Healer* (1923)—Turner claims that "her later fiction exposed a more liberating aesthetics of female power in the context of post-war Britain" (173). While arguing that Hull's novels develop an appreciation for political liberation, female liberation, and sexual liberation, Turner nevertheless concedes that the gender reversals she employs to explore such liberatory themes ultimately reinforce the gender binary because Hull gives her heroines "masculine" characteristics to signal their strength/power. While Turner seeks to recuperate Hull for her contributions to the literary canon, she ultimately reinforces an early feminist critique of romance: "Power, in Hull, always belongs to the masculine and in this sense her novels remain a tool of the imperialist patriarchy" (179).

Clare Deal similarly takes up the question of gender fluidity in Hull's novel, though she ultimately sees more promise in the potential for transgressing the rigidity of the gender binary. Deal's major claims closely parallel earlier scholarship on gender and orientalism, much of which she does not cite. For example, she explores *The Sheik* as a novel through which gender identity can be understood as a fluid, in-between state, a state that is mirrored and echoed in the space of the desert (90). Deal's argument seems to rest on the pre-conception that the desert is "naturally" liminal, and, in doing so, she perhaps unwittingly echoes orientalist themes. Despite this orientalist take on the desert, the idea of the desert as a barren space ripe for self-exploration is a prominent one in film theory focused on a critique of orientalism (see especially Shohat and Stam).

Moreover, Deal argues that the "transient space of the desert and the liberation offered to women within this liminal space opened up alternative ways in which to understand the relationship of the West with the East to those offered by Edward Said" (93), seemingly without knowledge of the fairly wide swath of scholarship on this very topic, particularly scholarship on women's travel writing (Lewis, *Gendering Orientalism* and *Rethinking Orientalism*; Roberts; Lowe). Nevertheless, her article does offer a new take on these old themes both by contributing to scholarship complicating the orientalism thesis and by theorizing the body as a "text through which the subjective self is revealed" (80), therefore disrupting the usual mind/body binary. Indeed, the critical importance of such a disruption of the mind/body dichotomy reaches beyond desert romances and could be applied more generally to the romance industry. Though not the main focus of her article, Deal's argument also provides a link to a key debate within romance studies more broadly: in referencing the attention that Hull's novel received due to its rape narrative, she draws our attention to the tensions between sexual violence and fantasy in the romance industry.

E. M. Hull's *The Sheik* can be understood as a quintessential "bodice ripper" novel, a term that itself points to fraught tensions around discussions of sexuality between members of the romance industry and feminist researchers. As several feminist scholars have argued, the "bodice-ripping" type of sex in romance novels (sometimes labeled as "rape fantasy" or "rape saga" and sometimes described as sadomasochistic) actually represents a complex relationship between the reader and notions of sexuality (see Creed and Wardrop). Rather than simply perpetuating patriarchal oppression, these scholars argue, romance novels may open up a different kind of space in which readers can positively identify with their own sexual agency; in this space readers can experience a fantasy of sexual pleasure unmediated by social scripts that attach guilt to female sexual agency and desire. For example, Patricia Raub reads Hull's *The Sheik* as the first romance novel to establish the theme of the white heroine as a liberated and powerful female character who embraces her own sexuality. This type of analysis of Hull's novel complicates the temptation to read romance solely as patriarchal fantasy. In relation to the central theme of women's sexual desire and liberation in romance novels, then, scholarship on desert romances continues to play a key role.

Contemporary feminist scholarship on romance novels has a lot to say about the way that the genre of romance uniquely focuses on themes of female liberation, particularly because it foregrounds and centralizes female sexual pleasure. In the desert romance landscape, the role of women's liberation plays a heightened role perhaps because popular perception of the Middle Eastern setting is that it is a space of oppression and even violent submission for women. If, as Joyce Zonana argues, twentieth-century Anglo writers produced a version of "feminist orientalism" (594), using an orientalist idea of the East as a foil to argue for the importance of feminism at home, contemporary desert romances build on this idea by suggesting that the Western (white) heroine is the antidote to Eastern sexism (Teo "Orientalism" 253, *Desert Passions* 232–3). As Fang-mei Lin argues, desert romances in Taiwan offer an interesting angle on this phenomenon. In their portrayal of a triangular relationship between the West (Western Europe and the U.S.), the Orient (the Middle East), and the East (Taiwan), Taiwanese heroines, like their Anglo counterparts, advocate a progressive stance on gender justice even as they are portrayed as "Eastern dolls" who rely on the authority of the sheikh-hero to enact the ideology of progress and development (11). In desert romances, white heroines "de-Orientalize" the sheikh (Teo *Desert Passions* 232), reforming them into modernized subjects who want to introduce women's rights and equality to their people (see also Jarmakani 107–12). In this respect, some authors have argued that desert romances call into question and revise traditional orientalist constructions of the East as feminized (Taylor; Holden). One trend in recent scholarship on desert romances then, is to look at the way that they construe feminist themes. While Teo argues that "the modern sheik novel is nothing if not a vehicle for liberal feminist concerns" (*Desert Passions* 267), I identify this use of the theme of liberal feminism as a "technology of freedom" in an otherwise imperialist project (79–115). In other words, I argue that "freedom" is adapted and re-deployed in a way that actually reinforces imperialist interests.

Given the way that romance novels track and reflect dominant social shifts—including feminist gains and interventions—it follows that overt rape fantasy themes are no longer supported in most contemporary romance. Nevertheless, desert romances sometimes pick up the somewhat similar themes of abduction and captivity. Echoing, again, the tricky balance between fantasy and reality in contemporary desert romances, several scholars have addressed the way that political abductions in the war on terror are reflected in desert romances set in the contemporary context (Haddad; Jarmakani; Burge). Though captivity has long been a theme in desert romance, traceable at least to piracy and the Barbary Coast narratives at the turn of the eighteenth century (Teo *Desert Passions* 111–14), contemporary realities, combined with mainstream reader perceptions that abduction is a common and barbaric practice in Middle Eastern countries (Jarmakani 68), mean that authors must be more nuanced about their incorporation of this theme.

One key strategy writers use is to normalize and de-politicize captivity, even if forced, framing it as "protection or rescue" (Burge 143). Under the semblance of rescue, abduction, or forced captivity then provides a convenient setting in which to explore romantic and erotic themes. Indeed, the trope of abduction echoes—or perhaps extends through another guise—the classic "rape fantasy" characteristic of earlier romances since it exploits the "fine line between rape and violent abduction, and the erotic potential of romantic abduction" (Burge 168). While demonstrating how desert romances must carefully balance the traditional tropes of orientalist fantasy with perceptions of the contemporary war on terror, the captivity narrative also exemplifies the compelling aspects of desert romance—in particular, the ways that desert romances still provide a refuge for some of the most important themes of romance, like a luxurious setting, an uncompromised model of alpha-male masculinity, and the basic elements of the traditional rape fantasy insofar as the cultural alibi can function as a license for the heroine to explore her own sexual desire.

Gender fluidity: the ambivalent alpha-male

Contemporary scholarship has built on early themes of gender anxiety as reflected in the powerful reactions to Valentino's portrayal of masculinity in *The Sheik*. Though mostly focused on the Rudolph Valentino's depiction of Ahmed in the film representation of *The Sheik* (1921), the representation of masculinity portrayed by Valentino ironically raised questions and anxieties about gender fluidity, and the feminization of modern U.S. culture at a time when women's rights (and particularly women's suffrage) had gained traction. A considerable body of film studies scholarship (most notable among these is Gaylyn Studlar) has linked modern anxieties about the feminization of men to contemporaneous attacks of Valentino as effete and emasculated. The irony of attributing an alpha-male sheikh-hero with a feminized presentation demonstrates the way that gender fluidity perhaps inadvertently defines the sub-genre of desert romances.

Considering the primacy of the logics of sexuality–eroticism–gender within orientalism, though, it is unsurprising that desert romances both reinforce and unsettle heteronormativity at the same time. As Amy Burge explains, "The gender blurring, or queering, that can occur in an Orientalized space disrupts the linear logic of gender, suggesting the possibility of gender identification that is more subversive and more troubling to the romantic structures of heteronormativity" (71). In other words, because of the way that an orientalist frame both relies on a traditional gender binary and simultaneously reverses that binary, it also provides a potentially gender-fluid space (thereby invoking queer theory through the central concept of gender fluidity) through which to play with or interrogate traditional notions of gender. In *An Imperialist Love Story*, I likewise analyze the fictional character Lawrence of Arabia as well as the historical character of T. E. Lawrence on which he is based, to argue that the instability (or fluidity) of gender is a key submerged theme in desert romances. In desert romances, the heroine's fierce independence often casts her as transgressing toward masculinity, while the sheikh's billowing and flowing robes threaten to feminize him away from his alpha-male characterization. Reading desert romances carefully demonstrates that there is a profound anxiety about the instability of gender that the romantic narrative ameliorates by re-stabilizing the expected gender binary through the narrative of achieving wholeness and the romantic coupling of the two gender-dichotomous characters (Jarmakani 171–7).

Despite the room for gender fluidity in desert romances, then, both Burge and I conclude that the overall function or resolution of the desert romance subgenre is to reinforce and stabilize gender binaries. Focusing on the trope of virginity, for example, Burge argues that "ultimately these romances do not seriously challenge the undergirding structures of heterosexuality. Gender identity, then, remains binary" (101). As a relatively new topic in desert romances, the application of queer theory as well as exploration of gay desert romances is undoubtedly a future direction for growth.

Race and miscegenation in desert romance

If gender and sexuality are central themes of Hull's foundational text, so too is that of race and miscegenation. While Elizabeth Gargano acknowledges the mixed gendered messages at the heart of desert romances, with their "unsettling brew of feminine victimization and female sexual empowerment" (171), her article also demonstrates the colonialist logic of *The Sheik*, whereby "an Englishman raised by Arabs makes a 'better' Arab than the Arabs" (182). As indicated in this quote, Hull dealt with miscegenation fears by revealing Sheik Ahmed's European ancestry at the end of the novel; he was therefore portrayed as culturally Arab yet ethnically white. Subsequent scholarship on desert romances has continued to foreground the issues of racial miscegenation and hybridity since the majority of heroines in desert romances continue to be ethnically and culturally white. Because race is historically and socially constructed, Arab, or sheikh, heroes are often portrayed as ethnically or culturally (but not racially) distinct from the white heroines. Nevertheless, they can be analyzed as interracial romances because of the way that the constructed differences between sheikh and heroine often serve as central plot devices through which their romance will be tested and strained before resolving into the HEA ending. Even if they are sometimes portrayed as, or associated with, Mediterranean heroes, then, sheikh-heroes continue to represent an "anxious hybridity" (Burge 134) or even a form of "cultural schizophrenia" (Teo "Orientalism" 250) that is narratively resolved through the ultimate union between sheikh-hero and white heroine.

Arguing that the sheikh and heroine ultimately end up demonstrating a "sameness in hybridity" (122), Burge investigates the role of fashion and fabric in the ethnic and religious constructions of the sheikh, a line of inquiry that allows Burge to advance the idea that ethnic and religious identities are literally "fabricated" through fashion, fabric, and ornament (103). In my own work on contemporary desert romances, I make a similar point about the significance of clothing as a marker of race, ethnicity, and/or religion, and as one that serves as a flexible code of racialization for the sheikh in a context in which he must have access to exotic difference while reserving recourse to the safety of racial (if not ethnic) whiteness by changing into Western dress (Jarmakani 147). Both Burge and I also explore the importance of the kind of racial cross-dressing exhibited by a number of white heroines who adopt Eastern dress as a way of getting in touch with their own sexuality through exoticism and of demonstrating their willingness to adopt elements of the sheikh's culture (Burge 121, Jarmakani 103–6). Interestingly, Burge notes that the use of clothing as a signifier of ethnic/racial/religious identity has an antecedent in the medieval context: "The use of clothing to mark religious identity was an established practice in the Middle Ages, encoded in contemporary legal regulation of Saracens and Jews" (122). Indeed, the legacies of marking religious difference through sartorial choices during the Crusades continues to resonate in contemporary popular notions of what Muslims look like (notions that often rely on clothing and hair). In arguing that race is not an "insurmountable barrier to union," even though marked in clothing, Teo also touches on these themes (Teo *Desert Passions* 35).

The importance of this legacy as reflected also in comparative historical considerations of the romance genre is something to which I will return in a future section. Given the growing demand for multiethnic and multiracial romance, further inquiry into the racial dynamics of desert romances is likely; an area for growth would be a study of the comparative racialization of differently marked heroes and heroines. Within the subgenre of desert romances, it would also mean closer consideration of both multiracial and multiethnic romances (e.g., *Delaney's Desert Sheikh*, featuring an African American heroine) as well as what we might call heritage heroines (e.g., Linda Conrad's half Iranian heroine in *Secret Agent Sheik* and Olivia Gates's Arab American heroines).

In her article on Suzanne Brockmann, particularly the novels featuring Navy SEALS, Kecia Ali also takes up the thread of research on race and miscegenation in desert romances to note the often-complex ways in which it can play out in Brockmann's oeuvre. Though Brockmann's novels are not necessarily desert romances, her incorporation of a range of multiracial relationships, including with characters of Middle Eastern and/or Muslim descent, puts her in conversation with sheikh novels. Noting that Brockmann's romances often focus on terrorists in ways that "flip the script" of the typical sheikh novel, Ali also demonstrates that a notable aspect of Brockmann's novels is the fact that they are set in the United States (Ali 17). Since they focus on the U.S., rather than a fictionalized "Arabiastan" (Jarmakani) or "Islamland" (Abu-Lughod), Ali shows that by putting the white heroine in a U.S. context, they focus on a social need to reform mainstream stereotypes about Muslims and/or the Middle East. Ultimately, Ali argues that Brockmann's novels advance the notion that stereotypes and racism are crucial threats both to U.S. national security and to individual well-being, since they block intimacy and human connection.

Ali's conclusions here echo some of the other contemporary scholarship on desert romances, particularly those that see some value in romantic representations of a lovable sheikh in a context in which Arab and Muslim masculinities are generally popularly constructed as hyper-aggressive, oppressive to women, and even evil. Drawing a complex picture of the way that desert romances reflect the geopolitical realities of the colonialist and neocolonialist interventions in the countries they represent (even if imaginatively), Teo notes that desert romances (and their authors) portray increasingly scarce "ameliorative representations" of the Middle East (*Desert Passions* 302). While she acknowledges the often orientalist "representational failings of sheik romance novels," Teo nevertheless argues that desert romances, like "no other genre of American popular culture has determinedly and repeatedly attempted to humanize the Arab or Muslim other—even if, out of ignorance or incomprehension, imaginary Orients had to be created in order to do so" (*Desert Passions* 216).

Stacy Holden similarly argues that desert romances offer a challenge to dominant narratives about the Middle East. Basing her argument on romance writers' own characterizations of the strategies they use to represent the usually imaginative sheikhdoms of the heroes, she writes that "sheikh romance authors often see themselves as putting forward an alternative fantasy of the Middle East: one that emphasizes attraction, rather than fear, and one that implicitly contradicts Huntington's contention of a perpetual Clash of Civilizations" (13). I argue in *An Imperialist Love Story* that such an appreciation of a positive representation of Arab/Muslim masculinity depends on the framework of liberal multiculturalism, which may not significantly shift, change, or even confront the negative representations in popular culture. In short, the debate about the extent to which desert romances speak back to and even potentially shift dominant negative stereotypes about the Middle East in U.S. popular culture offers much room for further scholarship.

Romancing the war on terror and its legacies

Contemporary research on desert romances must fundamentally grapple with the increased interest post 9/11 in addition to its relationship to the war on terror, yet such a focus does not lead the scholarship entirely in a new direction so much as it generates a development of and building on themes already well established. As already mentioned, there has always been a dialectical relationship between desert romances and their attending contexts of war, military intervention, and colonialism.

Perhaps because of the media attention devoted to the increased popularity of desert romances after 9/11, contemporary research about desert romances tends to address the context of the war on terror (for an analysis of the media coverage relative to the claim about the increased popularity of desert romances see Jarmakani x). However, desert romance-related research focused on the war on terror can suffer from a presentist perspective in the sense that it tends to overemphasize the impact of 9/11 as a radical rupture, while undervaluing or underestimating the longer legacy of orientalist representation. Here, recent work by Amy Burge and Hsu-Ming Teo (*Desert Passions*) makes a critical intervention in the field by demonstrating the need to look much further back than the twentieth century, at least back to the medieval era and the context of the Crusades. Indeed, one of the defining characteristics of recent scholarship is this longer historical reach, and it is an area that promises to deepen analysis of themes such as the dialectical relationship between romantic representations of the Middle East and the concurrent geopolitical constructions of it; the construction of difference through race and religion; the casting of difference as erotic and/or sensual; and the romantic incorporation of war and militarism as an obstacle to be overcome.

Burge's claim that "the touching points between medieval and modern romance audiences are closer than we might think" (180) echoes Teo's analysis of the Crusades as a crucial early context for the theme of cross-cultural love between the "Orient" and the West (Teo *Desert Passions* 31–7). Tracing this theme into the Renaissance, Teo also offers a trenchant analysis of the way that the themes of the "Barbary" coast would resonate even into more contemporary desert romances. Indeed, what is perhaps most exciting about the longer historical reach of contemporary research on desert romances is the way they trace familiar themes through the vicissitudes of both literary representation and historical context. Contrary to a myopic view that locates the dominant themes of desert romances in a purely contemporary context, these works enable a more sophisticated consideration of contemporary discourses—for example, in popular vernacular usage of "medieval" to simply mean backward, particularly given the irony that, during the medieval period, Europe could be construed as the backward region looking upon (Islamic) Andalusia as more advanced (technologically and otherwise).

Audience reception and beyond

On a final, methodological, note, a consideration of contemporary research on desert romances would not be complete without acknowledging the ethnographic turn as an important critical innovation. Janice Radway revolutionized the field of romance studies in the 1980s by incorporating reader response. Radway's study focused on a relatively small and homogenous group of women in a small town, and scholarship since then has sought to expand the bounds of audience reception. One way of doing so in the contemporary context is to utilize digital modes of reader response, like online discussion forums and book review sites. Initial forays into this mode of inquiry include Teo's analysis of Amazon book reviews ("Bertrice Teaches You History"; *Desert Passions*), and my analysis of comments and discussions on popular romance blogs like "Smart Bitches, Trashy Books" (Jarmakani). If tracking readers' responses to romance novels falls on the "decoding" side of the producer/consumer spectrum, there has also been research that focuses on unpacking the way that desert romances are framed or encoded (Hall). On this "encoding" side of research, Stacy Holden focuses on interviews with romance writers, arguing that "authors of sheikh romances consciously and deliberately struggle against the negative stereotypes of Arabs perpetrated by the media and other vehicles of popular culture" (3). In *An Imperialist Love Story*, I also incorporate interviews with popular desert romance authors, as they were able to both confirm the increased marketability of sheikhs after 9/11 (Jarmakani x) and speak to the ways that they imaginatively constructed the sheikhs' countries (see the reference to my conversation with Linda Conrad, above).

The future of the sheikh

Returning again to the framework of cartography, by way of conclusion I would draw our attention to the way that contemporary scholarship on desert romances demonstrates that the allure of the desert supersedes the spatial realm. In spite of—or perhaps because of—the orientalist stereotypes that dot the landscape of desert romances, these novels map a pattern of associations between the "West" and the "East," however much these configurations may shift over time, and they demonstrate the centrality of gender, sexuality, and race to geopolitical questions of war and empire.

Given the history of desert romances, one thing we can say with relative certainty is that even though the popularity of the sheikh will likely wane again, the sheikh as both romantic, erotic, and virile hero and as aggressive, threatening, and violent antagonist is unlikely to disappear from the romance scene.

Note

1 Melissa August, "Sheikhs and the Serious Blogger," *Time*, Monday, August 22, 2005 http://content.time.com/time/nation/article/0,8599,1096809,00.html; Patrick T. Reardon, "The Mystery of Sheik Romance Novels," *Chicago Tribune*, April 24, 2006 http://articles.chicagotribune.com/2006-04-24/features/0604240223_1_romance-readers-romance-novel-sheik; Dave Gilson, "Lust in the Dust," *Mother Jones*, March/April 2006 http://www.motherjones.com/politics/2006/03/lust-dust; Brian Whitaker, "Those Sexy Arabs," *The Guardian*, March 23, 2006 http://www.theguardian.com/commentisfree/2006/mar/23/thosesexyarabs.

Works cited

Abu-Lughod, Lila. *Do Muslim Women Need Saving?* Harvard University Press, 2013.

Alexander, Jacqui and Chandra Talpade Mohanty. "Cartographies of Knowledge and Power: Transnational Feminism as Radical Praxis." *Critical Transnational Feminist Praxis*. edited by Amanda Lock Swarr and Richa Nagar. State University of New York Press, 2010, pp. 23–45.

Ali, Kecia. "Troubleshooting Post-9/11 America: Religion, Racism, and Stereotypes in Suzanne Brockmann's *Into the Night* and *Gone Too Far*." *Journal of Popular Romance Studies*, vol. 6, 2017, n.p. http://jprstudies.org/2017/09/troubleshooting-post-911-america-religion-racism-and-stereotypes-in-suzanne-brockmanns-into-the-night-and-gone-too-farby-kecia-ali/

Anzaldúa, Gloria. *Borderlands/La Frontera: The New Mestiza*. Aunt Lute Books, 1987.

Bach, Evelyn. "Sheik Fantasies: Orientalism and Feminine Desires in the Desert Romance." *Hecate: An Interdisciplinary Journal of Women's Liberation*, vol. 23, no. 1, 1997, pp. 9–40.

Blake, Susan. "What 'Race' is the Sheik? Rereading a Desert Romance." *Doubled Plots: Romance and History*. edited by Susan Strehle and Mary Paniccia Carden. University Press of Mississippi, 2003, pp. 67–85.

Burge, Amy. *Representing Difference in the Medieval and Modern Orientalist Romance*. Palgrave MacMillan, 2016.

Cannadine, David. *Ornamentalism: How the British Saw Their Empire*. Allen Lane, 2001.

Conrad, Linda. Telephone interview with the author, March 5, 2012.

Creed, Barbara. "The Women's Romance as Sexual Fantasy: 'Mills and Boon.'."*All Her Labours Two: Embroidering the Framework*. edited by Women and the Labour Publications Collective, Hale & Iremonger, pp. 47–67.

Deal, Clare H. "'Throbb[ing] with a consciousness of a knowledge that appalled her': Embodiment and Female Subjectivity in the Desert Romance." *Women: A Cultural Review*, vol. 26, nos. 1–2, 2015, pp. 75–95.

Dixon, jay. *The Romance Fiction of Mills and Boon, 1909–1990's*. University College London Press, 1999.

Flesch, Juliet. *From Australia with Love: A History of Modern Australian Popular Romance Novels*. Curtin University Books, 2004.

Garland, Sarah. "Ornamentalism: Desire, Disavowal, and displacement in E.M. Hull's *The Sheik*." *Must Read: Rediscovering American Bestsellers: From Charlotte Temple to The Da Vinci Code*. Edited by Sarah Churchwell and Thomas Ruys Smith. Continuum Books, 2012, pp. 197–216.

Haddad, Emily. "Bound to Love: Captivity in Harlequin Sheikh Novels." *Empowerment versus Oppression: Twenty First Century Views of Popular Romance Novels*. Edited by Sally Goade. Cambridge Scholars, 2007, pp. 42–64.

Hall, Stuart. "Encoding, Decoding." *The Cultural Studies Reader*, 2nd ed. Edited by Simon During. Routledge, 1999, pp. 507–517.

Holden, Stacy. "Love in the Desert." *Journal of Popular Romance Studies*, vol. 5, no. 1, 2015, pp. 119.

Jarmakani, Amira. *An Imperialist Love Story: Desert Romances and the War on Terror*. NYU Press, 2015.

Lewis, Reina. *Gendering Orientalism: Race, Femininity and Representation*. Routledge, 1996.

————. *Rethinking Orientalism: Women, Travel and the Ottoman Harem*. Rutgers University Press, 2004.

Lin, Fang-mei. "Desert Romance in Taiwan: From Violence to Gender (In)Equality" paper presented at The Fifth International Conference on Popular Romance Studies: Rethinking Love, Rereading the Romance. Thessaloniki, Greece, June 19–21, 2014.

Lowe, Lisa. *Critical Terrains: French and British Orientalisms*. Cornell University Press, 1991.

Patai, Raphael. *The Arab Mind [1973]*. Long Island City, NY: Hatherleigh Press, 2007.

Raub, Patricia. "Issues of Passion and Power in E.M. Hull's *The Sheik*." *Women Studies*, vol. 21, 1992, pp. 119–128.

Regis, Pamela. *A Natural History of the Romance Novel*. University of Pennsylvania Press, 2003.

Roberts, Mary. *Intimate Outsiders: The Harem in Ottoman and Orientalist Art and Travel Literature*. Duke University Press, 2007.

Said, Edward. *Orientalism: Western Conceptions of the Orient*. Penguin, 1978.

Shohat, Ella and Robert Stam. *Unthinking Eurocentrism: Multiculturalism and the Media*. Routledge, 1994.

Snitow, Ann Barr. "Mass Market Romance: Pornography for Women is Different." *Powers of Desire: The Politics of Sexuality*. Edited by Ann Snitow et al. Monthly Review Press, 1983 (1979), pp. 245–263.

Studlar, Gaylyn. "Discourses of Gender and Ethnicity: The Construction and De(con)struction of Rudolph Valentino as Other." *Film Criticism*, vol. 13, no. 2, Winter 1989, pp. 18–35.

Taylor, Jessica. "And You Can Be My Sheikh: Gender, Race, and Orientalism in Contemporary Romance Novels." *The Journal of Popular Culture*, vol. 40, no. 6, 2007, pp. 1032–1051.

Teo, Hsu-Ming. "Orientalism and Mass Market Romance Novels in the Twentieth Century." *Edward Said: The Legacy of a Public Intellectual*. Edited by Debjani Ganguly and Ned Curthoys. Melbourne University Press, 2007, pp. 241–262.

———. "'Bertrice Teaches You History and You Don't Even Mind!': History and Revisionist Historiography in Bertrice Small's *The Kadin*". *New Approaches to Popular Romance Fiction: Critical Essays.* Edited by Sarah S. G. Frantz and Eric Murphy Selinger. McFarland, 2012, pp. 21–32.

———. *Desert Passions: Orientalism and Romance Novels.* University of Texas Press, 2012.

Turner, Ellen. "E.M. Hull and the Valentino Cult: Gender Reversal after *The Sheik.*" *Journal of Gender Studies* vol. 20, no. 2, June 2011, pp. 171–182.

Wardrop, Stephanie. "The Heroine Is Being Beaten: Freud, Sadomasochism, and Reading the Romance." *Style*, vol. 29, no. 3, 1995, pp. 459–474.

Zonana, Joyce. "The Sultan and the Slave: Feminist Orientalism and the Structure of *Jane Eyre.*" *Signs: Journal of Women in Culture and Society*, vol. 18, 1993, pp. 592–617.

Part III

Methodological approaches

12 Romance in the media

Jayashree Kamblé

> For years I have been bumbling along in the naïve belief that the women's magazines were devoted solely to such matters as how to chintz up the living room and get a cake to rise. But it seems I was wrong—the most worrisome problem facing milady's monthly gazettes is how to muss up the marriage bed and keep one's mate aroused.
>
> (Williams *Playboy*)

On any given day, an online search for the phrase "romance novel" will easily garner several hits, at least a couple of which laugh or rant about the genre's alleged formulaic nature. It's often implied or stated that said nature, with its seeming opiate-like hold on readers, gives them unrealistic ideas of sex and love and lulls them into loving the patriarchy instead of smashing it. At the time of this writing, such an online search led to a 2016 article titled "Dresses Made From Romance Novels Challenge Myth of Feminine Ideal," which conflated fashion (and its detrimental influence on women) with romance:

> [According to Schumacher] "Generation after generation of females have been programmed to buy into [the fashion magazine] culture of unrealistic beauty.
>
> Schumacher, a Chicago-based multi-media artist, said romance novels amplify the illusion, presenting an alternate reality where love is all-consuming and eternally passionate.
>
> (Stoner)

The article says nothing about the artist's credentials in evaluating the content of romance novels. No romance reader would be surprised by this. The most enduring feature of romantic fiction (even before mass-market romance novels became a genre) is its history as a target of disapproval.

The twentieth-century discourse bemoaning romance fiction's promiscuity and weaknesses (i.e., its lack of fidelity to any literary standards in favor of sexual frissons and sentiment) has appeared in newspapers, magazines, television, and movies, starting as early as the 1930s (as in the 1957 *Playboy* article in the epigraph, which lumped together excerpts from love stories and sexual health advice columns in women's magazines). Gradually, this condemnation of romance fiction through parody has taken on a life of its own. It has become its own genre—the "Media Romance," a fantastic combination of sexual comedy and literary tragedy. In large part, this simulacrum is a creature stitched together from bits of romance novel covers, whose design elements were standardized by publishers like Harlequin Mills & Boon and Avon over the last century, the most recognizable of which is a couple frozen forever in romantic contact. Judith McKnight-Trontz lists some of the elements, including the colors, font style, and motifs like flowers in her romance cover history in *The Look of Love*. The final section of the chapter describes the few studies, including mine, that have analyzed the history and the components of this standardization, though much remains to be done.

To start, the chapter surveys a range of popular representations of romance fiction in print and audio-visual media and documents how the genre's appearance becomes a springboard from which news, magazine, television, and movie writers (and some academics) have insisted on or alluded to its allegedly formulaic content without making much effort to research a fair sample of texts. Their dependence on the clichéd novel *covers* as forensic evidence of silly plots and overblown prose creates the parodic Media Romance. It is a maneuver through which the cover, a paratextual sign that means carnal and emotional love to romance readers, is mythologized into a new sign: intellectual vapidity and infantilized sexual desire.

As Roland Barthes has observed, sign systems are mythologies, where the unit of image and content, i.e., signifier/signified, is attributed a meaning not necessarily tied to that unit; this is the sign formation that occurs when it comes to the Media Romance as well. The Media Romance, in other words, is a myth. In its creation, critics assign romance novel covers, which are ubiquitous, an imagined meaning (escapist and titillating sexual fantasies); subsequently, they create a sign (romance fiction is formulaic soft porn), which is then reinforced with every news article, movie, and TV show that repeats that mythology. In other words, Media Romance mythologists appropriate what genre insiders receive primarily as the sign for love and equitable partnerships (alongside other marketing elements, such as a sub-genre indicator) and turn it into a signifier of porn, erasing its pre-existing life as a sign to make room for a new one. To be clear, the cover's connotation of love and partnership that exists for readers derives from the happy endings that all romances demand, rather than something organic or congenital in a cover itself. But in every case where a Media Romance appears, the fact that each novel has its own individual plot and its author a distinctive style is ignored in favor of reading the cover. In this way, critics have parodied the genre for the sins that they have attributed to it based on images that signify immorality or poor writing to them (though they signify a sexualized love story to romance readers).

Admittedly, the treatment of romance novels in popular discourse has tended to emphasize their status as commodities rather than literature because they resemble mass-produced, uniformly packaged objects. In *A Critique of Commodity Aesthetics*, Wolfgang Haug credits packaging with being the prime mover of consumer capitalism, and argues that branding not only begins eliminating the appearance of individual uniqueness, it eventually divests an object of its varied uses while teaching consumers to desire one single use in relation to that object. The creators of the Media Romance appear to think along the same lines about the romance genre, but while Haug's analysis is accurate when it comes to his example of a brand of laundry detergent, critiques of genre fiction that foreground this phenomenon are far from accurate; romance novels are not clones and while some romance novels may be poorly plotted or stylistically weak, the genre at large contains a vast spectrum of narratives.

Due to the focus in romance cover art on the heterosexual couple (at least till very recently) and on elements that suggest a clichéd setting, however, Media Romance writers equate all romance novels with their narrow form. They fold in the novels' individuality into one tale of sexual promise, and report this perspective to the broader public. The Media Romance has thus evolved out of the belief that the genre's exchange value (inexpensive standardized paperbacks sold at grocery stores and airports) has created a single-use value (escapism through sexual stimulation) and nurtured a readership that craves it alone. In other words, branding and its effect on *uninformed* readers (those with a minimal acquaintance with the actual content of romance novels or little interest in knowing more), has birthed the Media Romance. While few critics/Media Romance writers appear to be aware of their own susceptibility to the packaging of romance novels, the hackneyed popular assumption that one of these novels is basically the same as another thus stems from the uniform look of romance novel covers.

The critics' behavior is rooted in a long tradition. As Paula Rabinowitz documents in her 2014 study *American Pulp*, the first paperbacks were either reprints of works that had already been published in the more expensive hardcover format and bore sexually titillating covers (copying detective and romance magazines) or were PBOs, i.e., "paperback originals" that were short and inexpensive—critique and censorship ensued (191). (Also see Chapters 1, 7, 8, and 9 in particular, and for more pulp reprints of literary works; see the *Literary Hub* blog post "50 Pulp Cover Treatments.") *Pioneers, Passionate Ladies, and Private Eyes* offers a detailed look at dime novels and pulp (including cover illustrations) starting after the American Civil War (as does the "Pulp Magazines Project" website for pulp between 1896–1946) and shows how certain genres became associated with paperbacking and with unoriginality and immorality.[1] Furthermore, as Kenneth Davis has pointed out, their lower costs increased the potential readership, inciting fears about a possible drop in the novels' quality since they aimed at a poorer (and by extension, less cultured) audience (228).[2] My dissertation *Uncovering and Recovering the Romance* charts some of the moral panic around paperbacking after World War II. Though such hysteria over the paperback should be a thing of the past, it is alive and well in connection with romance fiction.

While romance novels in the first half of the twentieth century escaped such censure, possibly due to their hard binding and "glamorous, subdued" illustrations (some of which hinted at grim World War II plots), their descendants have been mocked for sentimentality or sexuality, likely because of their increasingly standardized covers (most recognizably the 1960s Gothic wave of a woman "at the fore and a mansion with a single light on in the background" and the semi-naked bodies and their paperback format in the 1970s and 1980s) (McKnight-Trontz 18–20).[3] Media critics' digs at the genre frequently reference its paraliterature: the material body of romance novels and their cover images. In this dilettantish understanding of the genre, references to textual details are infrequent and dismissive, or concocted to match the romanticized eroticism of the covers. The Media Romance is thus but the conflation of the appearance of romance novels with their content, and it exists because of the perpetuation of that perspective by various media, even in the face of contradictory evidence. As the genre's paraliterature changed over the twentieth century, it was accompanied by the growth of the Media Romance, starting with critiques of pulp romance and then of mass-market romance fiction in hardback as well as paperback.

Pre-World War II

Paperback publishing was on the rise in the 1930s on both sides of the Atlantic (though not at British romance publisher Mills & Boon) as was the tide of adverse criticism toward any fiction that appeared in that form. Kenneth Davis notes that even though paperbound books had begun to be printed in the eighteenth century, the trend only took off with the establishment of Penguin Books in England and Pocket Books in the United States in this decade (32–4). It was in this climate that critiques of romantic stories began to appear, aimed mostly at women's magazines and pulp novels. The news media denounced both the format and the illustrations that accompanied it, in a conflation of the two elements with allegedly poor content. In the case of romance fiction in particular, the identification of paperback and pulp forms with lowbrow taste, and of romantic tales with either form, condemned the genre as well. A look at the popular press's treatment of the genre shows how the commentary (calling the genre formulaic and/or sexual) was nominally based on the text's content but hugely influenced by its visual markers.

In a 1937 issue of *Literary Digest*, the article "Big Business in Pulp Thrillers: Love and Adventure Stories Gross $25,000,000 a Year" reviewed the workings of the pulp fiction business and emphasized its devotion to quantity. Aimed at appealing to the literary morality of its discerning readership, it warned against the evils of tacky, assembly-line books put out by those lacking literary-moral fiber. The *Digest* staff writer focused on the profit-driven aspects of pulp (as the dollar amount in the title shows) and though he admitted that Harry Steeger of Popular Publications had contested the notion of a "formula," he nevertheless portrayed this fiction as reliant on a cookie-cutter method aimed at low production costs and low returns from distributors. Most significantly, the article also referred to love stories in the pulp format, mocking their accompanying illustrations; in this case, it is a sketch of a young woman climbing down a tree with the help of a young, smartly-dressed man. Both the article and the illustration's caption ("Romance illustrations gush suggestively: 'Kit quivered at her rescuer's nearness'") ridicule the sentiment and sexuality of the romance—along with, or perhaps because of, its visual representation and pulp identity. The genre is already being treated as a sign of immature sexuality, with the image (man and woman) and its caption portrayed as a signifier for purple prose passages.

Post-World War II into the 1970s

The trickle of critique was to become a flood around World War II, when there was increased book demand, especially for soldiers overseas, and price wars that brought paperbacks into the public eye and resulted in censorious debates. Kenneth Davis's argument that it was the *covers* of the paperbacks that incited the moral brigade's ire is relevant here. Davis says of paperbacks, "[a] book that did not feature a woman in some state of undress—and preferably reclining—was difficult to find" (135). While hardcovers rarely employed illustrations, paperback publishing, especially in the 1940s and 1950s, resorted to covers that mimicked the sexualized look of mass publishing forms. Once the tie between paperbacks and sex became accepted as innate, it established indignation and contempt as the correct attitude toward this fiction, an attitude visible in lawsuits against pulp writers and cover artists.[4]

In the years that followed, news articles continued to address the new wave of publishing as well and played a key role in shaping their readers' opinions of the works that took this form. For instance, in 1967, Bernard Weinraub of the *New York Times* reported on the publishing industry's shift away from stereotypical covers but singled out romance fiction for a dig, critiquing it and paperback covers in one shot, remarking, "In the feverish, highly competitive paperback book market, more labor, more care, more anxiety, and more delicious enticements are placed on the cover than in the creation of one of those mystery romances that women adore." To see this pronouncement in the *New York Times* is to see the creation of the aristocracy of taste; a venerable cultural entity tells the nation to equate sexy covers with "those" books—carelessly written stories "adored," i.e., loved without reason, by women.

Weinraub not only labels romances as the reading choice of silly teens and idle women, but also implies that their content has little but sex and violence, saying, "For publishers, the clichés [cover illustrations suggesting sex or violence] remain strongest in gothic romance novels that appeal so strongly to young girls and middle-aged women"; Weinraub elects to put his claim directly on the heels of New American Library's William Gregory saying that he avoids clichés unless the book has "nothing else" going for it. Interestingly, Gregory also directly contests the conception of the genre as pornographic.

> "In gothic romance books, like high adventure, there's never any sex," says Mr. Gregory. "The girl is always looking longingly. She's always walking up or down a staircase. She's always holding a candle and there's always a room that no one unlocks."
>
> . . .
>
> Mr. Gregory said with a laugh: "There may be a man's hand on her shoulder, but it won't lead to the bedroom."
>
> "Until they get married." said Miss Temple.
>
> "Until they get married." Mr. Gregory repeated.

Even as Weinraub includes Gregory's claim of the Gothic's chaste narrative, which makes evident a disjuncture between the fiction and its marketing, he nevertheless identifies the genre with sex and stupid readers. In other words, Weinraub ignores Gregory's remark that Gothic romance is not about sex and violence, emphasizes the fact that the publisher himself treats the Gothic as formulaic, and then falsely implies that the formula is of a young girl's sexual adventure. In fact, his article begins with a series of quotes that are meant to cement the tie between paperbacks and love stories (such as "Her fierce love was a fortress in the midst of murder and revenge!") Articles like Weinraub's participated in fostering the myth that the sexualized covers are a sign of sexual content, presenting as content what was in fact marketing. If publishers' use of cover illustrations hinted at the idea that romance novels include some sexually suggestive passages, the idea was fully embraced by critics like Weinraub and disseminated to their non-romance-reading readers as the *only* meaning of the sign.

At least some of this insistence on labeling the genre as a recycled narrative of romanticized sexuality stems from the rise of Harlequin as a series romance publisher in North America. Harlequin's marketing strategy was to erase any suggestion of story-telling differences or authorial specificity, and use familiar packaging (such as the "clinch" image) to move its "product." The news media, functioning as the popular arbiter of good taste responded to this commodity packaging predictably. Numerous newspaper articles continued the trend of disparaging romance fiction's apparent formulaic nature and attributed Harlequin's high sales figures to it. In several accounts, the genre was equated with sexuality and its plots dismissed (with little evidence) as a formula that allows for sexual thrills. Contempt for romantic sexuality (and its market value as created by the packaging) appeared frequently in these hatchet jobs. For instance, Eric Pace's 1973 *New York Times* article "Gothic Novels for Women Prove Bonanza for Publishers" begins with the description of an embracing couple in Jane McIlvaine McClary's 1972 novel *A Portion for Foxes*:

> Reaching out, he pulled her to him. He saw the stars twinkling beyond her head and smelled the odor of her hair and skin, sweet-smelling and clean, like good soap and new-mown hay . . .
>
> (31)

Though Pace later identifies *Portion* as a family saga novel (a category that is distinct from romance fiction and of the Gothic romance subgenre he evokes in the title of his article), he has no qualms about using it to represent "salable, romantic writing" and the allegedly sexual Gothic romance referred to in the article's title; his intent is to identify the romance genre with sexuality, even if that means using bad evidence. Beyond quoting the above lines, Pace says nothing about *Portion*'s interrogation of the American South during the Civil Rights Movement, convinced as he is that any "romantic writing" is worth little analysis. His article is thus not about a romance novel but the fictitious Media Romance he perpetuates.

Even when Pace is informed about the textual diversity behind the uniform look of Gothic romance (and quotes editors who point out the feminist impulses in the novels) he ignores these interpretations. The article highlights stereotypical covers of Harlequin romances and of a Gothic, and ends by noting that Gothic covers "always showed a frightened girl, generally in a white negligee, under a lowering sky, in front of a castle or mansion with a mysterious light in a window." The images in this conclusion homogenize all the women's fiction he is surveying (and which the article earlier acknowledges contains more "ambitious" works) into one silly horror. Pace consolidates the Media Romance by equating the Gothic romance with Harlequin novels *and* with the family saga genre based on the fact that they all have a romantic element, with cover illustrations suggesting women-centered narratives. The grouping reveals a predisposition to misconstrue the genre and to devalue any narrative that is seen to involve women, love, and sexuality.

Over the years, this belief that romances are formulated to describe only sexual narratives appears repeatedly, such as in Joyce Maynard's 1976 *New York Times* article "Harlequin Novels: A Romance Between Stories and Readers." Like Pace, Maynard begins the article with an excerpt (from Rozella Lake's *If Dreams Came True*) of a couple kissing:

> With a murmur she twined her arms around his neck and placed her mouth on his. In her diaphanous costume her body was as transparent as her feelings and Daniel's hands gently moved her away from him ...
>
> She pulled his head on to her breast. "I want you, Daniel. So much that I can't find the right words."
>
> (44)

The quotation serves to categorize the genre as focused on sexuality and sentiment, eclipsing Maynard's later documentation of readers' claims that the novels are attractive because they are "clean." The article contains other contradictions—always a clue that the journalist is writing a Media Romance; even as Maynard notes that "[m]ost Harlequin readers, questioned about the books, remember the plots and characters' names with amazing clarity, although, to one not initiated, the novels might *appear* very interchangeable," she emphasizes that "[e]very [novel] is exactly 190 pages long, with the somewhat more sophisticated Harlequin Presents series running a little longer" (44, emphasis mine). Between this observation and her later focus on the Harlequin formula, she describes the book covers:

> The cover of a Harlequin Romance always shows a young woman, drawn in the style of the 1950s, with a small nose and long eyelashes and a faintly wistful expression. There is usually a strong-jawed man in the background, and often an exotic-looking foreign setting ... Inside, too, the stories vary only within a firmly set formula.
>
> (44)

It is reasonable to conjecture that her conviction in the romance "formula" is thus influenced by the *images* (since she doesn't offer any evidence that she read a fair sample). It is also noteworthy that the cover of *If Dreams Came True* does not have "an exotic-looking foreign setting," so though Maynard is accurate in noting some standard elements of the cover design, she ignores any signs of deviation.

By mentioning sexual content and covers, Pace and Maynard each betray the fact that they understand the genre by equating the two, even though the Gothic's plot involves a suspenseful female *Bildungsroman* while the family saga novel narrates several generations of a family. Both these kinds of fiction are distinct from the genre published by Harlequin, which itself involves different scenarios in which the romantic narrative unfolds; but so taken are Pace and Maynard by the recurrence of certain images, that Pace conflates different kinds of romantic fiction while Maynard denies the multiple narrative possibilities within the "firmly set formula." By the 1960s then, writers for such august platforms as the *New York Times* had invested the cover image of a man and woman on romance novels with the meaning "flimsy stories of sex" for its readers. It was becoming the sign for unoriginal, sentimental pornography. Maynard, writing in the late 1970s, may have had even more visual cues to assume that romance was sex—this was the decade that launched the bodice-ripper romance.

The bodice-ripper years

Avon Books' paperback printing of Kathleen Woodiwiss's *The Flame and the Flower* (1972) strengthened the existing media conviction in romance fiction's uniformity because *Flame* spawned a trend in terms of both plot and packaging. The cover of this breakout novel (designed by Robert McGinnis) indicated that its subgenre was historical romance, and while it was quite demure compared to later cover art, the components of the "clinch," such as the couple and the stylized font, were present. It bore some resemblance to earlier art, but as McKnight-Trontz observes of the wave that followed in its wake,

> the mood was different—more passionate and erotic—with full-fledged embraces. While sentimentality and innuendo had once been an integral part of romance cover art, the new formula consisted of a bare-chested hero forcing a long-haired heroine into a steamy embrace.
>
> (23–4)[5]

This design became indelibly linked to the apparent masochism as well as seeming eroticization of abuse in novels like *Flame*, so that from here on, elements such as the embrace, and the appearance and tone of the titles, were irrevocably associated with the genre—and with gender inequality and sexual titillation. Carol Thurston, in her study of the erotic content in romance over the 1970s and 1980s, mentions this dual meaning of "bodice-ripper," stating that it was a "tongue-in-cheek sobriquet said to derive either from the bodice-ripping sexual encounters described in these stories or the hyperventilation women suffered while reading about them" (19). A 1979 *New York Times* profile of a male romance novelist evokes this as well: the romance novel *Flames of Desire* is said to be one of "the sort of breathless historical romances … that are known in the publishing trade as bodice-rippers"—*Flames of Desire*'s cover shows the above-listed elements, albeit with a clothed male model (Van Gelder).

While readers of the genre came to expect the mythology of love and marriage when seeing these covers, critics and detractors understood these novels to be sexual (leaving readers gasping in arousal) and also in service of gendered violence. Though rape narratives faded out over the 1980s (due to reader dislike), the covers continued to feature a woman whose breasts and limbs overflow her clothes, crushed against a partially undressed muscular man—more often than not, the Italian model Fabio Lanzoni.[6] This increased the critical tendency to associate romance—all romance—with that old, short-lived narrative of sexual abuse. Case in point is Carolyn See's 1980 review of Beatrice Faust's *Women, Sex, and Pornography* (1980). While Faust expressed the classic early critique of erotic romances or bodice-rippers as romanticizing rape in her "Caution—Bodice-Rippers at Work" chapter, See's review ignored much of the remaining book, focused largely on this chapter, and collapsed all distinctions within the genre, writing that Faust associates "Harlequin romances, novels of 'sweet savagery,' bodice-rippers" with "rape, usually painless, and sex and more sex" and "dashing men in silk shirts and girls in tight corselets." This false conflation is especially notable because Faust did not mention "silk shirts" or "corselets" or use the word Harlequin—instead, she said that unlike in the sexually explicit historical romances, "Mills and Boon girls save their yes until after marriage" (156).

Perceived through the veil of the "bodice-ripper" cover—forcefully embracing couples in various stages of undress—since the 1970s, and of others bearing some resemblance to it, romance novels began to be solely regarded as sexual fantasies, or unrealistic, even comical, melodramas. The campiness of the image—period clothing, windblown hair, photoshopped voluptuous semi-clothed bodies and skin—was amplified by the glittering title that serves as a label for the embrace, often in language that alluded to sexuality and sentiment. As a result, sexual desire and farcical plots have become the inalienable characteristics of the Media Romance, a genre based on an outdated image, though admittedly one whose vestiges linger. Irrespective of what happens in individual romance novels, the Media Romance has bodices routinely shed by the heroines or ripped off them in an endless loop of sexual surrender. For the viewer who is not a romance reader, the images therefore act as signifiers of tawdriness or banality.[7]

During the 1980s, the media continued to emphasize Harlequin's strategy to sell its brand and some reports on romance publishing and authors dwelt on sex and sales, portraying it as an industry that has created a product with one use value and is focusing the efforts of its assembly-line on mass producing it.[8] In "Sex Still Sells in the Romance Novels Industry" (1985), which reports on the fifth conference of the Romance Writers of America, Karen Bennett hones in on a workshop titled "Does Sex Still Sell?" Though the article observes in an ostensibly objective reportage style that several authors caution against sexual explicitness, it contains phrases like "heroines ... usually end the last chapter in a blaze of passionate glory with their one true love," telling its readers to view the genre as overly sexual and corny. That Bennett's choice of such phrases arguably owes less to actual plots and more to the genre's paraliterature can be inferred from the fact that the workshop she describes is debating *whether* romances should go in the direction of routinely including passionate scenes. The slant of the report, however, would lead Bennett's readers to think that all romance novels are already full of rampant sexual activity.

In the late 1980s, as individual novelists begin to come to prominence, the media finally begins acknowledging their oeuvre but does not admit that the Media Romance it has created is a fake genre. *Toronto Star*'s Susan Kastner writes on Nora Roberts in the 1988 article "Romance Writer found her own ka-BOOM" (adopting the allegedly clichéd prose of novels like the ones Roberts writes). The title's cheekiness is continued in the article's descriptions of romance fiction, which it claims revolves around sex, especially where Roberts's novels are concerned:

> Why, in this liberated, hardboiled world, is the romantic phoenix rising from the ashes?
>
> Have you read a romance novel lately? ...
>
>> Impatient, he pulled off his shirt so he could feel his skin against hers. His torso was hard as iron. ... Passion. She'd wanted it, craved it ... Here it was, wrapped around her, burgeoning inside her. He moaned her name, and she was dizzy from the sound of it. His lips were on her breast. The muscles in her stomach contracted as he ...
>
> Let us discreetly close the boudoir door. And meet the woman behind the prose of *The Last Honest Woman*: a woman who creates volumes of prose like this, at the rate of seven volumes a year, the first author to publish 50 Silhouette romances: the woman who calls herself Nora Roberts.

Having panned the content of romances—both the "delicate tea-rose kind of thing" in which the relationship was unconsummated as well as new ones in which it is consummated—Kastner associates it with readers who have little choice of reading matter, or lack intellect, time, and money. She calls attention to Roberts' suspicious prolificacy and then repeatedly points out that some elements keep resurfacing in Roberts's work:

> [T]he bigger the mountain of misunderstandings at the start, the bigger the ka-BOOM that always took place, after a couple of false starts, around page 155.

This is the extent of Kastner's content analysis of Roberts's novels. When she chooses to actually talk about texts, she quotes—no surprise—sexual phrases.

> [I]n *All The Possibilities*, Shelby Campbell and Senator Alan MacGregor had striven "flesh against flesh, sigh for sigh, need for need." Anna and Daniel in *Now And Forever* cleaved "mouth against mouth, flesh to flesh," Mitch and Hester in *Local Hero* grappled "side by side ... flesh against flesh", while in *Dance To The Piper*, Maddy and Reed fuse "flesh to flesh, mouth to mouth."

The article abounds with sentences from the love scenes of Roberts's novels and from the works of other writers in order to argue that the writing is formulaic and sexually explicit. But at no point does Kastner present such evidence of formulae in the scenes that do not involve sex; she keeps the Media Romance's identity as a clichéd genre intact.

The 1990s and the disappearing clinch

As cover design outside series imprints like Harlequin continued to evolve, the early 1990s saw a trend to erase the cover images of the clinch. But the image did not disappear completely, in some instances merely migrating to the page behind the cover (a device called the "stepback"). Despite these changes, the Media Romance has a firm hold on the popular imagination and the continued presence of the stylized fonts that have become associated with the genre, along with printing techniques like foil and embossing, appear sufficient for the media to sustain the image of the clinch-cover romance in public memory. In fact, criticism that draws on this image of the genre and labels it as formulaic has now found a new avenue in electronic media.

Besides using the covers themselves, the new media coverage resorts to additional visual cues to simulate the alleged clichéd sexuality of the genre, reinforcing the existing sign. This was the tack in a 1995 CNN story on Cindy Guyer, who has appeared on many historical romance covers. In the story, the anchor's preliminary remarks, the reporter's voiceover, and the clip itself work to add to the impression of the genre as bubble-headed and raunchy. News anchor Natalie Allen introduces the story with

> Well, when it comes to romance novels, Cindy Guyer is known as "the queen of [the] clinched cover." CNN's Jeanne Moos reports on a woman whose love life appears to be hot, even steamy, not under the covers but on them.
>
> ("Female Fabio")

Allen's introduction performs the typical maneuver of employing derogatory terms that are supposedly universally accepted. While Guyer is filmed in various poses with male model John DeSalvo, Moos gleefully announces that "Cindy Guyer has had her neck nuzzled hundreds of times. She's cavorted with outlaw Vikings. She's been a gypsy dancer. She's been a blonde, a brunette, a redhead." Stressing the repetitious nature and the faux-sex aspect of Guyer's work, Moos implies that the stereotypical visual representation of romance novels is a perfect reflection of the genre's formulaic nature. The conversation between the photographer and the model that viewers hear includes references to Guyer's lips and breasts, reminding them of the sexuality in the novels. When the photographer tells Guyer not to jut out her chin, Moos jokes "[I]t wasn't Cindy's chin they wanted jutting out." The clip ends with Moos herself posing for the photographer and as we hear him asking her to loosen her lips, she signs off saying, "If you want to know what happens next, well, you're going to have to read the novel. In her lust for news, [this reporter] stumbles on the hottest story she's ever covered." The clip treats the genre as it is depicted on the bodice-ripper cover—a bawdy, prostituted form of fiction that one purchases for a fleeting sexual thrill.

By the mid-1990s, the press began to feature articles tracking the expansion of the romance publishing market into post-communist countries. Many of these write-ups attribute the genre's growth to the appeal of escapist sexual fantasies peddled to a downtrodden, fun-deprived people. In "Booked up for Knights of Polish Passion: Harlequin's Eastern Promise" Chrystia Freeland treats romance fiction as if it is an aggressive man who is seducing vulnerable women all over the former Soviet bloc. Her conviction that romance fiction is just vast numbers of a soft-core porn commodity shows the unmistakable influence of the novel-packaging phenomenon: "Harlequin paperbacks, with their covers of couples locked in romantic embraces, are now a common sight in Polish bookstores," she observes, using just one brand and its image to define the entire genre. In the same vein, in "Russian Readers Swept Away by Steamy Sagas" Angela Charlton of the Associated Press notices the increased visibility of romance novels in Russia and remarks on their seemingly absorptive quality. Her "analysis" is limited to book titles, one of the signifiers of the bodice-ripper:

> On Moscow's crowded subway, a woman sits reading intently, locked in "The Never-Ending Embrace." Nearby stands a teen-age girl, swept away in "A Hurricane of Temptation."
>
> These absorbed readers have caught on to Russia's latest, if less than greatest, literary trend: the romance novel.

No record exists of novels with these titles (in English), making the article a stellar example of how the media manufactures its fictional, farcical version of the genre as one given to emotional and sexual immaturity and dramatics. Charlton defines it as "formulaic, quickly written novels," and claims that it provides economically depressed readers an escape, but her evidence is little more than a quote from one romance and references made to a couple of others by some readers. Even as the article quotes readers who insist the novels' draw is not sex but romance, Charlton employs descriptors like "realm of unbridled passions," her purple prose creating the impression that romance fiction is badly written sexual fantasy. Underlying the article is the implication that the fantasy is escapist and its characters one-dimensional; the irony here is that the report is itself a fabrication to some extent. Written by an Associated Press reporter, however, it is printed in several news sources as gospel.

The impact of packaging in sustaining the Media Romance becomes most evident when the monolithic/iconic romance look crops up as a butt of jokes in other popular culture forms. While the 1984 movie *Romancing the Stone* is a prominent example of satirizing the genre by portraying romance authors as sexual fantasists, sitcoms routinely contain derogatory references to romance novels based on the covers. They enact the signifiers of that sign in a way that ratifies the Media Romance. In several episodes on NBC's popular *Friends* (1994–2004), the appearance of Nora Bing, a character's famous romance novelist mother leads to a number of jokes about her profession. She is played by voluptuous actress Morgan Fairchild, whose real-life history as a sexy day-time star as well as her body and purring voice are used to align her character and her profession with unbridled sexuality—she acts as if she is on a romance novel *cover*. In an interview, Fairchild speaks of her role as similar to the other "aggressive vixens" on her resume; referring to the scene in which she kisses her son's friend as "molesting young guys," and accepting her typecasting as "a deep-voiced, sex-symbol, gravelly seductress," she captures exactly what the show's writers intend their viewers to associate with romance novelists and their genre. Fairchild also describes Nora Bing as "this bigger than life, Jackie Collins, having-a-great-time character out of one of her own books," an indication that she (and/or the show's writers) see romance novels as just cheap bestsellers that includes sexual episodes ("Friends of *Friends*").[9]

Not only is Nora Bing's career presented as sleazy or risqué, she herself treats it as intellectually undemanding. She tosses out a "formula" for writing a successful romance, a clear statement that these novels are assembly-line products, and the resultant laugh track cues the audience to agree with the show's conviction that this fiction only deserves ridicule. Even when she is not being facetious, the joke continues:

NORA: I have sold a hundred million copies of my books and you know why?
ROSS: The girl on the cover with her nipples showing? ("The One with Mrs. Bing")

There is no escaping the nipples of romance novels—not the author's, not the characters'.

Another episode of the show identifies romance fiction with illicit sex and seduction when the character Joey Tribiani finds one of his female roommate's romance novels hidden under her mattress (an unsubtle signal that the text has a masturbatory function) ("The One With Rachel's Novel"). When he reads a page at random (a sex scene that mentions that the heroine's "loins were burning"), he smirks and says, "This is a dirty book!" resulting in hilarity on the laugh track. (The "quote" is made up by the show's writers and constructs a fake romance novel). Throughout the episode, Joey acts intensely macho toward Rachel and propositions her, presumably in imitation of the hero in her book, but he is in fact enacting a Media Romance. His behavior reinforces the popular belief that romance heroes are absurd characters, written with just one dimension—the lecherous seducer. The disjuncture between Joey's character on the show (a somewhat clueless flirt) and the swaggering Lothario of Rachel's text that he tries to play intensifies the absurdity of that alleged romance hero's actions. Rachel is embarrassed when she recognizes some of the characters—a vicar's daughter, a chimney sweep she wants to seduce—he mentions. She tries to justify her reading material as a "healthy expression of female sexuality" but Joey dismisses her with "You got porn!" and laughter erupts, cuing home viewers to be skeptical of her claims, too. When Joey tells her ex-boyfriend about it, he, too, mocks her "burning loins" and suggests that she started reading romances after they broke up (suggesting that the genre is a substitute for a boyfriend and a sex life).

Toward the end of the episode, Joey continues to tease Rachel with his role-playing. She finally puts an end to this harassment by donning the role of a horny butcher's wife (from the alleged novel) who wants to seduce the hero, and her aggressive sexual advance results in Joey's retreat. When she insists that they have sex, he whimpers, "I don't want to—I'm scared." The episode thus not only constructs the Media Romance as masturbatory fiction, but as peopled with sex-starved characters who turn readers into sexual predators to be feared by men.[10] Even if one argues that Rachel's aggressive heroine shows that romances are actually a narrative about the power women may have in sexual situations, the genre does not stage that fantasy in the farcical way the episode does. The seductive woman who aggressively pursues a chaste man is not one of the many formulas of the genre. The episode thus constructs a scenario that contradicts the actuality of romance fiction, a scenario that is actually modeled on the "Letter to Penthouse" genre.

A closer look at the role(s) that Joey plays in the episode reveals that they are doctored to add to the impression that romances are absurd and inconsistent. While he is the aggressor at the beginning, he is later seen as a victim of lust. This disparity is symptomatic of the skewed image of the romance that the sitcom offers. But the show chooses to ignore the unevenness in his roles, and attempts to portray romance novels as illogical and poorly plotted. This move is actually evidence of the show's sleight of hand in constructing a stereotype of the genre and erroneously conflating the aggressive hero (who can be found in romances) with a chaste male (a trait found infrequently in the genre and never in the same character). In either case, the scene that is staged evokes the farcical clinch cover.

Furthermore, the implied content of Rachel's novel, which includes the seduction of a chimney sweep by a vicar's daughter and of a vicar by a rapacious married woman, is another way that the media misrepresents romance novels as naughty tales of sexual misdemeanors—the kind that dwell on the transgression of boundaries that is actually the defining quality of pornography. The episode thus erases any distinction between romance and porn and perpetuates the idea that romance is devoted to the illicit sexual antics of random couples.

The sitcom *Dharma and Greg* also used the popular romance genre for laughs in an episode where a group of women, most of whom are aging hippies, gather to read aloud their own erotic writing—which consists of love scenes that resemble the *covers* associated with historical romances. The show's writers thus ignore romance fiction's interest in courtship and marriage, and they conflate erotica and romance since both have sexual content. They also suggest that romance novels can be written by anyone and do not require any art or craft, just personal diaries of sexual fantasy. Moreover, by titling the episode "The Story of K," a reference to *The Story of O* (an erotic novel of a woman's desire for sexual enslavement and objectification), they imply that sadomasochism is a necessary component of romance novels.

Each scene unfolds with the women playing swooning maidens to their real-life spouses (themselves cast in the role of romance hero). This role-playing is parodic since the characters do not resemble romance novel cover models. The viewers are also shown how the attendant listeners (all women) imagine the story in their own minds, each one casting herself in the role of the heroine, implying that romance readers identify fully with heroines and participate in the sexual pleasure experienced by the character; it's a portrayal that denies romance reading to be an individualized and complex act.[11]

The humor in the episode is also generated through the improbable scenarios (such as a seduction in a stable) that supposedly fill the romance genre. In Dharma's fantasy, her husband lifts her up along with a "flagon of ale," and they both puzzle over how he can do so even though he is using both arms to hold her. The scene thus reduces the genre to a romp in the hay, and pokes fun at the physiologically improbable lovemaking that romances apparently stage. Further, one of the listeners (who has already read a poem that has established her as an occasional lesbian) casts Kitty, one of the writers, as the masculine partner in her fantasy—complete with breeches and a riding crop. This is treated as amusing not only because it makes the straight White Anglo-Saxon Protestant Kitty the focus of queer desire, and disrupts the heterosexuality that is often a given in popular romances, but also because the fantasy is a parody of the bondage scenes that are supposedly a staple in romance novels (again conflating different genres, as the episode title does).[12]

Greg, who is Kitty's strait-laced lawyer son, is appalled to discover that his mother writes about sex and might publish it. But his worst fears never come to pass because Kitty (encouraged by Dharma, Greg's wife) uses her imagination to improve her sex life, and that takes all the zing out of her writing. The plot development implies that Kitty is just sexually frustrated and has channeled her longings into her diary—a direct hit at romance novelists. While *Friends* implies that the romance reader is sex-deprived and the romance writer is over-sexed, *Dharma and Greg* portrays writers of romances as women forced to sublimate sexual desire in the absence of an exciting sex life. Romance fiction is thus routinely represented as a substitute for sexual activity.

The true motivation behind this tendency of one kind of entertainment to mock another is that it is a strategy for improving one's stock through the deprecation of a fellow cultural form. Television shows (and movies), the poor cousins of literary fiction, often attempt to erase some of the stigma of being lightweight narratives by mocking other mass-market forms—even more so if they share a thematic similarity. This critique differs somewhat from that in the print media cited earlier, where the Media Romance emerges out of a belief that they have a duty to uphold cultural standards and keep out the lowbrow. But other media forms—CNN news magazines, sitcoms, movies—hope to show *themselves* in a better light by using familiar signifiers to disparage the genre. The 2001 romantic comedy *Kate & Leopold*, starring Meg Ryan and Hugh Jackman, takes this tack. Ryan plays Kate, an advertising executive in New York, who falls in love with a European aristocrat—who happens to be from the nineteenth century and has slipped into the twenty-first through a "crack in time." This is a plot that could have been lifted straight from a time-travel romance novel. Despite its evident origins, however, the movie takes pains to mock the very genre it echoes.

Early on in the movie, we see Kate's secretary reading a novel at her desk, one easily identified as a romance by the cover. She neglects her work to read and is shown sobbing as she reaches the end. Sniffling, she narrates the story of a man who waited on an island for the woman he loved for so long that he lost his leg to gangrene but eventually managed to get the heroine. Both the book and its reader come across as ridiculous. Again, the entire plot is an invention of the movie's scriptwriters, playing off the bodice-ripper inspired cover of the novel and building on what earlier media reports made of the signifiers of flourished font, unclothed bodies, and a sexualized pose. The actual plot of the novel used in that scene, Christine Feehan's *Dark Challenge* (2000), is completely different. While the story does not conform to realism—the book falls under the "paranormal romance" subgenre—it bears little resemblance to the melodrama and sentimentality that the movie ascribes to all romances. Instead, it tells the story of two supernatural beings (who are nowhere near an island). Moreover, the heroine is not the unattainable Laura-figure that the secretary describes. She is like a Valkyrie who can hold her own in a fight, and the novel ends with a battle, not an island sunset.

Kate & Leopold's scriptwriters write their own Media Romance, choosing to reiterate one stereotype of the genre (the sentimental tearjerker) in order to make their own fantasy-based plot more "real." Consequently, viewers unfamiliar with the novel or genre might leave the movie convinced that novels with such covers have nonsensical plots and that the genre is absurd. The movie perpetuates the mythologizing of the romance novel cover as the sign for a purely sexual, or ridiculously emotional and unbelievable caricature of "real" human relationships and this Media Romance is what the viewers of the above television shows or movies are left with. (Other instances of such portrayals are found in movies like *As Good As It Gets* (1997) and *Alex and Emma* (2003).)

A different example of discussing the covers alongside the ridicule with which they are associated involves the romance reading community itself. In "The Interactive Romance Community: The Case of 'Covers Gone Wild,'" Greenfeld-Benovitz writes about the blog "Smart Bitches Who Love Trashy Books" (SBTB) and a particular section of it in which the site's owners and other readers poke fun at romance covers. The article studies the online community through the lens of speech act theory and reports on some discussions that occurred on the site and in interviews that the author did with a few of the reader/commenters. In other words, it does not attempt close readings of the covers themselves but documents an online romance reading subculture—enacted through what the author identifies as asynchronous online participation practices and rituals—that exists around acknowledging that some covers are disliked by readers, too. Greenfeld-Benovitz points out, however, that the readers do not conflate the covers with an individual book's content, and are supportive of writers who participate in these discussions to bemoan how little control some have over the cover art.

This critique is on the other end of the spectrum from those like Deborah Phillips's "Mills & Boon: The Marketing of Moonshine." She is an example of a critic who embodies the prejudices of early academic romance criticism, but unlike many of that generation, she consciously equates the books with their covers. In effect, she generalizes about the genre by insisting that the nature of the texts can be better explored by studying Mills & Boon, Harlequin, and Silhouette packaging. Writing in 1984, she approves of Modleski's take on the genre but insists that "analyses of textual pleasures are not enough" and that context, i.e., marketing and distribution, must be studied. Accordingly, her essay does no close readings, noting instead the covers of two novels (from 1910 and 1934), and pointing out that the image and title "work towards a paradoxical suggestive propriety," balancing an erotic charge with a coy morality (141). She argues that the "basic structuring of the iconography" of Mills & Boon novels stayed "remarkably consistent" between 1910 and 1984, with its brand being linked to a stylized image of a man and a woman that frequently called on other popular culture images from movies and titles that recall popular song lyrics. The essay draws on unusual primary sources, such as a visit to a 1984 exhibition of Mills & Boon covers. It notes that the "company image, 'the rose of romance'" has lasted over seven decades and also uses the company's editorial tips and press releases to back up its Marxist reading of the genre as exemplifying the production of a commodity made by unknown laborers and sold on the basis of its brand and of subgenre indicators (such as Silhouette's *Desire* line) (140, 145). Even a more sympathetic early critic like Margaret Ann Jensen references a *Publisher's Weekly* article in her writeup of category romance covers and reinforces the idea of romances being formulaic tales of varying sexual explicitness (58–9, 62–3).

A better model for analyzing romance novel covers themselves lies in recent work that has been influenced by semiotics. In "Hidden Codes of Love: The Materiality of the Category Romance Novel," An Goris explains the term and the concept of the "clinch" (embrace) that is prominent in cover design. She explains the "material uniformity" of the category or series romance (or "imprint") as a coefficient of how widely the books are sold and thus encountered by both a "public" that is unfamiliar with them and only sees their "paratext," as well as by "readers" who engage with the complete book. (She draws on Gérard Genette's concept of the "paratext" and the public/reader distinction, and spends some time explaining his contention that the material body of a text is more about function—reaching an audience and controlling its interaction with the content—than aesthetics.) Goris argues that the potential dual audience for romance fiction leads to a "double semiotic code" in the material structure, with

> two different messages about the book's identity and its desired interpretation. The public code consistently suggests a uniformly generic interpretation of the text as a popular romance novel. This interpretative suggestion is created by the repeated invocation of a number of stereotypical images of and associations with the genre, which in turn perpetuate the public image of the romance genre as homogeneous, formulaic and clichéd. The reader code, by contrast, advocates a more specific and even idiosyncratic interpretation of the text that aims to distinguish the individual text from the generic group in which it is situated.

In breaking down the elements of the category romance's paratexts, she identifies three as standard features: "the front cover iconography, the line template in the design of the category romance's material packaging and the preview scene that is routinely printed on the first page of a category romance novel." Importantly, Goris points out how the same front cover image is interpreted as "typical" or clichéd by the "public" but parsed for slight variations that indicate sub-genres/plots by "readers" using "nuclear elements" such as the clothing worn by the models. In reviewing line templates (e.g., the line "Harlequin *Desire*") for both front and back cover, she observes that "[c]ategory romances published in the same line consequently share the same font, font size, composition of the title page, foreword, etc." Due to this, Goris argues, the "public" will see standardization/uniformity alone, but "readers" will see positive aspects of the line, a "codification of difference."

Goris also discusses the paratextual element of the preview scene, which she defines as

> a scene (or more often part of a scene) printed on the first page of the category romance novel. It is a brief piece of text (usually about five to ten lines) that is placed before the title page, colophon, foreword or any other kind of introductory page. Following immediately on the book's front cover, the preview scene is usually the first page of the book the reader encounters.

She believes that the scene functions to allow "readers" to understand how the particular novel fits the category even as it contains a special take on the imprint's expected conventions, most directly though the author's unique voice. The article concludes by arguing that if the highly conventional paratextual elements can contain subtle cues to trigger specialized interpretive strategies on the part of readers already in the know, there is room to imagine that the image of the genre as being clichéd and standardized should be reevaluated since its content, too, contains a similar second layer of codification and narrative. With numerous images and a solid conceptual foundation in semiotics, the article provides a strong starting point for anyone interested in extending the interpretation of the material body of romance novels, whether it be category romance or single titles.

In the same vein, George Paizis draws on the principles of semiotics and commodity packaging (referencing Roland Barthes and Genette) to analyze the covers of category romance novels. In a brief section titled "The Book" in the first chapter of his book *Love and the Novel*, he summarizes Harlequin's application of the "strategy of brand-name consumer goods" by reviewing design features and variances meant to sell the series (which he says is akin to magazine publishing), including colors, titles, author names, illustration styles, or logos/signposts indicating certain themes. He categorizes the material into "editorial, advertising and commercial information" and associates the standardized packaging with cultivating "brand fidelity" among readers and higher profits for the company (19, 21–2). In the chapter "The Cover, Time and Place" (whose premise is that the cover represents a contractual offer to the reader), he briefly looks at a few book titles as well as images, and claims that there is a tension, even a contradiction, between them, and the anxiety this creates is relieved by the narrative. He applies tenets from advertising and magazine illustrations to romance cover variations of heroines' facial angles, body placement vis-à-vis the hero, and gaze, as well as of the clothing and background elements. In the process he references the work of sociologists Marjorie Ferguson and Erving Goffman and the "grammar of images" suggested by D. Victoroff. While the analysis is somewhat universalizing and extrapolates from the small data set to claims about all category romance art, it is a useful model of how to break down the cover into component parts and interpret them using vocabulary developed in fields with a stronger history in visual analysis, such as film and marketing, as well as linguistics.

Another example of this mode is "'A Very Glamorized Picture, That': Images of Scottish Female Herring Workers on Romance Novel Covers," in which Jane Liffen examines the covers of two novels, *The Fisher Lass* (Dickinson) and *The Shimmer of the Herring* (Hood), featuring heroines working in the Scottish herring industry, in order to evaluate their verisimilitude. Her intent is to discover if the main protagonists are represented as the authors describe them and to check if there are design elements that stray from the reality of the profession and herring workers' actual lives. In addition, she aims to provide a psychoanalytic explanation for any truths that are left out of the images "in an effort to understand the cultural choices made by publishers in the marketing of these novels" (349–50). While the semiotic analysis provides another useful model for anyone interested in pursuing a similar method to study cover art, Liffen's article does not explain what makes her two selections (whose publishers are Macmillan and Warner, respectively) exemplary romance novels. Neither is strictly a mainstream romance novel, either in terms of imprint, publishing house, or author.

Liffen also surveys some romance scholarship, particularly one that distinguishes between "strong" and "soft" romances based on the prominence given to women on the covers. In her survey, she discusses reader identification using Janice Radway and Nancy Chodorow, as well as Paizis and M. Owen. She claims that her covers' mix of artistic and realistic style makes reader identification in the fantasy possible, while photographic realism is reserved for erotic texts. She also argues that the back cover of *The Fisher Lass* hints at a conflict that occurs in the plot, which the front cover ignores. She continues her negative evaluation of the cover design with the claim that even the realism that is present in the covers is romanticized, inaccurate, and impractical (using interviews with herring workers to back her assessment). While Liffen's method seems solid, albeit a bit mechanical at times, some of her close reading of the colors used on the covers is farfetched:

> The red lips of the main protagonist show they are blood-filled and connotative of passion, yet that passion corresponds with the dead fish she carries through their shared colour, suggesting her desire will not be sustained or allowed to flourish.

Similarly, when she critiques the absence in the cover design of the grit/dirt/guts/blood that is the reality of the herring industry, she convincingly argues that it is meant to maintain the idea of women as pure, but then she jumps to equating it with taboos about menstruation. The remainder of the article is given over to a Kristevan psychoanalytic feminist critique of women's representations, visually and textually.

If Liffen's article seems to go far afield in terms of romance covers, the most recognizable images of romance in the 1980s, as mentioned earlier, involved Fabio. In "'I Am Not a Bimbo': Persona, Promotion, and the Fabulous Fabio," Rosemary E. Johnson-Kurek does a first-person essay on him and artist Elaine Duillo's illustrations of him on the covers of Johanna Lindsey's historical romance novels. Writing in the New Journalism style, she recalls memories of her quest for discovering his identity after seeing him on numerous novels she read. Along the way, she quotes/ventriloquizes friends and his fans who shared her fascination, both before and after she discovered that he was an actual person. The essay documents her search for more data on him, a seemingly non-academic process that nevertheless includes sources that are now quite standard in pop culture studies (such as TV shows and magazines). In the process, she also notes the many "Fabio bashing" sessions in which her male acquaintances indulged as his fame spread and speculates that the specific combination of his good looks, muscularity, and romantic image made him particularly threatening to the men who were witnessing women's adoration of his image. She analyzes the potential misogyny that this response suggests and also proposes that his fame is galling for a patriarchal culture that believes that "looking good" is not a proper way for a man to get fame, and that a real man should sell something other than himself—pretty much the opposite of what he was doing by being a romance cover model (40). In describing his work, she also offers an insightful observation that the erotic charge of romance cover art comes from the embrace and does not involve naked models or unclothed representations of them—"But it wasn't truly Fabio who was naked—Fabio doesn't pose in the nude; it was his image and likeness. Actually, most of the heroes' bodies are effectively screened by the clothed heroine"—but doesn't follow up with more analysis (40–1).

Instead, she documents how he has to deal with the same dumb bimbo comments that are aimed at women models, briefly touches on his own (co-authored) romances, and terms him as unique for garnering fame through an art form that is unknown outside the romance reader community. She also attributes the rise of romance sales to readers' interest in him. Johnson-Kurek notes that though Fabio modeled for many genres, he is largely associated with historical novels and is thus a fantasy of the "man out of time." Further, she connects his fame to his reported courteousness, suggesting that he possesses the emotional qualities that are valued in romance heroes:

> [N]o amount of physical attractiveness or prowess would be able to compensate if he lacked the quality of a romantic soul. His romantic sensitivity toward women is critical in endearing him to his fans. So, more importantly, the success of Fabio the person required that he actually embody some of the qualities of the fictionalized characters that he has portrayed on a multitude of covers. His image is so enmeshed with the romantic hero, fans would probably invest him with these qualities whether he possessed them or not."
>
> (42–3)

In addition to his model good looks, she claims, his self-deprecating kindness is "what transcended the anonymity of the cover art" (44). In other words, she hypothesizes that his first-name only fame, unusual for someone who modeled mainly for a non-literary genre, rests on the alignment between the heroes he portrayed and his real-life self. To depict the latter, she quotes him several times on his views about love and women and provides some background on his Italian Catholic upbringing. Johnson-Kurek then documents her quest to find out if he was a good guy in person, despite the worry that he might be better as a figment of Duillo's imagination. While not academic (though she repeatedly says that her quest was an academic one for knowledge and it does use ethnography as a methodology, including interviews and participant observation), the article is a piece of creative non-fiction that will be useful to graduate students who, more and more, are seeking to write dissertations that are a hybrid of traditional exegesis and creative writing.

Another somewhat unusual look at romance covers is found in "The Success Behind the Candy-Coloured Covers: An Evolutionary Perspective on Romance Novels," from a 2012 issue of the *Evolutionary Review*. This study of Harlequin romance covers from the 1950s to the present is co-authored by a psychologist and mathematician who state that literary artifacts produced over time provide data on evolutionary behaviors and preferences. The writers suggest that the covers of Harlequins reveal a marked predominance of what might be considered a genetically viable male partner per certain markers of financial and biological strengths. Fisher and Meredith do not disparage the genre (though they seem to believe most romance novels are all the same and therefore interchangeable to readers). But the article's central argument feels essentialist, which is unsurprising, since it is based in "Darwinian literary study":

> Why are romance novels so popular and enduring? We propose that romance novels "hit" evolved triggers pertaining to a critical part of women's reproductive lives: selecting and acquiring high-quality mates. We speculate that reading these novels simulates the act of finding a high-quality mate. Thus, romance novels reflect and stimulate evolved female mating psychology in specific cultural contexts. (156)

The writers thus draw conclusions about the desires of women readers based on the composition of romance cover images by Harlequin's design department (a leap that leaves out male or male-identified or queer readers, and traces fantasy to biological imperatives). They insist that their perspective attends to universal biological mate preferences on the part of women and thus fills out the gaps left in romance critiques based on socio-cultural factors alone.

After this theoretical set-up, the article includes one paragraph per decade of Harlequin cover art, beginning with the 1950s, but oddly, there are no visual examples or even a mention of exemplary titles. Even stranger is the fact that the only cover they include as an example of the most recent version of romance novel cover design is the single-title novel *Master of Desire* by Kinley MacGregor—not a Harlequin series publication. In the subsequent section, there is a summary of the physical and financial characteristics of the men and women featured on the covers (though the data set's date range is unclear); the writers believe that these traits prove their belief in romance fiction as appealing to evolutionarily beneficial preferences. They cite a Harlequin designer on images of couples and families in cover design and an Avon executive to further validate their analysis about the cover art being evidence of "evolved female mate preferences" within existing social norms (162). While the article seems to rest on the faulty premise that romance novels are indistinguishable from each other to their readers and has a cherry-picking bias, it does provide a lens that fuses science and humanities perspectives ("evolutionary approaches to literature") that some scholars might want to pursue.

Less directly about romance novels but perhaps more familiar in methodology is Bill Gleason's article "Belles, Beaux, and Paratexts," which questions previous theories of the causes of the failures of nineteenth-century dime romances and papers by analyzing their paratext. Focusing on three romance story papers (*Belles and Beaux*, *Girls of Today*, and *The New York Weekly Story-Teller*), Gleason argues that they failed despite focusing on romance because they did not provide a "coherent reading environment." While he allows that the papers did declare an interest in love through both text and images, he suggests that there was too much other material that detracted from it. He describes *Belles and Beaux*'s cover as follows:

> The cover of the first issue announces the special focus of the periodical through a dramatic combination of image and rhyme ... In the middle of the page, occupying approximately two-thirds of the sheet, appears a collage-like illustration of the phases of heterosexual courtship, featuring a single couple in snapshots from preadolescence to young adulthood and culminating in the prominently centered image of the newly married pair taking their wedding bow.

Gleason also includes illustrations from the issue. But he subsequently enumerates the hodgepodge of non-romance items in the papers (such as clinical articles on topics like fake jewelry and military songs), and suggests that the paratext showed contempt for the romance stories the paper claimed to want to sell (despite other seemingly coherent efforts such as "practical romance" tips). He provides a survey of other material as examples of misogynistic, anti-romantic paratext, most notably illustrations that invite the reader to question the notion of happy-ever-after. Gleason's article is meticulously researched and illustrated and provides one of the few models for romance scholars wishing to study the popular roots of American romance fiction via adjacent genres.

Scholars interested in studying representations of people of color have even less to go on. Gwendolyn E. Osborne's 2004 essay is the only study that briefly touches on romance covers with African American characters. (The "Whiteness" chapter in my 2014 book focuses on analyzing the white body on romance covers.) Osborne interviewed several African-American romance readers and notes that each respondent stated that "she liked stories about 'women who looked like me'" (62). The essay provides an overview of how White ideals of beauty and who is deserving of love spread from movies to fiction and limited the space offered to other visions, including in themes and cover art at Harlequin. While describing a reader who was happy to see the start of the Black romance imprint Arabesque, Osborne quotes her as saying "You no longer had to pretend that you were the character with long, flowing, blonde tresses or steamy blue eyes," a comment that reveals a desire for Black representation in romance (63). In the final section of the essay, Osborne brings in the opinions of African-American romance authors, readers, and others in publishing about romance cover art that represents the reading demographic's varied identities more accurately. The sticking point, she notes, is that certain players in the industry believe that Black characters on romance covers alienate some readers but others are demanding that the industry change. A 2018 Buzzfeed article on Kensington Publishing's art department and the novel covers of romance author Alyssa Cole tells us that the industry is inching its way toward parity in cover art, and the issue needs more analysis from a variety of perspectives, critical race studies being the most obvious.

In addition to Media Romance or accurate analyses of covers, two short collections merit a mention at the end of this survey: *The Art of Romance* is a slim volume of 30 postcards issued by Harlequin on its 50th anniversary, and editor Marsha Zinberg writes a brief introduction that reviews decades of romance cover design, starting with some of the earliest covers done by its British predecessor, Mills & Boon. The 30 postcards are in vivid color and apart from being a collector's item, can provide a quick look at a century of visual representations of mass-market romance. Similarly, *The Art of Romance: Mills & Boon and Harlequin Cover Designs* has a short history of the companies and some descriptions of the covers. The rest of the book consists of photos of Mills & Boon and Harlequin book covers, many of which can be viewed on various sites such as the *Independent*, the *Guardian*, and the *Telegraph*. Both books are a useful place for a fledgling cover researcher to begin getting a lay of the land and reporting on it with more thoughtfulness.

Another place for more study of the genre's representation lies in examining documentaries like "Guilty Pleasures" (which repeats numerous clichés about the genre) and "Love Between the Covers," which focus on the genre's authors and some scholars, as well as TV shows like "Jane the Virgin," with its aspiring romance novelist protagonist and telenovela structure. The last territory that might prove fruitful for a romance cover researcher is the considerable body of work done on romance comics. Hayton and Hayton's "The Girls in White: Nurse Images in Early Cold War Era Romance and War Comics" and Nolan's *Love on the Racks: a History of American Romance Comics* might provide a new material culture approach to the romance cover, situated as they both are in a long and colorful history of popular art forms in which image is as key to the reading experience as text, and where a gulf lies between readers' and the wider public's perceptions of what is being read.

Notes

1 The collection ends with an essay that draws a through line from the successive reprintings of the work of a late nineteenth-century American romance author to 1980s romance and Jayne Anne Krentz's novel covers.

2 Davis provides a comprehensive look at the controversy surrounding paperbacking and reveals how it contributed to the disapprobation directed at the romance genre as well.

3 For a review of romance novel dust jackets and covers, see my chapter "Branding a Genre: A Brief Transatlantic History of Romance Novel Cover Art" in the essay collection *Romance Fiction and American Culture.*

4 As paperback sales rose, there was a book-banning wave across the United States, beginning with the hearings of the House of Representatives Select Committee on Current Pornographic Materials in 1952. The committee declared its intent to investigate "filthy sex books" with their "lurid and daring illustrations of voluptuous young women on the covers" (Davis 220). There were other legal hurdles in some cases, such as in Texas, which imposed fines not only on the authors of supposedly obscene books but also on cover artists.

5 See my "Branding a Genre: A Brief Transatlantic History of Romance Novel Cover Art" for more on bodice-rippers and the association of romance fiction with the normalization of sexual violence.

6 Oddly enough, this has less to do with what the sign meant to readers and more to do with romance publishers' belief that it would be easier for male salesmen to sell novels that featured undressed women to male booksellers. Consequently, novels with such covers (especially the paperbacks that were sold in airports and grocery and drug stores) dominated the marketplace. While as early as 1981, in the *New York Times* column "Paperback Talk," Ray Waiters reported that per an industry insider, "bodice-rippers, those stories of rape and violence that crowded the best-seller list not long ago, are definitely out," they appeared to be everywhere.

7 This is not to suggest that the sign does not have such a meaning for many romance readers. I have tracked online discussions in which readers express a preference for just such a sign (see *Uncovering and Recovering the Popular Romance Novel*). But the covers are polyvalent signs and the Media Romance grew by ignoring the other meanings and fixing on the one that would be most derogatory.

8 See Philip K. Dougherty's 1980 *New York Times* article "Selling Books Like Tide" or Waiters's abovementioned column, which reports on the first RWA conference and says that romance novels are "marketed like brands of cornflakes."

9 Collins's oeuvre falls far outside the romance novel genre; it edges toward soaps like *Dynasty*, a genre more rightly called glam or vamp fiction for its focus on the promiscuous rich.

10 This apprehensiveness has been an undercurrent in much anti-novel discourse. William Warner notes that "The figure of the woman reader eroticizes reading through the presumption of an automatic relay: if a reader reads erotic novels, then she will act out by having sex" (141).

11 That women readers cannot distinguish between fiction and reality, lose aesthetic distance, and overidentify with characters is an old critique, going back to the rise of the novel as a form and evident in romance criticism. I have noted this in Chapters 4 and 5 of *Uncovering and Recovering the Popular Romance Novel*; see also, in particular, Aliaga-Buchenau, Davis, Jensen, Leavis, and Warner.

12 Several romances now acknowledge that sexuality covers a spectrum and have characters that participate in kink (such as having a partner's hands restrained) or identify as kinky but BDSM/kink is a genre in its own right.

Works cited

Adewunmi, Bim. "An Extraordinary Romance: Meet The Black Women Upending The Romance Novel Industry." *Buzzfeed News*, www.buzzfeed.com/bimadewunmi/meet-the-black-women-upending-the-romance-novel-industry?utm_term=.ctejBWRMA. May 1, 2018.

Alex and Emma. Dir. Rob Reiner. Perf. Luke Wilson and Kate Hudson. Warner, 2003.

Aliaga-Buchenau, Ana-Isabel. *The "Dangerous" Potential of Reading: Readers and the Negotiation of Power in Nineteenth Century Narratives*. Routledge, 2004.

Anon. "Big Business in Pulp Thrillers: Love and Adventure Stories Gross $25,000,000 a Year." *Literary Digest*, vol. 123, 1937, pp. 30–31.

As Good As It Gets. Dir. James L. Brooks. Perf. Helen Hunt and Jack Nicholson. Tristar, 1997.

Barthes, Roland. *Mythologies*. Translated by Annette Lavers. Hill and Wang, 1972.

Belk, Patrick Scott and Nathan Vernon Madison, editors. *The Pulp Magazines Project*. www.pulpmags.org, April 25, 2018.

Bennett, Karen. "Sex Still Sells in the Romance Novels Industry." *Associated Press*, June 28, Domestic News, 1985.

Bowring, Joanna and Margaret O'Brien. *The Art of Romance: Mills & Boon and Harlequin Cover Designs*. Prestel, 2008.

Charlton, Angela. "Russian Readers Swept Away by Steamy Sagas." *Associated Press*, August 17, AM cycle, sec. International News, 1995.

Davis, Kenneth. *Two-bit Culture*. Boston: Houghton Mifflin, 1984.

Dougherty, Philip K. "Selling Books Like Tide." *New York Times*, February 26, D17, 1980.

Feehan, Christine. *Dark Challenge*. Lovespell, 2000.

Fisher, Maryann L. and Tami M. Meredith. "The Success behind the Candy-Colored Covers: An Evolutionary Perspective on Romance Novels." *The Evolutionary Review*. vol. 3, 2012, pp. 154–167. www.maryannefisher.com/wp-content/uploads/2013/09/Fisher_Meredith_Covers_TER.pdf.

Freeland, Chrystia. "Booked up for Knights of Polish Passion: Harlequin's Eastern Promise." *Financial Times*. June 7, p. 19, 1994.

Goris, An. "Hidden Codes of Love: The Materiality of the Category Romance Novel." *Belphégor*, vol. 13, no. 1, 2015. May 9, 2015. http://journals.openedition.org/belphegor/616; DOI: 10.4000/belphegor.616. Accessed April 24, 2018.

Greenfeld-Benovitz, Miriam. "The Interactive Romance Community: The Case of 'Covers Gone Wild.'" in *New Approaches to Popular Romance Fiction*, edited by Sarah S. G. Frantz, and Eric Murphy Selinger, McFarland, 2012, pp. 195–205.

Haug, Wolfgang. *A Critique of Commodity Aesthetics: Appearance, Sexuality, and Advertising in Capitalist Society*. University of Minnesota Press, 1986.

Hayton, Christopher J. and Sheila Hayton. "The Girls in White: Nurse Images in Early Cold War Era Romance and War Comics." in *Comic Books and the Cold War, 1946-1962: Essays on Graphic Treatment of Communism, the Code and Social Concerns*, edited by Chris York, and Rafiel York, McFarland, 2012, pp. 129–145.

Jensen, Margaret Ann. *Love's $weet Return: The Harlequin Story*. Bowling Green State University Popular Press, 1984.

Johnson-Kurek, Rosemary E. "'I Am Not a Bimbo': Persona, Promotion, and the Fabulous Fabio." in *Romantic Conventions*, edited by Anne K. Kaler, and Rosemary E Johnson-Kurek, Bowling Green State University Popular Press, 1999, pp. 35–50.

Kahn, Laurie. "Love between the Covers." Blueberry Hill Productions, 2015.

Kamblé, Jayashree. *Uncovering and Recovering the Popular Romance Novel*. Dissertation, University of Minnesota, 2008. UMI, 2018.

———. *Making Meaning in Popular Romance Fiction: An Epistemology*. Palgrave, 2014.

———. "Branding A Genre: A Brief Transatlantic History of Romance Novel Cover Art." in *Romance Fiction and American Culture: Love as the Practice of Freedom?* edited by William Gleason, and Eric Murphy Selinger, Ashgate, 2016.

Kastner, Susan. "Romance Writer Found Her Own ka-BOOM." *Toronto Star*. May 8, 1988, Second ed., Sec. People: D1.

Mangold, James, director. *Kate and Leopold*. Konrad Pictures, 2001.

Maynard, Joyce. "Harlequin Novels: A Romance between Stories and Readers." *New York Times*, October 22, 1976, p. 44.

McAleer, Joseph. *Passion's Fortune: The Story of Mills & Boon*. Oxford University Press, 1999.

McKay, Louisa. "Mills & Boon: The Art of Love." *The Telegraph*, August 17, 2008. www.telegraph.co.uk/culture/donotmigrate/3558711/Mills-and-Boon-the-art-of-love.html. Accessed May 15, 2018.

McKnight-Trontz, Jennifer. *The Look of Love: The Art of the Romance Novel*. Princeton Architectural Press, 2002.

"Mills & Boon—a Literary Love Affair." *The Independent*, May 29, 2008. www.independent.co.uk/arts-entertainment/books/features/mills-amp-boon-a-literary-love-affair-835616.html. Accessed May 15, 2018.

"Mills & Boon: The Art of Romance." *The Guardian*, December 3, 2008. www.theguardian.com/books/gallery/2008/nov/27/mills-and-boon-covers?picture=340129693. Accessed May 15, 2018.

Moggan, Julie. "Guilty Pleasures." Bungalow Town Productions, 2010.

Moos, Jeanne. "Female Fabio Has Book Cover Corner on the Market. *News*. CNN. Sec. Entertainment. July 27, 1995.

Nolan, Michelle. *Love on the Racks: A History of American Romance Comics*. McFarland, 2008.

Osborne, Gwendolyn E. "'Women Who Look like Me': Cultural Identity and Reader Responses to African American Romance Novels." in *Race/Gender/Media: Considering Diversity Across Audiences, Content, and Producers*, edited by Rebecca Ann Lind, Pearson, 2004, pp. 61–68.

Pace, Eric. "Gothic Novels for Women Prove Bonanza for Publishers." *New York Times*, June 18, 1973, pp. 31–32, ProQuest Newstand. University of Minnesota Lib. Accessed November 20, 2007.

Paizis, George. *Love and the Novel: The Poetics and Politics of Romantic Fiction*. Macmillan, 1998.

Phillips, Deborah. "Mills & Boon: The Marketing of Moonshine." in *Consumption, Identity, and Style: Marketing, Meanings, and the Packaging of Pleasure*, edited by Alan Tomlinson, Routledge, 1990, pp. 139–152.

Rabinowitz, Paula. *American Pulp: How Paperbacks Brought Modernism to Main Street*. Princeton University Press, 2014.

Radway, Janice. *Reading the Romance: Women, Patriarchy, and Popular Literature*. Chapel Hill: University of North Carolina Press, 1984.

Romancing the Stone. Dir. Robert Zemeckis. Perf. Kathleen Turner and Michael Douglas. Twentieth Century Fox, 1984.

Salmans, Sandra. "What's New in Romance: Passionate, Epic Tales that Make for Big Sales." *New York Times*. December 4, 1988, Late City Final Edition, sec. 3, p. 13. Lexis Nexis. University of Minnesota Lib., Minneapolis, www.lexisnexis.com. Accessed November 20. 2007.

See, Carolyn. "Angry Women and Brutal Men." *New York Times*, December 28, 1980, Late City Final Edition, sec. 7, p. 4. Lexis Nexis. Accessed April 27, 2018.

Stoner, Kayla. "Dresses Made from Romance Novels Challenge Myth of Feminine Ideal." *Northwestern Now*. October 10, 2016, https://news.northwestern.edu/stories/2016/10/dittmar-build-her-a-myth/. Accessed October 17, 2016.

Sullivan, Larry E. and Lydia Cushman Schurman, editors. *Pioneers, Passionate Ladies, and Private Eyes: Dime Novels, Series Books, and Paperbacks*. 1996. Routledge, 2007.

Temple, Emily. "50 Pulp Cover Treatments of Classic Works of Literature: Guns, Broads, Beefcake, Literariness." *The Literary Hub*. May 2, 2018, lithub.com/50-pulp-cover-treatments-of-classic-works-of-literature/. Accessed May 3, 2018.

"The One with Mrs. Bing." *Friends*. Created by David Crane and Marta Kauffman, season 1, episode 11, NBC, January 5, 1995.

"The One with Rachel's Book." *Friends*. Created by David Crane and Marta Kauffman, season 7, episode 2, NBC, October 12, 2000.

"The One with the Thanksgiving Flashbacks." *Friends*. Created by David Crane and Marta Kauffman, season 5, episode 8, NBC, November 19, 1998.
Thurston, Carol. *The Romance Revolution: Erotic Novels for Women and the Quest for a New Sexual Identity*. University of Illinois Press, 1987.
Urman, Jennie Snyder. "Jane the Virgin." Poppy Productions, 2014.
Van Gelder, Lawrence. "She . . . Uh He, Writes Romantic Novels." *New York Times*. September 2, 1979, p. LI2. *ProQuest*. Accessed April 27, 2018.
Waiters, Ray. "Paperback Talk." *New York Times*, July 19, 1981, p. 1. *ProQuest*. Accessed April 27, 2018.
Warner, William Beatty. *Licensing Entertainment: The Elevation of Novel Reading in Britain, 1684–1750*. University of California Press, 1998.
Weinraub, Bernard. "Cover Story." *New York Times*, February 26, 1967, p. BRP4. ProQuest Newstand. University of Minnesota Lib. Accessed November 20, 2007.
Williams, Ivor. "The Pious Pornographers: Sex and Sanctimony in the Ladies Home Journal." *Playboy*. October. 1957, p. 24.
Woodiwiss, Kathleen E. *The Flame and the Flower*. Avon-Harper Collins, 1972.
Zinberg, Marsha, ed. *The Art of Romance*. Harlequin, 1999.

13 Literary approaches

Eric Murphy Selinger

Consider the following passage from Sherry Thomas's historical romance *My Beautiful Enemy* (2014), which comes when the novel's half-Chinese, half-English heroine, Catherine Blade (AKA Bai Ying-Hua, AKA Ying-Ying, AKA "The Kazakh"), finds the jade tablet that she has been sent to England to recover.

> When she had pulled aside the protective tissue paper, nestled inside was the exact object she sought. At its center was a goddess, her eyes half closed in joy, her pliant back arched, and the ribbons on her flowing robe dancing all about her, as if lifted by a gentle breath. To her left and right were the famous words of the *Heart Sutra. Form is no other than emptiness; emptiness is no other than form. Form is exactly emptiness; emptiness is exactly form.*
>
> (107)

In terms of the novel's adventure plot, the only significant part of this passage comes in the opening sentence: here, at last, is the "object she sought." Likewise, its love plot hinges only on the fact of discovery, since the search for the tablet has brought Catherine, a Chinese spy, back into contact (and back at odds) with British spy Leighton Atwood. In what "plot," however—what system, what pattern, what design, what compositional logic—does it matter that the tablet is "nestled," and not simply wrapped, in the paper? That the eyes of the goddess on the tablet are "half closed in joy," her back "pliant" and "arched" while her robe is "dancing" (she's not stern or placid, sitting up straight or standing tall)? That this goddess is framed by a quote from the *Heart Sutra* (not the *Diamond* or *Lotus* or some other sutra), and that the quoted passage is those "famous words" about form and emptiness rather than, say, the sutra's equally famous closing mantra, *Gate, gate, paragate, parasamgate, bodhi svaha*?

To ask such questions of a popular romance novel is to assume, however provisionally, that the book is an aesthetic object: one whose "deep individuality" (Cappella and Wormser 15) rewards our attention; one whose particularities *signify*. This is not now, nor has it ever been, the dominant practice in romance reading, at least not in scholarly circles. As recently as 2018 an Australian research team investigating the "genre world" of popular romance observed that even when the close textual study of romance novels has occurred—still a rare phenomenon, though growing—it has "almost without exception" been in the service of ideological analysis rather than focused on anything related to poetics, aesthetics, or artistry (Fletcher, Driscoll, and Wilkins 1000). This chapter will survey the exceptions: the contrapuntal strain in popular romance scholarship that takes what we might call "literary approaches" to the genre.

By "literary approaches" I do not mean simply "the way that literature is treated." Literature is treated in many ways, and post-New Critical versions of "close reading" share a departmental hallway with sharply contrasting modes of inquiry, including ideological and philosophical investigations, material histories of the book, and computer-assisted analyses of vast digitized corpora.[1] Rather, this chapter will focus on approaches to popular romance that are "literary" in the sense that they emphasize what are still generally thought of as literary qualities or attributes of texts, no matter their genre or medium: telling details; compositional patterns and choices; references to and engagements with the history of the genre; formal decisions that can be said to act out or comment on content; adept variations on established conventions; metafictional winks and intertextual nods; in sum, all of the ironies, insights, and complexities, global and local, that make up a romance novel's "unlikeness" from others in its genre or subgenre (Rushdie 426). To paraphrase a famous quip from Terry Eagleton, the scholarship explored in this chapter either argues, or simply assumes, that some popular romance novels have been "born literary," that some may yet "achieve literariness," and that more than a few will reward the effort to "thrust literariness" upon them (7).[2] None *prima facie* belongs to a "subliterature of love" (Anderson).

Some doxa and their discontents

Laura Vivanco dedicates *For Love and Money: The Literary Art of the Harlequin Mills & Boon Romance* (2011) to "every Harlequin Mills & Boon author who has ever been asked, 'When are you going to write a *real* novel?'" (5). (Like Vivanco, I will shorten the publisher's name to HMB.) In the classroom, this epigraph can be used to tease out doxa—received ideas, social truths, assumptions which *go without saying*—about what, precisely, constitutes a "real" novel, how a romance might be different, and why it might seem so endlessly necessary to mark out the contrasts between them.[3] As those discussions often reveal, and as Vivanco's Introduction makes clear, much of that urgency springs from anxieties about class and social distinction. Sometimes the subtext is obvious, as when a writer for the *Yorkshire Post* sniffs that "to call them novels is to raise them far above their station" (2008; qtd. in Vivanco 15). More subtly and pervasively, however, the brand name "Mills & Boon" (or Harlequin, in the U.S. and Canada) gets invoked metonymically for the genre in general as, in Ann Curthoys' and John Docker's words, "a negative icon, what not, what never to be" (qtd. in Vivanco 15). What these Australian cultural historians observed in 1990 about much of the twentieth century has remained true in the early twenty-first:

> Newspaper critics in reviews, journalists in their columns, good professional-middle-class people in their conversation, would casually snap at a book or passage by saying things like "it unfortunately smacks of Mills and Boon," or, "in certain parts of the novel it lapses into pure Mills and Boon." "Mills and Boon" was a roaming, punitive signifier, a terrier running around and around the boundary that separates serious writing from the low, from sub-literature, para-literature, trash, schlock.
>
> (Curthoys and Docker 1990; qtd. in Vivanco 15)[4]

Since the category of "serious writing" or "Literature" depends, in no small part, on its communally-recognized opposition to something *else* (see Fish 14–15, 171–2; Eagleton 14; Gelder 11–17), the shorthand signifiers "Mills & Boon," "Harlequin romance," "bodice-ripper," and so on, do deeply needed cultural work, standing for any needed instance of the trivial, hackneyed, or "always already familiar" (Silliman). If such a term did not exist, it would be necessary to invent one.

To witness this boundary marking in action, one need look no further than the review of Vivanco's study by literary historian Kate MacDonald, who describes herself as the author of "tiny, hand-crafted essays on why she really likes a book" (MacDonald). Alas, she did not like this one. Unpersuaded by Vivanco's arguments, MacDonald declares herself "appalled" by the prose of HMB novels; she describes them as "manufactured to a carefully worked out formula"; she calls the publishing house a "prison" where books are "policed rather than edited"; and she contrasts HMB books, all "clones of the same hive mind," to the individualized voices and visions of books in science fiction. Although she allows that romance novels might be of interest from a socio-historical perspective, she scoffs at Vivanco's claims about the aesthetic self-consciousness of one HMB text she discusses. Observing that the line this romance quotes from a seventeenth-century poet is, in fact, just a cliché, and that the poet quoted "is not obscure, but regularly anthologised and taught," MacDonald takes pains to highlight her superior cultural capital: explicitly superior to the novel's heroine, who gets the quote wrong (the hero corrects her) and implicitly superior to Vivanco, who reads the protagonists' allusive dialogue—which includes complaints about being "written off" and unfairly "labeled"—as a metafictional "response to those who would be astonished to discover a quotation from Richard Lovelace in one of the novels they consider to be 'factory-produced hackwork'" (116). Clichés do not allusions make, MacDonald implies, nor echoes, metatexts; or, to switch poets, we might say that to find value in such a passage is to confess a critical heart too soon made glad, too easily impressed, leaving literature and the subliterary "all one!" (Browning 199).

As Thomas J. Roberts observes in *An Aesthetics of Junk Fiction*, "the conventions for talk about the popular arts are more restrictive by far than the conventions for the stories themselves" (124), and MacDonald's review is a conventional, even formulaic piece. As such, however, it reveals what Lynne Pearce calls the "deep structures . . . conventions, and clichés" of its genre, the critical dismissal of popular romance (521). Three structuring concepts stand out: first, that romance novels are badly written, both in their "appalling" prose and in their thoughtless, trivial deployment of allusions and other literary gestures; second, that romance novels are subject to corporate control and commodity standardization, such that they lack the individuating "unlikeness" that characterizes both high-art fiction and other popular genres; and, finally, as a corollary of the other two, that popular romance fiction will only really be interesting when approached from a socio-historical framework, read as a "register of popular feeling" and a "barometer of the ethos of its times" (Kamblé *Making Meaning* 23). Literary scholarship on popular romance has addressed each of these structuring concepts, whether to document how these doxa developed or to dispute them, and in the remainder of this chapter I will use them as a framework to organize an overview of this scholarly record.

Bad writing and other shibboleths

It is a truth, as they say, universally acknowledged that romance novels are badly written. This badness is fractal, appearing from the global levels of story, character, and theme down to sentence level issues of syntax, imagery, and word-choice. "Romance writers are often criticized for the lack of originality of our plots (which are regarded as contrived and formulaic) and the excessive lushness or lack of subtlety of our language," Linda Barlow and Jayne Ann Krentz explain in "Beneath the Surface: The Hidden Codes of Romance," the first extended response by romance authors to this charge against the genre (18–19). This criticism sometimes takes a public, ritual form. "Descriptive passages are regularly culled from romance novels and read aloud with great glee and mockery by everybody from college professors to talk show hosts" (24), and the fact that romance authors persist in deploying "rich, evocative diction that is heavy-laden with familiar symbols, images, metaphors, paradoxes, and allusions" (18) might well lead one to wonder whether these authors are "woefully derivative and unoriginal," whether "our editors force us to write this way," whether a lack of education or training has left them "incapable of expressing ourselves in any other manner," and so on (25). Any critic or scholar interested in taking a literary approach to popular romance fiction will need to disarm these objections—and, with them, the genre's reputation as either unworthy of, or unresponsive to, close reading.

One scholarly approach to this doxa has been to treat the ostensible maladroitness of romance as, itself, a subject for investigation. In *Love and the Novel: The Poetics and Politics of Romantic Fiction*, George Paizis nods to the notion that "the literary style of the novels is neither complex nor surprising" (33) but goes on to investigate that style from a variety of formal, theoretical, and other viewpoints, including Kitsch theory, a Proppian functional analysis, rhetorical and game-analogy perspectives derived from Umberto Eco's analysis of James Bond novels, and a brief but extraordinarily useful excursion into literary history. "Rather than being a reaction against 'literary style,'" Paizis explains,

> the romance borrows heavily from its most worn clichés to gain its effects ... Archaic elements litter its pages, both in style and in the images of society it employs. It is these which make the fantasy potential of the stories so powerful because they evoke the deep-seated and internalized codes of signification picked up at school.
>
> (36)

Like Barlow and Krentz, Paizis finds that both the plots and the prose of romance depend on "collectively recognized elements, deep-seated messages and encouragements, fears and aspirations" (34). In the authors' words, romance readers have a "keyed-in response to certain words and phrases" (Barlow and Krentz 25): "stock figures" (25) which draw forth what one might well assume to be stock responses.

To speak of stock figures and stock responses is, of course, to conjure a forbidding figure from the dawn of modern literary criticism: Q. D. Leavis. In *Fiction and the Reading Public* (1932), Leavis condemns the "consistent use of clichés (stock phrases to evoke stock responses)" that distinguishes popular fiction from real art (194). Authors of popular fiction deploy "the key words of the emotional vocabulary which provoke the vague warm surges of feeling associated with religion and religion substitutes—

e.g., life, death, love, good, evil, sin, home, mother, noble, gallant, purity, honour," she writes, warning that "these responses can be touched off with a dangerous ease," so that "every self-aware person finds that he has to train himself from adolescence in withstanding them" (64–5). The mockery of popular romance that Barlow and Krentz describe marks a ritual exorcism, or at least an attempt to demonstrate that we (the mockers) are the "self-aware" people who have learned to withstand the allure of romance fiction's key words and stock figures, whether of gender, of heteronormativity, of sexual experience, or of what constitutes romantic love. Likewise, the precision tools of close reading that Q.D. Leavis and her husband F.R. Leavis advocated from the 1930s onward can be read not simply as ways to appreciate and analyze "good writing," but as a set of counter-spells designed to break the dangerous hold of "bad writing" over our collectively socialized, and thus manipulatable, psyches.

The first pages of my essay "How to Read a Romance Novel (and Fall in Love with Popular Romance)" touch on Leavis and her legacy. As I argue there, when romance historian jay Dixon insists that "to enter the world of the romance, the method of analyzing literature which is taught in schools must be abandoned" (Dixon 10), this is because the "method" she has in mind "was designed, in no small part, to debunk, disarm, and dismiss" the rhetorical appeals and reading strategies with which popular romance is generally associated, including by its authors (Selinger 35). A longer, more elaborate consideration can be found in Laura Frost's essay "The Romance of Cliché: E. M. Hull, D. H. Lawrence, and Interwar Erotic Fiction" (2006) and her monograph *The Problem with Pleasure: Modernism and Its Discontents* (2013). Frost adds Lionel Trilling's essay "The Fate of Pleasure" as a second critical context for understanding when and why the pleasures offered by popular romance came to be seen as shameful, indeed "the essence of philistinism" (Trilling 435). Much more work, however, needs to be done on the implicit *rebuttal* to Leavis and Trilling offered by the Barlow/Krentz essay and seconded by Paizis: that is, that the overt, even over-the-top deployment of stock figures in romance also invites an active, specifically *intellectual* engagement with the text.

> "The [emotional] experience can be quite intense," the authors explain, yet, at the same time, the codes that evoke the dramatic illusion also maintain it *as* illusion (not delusion—romance readers do not confuse fantasy with reality) ... Because the language of romance is more lushly symbolic and metaphorical than ordinary discourse, the reader is stimulated not only to feel, but also to analyze, interpret, and understand.
>
> (Paizis 25–6)[5]

This collective "sharing of the fiction *as illusion*" (Paizis 34; my emphasis) makes the act of romance reading complex, not simplistic; alert, not languid or passive; and rather than naïve or naively sincere, it is fundamentally *ironic*, at least in the sense developed by Michael Saler in his discussion of the "ironic imagination," "as-if" perspective, and "double consciousness" employed by readers of detective fiction, horror, and fantasy: readers who are likewise "enchanted, not deluded" by what they read (22). One finds here, then, the foundations of a much-needed comparative analysis of popular romance *among* the genres, and more scholarship is sorely needed on popular romance novels as novels of ideas, whether along the lines laid out by Saler's *As If* or those articulated by the many scholars of science fiction and detective/mystery fiction who have approached their genres as the sites of readerly and authorial thinking and communal debate.[6]

If Paizis illustrates the power of a historicist response to the doxa of "bad writing," Vivanco's *For Love and Money* shows the effectiveness of rejecting the premise behind it. Trained as a Hispanomedievalist, Vivanco recalls the comparable disparagement of late medieval *cancionero* poetry as "vacuous and insipid" and the efforts of scholars, notably Keith Whinnom, to demonstrate the "exacting" aesthetics of the form and the "expertise" of its poets (qtd. 16). Citing Northrop Frye's reminder that "Value-judgements are subjective . . .," and that "when they are fashionable or generally accepted, they look objective, but that is all" (20), Vivanco ably articulates her own subjective sense that many romance novels "are well-written, skillfully crafted works which can and do engage the minds as well as the emotions of their readers, and a few are small masterpieces" (15). Two of Vivanco's four chapters draw on Frye's terminology—one discussing the deployment of Myth, Romance, and the High Mimetic, Low Mimetic, and Ironic modes in romance novels; the other the rewriting and adaptation of pre-existing story archetypes, which Frye calls "mythoi"—while the remaining pair offer extended discussions of romance as metafiction and the genre's deployment of overarching metaphors (Building a Romance, the Flowering of Romance, The Hunt of Love, and Love as a Journey) as a way for romance novels to propose, elaborate, and think through the nature of romantic partner love.[7]

Of Vivanco's four key concepts, the most influential has been the idea of metafiction, perhaps because it has allowed scholars to highlight how frequently and effectively romance novels defend, explore, and theorize the genre. I will return to metafiction in the final section of this chapter, since it illustrates one strong alternative to socio-historical readings of romance; her chapters on mythoi and extended metaphors will be addressed there as well. In addressing the doxa of "bad writing," however, the chapter on "Mimetic Modes" may be most applicable. Vivanco reviews Frye's taxonomy of literary modes, from myth, romance, and high mimesis down to irony, and also his notion of "modal counterpoint" as an aesthetic strategy: that is, the juxtaposition of various modes to produce literary effects (Frye 51; qtd. Vivanco 66). As she shows, the lush, evocative diction that characterizes "higher" modes such as myth or romance does not pervade romance novels, nor does it crop up at random; rather, such passages are, or can be, set in dynamic tension with crisper diction, everyday imagery, and other features of "lower" modes. A sense of modal counterpoint enables the nuanced perception and appreciation of popular romance styles—not just the purple passages, but the khaki, charcoal, royal blue, and emerald ones as well—and of one of the ways in which repetition and variation function within single-story and multi-narrative romance novels. As Vivanco shows, the different Frygian "modes" of parallel scenes can capture, in prose style, a character's emotional arc, a relationship's development, or the differences (thematic, emotional, ideological, etc.) between multiple relationships within a single text.

The focus on individual novels implied by Vivanco's approach marks a clear division between her work and that of Paizis, who is quite forthright in admitting that his study will not attend to "the particular internal dynamic, the aesthetic significance of the rhythms of individual narratives" (7). Such internal dynamics and rhythms are of necessity one of the topics that arise in the popular romance classroom, and Vivanco's terminology has proven helpful in pedagogical contexts (see Selinger, "Teaching with *For Love and Money*"). It would reward further development—both practical and theoretical—by future researchers, especially given Vivanco's brief but provocative association of modal counterpoint with the psychology of romantic idealization, a topic of considerable research in the field of relationship science (69).

Depending on the rhetorical or research situation, it may be more helpful to deploy either Paizis's historicist or Vivanco's formalist insights into popular romance aesthetics. In an off-the-cuff context, however—when answering an advisor's objection, a student's challenge, a friend's bewilderment—the simplest move may be to invoke Sturgeon's Revelation, often called Sturgeon's Law. As SF author Theodore Sturgeon explained in a 1957 book review,

> Sturgeon's Revelation ... was wrung out of me after twenty years of wearying defense of science fiction against attacks of people who used the worst examples of the field for ammunition, and whose conclusion was that ninety percent of SF is crud. Using the same standards that categorize 90% of science fiction as trash, crud, or crap, it can be argued that 90% of film, literature, consumer goods, etc. is crap. In other words, the claim (or fact) that 90% of science fiction is crap is ultimately uninformative, because science fiction conforms to the same trends of quality as all other artforms.
>
> (78)

Invoking Sturgeon's Law allows the would-be literary scholar of romance to sidestep the question of quality in the genre *overall* and focus instead on the task of making claims on behalf of this or that *individual* romance novel. One can ignore the questions of whether a particular novel is "representative" of the genre (it need not be) and whether it was embraced by the romance readership (a niche-published text or market failure might be an artistic success), and one can let the novel at hand dictate the terms of critical engagement and the topics to be explored.

What does such scholarship look like in practice, and what are its critical methods? The first of these is easier to answer: since the early 1990s, a cluster of instances has accrued around the works of Georgette Heyer, whom A.S. Byatt singled out as "a superlatively good writer of honourable escape" (Byatt 233). In deftly descriptive evaluative gestures Byatt goes on, as such readings will, to "distinguish between her books" (234), and essays have followed on individual Heyer novels (see, for example, Barr, Bell, Fletcher, Gillis, Vivancom, and Westman); more recently conferences have been devoted to her work, and a literary biography has been published. All of this effort is premised on the idea that *this* romance author differs from others, whether because of the "*precise* balance she achieves between romance and reality, fantastic plot and real detail" (Byatt 239), because of her "desire to transcend the type of historical romance formula(s) she invented and practically patented" (Barr 2), or some other cause. The grounds of distinction vary, but the *gesture* of distinction is the same, and the *Journal of Popular Romance Studies* special issue on Jennifer Crusie makes a series of comparable gestures toward distinguishing, if not canonizing, this American romance novelist of the 1990s. Each of its six essays claims, on behalf of Crusie, some distinctive artistry or insight into the genre: its history, its impact on the reader, its relationships to gossip, lies, and con-artistry, and more (see Baldus; Kramer; Moore and Selinger; Valeo; Vivanco; Zakreski; "Editor's Introduction").

In addition to these author-focused instances, and as a model of novel-specific scholarly methods, I would point to my essay in praise of Laura Kinsale's historical romance *Flowers from the Storm* ("How to Read a Romance Novel"). The method, here, was to start with a pair of nonce but nagging details in the text and to search out the thematic and compositional logic that would allow the novel's oddly specific references to non-Euclidean geometry and the cottage where Milton wrote *Paradise Lost* to fit into some overarching compositional and intellectual design. Treating these references as though they had occurred in a high-art text, the essay works its way from detail to design, finding in the process not only multiple geometric patterns—chiasmus, parallel lines that meet (it's a non-Euclidean textual universe), etc.—but an assortment of other allusions to *Paradise Lost* and other texts and developments from the "love revolution" of the seventeenth century which the novel links to its Regency setting and to its own late twentieth-century contexts of "the death of Eros" (Alan Bloom) and "the end of the novel of love" (Vivian Gornick) (38–43).

In effect, my "How to Read" essay applies to a popular romance novel some of the principles of "aesthetic criticism" articulated by poetry scholar and famed close reader Helen Vendler: first, "that no significant component can be left out of consideration," second, that "the significant components are known as such by interacting with each other in a way that seems coherent, not haphazard" (3), and finally that criticism should

> investigate *how* and *why* the art work is as it is, using its propositions and values as a bridge to its individual manner, its texture, its temperament, the experience and knowledge it makes possible, and its relation to other art works.
>
> (5)[8]

Stanley Cavell's *Pursuits of Happiness*, a philosophical reading of 1930s Hollywood comedies of remarriage, also underpins this essay's project: in particular, in Cavell's insistence that he is not merely demonstrating "our capacity for bringing our wild intelligence to bear on just about anything," but rather "the intelligence that a film," or in this case a romance novel, "has *already* brought to bear in its making" (10).

Novel-specific romance scholarship need not depend on tracking down or tracing out the implications of allusions, although these are more common—and more pertinent—than casual readers and reviewers generally observe. It will, however, always entail attention to moments of excess, oddly specific details, or puzzles of diction or phrasing—e.g., Piper Huguley's repeated reference to "chains of liberty" being struck from Africans who are being enslaved, and then restored with their liberation (195)—in the hope of articulating some textual logic that explains or compels them. *Pace* jay Dixon, who has claimed that HMB romance novelists of the twentieth century do not "play games with their readers" (10), such investigation treats reading the romance as something quite similar to playing a game or solving a puzzle, with patterns emerging as chains of connection are revealed.[9] In such an approach, it is worth noting, no *general* claim about the romance genre is made, other than the underlying claim (whether spelled out or implied) that the genre contains individual novels which reward being read "with the same demanding, passionate precision that we bring to any other text" ("How to Read" 44). Popular romance is thus brought in line with other forms of genre fiction, where the singling-out of particular texts and authors has long been a regular feature of book reviews, critical essays, and scholarly works.

To understand why it has taken so long for such disaggregating treatment to be accorded popular romance, we must turn to a second critical doxa: the notion that romance novels are not just "badly written," book by book, but are *standardized* products, and thus quite different not simply from literary fiction, but from books in other mass-market genres.

Standardization; or, the anxious othering of romance

The belief that romance novels are standardized products is a commonplace of what Jayashree Kamblé calls the "media romance": an account of the genre that asserts a *textual* sameness based on sameness of packaging rather than on any actual reading.[10] Yet we cannot dismiss the idea of standardization as simply a matter of judging the books by their covers. Reputable scholars have discussed the impacts of corporate control, genre conventions, and reader expectations on the genre, each of which might well seem at first blush to complicate any treatment of these books as art.[11] Romance authors, too, have written—often in asides, tweets, and other brief or ephemeral forms—about the need to negotiate, resist, or work around such guidelines: not only the explicit ones promulgated by publishers, but also the tacit advice that they are given about (for example) which historical settings will sell, and which should be avoided.[12] That said, from a literary standpoint, any account of the genre as a standardized product needs to be contested, or at least supplemented, by approaches that investigate the sources of this account and/or call it into question.

To begin, it helps to recall that popular romance is far from the only genre to be dismissed for its sameness. The same has been said at various points about science fiction, the western, and the detective story (Roberts 162); as for epic "sword and sorcery" fantasy, which vies with romance for the title of "most despised sub-genre of paraliterary production" (Delaney 129), the overall charge of uniformity contains a subsidiary litany of romance-like offenses, including puerile content, purple prose, and palpitating readers.[13] No wonder, then, that much of the most useful scholarship to address the doxa of standardization does so by addressing it as an issue related to genre fiction in general, or even to *genre* in general, rather than as a problem peculiar to romance.

In "On Popular Romance, J. R. Ward, and the Limits of Genre Study" (2012), for example, Mary Bly begins by wondering why the very existence of genre norms—whether imposed by a publisher, by a reading public, or by genre tradition—should seem so alarming. As Bly observes, the "perception that romance novels are 'mass produced,' so that like automobiles, it doesn't really matter which factory (or author) produces the text" (62) derives from concerns about the mass production and mechanical reproduction of art raised by thinkers in the 1930s, notably Walter Benjamin and Theodore Adorno. When Radway refers in passing to romance novels as "factory-produced commodities" (11), Bly explains, she draws indirectly on this critical tradition, and Modleski does so quite explicitly, as when she critiques her own earlier work for thinking that any local variation on or evolution within the romance "formula" was no more than "what the philosopher and culture critic T. W. Adorno called 'pseudo-individualization'" (Modleski "My Life as a Romance Reader" 57).[14]

Against such approaches, Bly throws down a historicist gauntlet. That great works should be *sui generis* would, she writes, have sounded absurd to a Renaissance artist—as, indeed, it would to any Neoclassical or early Romantic one (63). This is, therefore, a peculiarly *modern* anxiety: one with roots in the "crisis of indistinction" surrounding the novel in the middle of the nineteenth century, the period when high-art and mass-market fiction began to diverge in authorship, audience, reputation, and aesthetics (McGurl 4). As Mark McGurl explains in *The Novel Art*, some authors in this period wanted the novel—or, at least, a certain *kind* of novel—to be granted the status of "fine art" and the novelist—or at least a certain *kind* of novelist—the corresponding title of "artist" (3). For this to happen, the art-novel had to be distinguished from mass-market fiction, and a discourse emerged disparaging the latter as not only "worthless for any purpose of intellectual stimulus" but also a mass-produced, fungible product, churned out by an anonymous "process of manufacture" (qtd. in McGurl 5). Ken Gelder's account of the period concurs, adding that for a would-be art-novelist such as Henry James "the biggest threat to Literature's future was in fact popular fiction itself, the kind of fiction sold at the time at railway bookstalls, circulated through the commercial lending libraries, advertised in the newspapers and read or 'absorbed,'" as the novelist laments, "by those 'millions for whom taste is but an obscure, confused, immediate instinct'" (Gelder 18; for more on James and popular romance fiction, see Chung).[15]

In Gelder's *Popular Fiction: the Logics and Practices of a Literary Field* (2004), the split between capital-L "Literature" and popular fiction seems right and just. Each of these literary "fields," as he calls them, has its own aspirations and terms of praise, and although "one is inevitably disposed (for a range of social and cultural reasons, and for better or worse) towards some cultural forms and practices and not others," it is "perfectly possible to enjoy both," albeit "on different terms and under quite different logics" (19). McGurl, by contrast, presents the relationship as fraught and more complex. Across the 1920s and 1930s, he argues, art-novelists drew, however conflictedly, on popular modes and models: a point developed at length in terms of high modernism and "low modern" popular romance in scholarship (Hipsky, Frost) on D.H. Lawrence and (perhaps more surprisingly) Virginia Woolf.[16] Likewise, (some) popular authors saw in modernist themes and stylistic moves the "opportunity to produce intellectual social distinctions within the 'common' place of mass culture" (175). McGurl's example of the latter is Dashiell Hammett, who declared to his publisher the aspiration to "make 'literature'" (qtd. in McGurl 164) out of pulp detective fiction. As McGurl observes, such fiction was already "marked both as a *masculine* and as an *intellectualist* genre," safely located at a distance from "sticky swamps of 'feminine' sentiment" (McGurl 158): a reputation it retains, and one which helps to account for the respect it receives in academia. Dorothy Sayers's Lord Peter Wimsey/Harriet Vane novels from the 1930s, which hybridize mystery and romance, warrant future research along the lines McGurl suggests, as do more recent mystery and noir romances, notably Jennifer Crusie's homage to Hammett, *Fast Women*; comparable work is needed on romance and SF/fantasy.

Unlike McGurl or Gelder, however, Bly reaches back to the Renaissance for her historical contextualization, and this broader perspective leads her to a correspondingly broader, more provocative conclusion. To Bly, the charge of industrial standardization in romance fiction serves to localize, and thus contain, the general anxiety of living "in an age in which mechanical reproduction is not only possible, but ubiquitous and inevitable" (Bly 64). Yet pre-industrial visions of genre persist, routinely deployed in reading works from Bly's primary area of scholarly expertise, Renaissance drama. Although popular romance emerges as a distinct form in the modern period, she suggests, the genre's aesthetics might more profitably be read in this older, pre-modern way: that is, scholars can treat the ubiquity of genre frameworks as a literary *given*, an unproblematic matter of course, and thus free themselves to look for originality in what Bly, following Adorno, names simply "*parts*": the local compositional decisions, scenes, and details where novelty resides.[17] Indeed, Bly argues, genre frameworks do not constrain local originality so much as they shine a spotlight on it, since whether in a romance novel or Renaissance revenge tragedy, it is precisely the formality and familiarity of the framework which allows for the production (for authors) and the recognition (by readers) of an "unscripted" freshness, either in content or in structure (63–4).

Bly's insistence on the originality to be found in a romance novel's "unscripted" negotiations with, and departures from, the conventions of its genre echoes arguments found in earlier scholarship—albeit ones that did not gain traction or establish a continuing tradition of critical discourse. John Cawelti advanced similar ideas in his foundational essays "The Concept of Formula in the Study of Popular Literature" (1969) and "Notes Toward an Aesthetic of Popular Culture" (1971) and in his groundbreaking monograph *Adventure, Mystery, and Romance* (1976), which proposed that all popular genres be seen as "a set of artistic limitations and potentials" and "standard characteristics" that particular texts then vary to achieve literary interest (*Adventure* 7).[18] Likewise, almost a decade later, Radway's *Reading the Romance* offered not only a 13-part Proppian list of the "standard characteristics" of the romances admired by the Smithton readers—a roadmap to what she calls "*The* Narrative Logic of *the* Romance" (my emphasis)—but also an extended discussion of how one novel, Leigh Ellis's *Green Lady* (1981), defies its standardized packaging and treats that narrative logic as "an alterable set of generic conventions rather than a natural and immutable organic form" (152).[19] In *A Natural History of the Romance Novel*, published 20 years after Radway's study and nearly ten years before Bly's, Pamela Regis proposed a list of eight narrative elements that define the romance novel as a recognizable form, not in order to lump together or demystify the texts she studies (five literary novels—*Pamela*, *Pride and Prejudice*, *Jane Eyre*, Trollope's *Framley Parsonage*, and E.M. Forster's *A Room With a View*—and multiple works by half a dozen popular romance authors, including Hull, Heyer, Stewart, Krentz, and Roberts), but rather to establish a shared terminology or genre-prosody that each text distinctively varies in terms of when and how each element appears, how many times it appears, and whether its appearance is diegetic or offstage (or implied, or symbolically replaced, or otherwise elided by the narrative).

As my use of the word "prosody" should suggest, the experiences of reading and writing in a genre system resemble those of reading and writing formal verse. Vivanco compares the genre's aesthetics and reception to those of late-medieval *cancionero* love poetry (16–17, 149–50); some romance authors, notably Jennifer Cruise, invoke English Renaissance sonnets as an analogy for the genre's interplay between constraint and creativity ("So, Bill," Crusie imagines a courtier asking: "—when are you going to write a real poem?"). Roberts gives the analogy a temporal dimension. Not only does the existence of a metrical scheme, stanzaic norm, or genre system allow an author to "demonstrate . . . mastery of that formula" by "ringing changes on it" (166), but every change is potentially "an invitation to further variation in the books that will follow" (167). The essays of An Goris document this principle in action. In her early work, Goris applied the postmodern theoretical model of "constrained writing" generally associated with experimental texts (e.g., the works of OULIPO authors) to popular romance, with particular attention to how handbooks for aspiring romance authors teach them to negotiate the exigencies of convention and innovation (Geest and

Goris; Goris "Loving"); in later work, Goris documents and theorizes one such innovation: the emergence of a new "narrative space" in series romances, where the achieved romantic couple from one volume returns at length as secondary characters in another. "Analyses of post-HEA scenes reveal the genre is not merely representing a clear-cut, pre-fixed fantasy of a romantic Happy Ever After," Goris concludes, "but actively exploring and negotiating what such a fantasy might look like beyond the climactic yet inevitably formulaic moment of the HEA," with different authors (her examples are Nora Roberts and J. R. Ward) responding to the invitation of the post-HEA in radically different ways ("Happily Ever After").

Although it can be done with nuance and insight (e.g., Paizis's *Love and the Novel*), structuralist scholarship has done a great deal to perpetuate the notion that romance novels are "schematic texts" (Bowman 69), best read and understood in terms of a few enduring, if not immutable, narrative schemes. From a literary perspective, however, such insights into the "narrative logic" (Radway), "elements" (Regis), or "framework" (Bly) of romance must be the first word in an analysis, not the last—otherwise, they come perilously close to claims about the fundamental sameness of blues guitar solos, Scarlatti sonatas, or, for that matter, sonnets, about which William Carlos Williams scoffed that they all "say the same thing of no importance" (54). In each case, what's being said purports to be something like "to the educated ear these sound the same," but is in fact some ratio of "I lack the genre-specific competence that would let me hear the differences" and "I refuse to be the kind of person who *cares* about such differences, let alone who gives the artist credit for them."[20] More research is needed as to why the notion that "all the stories in [this] genre are effectively the same" (Roberts 162) remains viable in romance contexts when it has faded elsewhere, but such metacritical work on the genre's critical reception[21] is, perhaps, less important for literary studies than other tasks at hand: comparative work that draws on methodological and theoretical models developed for other, more thoroughly researched genres and artforms (e.g., Freedman's *Critical Theory and Science Fiction*; the accounts of "the cute," "the interesting," and "the zany" by Sianne Ngai; the various "uses of literature" enumerated and articulated by Rita Felski in her manifesto of that name); efforts to disaggregate the genre by testing critical claims about its structures or tropes against the practice of individual novelists (e.g., Goris "Mind, Body, Love"), of queer romance authors (e.g., Betz on lesbian romance novels), and of ethnically and racially diverse texts (e.g., Weisser on African American romance imprints or Young "Saving China"). Even fresh, revisionist looks at Adorno might be useful, since the same theorist who critiques industrial "pseudo-individualization" also insists on "the importance of the *tour de force* in art" (qtd. in Vendler 5; see Adorno *Aesthetic Theory* 106–7, 185), and an interpretive community prepared to imagine that a *tour de force* might exist in popular romance will likely be able to see and describe them.[22]

Beyond the socio-political

Of the doxa surrounding popular romance novels, perhaps the most positive—at least at first glance—is the assumption that they will be of most interest to scholars as records of shifting courtship mores, ideas about love, sex, gender, and relationships, public attitudes toward war and economics, and other types of socio-historical change. Indeed, when Bly advocates for scholars to take an interest in the originality of "parts" of romance novels, she does so explicitly in the hope of inspiring a more "historically specific" criticism, rather than a more aesthetically sensitive kind. Such work had already begun nearly a decade before her piece, as the essays gathered in Susan Strehle and Mary Paniccia Carden's *Doubled Plots: Romance and History* (2003) demonstrate;[23] published alongside the Bly essay, Hsu-Ming Teo's "Bertrice Teaches You About History, and You Don't Even Mind!: History and Revisionist Historiography in Bertrice Small's *The Kadin*" offered a compelling model of how attention to "parts" could be integrated with reception research; and many of the essays gathered in the *Romance Fiction and American Culture*, edited by William Gleason and myself, advance this historicist agenda (see particularly Matelski, Lyons and Selinger, Moody-Freeman, and Barot). In her monograph *Making Meaning in Popular Romance Fiction* Jayashree Kamblé offers a helpful evolutionary metaphor to articulate the assumptions behind this scholarly approach. "What may be acceptable as romantic alters over time," Kamblé explains, "not just in terms of archetypes but in terms of the constructed reality in which the relationship can be apprehended/enjoyed, that is, considered 'romantic'" (21). Because it must be perceivable as "romantic," the romance novel must change; because it is a novel, "a form that promotes evolutionary adaptation, linguistically and structurally," it has the capacity to do so in a radical way that other literary forms (say, the sonnet) may not (21). As a result, these novels are, for Kamblé, "lenses through which economic and sociopolitical dramas of immediate relevance to readers come into focus," offering "a glimpse of existing in the twentieth and twenty-first century under (and in conflict with) the spread of capitalism and the intensification of neo-conservatism" (21).

Given both the quantity and the quality of these historical/socio-political inquiries, some literary scholars have felt obliged to set such ends explicitly aside. "Questions regarding the cultural, psychological, and sociological resonance of rape scenes, while interesting and important, do not allot to the trope a literary significance beyond the purely mimetic," Angela Toscano observes near the start of "A Parody of Love: the Narrative Uses of Rape in Popular Romance," which attempts to take a more purely "narratological" approach to the topic. Toscano distinguishes three varieties of rape in popular romance—"the Rape of Mistaken Identity, the Rape of Possession, and the Rape of Coercion or 'Forced Seduction'"—but her argument is ultimately not structuralist but epistemological and ethical, framed in terms drawn from Emmanuel Levinas, Roland Barthes, and Georges Bataille. A comparable itch to "anatomize" a recurring feature of popular romance marks Jonathan Allan's "Theorizing Male Virginity in Popular Romance Novels," where representations of male virginity (and its loss) are seen as narrative tropes rather than as barometers of social sentiment; Toscano's deployment of philosophy, meanwhile, resonates with Deborah Lutz's earlier monograph *The Dangerous Lover*, where "through the theories of time, being, and selfhood of Heidegger and others we see how the outcast hero and the attraction to him represent ontology itself" (88).

Although they differ in topic and critical idiom, Toscano, Allan, and Lutz share a desire to reframe "sociopolitical dramas" (Kamblé 21) in aesthetic and/or philosophical terms. Rather than an object of inquiry to be thought *about*—one which reveals the contours of readers' desires or a historical moment's discourses surrounding some issue or concern—the romance novel becomes something to think *with*, the occasion for engaging with ideas that have already been engaged by the author and/or woven into the text's compositional fabric.[24] Often these are ideas about love: as Vivanco shows in *For Love and Money*, romance novels routinely propose and elaborate extended metaphors for what love is or is like (a hunt, a journey, a garden's cultivation, building a home) (151–98); they engage the "conundrum" of romantic love as "an ambiguous—and sometimes dangerous—practice of freedom *and* bondage" (Roach 120); and they foreground the complex relationship between love and repetition, which is for Lynne Pearce

> the seemingly inexhaustible, yet infinitely exhausting, life-blood of romance, regardless of whether the story in question is bound for tragedy (where death is invoked to vouchsafe love's non-repeatability) or a "happy ending" (where past relationships, as well as new ones glimmering darkly on the horizon, are temporarily dazzled and silenced by an all-consuming present).
>
> (Pearce "Romance and Repetition")

Yet as Kecia Ali demonstrates in *Human in Death: Morality and Mortality in J. D. Robb's Novels*, love is far from the only topic explored in, and explorable through, a close and thoughtful reading of popular romance novels. Ali's chapters explore intimacy, friendship, vocation, violence, and the dangerous allure of perfection, whether individual or social, as represented in the series' fictive future world; her study is the first monograph to treat a romance author (Nora Roberts, writing under a separate, series-specific nom de plume) as a novelist of ideas, and offers a useful model for future work along those lines.

The *In Death* series by J. D. Robb stands at the crossroads of multiple genres: police procedural, science fiction, and romance. Scholarship on the relationships between other genres and romance—and between romance and more canonical literature, and romance and the non-verbal arts (music, painting, etc.)—has offered a range of alternatives to socio-historical readings of the genre. Vivanco's chapter on "Mythoi" builds on her discussion of Frygian "narrative modes" to explore high mimetic, low mimetic, ironic, and other retellings of canonical narratives (e.g., the Pygmalion mythos, Sir Gawain and the Loathly Lady, Odysseus and Circe) and fairy tales, with ample notes to earlier scholarship on the latter as it bears on popular romance (e.g., Bettelheim; Crusie "Not Your Mother's Cinderella"; Lee). Using a theoretical model informed by Judith Butler, Lisa Fletcher reads popular, middlebrow, and high-art instances of historical romance fiction side by side in *Historical Romance Fiction: Heterosexuality and Performativity*; her subsequent *Island Genres, Genre Islands*, co-written with Ralph Crane, shows how an expansive, "Island Studies" framework allows one to read island-set romance novels, crime fiction, thrillers, and fantasy novels as co-equal branches of popular fiction, each with its own characteristic set of geographies and spatial logics. In "When I Paint My Masterpiece: Bob Dylan, Ekphrasis, and the Artistry of Susan Elizabeth Phillips" I attend to the significant narrative presences in Phillips's *Natural Born Charmer* of Bob Dylan's *Blood on the Tracks* and of elaborately described paintings by the novel's heroine. Phillips uses these artforms, I argue, to reflect on the pleasures and complexities that are possible in popular romance, ably demonstrating that it (like the heroine's paintings) cannot be brushed off as "sentimental bullshit" (Phillips 307).

More research is needed on how romance authors use references to other media (film, TV) and to texts by canonical authors (Austen, Shakespeare, Flaubert, any number of poets) to defend the romance genre, to analogize and theorize its practices, and to think through generic differences (e.g., how lyric poetry and narrative romance depict romantic love).[25] As Vivanco's chapter on Metafiction in *For Love and Money* demonstrates, such gestures are far from rare (110–50). They align romance with other forms of popular culture, which often offers "pointed commentary on, and even pastiche or parody of, its status as cultural item" (Polan 175; qtd. in Vivanco 110), and as with other metafiction, these gestures readily blossom into more elaborate investigations of the relationships between fiction and reality and any number of comparable pairings (the romantic and the real, the worlds of desire and experience, the world imagined and the world as suffered, etc.) (112). Romance novels also use metafictional gestures to consider the genre's unsettling status as both art and commodity, not least in plots that involve other products positioned between mass-produced and handmade status: artisanal chocolates, craft/micro-brewery beers, popular music, etc. No significant work has been done on this topic, yet many such novels exist, and they would reward investigation along both literary and historicist lines.

Conclusion: of criteria, canons, and classrooms

Debate has long since ended over the existence of "real novels" in detective fiction, science fiction, fantasy, and other popular genres. Reviews extol these exceptional cases; essays and monographs explore them; and publishers mark their merit through paratextual gestures. Pick up the handsome hardcover anthology *The Best of Gene Wolfe: A Definitive Retrospective of His Finest Short Fiction*, for example, and you'll find this breathless back cover blurb from the *Washington Post Book World*: "If any writer from within genre fiction ever merited the designation Great Author, it is surely Wolfe," a novelist who "reads like Dickens, Proust, Kipling, Chesterton, Borges, and Nabokov rolled into one" (Gevers). No matter how humble its origins—an Ace paperback with a lurid cover; a pulp magazine like *Black Mask*, *Weird Tales*, or *Fantasy Fan*—a work in any popular genre *other* than romance might well aspire to be enshrined, or perhaps entombed, in an authoritative edition that certifies its value.[26]

Will such editions someday exist of popular romance fiction? Several factors will affect the outcome, each of which needs more scholarship from a literary perspective. The first concerns how differently romance authors and authors from other genres discuss the literariness—potential or extant—of their own work and of their colleagues. Is it, in fact, the case that few romance authors have claimed that they are, in Hammett's phrase, "making 'Literature' of it" (qtd. in McGurl 164), even privately? (The Hammett quote is from a letter to his publisher.) As I have noted elsewhere, Kathleen Gilles Seidel may note, with justified annoyance, that scholars "seem unable to distinguish one book from another," but the central demand of her essay for the *Dangerous Men, Adventurous Women* anthology, announced in its title, is "Judge Me by the Joy I Bring," not "judge me by my mastery of language, dazzle of imagination, elegance of structure, deftness of allusion, strategic use of symbol, image, and ambiguity, fit between form and theme," and comparable criteria (212). More scholarship is needed on the institutional and epitextual logics behind this preference for an affective, rather than formalist, mode of advocacy: a preference whose history dates, as Rita Felski has described, to the highly gendered rejection of sentimentality in modernist aesthetics (see Felski *Gender*). Likewise, a scholarly eye should be kept on whether this preference persists in twenty-first-century author statements (the Seidel essay dates from the mid-1990s) and on the terms of praise that are deployed in the emerging corpus of romance reviews in mainstream newspapers and magazines, including the *New York*

Times, the *Washington Post*, and the *Seattle Review of Books*. (It says a great deal about both the cultural status and the assumed readership of SF/Fantasy, for example, that the a reviewer for the *Boston Globe* praises Gene Wolfe's novels for being "filled with arcane language, heavy with double meanings ... layered with allusion on top of metaphor on top of symbolism," textual strategies that modernism made the hallmarks of literariness (Bebergal).[27])

A second issue relevant to the genre's literary status concerns the contents, nature, and even existence of a popular romance canon. Writing in *Salon* in 2014, popular culture critic Noah Berlatsky observed that although he had "poked around online to find 'best of' lists or other recommendations," he soon realized that "there wasn't even a provisional consensus on which books were the best or essential romance novels": books which were "clearly central, or respected, or worth reading." Familiar with such discussions from other genres of fiction, comics, popular music, and film, Berlatsky concluded that "the genre is so culturally maligned that there has been no concerted effort to codify it. There is, in short, no romance canon."

To Berlatsky, this claim said more about the institutional occlusion of the genre than it did about romance itself, since it signaled the lack of any "group of experts who considers these works in particular, and the genre or medium in general, to be capable of greatness." Because they believed themselves to belong to precisely such a "group of experts," because they thought that a romance canon did exist—Berlatsky had been looking for it in all the wrong places—and/or because they saw the lack of such codification as a distinctive, egalitarian attribute of the romance genre world, many readers, reviewers, bloggers, and authors took issue with Berlatsky's essay. So did a handful of scholars (see McAlister). More work needs to be done on whether a popular romance canon does, in fact, exist; whether one is coming into existence as scholarship develops; whether several may be coexisting without competing (academic canons, reader canons, author canons, etc.); and whether the discourse of the romance "genre world" has indeed avoided talk of canonicity (and if so, how and why).

The final issue affecting the literary status of popular romance concerns its place in the classroom. As Roland Barthes mordantly observes, "Literature is what is taught, period" (*Rustle* 22), and the arrival of college and university literature courses including popular romance novels—or even, sometimes, exclusively focused on them—may bestow "literary" status on the genre, or at least those texts which are repeatedly put on syllabi. Scholarship is needed, therefore, not only on where and how popular romance novels are taught, but also on *which* novels are taught, and why. A few such pieces have already appeared in the *Journal of Popular Romance Studies*, written by those doing the teaching (Driscoll; Fletcher, Gaby, and Kloester; Dugger; Heiss). That said, the relatively small number of such courses being taught around the world would also make it possible for someone to investigate them from the outside, documenting the emergence and spread of popular romance pedagogy practices and, perhaps, of an academic or teaching canon.

Whether explicitly or implicitly, literary scholarship on popular romance fiction resists and refutes the genre's reputation for being poorly written, standardized, and primarily of interest from a socio-historical perspective. It also resists and refutes, or at least complicates, the way the genre talks about itself. Romance authors, reviewers, and readers tend, by and large, to reject the scholarly "doxa of difficulty" in which "discomfort, confusion, and hard cognitive labor" (Frost *Problem* 6) are terms of praise, and to espouse instead a set of goals that have long since fallen out of academic favor:

providing joy, consolation, instruction, and delight to readers, and, for authors, perhaps achieving a measure of fame and fortune in the process.[28] Such scholarship would seem perverse—an obstinate, headstrong practice—were it not for the fact that so many romance *novels*, whatever their authors may say, invite an attitude of "productive attentiveness" to their textual details, intertextual echoes, metafictional reflections, and other signs of artistry (Bialostoky 113). The sheer number of romance novels which have yet to be looked at through a literary lens makes this a promising area for future research. Already, though, it seems clear that although not every romance novel will reward literary investigation, every mode of literary reading can find a suitable text somewhere in popular romance.

Notes

1 For digital humanities scholarship on popular romance fiction, see Jack Elliott's "Patterns and Trends in Harlequin Category Romance," "Vocabulary Decay in Category Romance," and "Whole Genre Sequencing."

2 By "born literary" Eagleton would seem to mean that some texts are written and disseminated in ways that invite us to talk about the artfulness and insight of the author, the complexity and patterning of the text, the nuance or depth of its characters, the beauty of its language, and so on. A text that "achieves literariness" would be one that was written with some other set of hopes and expectations—to teach, to save souls, to entertain, to shape a debate–but which comes in time to be treated as literature in some ongoing fashion, not only because of what people say about it, but in terms of who does that saying and where it takes place: in the academy, in publications aimed at educated readers, in the conversation of poets, novelists, playwrights, etc., and in critical and canonical editions, but *not* in entertainment magazines, at church book groups, on Oprah's book club, or in paperback reprints with covers from film adaptations. As for texts' having literariness "thrust upon them," it is perhaps worth recalling the source of Eagleton's allusion. In it, Shakespeare's Malvolio reads with delight about having greatness thrust upon him in a letter purporting to be a declaration of Olivia's love—but which in fact advises him to behave in ways that will incur her displeasure. The scholar who "thrusts literariness" on a romance novel may not, in fact, be doing it a favor, at least if it leaves the text looking smug, self-important, and cross-gartered (*Twelfth Night* 2:5, 155).

3 The term "doxa" was popularized in literary studies by Roland Barthes. For a useful introduction to the term, its meanings, and its use in literary and rhetorical studies, see Amossy.

4 For more on popular romance as a signifier—both in its Mills & Boon and single-title historical varieties—see Jayashree Kamblé's chapter (Chapter 12) in this volume on media romance.

5 To be sure, not all romance novels flaunt the lushness of their prose. Jayashree Kamblé notes, for example, the "staccato prose" of Nora Roberts, which "lends her work a spartan charm, an unromantic kind of romantic storytelling" ("What's Love" 23): a quick, qualitative, memorable description that is rare in both the scholarship and reviewing of the genre.

6 For more on genre fiction as a technology that facilitates "thinking with tired brains" about substantive topics see Roberts (127–149); for SF as the site of "cognitive estrangement" see Suvin (7–12). The bibliography on mystery/detective fiction and moral issues is extensive; for a good introduction, see Berges.

7 Vivanco's account of how romance fiction uses these overarching metaphors draws on the scholarship of psychologist Robert Sternberg, whose *Love is a Story: a New Theory of Relationships* explores the range of metaphors through which individuals and couples articulate their expectations and understandings of love. Although this is a volume for the general public, Sternberg's discussion of metaphor as a mode of cognition seems a promising and under-studied resource for Popular Romance Studies.

8 Vendler distinguishes such "aesthetic criticism," the core of her own practice, from "ideological criticism," which "is not interested in the uniqueness of the work of art, wishing

always to conflate it with other works sharing its values" (2). She also notes in passing that, from her perspective, "one cannot write properly, or even meaningfully, on an art work to which one has not responded aesthetically" (5): a useful challenge for the romance scholar to keep in mind.

9 For a discussion of this reading method as a classroom practice, see Selinger, "Use Heart in Your (Re)Search."

10 For accounts of the "Media Romance" see Kamblé's *Making Meaning* (21), "Branding a Genre," and Chapter 12 in this volume.

11 The keynote for this scholarly tradition was struck by Tania Modleski's *Loving with a Vengeance* (1982), which addresses the issue of standardization briefly, in a clipped, disapproving discussion of the "strict set of rules" that Harlequin novelists must follow, which "even dictates the point of view from which the narrative must be told" (32). In the opening chapter of *Reading the Romance* (1984) Janice Radway seems more impressed, not only by "the effectiveness of commodity packaging and advertising" (20) in this segment of the publishing industry but also by the market research, focus group interviews, and other forms of "consumer testing" that stand behind it (42). If this leads to "authorial initiative and decision-making power [being] curtailed," Radway writes, this is simply the logical consequence of a shift by publishers from "locating or even creating an audience for an existing manuscript" to "locating or even creating a manuscript for an already-constituted reading public" (43). For more recent work on what romance publishers have told authors and how those guidelines have developed, see John Markert's chapter (Chapter 16) in this volume.

12 Madeline Hunter, in a book review, thus describes the "common wisdom" among authors that historical novels set outside the U.K. "don't sell" (Hunter). More research is needed on the impact of self-publishing on where and when romance novels are set in the twenty-first century.

13 "The popular imagination holds that sword and sorcery is the paradise of arrested male adolescence," Mark Scroggins explains: a genre where "broad-thewed and dim-witted barbarians stride across pseudo-medieval landscapes, fighting wizards and giant snakes, rescuing (and bedding) grateful but sketchily characterized young women—all for the entertainment and titillation of socially maladapted teenaged boys" (23).

14 Although Bly does not mention her foundational essay "Mass Market Romance: Pornography for Women is Different," Ann Barr Snitow is another early romance scholar indebted to this critical tradition, as we can see when Snitow avers that "to analyze Harlequin romances is not to make any literary claims for them," because "they are not art but rather what Lillian Robinson has called 'leisure activities that take the place of art'" (142).

15 Accusations of sameness often enter critical discourse with a whiff of superiority, as though they were trying to establish and defend the primacy of academic training or critical taste over the interest and expertise of those "millions." (In the case of Modleski, who grew up as a romance reader, the distinction is between the younger self, "an addict," and the adult investigating and resisting that addiction ("My Life,"53).) Often, however, a nervous recognition of the superior knowledge of pleasure readers reasserts itself. Thus, for example, in the very sentence where Radway refers to romance novels as "factory-produced commodities" she offers a contrasting view of these texts: the Smithton readers "understood themselves to be reading particular and individual authors, whose special marks of style they could recount in detail, *rather than* identical, factory-produced commodities" (11, my emphasis).

16 Scholars adjacent to popular romance studies have persuasively recast much of the romantic fiction of the late-nineteenth and early twentieth centuries—the same material that Rachel Anderson dismissed as the "subliterature of love"—as a "low modern" literary form. Martin Hipsky reads romantic fiction by Mary Ward, Marie Corelli, Emma Orczy, Florence Barclay, and Elinor Glyn alongside Woolf and Lawrence in order to explore their common interests in love, desire, ecstasy, and "the imperative to loft us [as readers] … into a refashioned symbolic order that would bridge us across the pain of the historical Real" (Hipsky, xxi). Laura Frost's work on "The Romance of Cliché" explores how Lawrence approaches, appropriates, and disavows the depictions of female desire and erotic transcendence espoused in bestselling love stories by female authors, notably E.M. Hull's *The Sheik.*

17 For a contrasting account of genre as a given of all textuality, see Derrida, "The Law of Genre," especially his assertion that "there is no genreless text, there is always a genre and genres, yet such participation never amounts to belonging" (230).

18 As Cawelti ruefully noted in the early 1990s, *Adventure, Mystery, and Romance* supplied extended discussions of exemplary figures from the Western, detective fiction, and social melodrama, but none of the authors discussed was a woman, and despite its title, the book contains "almost nothing about romance" ("Masculine Myths and Feminist Revisions," 123).

19 Radway presents *Green Lady* as an outlier text, and she distinguishes the authorial team writing as "Leigh Ellis," Anne and Louisa Rudeen, for their university educations (the latter went to Yale, she notes) and for what she sees as their atypical awareness of "literary history and generic conventions" (152). These gestures *ought* to have inspired the scholars who followed her in the 1980s to seek out other, equally savvy authors and novels. That few were, in fact, inspired to do so says a good deal about the academic reputation of popular romance and the hurdles faced by popular romance studies, but many such authors exist, and it is never too late to start.

20 That genre-incompetence and the *refusal* of such competence are two different issues can be seen in Robyn R. Warhol's discussion of the film *Pretty Woman* in *Having a Good Cry: Effeminate Feelings and Pop-Culture Forms*. Warhol has clear mastery of the genre-systems to which the film belongs, but she confesses herself ashamed of her own pleasurable reaction to the film, and when she notices wit, insight, complexity, intelligence, or nuance in it, she attributes these to the activity of a "perverse" and "self-conscious" viewer, rather than to the film or its makers (67; see Selinger, "When I Paint," 297–299).

21 For examples of such metacritical research, see Frantz and Selinger ("Introduction"), Regis ("What Do Critics Owe the Romance"), and Goris ("Matricide)

22 For a discussion of the power of communal expectations to shape interpretive activity, see Stanley Fish's essay "How to Recognize a Poem When You See One" (Fish, 322–327).

23 Of particular note in *Doubled Plots* are groundbreaking essays on race in romance—pieces on *Miss Numè of Japan by* Onoto Watanna [Winnifred Eaton] (Ouyang), on race in E. M. Hull's *The Sheik* (Blake), and on African American women's historical romances (Dandridge)—on the queerness or queer potential of heterosexual romance (Burley), and on the economic ideology underpinning Kathleen Woodiwiss's *The Flame and the Flower* (Hinnant).

24 I paraphrase Sumita Chakravaty's essay "Teaching Indian Cinema," which closes with the statement that "a Bollywood film is something to think *with* even more than something to think *about*" (108, emph. Chakravaty's). For more on the notion of aesthetic criticism treating a text's ideas as functional and structural rather than ideological features, see Vendler (4).

25 For more on Shakespeare in popular romance see Osborne and Whyte; for more on Austen and popular romance see Frantz ("Darcy's Vampiric Descendents"), Gillis ("Manners"), Kroeg, and Tyler. The relationships between poetry and popular romance have yet to be studied in published scholarship.

26 The Library of America, which "champions our nation's cultural heritage by publishing America's greatest writing," thus includes handsome hardcover editions of Hammett, H.P. Lovecraft, Philip K. Dick, Ursula LeGuin, and an anthology of Crime Novels from the 1930s and 1940s ("Library of America").

27 Despite Paizis's assertion that "the criteria used to judge 'high' literature make little sense when applied to products of mass culture" (35), a review like this one makes it clear that the invocation of those "higher" criteria remains a crucial strategy in claiming literary value for authors and works of popular fiction.

28 As Lionel Trilling points out in "The Fate of Pleasure," to the young Keats, the chief end of poetry was "to soothe the cares, and lift the thoughts of man" ("Sleep and Poetry"), but since the late nineteenth century this aspiration has struck critics and sophisticated readers as "the essence of philistinism" (435). For an extended discussion of Trilling's essay and the emergence of "doxa of difficulty" see Frost (*Problem* 3–12). Andreas Huyssen's account of modernism as "an aesthetic based on the uncompromising repudiation of what Emma Bovary loved to read" is relevant to this history (45), as is John Guillory's discussion of how the foundational New Critics taught their acolytes to flinch at sentiment, encouragement, emotional identification with characters, and other traits routinely marked as feminine or effeminate (173).

Works cited

Adorno, Theodor W. *Aesthetic Theory*. Trans. Robert Hullot-Kentor; edited by Gretel Adorno and Rolf Tiedemann. Continuum Books, 1997.

Ali, Kecia. *Human in Death: Morality and Mortality in J. D. Robb's Novels*. Baylor University Press, 2017.

Allan, Jonathan A. "Theorising Male Virginity in Popular Romance Novels." *Journal of Popular Romance Studies*, vol. 2, no. 1, 2011, n.p.

Amossy, Ruth. "Introduction to the Study of Doxa." *Poetics Today*, vol. 23, no. 3, Fall 2002, pp. 369–394.

Anderson, Rachel. *The Purple Heart Throbs: The Sub-literature of Love*. Hodder and Stoughton, 1974.

Baldus, Kimberly. "Gossip, Liminality, and Erotic Display: Jennifer Crusie's Links to Eighteenth-Century Amatory Fiction." *Journal of Popular Romance Studies*, vol. 2, no. 2, 2012, n.p.

Barlow, Linda and Jayne Ann Krentz. "Beneath the Surface: The Hidden Codes of Romance." *Dangerous Men and Adventurous Women: Romance Writers on the Appeal of the Romance*, edited by Jayne Ann Krentz. University of Pennsylvania Press, 1992, pp. 15–30.

Barot, Len. "Queer Romance in Twentieth- and Twenty-First-Century America: Snapshots of a Revolution." *Romance Fiction and American Culture: Love as the Practice of Freedom?*, edited by William A. Gleason and Eric Murphy Selinger. Ashgate, 2016, pp. 389–404.

Barr, Elizabeth. "'Who the devil wrote that?': Intertextuality and Authorial Reputation in Georgette Heyer's *Venetia*." *Journal of Popular Romance Studies*, vol. 3, no. 2, 2013, n.p.

Barthes, Roland. *The Rustle of Language*. Trans. Richard Howard. Hill and Wang, 1986.

Bebergal, Peter. "Wolfe's Exemplary Literary Fiction." *The Boston Globe*, June 8, 2009; http://archive.boston.com/ae/books/articles/2009/06/08/gene_wolfes_exemplary_literary_fiction/.

Bell, Kathleen. "Cross-dressing in Wartime: Georgette Heyer's The Corinthian in its 1940 Context." *War Culture: Social Change and Changing Experience in World War Two Britain*, edited by Pat Kirkham and David Thoms. Lawrence and Wishart, 1995, pp. 151–160. Reprinted in *Georgette Heyer: A Critical Retrospective*, edited by Mary Fahnestock-Thomas. Saraland AL: Prinny World Press, 2001, pp. 461–472.

Berges, Sandrine. "The Hardboiled Detective as Moralist: Ethics in Crime Fiction." *Values and Virtues: Aristotelianism in Contemporary Ethics*, edited by Timothy Chappell. Oxford University Press, 2006, pp. 212–225.

Berlatsky, Noah. "I'm a Guy Who Loves Romance Novels—and Jennifer Weiner is Right About Reviews." *Salon*, April 22, 2014.

Bettelheim, Bruno. *The Uses of Enchantment: The Meaning and Importance of Fairy Tales*. Alfred A. Knopf, 1976.

Betz, Phyllis. *Lesbian Romance Novels: A History and Critical Analysis*. McFarland, 2009.

Bialostosky, Don. "Should College English Be Close Reading?" *College English*, vol. 69, no. 2, Nov 2006, pp. 111–116.

Blake, Susan L. "What 'Race' Is the Sheik? Rereading a Desert Romance." *Doubled Plots: Romance and History*, edited by Susan Strehle and Mary Paniccia Carden. UP of Mississippi P, 2003, pp. 67–85.

Bly, Mary. "On Popular Romance, J. R. Ward, and the Limits of Genre Study." *New Approaches to Popular Romance Fiction: Critical Essays*, edited by Sarah S. G. Frantz and Eric Murphy Selinger. McFarland, 2012, pp. 60–72.

Bowman, Barbara. "Victoria Holt's Gothic Romances: A Structuralist Inquiry." *The Female Gothic*, edited by Julian E. Fleenor. Montreal: Eden, 1983, pp. 69–81.

Browning, Robert. "My Last Duchess." *Robert Browning: Selected Poems*, edited by John Woolford, Daniel Karlin and Joseph Phelan. Routledge, 2013, pp. 197–200.

Burley, Stephanie. “What’s a Nice Girl Like You Doing in a Book Like This? Homoerotic Reading and Popular Romance.” *Doubled Plots: Romance and History*, edited by Susan Strehle and Mary Paniccia Carden. Jackson, MI: UP of Mississippi P, 2003, pp. 127–146.

Byatt, A.S. “An Honourable Escape: Georgette Heyer.” *Passions of the Mind: Selected Writings*. Vintage International, 1993, pp. 233–240.

Cappella, David and Baron Wormser. *A Surge of Language: Teaching Poetry Day by Day*. Heinemann, 2004.

Cavell, Stanley. *Pursuits of Happiness: The Hollywood Comedy of Remarriage*. Cambridge, MA: Harvard University Press, 1981.

Cawelti, John G. “The Concept of Formula in the Study of Popular Literature.” *The Journal of Popular Culture*, vol. 3, no. 3, Winter 1969, pp. 381–390.

———. “Notes Toward an Aesthetic of Popular Culture.” *The Journal of Popular Culture*, vol. 5, no. 2, Fall 1971, pp. 255–268.

———. *Adventure, Mystery, and Romance: Formula Stories as Art and Popular Culture*. Chicago: University of Chicago Press, 1976.

———. “Masculine Myths and Feminist Revisions: Some Thoughts on the Future of Popular Genres.” *Eye on the Future: Popular Culture Scholarship into the Twenty-First Century in Honor of Ray B. Browne*, edited by F. Motz Marilyn, John G. Nachbar, Michael T. Marsden and Ronald J. Ambrosetti. Bowling Green, OH: Bowling Green State University Press, 1994, pp. 121–132.

Chakravaty, Sumita. “Teaching Indian Cinema.” *Cinema Journal*, vol. 47, no. 1, 2007, pp. 105–108.

Chung, June Hee. “Henry James’s ‘The Velvet Glove’ and the Iron Fist: Transatlantic Cultural Exchange and the Romance Tradition.” *Romance Fiction and American Culture: Love as the Practice of Freedom?*, edited by William A. Gleason and Eric Murphy Selinger. Ashgate, 2016, pp. 225–240.

Crane, Ralph and Lisa Fletcher. *Island Genres, Genre Islands: Conceptualisation and Representation in Popular Fiction*. London: Rowman & Littlefield, 2017.

Crusie, Jennifer. “This is Not Your Mother’s Cinderella: The Romance Novel as Feminist Fairy Tale.” *Romantic Conventions*, edited by Anne Kaler and Rosemary Johnson-Kurek. Bowling Green, OH: Bowling Green State University Press, 1998a, pp. 51–61.

———. “So, Bill, I Hear You Write Those Little Poems: A Plea for Category Romance.” *Romance Writer’s Report*, vol. 18, no. 5, May 1998b, pp. 42–44. Reprinted on Crusie’s website, https://jennycrusie.com/non-fiction/so-bill-i-hear-you-write-those-little-poems-a-plea-for-category-romance/

Curthoys, Ann and John Docker. ““Popular Romance in the Postmodern Age. And an Unknown Australian Author”.” *Continuum*, vol. 4, no. 1, 1990, 22–36.

Dandridge, Rita. “The Race, Gender, Romance Connection: A Black Feminist Reading of African American Women’s Historical Romances.” *Doubled Plots: Romance and History*, edited by Susan Strehle and Mary Paniccia Carden. Jackson, MI: University press of Mississippi, 2003, pp. 185–202.

Delaney, Samuel. “Sword & Sorcery, S/ M, and the Economics of Inadequation: The *Camera Obscura* Interview.” *Silent Interviews: On Language, Race, Sex, Science Fiction, and Some Comics*. Hanover, NH: Wesleyan University Press, 1994, pp. 127–163.

Derrida, Jacques. ““The Law of Genre.”.” Trans. Avital Ronell. *Critical Inquiry*, vol. 7, no. 1, Autumn 1980, pp. 55–81.

Dixon, jay. *The Romance Fiction of Mills & Boon, 1909–1990s*. University College London Press, 1999.

Driscoll, Beth. “Genre, Author, Text, Reader: Teaching Nora Roberts’s *Spellbound*.” *Journal of Popular Romance Studies*, vol. 4, no. 2, 2014, n.p.

Dugger, Julie M. ““I’m a Feminist, But . . .” Popular Romance in the Women’s Literature Classroom.” *Journal of Popular Romance Studies*, vol. 4, no. 2, 2014, n.p..

Eagleton, Terry. *Literary Theory: An Introduction*. Anniversary Edition. Minneapolis: University of Minnesota Press, 2008.

Elliott, Jack. "Patterns and Trends in Harlequin Category Romance." *Advancing Digital Humanities: Research, Methods, Theories*, edited by Katherine Bode and Paul Longley Arthur. London: Palgrave Macmillan, 2014a, pp. 54–67 .

———. ""Vocabulary Decay in Category Romance." *Digital Scholarship in the Humanities*, Online, December 2014b.

———. "Whole Genre Sequencing." *Digital Scholarship in the Humanities*, Online, August 2015.

Felski, Rita. *The Gender of Modernity*. Cambridge, MA: Harvard University Press, 1995.

———. *Uses of Literature*. Malden, MA and Oxford: Blackwell, 2008.

Fish, Stanley. *Is There a Text in This Class? The Authority of Interpretive Communities*. Cambridge, MA and London: Harvard UP, 1980.

Fletcher, Lisa. "'Mere Costumery'? Georgette Heyer's Cross-Dressing Novels." *Masquerades: Disguise in English Literature from the Middle Ages to the Present*, edited by Pilar Sánchez Calle and Jesús López-Paláez Casellas. Gdansk: University of Gdansk Press, 2004, pp. 196–212.

———. *Historical Romance Fiction: Heterosexuality and Performativity*. Aldershot, U.K.: Ashgate, 2008.

Fletcher, Lisa, Beth Driscoll and Kim Wilkins. "Genre Worlds and Popular Fiction: The Case of Twenty-First-Century Australian Romance." *Journal of Popular Culture*, Online First July 16, 2018.

Fletcher, Lisa, Rosemary Gaby and Jennifer Kloester. "Pedagogy Report: Embedding Popular Romance Studies in Undergraduate English Units: Teaching Georgette Heyer's *Sylvester*." *Journal of Popular Romance Studies*, vol. 1, no. 2, 2011, n.p.

Frantz, Sarah S. G. ""Darcy's Vampiric Descendants: Austen's Perfect Romance Hero and J. R. Ward's Black Dagger Brotherhood."." *Persuasions On-line*, vol. 30, no. 1, 2009, n.p.

Frantz, Sarah S. G. and Eric Murphy Selinger, editors. *New Approaches to Popular Romance Fiction: Critical Essays*. McFarland, 2012.

Freedman, Carl. *Critical Theory and Science Fiction*. Middletown, CT: Wesleyan University Press, 2000.

Freeman, Sarah. "100 Years of Romancing the Readers." *Yorkshire Post*, January 1, 2008.

Frost, Laura. "The Romance of Cliché: E. M. Hull, D. H. Lawrence, and Interwar Erotic Fiction." *Bad Modernisms*, edited by Douglas Mao and Rebecca Walkowitz. Durham: Duke University Press, 2006, pp. 443–473.

———. *The Problem with Pleasure: Modernism and Its Discontents*. New York: Columbia University Press, 2013.

Frye, Northrop. *Anatomy of Criticism: Four Essays*. Princeton, NJ: Princeton University Press, 1957.

Geest, Dirk de and An Goris. "Constrained Writing, Creative Writing: The Case of Handbooks for Writing Romances." *Poetics Today*, vol. 31, no. 1, 2010, pp. 81–106.

Gelder, Ken. *Popular Fiction: The Logics and Practices of a Literary Field*. Abingdon, Oxon: Routledge, 2004.

Gevers, Nick. "Could a Former Engineer Who Helped Invent Pringles Be Our Greatest Living Writer?" *Washington Post*, April 7, 2002.

Gillis, Stacy. "The Cross-Dresser, the Thief, His Daughter and Her Lover: Queer Desire and Romance in Georgette Heyer's *These Old Shades*." *Women: A Cultural Review*, vol. 26, no. 1–2, 2015, pp. 57–74.

———. "Manners, Money, and Marriage: Austen, Heyer, and the Literary Genealogy of the Regency Romance." *After Austen: Reinventions, Rewritings, Revisitings*, edited by Lisa Hopkins. Palgrave Macmillan, 2018, pp. 81–101.

Goris, An. "Matricide in Romance Scholarship? Response to Pamela Regis' Keynote Address at the Second Annual Conference of the International Association for the Study of Popular Romance." *Journal of Popular Romance Studies*, vol. 2, no. 1, 2011, n.p.

———. "Loving by the Book: Voice and Romance Authorship." *New Approaches to Popular Romance Fiction. Critical Essays*, edited by Sarah S. G. Frantz and Eric Murphy Selinger. McFarland, 2012a, pp. 73–83.

———. "Mind, Body, Love: Nora Roberts and the Evolution of Popular Romance Studies." *Journal of Popular Romance Studies*, vol. 3, no. 1, 2012b, n.p.

———. "Happily Ever After. And After: Serialization and the Popular Romance Novel." *Americana: The Journal of American Popular Culture (1900–present)*, vol. 12, no. 1, 2013, n.p.

Guillory, John. *Cultural Capital: The Problem of Literary Canon Formation*. University of Chicago Press, 1993.

Heiss, Karin. "14 Weeks of Love and Labour: Teaching Regency and Desert Romance to Undergraduate Students." *Journal of Popular Romance Studies*, vol. 5, no. 1, 2015, n.p.

Hinnant, Charles H. "Desire and the Marketplace: A Reading of Kathleen Woodiwiss's *The Flame and the Flower*." *Doubled Plots: Romance and History*, edited by Susan Strehle and Mary Paniccia Carden. UP of Mississippi, 2003, pp. 147–164.

Hipsky, Martin. *Modernism and the Women's Popular Romance in Britain, 1885–1925*. Ohio University Press, 2011.

Huguley, Piper. "A Sweet Way to Freedom." *The Brightest Day: A Juneteenth Historical Romance Anthology*. CreateSpace Independent Publishing, 2015, pp. 153–230.

Hunter, Madeline. "Romance Unlaced: Beyond Britain's Shores." *USA Today*, September 24, 2014.

Huyssen, Andreas. *After the Great Divide: Modernism, Mass Culture, Postmodernism*. Indiana University Press, 1986.

Kamblé, Jayashree. *Making Meaning in Popular Romance Fiction: An Epistemology*. Palgrave Macmillan, 2014.

———. "What's Love got to do with it? In Romance Novels, Everything!" *Oklahoma Humanities Council Magazine*, Winter 2015, pp. 20–23.

———. "Branding a Genre: A Brief Transatlantic History of Romance Novel Cover Art." *Romance Fiction and American Culture: Love as the Practice of Freedom?*, edited by William A. Gleason and Eric Murphy Selinger. Ashgate, 2016, pp. 241–272.

Kramer, Kyra. "Getting Laid, Getting Old, and Getting Fed: The Cultural Resistance of Jennifer Crusie's Romance Heroines." *Journal of Popular Romance Studies*, vol. 2, no. 2, 2012, n.p.

Kroeg, Susan M. "'Truly Our Contemporary Jane Austen': Thinking Like an Austen Fan about Regency Romances." *Kentucky Philological Review*, vol. 27, 2012, pp. 50–58.

Leavis, Q. D. *Fiction and the Reading Public*. 1932. Reprint, Chatto and Windus, 1939.

Lee, Linda J. "Guilty Pleasures: Reading Romance Novels as Reworked Fairy Tales." *Marvels & Tales*, vol. 22, no. 1, 2008, pp. 52–66.

Library of America. "Overview." www.loa.org/about

Lutz, Deborah. *The Dangerous Lover: Gothic Villains, Byronism, and the Nineteenth-Century Seduction Narrative*. Ohio State University Press, 2006.

Lyons, Sarah Frantz and Eric Murphy Selinger. "Strange Stirrings, Strange Yearnings: *The Flame and the Flower, Sweet Savage Love*, and the Lost Diversities of Blockbuster Historical Romance." *Romance Fiction and American Culture: Love as the Practice of Freedom?*, edited by William A. Gleason and Eric Murphy Selinger. Ashgate, 2016, pp. 89–110.

MacDonald, Kate. "*For Love and Money* [review]." *Vulpes Libris*, April 9, 2013. https://vulpeslibris.wordpress.com/2013/04/09/for-love-and-money/

Matelski, Elizabeth. "'I'm Not the Only Lesbian Who Wears a Skirt': Lesbian Romance Fiction and Identity in Post-World War II America." *Romance Fiction and American Culture: Love as the Practice of Freedom?*, edited by William A. Gleason and Eric Murphy Selinger. Ashgate, 2016, pp. 71–88.

McAlister, Jodi. "Boom Goes The Canon: Romance, the Canon Problem, and Iconic Works." *Momentum Moonlight*, April 30, 2014. https://web.archive.org/web/20160316230747/http://momentummoonlight.com/blog/boom-goes-the-canon/

McGurl, Mark. *The Novel Art: Elevations of American Fiction after Henry James*. Princeton University Press, 2001.

Modleski, Tania. *Loving with a Vengeance: Mass-Produced Fantasies for Women*. 1982. Reprint, Routledge, 1988.

———. "My Life as a Romance Reader." *Paradoxa: Studies in World Literary Genres*, vol. 3, 1–2, 1997, pp. 15–28. Reprinted in *Old Wives' Tales and Other Women's Stories*. NYU Press, 1998, pp. 47–65.

Moody-Freeman, Julie E. "Scripting Black Love in the 1990s: Pleasure, Respectability, and Responsibility in an Era of HIV/AIDS." *Romance Fiction and American Culture: Love as the Practice of Freedom?*, edited by William A. Gleason and Eric Murphy Selinger. Ashgate, 2016, pp. 111–127.

Moore, Kate and Eric Murphy Selinger. "The Heroine as Reader, the Reader as Heroine: Jennifer Crusie's *Welcome to Temptation*." *Journal of Popular Romance Studies*, vol. 2, no. 2, 2012, n.p.

Ngai, Sianne. *Our Aesthetic Categories: Zany, Cute, Interesting*. Harvard University Press, 2015.

Osborne, Laurie. "Sweet, Savage Shakespeare." *Shakespeare without Class: Misappropriations of Cultural Capital*, edited by Donald Hedrick and Bryan Reynolds. Palgrave, 2000, pp. 135–151.

———. "Romancing the Bard." *Shakespeare and Appropriation*, edited by Christy Desmet and Robert Sawyer. Routledge, 1999, pp. 47–64.

———. "Harlequin Presents: That '70s Shakespeare and Beyond." *Shakespeare after Mass Media*, edited by Richard Burt. Palgrave, 2002, pp. 127–149.

Ouyang, Huining. "Behind the Mask of Coquetry: The Trickster Narrative in *Miss Numè of Japan: A Japanese-American Romance*." *Doubled Plots: Romance and History*, edited by Susan Strehle and Mary Paniccia Carden. J. University Press of Mississippi, 2003, pp. 86–106.

Paizis, George. *Love and the Novel: The Poetics and Politics of Romantic Fiction*. Macmillan, 1998.

Pearce, Lynne. "Popular Romance and Its Readers." *A Companion to Romance: From Classical to Contemporary*, edited by Corinne Saunders. Blackwell, 2004, pp. 521–538.

———. "Romance and Repetition: Testing the Limits of Love." *Journal of Popular Romance Studies*, vol. 2, no. 1, 2011, n.p.

Phillips, Susan Elizabeth. *Natural Born Charmer*. Avon Books, 2007.

Polan, Dana. "Brief Encounters: Mass Culture and the Evacuation of Sense." *Studies in Entertainment: Critical Approaches to Mass Culture*, edited by Tania Modleski. Bloomington, In Indiana University Press, 1986, pp. 167–187.

Radway, Janice. *Reading the Romance: Women, Patriarchy, and Popular Literature*. 1984. Reprint with a new Introduction Chapel Hill: University of North Carolina Press, 1991.

Regis, Pamela. *A Natural History of the Romance Novel*. University of Pennsylvania Press, 2003.

———. "What Do Critics Owe the Romance? Keynote Address at the Second Annual Conference of the International Association for the Study of Popular Romance." *Journal of Popular Romance Studies*, vol. 2, no. 1, 2011, n.p.

Roach, Catherine M. *Happily Ever After: The Romance Story in Popular Culture*. Indiana University Press, 2016.

Roberts, Thomas J. *An Aesthetics of Junk Fiction*. University of Georgia Press, 1990.

Rushdie, Salman. *Imaginary Homelands: Essays and Criticism 1981–1991*. Granta Books, 1991.

Saler, Michael. *As If: Modern Enchantment and the Literary Prehistory of Virtual Reality*. Oxford University Press, 2012.

Scroggins, Mark. *Michael Moorcock: Fiction, Fantasy and the World's Pain*. McFarland, 2016.

Seidel, Katherine Giles. "Judge Me By the Joy I Bring." *Dangerous Men and Adventurous Women: Romance Writers on the Appeal of the Romance*, edited by Jayne Ann Krentz. University of Pennsylvania Press, 1992. Reprint, New York: HarperPaperbacks, 1996, pp. 199–226.

Selinger, Eric Murphy. "How to Read a Romance Novel (and Fall in Love with Popular Romance)." *New Approaches to Popular Romance Fiction: Critical Essays*, edited by Sarah S. G. Frantz and Eric Murphy Selinger. McFarland, 2012a, pp. 33–46.

———. "Nothing But Good Times Ahead: A Special Forum on Jennifer Crusie (Editor's Introduction)."." *Journal of Popular Romance Studies*, vol. 2, no. 2, 2012b, n.p.

———. "Teaching with *For Love and Money*." *Teach Me Tonight*. January 22, 2012c. http://teachmetonight.blogspot.com/2012/01/teaching-with-for-love-and-money.html

———. "Teaching with *For Love and Money*, part 2." *Teach Me Tonight*. January 27, 2012d. http://teachmetonight.blogspot.com/2012/01/teaching-with-for-love-and-money-part-2.html

———. ""When I Paint My Masterpiece: Bob Dylan, Ekphrasis, and the Art of Susan Elizabeth Phillips's *Natural Born Charmer*."." *Romance Fiction and American Culture: Love as the Practice of Freedom?*, edited by William A. Gleason and Eric Murphy Selinger. Ashgate, 2016, pp. 297–319.

———. "Use Heart in Your (Re)Search." Presentation at "Researching the Romance." Bowling Green State University, April 13, 2018. https://scholarworks.bgsu.edu/cgi/viewcontent.cgi?article=1012&context=researchingromance

Selinger, Eric Murphy and Sarah S. G. Frantz. "Introduction: New Approaches to Popular Romance Fiction." *New Approaches to Popular Romance Fiction: Critical Essays*, edited by Sarah S. G. Frantz and Eric Murphy Selinger. McFarland, 2012, pp. 1–19.

Shakespeare, William. *Twelfth Night: Or What You Will*. Edited by Barbara Mowat and Paul Werstine. Folger Shakespeare Library, 1993.

Silliman, Ron. *Silliman's Blog: A Weblog Focused on Contemporary Poetry and Poetics*. http://ronsilliman.blogspot.com/2003/06/so-what-do-poets-from-school-of.html

Snitow, Ann. "Mass Market Romance: Pornography for Women Is Different." *Radical History Review*, vol. 20, Spring/Summer, 1979, pp. 141–161. Republished in *Women and Romance: A Reader*. Edited by Susan Ostrov Weisser. NYU Press, 2001, pp. 307–322.

Sternberg, Robert. *Love is a Story: A New Theory of Relationships*. Oxford University Press, 1998.

Sturgeon, Theodore. "On Hand: A Book." *Venture: Science Fiction Magazine*, vol. 49, September 1957.

Suvin, Darko. *Metamorphoses of Science Fiction: On the Poetics and History of a Literary Genre*. Yale University Press, 1979.

Teo, Hsu-Ming. "'Bertrice teaches you about history, and you don't even mind!': History and Revisionist Historiography in Bertrice Small's *The Kadin*." *New Approaches to Popular Romance Fiction: Critical Essays*, edited by Sarah S. G. Frantz and Eric Murphy Selinger. McFarland, 2012, pp. 21–32.

Thomas, Sherry. *My Beautiful Enemy*. Berkley Sensation, 2014.

Toscano, Angela. "A Parody of Love: The Narrative Uses of Rape in Popular Romance." *Journal of Popular Romance Studies*, vol. 2, no. 2, 2012, n.p.

Trilling, Lionel. "The Fate of Pleasure." *The Moral Obligation to Be Intelligent: Selected Essays by Lionel Trilling*. Edited and with an Introduction by Leon Wieseltier. Farrar Straus and Giroux, 2000, pp. 427–449.

Tyler, Natalie. "Jennifer Crusie on Jane Austen as the Mother of the Modern Romance Novel." *The Friendly Jane Austen: A Well-Mannered Introduction to a Lady of Sense & Sensibility*. Viking, 1999, pp. 240–242.

Valeo, Christina A. "Crusie and the Con." *Journal of Popular Romance Studies*, vol. 2, no. 2, 2012, n.p.

Vendler, Helen. *The Music of What Happens: Poems, Poets, Critics*. Cambridge and London: Harvard University Press, 1988.

Vivanco, Laura. *For Love and Money: The Literary Art of the Harlequin Mills & Boon Romance*. Tirril, Penrith: Humanities-Ebooks, 2011.

———. "Jennifer Crusie's Literary Lingerie." *Journal of Popular Romance Studies*, vol. 2, no. 2, 2012, n.p.

———. "Georgette Heyer: The Nonesuch of Regency Romance." *Journal of Popular Romance Studies*, vol. 3, no. 2, 2013, n.p.

Warhol, Robyn R. *Having a Good Cry: Effeminate Feelings and Pop-Culture Forms*. Ohio State University Press, 2003.

Weisser, Susan Ostrov. *The Glass Slipper: Women and Love Stories*. Rutgers University Press, 2013.

Westman, Karin E. "A Story of Her Weaving: The Self-Authoring Heroines of Georgette Heyer's Regency Romance." *Doubled Plots: Romance and History*, edited by Susan Strehle and Mary Paniccia Carden. University Press of Mississippi, 2003, pp. 165–184.

Whyte, Tamara. "'A consummation devoutly to be wished': Shakespeare in Popular Historical Romance Fiction." *New Approaches to Popular Romance Fiction: Critical Essays*, edited by Sarah S. G. Frantz and Eric Murphy Selinger. McFarland, 2012, pp. 218–228.

Williams, William Carlos. "Author's Introduction." *The Collected Poems of William Carlos Williams, Volume II: 1939–1962*. edited by MacGowan. Christopher. New Directions, 1988, pp. 53–55.

Wolfe, Gene. *The Best of Gene Wolfe: A Definitive Retrospective of His Finest Short Fiction*. Tor, 2009.

Young, Erin S. "Saving China: The Transformative Power of Whiteness in Elizabeth Lowell's *Jade Island* and Katherine Stone's *Pearl Moon*." *Romance Fiction and American Culture: Love as the Practice of Freedom?*, edited by William A. Gleason and Eric Murphy Selinger. Ashgate, 2016, pp. 205–221.

Zakreski, Patricia. "Tell Me Lies: Lying, Storytelling, and the Romance Novel as Feminist Fiction." *Journal of Popular Romance Studies*, vol. 2, no. 2, 2012, n.p.

14 Author studies and popular romance fiction

Kecia Ali

This chapter attempts to answer five questions. First, what is an author study? Second, why are there so few author studies for popular romance fiction? Third, what literature currently exists? Fourth, what are promising avenues for future research? Fifth, how might considering popular romance fiction help reimagine the field of author studies?

Defining author studies

An author study is a bibliographic assembly and critical interpretation that puts forth an account, ideally comprehensive, of an author's contributions. Unlike approaches focused on a genre, theme, individual work, or group of works, author studies focus on specific writers and their oeuvres. Author studies often proceed chronologically, identifying themes, concerns, and shifts in genre over the course of a career. Such, at least, is the traditional notion of an author study, which assumes that an author is a significant figure to be taken seriously as an artist or thinker; such works may deal more or less extensively with an author's biography as a relevant element in interpreting their work. In the latter half of the twentieth century, theorists including Michel Foucault and Roland Barthes pushed back against this approach, emphasizing collective elements of texts' production and reception (the "author function") over the individual genius of their authorship. Studies which focus on the author function explicitly reject "the (Romantic) conceptualization of the author as the creative genius who is both the origin and the master of the meanings of and in the text." (Goris "From Romance to Roberts" 3)

For popular romance, author studies raise a number of questions about the association of a named author with a given body of work. If an oeuvre is "a group of texts that via a shared author's name are attributed to one and the same author" (Goris "From Romance to Roberts" 5), how does one grapple with pseudonymous work?

Pseudonyms are common in romance, as in all genres of popular fiction. Some romance writers use more than one pen-name simultaneously or over the course of a career. Nora Roberts (itself a pseudonym) has published well over 200 books since 1981, more than a fifth of them as J.D. Robb. Jayne Ann Krentz currently publishes under three names, each associated with a specific subgenre; she has used four others since she published the first of her 181 (as of early 2019) historical and contemporary novels in 1979. Susan Macias published several books under that name in the 1990s, followed by a baker's dozen as Susan Macias Redmond; she has since published scores of category novels and series bestsellers as Susan Mallery. Should the works under different names be studied as separate oeuvres?

Pseudonyms also lend themselves to other arrangements. Some collaborators share a pseudonym. Kit Rocha's post-apocalyptic dystopian oeuvre is co-written by Donna Herren and Bree Bridges; the pair has also published together under other pseudonyms and each has published individual works under their own name. Other arrangements may characterize husband-and-wife writing teams, of which the Romance Wiki—a collaborative online venture gathering information about the genre—lists more than 20. Of the scores of romances published under the name Emma Darcy, the first decade's worth were jointly written by Frank and Wendy Brennan; after Frank's death, Wendy wrote the remainder alone. (I am unaware of romance novelists whose work is produced by different authors under the same pseudonym, as was the case with the Nancy Drew children's books by "Carolyn Keene" and the Hardy Boys series by "Franklin W. Dixon.")

How one approaches a co-authored oeuvre under a single author name, or a body of work by one individual writing under multiple names, will depend on what elements one seeks to emphasize. An investigation focused on biography, linking individual experience and sensibilities to an oeuvre, will necessarily focus on the person or people "behind" the name(s). The introductory essay to the *Journal of Popular Romance Studies* special forum (Selinger "Nothing but Good Times Ahead") on Jennifer Crusie takes this tack, moving back and forth between the author and her works. To the extent one is interested in the author function the focus will be on the named author and the ways in which they are presented and received rather than on understanding the individual(s) behind the name; biography will be correspondingly less central. (Similar distinctions in approach apply even to authors who publish under their own names.)

Nora Roberts/J. D. Robb provides a good case for exploring these questions of authorship. She is the contemporary romance author about whom the most scholarship exists, although to date there has been no book-length traditional author study for Roberts. An Goris' doctoral dissertation ("From Romance to Roberts") explores how authorship functions in Roberts' oeuvre. My monograph *Human in Death: Morality and Mortality in J.D. Robb's Novels* explores the futuristic romantic suspense *In Death* series—an oeuvre study for Robb. As of this writing, roughly a dozen articles and book chapters focus on Roberts' and/or Robb's work. Regis ("Complicating Romances") discusses the "barrier" and "point of ritual death" in nine of Roberts' category novels to make the case that romances are not interchangeable. In her chapter on Roberts in her longer survey of romance, Regis addresses her skillful management of tone, emphasizing the role of "wills and wit" in courtship (*Natural History* 204). John Lennard writes about Robb and Roberts and their respective genre constraints. Christina Valeo divides Roberts' work usefully into three types: everyday, mystical, and magical, focusing on Roberts' use of magic ("Power of Three"). Goris explores Roberts's depiction of the relationship between mind and body ("Mind, Body, Love") and analyzes how serialization functions in Roberts' and J. R. Ward's novels ("Happily Ever After ... and After"). Beth Driscoll writes about teaching one of Roberts' novellas in a course on genre fiction. Jayashree Kamblé (*Making Meaning*) uses a Roberts novel to discuss book-to-television movie adaptation and uses *In Death's* billionaire protagonist Roarke to explore the seductions and seedy underbelly of consumer capitalism; she also explores Robb's approach to New York ("From

Barbarized to Disneyfied") in the series' first installment. Laura Vivanco (*Pursuing Happiness*) echoes that focus on place, comparing one of Roberts' series to that of another writer in their treatment of ideal community in one chapter. Ralph Crane and Lisa Fletcher devote one chapter in their book on islands in genre fiction to an exploration of Roberts' Three Sisters Island trilogy. Outside the field of popular romance studies, Putri Mayangsari and Ratna Asmarani psychoanalyze the villains in one *In Death* novel. Most recently, Jarlath Killeen gives an overview of Roberts in the context of popular romance, with brief explorations of three post-2000 novels. In addition to these focused works, a variety of scholars devote a few pages in passing to one or another of her novels. Yet the sum total of pages published about Roberts/Robb to date, including a book-length overview written for a lay audience (Snodgrass) and the sizeable, non-scholarly *Official Nora Roberts Companion* (Little and Hayden), barely equals a single year's worth of her formidable output.

Between 1981, when her first category romance was published, and early 2019, Roberts has published over 180 novels and novellas under that name. Starting in 1995, she has published another 48 novels plus a dozen novellas in Robb's police procedural series. At first there was no acknowledgment of the connection. Then, for a while, the *In Death* covers read "Nora Roberts writing as J. D. Robb." More recent covers acknowledge that Robb is a pseudonym but do not name Roberts.

Some works have addressed Robb and Roberts' work together. Lennard's "Of Pseudonyms and Sentiment: Nora Roberts, J.D. Robb, and the Imperative Mood" posits that writing as Robb liberated Roberts from the romance genre's expectations of objectified, passive women. (Though Lennard notes cultural disdain for genre fiction generally, he nonetheless denigrates romance in comparison to less feminized genres.) Like the *Official Nora Roberts Companion*, which includes entries for each of the Roberts and Robb novels published as of its appearance, Mary Ellen Snodgrass's *Reading Nora Roberts*, which aims to orient the lay reader to Roberts' oeuvre, treats the Roberts and Robb novels as part of the same corpus, though it devotes only one chapter to the *In Death* books. It offers useful information and suggestive analyses of various novels but is uneven in her treatment of the works. Her palpable disdain for much popular romance and the lack of engagement with extant scholarship in the field hamper this book's utility for scholars, since she fails to situate Roberts within a broader survey of the genre or in relation to her peers. (Goris ("Review") calls the book "ultimately disappointing" with an "apparently haphazard approach to Roberts' oeuvre").

Taking a different tack, Goris ("From Romance to Roberts") explores the "author function" in Roberts' oeuvre. She attends to works authored by Robb only insofar as the books and the publicity surrounding them invoke Roberts' authorship ("Nora Roberts writing as J.D. Robb"). What interests Goris is not the biographical study of Roberts as author but rather the "the literary concept 'author,'" which is "never completely separate from the person of the author" but also never "fully coincide[s] with this person." Thus, she attends to the ways in which the two personas coincide and diverge in the novels' paratexts and in publisher publicity campaigns. According to Goris, while "Roberts' authorial identity is strongly developed over the course of the last thirty years," and for romance readers "her name has developed into a commercially powerful brand name in its own right" outside of this context, "she is predominantly known as a popular romance author. To that extent the generic and authorial identity merge."[1]

In *Making Meaning in Popular Romance Fiction*, Kamblé treats both Roberts and Robb novels in her study which analyzes shifting representations of the romance hero to understand how romance novels make meaning and negotiate social change; she does not explicitly compare the two oeuvres or focus on authorial decisions. The other analyses mentioned above treat either a subset of the Roberts novels *or* a subset of the *In Death* novels.

My monograph *Human in Death* is a study of Robb's work. I refer to the author as Robb. I mention Roberts only in passing, making brief introductory biographical remarks and occasional comparisons to the novels published under that name. Because Robb's oeuvre is coextensive with the *In Death* series one might consider it less an author study than a study of that series. However, as I address *Human in Death*'s implicit ethical ideas and world-building, I attribute to Robb a set of coherent concerns—treating her as an author with "ideas" (to use Regis' ("Complicating Romances") formulation).

With the possible exception of Georgette Heyer, discussed further below, Roberts is the best-studied popular romance author. Nonetheless, the relative paucity of scholarship on her oeuvre is remarkable, given the hundreds of millions of books she has sold over the course of her career. This lack raises the question of why there are so few author studies in romance.

Why are author studies so rare for popular romance?

In 1997, Pamela Regis pointed out that studies of single authors were "standard critical practice" in literary studies generally but atypical—indeed, practically nonexistent—for popular romance. Despite the fact that conference papers, journal articles, and anthology contributions often "address the work of one or more particular romance author(s)," there are "few, if any, sustained and comprehensive studies of the entire oeuvre of a contemporary popular romance author" ("Complicating Romances"; qtd. in Goris "From Romance" 18) For Goris, this "apparent scholarly reluctance to focus on oeuvre and author studies" (18) "ignores and even obscures the increasing prominence of the individual author in the romance genre itself" (19) since the 1980s. That is to say, at least in the United States, romances have increasingly been marketed as single-title works by author name rather than in category lines. Yet despite the burgeoning of popular romance studies broadly, and the increased relevance of named authors for the romance industry, author studies remain scarce. Why?

The increased importance of named authors in popular romance marketing and reader reception runs counter to dominant trends in literary criticism, in which author studies comprise a smaller proportion of scholarly work. Moreover, in fields such as English there is deep skepticism about the literary status of popular romance. To the extent that scholars of literature do author studies, they focus on respected writers. For example, Routledge maintains an ongoing series entitled *Studies in Major Literary Authors*. The series emphasizes the importance of its chosen subjects who must be not only recognizably literary but also "major" figures. To the extent that authors of popular fiction attract critical interest, they tend to write in male-identified genres such as detective fiction and, to a lesser extent, speculative fiction. Still, author studies remain relatively uncommon for any popular fiction. (Interestingly, prominent search engine results for "author study" and "author studies" relate to classroom use in lower grades; books with author studies in the title are similarly aimed at elementary and middle grade students.)

In contrast to English and Literary Studies, where authors matter but popular romance does not, in fields such as Cultural Studies, Media Studies, or Women's and Gender Studies, where popular romance is a legitimate object of study, a focus on an individual (genius) author is suspect. Instead of author studies, scholars in these fields have tended to produce accounts of the reception of works or the novels' treatment of certain socially relevant patterns and themes (see Chris).

In many people's estimation, the romance author doesn't really exist. Popular romances are books but not literature; they have writers (considered laborers, even hacks), not authors (understood as creative, literary, and unique) (Lois and Gregson). Despite substantial evidence to the contrary, romance novels tend to be perceived, except by their loyal readers and scholars who study them, as a formulaic, interchangeable product: "one of the things that literature is, apparently, not" (Goris, "From Romance to Roberts" 1). Romance authors appear as homogeneous groups of more or less talented women (usually) but not as creators, artists, or thinkers. A negative feedback loop reinforces the situation. Because of romance's reputation as unauthored, scholars never produce the studies to explore and establish romance writers' significance. Scholars assume, probably correctly, that they will not earn tenure in an English department with a monograph on Barbara Cartland or Beverly Jenkins. Later career scholars, who have more flexibility to choose their projects, have also largely left romance to the side—and those who have worked on romance have typically worked on specific novels or specific themes.

A small cadre of romance scholars has worked to alter these perceptions of romance as simplistic. They have attended to the genre's constitutive elements. Regis (*Natural History*) has formulated a widely adopted definition of eight essential elements of the romance novel and explored them through a handful of author-centered chapters (see below). Other scholars have supplemented Regis's definition (see Roach 21–7) or investigated particular elements of it (Allan). In doing so, they have refuted the notion that romance works are fungible (e.g., Regis "Complicating Romances"). Early scholarship on romance often asked big questions and drew broad conclusions from small, haphazardly chosen samples. More recent scholarship has focused on work selected by publisher/category (e.g., Burge, Holden, Jarmakani ("The Sheik" and *Imperialist Love Story*), Teo, and others on the sheikh novel) or by a thematic element (Kamblé (*Making Meaning*) on the hero; Vivanco (*Pursuing Happiness*) on work). These studies reveal far more variation and nuance than the first generation of studies. Few, however, use the author as the unit of organization.

In addition to being dissuaded by questions of prestige or significance, logistical difficulties confront scholars who would undertake author studies: the ephemeral nature of popular romance publications and the sizeable nature of many authors' corpora.

First, preservation and access. Popular romances are often ephemeral. Few libraries collect them. Bowling Green State University's Popular Culture Library is one exception; it collects category lines as well as individual titles. The Nora Roberts American Romance Collection at McDaniel College's Hoover Library is also substantial, though less comprehensive. In addition to Nora Roberts/J. D. Robb's entire oeuvre, it has most or all of the publications through 2015 for a group of 19 authors deemed "important" (all are white). As it seeks to expand and diversify its collection while respecting budgetary and space constraints, the library has also begun collecting books that have won the Romance Writers of America's RITA awards in most categories along with three significant books from each Lifetime Achievement Award winner.[2] (These winners are also disproportionately white; see below.) Books that have not won awards or become bestsellers are likely to prove difficult to find. Category romances are seldom reprinted unless their authors prove, like Roberts, extremely popular. Although electronic books have made some more recent publications more widely accessible, access to mid and even late twentieth-century romances remains a challenge. The disparity in accessibility of work by authors of color is magnified as disproportionately more have self-published, owing in part to discrimination by major publishing houses. Fewer libraries, including local public libraries, acquire self-published books. And regardless of the prominence of the author, for those who wish to study paratextual elements of an author's oeuvre, e-books are unsatisfactory and reprints and omnibus editions reveal much about later contexts but not necessarily about the original publication.

The sheer prolificness of some popular romance authors poses another obstacle to studies of their oeuvres. It is not unusual for popular authors to have published dozens or scores of novels. Few write as much as Roberts or Krentz, who, respectively, exceed and approach 200 novels, though Brenda Jackson (see below), who has published over 130 stand-alone and connected novels, including in category series, comes close. No one matches Cartland, who published 723 novels over the course of a nearly eight-decade career (Harris). Still, the corpus of Roberta Gellis (1927–2016), LaVyrle Spencer, or Nalini Singh—to give only a few examples—is enough to give anyone pause.

Roberts presents a good illustration of the things that facilitate or impede an author study. Volume is an obstacle: her oeuvre runs to tens of thousands of pages. On the other hand, because of her prominence and popularity, few other logistical difficulties confront scholars who wish to explore the content of her work. Her website provides a chronologically ordered list of original publications. With the exception of the never-republished *Promise Me Tomorrow* (1984), all of Roberts' work, including her 100 category novels, remains in print or easily available secondhand. McDaniel College's library has a complete collection of her works, which circulate. Moreover, many of her books are in public library collections—in the case of her category novels, often in reprints or as e-books. These are all adequate for a study of the content of her novels. However, to study how her work has been marketed, as Goris does ("From Roberts to Romance"), is a complex task. Her books have been re-released many times, with different covers, in varying combinations, in numerous, variously titled omnibus editions.

Extant scholarship

Studies of individual novels, particular subgenres or themes, and specific category lines or publishers form part of a larger shift in popular romance studies away from large-scale claims to more focused investigations. In part, this shift is a reaction to foundational works that made large claims about the genre on the basis of limited samples (e.g., Modleski, Radway). However, relatively little of this work—for the reasons laid out in the previous section—focuses on individual authors. This section outlines what scholarship does exist, in addition to that on Roberts/Robb already discussed.

A few surveys provide information on individual authors. In addition to scattered entries for romance authors in works such as *Contemporary Authors* or the *Dictionary of Literary Biography*, Kay Mussell and Johanna Tunon's *North American Romance Writers, 1985–1995* provides introductions to the work of fifty authors; John Charles and Shelley Mosley's *Romance Today: An A-Z Guide to Contemporary American Romance Writers* (2007) doubles that number. *Romance Today*'s essays are based primarily on the authors' responses to "lengthy questionnaires" as well as some analysis of their work (xii); authors, all of whom were living at the time the work was compiled, were given final approval. Most entries are three or four pages long, including bibliography; only the entry for Krentz stretches to eight pages.

More substantial, and unsurprising given her prominence as an influential figure, two book-length studies of Georgette Heyer (1902–74) exist (Hodge; Kloester). There is also a book chapter (Regis, *Natural History*), at least one journal article exploring a specific title (Vivanco, "Nonesuch"), and an appreciative assessment by novelist and critic A.S. Byatt of Heyer as "a superlatively good writer of honourable escape" (Byatt). Heyer mostly wrote historical romances and detective fiction. With her careful attention to period slang and historically accurate details of dress and décor, she has been a significant influence on the historical subgenre, especially Regency romances. Even critics who denigrate popular romance generally may praise Heyer—although this, too, may be an artifact of distance; despite "phenomenal" sales, during her lifetime "she never had a review in a serious paper" (Byatt 297).

Publicity-shy seems to understate the case; Heyer was "reticent" if not reclusive, according to Byatt's short posthumous biography ([2001]1975). Heyer wanted the focus firmly on her books rather than her private life, as Jane Aiken Hodge acknowledges in the most thorough exploration of Heyer's oeuvre to date (1984). The title of *The Private World of Georgette Heyer* alludes both to Heyer's own family life and to the impeccably researched, lovingly limned, glossy, and sanitized Regency within which her novels are set. (As Regis' chapter on Heyer shows, her heroines and heroes "inhabit a Regency setting without being of it" (*Natural History* 112); instead, the heroines in particular affirm the twentieth-century bourgeois values Regis finds in romances broadly: "affective individualism, property or the means to get it, and companionate marriage" (140).)

Hodge had access to Heyer's papers and used them to set her novel-writing within the context of her marriage and family life. Laura Vivanco, too, brings biography to bear on Heyer's fiction, arguing that Heyer draws on her own experiences in *The Nonesuch* (1962) and that there "are parallels between Heyer's life and work and that of her eponymous hero" ("Nonesuch" n.p.).

In Hodge, the focus remains on Heyer's works, each of which receives a more or less extensive treatment. Hodge considers continuities and recurring themes and plot elements among the novels, including the appearance of what Heyer terms Mark I and Mark II heroes (59). (Mark I = domineering and remote, exemplified by Alastair from *These Old Shades*; Mark II = impeccably attired and mannered, such as the titular Corinthian.) Hodge concludes her study with the possibility that "a reappraisal in the next few years" might "give her work the critical acclaim it never achieved in her lifetime" (208).

Jennifer Kloester's *Georgette Heyer* is more literary biography and less oeuvre analysis. Drawing on extensive correspondence and archives not available to Hodge, Kloester explores the sales, marketing, and reception of Heyer's novels as well as Heyer's own feelings about them, and about their influence. Particularly valuable elements include her illuminating treatment of Heyer's response to perceived plagiarism by Barbara Cartland (275–9) and Heyer's self-deprecating assessment (247) that some of her books are "nonsense" but also "unquestionably good escapist literature." There remains more to be said, of course, about Heyer's impact on the sub-genre of Regency romance.

There is also one author study of Danish-Australian romance writer Marie Bjelke Petersen (1874–1969), who was about a generation older than Heyer. Bjelke Petersen became "a popular and respected novelist" (Carter and Osborne 120) whose work, well known in Australia, also sold well in the United States and United Kingdom. Alexander's biography is a precursor to an ongoing project to recuperate Australian authors, discussed further below. *A Mortal Flame* evinces more interest in Bjelke Petersen's life and her novels' settings than their romance elements; Alexander, reflecting on the project in 2013, asserts that "they're really trashy romances, not well written, only saved by their interesting backgrounds and characters."[3] Jeannette Delamoir examines cross-dressing and gender instability within one Bjelke Petersen novel—a device also used to good effect by Heyer. Roslynn Haynes situates Bjelke Petersen within the Australian canon, noting her exclusion from Australian literary studies because of her status as romance novelist while examining how her novels describe and monumentalize the Tasmanian wilderness.

A more traditional author study is Sarah S. G. Frantz [Lyons] article-length survey of Suzanne Brockmann's oeuvre ("Suzanne Brockmann"). Originally intended for a volume for the *Dictionary of Literary Biography* that never came to fruition, Frantz's brief overview of Brockmann, who has published extensively in category and single-title series romance and romantic suspense, lays the foundation for further scholarship on Brockmann's novels. While it does not report on each book in depth, it provides a chronological survey of her work, including at least a brief synopsis of every novel, along with information on recurring themes and concerns as well as character types and authorial techniques. (Other studies of Brockmann's work include Frantz, "I've Tried" and Ali, "Troubleshooting"; both focus on thematic elements in novels from the Troubleshooter series, as does Kamblé's *Making Meaning*.) Brockmann is one of the authors whose work McDaniel College's library collects.

As this discussion of Brockmann indicates, in addition to the quite limited number of extant author studies, scholarship which focuses on other elements of authors' work could be used to round out critical explorations of authors' oeuvres. Regis' *Natural History* includes chapters on Heyer, Mary Stewart, Krentz, Janet Dailey, and Roberts. Each chapter offers a very brief overview of the author's work, emphasizing certain salient points of that author's oeuvre which illustrate Regis's overarching arguments about the genre's main emphases: "affective individualism, property rights, and companionate marriage" (*Natural History* 205). Although these are not author studies, these and other studies of individual books, groups of works, or comparisons of authors would be useful for scholars looking to do studies.

A special issue of the *Journal of Popular Romance Studies* (2012) focuses on the oeuvre of Jennifer Crusie. Crusie, like authors including Krentz and Mary Bly/Eloisa James, is a thoughtful exponent of the genre as well as one of its best-known authors; materials for an author study are plentiful. In addition to Eric Selinger's introduction, which as noted above merges an overview of Crusie's work with a biographical account, six essays treat a variety of themes. One tracks the varied meanings of lingerie across four novels (Vivanco, "Literary Lingerie"), another the role of con artist protagonists (Valeo, "Crusie and the Con"). Three essays focus specifically on heroines: the relationship between storytelling and non-essentialist notions of female identity (Zakreski), the valorization of the "imperfect female body" (Kramer), the parallel between romance reader and romance heroine (Moore and Selinger "The Heroine as Reader, the Reader as Heroine"). A final essay treats parallels between Crusie's work and that of an author of eighteenth-century "amatory fiction" in how they deploy "voyeuristic images and gossip" (Baldus). With the exception of Kate Moore and Selinger, who focus on a single novel, these essays treat three or four of Crusie's novels. Complementing this special issue is William Gleason's thematic approach to domestic interiors in Crusie's novels ("Inside Story"). Although there remains much to be done—perhaps using the multimedia collages Crusie has made as part of her work on each book, eight of which are in the McDaniel library collection—this is a substantial body of critical literature. Most of it engages the ideas and literary strategies Crusie uses throughout her work, as well as her metatextual engagements with discourses around the romance novel.

Also concerned with the relationship of author to context, Regine Künne's *Eternally Yours* (2015), a published doctoral dissertation, focuses on the oeuvres of Jayne Ann Krentz and Barbara Delinsky. Situating Krentz and Delinsky's work in the broad field of romance publishing, and in its American cultural context, Künne analyzes three novels by each from different phases in their decades-spanning careers (1982, 1992, and 2007). She concludes that despite the relevance, especially in the early category-writing phase of their careers, of industry formulas, each has recognizably individual themes and concerns. Another comparative study is Deborah Chappel Traylor's doctoral dissertation, which treats Janet Dailey, Jude Deveraux, and LaVyrle Spencer (Chappel, "American Romances"); an excerpt on Spencer was published ("LaVyrle Spencer and the Anti-Essentialist Argument") but the remainder remains unpublished.

What can be done?

This section suggests the kinds of work that remain to be done in author studies and some potential criteria for discerning which authors might be especially important to study. Desiderata for author studies in popular romance fiction include coverage across the second half of the twentieth century and into the twenty-first, across the spectrum of sub-genres that comprise popular romance, and across regions, as well as coverage of authors whose work has been understudied to date.

Most scholarship in popular romance studies has focused on British, Australian, and US-based authors. Australian scholars have been particularly interested in Australian authors. Part of their focus has been the broad context and specific themes of those works (e.g., Flesch). Some attention is going to authors. Under the rubric of Australian Research Council Discovery Project "Genre Worlds: Australian Popular Fiction in the Twenty-First Century,"[4] Beth Driscoll, Lisa Fletcher, and Kim Wilkins received a Romance Writers of America grant in 2015 "to develop case studies of authors at different stages in their careers, exploring the creative processes whereby works of genre fiction are created, published, and marketed."[5] The research will focus on one book per author. So far, the project has focused on quantitative data, but it is possible that author studies will be among their approaches.

The Genre Worlds project makes nationality and career-stage explicit selection criteria. Author studies more generally rely on criteria of importance as well as feasibility. Relevant factors that might determine importance include number of works published, sales rankings, innovation (or, conversely, "representativeness"), impact on genre and form, name recognition, diversity, and/or literary merit. Some of these factors will be more important than others, depending on the scholar's discipline.

In popular culture studies, *popularity* matters, though the popular romance authors who have garnered the most scholarly and critical attention are not necessarily those who have sold best. (Roberts is, in numerous respects, exceptional.) Sales figures are difficult to obtain. Media coverage; awards (media, industry, and organizational); and film, television, and magazine adaptations are potential sources of information. Bestseller lists are more inclusive than book review pages. In the 1980s, the Romance Writers of America newsletter regularly printed short answers from booksellers to questions of what was selling well in their stores; store owners often remarked on the type of book and sometimes mentioned specific authors. One cannot draw quantitative conclusions from scattershot evidence, but it is, nonetheless, relevant to assessing impressions of specific works and writers.

The Romance Writers Association archives and website provide information on its award nominees and winners, both for individual books (RITA) and for longer-term accomplishments. An obvious place to search for appropriate candidates for author studies would be its Lifetime Achievement Award recipients, which stretches back to 1983. Romantic suspense author Mary Stewart and historical romance writer Roberta Gellis, both of whom were RWA awardees, have significant oeuvres as well as name recognition. Other less well-known figures such as Edna Ferber were also important predecessors to contemporary authors.

The RWA and its awards, however, have not historically reflected the diversity of romance readers or writers.[6] In 2012, Brenda Jackson became the first African American author to win its Lifetime Achievement Award; Beverly Jenkins won in 2017. Studies of African American and other writers of color, Native American writers, and/or LGBTIQ authors will require somewhat different and additional resources than those for studying straight romances by cis white authors. Because of industry discrimination and barriers, underrepresented writers have been early, successful adopters of self-publishing. Book recommendation blogs such as WOC Romance provide information on recent books.

African American authors of popular romance are well-represented in the popular culture collection at Bowling Green State University library, in part because of the library's choice to collect category lines. Using materials from the Kensington imprint, the online exhibit "Romance in Color: Pioneering African American Romance Authors" showcases the work of Jackson, Jenkins, Shirley Hailstock, and Gwynne Forster.[7] An obvious candidate for an author study, Jenkins, who published 37 novels between 1994 and 2018, writes in several subgenres, including Westerns and romantic suspense.[8] Although she publishes contemporaries, she is best known for her historical novels, set in the nineteenth century—though never under slavery, featuring African-American protagonists. (Jenkins' innovation helped prepare the ground for Alyssa Cole's award-winning Civil War-era Loyal League novels.) Jenkins has also published two "sweet" young adult romances and her *Blessings* series (2009–) can be understood as Christian fiction. Her work, alongside that of authors such as Piper Huguley, disrupts the whiteness of "inspirational" fiction as it is typically published and studied.

For twentieth-century traditionally-published authors and independent presses, archival resources—some newly digitized—are essential. In some cases, these archives preserve works of authors excluded from mainstream publication. Writers of lesbian fiction, including press founder Barbara Grier, can be studied through the Naiad press archives.[9] Groundbreaking author Radclyffe (Len Barot), whose first book appeared in 1973, is now a publisher. Barot is among the authors featured in *Love Between the Covers*, an award-winning documentary about popular romance. Others include Jenkins, Roberts, and Mary Bly, who writes as Eloisa James.[10]

How might a focus on romance help shape author studies as field?

A 2013 Princeton University symposium on "The Popular Romance Author" illustrates competing tendencies in the field.[11] Although some presented assessments of underappreciated or well-known authors, 3 of 11 participants' abstracts mention Barthes and the "death of the author." Thus, even a conference explicitly about authors involves skepticism about the idea of orienting studies in this way. Doing author studies of popular romance writers requires situating author studies in the contexts of popular fiction studies, including its market elements; it also requires taking account of the particularity of gendered disdain for romance. An insistence on treating writers as authoritative creators may serve as a gendered corrective: it seems particularly cruel to proclaim the death of the author in a field dominated by women whose individual authority is already suspect.

At the same time, to insist on authoritative individual creators may obscure some of what is most interesting about popular romance and other genre fiction. In addition to considering the author function, author studies of popular romance might consider the variety of things authorship means. Topics might include constrained writing, author communities, professionalization, and the boundaries between readers and authors.

Although romance has been unfairly stigmatized as formulaic (Regis "Complicating Romances"), it is true that especially in category lines it remains heavily shaped by publisher and reader expectations. Dirk de Geest and Goris explore handbooks for romance authors as a window into constrained writing. More might be done along these lines, including investigation of the advice offered by romance authors through workshops sponsored by the Romance Writers of America (RWA) and in print and online forums.

Romance readers have been studied at some length, but communities of romance writers less so. Roach includes some participant observation at the annual RWA conference in her survey *Happily Ever After*, although the book is oblivious to racist dynamics at the event (see Snyder). Another subject ripe for investigation is how collaboration, critique groups, and organizational support structures—in person and online—figure in the production of works. Popular romance seems to have an unusually high proportion of readers-turned-authors. The archives of the Romance Writers' Association, hosted at Bowling Green State University, provide fascinating material to investigate how individuals make the transition from aspiring writers to published authors, as well as of local groups and support networks (Ali, "Romance Fiction in the Archives"). They would also support further research into the gendered dismissal of romance authors. Jennifer Lois and Joanna Gregson's sociological study of how outsiders' "sneering disapproval" and "leering 'approval'" "sexually stigmatize" romance writers (7, 11, 2) models ways of exploring how authors in this genre inhabit their roles—and ways that writers' communities provide emotional and cognitive resources to cope with the sneers. (21)

Although such research would neither focus on the author function nor on studies of oeuvres, it would provide a deeper and richer account of the full range of practices, meanings, and patterns associated with the process of becoming and being an author —in, and potentially beyond, popular romance.

Notes

1 Goris' dissertation, including the abstract from which this quotation is drawn, is publicly accessible at https://limo.libis.be/primo-explore/fulldisplay?docid=LIRIAS1808825&context=L&vid=Lirias&search_scope=Lirias&tab=default_tab&lang=en_US&fromSitemap=1. Accessed August 21, 2018.
2 For information about the collection, see https://lib.hoover.mcdaniel.edu/arc.
3 This characterization appears on Alexander's website. "The life of Marie Bjelke-Petersen." www.alisonalexander.com.au/books/mortal-flame, dated 2013, accessed February 14, 2019.
4 www.genreworlds.com/about.
5 https://www.rwa.org/p/cm/ld/fid=554%20-%20Driscoll#Driscoll.
6 https://www.rwa.org/p/bl/et/blogid=20&blogaid=1415.
7 https://digitalgallery.bgsu.edu/exhibits/show/romance_in_color.
8 She maintains a list of publications at www.beverlyjenkins.net/web/. For an overview, consult www.salon.com/2017/06/25/uncommon-ground-beverly-jenkins-diverse-romance-and-american-history-the-way-it-really-happened/.
9 http://www.oac.cdlib.org/findaid/ark:/13030/c8gt5rhv/admin/.
10 The page devoted to Barot at an earlier iteration of the Popular Romance Project website http://popularromanceproject.org/barot/ appears to be defunct. As of June 2018, the project has a new website, which includes a page on *Love Between the Covers* www.blueberryhillproductions.com/prp.
11 https://www.princeton.edu/prcw/.

Works cited

Alexander, Alison. *A Mortal Flame: Marie Bjelke Petersen, Australian Romance Writer 1874–1969*. Blubber Head Press, 1994.

Ali, Kecia. *Human in Death: Morality and Mortality in J.D. Robb's Novels*. Baylor University Press, 2017a.

———. "Troubleshooting Post-9/11 America: Religion, Racism, and Stereotypes in Suzanne Brockmann's *Into the Night* and *Gone Too Far*." *Journal of Popular Romance Studies*, vol. 6, 2017b, n.p. http://jprstudies.org/2017/09/troubleshooting-post-911-america-religion-racism-and-stereotypes-in-suzanne-brockmanns-into-the-night-and-gone-too-farby-kecia-ali/.

———. "Romance Fiction in the Archives." *Journal of Popular Romance Studies*, vol. 7, 2018, n.p.

Allan, Jonathan A. "Reading the Regis Roundtable: An Outsider's Perspective." *Journal of Popular Romance Studies*, vol. 3, no. 2, 2013, n.p.

Baldus, Kimberly. "Gossip, Liminality, and Erotic Display: Jennifer Crusie's Links to Eighteenth-Century Amatory Fiction." *Journal of Popular Romance Studies*, vol. 2, no. 2, 2012, pp 1–22.

Burge, Amy. *Representing Difference in the Medieval and Modern Orientalist Romance*. Palgrave Macmillan, 2016.

Byatt, A. S. "The Ferocious Reticence of Georgette Heyer." *Sunday Times Magazine* London, October 5, 1975, pp. 28–38. Mary Fahnstock-Thomas, *Georgette Heyer: A Critical Retrospective*. PrinnyWorld Books, 2001, pp. 289–303.

———. "An Honourable Escape: Georgette Heyer." *Passions of the Mind: Selected Writings*, New York: Vintage, 2012 [1991], pp. 233–240.
Carter, David and Roger Osborne. *Australian Books and Authors in the American Marketplace, 1840s–1940s*. Sydney University Press, 2018.
Chappel, Deborah Kaye. "American Romances: Narratives of Culture and Identity." Ph.D. diss., Duke University, 1992.
———. "LaVyrle Spencer and the Anti-Essentialist Argument." *Paradoxa: Studies in World Literary Genres*, vol. 3, no. 1–2, 1997, pp. 107–120.
Charles, John and Shelley Mosley, editors. *Romance Today: An A-Z Guide to Contemporary American Romance Writers*. Greenwood Press, 2007.
Chris, Cynthia. "Author." *Keywords for Media Studies*, Edited by Laurie Ouellette, and Jonathan Gray, New York UP, 2017, pp. 21–23.
Crane, Ralph and Lisa Fletcher. *Island Genres, Genre Islands*. New York: Palgrave, 2017.
De Geest, Dirk and An Goris. "Constrained Writing, Creative Writing: The Case of Handbooks for Writing Romances." *Poetics Today*, vol. 31, no. 1, 2010, pp. 81–106.
Delamoir, Jeannette. "Marie Bjelke Petersen's 'Virile Story': *Jewelled Nights*, Gender Instability, and the Bush." *Hecate*, vol. 29, no. 1, 2003, pp. 115–131.
Driscoll, Beth. "Genre, Author, Text, Reader: Teaching Nora Roberts's *Spellbound*." *Journal of Popular Romance Studies*, vol. 4, no. 2, 2014, n.p. http://jprstudies.org/2014/10/genre-author-text-reader-teaching-nora-robertss-spellboundby-beth-driscoll/.
Flesch, Juliet. *From Australia with Love: A History of Modern Australian Popular Romance Novels*. Fremantle Arts Centre, 2004.
Frantz, Sarah S. G. "Suzanne Brockmann." *Teaching American Literature: A Journal of Theory and Practice*, vol. 2, no. 2–3, Special Issue Spring/Summer, 2008, pp. 1–19.
———. "'I've Tried My Entire Life to Be a Good Man': Suzanne Brockmann's Sam Starrett, Ideal Romance Hero." *Women Constructing Men: Female Novelists and Their Male Characters, 1750–2000*, Edited by Sarah S. G. Frantz, and Katharina Rennhak. Lexington, Lexington Books 2009, pp. 227–247.
——— and Eric Murphy Selinger, eds. *New Approaches to Popular Romance Fiction: Critical Essays*. McFarland, 2012.
Gleason, William A. "The inside Story: Jennifer Crusie and the Architecture of Love." *Popular Fiction and Spatiality*, Edited by Lisa Fletcher, Palgrave, 2016, pp. 79–93.
Gleason, William A. and Eric Murphy Selinger, eds. *Romance Fiction and American Culture: Love as the Practice of Freedom?* Ashgate, 2016.
Goris, An. "Review: *Reading Nora Roberts* by Mary Ellen Snodgrass." *Journal of Popular Romance Studies*, vol. 1, no. 1, 2010, n.p.
———. "From Romance to Roberts and Back Again: Genre, Authorship and the Construction of Textual Identity in Contemporary Popular Romance Novels." Ph.D. diss., University of Leuven, 2011.
———. "Mind, Body, Love: Nora Roberts and the Evolution of Popular Romance Studies." *Journal of Popular Romance Studies*, vol. 3, no. 1, 2012, n.p.
———. "Happily Ever After … and After: Serialization and the Popular Romance Novel." *Americana: The Journal of American Popular Culture (1900 to Present)*, vol. 12, no. 1, 2013, n.p.
Harris, Paul. "Barbara Cartland Leaves Nothing in Will." *The Daily Mail*. Accessed June 15, 2018. www.dailymail.co.uk/news/article-14765/Barbara-Cartland-leaves-will.html
Haynes, Roslynn. "Marie Bjelke Petersen's Romances: Fulfilling the Contract, Subverting the Spirit." *Southerly*, vol. 70, no. 2, 2010, pp. 41–63.
Holden, Stacy E. "Love in the Desert: Images of Arab-American Reconciliation in Contemporary Sheikh Romance Novels." *Journal of Popular Romance Studies*, vol. 5, no. 1, August, 2015, n.p.
Jarmakani, Amira. "'The Sheik Who Loved Me': Romancing the War on Terror." *Signs*, vol. 35, no. 4, 2010, pp. 993–1017.

———. *An Imperialist Love Story: Desert Romances and the War on Terror*. New York UP, 2015.

Kamblé, Jayashree. *Making Meaning in Popular Romance Fiction: An Epistemology*. New York: Palgrave, 2014.

———. "From Barbarized to Disneyfied: Viewing 1990s New York City through Eve Dallas, J. D. Robb's Futuristic Homicide Detective." *Forum for Inter-American Research*, vol. 10, no. 1, May 2017, pp. 72–86.

Killeen, Jarlath. "Nora Roberts: The Power of Love." *Twenty-First Century Popular Fiction*, Edited by Bernice M. Murphy, and Stephen Matterson, Edinburgh UP, 2018, pp. 53–65.

Kramer, Kyra. "Getting Laid, Getting Old, and Getting Fed: The Cultural Resistance of Jennifer Crusie's Romance Heroines." *Journal of Popular Romance Studies*, vol. 2, no. 2, 2012, n.p.

Künne, Regine. *Eternally Yours - Challenge and Response: Contemporary US American Romance Novels by Jayne Ann Krentz and Barbara Delinsky*. Lit Verlag, 2015.

Lennard, John. *Of Modern Dragons and Other Essays on Genre Fiction*. Humanities-Ebooks, 2007.

Little, Denise and Laura Hayden, eds. *The Official Nora Roberts Companion*. Berkley, 2003.

Lois, Jennifer and Joanna Gregson. "Sneers and Leers: Romance Writers and Gendered Sexual Stigma." *Gender & Society*, vol. 29, no. 4, 2015, pp. 459–483.

Mayangsari, Putri and Ratna Asmarani. "An Analysis of Personality Disorder and Abnormal Sexual Behavior that Lead to Crime in *Seduction in Death* Novel by JD Robb." *LANTERN (Journal on English Language, Culture and Literature)*, vol. 6, no. 3, 2017, 1–24.

Modleski, Tania. *Loving with a Vengeance: Mass-Produced Fantasies for Women*. 1982. Reprint, Routledge, 1988.

Moore, Kate and Eric Murphy Selinger. "The Heroine as Reader, the Reader as Heroine: Jennifer Crusie's *Welcome to Temptation*." *Journal of Popular Romance Studies*, vol. 2, no. 2, 2012, n.p.

Mussell, Kay and Johanna Tuñón. *North American Romance Writers, 1985–1995*. Scarecrow Press, 1999.

Radway, Janice. *Reading the Romance: Women, Patriarchy, and Popular Literature*. 1984. Reprint with a new Introduction Chapel Hill: U of North Carolina P, 1991.

Regis, Pamela. "Complicating Romances and Their Readers: Barrier and Point of Ritual Death in Nora Roberts's Category Fiction." *Paradoxa: Studies in World Literary Genres*, vol. 3, no. 1–2, 1997, 145–154.

———. *A Natural History of the Romance Novel*. U of Pennsylvania P, 2003.

Roach, Catherine M. *Happily Ever After: The Romance Story in Popular Culture*. Indiana UP, 2016.

Roberts, Nora. *Promise Me Tomorrow*. Pocket Books, 1984.

Roberts, Thomas J. *An Aesthetics of Junk Fiction*. U of Georgia P, 1990.

Selinger, Eric Murphy. "Review: Rereading the Romance." *Contemporary Literature*, vol. 48, no. 2, 2007, 307–324.

———. "Nothing but Good Times Ahead: A Special Forum on Jennifer Crusie (Editor's Introduction)." *Journal of Popular Romance Studies*, vol. 2, no. 2, 2012, n.p.

Snodgrass, Mary Ellen. *Reading Nora Roberts*. Santa Barbara, Calif.: Greenwood, 2010.

Snyder, Suleikha. "RWA15 in NYC: A Tale of Two Conferences." July 26, 2015. www.suleikhasnyder.com/2015/07/rwa15-in-nyc-tale-of-two-conferences.html?m=1.

Teo, Hsu-Ming. *Desert Passions: Orientalism and Romance Novels*. University of Texas Press, 2012.

Valeo, Christina A. "Crusie and the Con." *Journal of Popular Romance Studies*, vol. 2, no. 2, 2012a, n.p.

———. "The Power of Three: Nora Roberts and Serial Magic." *New Approaches to Popular Romance Fiction: Critical Essays*, Edited by Sarah S. G. Frantz, and Eric Murphy Selinger, McFarland, 2012b, pp. 229–240.

Vivanco, Laura. *For Love and Money: The Literary Art of the Harlequin Mills & Boon Romance*. Humanities-Ebooks, 2011.

———. "Jennifer Crusie's Literary Lingerie." *Journal of Popular Romance Studies*, vol. 2, no. 2, 2012, n.p.

———. "Georgette Heyer: The Nonesuch of Regency Romance." *Journal of Popular Romance Studies*, vol. 3, no. 2, 2013, n.p.
———. *Pursuing Happiness: Reading American Romance as Political Fiction*. Humanities-Ebooks, 2016.
Zakreski, Patricia. "Tell Me Lies: Lying, Storytelling, and the Romance Novel as Feminist Fiction." *Journal of Popular Romance Studies*, vol. 2, no. 2, 2012, n.p.

15 Social science reads romance

Joanna Gregson and Jennifer Lois

Writing in the early 1990s, Janice Radway acknowledged that "it matters enormously what the cumulative effects of the act of romance reading are on actual readers. Unfortunately, those effects are extraordinarily difficult to trace" (16). Social science scholarship in the subsequent decades affirms Radway's observations, with a smattering of studies across a host of methodologies underscoring both the importance of this line of inquiry and the challenge of accomplishing it effectively. No study has had the influence on the field that Radway's seminal work has had, both because *Reading the Romance* broke new ground and because there are so few studies in the field. Indeed, social science contributions to the study of romance are scant.

This chapter examines romance fiction-related studies originating from sociology, psychology, and adjacent disciplines (such as education or communication) utilizing social science methods. Because the existing literature is sparse, our review spans contributions from the 1980s to the present, with research falling into three areas. First, social scientists have conducted content analyses of texts, studying messages about gender, sexuality, and romance within the books. A second strand of research draws upon surveys, interviews, and experiments to explore how romance novels influence readers. Finally, a third area of scholarship investigates romance authors themselves. We examine each type of study in turn, concluding with our reflections about the contributions and limitations of the cumulative body of social science work.

Content analysis studies

Content analysis is a social scientific method designed to illuminate the ideas communicated in a set of textual artifacts. Social researchers use scientifically valid practices when selecting the sample of their studies and employ logic-based analytic procedures to discern patterns across a collection of texts, ensuring that the trends they uncover are not based on selective observations of social phenomena. When actual observation of readers is lacking, the method makes no claims as to knowing how texts are actually read or how the content is understood, a principle that distinguishes it from scholarship outside the social sciences. With this in mind, we agree with Ménard's assessment that "given the different norms between the two fields, it seems meaningless to compare and contrast literary criticism to social science studies" (5) when it comes to the content of romance novels. It is worth noting that not all of the social science research conducted on popular romance has been conducted according to the recognized standards of the field; in this section, we focus exclusively on methodologically sound, social-scientific content analyses of romance novels.[1]

Examinations of gender roles

One of the central foci of content analyses of romance fiction is exploring how gender is depicted in the novels, particularly in the portrayals of male and female protagonists. As Clawson observed, "Romance novels are ideal for examining gender ideology, since they take masculinity and femininity as a central focus and treat as natural the opposition between the two" (463). The theme emerging from these studies is an adherence to traditional gender roles.

Radway's ground-breaking investigation into the romance genre was one of the first to employ some social scientific principles to the gendered messages in romance novels. For the content analysis portion of her research (we take up her investigation with romance readers in the next section), she assembled a sample of 20 "favorite" and 20 "failed" romances published between 1974 and 1981, recommended by her participants: a group of 42 Midwestern readers. To increase the representativeness of the genre, this sample of novels could have been selected far more systematically. However, Radway acknowledged this fact, discussed the logical problems of selection bias, and warned against unfounded generalizations to the entire genre. By doing so, her research constitutes the first social-scientific foray into the content of romance novels. Radway found that heroines in her participants' favorite novels rejected traditional femininity by being feisty, independent, and rebellious; heroes were "spectacularly masculine" (128) in their muscular physiques and (often violent) domineering personalities but had a tender side only the heroine could bring out. These gender role expressions, Radway argued, represented "ambivalent feelings about gender" (124), which symbolized a rejection of the feminine. Despite many of her participants' reports that romance fiction was empowering, Radway concluded the genre ultimately reinforced patriarchy (a claim that has since been challenged, see Regis "What do Critics Owe the Romance?").

Radway's training as a literary scholar, however, led to epistemological blind spots and methodological weaknesses in her research (a fact she discussed in the second edition of her book). Her sampling techniques and lack of supporting evidence call many of her claims into question. For example, she jumped from analyzing the content of the 40 novels to imputing psychological motivation to authors by suggesting "it seems possible that [for] certain writers [the] preoccupation with misogyny may be the mark of a desperate need to know that exaggerated masculinity is not life-threatening to women" (168). Throughout her work, Radway leaped from analyzing words on the page to making claims about readers' and writers' unconscious desires. Despite these methodological flaws, Radway's work was revolutionary, both for bringing social-scientific legitimacy to the content of the popular romance as well as for suggesting that a full cultural critique of the content must include readers' interpretations and experiences.

With Radway's work as a backdrop, we turn to more recent content analyses of gender roles in romance. Like Radway, contemporary scholars have also found resounding patterns of stereotypical and traditional gender role depictions. One such example is the work of evolutionary psychologists Cox and Fisher, who analyzed the titles of 15,019 Harlequin romances published from 1949–2009. In so doing, they identified the 20 most frequently occurring words, looking for evidence that the books may "appeal to women because they address evolved, sex-specific mating interests" (387). They found support for their hypotheses in that words relating to long-term committed relationships (such as "bride" and "wife") and reproductive success (e.g., "baby") were among the most frequently occurring, as were words reflecting men's available resources (e.g., the profession of doctor). Following that study, Fisher and Cox turned their attention to character development, analyzing how descriptions of protagonists change over the course of a book. In their sample of 72 Harlequin novels published between 1960 and 2007, they found "the focus of most novels is on the changes that occur within the hero. He typically starts as a 'cad,' and by the end, he has been transformed into a 'dad'" (313). Just as in their previous work, Fisher and Cox speculated that these changes reflect women's evolutionary desires for a stable, nurturing mate, though they caution readers to be mindful of the exploratory (rather than explanatory) purpose of their work.

Christian-Smith ("Gender, Popular Culture, and Curriculum") explored similar gender themes in her examination of 34 adolescent romance novels published between 1942 and 1982. Her analysis revealed that the books promoted three consistent themes representing adolescent femininity: romance, beautification, and sexuality. Perhaps most notably, Christian-Smith observed that the path to empowered womanhood was romance; problematically, though, "By having so many romances dissolve in the wake of girls' bids for power, these novels make a strong statement about the irreconcilability of feminine power and having satisfying relationships with males" ("Becoming A Woman Through Romance" 388). Taken together, Christian-Smith argues that adolescent romance novels simultaneously empower girls while holding them to patriarchal constraints and positioning them as "good girls" or "other girls" (384), an argument Radway also proffers in her research on romance novels aimed at adults. In this way, young adult representations of femininity are strikingly similar to those in adult fiction.

Content analyses of LGBTIQ romance are scant, but the extant literature aligns with hetero-focused research in its examination of gender roles. Wood analyzed the content of 49 romance fiction novels with straight, lesbian, and gay protagonists published between 1950 and 1965, which Wood calls the "'golden age' for lesbian and gay pop fiction" (374). Wood contends that an intersectional analysis of characters in terms of their gender and sexual orientation "reveals a great deal more about the power of gendered narratives" (390) than does a study of gender alone. In particular, her study highlighted the greater range of emotional development afforded to straight male, gay male, and butch female protagonists, while feminine (lesbian or straight) women protagonists "lack an existential biography outside of relationships" (390). Like heterosexual women in other studies (e.g., Cox and Fisher, Fisher and Cox, Radway), the feminine characters Wood studied conformed to a narrowly constructed type.

Taken together, content analyses tell a similar story about romance novels reinforcing traditional gender roles. However, the books from which these conclusions were drawn have publication dates ranging from 1942 (Christian Smith) to 1974 (Radway) as a starting point. Although they capture some of what is now considered popular romance—work published after Woodiwiss's *The Flame and the Flower* in 1972 (Regis)—their findings are confounded by including works from much earlier time periods. As such, we cannot assume that these patterns would be found in a sample of more recently published books.

Examinations of sexuality

A related area of interest for social scientists conducting content analyses of romance novels is the depiction of sexuality and sexual behavior. For example, drawing on Simon and Gagnon's conception of a Western sexual script as the cultural rules dictating "the who, what, when, where, and why of sexual behavior," Ménard and Cabrera coded 46 sex scenes from 20 romance novels for such qualities as protagonists' age, gender, and sexual orientation, as well as the nature of the sexual contact between them (242). They used as their sample the 1989–2009 contemporary romance[2] winners of the annual RITA contest sponsored by the Romance Writers of America.[3] The researchers observed statistically significant differences in the sexual agency of male versus female characters; female characters were more likely to be undressed by their partners than vice versa, and female characters were more likely to receive (rather than initiate) sexual touching than male partners. They found tremendous adherence to a Western sexual script in other ways, too: most (90.4 percent) sex scenes depicted sexual contact progressing from kissing and touching to sexual intercourse, and most (77.3 percent) protagonists resembled one another with respect to age, ethnicity, and other features. Although the sample of 20 books was small, the 20-year time-span allowed the authors to see change over time in one area: a larger number of female protagonists (42.1 percent) initiated sexual contact in the novels published from 2000–9 compared to those from 1989–99 (33.3 percent). In spite of this difference, Ménard and Cabrera conclude that their findings "highlight the rigidity of prescribed gender roles" (251) and an overwhelming conformity to Western sexual scripts. Following up on that work, Cabrera and Ménard analyzed orgasm scenes in the same 20 RITA award-winning novels, identifying a pattern whereby female characters orgasm first (from activities other than intercourse), followed by simultaneous orgasms from penile–vaginal intercourse, a pattern that was unchanged over the time span of the books. Cabrera and Ménard conclude that these findings aligned with those from their previous study, showing further evidence of an adherence to a Western sexual script.

One element of the sexual script of particular focus in content analysis is the use of condoms. Diekman et al. examined 86 contemporary romance novels published between 1981 and 1996, selecting as their sample every third book on the shelf at three bookstores with "a large romance section" (181). Their analysis revealed that only 10.3 percent of the novels included a discussion of condom use between the main characters before their first sexual encounter, with all of the conversations initiated by the male. Furthermore, "female characters rejected condom use in almost half of the discussions" (181), deeming them unnecessary if they were in love. As Diekman et al. observed in 1996, "the extremely small percentage of 'modern' romance novels that portray any discussion of condom use is surprising in this age of STD risk and awareness" (181). Similarly, in their sexual scripts study, Ménard and Cabrera found that books published between 1989 and 1999 depicted condom use in only a small proportion (18.5 percent) of sex scenes. However, given the more recent publication dates of the novels they analyzed, they also found notably more reference to condoms in the second half of their sample: books published between 2000 and 2009 depicted condom use in more than half (57.9 percent) of sex scenes. One of the strengths of content analysis is its ability to tap into how the communication of social norms change over time, as these studies have done.

In a similar way, studies in the 1980s and early 1990s examining the sexual content of young adult romance novels show the extent to which both texts and research agendas are a reflection of the times. In the 1980s, romance novels written for teens "ranked in the top three kinds of books read and purchased by girls" (Christian-Smith "Gender, Popular Culture, and Curriculum" 368). Bereska noted the rapid growth and subsequent decline of the teen romance market in the 1980s and wondered what distinguished successful (that is, still in business) romance publishing lines from those that failed. After analyzing the content of 39 novels (with the only detail being that ten titles each were selected from three "successful" publishers and nine from "failed" publishers), Bereska observed that "In the failed teen series romance novels, kissing was presented as an extreme in sexual behaviour, even as late as 1986" (39). In contrast, "the most successful teen line," the *Sweet Valley High* series, "brought with it the greatest degree of sexual content in the adolescent literary market at the time" (39).

Together, examinations of sexuality in romance novels mirror the studies on gender showing an adherence to traditional norms and roles. Despite changing sexual mores, depictions of sexuality remain consistent with traditional Western sexual scripts. The exceptions are in the area of increased condom use in more recent titles, and a burgeoning industry of adolescent novels with sexual content in the 1980s.

Gender and sexuality in Christian romance

A third body of content analysis research brings together themes of gender and sexuality in examining Christian romance novels. While researchers often describe their purpose as analyzing "religious" romance novels, the studies in this area are actually about one particular form of religion: evangelical Christianity. Neal observed that unlike "unisex" Christian media, such as Christian music, the "evangelical romance" is produced and consumed primarily by women and "utilizes a fictional formula and a sentimental piety designated as feminine" (38–9); these unique qualities, coupled with its being the most popular and highest selling form of Christian romance, make the evangelical romance ripe for study.

The main finding of Clawson's content analysis comparing 120 secular and Christian romance novels published between 1998–2000 relates to gender. Specifically, secular heroes were more likely than Christian heroes to have occupations that played up their individualism, such as managerial positions, and they were "the most likely to be independently wealthy, self-employed, and physically powerful" (469). Christian men, on the other hand, were "less assertively masculine" (475); instead of displaying masculinity through their professions, sexual conquests and worldly success, Christian heroes were depicted as masculine because of their moral and religious leadership, particularly in the context of their families.

Christopherson's research is the young adult companion to Clawson's study. Christopherson compared the depictions of family roles and gender ideologies in secular and Christian young adult romance novels, studying books "that gave the appearance of having romance as one of its themes" based on title or cover art (443). In his analysis of 16 recent releases (eight secular, eight religious), he found few differences in the hobbies or occupations of male and female characters across the two subgenres, but significant differences in terms of the depiction of romance. Secular books, he found, gave the reader "the impression that for a teenage girl having a boyfriend was the most important thing in life," whereas in Christian books, "the boyfriend relationship in the story was *not* the most important part of the character's life" (449). In these ways, Christian books portrayed a less traditional gender role ideology than Christopherson hypothesized they would, although he theorized that the rationale for such portrayals may have been "promot[ing] the virtue of physical innocence and female purity" (451).

Content analyses in the social sciences uncover messages about women, men, their respective places in society, and their sexual behavior that are remarkably similar across different subgenres. With varying samples and focal questions, the existing literature reveals depictions that consistently adhere to traditional gender roles and sexual scripts.

Research with readers

Because content analysis tells us what messages exist in books, but not how (or whether) those messages influence attitudes or behavior, different methodologies are employed to address these questions. Social scientists typically engage in such research by conducting surveys or interviews. Thus, a second strand of social science research examines romance readers themselves, with an overwhelming emphasis on exploring how romance novels influence readers' expectations for gender and sexuality in their own relationships.

Studies of gender roles and gender ideology

The seminal study of romance readers is the ethnographic portion of Radway's study, wherein she examines the interplay between romance novel content, readers' beliefs about gender and sexuality, and reading behavior. The women in her study read fiction to escape from the stressors of their roles as wives and mothers in a patriarchal culture, and they chose romance because heroines lived happily ever after with heroes who nurtured their emotional needs, something Radway's participants found immensely attractive because they lacked this attention from their husbands. These findings were well supported in Radway's study, as participants spoke for themselves on these issues. On other issues, however, Radway rejected readers' self-reports—in particular their claims that reading romance felt empowering—and instead inserted her own empirically bereft psychological analysis of readers' unconscious desires. By Radway's own admission in retrospect, she failed to prioritize participants' understandings of romance novels over her own "fairly rigid notion of patriarchy" (9). Applying a positivist paradigm to an ethnographic investigation in this way destroys the epistemological integrity of the research (Blumer); thus Radway's characterization of romance readers as possessing a false consciousness—as "patriarchy's dupes" (Regis "What Do Critics Owe the Romance?" 3)—is questionable.

Crane's findings resembled Radway's: the majority of the women in her combined survey and interview study wanted their male partners to display "more traditionally feminine qualities," such as "'caring,' 'understanding,' and 'affection'" (263), and were somewhat critical of the "forcefully aggressive" sex scenes (267); 46 percent found them to be "exciting," whereas 33 percent found them to be "unpleasant" (267). Crane explicitly asked about feminism, finding that while her respondents were overwhelmingly positive (94 percent) about the gains feminism had made, most (73 percent) had "reservations" (266) about feminism's threat to traditional gender roles. Though Crane's sample was broader and less homogenous than Radway's, it was certainly not representative of romance readers, and she advises that her findings be interpreted with caution.

Other explorations into romance readers' attitudes and behaviors have been primarily ethnographic. Researchers have immersed themselves in different subgroups of readers, including adolescents (Christian Smith), women in India (Puri, Parameswaran), and readers of Christian (Neal) and Amish (Weaver-Zercher) romance. A question guiding much of this qualitative work is readers' gendered motivation for selecting romance. Consistent with Radway's findings, these studies show that readers value romance novels as both an escape from the challenges of daily life as well as for the connection they feel toward the stories and characters. Religious romances provided readers with "wholesome entertainment" (Neal 46), a heroine with whom they identify, and a diversion that aligned their values with their desire to escape from the stresses of everyday life (Neal, Weaver-Zercher). Puri's Indian readers found inspiration in heroines. Drawing on data collected through 90 surveys and 11 in-depth interviews, she found that about half of her respondents used words like "'successful,' 'independent,' 'strong,' and 'feminine' [to describe romance heroines] ... qualities that implicitly or explicitly challenge the socialization of women in India" (442). In a qualitative study of 30 young Indian women, Parameswaran located the practice of reading English-language romance novels in a global context, tracing the ways in which her participants considered themselves similar to and different from the white heroines in books—and how drawn they were to the freedom (symbolic or otherwise) these heroines enjoyed ("Reading Fiction").

In contrast to quantitative studies, most of which have tried to assess whether readers accept or reject the gendered and sexual messages of romance novels, qualitative studies reveal the complexity with which readers accept some messages but reject others. For example, Christian-Smith ("Voices of Resistance," "Becoming a Woman Through Romance") drew on interviews, surveys, and observations of 29 teens at three middle schools in the Midwestern United States, as well as interviews and observations with the girls' reading teachers. Contrasting the popular conception that readers assume the fantasies in romances are attainable in real life, she found that "very few of the young women envisioned romance in everyday life as anything like romance fiction" ("Voices of Resistance" 177) and that the cliff-hangers at the end of each chapter allowed young readers to think critically and imagine what they themselves would do in similar situations ("Becoming A Woman Through Romance"). The result, Christian-Smith argues, is a simultaneous acceptance of traditional feminine stereotypes (e.g., valuing being pretty, like the novel's heroines) and a willingness to challenge the status quo (e.g., wanting to be seen as capable and assertive). Puri, too, found that reading romance novels fueled a "cultural resistance" (441) whereby the Indian college students in her study questioned and critiqued otherwise taken-for-granted elements of their culture. Similarly, Weaver-Zercher's Amish readers "held their appreciation for Amish fiction in tandem with critical or even oppositional reading" (175), and Neal's evangelical readers criticized romance heroes "rather than their husbands" (151). Studies like this offer support for the idea that readers do not passively accept everything they read. Indeed, Moody's ethnographic research reveals the ways in which readers actively participate in and "co-construct" (46) the romance genre, insofar as romance readers use "romantic fiction [to] make possible a variety of personal, collective, and civic engagements both online and offline" (21).

These findings from reader studies are especially noteworthy when considered in tandem with content analysis findings. While content analyses reveal conformity to traditional gender roles and sexual scripts, studies of readers show that these books serve important functions in women's lives, that they are read critically, and that their take-away messages (of independent and strong heroines, for example), may not be consistent with the themes uncovered by social scientists.

Studies of gender, sexuality, and sexual behaviors

Just as social scientists conducting content analyses of romance focused on gender and sexuality, so too have researchers examining romance readers. The most compelling studies in this area are ethnographic investigations examining the ways readers understand romance to be a complex interplay between gender and sexuality, as well as the intricacy with which they internalize some messages yet reject others. For example, Puri's Indian interviewees reported on the lessons they learned from romance novels about physical anatomy, the emotional aspects of a sexual relationship, and the relationship between sex and romantic love. Parameswaran found similar patterns among her sample of young Indian women. One participant told her that in romance novels, "women express their thoughts to men and feel close to their husbands. That's what I want" ("Reading Fictions of Romance" 844). Parameswaran contended that romance novels served as "instructional manuals on sexuality that prepared [readers] for the transition to womanhood in the absence of other resources and taboos that discouraged women from seeking out information on sex at schools, colleges, and in their homes" ("Reading Fictions of Romance" 844).

This is not to say that there have not been significant contributions from quantitative social scientists. With respect to reader research on sexuality, one study stands out for its methodological rigor. Diekman et al. used multiple methodologies within the same study to examine influences on readers' attitudes toward condom use. To begin, Diekman et al. surveyed a convenience sample of 97 female college students and found romance readers had more negative attitudes toward condom use and a lower reported frequency of condom use compared to readers of other genres. The second part of their study, an experiment, assessed a causal link between the sexual content of romance novels and readers' sexual attitudes and behaviors. The researchers provided 49 of the students with book excerpts to read over a period of three weeks—including a romance story featuring condom use, a romance story without condoms, a science fiction story, and a political story. Students who read the romance excerpt with condoms "had significantly more positive attitudes towards condom use" and "reported marginally greater intention to use condoms in the future" (184). Because the researchers assessed both correlation and causation, the work makes an important contribution to the social science research on romance readers.

Social-scientific studies of romance readers' sexual attitudes and behaviors can employ widely accepted methodologies yet still be problematic. For example, several studies test hypotheses reflecting stereotypical assumptions about romance readers, such as the idea that romance readers engage in significantly more sexual activity than non-romance-readers (Wu "Reading Romance Novels"), or that romance novels are an "erotic stimulus" equivalent to pornography (Wu "Gender, Romance Novels and Plastic Sexuality" 126). Muram et al. examined whether the pregnancy histories of a sample of Black high school girls correlated with their romance novel reading. It didn't, but the very question reflected stereotypes about both romance readers and Black teenage girls (see Luker).

Most studies basing their hypotheses on stereotypical assumptions about readers fail to find support for them. These studies have shown that, contrary to expectations, female romance readers actually had "fewer sex partners than non-readers, and were older when they had their first thoughts about sex and had their first sexual intercourse" (Wu "Gender, Romance Novels and Plastic Sexuality" 131), that "readers turn out to be less 'sexual' than non-readers" (Wu and Walsh 108), and that there is "no difference between the groups [of readers and non-readers] in the number who reported having a partner or in response to a question on whether or not they found sex to be satisfying" (Coles and Sharp 196). On the one hand, these studies refute stereotypes because their hypotheses about romance readers' heightened sexual appetites are not empirically supported; on the other hand, non-representative samples of readers and problematic definitions of key terms (e.g., equating romance with pornography) makes them methodologically suspect, and hence, not very useful.

More equivocal, however, have been findings from more recent investigations into how sexual relationships in romance novels correlate with readers' attitudes about gender roles, a topic of renewed interest since the publication of *Fifty Shades of Grey*. In the same vein as earlier studies, several researchers have explored whether readers of the *Fifty Shades* series behave differently than other readers. For example, Bonomi and colleagues conducted survey research with 715 female undergraduate students and found statistically significant differences, such that young female readers of the series "were at increased risk of [experiencing] ... behaviors that are consistent with definitions of verbal/emotional abuse and stalking ..." (724), although Bonomi et al. acknowledge their cross-sectional study design (that is, capturing their data at one point in time versus assessing attitudes and experiences both before and after exposure to romance novels) was unable to move beyond correlation to determine causality.

Also inspired by the popularity of *Fifty Shades*, Harris et al.'s experiment was designed to examine a causal link between readers' attitudes and the content of the books they read. A sample of 481 heterosexual participants were randomly assigned to one of four conditions to assess whether characters' gender roles influenced readers' perceptions of sexually dominant/submissive stories. Harris et al. found small but statistically significant differences between readers of the different types of erotica along gender lines, such that "reading about male sexual dominance led women to report more benevolent sexism than men, and men to endorse rape myths more than women" (8). Both male and female readers of the female dominant/male submissive story "valued dominance equally in a potential partner, whereas in all other conditions women valued dominance significantly more than men" (8). They point out, however, that it is impossible to know whether the differences their measures revealed would be replicated in the days or even months after exposure to the different stories.

Studies of stigma

Despite the evidence that romance readers often read critically, the stigma of the genre persists. Fowler's study of the consumption of popular romance revealed a cultural hierarchy of reading material that speaks to this stigma. Drawing on the work of Bourdieu, Fowler interviewed 115 Scottish women about their reading preferences and motivations, ultimately creating a typology of five readership groups. The "formulaic romantic fiction" readers group represented the lowest form of consumption; at the other end of the spectrum were the readers with "legitimate taste"—that is, readers who identified titles and authors that were considered "the official literary culture of modern Britain" and who emphasized the style of the book (rather than the content) as driving their interest (122). The connection between the two reader groups was seen in their contrast: "Pleasure in legitimate works is most often linked to disdain for romantic fiction and the expression of a sense of pollution by it" (Fowler 123). Indeed, one legitimate taste reader described romance fiction as "the epitome of all that I hate" (Fowler 124). The stigma was not contained to this group; even the women who reported reading romantic fiction exclusively "parodied" the genre, "using terms like 'lovey-dovey' or 'mushy' to indicate their disgust" (Fowler 129).

Several qualitative studies have examined how readers experience and manage the stigma associated with romance fiction. For example, the romance-reading middle school students in Christian-Smith's ("Becoming A Woman Through Romance," "Voices of Resistance") study were classified by school staff as "reluctant readers" who were "tracked into remedial or low-ability reading classes" ("Voices of Resistance" 174). Their teachers declared that "any reading is better than no reading" ("Voices of Resistance" 174), but consistently disparaged the books as "mindless drivel" ("Voices of Resistance" 178; see also Parameswaran "Reading Fictions of Romance" and Radick). In a more extreme example, Puri observed that more than 40 percent of the Indian women in her sample reported being either "directly or indirectly forbidden by family members to read romance novels" (439).

Because romance is regarded as "mindless drivel," the time spent reading it is seen as unproductive. As Neal observed, Christian romance is the "'stepchild' of Christian fiction" (34); her respondents felt compelled to justify the time they spent reading romance because it was time they weren't "doing the laundry or cleaning house" (57) or otherwise fulfilling their expected roles as "wives, mothers, and workers" (58). Like Radway, Neal observed how frequently her participants described their reading in compulsive terms, using "the language of compulsion ... [to] mitigate their guilt ... [and] claim their leisure time ... transferring responsibility for their behavior from the self to the story" (59). Romance readers could also justify this leisure activity by using "corrective" stigma-management strategies, such as talking about the intellectual merits of the books (Brackett), the books' capacity for helping them learn a new language (Parameswaran "Western Romance Fiction"), or the lessons they taught readers about history (Radway). In one particular example, Parameswaran's sample of Indian readers "contrast[ed] the superior value of reading Mills & Boon [romance novels]" with "derisive comments about 'useless Indian films'" (96), asserting their privileged class position by comparing their leisure activity to a popular medium in mass culture.

Romance readers further manage the stigma cast upon them by distancing themselves from other romance readers, one of the "preventative" stigma-management strategies Brackett identified in her study of 12 romance readers. Similarly, Neal's Christian readers described secular romances as "perverted," "taboo," and "degraded" (76), referencing the chaste cover art of Christian books as "a visible marker of the purity of evangelical romance" and clearly distinguishing "their romance reading from its secular counterpart" (79). Likewise, Christian-Smith's ("Voices of Resistance") adolescents described their selectivity in choosing titles to prove they were discerning readers, while Parameswaran's Indian readers contrasted themselves with less-informed readers by mocking the notes previous readers of library copies had scribbled in the margins. In her study of legitimate taste readers who admitted to reading romance, Fowler observed, "They exonerated their occasional incursions into commercial culture with reference to illness, fatigue or the need for light reading on holiday or when travelling" (124); in other words, their reading was justified because it was an exception.

Finally, several studies demonstrate that readers manage the stigma of romance by concealing their reading material. Puri and Parameswaran both found that their Indian readers covered their novels with newspaper, read them in the restroom, and hid them behind their schoolbooks. These examples demonstrate the extent to which romance readers across sub-genres experience and respond to stigma.

Some studies have demonstrated readers' acknowledgment of the sexism underlying the stigma against romance novels and their readers. Basing her argument on her four years of fieldwork in the romance-writing subculture (which included readers), Roach provided an extended discussion of the gendered nature of the stigma. In a conclusion in line with Radway's, she argued that readers use romance fiction as a "reparation fantasy" (167) to deal with the constraints of patriarchy, and, in a finding at odds with Radway's portrayal, that readers view the novels as a potent source of sex-positive feminism. In an empirical example of these theoretical ideas, Christian-Smith's adolescents used their comprehension of romance novels to shape an identity that contrasted with the label of reluctant reader and "confirmed . . . their desire to be seen as competent young women" ("Becoming A Woman Through Romance" 115). In these ways, researchers argue that romance reading is an act of "cultural resistance" (Puri 441; see also Roach).

In contrast to the rich, vibrant, and methodologically sound body of qualitative research on readers, the quantitative literature comes up short. Indeed, a critique of reader research worthy of further discussion is the question of causal order. Does reading romances cause the behaviors described by Wu, Puri, and Diekman et al., or are the people drawn to romance the type of people who would hold these attitudes or engage in these behaviors regardless of their exposure to romance novels? This is one of the most significant gaps in the quantitative survey-based literature studying readers.

Research with authors

With a relatively scant body of work examining romance fiction, in general, it is perhaps not surprising that social science has virtually ignored the people who produce this work. The third area of scholarship investigates romance authors as a distinct occupational subculture.

Studies of writers' careers

One of the threads running through research with authors relates to how and why they became romance authors and the sources of inspiration for their work. Kirkland's interviews with 55 authors in the early days of RWA explored why women choose to write romance, with writers sharing stories of being readers first and then finding their way to writing; romance was just one (and sometimes not the optimal) option (see also Roach). Our longitudinal sociological research examines both the craft and the career of romance writers, drawing upon interviews with 43 writers and 12 romance-industry insiders, as well as attendance and observations at local and national meetings of the RWA and other industry events. In one facet of this larger project, we explore how writers' careers unfold and how writing romance shapes their identities (Lois and Gregson "Aspirational Emotion Work"). Just as Neal's evangelical authors described writing as a vocational call from God, many of the writers we interviewed described writing as their "calling" (10) and expressed a desire to turn their passion into a paid career; however, frequent rejections and harsh critiques affected authors' ability to think of themselves as "real writers" (10). We call this process "aspirational labor" because of the significant emotion work writers performed to sustain their sense of calling without knowing if they would ever realize their dream.

While those outside the industry assume romance is easy to write (Gregson and Lois) and autobiographical (Lois and Gregson "Sneers and Leers"), several studies underscore the amount of effort and talent required to be successful in the industry. For example, Radick conducted survey research with 200 published and aspiring romance authors to understand their use of libraries and archives, finding that 75 percent of writers use libraries and 42 percent use archives to inform their work. Neal's evangelical authors demonstrate business savvy as they negotiate making the leap from Christian to mainstream publishing. Indeed our work (Lois and Gregson "Negotiating the Professional Artist Identity") on how writers try to sustain their careers in the highly volatile publishing industry illustrates that authors need a great deal of business savvy to create and sustain stable careers. Even so, our data show that authors' careers remain extremely precarious, which causes a great deal of stress and undermines their professional identities. Larson's survey of 4720 members of the Romance Writers of America, in which a subsample of 802 participants provided their writing income from immediately before (2009) and during (2014) the self-publishing revolution, reveals that many romance authors' careers became less precarious; self-publishing helped them increase their writing earnings, gain a greater degree of career stability, and provided more opportunities to publish diverse work (a finding our research revealed as well).

The romance author identity is a relational identity, characterized by its community of authors and readers whose shared appreciation for the genre fosters deep affective bonds with one another. Kirkland described the romance writing community as "tightknit and insular" (40) and the authors as possessing complex author–reader identities, a finding Roach noted 30 years later in her discussion of how studying, reading, and writing about the genre led her to juggle her multiple identities as an "aca[demic]-fan-author" (38). Neal learned about authors' relationships with readers by analyzing hundreds of fan letters her evangelical authors shared with her. For readers, the letters served the purpose of connecting them with their favorite authors as friends and spiritual guides; for authors, they validated their calling, a process we found among the writers we studied as well (Lois and Gregson "Aspirational Emotion Work"). For both groups, the letters fostered an "affirm[ation of] the bonds of this female interpretive community" (Neal 125), similar to what Larson referred to as a "feminist ethic of care" (21) among writers themselves.

Studies of writers experiencing stigma

Research with romance authors also explores how writers experience working in "the most popular, least respected literary genre" (Regis xi). Kirkland's respondents mostly confronted the charge of writing books with little literary value. The authors she interviewed "cited the need to develop imaginative defenses in order to counter implications that romance writing is more properly considered a titillating hobby than a demanding investment of time and skill" (239). The 20 evangelical Christian authors Neal interviewed confronted the dual stigma of writing romance (disparaged by mainstream society) and an association with sex (looked down upon by evangelical critics). Our research (Gregson and Lois) revealed that writers often had both the process and the product of their work trivialized and devalued. With respect to the (perceived) sexual content of their work, the authors we studied (Lois and Gregson "Sneers and Leers") paradoxically encountered blatant disapproval and invitations to engage in sexually charged encounters from those outside the romance industry, experiences we likened to slut-shaming.

Writers engage these stigmas head-on. Neal observed that evangelical authors drew upon two justifications for writing romance: they were simply answering God's vocational call, and, "Like Jesus, [they] would use stories to minister" (108–9). The writers in our study (Gregson and Lois) attempted to neutralize the stigma that they were not writing "real books" by defending their writing process, contrasting the goals of literary and commercial fiction, demonstrating the impact of their work on readers, and pointing out the sexism implicit in the stigma. Like Kirkland, whose authors' "most significant source of immunity to such critical impugnations is financial success" (239), our authors, too, touted their financial success when those outside the industry stigmatized them through "sneering" or "leering" at the (perceived) sexual content of their work. In these interactions, authors took three tacks: contesting the stigma of women's sexuality, personalizing the stigma by playing up a sexual persona, or professionalizing the process by emphasizing why sex scenes were pivotal to story development (Lois and Gregson "Sneers and Leers").

Of note, many of Kirkland's interviewees reported ambivalence about writing romance; some authors felt shame for writing in a disparaged genre while others felt popular romance was beneath them. Similarly, many of her authors felt conflicted about writing in a genre they perceived to be in conflict with their feminist ideals. The contrast between her findings and later studies (Lois and Gregson "Aspirational Emotion Work," Gregson and Lois, Neal) is striking, insofar as her study shows authors being complicit in the stigmatization of the genre, whereas more recent work shows authors reacting to and rebuffing the stigma.

Limitations and directions for future research

A troubling, but not surprising, thread throughout much of the existing social science literature is a perpetuation of stereotypes about romance novels and the people (that is, women) who read them. One of these stigmas relates to the books being formulaic. In their content analysis, Ménard and Cabrera explained the lack of statistically significant differences in orgasm scenes between 1989 and 2009 by noting "the formulaic nature of these contemporary romance novels" (208). Bereska drew upon this stereotype in her study of adolescent romance publishers, justifying her content analysis sample by noting, "Due to the formulaic nature of novels in these genres ... the books chosen with each category are believed to be representative of other books in those same categories" (39). Likewise, in describing the challenges facing readers and authors of evangelical romance is the content of the books, Neal writes: "The novels do not exhibit literary excellence, embrace a feminist politics, or encourage a liberal faith. Rather, they rely on formulaic plots, reaffirm heterosexual marriage, and revere evangelical piety" (38). While arguing that this combination of factors is what makes the subgenre worthy of study, it nevertheless reifies the stigmas. Crane's research similarly perpetuates some of these biases when she explains that she developed her survey in collaboration with "two women writers puzzled by and interested in the popularity or romance novels" (259), as if a preference for the genre is a baffling mystery that must be explained by social science.

A second stereotype these studies play up is the connection between romance novels and sex. Of course, some romance novels include explicit sex scenes, but that is certainly not the case for the entire genre. Just as outsiders buy into this stigma, assuming romances and the people who produce them are hypersexual (Lois and Gregson "Sneers and Leers"), so, too, do social scientists—although they apply the stigma to readers. As Ménard observed, "romance novel research within the social sciences has been extremely limited in its focus, which may perpetuate unwanted stereotypes about romance novels (e.g., they are 'pornography for women')" (9). Implicit in many social science research agendas is a negative perception of women's rationality, morality, and sexual agency. With this in mind, we must critique our discipline's almost single-minded focus on gender and sex as topics of inquiry in studying romance fiction. As Ménard wrote, the field would benefit from studies of "portrayals of religion, politics, family, children, physical and mental illness, employment, leisure activities, communication styles, interpersonal relationships, etc." (16).

A further weakness of much of the social science literature on the romance genre comprises the lack of methodological sophistication in the research. Crane's survey of 80 female respondents and follow-up interviews with 24 of them, for example, result in descriptive findings based on frequencies in the quantitative and qualitative data. By contrast, a more rigorous approach would include inferential statistics for the quantitative data and a richer theoretical analysis of the qualitative data. Likewise, Radway's ethnography with romance readers had many methodological limitations, most notably her lack of recognition that the ethnographer's subjective experience must be taken into account when analyzing data—a critique she leveled against herself when she explained that if she were "writing *Reading the Romance* today, I would differentiate much more clearly between the remarks actually made by my respondents and my own observations about them" (5).

There are countless issues with the sampling procedures utilized in these studies, from an overreliance on white, heterosexual college students in survey and interview-based research (e.g., Bonomi; Wu "Gender, Romance Novels, and Plastic Sexuality"; Coles and Sharp) to a startling array of acceptable sample sizes for peer-reviewed published content analyses—ranging from 16 books (Christopherson) to 120 (Clawson). With two exceptions (Wood; Wu "Reading Romance Novels"), the existing literature uses a heteronormative frame in the sample of books selected for content analysis or readers recruited for behavior research. Similarly, using small, non-representative samples of romance novels shows a lack of appreciation for the diversity of plot lines and levels of sensuality that exist across the different sub-genres. There is simply too much variation within the genre for findings from one sub-genre to be generalized to another, a notion Ménard addressed in an article responding to critiques by the romance community about one of her studies (Ménard and Cabrera).

The rapidly expanding markets for "diverse" and "multicultural" romances are ripe areas for intersectional feminist analyses. We point to Christian-Smith's content analysis of how gendered messages differed for characters with varying racial and social class backgrounds and Wood's research on the gendered portrayals of characters with different sexual identities as examples of the intersectional work contemporary scholars ought to engage in. Additionally, we see a need for further research into the experiences of diverse authors, whose work has been largely excluded from the mainstream, white, heterosexual genre, both in terms of what their unique perspectives bring to the genre and how people who read these books experience them. These questions beg methodologically rigorous, theoretically-steeped analyses.

As a final comment, we note that we had to reach back four decades to find studies to review for this chapter. Much of what we did find was plagued with methodological shortcomings, such that some research didn't even make the final cut for our review. Rather than be discouraged, we regard this deficit as a call to action. There is clearly much work to be done, and great potential for colleagues in the social sciences to contribute to this important field.

Notes

1 We exclude Jayne Ann Krentz's (1992) *Dangerous Men and Adventurous Women* from our analysis for this reason. While the book examines many of the issues of interest to social scientists, the work represents literary criticism and analysis, not social science.
2 Contemporary romance is the subgenre of novels "set from 1950 to the present that focus primarily on the romantic relationship" (www.rwa.org).
3 The Romance Writers of America is the leading professional trade organization for romance authors; the RITA award for excellence is given annually to one book in each of 12 subgenres within romance (https://en.wikipedia.org/wiki/RITA_Award).

Works cited

Bereska, Tami M. "Adolescent Sexuality and the Changing Romance Novel Market." *The Canadian Journal of Human Sexuality*, vol. 3, no. 1, 1994, pp. 35–44.
Blumer, Herbert. *Symbolic Interactionism: Perspective and Method*. University of California Press, 1969.
Bonomi, Amy E., et al. "Fiction or Not? *Fifty Shades* Is Associated with Health Risks in Adolescent and Young Adult Females." *Journal of Women's Health*, vol. 23, no. 9, 2014, pp. 720–728.
Bourdieu, Pierre. "The Production of Belief." *Media, Culture and Society*, vol. 3, no. 2, 1980, pp. 261–293.
Bourdieu, Pierre. *Distinction*. Routledge, 1984.
Brackett, Kim Pettigrew. "Facework Strategies among Romance Fiction Readers." *The Social Science Journal*, vol. 37, no. 3, 2000, pp. 347–360.
Cabrera, Christine and Amy Dana Ménard. "'She Exploded into A Million Pieces': A Qualitative and Quantitative Analysis of Orgasms in Contemporary Romance Novels." *Sexuality & Culture*, vol. 17, 2013, pp. 193–212.
Christian-Smith, Linda K. "Gender, Popular Culture, and Curriculum: Adolescent Romance Novels as Gender Text." *Curriculum Inquiry*, vol. 17, 1987, pp. 365–406.
Christian-Smith, Linda K. *Becoming A Woman Through Romance*. Routledge, 1990.
Christian-Smith, Linda K. "Voices of Resistance: Young Women Readers of Romance Fiction." *Beyond Silenced Voices: Class, Race, and Gender in United States Schools*, edited by Lois Weis, and Michelle Fine, State University of New York Press, 1993, pp. 169–189.
Christopherson, Neal. "Accommodation and Resistance in Religious Fiction: Family Structures and Gender Roles." *Sociology of Religion*, vol. 60, no. 4, 1999, pp. 439–455.

Clawson, Laura. "Cowboys and Schoolteachers: Gender in Romance Novels, Secular and Christian." *Sociological Perspectives*, vol. 48, no. 4, 2006, pp. 461–479.

Coles, Claire D. and M. Johnna Sharp. "Some Sexual, Personality, and Demographic Characteristics of Women Readers of Erotic Romances." *Archives of Sexual Behavior*, vol. 13, no. 3, 1984, pp. 87–209.

Cox, Anthony and Maryanne Fisher. "The Texas Billionaire's Pregnant Bride: An Evolutionary Interpretation of Romance Fiction Titles." *Journal of Social, Evolutionary, and Cultural Psychology*, vol. 3, no. 4, 2009, pp. 386–401.

Crane, Lynda L. "Romance Novel Readers: In Search of Feminist Change." *Women's Studies*, vol. 23, 1994, pp. 257–269.

Diekman, Amanda B. et al. "Love Means Never Having to Be Careful: The Relationship between Reading Romance Novels and Safe Sex Behavior." *Psychology of Women Quarterly*, vol. 24, 2000, pp. 179–188.

Fisher, Maryanne and Anthony Cox. "Man Change Thyself: Hero versus Heroine Development in Harlequin Romance Novels." *Journal of Social, Evolutionary, and Cultural Psychology*, vol. 4, no. 4, 2010, pp. 305–316.

Fowler, Bridget. *The Alienated Reader: Women and Popular Romantic Literature in the Twentieth Century*. Harvester Wheatsheaf, 1991.

Goffman, Erving. *Interaction Ritual: Essays on Face-to-Face Behavior*. Pantheon, 1967.

Gregson, Joanna and Jennifer Lois. "Legitimating Romance: Neutralizing the Stigma of Romantic Fiction." Paper presented at the Annual Meeting of the Popular Culture Association, April 1, 2015, New Orleans.

Harris, Emily Ann. et al. "Fifty Shades Flipped: Effects of Reading Erotica Depicting a Sexually Dominant Woman Compared to a Sexually Dominant Man." *The Journal of Sex Research*, vol. 2, 2016, pp. 1–12.

Larson, Christine. "Writing the Romance: Precarity, Solidarity, and the Ethics of Care in E-books and Digital Self-Publishing." Unpublished manuscript. 2016.

Lois, Jennifer and Joanna Gregson. "Sneers and Leers: Romance Writers and Gendered Sexual Stigma." *Gender & Society*, vol. 29, no. 4, 2015, pp. 459–483.

Lois, Jennifer and Joanna Gregson. "Negotiating the Professional Artist Identity: Romance Authors, Emotions, and Precarious Work in the Arts." Unpublished manuscript. 2016.

Lois, Jennifer and Joanna Gregson. "Aspirational Emotion Work: Calling, Emotional Capital, and Becoming a 'Real Writer'." *Journal of Contemporary Ethnography*, vol. 48, no. 1, 2019, pp. 51–79.

Luker, Kristin. *Dubious Conceptions: The Politics of Teenage Pregnancy*. Harvard University Press, 1996.

Ménard, A. Dana "Notes from the Field: Reflecting on Romance Novel Research: Past, Present and Future." *Journal of Popular Romance Studies*, vol. 3, no. 2, 2013, pp. 1–19.

Ménard, A. Dana and Christine Cabrera. "'Whatever the Approach, Tab B Still Fits into Slot A': Twenty Years of Sex Scripts in Romance Novels." *Sexuality & Culture*, vol. 15, 2011, pp. 240–255.

Moody, Stephanie Lee. *Affecting Genre: Women's Participation with Romance Fiction*. 2013. University of Michigan, Ph.D. Dissertation.

Muram, David, et al. "Teenage Pregnancy: Dating and Sexual Attitudes." *Journal of Sex Education and Therapy*, vol. 18, no. 4, 1994, pp. 264–276.

Neal, Lynn S. *Romancing God: Evangelical Women and Inspirational Fiction*. University of North Carolina Press, 2006.

Parameswaran, Radhika. "Western Romance Fiction as English-Language Media in Postcolonial India." *Journal of Communication*, vol. 49, 1999, pp. 84–105.

Parameswaran, Radhika. "Reading Fiction of Romance: Gender, Sexuality, and Nationalism in Postcolonial India." *Journal of Communication*, vol. 52, 2002, pp. 832–851.

Puri, Jyoti. "Reading Romance Novels in Postcolonial India." *Gender & Society*, vol. 11, no. 4, 1997, pp. 434–452.

Radick, Caryn. "Romance Writers' Use of Archives." *Archivaria*, vol. 81, 2016, pp. 45–73.

Radway, Janice. *Reading the Romance: Women, Patriarchy, and Popular Literature*. 1984. University of North Carolina Press, 1991.

Regis, Pamela. *A Natural History of the Romance Novel*. University of Pennsylvania Press, 2003.

Regis, Pamela. "What Do Critics Owe the Romance? Keynote Address at the Second Annual Conference of the International Association for the Study of Popular Romance." *Journal of Popular Romance Studies*, vol. 2.1, 2011, n.p. jprstudies.org/issues/issue-2-1. Accessed June 29. 2016.

Roach, Catherine M. *Happily Ever After: The Romance Story in Popular Culture*. University of Indiana Press, 2016.

Weaver-Zercher, Valerie. *Thrill of the Chaste: The Allure of Amish Romance Novels*. Johns Hopkins University Press, 2013.

Wood, Christine V. "Tender Heroes and Twilight Lovers: Re-Reading the Romance in Mass Market Pulp Novels, 1950-1965." *Journal of Lesbian Studies*, vol. 18, 2014, pp. 372–392.

Wu, Huei-Hsia. "Gender, Romance Novels, and Plastic Sexuality in the United States: A Focus on Female College Students." *Journal of International Women's Studies*, vol. 8, 2006, pp. 125–134.

Wu, Huei-Hsia. "Reading Romance Novels and Female Sexuality among American Heterosexual and Lesbian College Students." *International Journal of the Diversity*, vol. 6, no. 6, 2007, pp. 31–38.

Wu, Huei-Hsia and Anthony Walsh. "Romance Novels and Female Sexuality: Vicarious Participation." *Free Inquiry in Creative Sociology*, 2005.

16 Publishing the romance novel

John Markert

Individuals who are strategically placed within an organization to decide the fate of product/ideas are called gatekeepers. These individuals, by virtue of their key position, screen and selectively choose from an array of products/ideas what to offer the public. The crucial role played by gatekeepers has been observed in a wide variety of disparate organizations and markets (White "Gatekeepers"; Becker; Reagan; Di-Capua; Fernald et al.). In book publishing, the editor is viewed as the key gatekeeper because it is the editor who decides what books to filter into the production cycle and which to exclude (Coser; Coser et al.; Powell; Greco 123–6). The importance of upper-level management in providing input and direction, however, is seldom given more than cursory attention in these works.

The role of the editor cannot be overstated; nevertheless, the editor is given directions by upper-level management on the houses' direction, and this can shape the decision of the editor as to what books they will select, as we will see with the selection of Woodiwiss's now-classic *The Flame and the Flower* at Avon in 1972 and the debut of Ecstasy at Dell Candlelight in 1980. We will also see that the failure of a number of romance lines in the 1970s and 1980s was largely (though not exclusively) the fault of management who set arbitrary production figures and forced editors to take manuscripts they might otherwise have rejected because they were poorly written or poorly plotted. In short, editors do not work in a vacuum. They are under directive from upper-level management to proceed along certain lines. The relationship is not unidirectional. Editors at staff meetings also provide input to upper-level management regarding trends and try to convince management to go in this or that direction, as was the case when Mary Ann Stuart at *Playboy* successful talked reluctant managers into venturing into women's fiction and launched a line of sensual historical romances (Markert *Publishing Romance*). The type of romance content that is offered to the public is, then, a complicated process and one that is not totally in the hands of the editor, as much attention as the editor deservedly gets for "discovering" new talent.

Research on the romance novel tends to revolve around its content, and even though many critics acknowledge the structure of the industry shapes content, the dynamics within the industry are often only briefly touched upon. When the industry is critiqued, the discussion often justifiably revolves around the two giant romance publishers: Harlequin and Mills & Boon. Margaret Jensen and Paul Grescoe both critique Toronto-based Harlequin in some detail. Jensen follows the traditional path by examining nuances in Harlequin content, though in the first third of her analysis she does sketch the early organization years at Harlequin; Grescoe picks up the story and though he retreads the early history of Harlequin for those unfamiliar with Jensen's work, he goes on to provide insights about developments at Harlequin during the first half of Brian Hickey's tenure as CEO (1988–2001).[1] Both Jensen and Grescoe are leaned on heavily in my own analysis of Harlequin's early years (Markert, *Publishing Romance*), which threads together a few missing pieces from the 1970s, 1980s, and 1990s, and continues the story of Harlequin after Hickey resigned and Donna Hayes took over (2001–13), leaving Craig Swinwood to finalize Harlequin's sale to HarperCollins in 2014.

Two other works examine internal dynamics within Mills & Boon in Richmond, outside London. Joseph McAleer goes into great detail on the early years of Mills & Boon, from its inception in 1908 through 1972 when Mills & Boon was purchased by Harlequin. Jay Dixon also looks at the early years of Mills & Boon but continues the story through the 1990s. Her analysis, like Laura Vivanco's, largely focuses on the novels' content and clearly shows how Mills & Boon novels kept pace with evolving social trends; Dixon's critique of organizational dynamics is woven into the story of content, but her long association with Mills & Boon colors her lens of Harlequin's contribution. My own analysis examines Mills & Boon from the vantage point of its distributor, Harlequin, in Toronto, and some of its owner's views are distinct from those sketched by Dixon. This difference is largely a matter of perspective: Grescoe and I focus on internal organizational dynamics and the rationale by key insiders that influenced the positioning of the romance novel in the marketplace, which means our critique of Mills & Boon is viewed through the lens of key decision-makers at Harlequin, whereas Dixon views Harlequin through the eyes of insiders at Mills & Boon.[2] Another variation in these studies is the focus of the various authors: Grescoe, McAleer, and I concentrate more on internal developments shaping the romance novel and thus only summarily critique changes in the content of the romance novel, while Jensen, Dixon, and Vivanco focus more on how the content of the romance novel changed over time and only sketch the influence of organizational dynamics in shaping content. The two approaches marry nicely by providing a holistic account of developments of the novel at both Harlequin and Mills & Boon.

The Harlequin-Mills & Boon story is taken overseas by a number of authors who look at how the novels originating elsewhere are adapted to local exigencies: McWilliams, Thomas, and Driscoll et al. have all independently looked at how the romance novel is adapted to social conditions within New Zealand and Australia; Eva Hemmungs Wirtén dissects how and why the editors at Förlager Harlequin in Stockholm modify content to make it "digestible" for the Scandinavian reader. The importance of the international development of the romance novel is traced in my analysis, but beyond the scope of this brief review of the industry.[3] Olivia Tapper is correct to point out that the international, which has always been there to some degree, is even more pronounced to developments with the romance field at the outset of the twenty-first century. All this attention to Harlequin-Mills & Boon tends to detract from industry developments outside these two monolithic organizations. My contribution departs from the straightforward history of the dominant romance producers by taking into account how others in the industry responded to the dominant publisher's product. The present analysis builds on the theoretical framework suggest by White ("Where") and DiMaggio and Powell: publishers survey the competition and niche their product to compete with the dominant producer and, in turn, the dominant publisher, whether it be Harlequin or Mills & Boon, need to stay competitive by offering a similar but slightly different type of content.

Susan Palmer takes social developments that impacted the industry into account when she traces the current state of the romance novel (1960s–80s) to earlier developments (1930s–50s) in mass-market publishing.[4] Palmer is right to start with the development of mass-market publishing, which, as John Tebbel points out in his seminal study of the book publishing industry, had its origin in the United Kingdom when Sir Allen Lane introduced Penguin Books in 1936 and when Robert Fair de Graff adapted the new mass market paperback to the U.S. market and launched Pocket Books in 1938. The incipient paperback revolution was stalled by the advent of World War II. The paper shortage of the war years ended not long after the war did, but this was offset by a rapid rise in manufacturing costs. Paperback reprints thus "offered the best chance to keep a wide range of books available to the public at prices that large numbers of people could afford to pay" (Tebbel 348). The result was a boom in mass-market publishing between 1948 and 1955. Among the new paperback houses were New American Library (1948), Harlequin (1949), Pyramid (1949–-77), Fawcett (1950), Ace (1952), Ballantine (1952), and Berkley (1955). Many of these houses continue to be dominant mass-market publishers today, though some, like Penguin, have shifted their emphasis to "quality" paperbacks, and others, such as Berkley, Jove, Fawcett, and, more recently, Harlequin, have merged with other firms but continue to publish paperback books under their original names.

The world of Harlequin: 1949–79

Harlequin Enterprises Limited[5] was founded in 1949 by the former mayor of Winnipeg, Richard Gardyn Bonnycastle. Prior to launching Harlequin Enterprises—a name chosen to convey light entertainment—Bonnycastle owned a company that produced American paperbacks for distribution in Canada. This company provided the base for Bonnycastle's publishing venture.

Harlequin was not much different than other paperback houses of the day. Between 1950 and 1959, Harlequin published an average of 50 books a year: some years it offered as few as 25 (1955) to 28 (1956) titles and some years as many as 61 (1953) to 65 (1950). Most of these titles were reprints of westerns, mysteries, and thrillers, and included books by such authors a W. Somerset Maugham, Arthur Conan Doyle, and Edgar Wallace. The list was lightly peppered with romances. The first decade was unmarked by any notable success.

The romance stage of Harlequin's enterprise began in late 1957 when it published its first British romance, a Mills & Boon reprint entitled *Hospital in Buwambo.* This transcontinental arrangement and the consequent domination of Mills & Boon romances among Harlequin's titles was prompted by Mary Bonnycastle, then editor of the house and the publisher's wife, who considered the Mills & Boon romances to be "fiction of good taste" (Guiley 84). That Mary Bonnycastle would decide to focus increasingly on romance because she enjoyed the books should not be considered unusual: editors tend to select novels they personally enjoy, assuming that their enjoyment reflects the consumer's taste (Coser 14–22; Coser, Kadushin, and Powell; Simon and Fyfe).

Mary Bonnycastle's personal preference for the genre may have been one reason for Harlequin's decision to increase its romance line, but it is not the only one. The arrangement with Mills & Boon was also financially sound for both publishers. For

Mills & Boon, it provided an outlet for its hardcover romances that had traditionally been marketed to libraries at a time when this market was drying up in the United Kingdom. For Harlequin, the reprint agreement would provide a steady stream of fiction titles that would already have established themselves as proven sellers in Britain. The decision must have proved satisfactory because between 1957 and 1963 Harlequin's list of Mills & Boon romance titles increased steadily from 33 to 78. Yearly romance production rose to 96 titles in 1964, the year Harlequin began publishing Mills & Boon romances exclusively; it remained at this level until 1973, when Harlequin debuted Presents and added another 48 Mills & Boon titles to its list.

Harlequin vastly expanded its market when it entered into an arrangement with Pocket Books in 1970 to have its books distributed in the United States. The only real thematic difference between Harlequin's product and that being released by American mass-market houses in the 1950s and 1960s was that Harlequin's novels were all set in the contemporary world while American romances were predominantly historical romances, which are set in some bygone era: Gothic (circa 1700), Regency (1811–20), Victorian (1837–1900), Edwardian (1901–10), and the like. The novels of the period, whether contemporary or historical, were otherwise very much alike: "sweet" with no overt sexual nuances, with stereotyped 1950s heroes and heroines.[6] To compete in the American marketplace, and to set its product apart from American-based romance publishers, Harlequin had to do something unique. It did!

The first major decision Harlequin made was to appoint W. Lawrence Heisey president in 1971. Heisey must have seemed an unusual choice in the publishing world since he had no background in publishing: he was a marketing executive at Proctor and Gamble. His marketing background would prove significant because he didn't try to sell each novel as it rolled off the presses; instead, he focused on selling the overall product—romance novels. He was able to do this because, unlike most publishers of the day, Harlequin did not have a range of fiction and nonfiction to promote. Heisey reasoned that if a publisher could arouse interest in one book, they could arouse interest in the series—a point, Heisey says, that "seems terribly obvious today, but it wasn't then" (Heisey). It was this insight that led Harlequin to emphasize its romance line, while most publishers were attempting to arouse interest in particular authors or titles.

To "hook" the consumer on its romance line, Harlequin employed numerous giveaways, which Heisey readily acknowledges as gimmicks. One of these was to distribute 2 million copies of the book *Dark Star* to dealers at no cost in 1973. The book was sold to the consumer for 15 cents. By giving them to dealers and allowing the dealers to sell the book for 15 cents dealers were assured a quick, straight profit on every paperback. In other introductory offers for readers who might be reluctant to spend even 15 cents, Harlequin gave away millions of other books outright, among them 5 million copies of Violet Winspear's *Honey Is Bitter*. These books were targeted to the audience Harlequin wished to attract, the housewife. One such targeted product was arranged with Heisey's old company, Proctor and Gamble: inside each box of P&G Bio-Ad laundry detergent was a free Harlequin novel. The success of these giveaways can be judged by the firm footing Harlequin established by 1976, when Heisey abandoned the gimmicks for the more traditional promotion of advertising. "We finally built a big enough business base," Heisey said, "that we were able to [begin] formal advertising" (Heisey). Their formal advertising campaign was also strongly focused: over 80 percent of their unprecedented $1.3 million was spent on the high-female daytime soap-opera viewer.

It was not all marketing and distribution, however. Harlequin made some innovative content changes during the 1970s. Its typically sweet romances were "notched up" a degree with the introduction of Presents in 1973. These books, though still sweet, did at least acknowledge that individuals in a committed relationship engaged in sexual activity before marriage, even if the novel did not venture into the bedroom. It was, interestingly, Heisey who decided to push for these books; the editors were reluctant to introduce them because they were so different from what they had been releasing. Heisey felt that since the novels were doing so well in the U.K., they would do well in the North American market. He was right. The Presents line was soon outselling the more traditional romance line (Heisey). Harlequin also introduced Janet Dailey in 1976. Dailey was Harlequin's first non-Mills & Boon author and, being American, she situated her romances in the United States instead of in the U. K., Australia, or on the Continent (Guiley 156).

Competing against Harlequin: American houses, 1949–79[7]

American romance publishers released a mix of contemporary and historical novels during the 1940s and 1950s. These novels were released in limited number to round out a house's list; they were not expected to generate any real profit. During the 1960s, American houses, while they continued to release some contemporary romances, increasingly shifted to historical romances since Harlequin was "flooding" the market with contemporary novels. This shift to historicals became even more pronounced after Harlequin gained wider distribution in the United States market in 1970 since few publishers in the United States felt they could compete head-on with the strong outpouring of contemporary romances by Harlequin. The shift to historical novels in the United States was accelerated by the successful entry of Avon's historical product in 1972, and Avon's new brand of romances moved the historicals from the sweet to the sensual (meaning sexual content that was more explicit and erotic), which to this point in time was markedly absent in either the contemporary or historical romances.

At the outset of the 1970s Avon was much like other mass-market publishers except for one key feature: they were looking for original paperback novels. The move from reprints to original releases took place shortly after 26-year-old Peter Mayer became editor-in-chief in 1964, then publisher in 1965. Prior to assuming the helm at Avon, Mayer acquired the rights to Henry Roth's long out of print 1934 novel *Call It Sleep*. Instead of having the novel reissued in traditional paperback release, Mayer prepared it as an original publication, with bound galleys sent to book reviewers in advance of publication—an unusual undertaking for a paperback house in 1964. Just as unusual was the front-page review by *The New York Times Book Review*, which helped send sales past the million-copy mark. The success of *Call It Sleep* proved that a paperback novel could be a commercial success without the stamp of hardcover bestseller status. By 1972, Avon could fill an entire month's list of 26 titles with paperback originals.

This search for original manuscripts prompted senior editor Nancy Coffey to read Kathleen Woodiwiss's unsolicited first novel. *The Flame and the Flower* was not a typical romance, and not only because the content was vastly different. At 400-plus pages, it was also nearly three times the length of romances being published at the time. Its length made it more likely that the manuscript would be read, since at the time Avon was seeking "good original novels rather than romances" (Coffey) and a shorter manuscript would immediately have distinguished it as a romance. Coffey took it home over the weekend to browse through and, so the story goes, couldn't put it down. She regarded her own reaction as a fairly reliable barometer of the book's potential success: "I figured that if I would keep reading this story, other women would too" (Coffey).

The book was certainly atypical in romantic content. Woodiwiss's novel was spicier and more sensual than any of the romance subgenres being published at the time: it's a historical novel set in early nineteenth-century London; it opens with an attempted rape followed by an actual rape. The heroine, Heather, has her virginity forcibly taken by Captain Brandon Birmingham, who makes her pregnant. Her relatives force them into a shotgun wedding. Afterward, they spend almost the entire book certain of each other's hatred and resentment, only to discover, some 400 pages later, that they are actually deeply in love.

The Flame and the Flower was submitted in 1971 and published as an Avon Spectacular, or lead title, in April 1972, by an "unknown author, without any review attention, and with no extra effort from Avon to promote it" (Guiley 65). Nevertheless, the book went on to sell one million copies within the year, touching what Kenneth Davis somewhat cryptically calls "a slumbering erogenous zone in the American heartland" (362). Soon thereafter, another "bodice-ripper," *Sweet Savage Love*, was submitted by another unknown author, Rosemary Rogers, to "the editor of *The Flame and the Flower*" (Guiley 65). Rogers' first novel notched up the sensual and resulted in the disparaging term that would mark the subgenre, since the heroine had her bodice ripped off numerous times during the course of the novel.[8]

Over the next few years another half dozen "Avon ladies" were introduced. Avon's success with the new subgenre did not go unnoticed, and before long others were rushing in to cash in on the new trend in sensual historicals. The first two came from unlikely sources—newly formed Zebra Books (1974), which was looking for a niche (Zacharius), and Playboy Press, which had never before published women's fiction (Stuart). Both houses quickly established a presence with their sensual historical romances. Management at other houses pressed their editors to replicate the success of these publishers and soon the field was awash with sensual historicals: production rose from only a handful of novels in the early 1970s to nearly 300 a year by mid-decade. These numbers were often mistakenly interpreted as an indication of the novel's success, even as many houses were dropping (or drastically reducing) the number of sensual historicals being released due to lack of sales. One reason for the lackluster sales was that the market was saturated with sensual historical novels. Another reason, tied to the first, was that in the rush to mimic the success of these early houses, many newly promoted female editors felt forced to meet management's arbitrarily contrived production quotas and accepted inferior products. Yet another reason, suggested by many of the seasoned editors in place in the late-1970s (Sullivan, Nichols, Edwards), was that by the close of the 1970s the rape theme had become politicized as the feminist concerns of the late 1960s took root in the wider society during the 1970s; it was no longer viewed as escapist literature. The proof to this latter proposition is that when the reader was offered an alternative, more thematically nuanced, sensual product in 1980 by Dell's new Ecstasy line, they rushed to embrace it (Markert "Unsated"; Thurston; Lyons and Selinger).

The two-front challenge to Harlequin's supremacy[9]

In early 1976, top executives at Harlequin were engaged in regular and serious deliberations over the Pocket Books distribution contract. These sessions, which often ran long into the night, eventually resulted in the decision to terminate. Fred Kerner, the newest member of Harlequin management's executive team, dissented, although his objection was less to the decision than the method (Kerner). He felt that they should not forewarn Pocket of their intention and only give them the required three-month termination notice. Kerner's advice went unheeded and senior management informed Dick Snyder at Simon & Schuster of their intention. Snyder was furious, and argued that they had a gentleman's agreement to stay with Pocket Books. Heisey called from Kennedy airport on his way back to Toronto and said, "We are men of honor and will honor our agreement with you" (Heisey; Snyder). Four years later, Harlequin's break was anticipated, and Simon & Schuster's Silhouette Romance was already in the pipeline. Silhouette was designed to go head-to-head with Harlequin in the sweet contemporary market.

Simon & Schuster's decision to compete with Harlequin was exclusively managerial, based on: 1) knowledge of the Harlequin product; 2) Pocket's extensive distribution system; and 3) an astute awareness of just how much income was generated by these slim volumes of love and marriage. The decision was reinforced by research between 1977 and 1979 that clearly showed that the romance reader consumption rate in America was below the norm: Canadian consumption was 1500 books per 1000 women, but in the United States it was only 800. Simon & Schuster also found growth potential among loyal Harlequin readers.

One of the few in the industry to have knowledge of Harlequin's closely guarded sales figures, Simon & Schuster pumped millions into starting the aptly named Silhouette Books—management directed its staff to emulate (i.e., shadow) Harlequin, to use it as their "role model." This strategy was clearly visible on Silhouette's pre-launch promotional material aimed at book retailers, which carried the bold print logo: "When It Comes to Romance, Experience Is the Best Teacher." It was also seen in their early post-launch retail advertising, which simply stated: "The only other line you need is Harlequin."

Simon & Schuster did three other things to make the new line Harlequin-competitive. First, it hired P.J. Fennell, Harlequin's vice president of marketing and sales in North America, as the President of Silhouette Books. Second, it secured the services of Janet Dailey, who had become one of Harlequin's bestselling authors, and used her name to help promote the new line, which even subsequent CEO of Harlequin David Galloway admitted was a "good strategy" (Galloway; Johnson),[10] even if she was a loss leader.[11] Third, they had a one-year inventory of novels ready to go when they launched because they were open to all those American women who had written contemporary romances set in the United States but had no outlet for their manuscripts. And fourth, Silhouette debuted Romances in 1980 with a $3 million advertising campaign, spending $1.1 million for airtime from mid-May to mid-June, when the line premiered. Another $1 million was spent on other forms of advertising; this burgeoned to $22 million by 1982—a figure comparable to Harlequin's increased advertising expenditure and more than the entire U.S. publishing industry spent in domestic advertising.

The battle for market share between Harlequin and Silhouette raged until 1984 when Silhouette threw in the towel and sold to Harlequin. The battle had simply become too expensive for generalist publisher Simon & Schuster, which had other ventures to shore up its bottom line, which Silhouette was draining (Snyder). Harlequin, being a specialist publisher, was fighting for its very survival. The battle for market share between these two rivals was compounded by Dell's introduction of radical new content in December 1980 and the mad rush by other American publishers to cash in on the new sensual contemporary romance theme debuted by Dell Ecstasy.

Dell's Candlelight romance line was an anomaly in the American market since it did not follow the trend in sensual historical romances; it continued throughout the 1970s to produce a mix of four sweet contemporary and two historical (Regency) romances a month. The production of these six romances at Dell had remained fairly consistent since 1967. The novels were churned out to meet what was perceived in-house as a limited demand. Indeed, the new editor of the Dell Candlelight line, Vivian Stephens, could say that when she came aboard in late-1979, "The line wasn't looked at to make any money or make a statement for Dell. It was just there" (Stephens).[12] Perhaps because no one internally was paying any attention to the content of the novels, Stephens had little resistance when she introduced radically different contemporary romance content in 1980.

Stephens was a researcher for Time-Life Books before joining Dell.[13] She acknowledges her limited experience probably helped her get the job since romance editing "is usually done by people who are just starting in publishing. It is used as a stepping stone to get into mainstream fiction." This didn't pose an issue for Stephens who was in her 40s, nearly twice the age of most romance editors at the time: "I just want to do something I could enjoy without any competition." At best, Stephens's plans were modest: "What I tried to do was just increase the quality of the work, to kind of stretch the line, to try new people." Her lack of experience in the romance field and her feeling that the contemporary romances being produced by Dell were a bit "dated" led her to be open to new manuscripts. One shortly arrived. The book by Joan Hohl was called *Morning Rose, Evening Savage*, and "it was very sensuous. I never read anything as sensuous without being explicit." So, she says, "What the hell. I'll put it out. And if I get *any* negative feedback saying it's too sensuous, then of course I wouldn't do any more books [like it]."

The lack of negative reaction reinforced Stephens's decision to put out another sensual contemporary. Two manuscripts crossed her desk at the time: another by the author she had just published, and an unsolicited manuscript submitted by Jayne Castle. This latter book, *Gentle Pirate*, surpassed the merely sensual and ultimately liberated the contemporary romance novel beyond the sexually liberated theme that Carol Thurston finds in the sensual historical novels.

The hero and heroine in Castle's romance more closely resembled real 1980s people than those in other novels of the genre, which is why, Stephens' says, she published the novel: "all the things that are in it are right now, [are] the world today."[14] The novel sold out of its first printing within weeks and paved the way for the growth of the Candlelight Ecstasy line. Between 1980 and 1982, the sweet contemporary (Candlelight) and historical (Regency) line faded away and the Ecstasy books took over. Ecstasy initially released two books per month; production rose steadily to peak at eight novels every month in 1983–4, after which the trend started to reverse itself.

Romance aficionados and industry sources credit Dell's Candlelight Ecstasy line with changing the content of the romance novel in the 1980s, much as Avon is credited with initiating changes that affected the content of romance novels in the 1970s (Markert "Romance Publishing"; "Publishing Decision"; Guiley). One key difference, however, is that while it took a half dozen years before the Avon novels started to be imitated in any number, the market was soon awash with Ecstasy-like romances. The rapidity with which publishers responded to Ecstasy's new romance theme was largely the result of management's changing attitude toward romances[15] and having women editors in place to monitor trends in the field. The problem was that many of the new newly promoted editors did not fully grasp just what it was about the Dell product that appealed to readers, in no small part because Dell, unlike Avon in the 1970s, introduced multiple themes. One editor did, however: Carolyn Nichols.

The idea for a line of sensual contemporary romances featuring a divorced heroine who finds love the second time around was originated by Carolyn Nichols who had actually conceived the idea for Second Chance at Love in 1978 and pitched it to management (Nichols; Edwards). The publisher, William Grose, did not feel the idea had merit: "It would take an enormously successful romance formula to bring it into the twentieth century" (Guisto-Davis 43). He appears to have had a change of heart after witnessing the success of Ecstasy: "Judging from how well some of our competitors have done, it seems the market for romances keeps growing and growing" (Guisto-Davis 43). Nichols, more seasoned than her 20-something-year-old fellow editors, honed in on one aspect of the Ecstasy book, and her success led others to focus on one nuance of the multiple Ecstasy themes without fully realizing just what it was that made the new sensual contemporary novels resonate with the reader.

Ecstasy introduced a heroine who was older, divorced, sexually experienced, and career-oriented. Love was still the *sine qua non* of the novel but Dell's content was more dramatic,[16] and the more unique the recombination of existing factors of production, argued the economist Joseph Schumpeter, the greater the amount of disruption that will occur in the task environment as producers scurry to imitate the latest innovations. Thus, Dell, unlike Avon a decade earlier, "recombined" the existing romance theme by introducing more than one content variation. Many editors appeared unsure exactly which innovation appealed most to readers, or even who the readers now were. The result was a potpourri of lines over the next few years that attempted to marginally differentiate themselves by focusing on a different dimension of the new themes; for example, Second Chance at Love featured divorced women; Intimate Moments and Finding Mr. Right focused on other thematic variations: Intimate Moments honed in on career-oriented females; Finding Mr. Right pivoted around the heroine's choice between two equally suitable males.

The rapidity with which publishers responded to Dell's innovations did not allow editors or writers time to grasp the reasons for Ecstasy's success, yet the editors were required to publish from two to eight romances a month in the new liberated style of Ecstasy. At the same time, few books in the new subgenre were available. Editors in the 1980s, then, could not point to other writers—as Mary Ann Stuart at Playboy did by simply telling her writers to read Woodiwiss, Rogers, or McBain—and say merely, "read so-and-so; that's what we want" (Stuart). Editors resorted to detailed guidelines to help delineate the new content for authors so that they would be able to fill their lists, while, at the same time, marginally differentiating their product from other lines. The result was similar to the reader disaffection that followed the surge of bodice-rippers in the late 1970s: too many sensual contemporary books on the market, many of which were poorly written in the frantic search for authors,[17] resulting, by mid-decade, in lines reducing their monthly output, or, more often than not, the line being terminated because of lackluster sales. By the end of the 1980s, the category romance market had settled down and returned to normal, which in this case means that Harlequin had regained market supremacy and other publishers, burned by the "romance revolution" of the first half of the decade, reverted to producing some romances for what they viewed as a limited market. The decline in category publishing during this period did open the door for some of the better-known category authors, such as Nora Roberts, Laura Kinsale, and Susan Elizabeth Phillips, among a handful of others, to move beyond category romances into publishing single-title romance novels,[18] which Avon pioneered with Woodiwiss and continued to mine, and Harlequin, as we'll see below, would subsequently move into with MIRA.

Line diversification: the byword of the new millennium

Harlequin returned to market supremacy with the purchase of Silhouette. It makes sure that it maintains its dominant share of the romance market by staying abreast of trends. Red Dress Ink is a good example of how Harlequin does this. Red Dress was developed by Harlequin's future CEO, Donna Hayes (2002–13). The line was positioned to take advantage of the chick-lit craze that followed the publication of *Bridget Jones's Diary* in 1996. Most major publishing firms jumped aboard this bandwagon and rushed to publish chick-lit novels as part of their mainstream press; a few even had dedicated chick-lit imprints, such as Kensington (Strapless) and Simon & Schuster (Downtown). Harlequin, whose expertise was in category fiction, was the only house to develop chick-lit as a category line, which means that while most houses were releasing a few novels every year in the chick-lit format as part of their overall program, Harlequin was publishing a new title every month. It was a contentious in-house issue because it didn't fit snugly into the Harlequin oeuvre, which explains why the line didn't launch until late in 2001. It lasted until January 2013, a pretty good run for a steady diet of books that Dianne Moggy deemed an unsustainable program: "It was really a victim of time" (Moggy). Chick-lit had simply run its course. Other lines that debuted to keep the Harlequin brand fresh include, among others, Love and Laughter (1996–9), which emphasized humor in relationships; Love Inspired (1997–present), inspirational romances; NEXT (2005–12), that accentuated the next stage of a woman's life; Kimani (2005–18), African-American romances; Spice (2006–11), Nocturne (2006–present), paranormal romances; NASCAR (2007–10), Teen (2009–present), Heartwarming (2011–present), that revolves around traditional values; and Kiss (2013–present) for the New Adult 20-something market.

MIRA was also developed by Hayes; it launched in 1994 and is unquestionably Harlequin's most significant product development because it moved Harlequin into direct competition with other mainstream publishers of women's fiction, not just category romance fiction. It is clearly a success. As early as 2001, just six years after launching MIRA, single-title sales represented 25.6 percent of Harlequin's revenue (Millot 16). The company's bottom line is also supported by Harlequin's extensive international presence: its romances appear in 111 countries in 31 languages. In 1982, sales outside North America accounted for more than half (54 percent) of all Harlequin book sales. This may have dropped recently (2012) but international sales still contribute a hefty 47 percent to Harlequin's bottom line ("Global Publishing"). Its primary international markets are the U.K., Australia, Germany, Scandinavia, France, and, more recently, Japan ("Global Publishing"). In fact, it was Harlequin's strong international presence that initially attracted HarperCollins as a suitor.

Mainstream publishers have not thrown in the towel and conceded domain to Harlequin to the degree they did in the 1960s and 1970s; all major houses publish romances, and many have dedicated romance lines, such as Berkley's Heat and Avon's Red. But publishing is a different world today: "What used to work is not working anymore," said Monique Patterson at St. Martin's (Patrick). The issue goes beyond St. Martin's and also affects Harlequin. Diane Patrick at *Publishers Weekly* summed up the problem: "most professions we contacted acknowledged that ... all the old rules [are] crumbling," and, she goes on to say, that to move ahead publishing houses have to "ignore former 'set-in-stone' publishing conventions, categories, and strategies" (17). This has opened opportunities for independent houses outside the Big Five,[19] such as Kensington, Scholastic, and Sourcebooks, which, because they are less bureaucratically entrenched, are able to respond more rapidly to shifting market conditions (Peters and Waterman; Hayes et al. 287). The challenge to mainstream publishing is exacerbated by the potpourri of digital publishers and rising ranks of self-published authors.

Niche publishing abounds today, both within and outside the mainstream. African American, Young Adult, Christian or Inspirational, and LGBTQIA romances, all of which have a long and well-established niche, have gained renewed vigor at the outset of the new millennium and are thriving as never before. These areas are all separately developed in this collection, as is the growing popularity in the surge in erotica and paranormal romances today.[20] This section will therefore sidestep these developments and conclude by briefly turning its attention to one of the key features that is driving niche romance publishing today: the digital age.

Most mainstream publishers were toying with digital at the close of the 1990s but abandoned their efforts after the dot.com bubble burst in 2001 (Thompson 314). This left the field open to small digital publishers who took advantage of the opportunity to establish a strong presence before mainstream houses started, belatedly and somewhat lackadaisically, to (re)enter the field after 2010. Independent digital publishers launched ventures mainly because 1) they had been shut out by the mainstream houses, who balked at their radically different content, and 2) the cost of entry was attractive since the monetary investment was relatively meager, at least in comparison to the capital outlay necessary to start a brick-and-mortar publishing house. Ellora's Cave, one of the early entries into what I call xrotica—erotica at the upper end of the erotic spectrum where sexual escapades are often graphically depicted—is an excellent case in point and illustrates what has happened elsewhere among the small digital publishers.

Tina Engler launched a website in 2000 to sell her self-published erotic romance e-books, which she penned under the name Jaid Black. Ellora's Cave (EC) was an outgrowth of that venture and officially incorporated in 2002. Romantica is a trademark name and EC's main imprint. The Romantica line delivers a classic romance story because it's a love story with a happy ending; it's just sprinkled heavily with lots of sex, "described in graphic detail, using the kind of language regular people use, rather than flowery euphemisms" (Brashear). Kink (sexual fetishes) moves beyond the traditional romance and focuses on no-strings-attached sexual adventures;

it is the only line under the Exotika imprint. There are six lines that appear under the Blush imprint which tones down the erotic element. Just as MIRA was a means of keeping Harlequin category writers with Harlequin, Blush is a way to keep those writers with EC who want to write "regular" romances. The other independent digital publishers—Siren (2004–present), Samhain (2005–16), Changeling Press (2004–present), and Totally Bound (2006–present), to name but four erotic houses—share similar start-up histories. They have similar imprints and lines and use digital as their primary method of distribution.[21]

Adding to the growing digital market are self-published authors.[22] Some self-published authors did not like the restrictions imposed on them by their publisher; others couldn't find a publisher. Some have been very successful, but their success does not necessarily represent the experience of the average self-publishing author. One recent study sheds some light on the self-publishing cottage industry. Beverly Kendall, who entered the self-publishing world after her second novel did not generate enough sales to warrant Kensington renewing her contract, conducted the study. She is one of the success stories: she published her third book herself and in less than a year had earned over $100,000. She posted a survey online in an attempt to get a reading on what other self-publishing authors were doing. The survey, conducted in 2013, received 822 responses and while Kendall makes no claim at the scientific merits of her study, it nevertheless sheds light on an area that receives little attention.[23] Responses came from across genres, with 61 percent of those responding writing romances. She found that 52 percent earned less than $10,000, 15.67 percent earned between $10,000 and $25,000, which Kendall thought was "a significant amount"; the remaining 32 percent earned over $25,000 a year, nearly half of whom (13.5 percent) earned over $100,000. Fifty-three percent of the authors who had 1 to 11 books out with a traditional publisher earned more by self-publishing. Only when the author had 12 or more books out did the percentages shift and more traditional published authors earn more with their publisher than they did self-publishing. Of those respondents (266) who did not have their books edited by an editor with a publishing background, sales dipped: 59.8 percent earned less than $10,000 compared to 49.2 percent who used a professional editor. Similar results were found among those who did not use a graphic artist or professional designer for their cover illustration compared to those who did. These and related findings are reflected among those self-published romance authors I interviewed for my study on the romance publishing industry, including what we've already seen: the advantage of having a professional editor and graphic artist, plus the importance of coming from a traditional publishing background—Kendall found no advantage "at *all* [emphasis original] if the author came from a digital-first publishing background".

Conclusion

The evolution of the romance novel and the derivation of the various romance subgenres tend to focus on content, even if it touches on the publisher or house that was responsible for introducing new romance content or varying subgenre themes. This gives a clear picture of the novel itself. The role of the industry in shaping content is more often than not glossed over. Even the seminal work done by jay Dixon on Mills & Boon romances tends to revolve more around content than the impact of the dynamics within the firm that are key factors in determining what is released to the public. The same holds with Margaret Jensen's work on Harlequin. Joseph McAleer's study of the emergence of Mills & Boon, however, leans heavily on internal and external factors that helped the firm rise to prominence, as does Paul Grescoe's analysis of Harlequin, which is especially illuminating about the impact the new CEO, Brian Hickey, had on extending Harlequin's reach during the 1990s. These two latter works, as well as my own, drift in the opposite direction: content is critiqued, ultimately because executives decide what books they want the house to focus on, but these same critiques are thin on capturing nuances of content within a line or by different authors within the house. In either case, the assessment of the industry, whether sketched or detailed, all show the importance of those working within the house in shaping what ultimately reaches the public.

The impact of the industry is widely cited by scholars, even those only tangentially working on aspects of the novel, when they recognize the dominance of Harlequin. Silhouette's key function in showing other romance publishers that Harlequin could be challenged on its own turf is largely forgotten in the aftermath of Harlequin's purchase of Silhouette after a few rough and tumble years. One of the lapses in recognizing Harlequin's hegemony is how others kept churning out romances that were different from Harlequin in order to maintain a slice of the market. These lines ultimately led to the debut of sensual historicals, first at Avon, then seemingly everywhere, and after these novels had run their course, sensual contemporaries were "discovered" at Dell, and soon the market was awash with similar themed novels. Decisions by management at houses that followed Avon and Dell were often (but not always) disastrous, if only because management pressed editors to go beyond their limits with arbitrary production quotes: the level of writing fell in both cases and this was followed by reader disenchantment. Today the market remains particularly vibrant and publishing houses are attempting to avoid the mistakes of the past by making sure they have the widest range of romantic fiction possible in order to cater to all tastes, leading to a stunning array of niched romance novels.

One content theme has largely, but not totally,[24] been neglected by mainstream romance houses is the growing interest in xrotica—love at the upper end of the erotic scale (Markert "Love"). At the outset of the twenty-first century, authors were writing highly eroticized romances novels that disdained sexual euphuisms and graphically detailed the sexual act. These novels were rejected by mainstream publishers as pornography. Not finding an outlet for their product, a number of xrotic authors started small independent publishing ventures. This would have been cost-prohibitive in the past, but the new digital world allowed these frustrated writers to get their product direct to the readers. These small independents were able to gain a foothold at the outset of the new millennium because mainstream houses backed off digital entry after the dot.com bubble burst in 2001, though they are now quickly (post-2010) establishing a digital presence and making the market more difficult for the small independents, in no small part because they have the financial clout to move forward quickly.

The rapid and ongoing change in digital romance publishing—and romances are at the forefront of the digital genres—offers a potpourri of research opportunities. A few areas of potential research are suggested. The small digital publishers, though they have been around for a decade or more, have not been examined in any detail. The content of their novels and how their content is different from or similar to one another and the mainstream houses deserves more attention. It would also be illustrative to determine if the readers of the small independents are any different from those who read mainstream romances.

The erotic aspect of some of the digital publishers has garnered a certain amount of attention. Mainstream editors also talk about the eroticism of their novels, but many erotic digital publishers scoff at the proffered eroticism offered by mainstream houses. "Erotic" is a widely used term in the marketplace today. It would be illustrative to determine just how erotic the proffered romances are between mainstream houses and the digital independents. Most digital publishers, such as Siren, Ellora's Cave, and Looseld, besides publishing erotica, as well as ManLoveRomances, also publish male/male romances for heterosexual women.[25] Just how these novels differ from those released by traditional LGBTQIA presses is unclear, though many of the editors of LGBTQIA houses in my study suggest their romances are more nuanced because they are written by gay authors for a gay audience.

It would be illustrative to ascertain specific genres that the digital publishers have developed that are not addressed by mainstream houses, such as Looseld's "Full-Figured Heroines" (69 as of 2016), Ménage and Polyamory (270), or Steampunk (10). If a difference is determined, as I expect it will be, it needs to be ascertained how successful these niched novels are and why mainstream publishers neglect them, or if, once developed by the independent houses, mainstream houses start publishing the new subgenre(s) and how they might alter content for a wider audience.

Mainstream houses often entice authors associated with digital publishers or who self-publish into their fold once they are seen generating sales on the internet. Since many mainstream editors have distinct ideas of what they want addressed in their books, it would be interesting to ascertain how the books change, if, in fact, they do, when the author becomes affiliated with a corporate entity.

Most publishers filter multicultural romances into their existing lines, but more often than not multicultural means intra-racial (same color hero/heroine) more so than interracial (opposite race hero/heroine). Jayha Leigh, co-owner of recently defunct (2016) Beautiful Trouble Publishing, who is in an interracial marriage and writes interracial romances, scoffs at the depiction of interracial relationships depicted in mainstream romance novels. She is particularly "appalled" by the stereotypes in mainstream multicultural romances: "If it's a white female with a black male, he must be Mandingo," says Leigh. "So disrespectful" (Leigh). Her assessment of mainstream multicultural romances is a fertile area of content analysis, including just how distinct intra-racial relationships are depicted in contrast to the distinct social issues challenging inter-racial couples.

And there is, finally, the consequence of the sale of Harlequin to HarperCollins, and whether this new relationship will affect content of any of the romance lines produced by HarperCollins, which also owns Avon, as well as two highly-regarded religious publishers of romance novels: Zondervan and Thomas Nelson.

Notes

1 Grescoe is much less critical of Hickey's tenure than I. The disparate views are largely the result of the time frame: Grescoe was immersed in developments at Harlequin under Hickey during the first few years of his tenure while I looked back at some of the issues that arose later in his career.

2 McAleer ends the story of Mills & Boon in 1972 before the London publisher was purchased by Harlequin. His contribution is to show the struggle to establish Mills & Boon as a major romance publisher in the United Kingdom.
3 See Chapter 24, "In response to Harlequin: global legacy, local agency," by Kathrina Mohd Daud for a discussion of the international development of the romance industry in the twenty-first century.
4 Palmer's attempt to link the contemporary romance industry with developments in mass-market publishing is filled with errors which undermine her connections. Two glaring ones is her statement that "the romance [novel] was born in 1972, and no sooner" (122) and shortly thereafter contradicting this statement by negating any contribution by others in the United States to the production of romances in her assessment that in 1970, "Harlequin held 100% of the romance market" (124).
5 The history of Harlequin is traced in the three books that detail developments at Harlequin that were discussed at the beginning of this article, regardless of the years that are the focal point of the analysis: Jensen, Grescoe, and Markert. Most of the historical critique in these works, as well as Dixon's and McAleer's on Mills & Boon, are based, in part, on extant articles in popular newspapers and magazines accounts, such as *Publishers Weekly*, and on authorial interviews with those in the industry. The historical information in this section is based on my earlier works, unless otherwise cited (Markert "Publishing Decision"; "Romance Publishing"; *Publishing Romance*; see also *Thirty Years of Harlequin*).
6 I have chosen to use the term "fifties" romances for these novels produced in the 1960s to avoid confusion. The term "sixties" often connotes changes in attitudes taking place on college campuses during this period; "fifties" more adequately reflects the content of these early, sweet romances. Betty Friedan, writing for *TV Guide* in 1964, takes the television shows of the 1960s (*The Donna Reed Show*, 1958–66; *The Adventures of Ozzie and Harriet*, 1952–66; and *Leave It to Beaver*, 1957–63) to task for promoting dated "fifties" values. Her lengthy commentary is just as applicable to the romance novel as it is the television shows of the period.
7 Information in this section is based on extant articles in popular newspapers and magazines accounts, such as *Publishers Weekly*, and on authorial interviews with those in the industry, unless otherwise cited (Markert "Publishing Decision"; "Romance Publishing"; *Publishing Romance*).
8 Despite the sensuality of the so-called bodice-rippers, the sexual escapades were rather quickly glossed over and not dwelt on. Roger's first sexual tryst is over in a few sentences: "She felt her body bending backward, felt the length of his hard body against her, and then somehow, they had almost fallen on the rough, dirty stone floor together still kissing. Their hands found and uncovered each other, and then, without preliminaries, he was over her, penetrating her roughly and deeply and, after her first cry of despair completely satisfying" (*Sweet Savage Love* 14). See also the discussion of these early sensual historicals by Thurston as well as Lyons and Selinger.
9 Information in this section is based on extant articles in popular newspapers and magazines accounts, such as *Publishers Weekly*, and on authorial interviews with those in the industry, unless otherwise cited (Markert "Publishing Decision"; "Romance Publishing"; *Publishing Romance*).
10 Heisey, who was responsible for the break with Simon & Shuster, was promoted to the honorary position of chairman when Galloway took over the reins to become president and CEO of Harlequin in 1983. Galloway faced a formable task: recapturing Harlequin's dominant market position. He accomplished this in fairly short order: by the time he was promoted to president and CEO of Harlequin's parent, Torstar, in 1988, he had shepherded to fruition the purchase of its major rival, Silhouette, and moved sales from a low point of $11 million to $52 million (Kearns "David Galloway").
11 A loss leader is when a product (e.g., Janet Dailey) actually loses money because the cost (royalties) outweighs the sales. Loss leaders, however, are widely used because they bring in consumers who might purchase other products. In the case of Dailey, her name would generate interest in the Silhouette line because of her fans, and once familiar with Silhouette, her fans were likely to buy other Silhouette novels.
12 For more on Vivian Stephens see Chapter 10.

13 Time-Life put out a number of nonfiction series books on a range of subjects from cooking to the Civil War. Stephens was one of a number of individuals who researched background information used in the books. Her Time-Life position was her first job in publishing.

14 The hero lost an arm in Vietnam. He is 28, not perfect, not extraordinarily handsome, but with a keen sense of humor. The heroine is the widow of a Marine killed in combat. The heroine's relationship with her deceased husband had been less than ideal: he was a wife abuser.

15 Management's attitude was still condescending, but they were beginning to realize how lucrative the market was. The launch of Silhouette also showed others in the field that Harlequin was vulnerable to direct competition in the contemporary market.

16 Both the hero and the heroine have more scars, both physically and mentally, than marked the contemporary pre-1980 pining-for-love heroine and the perfect (handsome and often wealthy) hero. See endnote 14.

17 This is my conclusion after interviewing editors and senior management at most of the major romance houses in the first half of the 1980s (Markert "Publishing Decision"; "Romance Publishing"). Support for the growing disenchantment of readers about the quality of books was remarked on by Vivian Jennings in her romance newsletter, *Boy Meets Girl* 1984.

18 Loveswept was one of the few houses to regularly release a series of noncategory romances. It is interesting to observe that Carolyn Nicholas was responsible for the first successful category challenge to Dell's Ecstasy line with Second Chance at Love (1982); she was also one of the first to realize category romances in the style of Second Chance were "dead" and introduced Loveswept as the "author's line" in 1983 (Nicholas; Edwards; Guiley 177–8).

19 Despite the wide range of houses, most are owned by one of five conglomerates: Bertelsmann (Germany) owns 34 houses in the United States; Hachette (France), owns 17; Rupert Murdoch's News Corporation (British) controls 25, if its recent acquisition of Harlequin is added to the mix. Rounding out the Big Five are and Holzbrinck (Germany) with 19 houses and Simon & Schuster (U.S.A.) with ten.

20 For African American romance, see Chapter 10 of this collection; for Young Adult, see Chapter 7; for Christian/Inspirational romance, see Chapter 8; for erotic romance, see Chapter 9; for paranormal romance, see Chapter 6. LGBTQIA romance is discussed in Chapter 18; a useful history of LGBTQIA romance publishing can be found in Barot.

21 Romance e-book sales have imploded since 2010 because of at least two interrelated issues, which could prove a fertile ground for study by those working in the digital humanities. The first revolves around Ellora's Cave, whose sales appear to have dropped from $6.7 million in 2006 to $5 million in 2010 ("Curious"). EC has garnered most of the attention because of a public spat between EC and Dear Author blogger Jane Little (the pen name of Jennifer Gerrish-Lampe), who suggested the EC's falling sales meant they would soon be out of business. The real problem affecting sales is one that I suspect is facing all the early small digital presses, who initially had the field to themselves. The internet is simply awash today with romance titles on sites like Amazon (Robinson; Reilly). One reason for the abundance of romance titles on internet sites since 2010 is that mainstream publishers have since entered the digital era. The outpouring of romances on internet sites is compounded by the growing problem of piracy, which is thriving today because a bevy of romance "authors" are rewriting, often minimally, books that have succeeded in print, and while legitimate sites like Amazon have a policy of reimbursing royalties if the author can prove plagiarism, it is a difficult (and laborious) process to prove (Lanzendorfer).

22 I am referring to those legitimate, often struggling, self-publishing romance authors and not the pirates mentioned in endnote 21.

23 I am indebted to Beverly Kendall for allowing me to discuss, often verbatim, her findings.

24 Kensington (formerly Zebra) is one of the few major houses outside the "Big Five" (see endnote 19) that is not owned by a conglomerate, which, less bureaucratically encumbered, gives it more freedom to respond to changing market conditions, and always being a maverick publisher, they are not afraid to delve into erotica (Markert, *Publishing Romance* 165, 167, 200, 202–3, 243–5, 247–8, 295, 297).

25 Dreamspinner Press also releases male/male romances largely written by heterosexual woman but their novels are marketed to gay men even though Elizabeth North at Dreamspinner recognizes that women devotees of m/m romances are a strong secondary market.

Works cited

Barot, Len. "Queer Romance in Twentieth- and Twenty-First-Century America: Snapshots of a Revolution." *Romance Fiction and American Culture: Love as the Practice of Freedom?* edited by William A. Gleason, and Eric Murphy Selinger, Ashgate, 2016, pp. 389–404.

Brashear, Christina. "Personal Interview." 2013.

Coffey, Nancy. "Personal Interview." 1983.

Coser, Lewis. "Publishers as Gatekeepers of Ideas." *The Annals of the American Association of Political and Social Sciences*, vol. 421, no. 1, 1975, pp. 14–22.

Coser, Lewis, Charles Kadushin and Walter W. Powell. *Books: The Culture and Commerce of Publishing*. Basic Books, 1982.

"David Galloway Named President of Torstar Corp." *Toronto Star*, September 1, 1988, p. A4.

Davis, Kenneth C. *Two-bit Culture: The Paperbacking of America*. Houghton Mifflin Harcourt, 1984.

Di-Capua, Yoav. *Gatekeepers of the Arab Past: Historians and History Writing in Twentieth-Century Egypt*. University of California Press, 2009.

DiMaggio, Paul and Walter W. Powell. "The Iron Cage Revised: Institutional Isomorphism and Collective Rationality in Organizational Fields." *American Sociological Review*, vol. 48, no. 2, 1983, pp. 147–160.

Dixon, jay. *The Romance Fiction of Mills & Boon, 1909-1990s*. University College London Press, 1999.

Driscoll, Beth, Lisa Fletcher and Kim Wilkins. "Women, Akubras, and Ereaders: Romance Fiction and Australian Publishing." *The Return of Print? Contemporary Australian Publishing*, edited by Aaron Mannion, and Emmett Stinson, Monash University Press, 2016, pp. 67–88.

Edwards, Ellen. "Personal Interview." 1983.

Faircloth, Kelly. "Erotic Romance Publisher Spins Torrid Tale of Defamation." *Jezebel*, September 30, 2014. www.jezebel.com/erotic-romance-publisher-spins-torrid-tale-of-defamatio-1640802815

Fernald, Kenneth, Ruud Hoeben and Eric Claassen. "Venture Capitalists as Gatekeepers for Biotechnological Innovation." *Journal of Commercial Biotechnology*, vol. 21, no. 3, 2015, pp. 32–41.

Friedan, Betty. "Television and the Feminine Mystique, Parts I and II." *TV Guide: The First 25 Years*, edited by Jay S. Harris, New American Library, 1980, pp. 93–100.

Galloway, David. "Personal Interview." 1983.

"Global Publishing Leaders 2013: Harlequin." *Publishers Weekly*, July 19, 2013. www.publishersweekly.com/paper-copy/by-topic/industry-news/financial-reporting

Greco, Albert N. *The Book Publishing Industry, 2nd edition*. Lawrence Erlbaum, 2005.

Grescoe, Paul. *The Merchants of Venus: Inside Harlequin and the Empire of Romance*. Vancouver: Raincoast Books, 1996.

Guiley, Rosemary. *Love Lines: A Romance Reader's Guide to Printed Pleasure*. Facts on File Publications, 1983.

Guisto-Davis, Joann. "Jove to Bid for Female Readers with 'Second Chance at Love' Romance Line." *Publishers Weekly*, January 16, 1981, pp. 43–45.

Hayes, Robert, Gary Pisano, David Upton and Steven Wheelwright. *Pursuing the Competitive Edge: Operations, Strategy, and Technology*. Wiley, 2005.

Heisey, W. Lawrence. "Personal Interview." 1983.

Jennings, Vivian. *Boy Meets* Girl, vol. III, no. 33, 1983, p. 1.

———. *Boy Meets Girl*, vol. III, no. 35, 1984, pp. 1–2.

Jensen, Margaret Ann. *Love's Sweet Return: The Harlequin Story*. Women's Educational Press, 1984.

Johnson, Arthur. "Heartbreak at Harlequin: New Entries Distorting Blissful Profit Picture at Romance Fiction Firm." *The Globe and Mail*, October 28, 1983, p. 1.

Kendall, Beverly. "The Self-Publishing Survey Results—It's a Brave New World." at www.theseasonforromance.com/wordpress/2014/01/the-self-publishing-survey-results.

Kerner, Fred. "Personal Interview." 1983.

Kerns, Robert. "Galloway Rekindles Flame at Harlequin." *Chicago Tribune*, April 26, 1986. www.articles.chicagotribute.com/1986-04-16/business/8601270954/romance-novels.

Lanzendorfer, Joy. "Stealing Books in the Age of Self-Publishing." *The Atlantic*, June 5, 2016. www.theatlantic.com/entertainment/archive/..age-of-self-publishing/485525.

Leigh, Jayha. "Personnel Interview." 2013, 2014.

Lyons, Sarah Frantz and Eric Murphy Selinger. "Strange Stirrings, Strange Yearnings: *The Flame and the Flower, Sweet Savage Love*, and the Lost Diversities of Blockbuster Historical Romance." *Romance Fiction and American Culture: Love as the Practice of Freedom*, edited by William A Gleason, and Eric Murphy Selinger, Ashgate, 2016, pp. 89–110.

Markert, John. "Romance Publishing and the Production of Culture." *Poetics: International Review for the Theory of Literature*, vol. 14, no. 1/2, 1985a, pp. 69–94.

———. "Unsated Demand: An Explanation for the Growth in Romance Publishing." Presented at the Modern Language Association Conference in Washington, DC. Dec. 1985b.

———. "The Publishing Decision: Managerial Policy and Its Effect on Editorial Decision-Making." *Book Research Quarterly*, vol. 3, no. 2, 1987, pp. 33–59.

———. "Love in the Extreme: Publishing the Erotic Romance Novel." Presented at the Popular Culture Association/American Culture Association Annual Conference in New Orleans, April 2015.

———. *Publishing Romance: The History of an Industry, 1940s to the Present*. McFarland, 2016.

McAleer, Joseph. *Passion's Fortune: The Story of Mills & Boon*. Oxford University Press, 1999.

McWilliams, Kelly. "Romance in Foreign Accents: Harlequin-Mills & Boon in Australia." *Continuum: Journal of Media & Cultural Studies*, vol. 23, no. 2, 2009, pp. 137–145.

Millot, Jim. "Harlequin Pushes to Boost Single-Title Sales." *Publishers Weekly*, February 4, 2002, p. 23.

Moggy, Dianne. "Personal Interview." 2013, 2014.

Nicholas, Carolyn. "Personal Interview." 1983.

North, Elizabeth. "Personal Interview." 2013.

Palmer, Susan. "Romance Fiction and the Avon Ladies." *Approval Plans: Issues and Innovations*, edited by John H. Sandy, The Haworth Press, 1996, pp. 119–131.

Patrick, Diane. "The State of African-American Publishing." *Publishers Weekly*, December 10, 2012, p. 17.

Peters, Thomas J. and Robert H. Waterman Jr. *In Search of Excellence: Lessons from America's Best-Run Companies*. Harper & Row, 1982.

Powell, Walter W. *Getting into Print: The Decision-Making Process in Scholarly Publishing*. University of Chicago Press, 1985.

Reilly, Phoebe. "Did Amazon Sink the Queen of Online Erotica?" *Vulture*, February 24, 2015. www.culture.com/2015/02/amazon-tina-engler-erotica.html.

Robinson, Sal. "Is Amazon Responsible for the Ellora's Cave Fiasco?" *MobyLives*, October 2, 2014.

Schumpeter, Joseph. *Theory of Economic Development*. Harvard University Press, 1934.

Simon, R. and J. Fyfe. *Editors as Gatekeepers: Getting Published in the Social Sciences*. Rowman & Littlefield, 1992.

Snyder, Dick. "Personal Interview." 1983.

Stephens, Vivian. "Phone Interviews." 1983-1984, 1987.

Stuart, Mary Ann. "Personal Interview." 1983.

Sullivan, Judy. "Personal Interview." 1983.

Tapper, Olivia. "Romance and Innovation in Twenty-First Century Publishing." *Publishing Research Quarterly*, vol. 30, no. 2, 2014, pp. 249–259.

Tebbel, John. *A History of Book Publishing in the United States, Vol. 4: The Great Change, 1940-1980.* R. Bowker, 1981.

Thirty Years of Harlequin 1949-1979. Harlequin Books, 1979.

Thomas, Glen. "Romance: The Perfect Creative Industry? A Case Study of Harlequin-Mills & Boon Australia." *Empowerment versus Oppression: Twenty-First Century Views of Popular Romance Novels*, edited by Sally Goade, Cambridge Scholars Publishing, 2007, pp. 20–29.

Thompson, John B. *Merchants of Culture, 2nd edition.* Plum, 2012.

Thurston, Carol. *The Romance Revolution: Erotic Novels for Women and the Quest for a New Sexual Identify.* U of Illinois P, 1987.

"The Curious Case of Ellora's Cave." *Dear Author*, September 14, 2014. www.dearauthor.com/ebooks/the-curious-case -of-elloras-cave.

Vivanco, Laura. *For Love and Money: The Literary Art of the Harlequin Mills & Boon Romance.* Humanities-Ebooks.

White, David M. "The Gatekeeper: A Case Study in the Selection of News." *Journalism Quarterly*, vol. 27, no. 3, 1950, pp. 383–390.

White, Harrison C. "Where Do Markets Come From?" *American Journal of Sociology*, vol. 87, no. 3, 1981, pp. 517–547.

Wirtén, Eva Hemmungs. *Global Infatuation: Explorations in Transnational Publishing and Texts: The Case of Harlequin Enterprises in Sweden.* Ph.D. dissertation. Department of Literature, Uppsala University, Uppsala, Sweden, 1998.

Zacharius, Stephen. "Personal Interview." 2014.

17 Libraries and popular romance fiction

Kristin Ramsdell

Genre romance fiction has long been one of the circulation mainstays of the American public library, as it has been in libraries in Australia, the U.K., and elsewhere. In *Library Journal*'s annual materials survey, a report that tracks U.S. library purchasing and circulation patterns for materials in various formats, romance typically comes in third or fourth in print popularity with a comparable ranking in ebooks, yielding only to mysteries and general fiction—and thrillers in the case of print (Hoffert 35–6). The genre is obviously popular with readers and, therefore, important to libraries, whether they be public, academic, or school. This chapter will review the most significant research to date on libraries and popular romance and, in the hope of sparking interest in the topic, it will highlight areas that would benefit from further research.

Research studies, dissertations, and theses

The formal research that has been done on libraries and popular romance tends to break down along several lines, first sorting itself by the type of library to be studied (public/community, academic, or school[1]) and then by the particular topic of interest (e.g., collections, circulation, library personnel, readers), each which may then be broken down further. While it is possible for a study to focus on more than one kind of library, this is rarely the case, primarily because the roles of these libraries are not the same. (Connie Van Fleet's article "Popular Romance Collections in Academic and Public Libraries," discussed later in the chapter, is one exception, but it is not a scholarly study per se.) While the main goal of all libraries is to acquire and maintain collections relevant to their clientele and to connect readers with the appropriate materials, it is there that the similarity ends.

To be specific, academic libraries exist to support both the curricular and research needs of students and faculty of the college or university; public libraries are charged with meeting the current leisure reading, media, and information needs of their communities; and school libraries provide supplemental materials for the school curriculum, including age-appropriate fiction and non-fiction. While there are academic libraries that maintain small popular reading collections (some of which could certainly contain romance fiction), especially if they are residential campuses, it is the public library where the vast majority of current romance titles are held. However, except in the case of large public systems such as the New York Public Library, most public libraries are not archival; and once a title is no longer popular and ceases to circulate, it will usually be weeded from the collection and is, therefore, unavailable to readers or researchers. On the other hand, academic libraries do have an archival function, and while research collections of romance fiction are relatively uncommon, some do exist (e.g., The Browne Popular Culture Library at Bowling Green State University, The Nora Roberts American Romance Collection at Hoover Library at McDaniel College).

All three types of libraries are represented in the studies that follow, although not surprisingly, school libraries (K-12 in the U.S. system) are far fewer in number. Most of these studies are specific to romance, although some are included that are broader in scope but have information that might be of interest to romance researchers.

Popular romance fiction in public or community libraries

Although there are numerous articles and books detailing the practical aspects of managing popular romance collections, providing readers' advisory services to library users, and dealing with staff issues in public libraries, as well as opinion pieces, on the topic, and these will be discussed later in the article, serious, systematic research into libraries and popular romance—the kind that makes use of vetted surveys of library staff, readers, and other relevant subjects; systematic analysis of library collections, review sources, publishers lists, and other materials; focus groups and interviews; and other methods of gathering and assessing the necessary information and data—is far less common.

Collection practices are often the topic of library research: specifically, how collections are acquired, managed, and accessed. Such practices are not uniform across genres, and even when similar practices are followed, results can differ. In a 2004 study of genre fiction collections in North Carolina public libraries, Amy Funderburk focuses on romance and asks the question, "Are all genres treated equally?" Because librarians normally rely on book reviews to select materials, her study set out to determine if "romance novel collection in public libraries is unbalanced as a result of the paucity of reviews in this genre" (Funderburk 12). Data was collected for five genres of popular fiction (romance, science fiction/fantasy, horror, Western, and mystery), each of which gives a major award, and the libraries' collections were analyzed for the presence of a selected list of award-winning titles in the various genres. The major book review sources used by most libraries were searched for reviews of these titles and those results were then correlated with which titles were held in library collections. The study found that romance—including award-winning romance—is reviewed far less frequently than the other genres, and since there is a significant correlation between review availability and titles held by the libraries, this leads to a structural handicap to the representation of popular romance in library collections. Funderburk suggested additional selection methods and resources be deployed, and it would be interesting to see what a follow-up study would reveal, given the wider availability of romance reviews both online and in respected mainstream outlets (e.g., *The New York Times*, the *Washington Post*, the *Seattle Book Review*, all of which now review romance on a regular basis).

Australian scholars have also explored library collection practices and popular romance. Ten years after Funderburk's study, Vassiliki Veros, in her 2012 article, "The Romance Reader and the Public Library," considers both impediments and potentials for improvement to readers' access to romance materials in public libraries in Australia. Data from a survey conducted by the Australian Romance Readers

Association revealed that half of the respondents never use the library and only one-quarter of them said new romance titles were available in their public libraries. Veros concludes that current library practices (e.g., poor acquisition practices, substandard cataloging, and a lack of legacy romances and academic library collections) marginalize romance readers by not meeting their needs, a situation that is currently "preventing a very popular aspect of contemporary culture, the reading of romance fiction, from becoming a part of the institutionalized culture of the future" (Veros "The Romance Reader" 305). Three years later Veros followed this up with "A Matter of Meta: Category Romance Fiction and the Interplay of Paratext and Library Metadata" (2015), a study that posits that libraries endorse cultural capital via their collection development and cataloging practices and explores the marginalizing effect of the lack of sufficient metadata in the catalog records of category romance paperbacks in Australian public libraries on romance novels and the readers' ability to access these materials. Lack of good cataloging data—and, therefore, reader access ability—also has a profound effect on the authors, both economically and in terms of their reputation.[2] This is an excellent study, and as Veros points out, much more could be done to document the relationships between metadata and "the creation of cultural capital in other forms of popular fiction," as well as the "importance in economic and cultural terms of the inadvertent withholding of Public Lending Right payments to authors of category romance and other categories of cultural objects which are not given full metadata records in public libraries" (Veros "A Matter of Meta" 11).[3]

The collection development practices in American public libraries are the focus of a nationwide study conducted by scholars Denice Adkins, Linda Esser, Diane Velasquez, and Heather L. Hill and partially presented in their 2008 article, "Romance Novels in American Public Libraries: A Study of Collection Development Practices."[4] The authors sent 1020 survey requests to library directors in 49 states and the District of Columbia and received 396 responses from a large mix (small, large, urban, rural, suburban) of libraries. (Missouri was not included because its data was gathered in a previous pilot study.) Although the study gathered other data, some of which is discussed in another article mentioned in this chapter, the results reported on in the 2008 article focus largely on library location, collection size and content, budgets, and acquisition practices. The results indicate that while a number of libraries have fairly large romance collections, there is not much information available on specific genre collection development practices (for any genre, including romance), and, among other things, suggests that library and information science education should emphasize the ways in which leisure reading functions for readers. This study was preceded by "Relations between Librarians and Romance Readers; A Missouri Study" (2006), a pilot study for the 2008 project that explored Missouri public librarians' attitudes about romance, as well as gathered data on collection development and cataloging practices. Some questions were slightly modified for the national survey and the percentages of urban to suburban to rural libraries varied a lot between the studies; however, the results were generally similar and supported the belief that more needs to be done.

In "Love in the Digital Library: A Search for Racial Heterogeneity in E-Books" (2009), Renee Bennett-Kapusniak and Adriana McCleer take a more narrowly focused approach to their analysis, limiting their research by topic and format in "an exploratory case study that examines the digital collection of the state-wide Wisconsin Public Library Consortium (WPLC) for its multicultural romance holdings in relation to the demographics of Wisconsin residents" and makes suggestions for potential improvements. The WPLC includes most of the public libraries in the state and its rapidly expanding digital collection (formats: Adobe PDF, Mobipocket, Adobe PUB, Overdrive READ, and Kindle library downloads) held almost 9500 romance ebooks at the time of the study. Consulting a wide variety of selection tools, the authors created a list of 151 racially and ethnically diverse authors and 153 titles to include in the study. The authors and titles were searched for in the digital library catalog individually and the results were tallied and compared with the racial and ethnic demographics of Wisconsin (15.5 percent identified as African American/Black, Hispanic or Latina/o, Asian, and/or American Indian or Alaska native in 2010). Access and accessibility issues were also considered. The study found that the WPLC digital library provides a decent "foundational" collection of romance ebooks (10.3 percent of the romance ebook collection) but that the results did not always line up with the precise demographics of Wisconsin. Although many states do not have a state-wide consortium as Wisconsin does, this study could still be a useful model for other, even smaller library systems/consortia to consider using to see how well their collections are meeting the needs of their digital readers.

In her Ph.D. dissertation, "Reading Infrastructures in the Contemporary City: A Study of Three Public Libraries in Sydney" [Australia] (2016), Jen Sherman looks broadly at the way in which libraries function within a governmental infrastructure, both as an integral, visible part of the local municipality and also as an institution that highlights and encourages reading and literacy. This research explores the various governmental, professional, and commercial forces that influence public libraries, helping to shape their spaces and collections, and also the ways in which "public libraries function as spaces that organize reading and readers, catering to different types, tastes and reasons for reading" (vii). Using semi-structured interviews with 16 librarians (as well as internal library documents and statistics) and 30 self-selected library users and readers from three socioeconomically diverse libraries, Sherman examines the role of librarians in shaping reading interests and tastes, examining the inherent tension between promoting literacy and "worthy" literature and providing readers with leisure reading materials, which are often less valued, and analyzing the rationale behind librarians' collection development choices and display methods. She specifically uses the "romance genre as a way to examine ideas of power and regulation inherent in discussions of popular fiction in libraries" (15) and considers the commercial forces that shape libraries (173). She also looks at the library from the viewpoint of the reader, using Bourdieu's theories of cultural capital and habitus to examine how "library users and readers sort themselves into different groups with varying levels of cultural competency and how these affect their reading habits" (15).[5] Although done in Australia, this study has implications for library systems everywhere. It would be interesting to see if the study repeated in, say the United States or the U.K., would have similar results, particularly when it comes to attitudes toward and the treatment of romance on the part of librarians and readers alike.

Noting that little research had been done on romance readers and the use of libraries, Mary Bryson goes directly to the readers in her masters' thesis, "Public Library Services to the Romance Reader: An Online Survey of Romance Readers" (2004), to assess the effectiveness of library services to romance readers, including collection development and access issues. Using an online survey of 16 questions that focused on the readers' romance reading practice and preferences and their use and opinion of their public library, Bryson distributed the questionnaire to selected groups of active reader and romance listservs and message boards. The survey was available for eight days and garnered 240 usable responses. The results were mixed but showed that the majority of respondents both purchased books and borrowed them from their local libraries, and that while almost all of their libraries had romances in their collections, the readers' opinions of their currency and comprehensiveness varied widely, indicating there was more that could be done. This was a relatively good survey that reflected the situation at the time; it would be useful to see a similar survey repeated now, considering the major technological changes affecting publishing, libraries, and romance that have taken place since 2004.

Quite different in their methodologies, approaches, and foci, nevertheless, all of these studies were concerned to some extent with the ways in which the romance collections meet the needs of their readers and ways in which that could be improved.

While collection development is the most frequent research topic of choice, readers' advisory and general readership issues, including the perception of the genre, are a close second.

In "Perceptions of Romance Readers: An Analysis of Missouri Librarians" (2004), a paper that presents some of their early research on librarian attitudes toward romance, Denice Adkins, Linda Esser, and Diane Velasquez find that feminist and library science scholarship of the 1980s and 1990s indicates a bias against the genre, and they examine some of the underlying reasons for this. (This is an ongoing issue that, as of this writing, continues to inform and impact all aspects of library service related to popular romance.) Several years later Adkins, Esser, and Velasquez addressed the various ways in which romance fiction was promoted and highlighted in public libraries, gathering data through a nationwide survey of U.S. public libraries and discussing the results in "Promoting Romance Novels in American Public Libraries" (2010), an article aimed at the larger public library community. The results show that libraries are indeed promoting the romance genre—half provide romance readers' advisory services and four in ten use displays—but more could be done in other areas, such as programming or book groups. This same survey, which was sent to 1020 library directors and yielded 396 usable responses, also provided data for the authors' research discussed in "Romance Novels in American Public Libraries: A Study of Collection Development Practices" (2008).

In "Reader's Advisory: Matching Mood and Material" (2001), Catherine Sheldrick Ross and Mary K. Chelton discuss the results of Ross's survey of 194 dedicated readers to determine what elements they look for when choosing books for pleasure reading. Mood is of primary importance, particularly in fiction selection, and is a key factor for readers' advisory librarians to consider when making suggestions. This study covers all fiction genres, including romance, and identifies five strategies readers use in choosing books for pleasure and suggests ways in which they may be used by readers' advisory librarians to make more successful recommendations. This article is a good example of how the results of an academic research study can be put to practical use in the day-to-day operations of the library.

Another reader's advisory study that includes romance as well as the other genres is Kathryn R. Gundlach's Masters thesis, "Patterns of Genre Fiction Readers: A Survey of Durham County Library Patrons" (2002). Noting that fiction readers don't always ask for suggestions from a librarian directly but more often are influenced indirectly by targeted displays, theme-focused booklists/bookmarks, shelving arrangement, and other non-interactive/passive forms of readers' advisory, Grundlach focused her research on finding ways to improve this indirect form of readers' advisory. An understanding of readers' perceptions of the various genres was important, so the researchers used a reader questionnaire to ascertain if local genre fiction reading interests reflected appeal characteristics generally common to the specific genres (e.g., believable plotline and justice achieved in mysteries, emotional engagement and happy endings in Romance), and if the language used by both librarians and readers to talk about the genres was the same. Ninety-five usable questionnaires, out of 100 returned by readers in the three Durham libraries surveyed, revealed that readers read across genres, especially if they had similar appeal characteristics, and also showed that readers were sometimes confused when identifying genres. (For example, participants might answer that they didn't read a particular genre and then, in another part of the survey, identify the corresponding genre description as something they would read.) This is the kind of information that would be useful to librarians in designing programs and indirect readers' advisory materials.

Emily Lawrence takes a look at the tension that exists between populism and elitism that has long existed in the library field. In "Is Contemporary Readers' Advisory Populist?: Taste Elevation and Ideological Tension in the *Genreflecting* Series" (2017), Lawrence traces the development of readers' advisory (RA) services from its inception in the 1920s, with special attention to its renewal in the early 1980s with the publication of the first edition of Betty Rosenberg's *Genreflecting* (1982). Lawrence concludes that although RA refuses to try to elevate readers' taste in books, it is not, in fact, a populist project. This is in part because "librarians simply defer to other cultural authorities for their aesthetic verdicts" (that is, they recommend books that have won prizes or been adapted for films/TV, etc.) and in part because RA tries to instill a preference for pleasure reading over non-reading leisure practices, and "insofar as *to prefer* is always *to prefer one thing over some alternative*, RA is essentially a project devoted to taste elevation in leisure activities" (491).

Readers and pleasure reading are the focus of "Reader on Top: Public Libraries, Pleasure Reading, and Modes of Reading" (2009), Catherine Sheldrick Ross' analysis of seven models of reading developed in various fields, including librarianship. The value placed on reading depends on the reading model one subscribes to and, as Ross posits, each model has different strengths and weaknesses and some are more appropriate to public library use than others, especially those that embrace the "model of the reader as an active meaning-maker who can be trusted to make choices" (654). Ross chose to use series books readers and romance readers as the test cases in her discussion, two groups that have been traditionally belittled because of their reading choices. This article is an informative introduction to reading model theory and practice, as well as librarianship.

In "The Ranges of Life Interests and Reading Interests Among Adult Users of Public Libraries of Various Sizes" (1980), a dissertation that strives to discover if there is a correlation between readers' life interests and reading interests regardless of the size of the community, Linda Sue Lucas analyzed questionnaires from readers in six Illinois libraries of varying sizes and in different kinds of communities. The results showed that there is indeed a relation between life and reading interests and that public libraries should consider the life interests and lifestyles of the local communities when building the collections. Of particular interest to researchers concerned with the romance genre is that while no attempt was made to statistically analyze the relationship between the individual subjects of the books borrowed and the life and reading interests of the borrowers because the numbers in each subject group were considered too small, "romances were the most frequently borrowed fiction books in all three community size types" (68). It would be worthwhile to see if a similar study done today would have the same, or very different, results.

As expected, most of the studies discussed above have a public library focus, and for those researching the intersection of romance and public libraries, they will probably be the most useful. However, the two studies listed below consider readers and reading interests in atypical settings and may thus indicate directions for future research outside the public library setting.

One of the earliest reader-focused studies (1953) to mention romance was Elizabeth Shelby Eaton's dissertation, "The Free-Reading Use of the Library by Patients in a Veteran's Hospital." The hospital library's circulation statistics and the book collection were analyzed to correlate subject reading to the patients by age, sex, race, and diagnosis; to see how reading interests related to the book collection; and to see how these results compared with public library statistics. Romance was one of the many subjects included in this study; and while it made up 18 percent of the female patients' reading, it accounted for only a tiny percentage of the total circulations, possibly because only 3.4 percent of the hospital's patients were women and romance titles were not popular with the men. Given the many cultural and societal changes in 60 years, it would be interesting to see the results of a similar study conducted today.

In her dissertation, "Public Images, Private Pleasures: Romance Reading at the Intersection of Gender, Class, and National Identities in Urban India" (1997), Radhika E. Parameswaran examines the popularity of Mills and Boon romances and how they are accessed and received by urban, young, middle- and upper-class women in a town in Southern India. Parameswaran used an ethnographic approach for her study and found her readers through women's colleges and lending libraries. At the time of this study, India did not have a public library system as in the U.S., and the romances the subjects of her study read often were obtained from small, neighborhood shops that functioned much as rental libraries.

Popular romance fiction in academic libraries

Unlike research on romance fiction in the public library, which is generally evenly divided between collection development and readers' advisory and other readership issues, the vast majority of research on romance in academic libraries focuses on collections. Some of this information is found in studies or surveys that include a range of fiction genres, but others focus on romance specifically. Jennifer K. Thompson's master's thesis, "Romance in the Stacks: The Prevalence of Romance Fiction in Academic Libraries" (2010), is one example of the latter. Using two lists—one of works included in Virginia Brackett's *Classic Love and Romance Literature: An Encyclopedia of Works, Characters, Authors, and Themes* (1999), the other of contemporary romance titles—she conducted a survey of the holdings of five North Carolina academic libraries. She found that while all of the libraries held 90 percent of the "classic" romance titles, the contemporary holdings were lacking, with only one library holding more than 20 percent of the titles. The make-up of the title lists was critical to this survey and deserves comment. The 69 titles included in Brackett's *Classic Love and Romance Literature* represent an eclectic mix of literary titles including *Daphnis and Chloe* (second century AD) by Longus, Jane Austen's *Pride and Prejudice* (1813), Charlotte Brontë's *Jane Eyre* (1847), Nathaniel Hawthorne's *The Scarlet Letter* (1850), E.M. Forster's *A Room with a View* (1908), Edith Wharton's *Ethan Frome* (1911), F. Scott Fitzgerald's *The Great Gatsby* (1925), Margaret Mitchell's *Gone with the Wind* (1936), E.R. Braithwaite's *To Sir with Love* (1959, and Amy Tan's *The Kitchen God's Wife* (1991), but, surprisingly, not Samuel Richardson's *Pamela* (1740). Although many of these titles would not pass the "happy/satisfactory ending" test expected of today's romances, most of them are staples in English literature classes, so it's not surprising to find them in the libraries' collections. For the list of contemporary romance titles, Thompson used the books in a popular romance website's reader survey, "All About Romance 2007 Top 100 Romances Poll," a list (not limited by date) which included several classic Austen titles. It's interesting that contemporary romance award winners were not specifically included.

This lack of primary source material noted in Thompson's survey is especially problematic for scholars of popular romance, particularly those interested in series romance. In an earlier article, "Romance in the Stacks; or Popular Romance Imperiled," in *Scorned Literature: Essays on the History and Criticism of Popular Mass-Produced Fiction in America* (2002), Alison M. Scott, former head of the Ray and Pat Browne Library for Popular Culture Studies at Bowling Green State University, Ohio, made that point, stating that academic libraries rarely collected popular romance because they were often considered unworthy of collection or study. (It is worth noting that the Popular Culture Library at BGSU has one of, if not the, largest research collections of popular romances in the country, including more than 10,000 series titles. It also houses the official archives of the Romance Writers of America.)

In recent years, however, romance has gotten a bit more academic notice, making it a more urgent topic for academic library collections to address. In "Creating a Popular Romance Collection in an Academic Library" (2015), librarians Sarah E. Sheehan and Jen Stevens discuss their rationale, methodology, process, and success in building a popular romance collection at George Mason University. The article speaks to the critical importance of collecting such primary source material and provides a road map for other libraries wanting to build similar collections.

In "Love in the Stacks: Popular Romance Collection Development in Academic Libraries" (2012), Crystal Goldman agrees with the importance of primary source collection. However, she acknowledges that it would be impractical for academic libraries to collect all of the romances themselves and, therefore, suggests that libraries interested in collecting in this area could work together in a coordinated effort that spreads the cost and collection responsibilities more broadly. She also makes a case for the establishment of a core list of popular romance scholarship titles that academic libraries should hold and argues for the necessity of the collection of these resources by academic libraries. She uses examples of the romance scholarship holdings of libraries in California's two state university systems [University of California (UC) and California State University (CSU)] to show that while no one institution owned all of the books on the list, all but one, the CSU's merchant marine focused Maritime Academy, owned some. Ready access to materials of this type is imperative for romance scholars, and a collaborative effort in acquiring and maintaining these materials would ensure access to important primary and secondary sources in at least one library in a cooperative.

However, research collections are not the only kind of romance collections that exist in academic libraries. Some college and university libraries, particularly those with large residential populations, maintain popular reading collections, many of which include romance fiction. Over the years, a number of studies of collections of this type have been done. For the most part these are surveys and are usually limited by region; however, their findings could have larger implications.

In one of the earlier studies of this kind, "Leisure Reading Collections in Academic Libraries" (1994), L.A. Morrissett's survey of 85 academic libraries in the southeastern United States showed that fewer than half had designated leisure or recreational reading collections, although several libraries were planning to establish one, and that private colleges and universities were far more likely to have them than public institutions. The results also showed that historical romances were second only to mysteries in popularity, a finding that would be useful for collection development purposes.

Several years later in a narrower study, "Recreational Reading Collections: A Survey of Tennessee Academic Libraries" (2001), K. Kerns and D. O'Brien reported that 70 percent of the 30 libraries (out of 40) that responded to their questionnaire maintained some kind of designated leisure reading collection. These collections were popular at the schools that had them, but they were more prevalent and considered "very important" by librarians in community colleges than in four-year institutions where the librarians rated them only "somewhat important." The results of this study led to the establishment of a leisure reading collection at Sherrod Library at Eastern Tennessee State University that included using a book leasing program for popular fiction. Unfortunately, this study did not break out circulation figures by genre, so there is no specific data for romance. However, since most fiction lease programs include current bestsellers in all genres, it is likely that there are romances in the mix.

As presented in "Recreational Reading Collections in Academic Libraries" (2005), B. Rathe and L. Blankenship chose a slightly different approach. Instead of surveying the collections in a number of libraries, they focused on the recently established small fiction and non-fiction leisure reading collection in Michener Library at the University of Northern Colorado at Greeley and its use and reception by students, faculty, and staff. In all, 55 surveys were returned with positive results, with circulation increasing by 40 percent from the first to the second year, with students accounting for most of the usage by the second year. Brodart's McNaughton book leasing plan was used to provide the majority of books for the collection, and while this study did not report circulation by genre, books by Nora Roberts and Jude Deveraux, both romance authors, were among the highest-circulating titles.

In order to better understand how the recreational reading collection at Sam Houston State University Library in Huntsville, Texas, was being used, librarians Kate Landry Mueller, Michael Hanson, Michelle Martinez, and Linda Meyer conducted a survey of the library's users. The results of this study, presented in "Patron Preferences: Recreational Reading in an Academic Library" (2017), revealed, among other things, that library users preferred print materials, although they felt that audio and ebooks were useful under certain circumstances, and that a number of them did not consider the library a major source of leisure reading. Although romance was not listed among the top five fiction genres preferred, young adult fiction and historical fiction both made the list, two genres that often include stories with strong romance elements. A copy of the survey, which would include the genre choices available for selection, would have proved helpful.

Mark Sanders took a two-pronged approach in his study, "Popular Reading Collections in Public University Libraries: A Survey of Thee Southeastern States" (2009). Focusing on the analysis of the leisure reading collections of 45 public university libraries in North Carolina, South Carolina, and Georgia, as well as the collection details and response from library users of the popular reading collection at his own university, East Carolina University (ECU), Greenville, North Carolina, Sanders learned that fiction is more popular than non-fiction, and students, as opposed to faculty and staff, account for most of the circulation. Best-seller fiction was especially popular, and staff reported anecdotally that there was high interest in mysteries and romances. Romance was also one of three genres that was specifically named in the "other" category of the reading survey given at ECU.

Tracking the number of fiction titles written by Australian authors between 1900 and 1970 that were currently held in Australian major academic and research libraries (as well as the British Library and the Library of Congress) was the focus of Robert Pymm's dissertation, "Australian Fiction in Australian Libraries: The Collection and Preservation of Titles Published between 1900 and 1970" (1996). The holdings of these libraries were compared with two lists, one of all Australian fiction produced during the period, the other of works that had received awards or critical acclaim for literary quality. The results showed that no one library owned them all, that the literary titles were far more likely to be held than titles in the total group (80 percent to 22 percent mean holdings of the totals possible), that a small number of libraries were responsible for the majority of the holdings, and that romance was one of the least collected genres. These findings point out the difficulty of finding titles within this time frame that were not considered literary.

But the link between romance and academic libraries is not always simply about the books. Caryn Radick's study, "Romance Writers' Use of Archives," examines a less studied aspect, the way in which romance authors make use of archives in doing research for their books. In a survey of 200 romance writers on the topic, Radick found that the majority of respondents used libraries and almost half had used archives in their research for their romances. While the writers like using archives—and need to do so for their work—barriers to use can include travel issues, lack of digitization, and the absence of adequate instruction or assistance in finding materials. Some writers reported a dismissive attitude on the part of archivists (but not on the part of librarians) and felt that they were not focused on meeting users' needs. As one respondent commented,

> Archivists often don't understand how to help you find what you need and are often wrapped up in the technical aspects of maintaining the archive rather than exposing that info to a wider audience. Then, there is a distinct bias against romance as well. The idea of the use of their material for one of "those tawdry romances" often offends their academic snobbery to the max unfortunately.
>
> (64)

The study considers the benefits of the use of archives by romance writers, examines the possible effect of archivists' views on what is considered serious research and what is trivial and the impact on romance researchers, and suggests that more should be done, both educationally and in outreach to the romance writing community. The fact that librarians have a strong relationship with the Romance Writers of America despite earlier biases was mentioned as an example of how a shift in attitude and understanding on the part of archivists might lead to better relationships with romance writers and other non-traditional archives users.

Of course, academic researchers of romance fiction use archives, as well. Often this is for research on a particular author or group of authors, which partly depends on the papers of romance writers, many of which are held in library archives in countries around the world. But for scholars looking for information about popular romance in general, as well as authors in particular, one of the best places to begin is the archives of the Romance Writers of America (RWA) at the Ray and Pat Browne Popular Culture Library (PCL) at Bowling Green State University in Ohio. In May 2017, Kecia Ali attended the second Summer Research Institute hosted by the Popular Culture Association and PCL and spent time exploring the RWA archives. She discusses her experience in "Romance Fiction in the Archives" (2018). While her initial purpose was to discover particular details about Nora Roberts and her career, Ali's dive into the RWA archives opened an unexpected wealth of new avenues for further research. The history of the organization, tracking technological shifts and their effects on the genre, the evolution of romance subgenres as indicated by award categories, diversity issues of all kinds (e.g., gender, race, ethnicity, sexual orientation, religion) within the genre—present and historically, tensions between author members (e.g., indie versus traditional/published versus unpublished), sexuality, and levels of explicitness, are only a few of the many suggested.

Popular romance fiction in school libraries

It must be said that school libraries are not usually treasure troves of popular romance fiction, nor do they generate many research studies on the genre. In addition, very few, if any, exist that are solely dedicated to the topic of romance fiction in school libraries. However, there are some studies that might be of tangential interest because they do have implications for young adult (YA) and school library collection development; a few of these are discussed briefly below and may spark ideas for future study.[6]

One very early study, Ivan Griffin's "Libraries and Reading Practices in Four Selected Schools" (1939), takes a look at the library holdings of four Utah junior high schools, to discover the preferences of seventh and eighth grade students, and to learn how the books were being selected. The importance of the school library is acknowledged at the outset and the results indicate that junior high students had definite reading preferences which indeed included books in "Adventure and Romance," a classification that was considered to be generally of a higher level and to include more mature themes and characters than some of the others. Its popularity varied among schools, but adventure and romance stories ranked high in both grade levels (second highest with seventh graders; first with eighth graders), especially with girls. This is a comprehensive, highly detailed study and was undoubtedly valuable to the schools in the survey. However, it is 80 years old and primarily of historical interest. It should be noted that the titles considered as "adventure and romance" in 1939 (e.g., *Little Women*, *Little Men*) are nothing like the YA romance titles of today, or even the sweet school and career romances of the mid-1940s through the early 1960s by writers such as Betty Cavanna, Maureen Daly, and Rosamund du Jardin discussed in the dissertation below. However, they are books of relationships, in some cases romantic, and as such, might appeal to those long-ago readers in the same way that YA romances would appeal today.

Several decades later, Kimberly Kay Foss takes a look at the romance novels that high school women read in an attempt to learn whether or not they are accurate representations of the roles and expectations of women in the then-current society. Her thesis, "An Analysis to Determine if Popular Romance Novels, Read by Today's High School Students, Reflect the Characteristics and Roles of Women in Current Society" (1997), focuses on the holdings of the Laramie (Wyoming) Senior High School Library and her study sample consists of 20 books identified as romances in the collection that had been checked out ten or more times by students in the last ten years. A vetted researcher-designed tool was used to examine the various characteristics and roles of the female protagonist through qualitative content analysis. The results showed a marked similarity among the fictional heroines (pretty, small, slim, Caucasian, from traditional upper-middle-class families, etc.) and, also, that their hopes, feelings, and concerns were generally on par with those of contemporary teens. However, the study concluded that these heroines did not represent the overall norm—racially, ethnically, physically, or socioeconomically—and this was a cause for concern. Because of the changes that have taken place in the romance industry in the past two decades, this is a study that would be worth redoing, perhaps expanding, today.

Amanda Kirstin Allen takes a dive into the past as she explores the often-ignored American teen romance novels of the post-World War II years in her dissertation, "The Girls' Guide to Power: Romancing the Cold War" (2010). Using a feminist material culture approach, Allen examines the adolescent female society found in these novels as well as authors, editors, and others who produced them and the librarians, critics, and others who provided them to the teens—almost all of whom were women. While not focused specifically on school libraries, references to school librarians and libraries flow throughout and her discussions of these novels' use in the classroom may be of particular interest. Allen is the author of the chapter on young adult romance (Chapter 7) in this guide.

In an effort to assess the reading preferences of adolescent students in India and the methods used by authors to promote their books to them, Fayaz Ahmad Loan and Refhat-un-nisa Shah surveyed 150 students (ages 14–16, equal numbers of boys and girls) in the Delhi Public School, Srinagar, India, using a questionnaire. The results, presented in "Survey of the Literature Reading Habits and Preferences of Adolescents: A Study of a Public School in India" (2017), showed that a majority of both boys and girls preferred reading in print as opposed to digital formats and that fiction was preferred over non-fiction. Crime/detective fiction was the most popular genre overall, with realistic teen fiction next in line. Romance and mystery/thriller tied for third place. Poetry was the least preferred. Not unexpectedly, romance, as well as poetry, proved more popular with girls, while crime detective, horror, and realistic teen fiction appealed more to boys. The questionnaire also revealed that students felt that the authors of the books they read used violence and aggression; romantic, slangy, and/or crude language; explicit sexual content; and other devices to varying degrees and with varying success in an effort to appeal to teenage readers. The researchers believe that this is a study that would be worth repeating with a larger student sample, perhaps at the state-wide level.

Libraries and popular Gothic romance in Regency and Georgian England

Although most of the scholarship discussed in this chapter is concerned with the romances and libraries of today and the relatively recent past, there are studies that discuss the Gothic and romantic fiction of earlier centuries and mention libraries, if only tangentially, in ways that may be of interest to contemporary researchers.

In his dissertation, "Twilight of a Genre: Art and Trade in Gothic Fiction, 1814–34" (2002), Franz Potter calls into question the ways in which the classic canon of the Gothic romance genre was defined and formed as he focuses on the waning years, or the "twilight," of the genre. The tension between the "good" or artistic as opposed to the popular and salable existed then, as it does now. As a result, the many popular, or "trade" Gothics, were not considered true Gothics and, therefore, ineligible for genre inclusion. For example, earlier works such as Horace Walpole's *The Castle of Otranto* (1764), Ann Radcliffe's, *The Italian; or, The Confessional of the Black Penitents* (1797), or Mary Shelley's *Frankenstein; or, The Modern Prometheus* (1818), or even Charles Maturin's *Melmouth the Wanderer* (1820) are almost always part of the Gothic literary canon, but best-selling works by popular trade authors of the day are rarely even considered. In the first section of this study, Potter uses data from circulating library catalogs and Gothic bluebooks and magazine stories to analyze the trade. The second section examines the lives and works of two popular trade authors, Francis Lathom and Sarah Wilkinson, to show readers' changing interest in the genre. The popularity of the circulating library was important to the rise of the trade Gothic; an appendix that includes the entire catalogs of two Norwich circulating libraries may be of particular interest.

In the dissertation, "Reading Books, Reading Life: The Cultural Practice and the Literary Representation of Reading in Jane Austen's Time" (2006), Young Leon Won examines the important role that books and reading played during the Regency and late Georgian periods in England and includes discussion of the critical role that lending and circulating libraries played in the practice. Their importance is borne out by the fact that these libraries are a common feature in many of Austen's books, as well as those by other authors of the period.

Opinion, commentary, practical accounts, and other relevant articles

Although rigorous studies on the relationship between libraries and popular romance fiction are not currently in grand supply, this is not true of less formal articles on the topic. Articles by scholars and practicing librarians have graced the pages of the professional library literature for decades and may serve as a window into the discourse that has bubbled and flowed around this topic for years. These range in content from the importance and value of popular romance—or the lack thereof—and its place in the library, to ones that present their institutions' collections development as a model for others.

There have long been two camps in the library world when it comes to what books should be included in library collections and which ones should be left out. Some argue for "literary quality" on the grounds that only the "best" (as determined by critical acclaim and awards) should be made available to readers, while others are of the opinion that libraries should serve the interests of their users and provide the books, often popular fiction titles and other bestsellers, that people actually want to read, as well. Over the years, the idea that libraries should provide access to the materials their communities demand has taken hold and most libraries now overflow with copies of the latest bestsellers and other popular fiction in multiple formats. However, the debate concerning the acquisition and treatment of popular romance has taken longer to resolve, and as these articles show, in some cases by their mere presence, the discussion still continues. While these pieces do not qualify as research studies in the technical sense, they are relevant, often classic, articles that any researcher considering pursuing this topic would want to be aware of. Several of the more important and/or interesting are discussed briefly below.

Rudolph Bold's 1980 article, "Trash in the Library," gives a clue into the some of the prevailing attitudes of the times and is one of the earliest to advocate for the inclusion of popular romance in the library collections. Bold's tone is elitist and intellectually superior, and his reasons for including romance appear to have more to do with acquiescing to the current trend of collecting more popular materials and then using romance as a lure to lead readers to what he and others in the profession consider quality literature than they have to do with providing access to romances because he considers them worthy books. Nevertheless, his article was a step in the right direction, a challenge to librarians to be more inclusive in their selection practices and not censor materials by simply not acquiring them.

The acquisition of young adult romances has been equally controversial. Publication of these texts exploded in the early 1980s as paperback romances aimed at the teen market (Scholastic's Wildfire, Bantam's Sweet Dreams, and Silhouette's First Love) hit the stands. In "Librarians and the Paperback Romance: Trying to Do the Right Thing" (1985), Roger Sutton gives a good rundown of the teen romance paperback situation of the day, complete with popular lines/series listings and review coverage. He obviously does not regard these books highly—the numbered series, in particular—nor does he think that they are worth the attention they're being given, including being reviewed, but his article does highlight the dilemmas librarians had to deal with and it documents a range of commentary from publishers, librarians, and other industry professionals.

The 1990s were a decade of profound change in the discourse of librarians about popular romance. Much of that change may be due to one woman, Mary K. Chelton, a persuasive advocate for both romance and YA fiction. In her ground-breaking article, "Unrestricted Body Parts and Predictable Bliss: The Audience Appeal of Formula Fiction" (1991), Chelton laid out the appeal and importance of popular romantic fiction to libraries and their constituents with lively precision and wit. This article explains the genre conventions and zeros in on romance's place in public libraries and how to select and handle materials and advise readers. Acknowledging the differences among the lines in category romance, Chelton includes a helpful chart that succinctly shows the differences among the lines (sweet, sexy, historical, contemporary, paranormal, suspenseful, futuristic, etc.) that would be of immense help to librarians unfamiliar with the complexities of the romance genre.

In 1994, *Library Journal* became the first mainstream trade publication to review romance on a regular basis with the inauguration of their romance column, a move that was not without resistance. (The executive editor of *Library Journal*, Francine Fialkoff, was obliged to defend the journal's decision to cover both romance and Christian fiction in a piece entitled "Are We Dumbing Down the Book Review?") The fact that there were definite quality differences among the books within the genres (i.e., they are not all alike) and librarians needed reliable reviews in order to acquire the best materials for their collections was key to *LJ*'s ground-breaking decision. That same year Shelley Mosley, John Charles, and Julie Havir weighed in with another memorably entitled essay: "The Librarian as Effete Snob: Why Romance?" This articulate article delivered a stinging rebuke of librarians' traditional superior attitude toward the romance genre and earned the trio the Romance Writers of America's first Veritas Award (1995) for articles that portrayed romance fiction in a positive light. The authors' systematic rebuttal of the classic reasons for *not* collecting romances has enduring value, as does their warning against censorship: "But censorship is censorship ... even if you don't like romances you have the professional obligation to defend the rights of others to read them. It is not part of our professional creed to deliberately hinder the reading of anything. Even romances" (Mosley et al. 115).

The mid-1990s were a pivotal period for this shift in attitude. The first Public Library Association Cluster Workshop on romance took place in March of 1995, and in her article "An Appetite for Romance: How to Understand, Buy, Display, and Promote Romance Fiction," Johanna Tuñon provides a detailed report on the day-and-a-half conference that covered everything from the history of the genre, its various subgenres, and its importance to the more practical aspects of selection and shelving, staff training, and working with readers. Presentations were made by authors (Nora Roberts and Diana Gabaldon were highlights), librarians well-versed in the genre and in readers' advisory, and editors and other romance industry professionals. As Tuñon concludes, "The wealth of practical tips, stimulating discussion, and informative handouts combined to make this workshop both stimulating and practical for attendees" (Tuñon *An Appetite for Romance* 475). Articles followed aimed at helping librarians deal with the practical side of collecting and promoting romance. "Exploring the World of Romance Novels" (1995) by librarians Cathie Linz, Ann Bouricius, and Carole Byrnes and "A Fine Romance: How to Select Romances for Your Collection" (1995) by Johanna Tuñon are two of the more useful, practical examples.

The following year, at the 1996 Public Library Association Conference in Portland, Oregon, best-selling romance author and former librarian Jayne Ann Krentz delivered a riveting address in defense of the genre, which was subsequently published as "All the Right Reasons: Romance Fiction in the Public Library" (1997). Building on the defenses of the genre in *Dangerous Men, Adventurous Women* (1992), the essay anthology Krentz had edited at the start of the decade, "All the Right Reasons" outlines the evolution of the popular romance from the paperback dime novels or "penny dreadfuls" of the nineteenth and early twentieth century to the fully-fledged bestselling hardcovers of today and its ultimate recognition as a legitimate literary genre: one to be valued in its own right because, like the other genres of popular fiction, it "preserves the heroic traditions and affirms our core values and beliefs" (Krentz 165). A powerful, articulate argument for genre fiction as a whole and for romance in particular, "All the Right Reasons" was and remains an indispensable work of advocacy, and should be read by anyone serious about the genre.

As most librarians know, young adults will often "read up"; and while many have no problem recommending adult sci-fi, mysteries, or fantasy for teens, suggesting romance titles is a problem for some for any number of reasons. In "Romancing the YA Reader: Romance Novels Recommended for Young Adults" (1999), John Charles, Shelley Mosley, and Ann Bouricius tackle this issue head-on with humor, common sense, selected reference sources, and a substantial list of recommended titles in the then-current subgenres. Charles and Mosley join forces once again to sort out another adult/YA romance issue in "Getting Serious About Romance: Adult Series Romances for Teens" (2002). This article details the value and wide diversity of the adult paperback series romances, dispels some common myths about them, discusses collection development issues unique to series (e.g., their limited window of availability), includes lists of relevant reference sources and websites, and concludes with a comprehensive list of recommended series titles. Although aimed at the YA market, this article is relevant to adults, as well as teens.

Using Catherine Sheldrick Ross's 2001 research study with adult readers on how mood relates to readers' book choices (discussed earlier in this chapter), in "What Kind of Romance are You in the Mood For?: A Recommended Reading List" (2001) Mary K. Chelton, Cathie Linz, Joyce Saricks, Lynne Welch, and Ann Bouricius put this research into practice by developing a series of recommended lists of romance titles based on mood, as opposed to subgenre or genre. "Adventurous," "heartwarming," and "tormented" are some of the highlighted moods. Lists like this are not easy to put together—much easier just to toss all historical or vampire stories into their requisite groups than to sort them out by the feelings they engender—and the authors believe that this is the first published of its kind.

In "Popular Fiction Collections in Academic and Public Libraries" (2003), Connie Van Fleet references current interdisciplinary research (including the Ross study mentioned a moment ago) to show that popular fiction is of critical importance to both its readers and students of popular culture, and, as such, deserves to be taken seriously and cared for appropriately. Stating that "Popular literature is the textual representation of popular culture," Van Fleet goes on to define terms, explain the relevant issues, and provide practical ideas and solutions for librarians interested in preserving these collections (65). Both academic and public library collections are included and while not the only fiction genre dealt with, romance is an important part of this article.

Librarian John Charles and author and RWA Library Liaison Cathie Linz set out to help libraries deal with a classic public service issue in "Romancing Your Readers: How Public Libraries Can Become More Romance-Reader Friendly" (2005). In addition to defining the genre and its appeal, the article points out common misconceptions and offers a useful discussion of current genre trends including changes in cover design and the growing interest in related or linked books. Lists of recommended titles and print and online references, statistics that show that at the time top-ranked romance was responsible for over 34 percent of the popular fiction sales, and a smart list of suggestions for how to become more romance-reader friendly made this a valuable resource in its time, and it remains worthy of attention as a snapshot of the discourse surrounding libraries and popular romance in the early twenty-first century.

Librarians are often looking for core collections in various subjects, and popular romance is no exception. Periodically, the library trade publications will include articles aimed at fulfilling this need. "Core Collections in Genre Studies: Romance fiction 101" (2007), edited by Neal Wyatt, is one of the better examples for the time. Dividing the genre into five broad categories—contemporary, historical, Regency, suspense, and paranormal—Wyatt enlisted the aid of five genre-savvy librarians to select five titles that highlight the important features of each subgenre. The resulting lists include titles that most libraries would want in their romance collections and provide a window into the romance tastes of the times.

Although public libraries are the primary places where romance fiction normally resides, as noted earlier, academic libraries cannot be left behind. In "Why Your Academic Library Needs a Popular Reading Collection Now More Than Ever" (2010), Pauline Dewan makes a timely and brilliant argument for having a popular reading collection on campus and details the steps necessary to make that happen. Romances are, of course, included, and the promotion and encouragement of literacy and lifelong learning are among Dewan's primary arguments.

Periodically, overview and preview articles highlighting the various fiction genres will appear in the trade publications. Aimed at keeping the library world up-to-date on the latest trends in genre fiction, *Booklist*, *Publishers' Weekly*, and *Library Journal* are prime sources for pieces of this type, and often publish one each year. *Library Journal*, for example, usually comes out with one on romance in October, while *Booklist*, has traditionally done a spotlight on romance in September. One good, recent example is "Love Changes Everything: The Need for Inclusiveness, the Strength of the #MeToo Movement, and the Power of Love" (2018) by Kathryn Howe. Typically, romance is quick to tie into the latest social and cultural trends, and this article shows that this is definitely taking place. Howe points out that publishers are finally beginning to realize the serious lack of romances written by authors of color and working to change that, and romances are beginning to include more multicultural characters and themes. Inclusivity also extends to the LGBTQIA community, as the subgenre's complexity deepens and gains readership in the process. In addition, romances focusing on characters with various neurological and developmental differences (e.g., dyslexia, ADHD, autism) are becoming a growing part of the mix. Although romance has long had strong female characters, the #MeToo movement has sparked a new breed of empowered heroine who will challenge injustice and marginalization, confront harassment, fight for the rights of others, and overcome past abuse in her own life. Humor is present and popular in most of the subgenres; shifters, sexy men, and characters (both heroes and heroines) with dangerous, life-threatening jobs are prominent; and diversity and inclusivity are helping the genre reflect the reality of the world we live in.

As these studies and articles show, romance has had a rather rocky path to navigate on its way to acceptance in both the literary and the library worlds. When Krentz declared in 1996 that "Romance Has Arrived!" (Krentz 162), in many ways it was true. Sales were strong, the genre was expanding, romance novels were appearing on bestseller lists and beginning to be regularly reviewed in mainstream professional sources, academic romance scholarship was entering its second decade, and the genre was catching the serious attention of librarians. With the increase in serious romance review coverage in respected publications (e.g., *The New York Times*), with the general, albeit sometimes grudging, acknowledgment that romance is both popular and important, and with the appearance of this volume, it seems that romance is even more firmly established today. This greater acceptance should open the door not only to fresh approaches to the acquisition and management of romance collections in libraries, but to research into popular romance library practices.

Suggestions for further research

Many of the studies discussed in this chapter include suggestions by the author(s) for additional research. I have mentioned some of these above; however, in the interests of time and space—and because anyone interested in a particular study will probably want to read the whole thing—I won't include them all here. There are, however, some general ideas and directions that stand out, as well as other areas that have been neglected and might be of interest that are worth mentioning.

First, although this is not a research topic per se, it is worth noting that if more scholars (faculty and students) at Library and Information Science (LIS) schools researched popular romance fiction topics, this might help with the persistent bias on the part of some librarians against the genre. This is an idea that is promoted by working "romance-friendly" librarians, and it might be adopted by scholars of popular romance fiction from English, Women's and Gender Studies, and other disciplines who are interested in collaborative work with colleagues in LIS.

Second, as I have observed at several points in this chapter, a number of the studies included above are quite old and have been included primarily for their historical perspective. Many are worth a second look to see if they contain anything that would be worth revisiting, if only to see if and how attitudes and situations have changed.

As an alternative to simply revisiting earlier topics and approaches, some of the older studies that were more narrowly focused—on a particular library, library system, type of library, area of the country, group of people, particular set of titles, for example—might be revived and expanded to broaden the scope of the study. Conversely, new scholarship seems warranted along the lines of some of the broader studies, especially those that focused on library materials, readers, and readers' advisory issues in connection with multiple genres of popular fiction (or sometimes even an entire library collection), as these could be narrowed to focus more closely on romance and romance readers.

More research is needed into library romance collection development practices both locally and on a comparative basis. What selection tools are used, how selector attitudes may or may not affect acquisition, how the romance collection compares with other fiction genres size and currency-wise, what percentage of the budget it has, how this all relates to circulation statistics and compares with community needs: all of these need further study. Likewise, as the romance genre continues to diversify, more research is needed into all aspects of access to multicultural and diverse romance books in all formats, including appropriate subject headings or tags.

As I have indicated, the presence of librarian/library staff bias against the romance genre has been well documented. Better and more rigorous scholarship is needed, however, on the impact of this bias on reader experience and circulation statistics. Is there any? If so, what? When such bias is absent or contested, libraries will display and promote their romance collections to readers, but the ways in which this happens are in need of documentation and analysis, and research is needed into the circulation results of these efforts. Few if any studies have been done on the ways in which libraries interact with romance *authors*, especially local ones, and it would be valuable to know what, if any, effect such interaction has on their collections, on circulation statistics, and on the cultural capital which accrues to the genre.

As digital technology evolves, research into romance readers' preferred formats—eBook, print, audio—would be useful. Also, do readers prefer to buy, borrow, or both? And why? These are questions that library and information science scholarship is well-suited to explore.

The suggestions in this section are only a small sample of possible ideas for further study, and there is much more to be done, especially when it comes to serious research on the relationship between romance and libraries. The studies I have elaborated on in this chapter cover significant ground but they leave open the door for refining methodologies, repeating analyses with new data, and taking on a more intersectional and inter-disciplinary approach to enduring topics. As the genre evolves, as do the platforms and media in which it is available, so must library scholarship on romance.

Suggested reference works

Bouricius, Ann. *The Romance Readers' Advisory: The Librarian's Guide to Love in the Stacks.* American Library Association, 2000.

Carpan, Carolyn. *Rocked by Romance: A Guide to Teen Romance Fiction.* Libraries Unlimited, 2004.

Genreflecting: A Guide to Reading Interests in Genre Fiction Ed. 1–5; Genreflecting: A Guide to Popular Reading Interests. Ed. 6–8. The various editions of this title, first one by Betty Rosenberg (1982) and the most recent one, the 8th edition by Diana Tixier Herald and Samuel Stavole-Carter (2019), provide readers' advisory and some collection development information for libraries and librarians about popular fiction and all have sections on romance.

Ramsdell, Kristin. *Happily Ever After: A Guide to Reading Interests in Romance Fiction.* Libraries Unlimited, 1987. One of the earliest guides to the romance genre specifically aimed at libraries and librarians who do readers' advisory.

———. *Romance Fiction: A Guide to the Genre.* Libraries Unlimited, 1999. A revised and updated version of *Happily Ever After.*

———. *Romance Fiction: A Guide to the Genre.* 2nd Ed. Libraries Unlimited, 2012.

———. ed. *The Encyclopedia of Romance Fiction.* Greenwood, 2018.

Wyatt, Neal and Joyce G. Saricks. *The Readers' Advisory Guide to Genre Fiction.* 3rd Ed. American Library Association, 2018.

Notes

1 A fourth type of library, the special library, is not included because it is a library, usually within a corporation or non-profit organization, that focuses exclusively on the needs of that entity. Since popular romance fiction would likely be out of its scope, it is not a common choice for studies of this kind.
2 In Australia the program Public Lending Rights provides a small compensation to authors when books are borrowed; a similar program does not currently exist in the United States.
3 For more on these studies and on the status of popular romance in Australia, see Chapter 3 of this volume.
4 Adkins and her fellow researchers received the Romance Writers of America Academic Research Grant in 2006 to help support the research for the national study; I should perhaps acknowledge that in 1996 I received a Librarian of the Year award from the RWA for my work in support of the genre and its readers.
5 Bourdieu's idea of cultural capital is also important to Veros ("A Matter of Meta," "The Romance Reader and the Public Library") discussed above.
6 For more on YA romance see Chapter 7 of this volume.

Works cited

Adkins, Denice, Linda Esser, and Diane Velasquez. "Perceptions of Romance Readers: An Analysis of Missouri Librarians." Library Research Seminar III, October 15, 2004, Kansas City, MO. mospace.umsystem.edu/xmlui/bitstream/handle/10355/46258/LRS3-2004-Paper-PerceptionsofRomanceReaders.pdf?sequence=1&isAllowed=y. Accessed June 22, 2018.

Adkins, Denise, Linda Esser, and Diane Velasquez "Promoting Romance Novels in American Public Libraries." *Public Libraries*, vol. 49, no. 4, 2010, pp. 41–48.

Adkins, Denice, Diane Velasquez, and Linda Esser. "Relations between Librarians and Romance Readers: A Missouri Study." *Public Libraries*, vol. 54, no. 4, 2006, pp. 54–64.

Adkins, Denice, Linda Esser, Diane Velasquez, and Heather L. Hill. "Romance Novels in American Public Libraries: A Study of Collection Development Practices." *Library Collections, Acquisitions, and Technical Services*, vol. 32, no. 2, 2008, pp. 59–67.

Ali, Kecia. "Romance Fiction in the Archives." *Journal of Popular Romance Studies* vol. 7, May 2018. n.p. jprstudies.org/2018/05/romance-fiction-in-the-archivesby-kecia-ali/. Accessed July 1, 2019.

Allen, Amanda Kirstin. "The Girls' Guide to Power: Romancing the Cold War." Dissertation. University of Alberta, 2010.

Bennett-Kapusniak, Renee and Adrian McCleer. "Love in the Digital Library: A Search for Racial Heterogeneity in Ebooks." *Journal of Popular Romance Studies*, no. 5.1, 2009, n.p. jprstudies.org /2015/08/love-in-the-digital-library-a-search-for-racial-heterogeneity-in-e-booksby-renee-bennett-kapusniak-and-adriana-mccleer. Accessed June 18, 2018.

Bold, Rudolph. "Trash in the Library." *Library Journal*, vol. 105, no. 10, 1980, pp. 1138–1139.

Bryson, Mary. "Public Library Services to the Romance Reader: An Online Survey of Romance Readers." M.S. in L.S. thesis, University of North Carolina at Chapel Hill, 2004.

Charles, John and Shelley Mosley. "Getting Serious about Romance: Adult Series Romances for Teens." *Voice of Youth Advocate*, vol. 25, June 2002, pp. 87–93.

Charles, John, Shelley Mosley, and Ann Bouricius. "Romancing the Y.A. Reader: Romance Novels Recommended for Young Adults." *Voice of Youth Advocate*, vol. 21, February 1999, pp. 414–419.

Charles, John and Cathie Linz. "Romancing Your Readers: How Public Libraries Can Become More Romance-Reader Friendly." *Public Libraries*, vol. 44, no. 1, 2005, pp. 43–48.

Chelton, Mary K. "Unrestricted Body Parts and Predictable Bliss: The Audience Appeal of Formula Fiction." *Library Journal*, vol. 116, no. 12, July 1991, pp. 44–49.

———. "What Kind of Romance are You in the Mood For?: A Recommended Reading List." *Booklist*, vol. 98, September 15, 2001, pp. 210–212.

Dewan, Pauline. "Why Your Academic Library Needs a Popular Reading Collection Now More than Ever." *College & Undergraduate Libraries*, vol. 1, no. 1, 2010. pp. 44–64.

Eaton, Elizabeth Shelby. The Free-Reading Use of the Library by Patients in a Veterans Hospital." Dissertation, University of Chicago, 1953.

Fialkoff, Francine. "Are We Dumbing down the Book Review?" *Library Journal*, vol. 120, no. 7, April 15, 1995. p. 60.

Foss, Kimberly Kay. An Analysis to Determine if Popular Romance Novels, Read by Today's High School Students, Reflect the Characteristics and Roles of Women in Current Society." Thesis. M. S. in Educ./Lib. Sci. University of Wyoming, 1997.

Funderburk, Amy. "Romance Collections in North Carolina Public Libraries: Are All Genres Treated Equally?" M. S. in L. S. Thesis, University of North Carolina at Chapel Hill, 2004.

Griffin, Ivan Albert. "Libraries and Selected Reading Practices in Four Selected Schools." Dissertation. M.S. in Education. University of Southern California, 1939.

Gundlach, Kathryn R. "Patterns of Genre Fiction Readers: A Survey of Durham County Library Patrons." M.S. in L.S. Thesis. University of North Carolina at Chapel Hill, 2002.

Hoffert, Barbara. "What's Hot Now." *Library Journal*, vol. 143, no. 2, 2018. pp. 34–36.

Kerns, Kerns and Debbie O'Brien. "Recreational Reading Collections: A Survey of Tennessee Academic Libraries." *Tennessee Librarian*. vol. 52, no, 2, 2001, pp. 6–16.

Krentz, Jayne Ann. "All the Right Reasons: Romance Fiction in the Public Library." *Public Libraries*, vol. 36, May/June 1997, pp. 162–166.

———, ed. *Dangerous Men and Adventurous Women*. University of Pennsylvania Press, 1992.

Linz, Cathie, Ann Bouricius, and Carole Byrnes. "Exploring the World of Romance Novels." *Public Libraries*. Vol. 33, no. 3, May/June 1995, pp. 144–151.

Lawrence, Emily. "Is Contemporary Readers' Advisory Populist?: Taste Elevation and Ideological Tension in the *Genreflecting* Series." *Library Trends*, vol. 65, no. 4, 2017, pp. 491–507.

Loan, Fayaz Ahmad and Refhat-un-nisa Shah. "Survey of the Literature Reading Habits and Preferences of Adolescents: A Study of A Public School in India. *LIBRES: Library & Information Science Research Electronic Journal*. vol. 27, no. 2, December 2017, pp. 80–96. www.libres-ejournal.info/2577/

Lucas, Linda Sue. "The Ranges of Life Interests and Reading Interests among Adult Users of Public Libraries in Communities of Various Sizes." Dissertation, University of Illinois at Urbana-Champaign, 1980.

Morrissett, Linda A. "Leisure Reading Collections in Academic Libraries: A Survey." *North Carolina Libraries*, vol. 52, 1994, pp. 122–125.

Mosley, Shelley, John Charles, and Julie Havir. "The Librarian as Effete Snob: Why Romance?" *Wilson Library Bulletin*, vol. 69, no. 9, May 1995. pp. 24–25+.

Mueller, Kate Landry, Michael Hanson, Michelle Martinez, and Linda Meyer. "Patron Preferences: Recreational Reading in an Academic Library." *Journal of Academic Librarianship*, vol. 43, no. 1, 2017, pp. 72–81.

Parameswaran Radhika, E. "Public Images Private Pleasures: Romance Reading at the Intersection of Gender, Class, and National Identities in Urban India." Dissertation, University of Iowa, 1997.

Potter, Franz. "Twilight of a Genre: Art and Trade in Gothic Fiction, 1814-1832." Dissertation. University of East Anglia, 2002.

Pymm, Robert Anthony. "Australian Fiction in Australian Libraries: The Collection and Preservation of Titles Published between 1900 and 1970. Dissertation. University of New South Wales, 1996.

Radick, Caryn. "Romance Writers' Use of Archives." *Archivaria*, vol. 81, Spring 2016, pp. 45–73.

Rathe, Bette and Lisa Blankenship. "Recreational Reading Collections in Academic Libraries." *Collection Management*. vol. 30, no. 2, 2005, pp. 73–85.

Ross, Catherine Sheldrick. "Reader on Top: Public Libraries, Pleasure Reading and Modes of Reading." *Library Trends*, vol. 57, no. 4, 2009, pp. 632–656.

Ross, Catherine Sheldrick and Mary K. Chelton. "Reader's Advisory: Matching Mood and Material." *Library Journal*, vol. 126, no. 2, 2001, pp. 52–55.

Sanders, Mark. "Popular Reading Collections in Public University Libraries: A Survey of Three Southeastern States." *Public Services Quarterly*, vol. 5, 2009. pp. 174–183.

Scott, Alison M. "Romance in the Stacks; Or, Popular Romance Fiction Imperiled." In *Scorned Literature: Essays on the History and Criticism of Popular Mass-Produced Fiction in America*, edited by Lydia Cushman Schurman and Deirdre Johnson, Westport, CT: Greenwood Press, 2002, pp. 213–231.

Sheehan, Sarah E. and Jen Stevens. Creating a Popular Romance Collection in an Academic Library. *Journal of Popular Romance Studies*, vol. 5, no. 1, 2015. n.p. http://jprstudies.org/wp-content/uploads/2015/08/CAPRC.08.2015.pdf. Accessed July 22, 2019.

Sherman, Jen. "Reading Infrastructures in the Contemporary City: A Study of Three Public Libraries in Sydney." Dissertation, Western Sydney University (Australia), 2016.

Sutton, Roger. "Librarians and the Paperback Romance: Trying to Do the Right Thing." *School Library Journal* vol. 3, no. 3, November 1985, pp. 25–29.

Thompson, Jennifer K. "Romance in the Stacks: The Prevalence of Romance Fiction in Academic Libraries." M.S. in L.S. thesis. University of North Carolina at Chapel Hill.

Tuñon, Johanna. An Appetite for Romance: How to Understand, Buy, Display, and Promote Romance Fiction." *Library Acquisition*, vol. 19, no. 4, Winter 1995, pp. 471–475.

———, "A Fine Romance: How to Select Romances for Your Collection." *Wilson Library Bulletin*, vol. 69, no. 9, May 1995, pp. 31–34.

Van Fleet, Connie. "Popular Fiction Collections in Academic and Public Libraries." *Acquisitions Librarian*, vol. 15, no. 29, 2003, pp. 63–85.

Veros, Vassiliki. "A Matter of Meta: Category Romance Fiction and the Interplay of Paratest and Library Metadata." *Journal of Popular Romance Studies*, no. 5.1, 2015, n.p. http://jprstudies.org/2015/08/a-matter-of-meta-category-romance-fiction-and-the-interplay-of-paratext-and-library-metadataby-vassiliki-veros/. Accessed June 25, 2018.

———. "The Romance Reader and the Public Library." *Australian Library Journal*, vol. 61, no. 4, 2012, pp. 298–306.

Won, Young Seon. "Reading Books, Reading Life: The Cultural Practice and Literary Representation of Reading in Jane Austen's Time." Dissertation. University of Nebraska, 2006.

Wyatt, Neal, ed. "Core Collections in Genre Studies: Romance Fiction 101." *Reference and User Services Quarterly*, vol. 47, no. 2, Winter 2007, pp. 120–125.

Part IV

Themes

18 Class and wealth in popular romance fiction

Amy Burge

Class has not generally been a central focus of popular romance research. However, there is a small but significant body of work on class and wealth in popular romance. This scholarship treats as suspect "the claim of romantic love's disinterestedness, of its being exempt from issues of hierarchy and inequality in class society" (Weisser 135): romance is not, in fact, universal and class *does* matter.

This chapter offers an overview of this scholarship on class and wealth in the popular romance as it has emerged over the past 30 years. My focus, following the majority of previous scholarship, is on the heterosexual romance novel as it is consumed and produced in Britain and the U.S.[1] I begin by offering a brief outline of sociological and cultural approaches to studying class and the ways these have informed criticism of the romance novel. I also provide a synopsis of the popular romance texts produced by and for specific audiences in Britain and the U.S. that form the basis for scholarship in this area. The chapter then focuses on four key themes that emerge from this scholarship: intersectionality; cross-class marriage and social mobility; romance as middle-class propaganda; and the implications of romance's escapist qualities. I end with some thoughts on where critical engagement with class and wealth in romance might go next.

Reading class

Over the last 30 years, scholarship on class in the popular romance has shifted in line with wider changes in approaches to the study of class. As Jennifer Haytock points out, "discussions of class used to start with Marx and hence with the connection between labor and capital, specifically the interplay between them labelled 'class struggle'" (7). In Marxist terms, class is understood in terms of its relation to the means of production. Early studies of the romance were influenced by materialist feminism and read romance through the twin lenses of capitalism and patriarchy; Jan Cohn's *Romance and the Erotics of Property* (1988) is an example of this kind of analysis. In the mid-1980s, the appearance of English-language translations of the work of Pierre Bourdieu prompted a shift away from conceptions of class based on social stratification and toward a more individual, self-determined view of class based on forms of capital, to borrow Bourdieu's term (1987). Bourdieu viewed class in terms of capital: economic capital (command over economic resources); social capital (resources based on group membership, relationships, networks of influence and support); and cultural capital (forms of knowledge, skill, education). Stuart Hall extends this further to propose that class is *active*—a performance of particular kinds of classed behavior—thus "class has come to be regarded as something between a fixed economic category and a social construction" (Hall, qtd. in Haytock 7).

From the mid-1980s onwards, romance scholarship echoed the "cultural turn" in approaches to class. Fowler's *The Alienated Reader: Women and Popular Romantic Literature in the Twentieth Century* (1991) uses Bourdieu's categories of taste—legitimate taste, "middle-brow" taste, and popular taste—to distinguish between her romance readers. Janice Radway's *Reading the Romance* (1984), a well-known study of popular romance fiction, describes the educational and cultural capital of her Smithton readers, in addition to their economic situation. Indeed, Bourdieu's work on *habitus*—"the set of bodily, linguistic, and cultural dispositions acquired during socialization" (Illouz *Why Love Hurts* 49)—has been influential in work on dating, love and romance; Eva Illouz draws on these ideas in her 1997 study *Consuming the Romantic Utopia*, where she aims to make class a more central issue in the cultural study of love. Paul Johnson and Steph Lawler point out how helpful these conceptions of class can be when dealing with something seen as "more 'cultural' than economic" (Johnson and Lawler n. p.). Twenty-first-century scholarship on class in the popular romance has also explored the neoliberal turn in world economics, and the endorsement of global free-market capitalism—an issue Jayashree Kamblé explores at length in her *Making Meaning in Popular Romance Fiction: An Epistemology* (2014).

In general, this work on class in popular romance takes one of two approaches: a focus on working-class readers and material produced and consumed by them; or analysis of the way class is represented in romance fiction more widely. Studies vary in their historical approach, with many tracing the roots of class issues in current romances from their ancestors in the eighteenth and nineteenth century. Given the wide range of sources discussed across this scholarship, I will briefly outline the romance novels discussed by critics that were published in Britain and the U.S. from the 1740s onward.

Class and romance reading in Britain and the U.S.

Romance in Britain

Several different genres and periods of British popular romance have been explored by scholars for their representation of, or relation to, class and wealth. Some critics begin with what Pamela Regis calls the "classic" romances of the eighteenth and nineteenth century: namely, Samuel Richardson's *Pamela* (1740), Jane Austen's *Pride and Prejudice* (1813), Charlotte Brontë's *Jane Eyre* (1847), and Emily Brontë's *Wuthering Heights* (1847). Social position is at the heart of these novels; in particular, the "magical social ascent of fairy-tales" evident in romance (Fowler 15). Lillian S. Robinson highlights how Austen's novels are rooted in an understanding of social change and how it was affecting people (215–16); for Austen's characters, everything they do is mediated by class (Robinson 220). As for *Pamela*, Fowler argues,

> however severe its critique of elitism, however much it softened the practices of a market economy with an appeal to charity or "caring capitalism," opposition to the desire for social reconstruction championed by the new working class was its secret centre.
>
> (17)

In *Pamela*, the heroine's ascent to become part of a ruling gentry class that governs justly is the fantasy (Fowler 15–17). Subsequent romance fiction was heavily influenced by these classics of the genre; Fowler posits that the birth of mass fiction in the 1840s and 1850s recycled the values of novels like this one.

The most obvious, although admittedly not historically chronological, successor to Austen was Georgette Heyer, whose *Regency Buck* (1935) heralded the start of the wildly popular Regency subgenre of romance. For Robinson, Heyer "shows a society articulated by class and one in which class feeling, especially snobbery and ambition, runs high" (220). The Regency has also influenced non-historical romances; Regis, in her diachronic survey of the popular romance, notes how American author Kathleen Gilles Seidel centers her novel around a Regency-era historical soap opera to create a society defined "by that period's rigid class structure" in *Again* (1994) (41). Many scholars have looked to the Regency romance, with its strict delineation of social strata, for their exploration of class and wealth (e.g., Osborne; Kamblé).

In the early twentieth century, Edwardian romance novels continued to be preoccupied with themes of class and wealth. Heroes were drawn from the aristocracy, and heroines came either from the upper classes, or the working middle classes (Dixon 6). Jay Dixon argues that these novels reflected the instability of the period in terms of class change and fears for the stability of the upper classes, with romance novels often containing an external menace reflecting this threat. She thus concludes "that from the earliest days of their history, Mills & Boon books have symbolically represented aspects of the society in which they were written" (Dixon 14–15). However, these "society" novels, concerned with the English upper classes and set in southern England, had largely disappeared by 1914 (Dixon 14). Dixon also points to a shift in the association of class and wealth. In society novels, class and wealth are combined—higher class means greater wealth—and the hero is often representative of England, with his country estate and aristocratic lineage (Dixon 46). But the heroes of current Mills & Boon romances are no longer associated with England or with the aristocracy; today's heroes are sheikhs, Spaniards, and wealthy entrepreneurs (Dixon 46, 48), indicating a movement away from class in strict social terms, toward a global, market-driven emphasis on wealth.[2]

It was after 1914 that the first publications specifically targeted at working-class women appeared: "the down-market, consumer-oriented periodical which was, none the less, a class paper" (Melman 107). These cheap, regularly-produced magazines, such as the mill-girl focused *Peg's Paper*, identified themselves with working-class women, represented working-class experiences, and invited readers to send in their "real" stories (Melman 109, 113). The periodical boom in the post-war era was predominantly associated with women and the working class; by the mid-1920s, "over half the fiction magazines for women catered for the adolescent and adult working-class market" (Melman 110, 112).

In terms of working-class readership, it is worth highlighting the work of Catherine Cookson—a hugely successful British writer of "social democratic" romances from the 1950s onward. Cookson's domestic romance novels focused on multi-generation stories set in the North of England and offer a microcosmic view of social relations (Fowler 91). Cookson places the domestic at the heart of her novels—"minute detail is included of women's domestic labour, so as to enhance its use-value" (Fowler 94)—and it has been argued that "the reformist adaptation of working-class radicalism to capitalism represented in the tradition of Methodist unionism is the hidden centre of all

Cookson's naturalist novels" (Fowler 78). Marriage for social advancement is a key motif in Cookson's novels (Fowler), but critics are divided as to how socially aware her novels are. For Janet Batsleer et al., the focus on "formulaic narrative devices" of romance obscures politics; "in Catherine Cookson's novels, heredity replaces and displaces class struggle as the motor of history" (87–8). However, in *The Historical Novel* (2010), Jerome de Groot argues that "Cookson's novels refuse to compromise their message about the privations suffered by women in the past, and in doing so they present a type of historical romance which is idealistic about relationships but clear-sighted about history" (56), thus refuting Batsleer's argument. For de Groot, Cookson's novels make apparent the function of hegemonic capitalism to indicate how it might be "challenged, subverted or questioned" (57). Fowler similarly argues that "it is striking how many of these novels are pastiches specifically of the Victorian 'condition of England' novels of the 1840s" and "therefore centrally concerned with the relations of labour and capital" (100). Fowler claims that Cookson's later novels are more explicit in their class politics and "opposition to 'Victorian values' can be detected within some recent romances, including the presentation of strikes as legitimate defences of workers' interests and the linkage of exploitation to high rates of profit" (Fowler 99).

Mills & Boon, the most successful British romance publisher, produced novels in the early twentieth century where the protagonists were both middle-class, white-collar workers (Kamblé 35). However, this changed with the growing popularity of the "capitalist hero" (Kamblé 36) where the hero is presented as the "wielder of bourgeois power" and the novel "dramatize[s]" his effect on the working-class heroine (Kamblé 29–30). Romance novels thus reflect changes in the British economy from Keynesian economics to the free market. From the mid-twentieth century, popular romance also shifted in response to social and historical changes. Batsleer et al. point to the increase in exotic settings that occurred alongside a rise in package holidays and the "transnationalisation of capital" (91). As women worked in a wider range of industries following World War II, romance novels began to feature more diverse working heroines. The career novel, "of which over 50 were published in the 1950s and 1960s, [was] aimed at young girls and designed to encourage the development of career aspirations" (Baum 1187). Thomas Baum focuses his analysis on flight attendants, but romance heroines were imagined in a range of occupations, although these remained predominantly feminized (secretary, teacher, governess) (Markert, qtd. in Liffen 350). A key subgenre in this period is the doctor–nurse romance that emerged in the 1950s in response to the establishing of the NHS in Britain. In these novels, "Mills & Boon authors brought their own work experience as nurses to bear in crafting a more realistic, sometimes gritty background for their love stories" (McAleer 174). Joseph McAleer notes that after World War II women were more interested in having jobs and not just being in the home—the doctor–nurse romances of the 1950s is an indication of Mills & Boon's editorial policy shifting to accommodate this (176).

Romance in the U.S.

While social changes in the U.S. and the U.K. were broadly comparable and many of the romantic texts mentioned circulated in both countries, there are two specifically American genres that appear in scholarship on romance and class.[3] The first is the domestic novel, popular in the mid-nineteenth century. Cohn notes that "the period directly following the Civil War saw a burgeoning market for women writers of popular fiction" (Cohn 49). Described by Nina Baym as "the story of a young girl ... deprived of the supports she had rightly or wrongly depended on ... [who] [b]y the novel's end ... has developed a strong conviction of her own worth" (19), the subgenre did not really focus on working-class women (Denning 187). Indeed, the demise of the domestic novel in the 1860s was partly predicated, according to Michael Denning, on a "new visibility of class, of working-women in the culture" (187). Denning focuses his analysis on the second genre, the dime novel, the first popular romance text produced for working-class women in the U.S. (Enstad 14). Emerging in the 1840s, the working-girl novel was a major subgenre of dime novels (Denning 185). Such a distinction, between the longer novel for and about the middle and upper classes, and the serial publication, for and, mostly, about the working class (Melman 148), is common to popular romance on both sides of the Atlantic. As Billie Melman points out, "working-class modes of feeling and thinking about women differed radically from those of the middle classes or élite audiences. The differences manifested themselves in both the form and the language of discourse" (147–8).

To some extent, the way class and wealth are represented in popular romance publishing has changed significantly. Works specifically aimed at working-class women emerged for the first time in the twentieth century, novels are now far more likely to represent women at work (and in a wider range of roles), and there has been a shift away from the domestic focus of nineteenth-century novels. But there are threads that can be drawn from the classic romances of the eighteenth and nineteenth century through to the present day. Kamblé points to a "changing economic milieu" as the "key thematic connection between classic and contemporary romance" (28–9); she traces the association of big business and capitalism with the modern romance hero back to these classic novels and their focus on society and entwining of a courtship narrative (32). Fowler argues that modern romance novels still have "recourse to such hegemonic gentry figures" as we see in novels like *Pamela* (15–17) (this is also clearly evident in the continuing popularity of Regency and Victorian historical novels). Regis similarly recognizes that the society consideration of earlier "classic" romances is not gone, but is simply less important in the popular romances of the twentieth century (123). It is to these common threads and themes that I now turn.

Key themes in the scholarship of class and wealth in romance

Intersectionality

Romance is a genre written and read by women. It is thus impossible to think about class without also thinking about gender; as Alison Light puts it, "class and gender differences do not simply speak to each other, they cannot speak *without* each other" (19). What's more, "by seeing that women are constituted not just by their difference from men, but by class differences that separate them from each other, we become more alert to the complex ways women relate to each other and to men" (Amireh xiii–xiv). Unlike much early scholarship on the romance, which focuses almost entirely on gender, all the studies discussed in this chapter are explicit about the way gender and class intersect in romance. The most obvious is the presentation of conflict between the hero and heroine as class conflict, where he is the one with more social *and* more gender power. In her analysis of Catherine Cookson's novels, Fowler notes how class preservation is related to control of sexuality and marriage (92–3); in a heterosexual romance novel whose end goal is monogamous marriage, while the heroine might gain social status through the marriage she remains subordinate to the hero, who has top billing in gender and in class (Osborne 145–6).[4] Such subordination is not new: Fowler argues that "the romance's promise of happiness originated in feudal female vassalage to husbands" (19).

The intersection of gender and class is evident in the way that women's work is depicted. I have outlined how the work women undertake in romance novels can be feminized—women are often nannies, secretaries, or teachers. Yet, even where women undertake different professions, or where working women are celebrated, heroines often, especially in older romance novels, end up ensconced in the domestic sphere through marriage by the end of the novel with the male hero re-established as the primary earner (Fowler 60). Baum notes that "typically, these novels depicted situations which gave their heroines a taste of independence within a conventional framework, but confirmed their ultimate domestic role through a successful romance" (1187). Romance novels are also revealing of differences between women based on their profession—this is evident in the doctor-nurse romances of the 1950s. McAleer notes that a key difference between romances where the heroine is a nurse and those where she is a doctor is that at the end of the novel the nurse is expected to give up her career immediately, but the doctor-heroine can carry on working (187–8). The distinction between work and the domestic is presented slightly differently in the "corporate romances" of the 1990s. Focusing on the work of Jayne Ann Krentz, Erin S. Young notes how the heroine domesticates the workplace meaning she does not have to give up work in order to share domestic bliss with the hero. However, as Young points out, the flexibility to manage both a successful career and romantic union is dependent on the privilege afforded by her status as a white upper-class woman. There is, therefore, a sharp difference in opportunities for women from different classes and ethnic and racial groups.

It is possible to read the representation of women's work as symbolic in a larger sense. In her reading of romance novels as allegories of economic change, Kamblé suggests that the double bind women found themselves in during the Thatcher administration (where jobs were lost and women were encouraged to stay at home by the "Tory emphasis on the family" but found themselves financially unable to do so) "is the concealed narrative in many Harlequin Mills and Boon romances of the time, though it is cased in a deceptively simplistic formula of the aggressive male faced down by the scrappy woman" (39). She argues that "the battle of the sexes (reflected in the hostile skirmishes that make up the hero and heroine's relationship) is the familiar signifier that is reinvigorated by its new meaning (class conflict), a meaning provoked by the growth of multinational capitalism" (Kamblé 40). For Kamblé, "the novels thus represent a socioeconomic drama of the way British national firms and the people in the workforce faced Britain's changing economic landscape" and "it signals the novels' response to a larger shift in the mode of production in Britain from social democratic welfare economics to liberal political economy and the doctrine of market order" (40). The gendered conflict between the hero and heroine thus represents wider shifts in British economic culture.

Looking at class alongside gender can also be revealing of other areas of intersection. Batsleer et al. highlight the presence of both "Society women" and working-class women in romance novels but, rather than pointing out their differences, attempt to show how they are connected through a focus on the family; both classes of women are excluded from "full-time work, trade-unionism, politics, the making of 'history'" (103), all of which are reserved for men. In these novels, "Englishness" is a common theme for "all (white) women" in romances that "place families—rather than class wealth or enterprise—at the heart of the nation" (Batsleer et al. 103). Batsleer et al.'s choice of language here—"all (white) women" is revealing of a glaring omission in much of this scholarship of any attention to race or ethnicity and the ways this intersects with class and gender.[5]

Fowler is one of very few scholars who takes a more intersectional approach to romance novels—she is quick to point out that 1970s and 1980s feminist scholarship on the romance novel failed to take class, ethnicity, and power into account (35). While she does not actually focus on ethnicity in her book-length study, Fowler does mention a Catherine Cookson novel, *Colour Blind* (1953) featuring a cross-racial relationship that shows tensions between working-class people in the North-East of England and immigrants from Africa and Asia. Fowler points out that this is Cookson's only romance that does not have a positive ending—the cross-racial relationship breaks up the family and, ultimately, can't be accepted. For Fowler, the morality and message of this book is aligned with native British workers (82–7). Susan Ostrov Weisser points to the interlinking of class and race in contemporary Harlequin Mills & Boon publications. She notices that Black romance series explicitly require "aspirational" protagonists, while in series containing predominantly white characters, like "Harlequin Presents," "most white heroes and heroines are middle-class or upper-class ... without the reminder or task of heavy-handed 'modeling'" (166–7).

In her contribution to the edited collection *Romance Fiction and American Culture*, Erin S. Young examines how race and class intersect in contemporary romance novels featuring mixed-race Asian heroines. She notes that contemporary China is often identified with the past, from which the Asian heroine is rescued by "the 'American dream' of economic independence and social or political power" (209): the "therapeutic power of white economic hegemony" (221). Young argues that rather than the white hero becoming more sympathetic to a "female worldview" over the course of the novel (as noted by earlier romance scholars), it is actually the Asian heroine who is transformed through her introduction to the "(white) British or American corporation" (206) that the white, Western hero represents. The happily ever after is thus the "success and security of an American corporation" (213) with attendant implications of whiteness. There are several potential reasons for the general elision of race/ethnicity from the discussion of class in romance (which I will outline at the end of this chapter), but it is clear that a fully intersectional approach to the study of popular romance is overdue.

Cross-class marriage and social mobility

In most romance genres, in most periods, the way for lower-class women to improve their social class and gain power is through marriage to the wealthy hero. As Cohn puts it,

> bourgeois, patriarchal society reduced women's economic function to her role in the marriage market. Upward mobility, promised at least in theory to all sober and industrious men, was denied her in her exclusion from the marketplace. Marriage was her only real economic resource; and marriage to a man socially and

> economically her superior, her only real chance for upward mobility, her only recourse to power.
>
> (8)

The heroine, almost always of a lower class or status than the hero, is not permitted access to wealth or upper-class identity in a genre where the hero's identity is so consistently defined by wealth, upper-class status, and power. Thus, "in the structures of contemporary romance there is no way for the heroine to acquire that power except by acquiring the hero" (Cohn 5). Cross-class marriage is also the most obvious way that class conflict, often the barrier between hero and heroine, can be removed.

Cross-class marriage is thus common in popular romance. Catherine Cookson, whose novels were popular throughout the second half of the twentieth century, used cross-class marriage as a major device (Fowler 82). Analyzing the Regency romances of Georgette Heyer, Robinson notes that Heyer's heroes are always drawn from "the first circles" of society, and heroines are usually from impoverished families to allow for the emergence of a Cinderella motif of upwardly mobile marriage (216–17). In the U.S., nineteenth-century dime novels regularly featured stories about the transformation of working girls into ladies through marriage (Denning 195–6). Cross-class marriage can even be used to side-step gender inequality. Laurie Osborne, exploring the way romance uses Shakespeare to mediate class, argues that "Shakespeare enables romance novelists to rewrite patriarchal gender inequalities as class or status obstacles" which is meaningful as "class differences can ostensibly be resolved through marriage; gender inequity cannot" (149). This means that apparently immutable gender inequalities can be side-stepped because "class is assumed to be flexible and fantasies of transcending class are particularly potent" (Osborne 149).

However, this interlacement of love, marriage, and power is complicated by the ideology of the romantic story that defines marriage as "based on emotional rather than economic considerations" (Cohn 8). The romance heroine is not permitted to be calculating in her pursuit of advantageous marriage; on the contrary, she must be seen as actively *not* seeking such an arrangement. Tania Modleski points out that while "it is socially, economically, and aesthetically imperative for a woman to get a husband and his money, she achieves these goals partly by *not wanting* them" (50). As Cohn puts it:

> the goal of this heroine is to find the right husband, the mature, successful, sensual hero. The problem for the heroine, of course, is that she cannot openly pursue this goal, that she must appear to be doing something else entirely.
>
> (95)

This dates back to nineteenth-century classic romance, where desiring a successful marriage to rise above one's station would be seen as vulgar (Robinson 219).

Thus, socially advantageous marriage is a realistic way for women (in romance and in reality) to gain access to social circles and commodities otherwise unavailable to her. There is, then, a tension between marriage as romantic endeavor, and marriage as social contract or bargain. Kamblé, analyzing late twentieth-century and twenty-first-century Regency historical romances, finds evidence of bargaining and negotiation in conversations around marriage, for instance in Loretta Chase's *Lord of Scoundrels* (1995) where the hero and heroine negotiate their marriage contract "in the register of the corporate takeover, with its characteristic demands and counteroffers of dividends and stock options" (43). For Kamblé, while this example does point to "the kind of wealth, monetary security, and financial reward that the heroes of Harlequin Mills & Boon promise as husbands" (43), it also indicates "the genre's immersion in, and suspicion of, business-speak and the ethos of late capitalism" (43). Kamblé writes:

> [it is not] that romance novels show marriage to be a system of commoditization and exchange but rather that they reflect the pervasive nature of industrial and postindustrial capitalism's worldview, with its constant threatening undercurrent of annexation and loss of economic autonomy.
>
> (45)

According to Kamblé, upwardly mobile marriage points to deeper issues in popular romance.

Romance as middle-class propaganda

Given the development of the working-class popular romance from its middle-class antecedent, it seems inevitable that romance would sometimes focus on middle-class experience to the exclusion of working-class lives. McAleer states that Mills & Boon were careful and deliberate about how they came across "to maintain a solidly middle-class moral worldview that maintained the status quo" (175). Indeed, Fowler argues that the romance magazines of the 1920s and 1930s were adapted from the middle-class romance form "to take account of the deprivations and the wish-fulfilment of an oppressed lower-class readership" (51). Yet, an accusation that has been leveled at popular romance read by working-class women is that it functions as middle-class propaganda.

It certainly seems as though popular romance aimed at working-class women has, at least in the past, been preoccupied with "besieging" working-class families with middle-class values; Fowler posits that from the 1850s onwards popular romance encouraged a halt to the working-class practice of taking in lodgers and encouraged middle-class measures, such as marriage before pregnancy and the surveillance of children (54–5). Equally, when key social conflicts are described (e.g., the great strike) they are usually represented from the point of view of the dominant classes (Fowler 103). Barbara Cartland, who wrote hundreds of novels read by working-class or lower-middle-class women, was herself a "Society" woman (Batsleer et al. 92–3) whose writing endorsed "conservative modes of cultural and social behaviour" (de Groot 59). Judy Giles notes that women represented in romance tend to be bourgeois, which is not particularly helpful as a role model or example for working-class women (289) and Batsleer et al. observe that lower-class and non-white protagonists are often subordinate to the main couple and reliant on them for the success of their own relationships (98). Admitting that many romance novels are "entirely permeated with the ideas of the dominant class and gender," Fowler points to the problematic desire for white, dominant class heroes by working-class romance readers (120, 145).

A key way this middle-class capitalist agenda is promoted, it has been suggested, is through the figure of the desirable, dominant class, capitalist hero. Sexual and economic dominance are located in the hero, who is often the focus of the romance novel (Cohn 8), with the connection between "male sexual and male economic power" dating "at least as far back as Richardson" (Cohn 49). The hero's wealth is a large part of his appeal; his "brand of capitalism—ambitious, go-getting, swift, ruthless" is connected with "his worth as a man, a husband, a social being" (Kamblé 33–4). The promise of no further economic hardship for the heroine is equally appealing. By making the hero's capitalist world, with its private jets, yachts, and mansions, the primary backdrop of the story the romance implicitly endorses it (Kamblé 36).

But, things are not quite as simple as they seem. While Raymond Williams argues that popular literature has a "moral regulation" function to "control the development of working-class opinion," popular romance readers are more "selective" in their taking on of "elements of dominant thought" (Fowler 40). Popular romance contains themes that criticize middle-class views of the working classes (e.g., that women are good for sex but not marriage; that they are criminals) and Fowler argues: "in these imaginary documents of social injustice there does surface a cry of pain against the 'injuries of class'" (67). In her study of the London shopgirl, Lise Shapiro Sanders argues that the late-nineteenth and early-twentieth-century romance novels she reads often critique "the politics of labour and capitalist production" (82). Equally, there is a limit to how far the dominant class's views can be "made palatable for a working-class readership"; for instance, the workhouse is often presented negatively in working-class romance novels (Fowler 53). Middle-class values are thus adapted to place them more in line with working-class ideals.

The capitalist hero, too, is not all he seems. Jayashree Kamblé argues that the romance hero wears a "mask" of the capitalist that allows romance novels to personalize the "abstract economic force of the free market" and make the love story about "big business and its impact on others" (Kamblé 32). She admits that in some cases, it seems as though the popular romance is endorsing capitalism, particularly in the celebration of the ambitious, wealthy hero. However, popular romance is more conflicted than it might at first appear about the capitalist hero, stopping short of outward idolizing. Reservations are expressed about "the capitalist's ethics, often as anxieties over his conduct in his sexual-romantic life" (Kamblé 36) and American novels show "a questioning of the hero's very nature through the portrayal of his emotions as identical to his economics—an equivalence that seems quite dangerous on occasion" (Kamblé 46). Kamblé points to Judith McNaught's Regency historicals *Whitney, My Love* (1985) and *Until You* (1994) where the traits that provide heroes success on the stock market are viewed more problematically when they are applied to the romantic relationship, particularly sexual aggression toward the heroine (Kamblé 46, 49). Indeed, Kamblé concludes that romance novels might not condemn current economic structures, but "they are not capitalist propaganda or blind affirmation either; instead, the romantic plot and the figure of the hero voice a terror of the American immersion in advanced capitalism" (47).

Kamblé's argument echoes Charles H. Hinnant's (2003) view that romance novels present a feminist critique of capitalism. Conceding that the romance hero is typically associated with "traditional masculine economic ideals of self-sufficiency, rationality, and rugged individualism" (149), Hinnant argues that the "taming" of the alpha male by the romance heroine modifies or overturns these characteristics "by a new commitment to the civilising and feminizing virtues of sociability, empathy, and interdependence" (149). Hinnant thus claims that romance novels—he focuses his analysis on the influential historical novel *The Flame and the Flower* (1972) by Kathleen E. Woodiwiss—"correspond … to a certain strain of feminist criticism of mainstream economics" (149) that insists the liberal individualism of capitalism must be tempered by the "virtues of liberality, sociality, and sentimentality" (160). Hinnant sees romance novels as the landscape where capitalism is "transformed from within" and "purged of its more brutal features" (164) recasting "commerce as a civilising process" (161). The romance novel is evidently able to support a more complex reading of capitalism than might at first be apparent.

Romance as escapism

> Only very immature people or girls whose tastes have begun to be perverted could endure the constant repetition of this kind of description: "Glyn Curtis was the only man who could make her heart throb with longing—the longing to be taken into his arms, to feel his lips upon hers. Not lightly, caressingly as he had kissed her before but—!"
>
> (Jephcott qtd. in Giles 283, her emphasis)

I turn, in this final section to working-class romance readers, exploring divergent arguments for and against romance reading. Working-class women are particularly susceptible to romance. Or, at least, that is what Pearl Jephcott claimed in her 1943 report *Girls Growing Up*. The growth in popularity of dance halls, as well as an emerging romance fiction market for working-class women and girls led critics to level such charges against romance novels (Giles 288–9). Scholarship on working-class readers of romance found that working-class women were very aware of this discourse and, in their real lives, actively refused romance "not because of a lesser sensibility, but because 'being swept off your feet' was a fate too dangerous, however seductive, to even contemplate, for a consciousness formed from poverty and exclusion" (Giles 290). Giles interviewed women who grew up before World War II and notes that respondents located "pleasure, romance, and sexual flirtation" in the upper classes where there was money, not the working classes, where you had to get married to advance socially or even get by and where reputation was vital (286).

Such messages were evident in romantic fiction. Pamela Fox, analyzing working-class fiction of the early twentieth century, notes its message that working-class women of the time did not have access to the codes of romance available to middle-class women—marriage was economic for them and any working-class women trying to be romantic would be chastised (141). Fowler notes that the sexualized "other" woman in working-class fiction is usually wealthy or from a wealthy family (63). Furthermore, Fowler claims that the femme fatale represents "stereotypes of the evil capitalist" so defeating her offers a "democratic" illusion "in which the negative elements of class conflict can be sealed off" (64). Working-class romance fiction thus contests the "subjectivities offered by middle-class observers which interpellated working-class women as over-burdened victims, sexual predators or peculiarly susceptible to the seductions of romance" (Giles 289). Indeed, Giles is prudent to caution against "applying a single understanding of women's relation to romance to all women regardless of social, cultural, and historical difference" (289).

A further charge has been laid against popular romance—that it is escapist. Such an accusation will not strike scholars of the romance as particularly surprising. However, escapism takes on a slightly different meaning when connected with class. The aims of popular romance novelists are, according to Fowler's reading of Leavis, to produce "anti-intellectualist panaceas" (Fowler 37). This is particularly pronounced for working-class romance and its readers. Indeed, Fowler locates a heightened desire for happy endings among lower-class readers, suggesting that "class shapes the pattern of needs to be satisfied in the personal leisure/pleasure economy so that the search for magical escapes via fantasy is more often found in the most exploited or oppressed groups" (139). In her interviews with readers, Fowler found that those who preferred romance did so because of its "reassuring pleasure in a familiar and benign world offered by the genre" (167).[6]

Escapism can be seen as detrimental to the working-class reader. Fowler argues that the "escapist literature of mass culture" is "favourable to market society" (66). This is problematic, Fowler argues, drawing on Gramsci and ideas about pleasure in popular reading, because it "extend(s) to mass culture the Marxist analysis of religion as an opiate" (31); it is "optimistic wish fulfilment at the cost of illusion" (Fowler 34). Gramsci suggests that where the lower classes are trapped by capitalism and denied control over their own lives, popular literature offers "compensatory satisfactions" (Fowler 31–2). In other words, romance novels function as "ideological elastoplasts" or band-aids to solve the problems raised by market society, such as the discontent of work (Fowler 67). This idea is echoed by Radway when she claims that reading romances provides women with "an important emotional release" from their role as primary familial nurturer, identifying "romantic escape" as "a temporary but literal denial of the demands women recognise as an integral part of their roles as nurturing wives and mothers" (95, 97). Osborne points out that romances like Mills & Boon "still engineer analogous fantasy solutions in which societal demands and individual happiness can coincide" meaning "societal contradictions are thus transcended" (14–15). So, romance is escapist for working-class readers because it elides the reality of class discrimination.

However, Robinson has refuted the argument that romance is escapist for working-class women (and that this is damaging). She argues that romance novels show how women are excluded from public life, thus reflecting rather than distracting from their reality. She argues that readers seek these novels out not to escape, but "to receive confirmation, and, eventually, affirmation, that love really is what motivates and justifies a woman's life" (Robinson 222). Sanders suggests a more complex mode of escapism for turn of the century working-class shopgirl romance readers, characterised by both absorption and distraction and signalling "alternative identificatory structures" (Sanders 168). Cohn also disagrees with the claim that escapism is harmful for working-class women by positing that romance goes *further* than other popular fiction:

> Like all popular formula fiction, romance exists to answer in fantasy needs that cannot be met in real life. But romance goes further; it answers desires that cannot be spoken, so powerfully would they subvert authority. Desire and authority are profoundly at issue in popular romance. Desire, however, must be heavily masked since, at the deepest level, what is desired is authority itself, the power and autonomy the social system denies women.
>
> (5)

For Cohn, romance novels constitute a fantasy fulfillment of power for women that they could not otherwise have; "romance fiction insists so heavily on the powerlessness of its heroine precisely because it exists to redress, in fantasy, the powerlessness of women in bourgeois society" (176). Cohn thus assumes not that working-class women are cultural dupes unable to recognize the nature of romance's fantasy, but that the fantasy romance offers—a satisfying, imaginary fulfillment of a perceived lack of power—serves to emphasize and draw attention to the gender inequalities experienced by women readers.

Reading class and wealth in romance today

Part of the draw of popular romance, at least according to publishers like Harlequin Mills & Boon, is that it appeals to everyone: it is "universal." In some ways, it is true that reading popular romance cuts across all classes (although, as Robinson notes, class will determine where you buy your books) (203). Yet, Fowler's interviews with readers demonstrate that taste is important to the reading choices women make and to the pleasures they gain from it. The emergence of romances targeted specifically at working-class women is indicative of a fracturing of romantic experience between different classes of women. Equally, Kamblé's reading of popular romance as an allegory for societal anxiety about capitalism reveals how class can be implicated at a deeper level in these texts. Clearly, class is important to popular romance and it is thus equally important to engage critically with the ways romance represents and expresses class, as the scholarship outlined in this chapter has done.

So, where next for scholars of class and wealth in romance? In the wake of the publication of E. L. James' *Fifty Shades* trilogy (2011–15) attention was paid to the novels' veneration of capitalism and consumerism (e.g., see Dymock et al. *Hard-Core Romance*) and to Christian Grey's role as a "billionaire hero" in particular. In the context of a post-industrial crisis of white masculinity, Claire Trevenen argues that "Christian is an emblematic model of the wounded white male reaping the symbolic power of being the 'subject-in-crisis,'" thereby permitting "this perception of crisis [to be] be rearticulated in such a way that it sets up the white male character as the victim, rather than the victimiser, in crisis situations" (13). Certainly, there is scope for further work on the intersection between masculinity and class, particularly in light of the development of Men's Studies as a field. A distinctive trend in romance, emergent in the U.S. in particular, is the "blue-collar" hero. Often described as a cop, mechanic, construction worker, or similar, the popularity of this hero is evident from several blog posts collating examples of blue-collar heroes, a podcast discussion on the popular reader site "Smart Bitches, Trashy Books" that attempts to define blue-collar romance heroes, and collated lists of blue-collar hero novels on sites such as Goodreads.com. But, despite this popular interest from romance readers, there has not been a similar interest among romance scholars on the demand for working-class and middle-class heroes.

Furthermore, as I've already mentioned, scholarship has been slow to engage in truly intersectional approaches to romance. While all the scholarship I have introduced deals with questions of class in the context of gender, race and ethnicity are largely absent from these discussions (Kamblé's brief treatment of class and whiteness, following Richard Dyer's equating of whiteness and capitalism, is a good starting point for further analysis (133–48)). If, as has been claimed, this lack of focus is due to a paucity of non-white protagonists in mainstream popular romance, then a critical focus on more specialist series (such as the soon-to-be canceled Kimani line) might be appropriate (as has indeed been done with non-heterosexual romance). Alternatively, if romance scholarship lacks the appropriate critical tools for engaging in intersectional research, it can start to build on and extend research on race and ethnicity in romance that does not already consider class.

In the conclusion to their chapter on class in romance, Batsleer et al. claim that romance novels will change only when society changes (105). To some extent, this chapter has shown that this is true; for instance, as society has become more accepting of women workers, romance novels have diversified their own representations of working heroines. However, I want to end this chapter by referring to Fowler's assertion that reading can have an effect on people's ideas. While Fowler, writing in the 1980s, does not see romance as "a weapon for human emancipation" (158), it might be possible for critical scholarship of the romance to further develop our understanding of the way class and wealth work in popular romance, making scholarship just the "weapon" that we need.

Notes

1 Phyllis M. Betz has explored class in lesbian romance novels. She notes that very few lesbian characters are working-class but where they are, novels make use of class conflict to provide a barrier to the relationship and to have the wealthy character provide comfort and luxury to allow the romance to happen, similar to the way it functions in heterosexual romance (see esp. 14, 86–96).

2 In a study of romance novel titles, Cox and Fisher (2009) found that words associated with wealth and resources (millionaire, billionaire, tycoon, fortune, wealth, money, diamond, dollar, inheritance, heir, gift, treasure, rich, and gold) appeared a total of 796 times in 15,019 Harlequin romance titles published from 1949–2009, suggesting that wealthy heroes continue to be present (although the authors do not indicate change over time nor do they analyze this data in any detail).

3 For examples of class as represented in the romance comic, popular in 1940s and 1950s America see Barson 153–203.

4 Ann Herendeen's article on her bisexual Regency romances offers an interesting corollary to these romances, with "the combination of high economic, social, and sexual status as desirable ingredients in the romantic hero" (n.p.) persistent in these non-heteronormative novels.

5 Weisser pays some attention to class in her examination of African American romance readers, where she notes that Black romances are as homogenous as Anglo romances in their representation of class.

6 An interesting perspective is offered by Jean Radford in her analysis of Susan Howatch's *Penmarric* (1971). Radford argues that the historical text presents class relations in a visceral, brutal fashion, but is cushioned by its historical distance: "at no point . . . is the reader invited to make connections between then and now; it is precisely because of such historical distancing that the text can summon up such an *exposé* while still securely endorsing the contemporary status quo" (180).

Works cited

Amireh, Amal. *The Factory Girl and the Seamstress: Imagining Gender and Class in Nineteenth Century American Fiction*. Garland, 2000.

Barson, Michael. *Agonizing Love: The Golden Era of Romance Comics*. HarperCollins, 2011.

Batsleer, Janet, Tony Davies, Rebecca O'Rourke and Chris Weedon. *Rewriting English: Cultural Politics of Gender and Class*. Methuen, 1985.

Baum, Thomas. "Working the Skies: Changing Representations of Gendered Work in the Airline Industry, 1930–2011." *Tourism Management*, vol. 33, no. 5, 2012, pp. 1185–1194.

Baym, Nina. *Woman's Fiction: A Guide to Novels by and about Women in America, 1820–1870*. Cornell University Press, 1978.

Betz, Phyllis M. *Lesbian Romance Novels*. McFarland, 2009.

Bourdieu, Pierre. *Distinction: A Social Critique of the Judgement of Taste*. 1979. Translated by Richard Nice, Harvard University Press, 1987.

Cohn, Jan. *Romance and the Erotics of Property*. Duke University Press, 1988.

Cox, Anthony and Maryanne Fisher. "The Texas Billionaire's Pregnant Bride: An Evolutionary Interpretation of Romance Fiction Titles." *Journal of Social, Evolutionary, and Cultural Psychology*, vol. 3, no. 4, 2009, pp. 386–401.

De Groot, Jerome. *The Historical Novel*. Routledge, 2010.

Denning, Michael. *Mechanic Accents: Dime Novels and working-class culture in America*. Verso, 1987.

Dixon, jay. *The Romantic Fiction of Mills & Boon, 1909–1990s*. University College London Press, 1999.

Dymock, Alex. "Flogging Sexual Transgression: Interrogating the Costs of the '*Fifty Shades* Effect.'" *Sexualities*, vol. 16, no. 8, 2013, pp. 880–895.

Enstad, Nan. *Ladies of Labor, Girls of Adventure: Working Women, Popular Culture, and Labor Politics at the Turn of the Twentieth Century*. Columbia University Press, 1999.

Fowler, Bridget. *The Alienated Reader: Women and Popular Romantic Literature in the Twentieth Century*. Prentice-Hall, 1991.

Fox, Pamela. "The "Revolt of the Gentle": Romance and the Politics of Resistance in Working-Class Women's Writing." *NOVEL: A Forum on Fiction*, vol. 27, no. 2, 1994, pp. 140–160.

Giles, Judy. "'You Meet 'Em and That's It': Working Class Women's Refusal of Romance between the Wars in Britain." *Romance Revisited*, edited by Lynne Pearce, and Jackie Stacey, New York University Press, 1995, pp. 279–292.

Haytock, Jennifer. *The Middle Class in the Great Depression: Popular Women's Novels of the 1930s*. New York: Palgrave Macmillan, 2013.

Herendeen, Ann. "The Upper-Class Bisexual Top as Romantic Hero: (Pre)dominant in the Social Structure and in the Bedroom." *Journal of Popular Romance Studies*, vol. 3, no. 1, 2012, n.p.

Hinnant, Charles H. "Desire and the Marketplace: A Reading of Kathleen Woodiwiss's *the Flame and the Flower*." *Doubled Plots: Romance and History*, edited by Susan Strehle, and Mary Paniccia Carden, University Press of Mississippi, 2003, pp. 147–164.

Illouz, Eva. *Consuming the Romantic Utopia: Love and the Cultural Contradictions of Capitalism*. University of California Press, 1997.

———. *Why Love Hurts: A Sociological Explanation*. Polity Press, 2012.

———. *Hard-Core Romance: Fifty Shades of Grey, Best-Sellers, and Society*. University of Chicago Press, 2014.

Johnson, Paul and Steph Lawler. "Coming Home to Love and Class." *Sociological Research Online*, vol. 10, no. 3, 2005. http://www.socresonline.org.uk/10/3/johnson.html

Kamblé, Jayashree. *Making Meaning in Popular Romance Fiction: An Epistemology*. Palgrave Macmillan, 2014.

Liffen, Jane. "'A Very Glamorized Picture, That": Images of Scottish Female Herring Workers on Romance Novel Covers." *Social Semiotics*, vol. 18, no. 3, 2008, pp. 349–361.

Light, Alison. "'Returning to Manderley'—Romance Fiction, Female Sexuality and Class." *Feminist Review*, vol. 16, 1984, pp. 7–25.

McAleer, Joseph. "Love, Romance, and the National Health Service." *Classes, Cultures, and Politics: Essays on British History for Ross McKibbin*, edited by Clare V. J. Griffiths, James J. Nott, and William Whyte, Oxford University Press, 2011, pp. 173–191.

Melman, Billie. *Women and the Popular Imagination in the Twenties: Flappers and Nymphs*. Macmillan, 1988.

Modleski, Tania. *Loving with a Vengeance: Mass-produced Fantasies for Women*. Routledge, 1982.

Osborne, Laurie. "Sweet, Savage Shakespeare." *Shakespeare without Class: Misappropriations of Cultural Capital*, edited by Donald K. Hedrick, and Bryan Reynolds, Palgrave Macmillan, 2000, pp. 135–151.

Radford, Jean. *The Progress of Romance: The Politics of Popular Fiction*. Routledge, 1986.

Radway, Janice. *Reading the Romance: Women, Patriarchy, and Popular Literature*. University of North Carolina Press, 1984.

Regis, Pamela. *A Natural History of the Romance Novel*. University of Pennsylvania Press, 2003.

Robinson, Lillian S. *'Reading Trash.' Sex, Class, and Culture*, edited by Lillian S. Robinson, Indiana University Press, 1978, pp. 200–222.

Sanders, Lise Shapiro. *Consuming Fantasies: Labor, Leisure, and the London Shopgirl, 1880–1920*. Ohio University Press, 2006.

Trevenen, Claire. "*Fifty Shades* of "Mommy Porn": A Post-Global Financial Crisis Renegotiation of Paternal Law." *Journal of Popular Romance Studies*, vol. 4, no. 1, 2014, pp. 1–20.

Weisser, Susan Ostrov. *The Glass Slipper: Women and Love Stories*. Rutgers University Press, 2013.

Young, Erin S. "Escaping the 'Time Bind': Negotiations of Love and Work in Jayne Ann Krentz's 'Corporate Romances.'" *Journal of American Culture*, vol. 33, no. 2, 2010, pp. 92–106.

———. "Saving China: The Transformative Power of Whiteness in Elizabeth Lowell's Jade Island and Katherine Stone's Pearl Moon." *Romance Fiction and American Culture: Love as the Practice of Freedom*, edited by William A. Gleason, and Eric Murphy Selinger, Ashgate, 2016, pp. 205–221.

19 Sex and sexuality

Hannah McCann and Catherine M. Roach

If sex belongs anywhere, it's in a romance novel.
—Anne Gracie

A feminism of desire would fit me, I think, like a corset. Instead of wondering why I'm corseted in the first place, and whether others have to wear a corset or what the corset means, or how I might remove it, I could instead focus on the intensity of the sensation afforded by the constraint, becoming increasingly aware of the boundaries of my own body.
—Jennifer Lutzenberger

Introduction

Popular romance fiction is about sex, even when it isn't. Sexual pleasure—and, most often, *women's* sexual pleasure—is a fundamental and telling concern of the genre.

While not all romance novels involve sex *explicitly*, sexuality plays a key role in romance, even if merely to function *implicitly* as an event on the future horizon. As the historical romance author Anne Gracie argues, sex need not be the prime purpose of romance relationship or storytelling but it is always part of the resolution of romance fiction, insofar as "part of the Happy Ever After promise is the promise of fabulous sex" (in Fletcher 15). Sexual satisfaction is inherent to the appeal of the genre for its mainly female readership. Even in m/m romance stories, where the lovers are men, these women fans get to enjoy stories of sexual desire and fulfillment. As Candice Proctor describes, in the early 2000s, when some romance writers attempted to gain greater mainstream credibility by removing sex scenes from their works, there was an angry backlash from fans (17). Whether represented explicitly, metaphorically, or through mere discreet allusion, sex is an integral feature of the romance genre.

This emphasis on sexuality and sexual pleasure in a genre read so disproportionately by women is not accidental—not prurient, voyeuristic, or "merely" pornographic: the stakes are too high for that to be the case. Sex is a deeply troubled topic for women, more so than for men, and the romance genre is one site in the culture where women work through the troubles of sex and desire. Carole S. Vance laid out this axis of "pleasure and danger" in her foundational 1984 anthology analyzing the complex status of sexuality for women. In sex, women are the more vulnerable. Women are more subject to rape, sexual abuse, and domestic violence. They suffer unwanted conceptions, the burdens—sometimes life-threatening—of pregnancy and childbirth, and a disproportionate share of childcare, all while earning lower wages and buffeted by enduring cultural sexism and misogyny. Even in consensual heterosexual sex, women are more vulnerable to inequalities in the relationship and their sexual pleasure is less assured. Romance novels dramatize this nexus of pleasure and danger, so central to female experience. Within the storytelling, the knot is untied: danger overcome and pleasure maximized. The romance genre exists as an attempt, in fiction, to solve—to resolve, to dissolve—the problems of sex.

Despite this centrality of sexuality to the romance narrative, sex is not always similarly central to discussions of the genre. No understanding of romance fiction is complete, however, that does not grapple with this status of sexuality within the genre: complicated and contested, central yet sometimes silent. When sexuality in the romance *is* addressed, the books' erotic content can lead to shaming accusations that the genre functions as pornography. In cultural contexts that equate proper femininity of "the good woman" with norms of ladylike passivity and male leadership in the bedroom or that differentiate the role of women as to *look sexy* and be sexually pleasing from the role of men as to *be sexual* and to receive sexual pleasure, the notion of women actively writing, buying, and reading their own overtly sexual and female-centered texts is especially transgressive. One way to control and shut down such transgressions is to call the writing "pornographic": a label of shame.

As has been widely discussed, although romance books are very popular in terms of sales and readership, they are not always celebrated, in part because of their gendered content and largely female authorship and readership (Armstrong, Byrski, and Merrick 258; Regis xi). However, we also read the "shame" attached to romance novels as related to the link of the genre to sex and sexuality. As Pamela Regis suggests, critics of romance novels often focus on the inclusion of sex scenes in the genre (6). However, Regis herself dismisses the centrality of sex, stating that such scenes are "widespread but not essential in a romance novel" (6). Here we see that even those who wish to defend romance novels must grapple with the question of sexuality that haunts the genre. When romance novels are dismissed, it often has to do with a deep-seated fear of women's desires and sexuality. The insight is long-standing within popular romance criticism; Janice Radway, for example, notes that "the struggle over the romance is itself part of the larger struggle for the right to define and to control female sexuality" (17). These are books about women wanting and getting great sex from partners who know how to deliver: an anxiety-provoking message for a culture more comfortable with male arousal and satisfaction than the pleasure of its female counterparts.

Some academics and other writers on the romance genre have successfully made the case that, since so many women enjoy mass-produced romance, scholarship should address these texts and not simply oppose them (Modleski). From this perspective, an angle of analysis opens on the possibilities of the romance genre as a means for exploring and navigating female desire. Examinations of sexually explicit material produced for women point out that these stories are not primarily about sexual release but rather about fantasy; as Clarissa Smith suggests, "When a story gets it right, readers are able to imagine sexual and emotional possibilities for themselves" (220). This latter view suggests that sex in romance allows for important inquiry into what "pornographic" means and how to reevaluate its stigma and that romance fiction offers a powerful and creative space to work through what are, for women, literally life-and-death questions of desire and sexuality.

Taking up this latter theory, this chapter presents an overview of representations of sex in romance. We outline a reparative view of the romance genre, following Eve Kosofsky Sedgwick, that reads romance as providing a means to explore the tensions of contemporary sexuality, particularly heterosexuality. Though romance fiction can be seen to reify hegemonic and gendered cultural scripts of what counts as appropriate sexuality, from a different angle the romance novel creates a collective fantasy space where women readers and writers explore the conundrum of female heterosexual desire in a man's world. We survey these approaches, not to set up an empowering/disempowering divide that ultimately disappoints as an unproductive interpretive strategy, but to offer a reading of the complexity of sex in the popular romance genre.

Sex in romance: pornographic, normative, anti-feminist?

Within both academia and the mainstream media there exists a moralism that associates sex in romance storytelling with the unseemly, if not the downright pornographic. Some feminist theorists in the 1970s analyzed the genre to argue that romance is akin to pornography for women; citing critic Peter Parisi, Ann Snitow agrees that romance novels are about "release ... specifically sexual release" (qtd. in Snitow 151). Offering an analysis of Harlequin romance novels, Snitow suggests that "sexual feeling is probably the main point," where sexual desire can only be fulfilled once heterosexual matrimony is secured (151). Snitow attempts to generously understand what these books offer to women in terms of fantasy, where sex and "deep feeling" somewhat impossibly meet. However, for Snitow, the emotional intimacy desired by women in these sexual fantasies renders them ultimately passive, as female characters cannot access the "spontaneity and aggression" sexually available to men (160). Sex in romance is marked from this perspective as inherently problematic because the sexist gender-divided world that informs these representations is, as Snitow suggests, "a cold, cold place" (160).

At other times, sex in romance is seen as simply laughable. Along these lines, recent mainstream discussions of romance books such as E.L. James's *Fifty Shades of Grey* often use the derisive term "mommy porn" to describe the series and to explain why women enjoy them (Trevenen 2). Indeed, it is sometimes assumed that the stories in romance only exist as filler around the sex scenes to help legitimize or obscure the crude details within. In the case of *Fifty Shades*, there has also been a focus on the sexual *markets* that have emerged around the series (Comella), rather than the content and broadly romantic appeal of the novels themselves. However, as Eva Illouz suggests on the topic of the *Fifty Shades* series, sex can function as a way to draw the reader into the larger romance narrative, rather than vice versa:

> *Fifty Shades of Grey* cannot be characterized as being simply and only mommy porn—unless one naively assumes that the romance is the "pretext" to wrap the sex in the pink paper of sentiments. In fact, the opposite is the case: it is the sex that is the pink paper in which the love story is wrapped.
>
> (35)

To understand the status of the sexual within the romance genre, it is important to clarify that while women's sexual pleasure is key to the overall romance narrative, sexual activity can be deeply off-page in individual novels. Some romance stories contain no sex scenes at all, some only imply sexual content, and others are overtly erotic. Erotic romance is considered a subgenre of romance fiction, and some publishing houses or imprints specialize in specifically sexy or high-heat romance stories (Thomas "Romance" 21). Leading category romance publisher Harlequin, for example, distinguishes between its books that have more frequent and explicit sexual content categorized as part of the "Blaze" line, those that focus on emotions in the "Presents" line, and those that use euphemisms in the "Desire" line (Harlequin "What Category Are You"). While reader studies show that category romance has lower status within the reader community than longer, single-title romances (Thomas "Romance" 24), these distinctions are helpful for understanding how levels of sexual content vary across the genre of romance as a whole. This "sweet to spicy" continuum of explicit content is occasionally signaled by a "heat meter" that publishers employ in website marketing or book jacket copy as a rough measure of a novel's sexual content and as a way to guide readers to the level of sensuality they seek. Scholars note how the sexual content of romance fiction has increased in recent years and the subgenre of erotic romance or mommy porn has become more mainstream (Phillips). The market change relates to a larger phenomenon that Cultural and Media Studies scholars describe as a "sexualization" of Western culture wherein sex itself becomes more mainstream (Attwood) or a "pornification" of the culture (Paasonen, Nikunen, and Saarenmaa; McNair). Although the initial sexualization of romance fiction predates *Fifty Shades* by several decades (Thurston), the *Fifty Shades* publishing phenomenon, along with the privacy and anonymity afforded by the meteoric rise of e-readers and digital books, has hastened this mainstreaming of sexy romance, quasi-respectable precisely because of its omnipresence.

Even in those romance stories with no explicit sexual content, the story arc itself encodes a kind of erotic tension and release. It does so in a key narrative moment, immediately recognizable to aficionados of the genre: the hero's climactic declaration of love typical to the happily-ever-after (HEA) ending. As Catherine M. Roach suggests, this HEA can be understood as a "money shot" akin to the image of male ejaculation as the climax in visual pornography (10–13). It is this ending that the romance narrative leads up to, where conflict is resolved, wishes are fulfilled, and the fantasy of the romance finds full closure. Where there is no sex but there is HEA, sexual pleasure still permeates and pinkens this release moment with—as Gracie contends—the implicit promise of future pleasure. Given that romance has a predominantly female readership it is no surprise that an intertwining of women's emotional and sexual satisfaction is central to its appeal. In this way, romance fiction—with or without explicit sexual content—reads as woman-centered and erotically charged storytelling with the narrative resolution as the peak moment of satisfaction and release of tension.

As Dana Ménard and Christine Cabrera demonstrate in their content analysis of award-winning romance titles from 1990 to 2009, where there *is* sexually explicit content, sex scenes largely adhere to normative Western sexual scripts (250). The majority of characters having sex in romance fit not only normative standards of attractiveness but they also frequently engage in "kissing, touching and penile–vaginal intercourse," with men typically represented as the initiators of sex (Ménard and Cabrera 243). On this level, the sex acts of romance can be understood as, for the most part, socially normative. As Illouz suggests, sexuality is not only about sex acts; it is the vehicle through which social norms take shape. She suggests that sex acts are social insofar as they occur in relation to the social mores of their time (37). When these boundaries and conventions are challenged in romance, the storylines operate as risqué relative to the social codes and breaking these standards becomes part of the stories' allure.

For the most part, however, the focus in popular romance studies has been on that which is shored up by these novels, rather than what boundaries are transgressed. For example, Claire Trevenen argues that texts like *Fifty Shades* use bondage and sadomasochism in ways that reify traditional gender roles and reflect a broader contemporary anxiety to keep the traditional gender binary securely in place (16). In other words, even where non-normative practices appear in the stories, many critics focus on the problematic norms reinforced through romance texts. In another example, speaking more broadly, Bridget Fowler comments that "the romance offers—like the good family photograph—an image of integration of the social group, with the harmonious couple at its center. In doing so, of course, its ideological elements continue to legitimate the existing order" (97). Along these lines, Talbot notes the "eroticized difference" represented in romance novels, that is, there is often a strong distinction made between a very feminine female heroine and the very masculine male hero (109). These scholars of romance are concerned with the dominant ideology that is reinforced through romance, particularly in relation to sex and sexuality.

The point made by many feminist commentators that romance novels participate in larger structural problems of sexism—that "they express primal structures in our social relations" (Snitow 143)—warrants attention. Some scholars have argued that the genre of chick lit, arising in the 1990s, functioned as an alternative form of romance fiction that portrayed heroines as more sexually assertive and as distinctly "post-feminist" (Gill and Herdieckerhoff 498). Post-feminism here can be defined as a milieu within which the wins of feminism have been embraced but the politics of feminism have been rejected (Tasker and Negra 171). Or, as Angela McRobbie describes it, post-feminism involves "anti-feminist sentiment" where words such as "empowerment" and "choice" are deployed to ensure the women's movement will not re-emerge and that it is seen as unnecessary (McRobbie 1).

The feminist critique of post-feminism focuses on contemporary female sexuality as a site for intense concern (see, e.g., Levy; Power; McRobbie; Walter). In relation to romance, this accusation of problematic contemporary sexuality as post-feminist found an epicenter around the *Fifty Shades of Grey* series, with feminist protests occurring at screenings of the first film around the world in 2015. Illouz suggests that *Fifty Shades* "obviously" isn't feminist because it does not challenge heteronormativity, yet it draws on a cultural code of feminism (56). These kinds of texts, particularly focused on women's sexual exploits, are understood as post-feminist because they adopt the rhetoric of liberation but still portray women who are sexually submissive to men. Often these women are independent and strong-willed but also virgins, or at least relatively inexperienced and under-satisfied; women who learn the ways of sex and pleasure from their male counterparts is an old trope of the romance genre (McAlister "You and I" 13) that persists even in this new "liberated" context.

Despite claims about the normative and potentially anti-feminist aspects of the romance genre, the actual ways that romance fiction influences readers and whether and how such reading reinforces dominant ideas continue to be debated. This is particularly the case in regards to scenes of sexual dominance or violence within romance. One recent study revealed that in showing readers stories that rendered either male or female sexual dominance, both forms of dominance were viewed as equally sexy but the representations of male dominance increased readers' sexist views (Harris, Thai, and Barlow). However, in this study by Emily Ann Harris, Michael Thai, and Fiona Kate Barlow, the effects of reading "erotic stories" were extrapolated out as significant to understanding the *Fifty Shades* phenomena, conflating the erotic and romantic, and the sexual part for the romantic whole. Other studies have sought to demonstrate that the low use of sexual health protection in romance novels has a negative impact on romance readers and that promoting safe sex behavior within the story-world can have a positive effect (Diekman, McDonald, and Gardner).

As Janice Radway famously argues, there is much at stake in determining how romance affects readers (17). Indeed, Radway argues that though a plethora of reader responses might exist, there is a great deal of similarity across readers because of commonly taught strategies of reading (Radway 8). Others have suggested that more research on the effects of romance fiction on readers needs to be undertaken in order to ascertain a clearer picture of the genre's influence. Even in "positive" reader studies that claim, for example, that romance readers enjoy better sex, the notion persists that readers are uncritical "dupes" who merely absorb the content they are given (Thomas "Happy Readers" 210). Yet as reader studies on *Fifty Shades* have shown, many readers read critically and in contradictory ways (Deller and Smith) or engage with the series as an "ironic" and "guilty" pursuit (Harman and Jones). Even in their research about the normative sexual scripts reproduced in romance, Ménard and Cabrera suggest that more "research on the impact of romance novel content on readers would help to clarify whether these books constitute sex education, sex entertainment or both" (253).

Sex in romance: a space for fantasy and exorcism?

So far this chapter has considered primarily negative assessments of romance novels as focused on the question of sex. Though we might agree that on one level romance novels and the sexual activity therein reflect and can reinforce traditional gender identities and sexual roles, another body of scholarship explores the question of romance fiction as a site of positive autonomy and views its treatment of sexuality as offering new possibilities of empowerment and liberation. Central scholarly texts interrogate this question in terms of a "practice of freedom" (Gleason and Selinger) or in terms of women's "empowerment versus oppression" whereby "women romance readers are simultaneously bound to a patriarchal system and emboldened by their own choice and creativity within that system" (Goade 10).[1] Similarly, Linda J. Lee notes the parallels between romance novels and fairytales and argues that the genre lends itself to a re-reading as "fantasies of female empowerment" (62).

Key to understanding romance is this *fantasy* aspect of the stories, which culminates in that all-important HEA climax. It is this element of fantasy that lends itself to understanding romance as a safe space of creative respite. Readers are able to project themselves into the characters' desires, to inhabit the fantasy space of the story and experience the events (sexual or otherwise) narrated therein. That romance functions as a fantasy space for women has been well documented. Glen Thomas' study of romance readers showed that "romance novels are perceived [by readers] to be pure escapism" (Thomas "Romance" 23). Illouz comments on *Fifty Shades of Grey* that, "without a doubt, the book enacts contemporary women's fantasies" (32). Further, as Kathryn Cheshire, an editor at Harlequin, explains, even if you are writing high fantasy works you need to "make sure that there is something there that readers can identify with so that they can imagine themselves in the place of your heroine" (Harlequin "Cheshire").

That romance functions as a fantasy space does not, however, easily recover the genre from accusations that its representation of sex and relationships is problematic. Ann Snitow argues that romances play some function in maintaining the dominant order, in conveying the possibility of a fantasy where there is no reality, or what Lauren Berlant now calls "cruel optimism" (Berlant *Cruel Optimism*). As Berlant further contends, cultural imaginings of desire and love involve "a utopian promise" (*Desire/Love* 112), and this promise can be cruel or even toxic when the wish fulfillment—that HEA climax—is never possible or at least not entirely so. However, as Jeff Sparrow argues in his investigation of pornography and the sexualization of culture, "If we could all just snap our fingers and choose what turned us on and what didn't, sex would be a far less complicated affair" (307). In application to romance, we can take Sparrow's point to mean that representations of "problematic" sex in romance show how the question of desire and pleasure in sexuality is much more complicated than any simple good/bad dichotomy. Or, as Jennifer Lutzenberger writes, "To take up desire as a feminist project is to take up *desiring feminists*, with all our complex urges and contradictory behaviors" (110, her emphasis).

To avoid an impasse of interpretation, a further point is needed here: that the broad genre of romance can be understood to offer a particular *type* of fantasy space, a space of imagination in which to negotiate the conundrum of living in patriarchal rape culture as a heterosexual woman. Here, we read romance as a way to explore the tensions and fraught desires of contemporary sexuality, as Gillian Beer suggests:

> Romance, being absorbed with the ideal, always has an element of prophecy. It remakes the world in the image of desire. At present, however such prophetic literature tends to resolve into images of dread. The function of romance in our own time may well prove to have been not wish-fulfilment but exorcism.
>
> (79)

Though Beer is speaking of "romance" broadly, this mention of "exorcism" evokes the power of the genre as a pathway to confront sexual demons. As Tania Modleski notes,

> An understanding of Harlequin Romances should lead one less to condemn the novels than the conditions which have made them necessary. Even though the novels can be said to intensify female tensions and conflicts, on balance the contradictions in women's lives are more responsible for the existence of Harlequins than Harlequins are for the contradictions.
>
> (49)

Here, Modleski acknowledges that romance novels reflect broader conditions of sexism.

Snitow makes a similar argument: "these Pollyanna books have their own dream-like truth"—again highlighting the element of fantasy—"our culture produces a pathological experience of sex difference" (144). Illouz pushes the point even further by suggesting that books like *Fifty Shades* are able "not only to encode the conundrums of heterosexuality but also to provide the tools to actually make it better" (72). As we will show below, romance fiction becomes diagnosis and treatment, if not cure, for the risky business engaged in by a woman who goes looking for love.

Reading the romance reparatively

In order to understand how romance fiction can function at once to replicate dominant ideology *and* to offer something more transgressive and transformative, we turn, as promised, to Sedgwick and her notion of the value of "reparative" versus "paranoid" ways of knowing. Sedgwick's theory, when applied to romance texts—and particularly to narratives of *sex* in romance—allows the genre itself to be read, or re-read, as a sex-positive space. Drawing on a psychoanalytic tradition through Freud, Paul Ricoeur, and the British object relations theorist Melanie Klein, Sedgwick argues that literary criticism and other critical cultural analyses can overemphasize *paranoid* readings of texts—readings that highlight the pain and negative effects of oppression in order to raise consciousness and rally against suffering; by contrast, Sedgwick proposes highlighting *reparative* reading strategies that offer resources of hope amid crisis ("Paranoid and Reparative" 20, 22).[2]

From this perspective, the representation of sex in romance is not recovered because it *is* definitely empowering, but because it can be viewed from another angle altogether that evades the need to settle on one side or the other of this empowerment/disempowerment binary. Sedgwick applies this reading strategy to the products of popular culture as a way to find queer sexuality in spaces where it would otherwise not exist. As she suggests, "for many of us in childhood the ability to attach intently to a few cultural objects ... became a prime source for survival" (*Tendencies* 3). The point of reparative reading is to find sustenance within a broadly problematic and oppressive world in order to survive, and indeed, to thrive ("Paranoid and Reparative" 31).

We apply Sedgwick's suggestion to the genre of romance fiction to understand how these novels offer room for both writers and readers to move through these broader issues of sexism and sexuality. To view romance fiction as a communal, woman-oriented realm of "reparative impulses, practices, and fantasies" does "better justice to the genre and to its creators and consumers" (Roach 178). The reparative perspective permits a less dismissive take on the popularity of romance fiction and the women who read it in such happy numbers, a more sympathetic take on the stratospheric sales of erotic romance. Applying this reparative and recuperative strategy to the interpretation of romance fiction uncovers an important aspect of how the genre functions for its legions of devoted readers: as a sex-positive and unruly exploration of the conundrum of female desire, heterosexual or otherwise, in a patriarchal world, rather than simply a consumer media product that reifies the dominant sexual hegemony (Roach 176–88; see also Allan *Reading from Behind* 9–18).

The sex-positive, feminist claim for representations of sex in romance is rooted in the fact that the genre is one of the few spaces in the culture that embraces the idea of women's authentic sexual pleasure and that delights in the depiction of female orgasm. In romance novels, "women can enjoy sex" (Wendell and Tan 158). Even in sweet novels devoid of all steamy love scenes and in the genre's nineteenth- and earlier twentieth-century precursors that by the conventions of their day did not feature on-page sex, readers can trust that the heroine enjoys the marriage bed. In a heterosexual romance novel, the hero is never indifferent; women authors depict their male characters as deriving excitement and pleasure from attending to and exploring their female lover's sexual needs. Whether the intimacy is cozy or spicy, the genre teaches that sexuality is not dirty or sordid and should never be forced or demeaning, but is natural, healthy, and empowering. As bestselling romance novelist and pop culture essayist Jennifer Crusie writes, romance fiction tells women "it's not wrong to want a full sexual life and show[s] them how to get one" (Crusie 38). Romance fiction affirms women's desire, unapologetically, and the genre helps the culture get past the slut-shaming notion that women aren't supposed to be sexual or make the first move.

This embrace of women's sexual pleasure remains one of the most challenging and potentially transformative aspects of romance fiction for the culture. As Mary M. Talbot points out, "Romance is a traditional source of erotic material for heterosexual women" as it fills the gap in broader society where women's sexuality and desire is so rarely affirmed or celebrated outside of a male gaze and the context of male sexual satisfaction (118). The necessity of filling such a gap gestures to a broader social issue of sexual inequality, including the gendered "orgasm gap" whereby men experience more orgasms through sex than do heterosexual women (Mintz, Orenstein, Wade). Representations of sex in romance fiction help negotiate this disparity for the women who engage with the genre. Romance novels help readers imagine ways to close this orgasm gap, partly by depicting relationships in which the gap doesn't exist. Indeed Illouz argues that *Fifty Shades* "is less pornographic than it is a self-help book" (73), in the sense that it literally offers the reader instructions for pleasurable sex.

Romance is sex-positive here in a different way than is, say, feminist porn. Romance may not be explicitly feminist, in the same way that feminist porn seeks to be, because the fiction genre offers a different kind of space not necessarily trying to align with feminist values. For example, Penley et al. argue that "feminist porn uses sexually explicit imagery to contest and complicate dominant representations of gender, sexuality, race, ethnicity, class, ability, age, body type, and other identity markers" (9) and that feminist pornography is about challenging dominant ideologies of sex (10). However, working from Sedgwick's point of view, romance need not be overtly feminist in trying to subvert or challenge dominant ideas in order for it to be of value. Rather, without making any overtly feminist moves, romance can be understood as a safe space for exploring sex in a sexist world. This view does not suggest doing away with the paranoid view—rather, the point is that the two approaches can and should coexist. Sex in romance novels is understood as problematic, and as problematizing, both at once.

This debate connects with representations in pornography and how we can acknowledge women's critical agency in creating pornographic images. As Celine Parreñas Shimizu argues, in pornography there is "space between bondage and freedom" (184), where women might at once reproduce fetishized stereotypical representations and also exercise freedom in choosing how and why to engage in this work. Both bondage and freedom are involved in romantic love as well (Roach, 119–32). In this difficult reparative work of finding resources for the self to aid in sustenance and survival, romance fiction does not have to offer up portrayals of perfectly egalitarian sex —whatever that ideal might be imagined to be. A better goal and way to understand the liberatory possibilities of the genre is to see romance fiction as offering a woman-centered imaginative space where normative constraints are worked through. As Kelly Faircloth writes,

> All the way back to those first so-called "bodice rippers," romance novels have been a quietly powerful stronghold of the notion that yes, women do deserve pleasure, and a series of thought experiments for individuals and communities attempting to determine what that pleasure looks like and how we can achieve it.

Here, Faircloth offers an understanding of the romance genre as an avenue for women to grapple with "sexual subjectivity" in a world that does not support women's sexual exploration or adventure. In a reparative reading—one less oriented around suspicion or accusation, and perhaps more loving—romance fiction is exactly this "thought experiment": an imperfect and messy space to experiment with all manner of imagined storylines, character types, power dynamics, and, yes, the fullest and most varied array of erotic couplings, all on our way to imagining ourselves into a queer, better, more just, more playful, and sexier future.

Writing the romance as reparative

This vantage point of the reparative perspective opens up room to acknowledge the overlap between those who read romance fiction and those who write it. We see that romance can be viewed not only as a space of survival for readers but also as a creative imaginative space where women quite literally express themselves in a powerful exercise of voice.

As Thomas notes about the cycle of the romance publishing industry, writers are always readers and readers are not infrequently writers; there exists "an almost symbiotic relationship" between the two groups in the romance community (Thomas "Romance" 28). Radway, too, observes how many women become romance writers after a period of time as readers, that "the cross-over rate from consumer to producer seems to be unusually high within this genre," and that women can gain real empowerment to express their voice through the genre (17). The key point is that the romance story can be particularly useful in developing a woman's sense of self and in allowing her to articulate her voice because the sheer act of crafting these stories—whether or not the writer ever publishes her work or achieves any particular success as an author—creates a means for her to explore contradictions and quandaries of female desire.

Writing is a very powerful act. For a woman writing can be, in and of itself, a feminist act. There is a long tradition in feminism of urging women to write as a means to forge a self. Dale Spender has a definitional notion of a feminist as "a woman who writes" (47). Hélène Cixous issues a rousing call for women to harness the power of wordcraft in order to exercise and develop their voice: "Write!" Cixous urges women. "Writing is for you ... Write, let no one hold you back, let nothing stop you ... Your body must be heard." Writing, she says of the woman author, will give "her access to her native strength" (876, 877, 880). By these definitions, a woman becomes a feminist by putting words on paper (or computer screen) in order to work her will, to pursue her pleasure, to further her sense of self. This tradition stretches back to the seventeenth-century precursor of today's romance novelists, Aphra Behn, the first Englishwoman to earn her living by her pen. Behn's plays and novels contain frank and erotic plotlines about feisty women who lead bawdy lives. In *A Room of One's Own*, that iconic text about the transformative power of the writing life for women, Virginia Woolf states, "All women together ought to let flowers fall upon the tomb of Aphra Behn ... for it was she who earned them the right to speak their minds" (69).

Women, socialized by the culture to put the needs of others before their own (Radway), find joy of voice, personal growth, agency, self-awareness, and sometimes even a lucrative living in the act of writing and in the power of their own words. From this perspective, romance novels have force to transform both self and world. Returning to Faircloth's notion of the genre as a decades-long and woman-oriented "thought experiment," romance is an attempt to figure out pathways to sexual pleasure and relationship satisfaction, carried out by women *who dare to write.* Romance authors dare to explore thoughts and fantasies that run contrary to patriarchal scripts for feminine docility, submissiveness, and sexual passivity; for mandatory heterosexuality; for a masculinity that denies gender equality. These scripts are still alive in the impossible contradictions and oppressive double standards that the culture mandates for women: *Be sexy but pure. Don't be a prude but don't be a slut. Stand up for yourself but make sure he still feels like a man* (Roach 88, 99–100).

Precisely because women writing lusty sex scenes is still not considered entirely seemly or "ladylike," these acts become feminist by opening up new space for their authors. Along these lines, the mommy porn label could be reclaimed as a badge of pride rather than embarrassment, a way of saying that women can be unafraid and unashamed in their sexuality. Romance as "mommy porn" points at the feminist liberatory potential of the genre.

Directions for future research

Much of the current wave of scholarship in popular romance studies is reparative, exploring these women-centered texts as sites of resistance and possibility. The question remains: how to reconcile the reparative and paranoid readings or how to hold them in an attendant and productive tension? What more can authors within the romance genre do and what new directions exist for researchers engaged in scholarship on sexuality in popular romance fiction? We review four areas.

1 *Sexual revolution*

The sexual revolution of the 1960s and 1970s helped inaugurate an era of unprecedented cultural acceptance and greater legal protection than ever before for diversity in gender expression and in consensual sexuality. In stories running the gamut from erotic to sweet, the genre works out, within the realm of fiction, and makes up, through the pleasures of the text, some of the inevitable cost to the psyche of toxic cultural ambivalences around sexuality and gender, even as these binds are slowly uncinched through ongoing developments of the sexual revolution (e.g., the mainstreaming of transgender and of same-sex romance and marriage, the #MeToo movement, activism against slut-shaming). The genre of romance—with its supportive and engaged online community of readers and writers—has staked out a claim as a prime site of imaginative solace to navigate these tensions. Many, although not all, of today's romances engage a new sex-positive emphasis on consent and safe sex, on storylines of inclusion and diversity that burst with independent heroines and egalitarian relationships. Romance fiction helps deepen awareness about shifting sexual and gender norms by staging these stories on the page for widespread discussion among its community of readers and authors, as part of the ongoing experiment of imagination in which the genre participates. New research combining textual analysis with gender studies, queer studies, sociology, and more will help determine where exactly and how far the genre is heading on these questions and what legacy it ultimately produces of opening up new liberatory space or propping up old limiting patterns.

2 *Sexual consent*

This point can be summarized as "the problem of the bodice-ripper." Much discussion, both popular and academic, about romance fiction has viewed as "old school" and as problematic scenes of non-consensual sex between main characters destined for true love. While many bodice-rippers from the 1970s and 1980s were hugely popular, today's romance novels much more often dramatize that a good relationship is egalitarian and that good sex is always consensual. As historical romance author Saralee Etter writes,

> Sometimes, romance novels are the only glimpse a reader might get of the way men and women build and sustain a healthy, intimate relationship. Therefore, it is a worthwhile effort for a romance novel to show how two people can treat each other right . . . A hero will stop, if his partner says no. The failure to ask, or failure to stop, is an excellent way to show when a character is *not* a hero.
>
> (her emphasis, 20, 21)

From this perspective, romance fiction functions as a descriptive and prescriptive narrative for how sexuality can be lived for justice and joy.

While the genre has generally distanced itself from bodice-rippery, romance authors do continue to play with the look or feel or meaning of non-consensual sex and what's sometimes called "dubious consent" or "dub-con" sex. Current BDSM romances represent a version of or a response to the earlier bodice-ripper, one in which partners gain trust and negotiate consent in advance before engaging in scenes of power exchange, including punishment and bondage. More widely, many romances continue to grant such masterful powers of seduction to the hero that sex scenes can sometimes read as disturbingly forced or as dub-con: the heroine's initial "no" yields to "yes" in the hero's magical embrace.

These storylines about consenting and not consenting and sort of consenting to love and sex represent an important appeal of the romance genre for its largely women readers who live in what is still a rape culture. The genre may need the latitude of staging force in various forms as a way to think through the problem of rape and the bedrock importance of consent. Scholars have analyzed the narrative uses of rape in romance fiction (Toscano). More work remains to be done in continued discussions about the meaning of consent, seduction, and BDSM and the relationship between fictional depiction and real-life experience around issues of assault, traumatic reenactment, healing, agency, and desire.

3 *Sexual climax*

Here, the genre's problem—and its potential—is one that may be described as *cliteracy* (Wallace, Mintz). Romance fiction is *cliterate* in that its stories are literate about the clitoris and, more generally, about women's sexuality and how it may differ from the male. Romance stories take abundant literary pleasure in women's abundant sensual pleasure, with scenes of endless foreplay, true love seductions, and earth-shattering orgasms. But it must be acknowledged that the cliteracy of romance fiction is not that of full realism. Nature seems to have endowed many a romance heroine with a fantastically responsive sexual physiology, such that she climaxes early (from the moment of defloration), often, and easily.

While acknowledging the compensatory appeal of an imaginary escapist romp wherein sex is easy and good, the more critical perspective nevertheless suggests that the romance genre and its critics could do more to actualize a fuller cliteracy. Romance scholarship could challenge stereotypical, false norms of female sexual response, and novelists, in their role as sexual advocates and educators, must continue to write beyond the trope of penis-in-vagina-intercourse-to-simultaneous-orgasm. The convention of such phallic penetration no longer dominates the genre but nor has it fully disappeared, despite its limitations as a pathway to pleasure for women, whose locus of sensation is the clitoris and not the vagina. Wallace notes the pernicious cultural blind spot and paradox of the "global obsession with sexualizing female bodies in a world that is maddeningly illiterate when it comes to female sexuality" (*Cliteracy*). To know how the body and its pleasures work—how to ask for, give, and receive pleasure; by oneself and in relationship—is a fundamental and transformative human right. The romance genre and its critics are uniquely positioned to render readers more cliterate and knowledgeable about female pleasure.

Of course, fantasy sex holds true for male heroes as well, typically portrayed as masterfully skilled lovers: no erectile dysfunction or premature ejaculation for these guys. Here, scholarship could productively push further into representations of male sexuality in the romance genre, both in heterosexual romances and in gay or m/m storylines. The construction of sexual masculinity and of masculine sexuality remains fertile ground for analysis (see, e.g., Allan, and Chapter 20 of this volume).

4 *Diversity*

How can the erotic aspect of romance storytelling reach fullest potential for inclusive, sex-positive, queer-friendly, feminist liberation? The genre has in recent years begun to embrace more racially and ethnically diverse love stories, as well as same-sex male love stories and the kink of BDSM erotica. Available but less mainstream are lesbian, bisexual, polyamorous, transgender, and asexual romance stories. Romance scholarship needs more analysis of such sexual diversity. For example, virginity studies draw attention to the under-examined male virgin (Allan "Virginity"). Asexual or "ace" romances can help us move beyond master narratives centered around not only penetrative sexuality but genital and orgasmic sexuality as well; indeed, ace romances challenge the genre's central love/sex nexus and its core value of sexual pleasure (Springer). Polyamorous romances expand the genre beyond its stories of "compulsory demisexuality" (McAlister *Romancing the Virgin*) where the heroine, in particular, only experiences desire, pleasure, and love with her One True Love. The status of the iconic happily-ever-after ending, the HEA, comes into question here. Some romance stories have already moved to the HFN: the "happy-for-now" ending, with a less compulsive focus on lifelong pair-bonding as the pathway to happiness and greater openness to other paths to fulfillment through celibacy, divorce, widowhood, serial romance, or casual sex. Such narratives pose questions for future scholarship regarding the very definition of "romance."

We see here the power of authors writing within the romance genre and critics writing about it. Romance genre professionals—novelists, editors, publishers, reviewers, bloggers—share responsibility to support new writing that breaks boundaries and celebrates diversity. Romance scholars must attend to this diversification in both mainstream and independent publishing. Ideally, all this storytelling opens up more space in the culture. It queers—questions, transforms—stifling and oppressive one-size-fits-all story norms. It leads us toward a goal of equity and inclusion in support of sexual and gender diversity.

Conclusion

Twenty-five years ago, Radway hoped that we might "learn how to activate the critical power that even now lies buried in the romance as one of the few widely shared womanly commentaries on the contradictions and costs of patriarchy" (18). This task of "activation" is happening now; this buried power erupts. The romance genre has emerged as a critical and fascinating frontier for sexual storytelling that creates new space for narratives and realities of a wider and more diverse, sex-positive future for us all.

We're not there yet, but the sexy stories of romance fiction help us on our way.

Notes

1 In another example, Pamela Regis argues strongly that romance novels are about women's freedom and not their enslavement (xiii). She suggests that the genre requires its heroines to overcome one or more significant barriers on their path to love and that the happy ending is a celebration of that overcoming and of the heroine's freedom (15). Regis emphasizes the agency of the women depicted in romance: "Romance heroines make their own decisions, make their own livings, and choose their own husbands" (207).

2 As Sedgwick writes, "The desire of a reparative impulse ... is additive and accretive. Its fear, a realistic one, is that the culture surrounding it is inadequate or inimical to its nurture; it wants to assemble and confer plenitude on an object that will then have resources to offer to an inchoate self" ("Paranoid and Reparative" 25).

Works cited

Allan, Jonathan A. "Theorizing Male Virginity in Popular Romance Novels." *Journal of Popular Romance Studies*, vol. 2, no. 1, 2011, pp. 1–14.

———. *Reading from Behind: A Cultural Analysis of the Anus*. University of Regina Press, 2016.

Armstrong, Jane, Liz Byrski and Helen Merrick. "Love Works: Reading and Writing Romance in the Twenty-First Century." *Australasian Journal of Popular Culture*, vol. 3, no. 3, 2014, pp. 257–261.

Attwood, Feona, editor. *Mainstreaming Sex: The Sexualization of Western Culture*. I.B. Tauris, 2009.

Beer, Gillian. *The Romance*. Methuen & Co Ltd, 1970.

Berlant, Lauren. *Cruel Optimism*. Duke University Press, 2011.

———. *Desire/Love*. Punctum Books, 2012.

Cixous, Hélène. "The Laugh of the Medusa." translated by Keith Cohen and Paula Cohen, *Signs*, vol. 1, no. 4, 1976, pp. 875–893.

Comella, Lynn. "Fifty Shades of Erotic Stimulus." *Feminist Media Studies*, vol. 13, no. 3, 2013, pp. 563–566.

Crusie, Jennie. "Defeating the Critics: What We Can Do about the Anti-Romance Bias." *Romance Writers' Report*, vol. 18, no. 4, 1998, pp. 38–39, 44.

Dana, Ménard, A. and Christine Cabrera. "'Whatever the Approach, Tab B Still Fits into Slot A': Twenty Years of Sex Scripts in Romance Novels." *Sexuality and Culture*, vol. 15, no. 2011, pp. 240–255.

Deller, Ruth A. and Clarissa Smith. "Reading the BDSM Romance: Reader Responses to Fifty Shades." *Sexualities*, vol. 16, no. 8, 2013, pp. 932–950.

Diekman, Amanda B., Mary McDonald and Wendi L. Gardner. "Love Means Never Having to Be Careful: The Relationship between Reading Romance Novels and Safe Sex Behaviour." *Psychology of Women Quarterly*, vol. 24, no. 2000, pp. 179–188.

Etter, Saralee. "The Dance of Consent." *Romance Writers Report*, vol. 35, no. 3, 2015, pp. 19–22.

Faircloth, Kelly. "The Sweet, Savage Sexual Revolution that Set the Romance Novel Free." *Jezebel*, 6 December, 2016, http://pictorial.jezebel.com/the-sweet-savage-sexual-revolution-that-set-the-romanc-1789687801.

Fletcher, Lisa. "Writing the Happy Ever After: An Interview with Anne Gracie." *Journal of Popular Romance Studies*, vol. 4, no. 2, 2014, pp. 1–17.

Fowler, Bridget. "Literature beyond Modernism: Middlebrow and Popular Romance." *Romance Revisited*, edited by Lynne Pearce, and Jackie Stacey, New York University Press, 1995, pp. 89–99.

Gleason, William A. and Eric Murphy Selinger, editors. *Romance Fiction and American Culture: Love as the Practice of Freedom?* Ashgate, 2016.

Goade, Sally, editor. *Empowerment versus Oppression: Twenty First Century Views of Popular Romance Novels*. Cambridge Scholars Publishing, 2007.

Gracie, Anne. "Myths of Romance." *www.annegracie.com/writer-resources/myths-of-romance/*. Accessed 24 April 2018.

Harlequin. "Assistant Editor Kathryn Cheshire on Relatable Contemporary Romance." www.youtube.com/watch?v=BSqA9aXKox0. Accessed 24 April 2018.

———. "What Category Are You." www.soyouthinkyoucanwrite.com/2014/09/what-series-are-you/. Accessed 24 April 2018.

Harman, Sarah and Bethan Jones. "Fifty Shades of Ghey: Snark Fandom and the Figure of the Anti-Fan." *Sexualities*, vol. 16, no. 8, 2013, pp. 951–968.

Harris, Emily Ann, Michael Thai and Fiona Kate Barlow. "Fifty Shades Flipped: Effects of Reading Erotica Depicting a Sexually Dominant Woman Compared to a Sexually Dominant Man." *The Journal of Sex Research*, vol. 54, no. 3, 2016, pp. 386–397.

Illouz, Eva. *Hard-Core Romance: Fifty Shades of Grey, Best-Sellers, and Society*. University of Chicago Press, 2014.

Lee, Linda J. "Guilty Pleasures: Reading Romance Novels as Reworked Fairy Tales." *Marvels & Tales: Journal of Fairy-Tale Studies*, vol. 22, no. 1, 2008, pp. 52–66.

Levy, Ariel. *Female Chauvinist Pigs: Women and the Rise of Raunch Culture*. 2005. Black Inc., 2010.

Lutzenberger, Jennifer. "Cutting, Craving, & the Self I Was Saving." *Jane Sexes It Up: True Confessions of Feminist Desire*, edited by Merri Lisa Johnson, Four Walls Eight Windows, 2002, pp. 107–125.

McAlister, Jodi. *Romancing the Virgin: Female Virginity Loss and Love in Popular Literatures in the West*. Ph.D. dissertation, Modern History, Politics & International Relations, Macquarie University, Sydney, Australia, 2015.

———. "'You and I are Humans, and There Is Something Complicated between Us': Untamed and Queering the Heterosexual Historical Romance." *Journal of Popular Romance Studies*, vol. 5, no. 2, 2016, pp. 1–21.

McNair, Brian. *Porno? Chic! How pornography changed the world and made it a better place*. Routledge, 2013.

McRobbie, Angela. *The Aftermath of Feminism: Gender, Culture and Social Change*. SAGE Publications, 2009.

Mintz, Laurie. *Becoming Cliterate: How Orgasm Equality Matters–And How To Get It.* HarperOne, 2017.

Modleski, Tania. *Loving with a Vengeance: Mass-Produced Fantasies for Women.* Second edition. Routledge, 1990.

Orenstein, Peggy. *Girls and Sex: Navigating the Complicated New Landscape.* Harper, 2016.

Paasonen, Susanna, Kaarina Nikunen and Laura Saarenma, editors. *Pornification: Sex and Sexuality in Media Culture.* Bloomsbury, 2007.

Parreñas Shimizu, Celine. *The Hypersexuality of Race: Performing Asian/American Women on Screen and Scene.* Duke University Press, 2007.

Penley, Constance, et al. "Introduction: The Politics of Producing Pleasure." *The Feminist Porn Book: The Politics of Producing Pleasure*, edited by Constance Penley, et al. The Feminist Press, 2013, pp. 9–20.

Phillips, Kristen, editor. *Women and Erotic Fiction: Critical Essays on Genres, Markets and Readers.* McFarland, 2015.

Power, Nina. *One Dimensional Woman.* O Books, 2009.

Proctor, Candice. "The Romance Genre Blues or Why We Don't Get No Respect." *Empowerment versus Oppression: Twenty First Century Views of Popular Romance Novels*, edited by Sally Goade, Cambridge Scholars Publishing, 2007, pp. 12–19.

Radway, Janice A. *Reading the Romance: Women, Patriarchy, and Popular Literature.* University of North Carolina Press, 1991.

Regis, Pamela. *A Natural History of the Romance Novel.* University of Pennsylvania Press, 2003.

Roach, Catherine M. *Happily Ever After: The Romance Story in Popular Culture.* Indiana University Press, 2016.

Sedgwick, Eve Kosofsky. *Tendencies.* Duke University Press, 1993.

———. *Novel Gazing: Queer Readings in Fiction.* Duke University Press, 1997.

Smith, Clarissa. *One for the Girls! The Pleasures and Practices of Reading Women's Porn.* Intellect, 2007.

Snitow, Ann. "Mass Market Romance: Pornography for Women Is Different." *Radical History Review*, vol. 20, no. 1979, pp. 141–161.

Sparrow, Jeff. *Money Shot: A Journey into Porn and Censorship.* Scribe, 2012.

Spender, Dale. *The Writing or the Sex? or. Why You Don't Have to Read Women's Writing to Know It's No Good.* Pergamon Press, 1989.

Springer, Elyse. "Why We Need Asexual Romances." *Just Love: Queer Book Reviews.* 15 January 2016. https://justlovereviews.com/2016/01/15/asexual-romances-are-necessary/.

Talbot, Mary M. "'An Explosion Deep inside Her': Women's Desire and Popular Romance Fiction." *Language and Desire: Encoding Sex, Romance and Intimacy*, edited by Keith Harvey, and Celia Shalom, Routledge, 1997, pp. 106–122.

Tasker, Yvonne and Diane Negra. "Postfeminism and the Archive for the Future." *Camera Obscura: Feminism, Culture, and Media Studies*, vol. 21, no. 2 (62), 2006, pp. 170–176.

Thomas, Glen. "Romance: The Perfect Creative Industry? A Case Study of Harlequin-Mills and Boon Australia." *Empowerment versus Oppression: Twenty First Century Views of Popular Romance Novels*, edited by Sally Goade, Cambridge Scholars Publishing, 2007, pp. 20–29.

———. "Happy Readers or Sad Ones? Romance Fiction and the Problems of the Media Effects Model." *New Approaches to Popular Romance Fiction: Critical Essays*, edited by Sarah S. G. Frantz, and Eric Murphy Selinger, McFarland & Co, 2010, pp. 206–217.

Thurston, Carol. *The Romance Revolution: Erotic Novels for Women and the Quest for a New Sexual Identity.* University of Illinois Press, 1987.

Toscano, Angela R. "A Parody of Love: The Narrative Uses of Rape in Popular Romance." *Journal of Popular Romance Studies*, vol. 2, no. 2, 2012, pp. 1–17.

Trevenen, Claire. "Fifty Shades of 'Mommy Porn': A Post-GFC Renegotiation of Paternal Law." *Journal of Popular Romance Studies*, vol. 4, no. 1, 2014, pp. 1–20.

Vance, Carole S., editor. *Pleasure and Danger: Exploring Female Sexuality*. Routledge & Kegan Paul, 1984.

Wade, Lisa. "Are Women Bad at Orgasms? Understanding the Gender Gap." *Gender, Sex, and Politics: In the Streets and Between the Sheets in the 21st Century*, edited by Shira Tarrant, Routledge, 2016, pp. 227–237.

———. *American Hookup: The New Culture of Sex on Campus*. Norton, 2017.

Wallace, Sophia. *Cliteracy: 100 Natural Laws*. 2012. www.sophiawallace.com/cliteracy-100-natural-laws. Accessed 18 June 2015.

Walter, Natasha. *Living Dolls: The Return of Sexism*. Virago Press, 2010.

Wendell, Sarah and Candy Tan. *Beyond Heaving Bosoms: The Smart Bitches' Guide to Romance Novels*. Simon & Schuster, 2009.

Woolf, Virginia. *A Room of One's Own*. 1929. Harcourt Brace Jovanovich, 1957.

20 Gender and sexuality

Jonathan A. Allan

The popular romance novel, perhaps more than any other genre, concerns itself with and explores the complexity of gender and sexuality. As scholars have shown, often romance novels essentialize both gender and sexuality; by contrast, this chapter is explicitly interested in gender and sexuality in popular romance novels as social constructs, rather than essential categories. Simply put, this chapter understands that gender and sexuality are something characters *do*, and it will explore how foundational works of popular romance scholarship have understood and theorized gender and sexuality, as well as pay attention to the lacunae in that scholarly record, which new generations of scholars have now begun to explore. The popular romance novel is a complicated archive that offers scholars of gender and sexuality much to think about, theorize, and critique. To these ends, this chapter will cover masculinity and femininity, as well as queer approaches to gender in the popular romance, while also providing something of a historical overview of the treatment of gender and sexuality in the scholarship.

The "Harlequin formula" and the pornographic

One of the most influential studies that has continued to frame debates about the popular romance novel is Ann Barr Snitow's "Mass Market Romance: Pornography for Women is Different" (1979). The value of Snitow's article is two-fold: firstly, she develops her idea of "the Harlequin Formula"; and secondly, she argues that romance is "pornography for women." This article, thus, sets up language that will be articulated, developed, critiqued, and applied throughout popular romance studies. What Snitow calls "the Harlequin Formula" has become a shorthand for romance novels more generally, especially outside of the study of popular romance, even as the meaning of that shorthand phrase has changed from Snitow's original formulation.[1] In Snitow's article, gender and sexuality are essential to both the formula and to how romance is framed as pornography. Snitow shows how these novels construct masculinity and femininity, and how these participate in sexuality, all of which is part of the patriarchal structure reflected in, and replicated by, popular romance.

Snitow begins by asking, "What is the Harlequin romance formula?" and she answers,

> The novels have no plot in the usual sense. All tension and problems arise from the fact that the Harlequin world is inhabited by two species incapable of

> communicating with each other, male and female. In this sense, these Pollyanna books have their own dream-like truth: our culture produces a pathological experience of sex difference. The sexes have different needs and interests, certainly different experiences. They find each other utterly mystifying.
>
> (143)

Later scholars have quarreled with Snitow's generalizations, which seem to be based on reading only a handful of Harlequin romances from the 1970s (see, for example, Dixon 29, 174). Her central theoretical points, however, remain of value. For Snitow, the romance novel "formula" reflects a broader cultural assumption that there are essential differences between "male" and "female," or "hero" and "heroine," and in so doing the genre, however upbeat (these are "Polyanna books") registers an unhappy and uncomfortable truth: "our culture produces a pathological experience of sex difference." This is not to say that the novels explicitly critique this "pathological" and even "erroneous" idea that men are from Mars, and women are from Venus, as the more recent cliché would have it.[2] Quite the contrary: in Snitow's account, they systematically reproduce this essentialist binary by insisting on "traditional" gender roles that associate heroines with consumer culture ("her time is filled by tourism and by description of consumer items: furniture, clothes, and gourmet food" (144)), with passivity ("the heroine is not involved in any overt adventure beyond trying to respond appropriately to male energy without losing her virginity" (144)), and with a happy ending that depends on her successful performance of patriarchal norms:

> the heroine gets her man at the end, first, because she is an old-fashioned girl (this is code for no premarital sex) and, second, because the hero gets ample opportunity to see her perform well in a number of female helping roles.
>
> (145)

Yet although the genre does not itself critique gender essentialism and heteropatriarchy, it does engage with the cultural situation they produce as a *problem*, since members of these two "species" must come to learn about one another and learn to love and exist with one another. In particular, this burden of learning falls on the heroine, for whom the hero appears as "the unknowable other, a sexual icon whose magic is maleness" (Snitow 144).

Snitow's account of the "Harlequin formula" anticipates twenty-first-century discussions about heteropatriarchy. When Mari Ruti critiques the emotional costs entailed by the "fantasy of complementarity"—the cultural fantasy which "perpetuates the idea that men and women are capable of rescuing each other: women, supposedly, are supported by men's ambition, activities, and protection whereas men are saved by women's tender sensibilities" (78)—we can hear echoes of the "Formula" that Snitow describes. Snitow's attention to the genre's construction of an "iconic" and "magic" masculinity is an early instance of what has been one of the most productive ways to explore the romance archive, one which I will return to throughout this chapter.

Snitow was also prescient in the sense that a comparison with pornography might offer a discourse, even a theory, for how to engage with romance. Pamela Regis has claimed that Snitow "branded romance with the dismissive label of porn" ("What Do Critics Owe the Romance?"), and equations of romance with pornography remain omnipresent in dismissals of the popular romance novel, a gesture which reached its climax, or its most recent climax, following the publication of *Fifty Shades of Grey* by E. L. James.[3] This is not, however, how Snitow proceeds. Rather, Snitow uses the word pornography "as neutrally as possible here, not as an automatic pejorative" (Snitow 151), and she pushes back against "an unpublished talk [by] critic Peter Parisi" in which the male critic characterizes Harlequin romances as "essentially pornography for people ashamed to read pornography" (151), and "a sort of poor woman's D.H. Lawrence" (151). Rather than being an anxious, second-rate version of what exists more authentically in male-authored literary fiction, romance *qua* pornography is "masterly," a "delicate miracle of balance" (158) in which "the barriers that hold back female sexual feeling are acknowledged and finally circumvented quite sympathetically" (160) and where the creation of a secure context in which a man might be trained to be a satisfying lover is given its due as part of the erotic fantasy (157). "A strength of the books," she writes,

> is that they insist that good sex for women requires and emotional and social context that can free them from constraint. If one dislikes the kind of social norms the heroine seeks as her sexual preconditions, it is still interesting to see sex treated not primarily as a physical event at all but as a social drama, as a carefully modulated set of psychological possibilities between people. This is a mirror image of much writing more commonly labeled pornography.
>
> (160)

As "sex books for people who have plenty of good reasons for worrying about sex" (160) romance novels are not dismissed by calling them pornography, but made available for richer and more nuanced investigation.

Snitow's discussion of Harlequin romances as a "different" form of pornography is part of a much larger narrative unfolding around sex, pornography, and popular romance in the late 1970s and early 1980s, and historicist readings of romance and pornography during those decades (and after) remain needed. Historian Carolyn Bronstein's essay "The Political Uses of Lesbian Romance Fiction: Reading Patrick Califia's Macho Sluts as a Response to 1980s Anti-Pornography Feminism" offers a useful model; others can be found in Kristen Phillips's anthology *Women and Erotic Fiction: Critical Essays on Genres, Markets and Readers*, most of whose contributors come from the fields of Queer Theory, Communications, and Porn Studies. Popular romance scholars have spent many years resisting the romance/pornography connection, but some have begun to return to it. In *The Glass Slipper: Women and Love Stories* Susan Ostrov Weisser devotes a chapter to the topic, encouraging us to think of these two concepts—romance and porn—as "parallel investments of meaning, permitting us to experience a need whose possibility of existence may not be fully recognized in social relations, reified in the body of desire" (172). Weisser is interested, then, in thinking through the "interdependence of porn and romance" and the ways in which "in recent cultural history" these terms

> seem to depend on each other, in the same way that an old married couple who have hated each other for decades organize their existence around that hatred and would be lost if they did not have one another define themselves against.
>
> (173)

In *Happily Ever After: The Romance Story in Popular Culture* Catherine Roach offers a more optimistic, reparative reading of this interdependence, based in part on her interest in "reclaiming porn and rehabilitating its definition in feminist and queer directions" (88).[4]

In *Loving with a Vengeance: Mass-Produced Fantasies for Women*, Tania Modleski developed Snitow's interest in the "Harlequin formula." Unlike Snitow, Modleski grew up as a reader of romances, although she did not reveal this fact until later in her career; as she explains in "My Life as a Romance Reader," she grew up in a household where both she and her mother struggled to navigate her father's "surly silence," "bursts of temper," and "bouts of ridicule" ("My Life" 50). Perhaps because of this context—the speculation is Modleski's—her account of the "Harlequin formula" is more fraught and conflictual than Snitow's. The hero is, again, an "unknowable other" (Snitow 144), but the mystery surrounding him depends on the contrast between his interest in the heroine and his behavior toward her, which is "mocking, cynical, contemptuous, often hostile, and even somewhat brutal" (*Loving* 28). This mystery will, as in Snitow, be resolved; but in Modleski, its resolution depends on the hero realizing that the heroine is "different from all other women, that she is not, in other words, a 'scheming little adventuress'" (*Loving* 30–1). Modleski also adds a crucial psychoanalytic turn to her interpretation of the "Harlequin Formula," attending to the potent, addictive dose of "latent content" it delivers to readers. "A great deal of our satisfaction in reading these novels comes, I am convinced, from the elements of a revenge fantasy," she writes, "from our conviction that the woman is bringing the man to his knees and that all the while he is being so hateful, he is internally groveling, groveling, groveling ..." (*Loving* 45). That this fantasy is "regressive" (*Loving* 32) and "infantile" (*Loving* 45) makes it no less potent: she uses such terms not to disparage it, but to relate it to psychoanalyst Karen Horney's work on women's "deep-seated desire for vengeance" (*Loving* 45).

By the 1990s, Modleski's emphasis on conflict and revenge in romance was known and debated by romance authors. As the essays written for Jayne Ann Krentz's *Dangerous Men, Adventurous Women* anthology attest, some embraced or even exulted in it (see the pieces by Krentz and Susan Elizabeth Phillips); others (see the essay by Laura Kinsale) fiercely contested its assumption that the romance reader always or inevitably identifies with the heroine, arguing instead that the appeal of the genre lies in its allowing women to identify across gender lines with the hero, especially in his moments of "emotional cataclysm," when he is finally *known* (52).[5] Authors also discussed Modleski's contribution to romance narratology, particularly the way she engages with Wolfgang Iser's notion of "advance retrospection." "Since the reader knows the formula, she is superior in wisdom to the heroine and thus detached from her," Modleski explains (*Loving* 33), and this detachment means that the "unknowable" hero may be, in fact, known to the reader—if not the heroine—all along. As Modleski explains, "since readers are prepared to understand the hero's behavior in terms of the novel's ending, some of the serious doubts women have about men can be confronted and dispelled" (33). In the genre's fantasy of assuagement, which is to suggest, its happy ending, the difference of gender is overcome by heterosexuality—but as Modleski observes in her retrospective later work on romance, the power of that ending depends on the seriousness of the doubts that have been raised before it arises, such that "the elements of the formula that most disturbed me were the very same ones I desired for my reading pleasure" ("My Life" 61).

Although the "Harlequin formula" that Snitow and Modleski discuss appears primarily in a period subset of category romance novels (1950s–70s), they inaugurate the study of romance novels more generally as an archive of cultural fantasies about gender and sexuality.[6] A third foundational scholar from the 1980s, Janice Radway, continued this investigation, but rather than focus on Harlequin novels, she explored the corpus of longer, single-title romance novels, mostly historical romances, that emerged in the 1970s. Radway's *Reading the Romance: Women, Patriarchy, and Popular Literature* (1984), is an ethnographic study of popular romance readers, and draws on publishing history, feminist method, and post-Freudian psychoanalytic theory to attempt to understand the "institutional matrix" in which readers, novels, publishers, and others are embedded (10). From the perspective of this chapter, Radway's most important contribution may be her deep consideration of the romance hero, not just as a character, but as a site in which masculinity can be theorized—and this happens *before* the rise of critical studies of men and masculinities.[7] In particular, Radway argues that the hero of romance is "always characterized by spectacular masculinity" (128), with the reader "told ... that every aspect of his being, whether his body, his face, or his general demeanor is informed by the purity of his maleness" (128).

In Radway's account, the romance hero's masculinity is not only affirmed but celebrated by the genre: it is "spectacular" in every sense of the word. The alien, intimidating, and oppressive elements of masculinity described by Snitow and Modleski are not absent from this spectacle. As Radway, too, observes, the "simple binary oppositions that are the basis for character differentiation in the romance are ... a useful clue to the things women most fear as potential threats to heterosexual love and traditional marriage" (131), and indeed "*all* popular romantic fiction originates in the failure of patriarchal culture to satisfy its female members" (151, my emphasis). Yet in contrast to what the Smithton readers thought of as "failed romances," where these negative elements of masculinity predominate, in the novels they preferred, the "terrorizing effect" of the hero's "exemplary masculinity" is inevitably "tempered by the presence of a small feature that introduces an important element of softness into the overall picture" (128). In a crucial innovation, Radway then reads this "softness" through a lens provided by Nancy Chodorow's *The Reproduction of Mothering*, such that this element of caregiving "softness" links between the romance hero not just with femininity, but more specifically with the female reader's nurturing, pre-Oedipal mother: the person who took care of her as she was socialized into becoming a caregiver herself. As Radway summarizes the argument, "it is the constant impulse and duty to mother others that is responsible for the sense of depletion that apparently sends some women to romance fiction," and "by immersing themselves in the romantic fantasy, women vicariously fulfill their needs for nurturance" by identifying with the heroine who is nurtured by the hero as she, the reader, is not (sufficiently) nurtured in her own heterosexual relationship (84).

Against the vision of gender in romance as something static, Radway offers a reading in which gender is a journey for both heroine and hero. A novel's heroine may initially be "aberrant" because she is not "feminine" or "feminine enough," but over the course of the novel, she will become more and more womanly (124); in turn, the hero who starts out excessively masculine (that is, performing only the more distancing and negative forms of "spectacular" masculinity) will ideally offer the heroine a "nurturant, essentially 'effeminate' attention"—not in *place* of his original masculinity, but as a complicating addition to it (155). Writing before the rise of post-structuralist feminist theories, queer theories, etc., all of which sought to destabilize the essentialism of gender, Radway nevertheless suggests that the gender binary of heterosexual popular romance is less clear-cut than it appears, at least where the hero is concerned. The spectacle of heteronormativity that appears on the pages masks a deeper same-sex love, that of the reader/daughter and the hero/pre-Oedipal mother. As such, "some romance fiction is as much about recovering motherly nurturance and affection as it is about the need to be found desirable by men" (151), and Radway goes so far as to claim that "the reestablishment of that original, blissful symbiotic union between mother and child ... is the goal of all romances, despite their apparent preoccupation with heterosexual love and marriage" (156).

Like Snitow's and Modleski's arguments about the "Harlequin formula," Radway's counterintuitive claim about the hero's maternal identity has been adapted, modified, and debated by later writers. In "Confessions of a Harlequin Reader: Romance and the Myth of Male Mothers" Angela Miles seems to combine all three of these foundational approaches. "Knowing the romance formula," an echo of Snitow, she baldly asserts that "the hero is in fact a mother figure for the reader/woman" (93), a reminder of Radway, but she goes on to argue that in reading a romance novel, women "are reenacting the emotionally demanding ambivalence of our relationship with an unpredictable, tender, threatening, all-powerful mother," a description more evocative of Modleski, albeit this time about a mother and not a father (101–2). Drawing on more recent queer theory, Stephanie Burley's essay "What's a Nice Girl Like You Doing in a Book Like This? Homoerotic Reading and Popular Romance" (2003) builds on Radway's suggestion that the search for the mother in romance masks, or at least hints at, the possibility of a homoerotic reading of the genre. I discuss this essay in detail below; here it is worth noting that in *Reading the Romance* the genre's investments in homosociality and homoeroticism are, and must remain, unconscious, visible more often through their anxious occlusion than through textual evidence.[8] Kate Moore and Eric Murphy Selinger have argued that romance authors sometimes nod to, joke about, or contest through parody Radway's arguments, especially about the romance hero (2012; see also Selinger 2007), and more work needs to be done to document her ideas' reception (as well as those of other scholars) in the romance community.

Post-Radway; pre-millennial

In the work of these three foundational analysts, popular romance is predicated on a commitment to heteronormativity. In it, men are men and women are women; the genre creates an essentialist space (conflicted but ultimately utopian) in which even when the hero becomes caring, and thus partially "effeminate" (Radway 155) he never loses his claims to heterosexual masculinity and masculine heterosexuality.[9] Between Radway's work and the end of the century, a handful of essays and monographs test this depiction of the genre against its late-century evolution and against its deeper literary history, deploying a variety of critical methods.

Building on Janice Radway's interest in the "Institutional Matrix" of romance publishing, but adding a vast array of new archival research into sales figures, publishers' guidelines, and reader feedback (including a reader survey aimed to update the ones in Radway), Carol Thurston provides a well-documented sociological study of feminist ideas and sexual representation in the genre during the 1970s and 1980s. As its title suggests, Thurston's *The Romance Revolution: Erotic Novels for Women and the Quest for a New Sexual Identity* (1987) accepts Snitow's assertion that romance novels can and should be read as "female sexual fiction" (10), but Thurston rejects many of Snitow's conclusions about the "Harlequin Formula," which she finds narrow and dated. Thurston's study considers a more adventurous, more self-determined heroine, who has become more and more present in the genre, she argues, since the 1970s. This "new heroine" is "both good and sexual, and she provides a passionate drive for self-determination and autonomy," such that the novels in which she appears "increasingly depict the relationship between a developing sense of self and sexual awareness and satisfaction" (124): a relationship between self and sexuality that vividly contrasts with the one described by both Snitow and Modleski, in whose accounts the sexualized woman was invariably the heroine's rival.

Both Radway and Modleski felt compelled to respond to Thurston's claims: Modleski indirectly, through her sometimes quite scathing critique of claims that the genre was not just feminist, but "revolutionary" (see "My Life as a Romance Reader" and "My Life as a Romance Writer"); Radway in an extended discussion that introduces intersectional questions about whiteness and class into Thurston's argument ("Romance and the Work of Fantasy: Struggles over Feminine Sexuality and Subjectivity at Century's End" esp. 408–12). Snitow does not seem to have responded. This is a pity, since Thurston specifically addresses the relationship between romance and pornography in the contexts of the Reagan administration's *Attorney General's Commission on Pornography* (1986) and of "feminist-led attempts to ban pornography by labelling it sex discrimination and defining it as any material that includes 'graphic, sexually explicit subordination of women'"—and, as Thurston explains, "in at least one of those cities, Minneapolis, that included paperback romance novels" (160).

Thurston's *Romance Revolution* also drew the attention of an emerging post-structuralist theorist of love literature, including popular romance, British scholar Catherine Belsey. In a review of Thurston (1990), Belsey writes that "the new confidence of the heroines and the new difference of their lovers reads to me more like wish-fulfillment than a reflection of a new social reality" and like Modleski in the "My Life" essays, she asks, rightly, "is it not rather an impoverished form of feminism which is satisfied with 'the full development of the heroine as an individual in her own right'?" ("Review" 907) (This question might be asked of more recent discussions of romance as a feminist genre, including Catherine Roach's *Happily Ever After*, discussed below.) In the popular romance chapter of *Desire: Love Stories in Western Culture* (1994), Belsey invokes then dismisses Thurston in less than a paragraph, pivoting to her own more subtly theorized discussions of mind and body in romance (which promises to suture the gap between these, and inevitably fails, she claims), of the pleasure of the romance text (with reference to Barthes and Brecht), and of the Smithton readers discussed in *Reading the Romance*, whose reactions to the genre she reads not in Radway's Chodorovian terms but through more strictly Freudian and Lacanian lenses (*Desire* 21–41). In a subsequent essay on popular romance and the "Feminine Masquerade"—a term she borrows from Joan Riviere's psychoanalytical essay "Womanliness as a Masquerade" (1929)—Belsey again refuses the notion that these novels are feminist in their own right, but she champions the nuance with which they nevertheless engage, asking feminist questions such as "Is there a single truth of woman? Can we usefully speak of 'the feminine'? And if so, is it an origin or an effect?" (343). The novels, she reports, sometimes frame and investigate these topics with "a complexity in excess of some of the existing academic feminist answers to these questions" (343).

Belsey ends her "Masquerade" essay with a brief reference to Judith Butler, and although Butler's work has begun to be used in the study of popular romance, notably by Lisa Fletcher (discussed below), much more could be done to explore the "work of instruction" in gender performance found in romance novels ("Masquerade" 346). Likewise, the tension Belsey traces between skeptical or debunking theoretical models of love and desire and the happy ending promised by the romance novel ("there are no *perfectly* happy endings," she insists (*Desire* 34)) warrants future investigation, perhaps along the lines suggested by Lauren Berlant's work in *The Female Complaint* and *Cruel Optimism*. As yet, the only twenty-first-century romance scholarship to revisit Belsey's work in detail is "Mind, Body, Love: Nora Roberts and the Evolution of Popular Romance Studies," by the Belgian scholar An Goris, which uses "Belsey's general(izing) claims about popular romance novels ... as a framework to study the work of Nora Roberts, the single most popular romance author of our time" (2).

While Belsey speaks of the psychological "price women have been expected to pay for our culture's conflation of romance and marriage" ("Masquerade" 346), more literal economics are central to Jan Cohn's *Romance and the Erotics of Property: Mass-Market Fiction for Women* (1988) and Bridget Fowler's Marxist study *The Alienated Reader: Women and Popular Romantic Literature in the Twentieth Century* (1991). In Cohn's account, beneath its "surface story of romantic and sexual love" (5) modern popular romance fiction is fundamentally "a story about how the heroine gains access to money—to power—in a patriarchal society" (3). Some of Cohn's arguments will be familiar, for instance that "the dominant character" in the romance novel is "always the hero" (41) and that the popular romance heroine's longings for "economic vengeance and appropriation" (173)—a version of Modleski's conflictual account of the genre—must remain "carefully coded" (16) and "heavily masked" (5) so that both the heroine and her reader retain their "economic innocence" (127). However, in Cohn's work, readers find an addition to these arguments, namely, that "the hero's work signifies his male energy and his power," and moreover, that "work is itself virile" (43). If Protestants gave work its ethic, men gave work its sex appeal, at least in the romance novel, where the work ethic that underpins his masculinity also speaks to his financial prowess. The romance novel eroticizes work, as well as wealth and capital, such that, as Cohn notes, "sexuality is never divorced from economic power" (42). Jayashree Kamblé's more recent discussion of capitalism and the romance hero (31–60) builds on Cohn's example, and a good deal of scholarship on E.L. James's *Fifty Shades of Grey* revisits these associations between eroticism, masculinity, and money-power, notably sociologist Eva Illouz's brief monograph *Hard-Core Romance: Fifty Shades of Grey, Best-Sellers, and Society*.[10]

Mixing cultural theory, ethnographic interviews, and close readings of texts from the 1930s, 1950s, and 1970s–80s, Fowler's ambitious text sets out to "elucidate the ideological structure of the romance," to "dissect representative popular texts in order to show both continuities and structural transformations within the genre," and to "assess cultural consumption ... passing from texts to readers" in order to "show how the reception of literature varies with social experience" (2). More influential in British popular romance studies than in the United States, *The Alienated Reader* is far more precise in its discussions of intersections between gender and social class than Cohn's study, or indeed than any American romance scholarship of the time. Likewise,

Fowler offers a more nuanced discussion than Cohn's of the emerging representation of female agency, both sexual and economic, in what Fowler calls "the new quasi-feminist romance" of the 1980s (104). In such books, she explains, "the repressed passivity of the traditional heroine has now been stripped away" (104) replaced by a "cult of entrepreneurial personality" (105) focused on sexually confident businesswomen for whom "the market-place ... is the new Arcadia" (106). Fowler's consideration of how late-twentieth-century British and American conservative thought reshaped romance in the Thatcher/Reagan era offers a useful model for future scholarship on gender, economics, and ideology in other periods of popular romance history, as does her attention to how socially situated female readers discuss the mix of realism, critique, and utopian fantasy in the genre.

For Pamela Regis, all of the works I have discussed so far would be part of what she calls "the first wave of romance criticism" and its immediate aftermath (2011). These works represent an early approach to the study of popular romance, especially along gendered lines, and while they might be faulted for any number of omissions, for instance engagement with queer texts, we would do well to remember that they appeared before many of the seminal works in gender theory that are now routinely called upon by scholars of popular romance. This point has been made by An Goris, who notes that "when these early critics started conducting their at-the-time highly innovative, ground-breaking studies, they were facing somewhat different conditions than we are today" (2011). For a variety of reasons, popular romance scholarship slows down significantly over the 1990s; indeed, in Regis's history of popular romance criticism, the second wave of criticism is referred to as "Millennial" (2011). During this slow-down, theories of gender are exploding and over the course of the nineties some of the most important works on gender and sexuality would be written, including, *Epistemology of the Closet* (1990) by Eve Kosofsky Sedgwick, *Gender Trouble* (1990) by Judith Butler, *Masculinities* (1995) by R.W. Connell, *Female Masculinity* (1998) by Judith Halberstam, *Making Things Perfectly Queer* (1993) by Alexander Doty, *Queer Theory* (1996) by Annamarie Jagose, *Inside/Out: Lesbian Theories, Gay Theories* (1991) edited by Diana Fuss, to name but some of the most obvious (and now canonical). The Millennial era in romance criticism is the beneficiary of this explosion of scholarship on gender and sexuality.

Millennial criticism

Twenty-first-century scholarship on gender and sexuality in popular romance has diversified considerably in both the texts and the topics it addresses. Not all of it draws on the theoretical models developed in the 1990s: for example, Juliet Flesch's *From Australia With Love* (2004) initiates an ongoing critical discussion of national difference in the representation of Australian heroines and heroes that is based more on archival work and the study of how Australian novels have been translated than it is on contemporary gender theory; likewise, the accounts of Black romance heroine construction and the politics of respectability offered by Rita Dandridge, Conseula Francis, and Julie Moody-Freeman are primarily engaged with understanding these heroines in the contexts of Black history, Black love, and intracommunal discourse than they are with viewing them through post-structuralist or queer theoretical lenses.[11] Australian scholar Lisa Fletcher, by contrast, draws heavily on such theories, notably the work of Judith Butler, in *Historical Romance Fiction: Heterosexuality and*

Performativity (2008). Quoting Butler's assertion that "heterosexuality is always in the process of imitating and approximating its own phantasmic idealization of itself—and failing" (Butler "Imitation" 21; qtd. 34), Fletcher sees historical romance novels, whether popular or literary, as caught up in the same anxious, hyperbolic effort to secure heterosexuality as an original, natural thing, not least through the "perpetual repetition" of performative gestures like the declaration "I love you" (81–2). Viewed in this light, "it becomes theoretically possible to conceive of even the most normative of cultural moments or practices as (inevitably) self-subversive," she argues (82): a possibility that she pursues through readings of cross-dressing in the popular romance novel. The motif of cross-dressing, especially by the romance heroine, shows the genre's capacity for "analytical self-reflection," she writes, as cross-dressing romance plots return again and again (anxiously) to two core questions: "(1) What are the implications of the heroine's (and to a lesser extent the hero's) recognition that gender norms are a social construct? (2) How then does the heroine come to own (and welcome) her gender?" (91). Fletcher's interest in cross-dressing and the popular romance has also been explored by Jodi McAlister in "'You and I are humans, and there is something complicate between us': *Untamed* and queering the heterosexual historical romance," which provides an analysis both of Anna Cowan's novel *Untamed* (2016) and of the sharply divided reception of this novel, in which the hero, while in disguise, all-too-successfully and enthusiastically (at least for some readers) performs normative femininity.[12]

As she herself notes, Fletcher's presumption that the declaration "I love you" functions as a "heteronormative call to order" (41) precludes any investigation of gay or lesbian romance. "Hopefully my work suggests the need for and importance of such a study" (42). She was not the first to notice this need. In the 1997 issue of *Paradoxa* devoted to popular romance, Kay Mussell called upon scholars to "incorporate analysis of lesbian and gay romances into our mostly heterosexual models" (12), and such texts had long since been available, if romance scholars had wished to discuss them. As Len Barot observes, the first press dedicated to publishing "almost exclusively lesbian genre fiction, mostly romance," Naiad Press, was founded in 1973, well before any of the foundational works of popular romance scholarship had been published; gay male romances appeared in both queer and mainstream presses in the 1970s as well (393). Indeed, the prehistory of both lesbian and gay romantic fiction stretches back well before the 1970s, including both literary and pulp novels. Most of these novels did not feature the happy ending for a central couple that has become the defining feature of the romance novel, but as scholars have documented, they could be and were read in resistant, optimistic ways, and have been seen by later authors as part of ongoing lesbian, gay, and other queer romance traditions.[13]

Scholarship on lesbian popular romance fiction had likewise begun to appear several years before Mussell's appeal. In 1992, two essays by Joke Hermes drew on the work of Modleski and Radway to explore the representation of sexuality in these novels and to distinguish the "subcultural phenomenon of lesbian romance reading" from the "mass phenomenon" those predecessors described ("Sexuality" 49). Two years later, Julie Abraham's *Are Girls Necessary? Lesbian Writing and Modern Histories* disputed such distinctions. As Suzanne Juhasz explains in a summary of Abraham's argument, for Abraham, "'plot' equals 'heterosexual,'" such that "even though the story is about romance between two women, Abraham insists that if they are narratively positioned as lovers, they must enact heterosexuality and heterosexual consequences" (Juhasz

65–6). Juhasz sees Abraham's argument as evidence that "the debate that began around heterosexual romance fiction has been rekindled around the lesbian romance," such that "to the specter of the totalizing patriarchal plot has been added the power of the heterosexual plot" (65). Against both specters, Juhasz insists that a close textual analysis of lesbian popular romance—her case study is of *Keep To Me, Stranger* by Sarah Aldridge, published by Naiad in 1989, a book from "the heartland of lesbian romance territory ... as 'mainstream' as they come" (67)—will show that it "disrupts rather than maintains dominant social structures: specifically, heterosexuality and phallocentrism" (80). To prove this, she draws on Adrienne Rich's well-known idea of a "lesbian continuum" and on then-recent feminist psychoanalytic criticism and queer theory (Jane Flax, Teresa De Lauretis, Eve Kosofsky Sedgwick) and argues that although "the plot of *Keep To Me, Stranger* uses a romance formula—girl meets girl, girl loses girl, girl gets girl—," it does so "to develop a fantasy in which a world structured by feminosocial bonding will become normative rather than aberrant, central rather than marginal" (78).

Drawing extensively on Juhasz, Radway, and Thurston, Phyllis M. Betz published the first and as yet only book-length study of lesbian romance novels. In *Lesbian Romance Novels: A History and Critical Analysis* (2009) Betz provides an historical overview of the subgenre, and a series of case studies of individual novels, such as *Patience and Sarah* by Isabel Miller or Jane Rule's *Desert of the Heart*, Katherine Forrest's *Curious Wine*, as well as the more recent work of Radclyffe, Karin Kallmakert, and Jennifer Fulton. Like Juhasz, Betz aims to show how lesbian romance modifies and transforms the literary strategies and tropes of the heterosexual romance novel: an approach she also pursues in *Lesbian Detective Fiction: Woman as Author, Subject and Reader* (2006) and *The Lesbian Fantastic: a Critical Study of Science Fiction, Fantasy, Paranormal, and Gothic Writings* (2014). These companion volumes will be of use to scholars wishing to study lesbian and other f/f[14] works from the detective/mystery romance and the SF, fantasy, Gothic, and paranormal romance subgenres. Paranormal (werewolf) lesbian romance is discussed in "Queering the Romantic Heroine: Where Her Power Lies" (2012), co-authored by romance author and literary scholar Katherine E. Lynch, romance editor Ruth E. Sternglantz, and award-winning author and publisher Len Barot (AKA L.L. Raand, AKA Radclyffe). Barot is the author of the werewolf novel discussed, making this essay a useful glimpse the thinking that went into the text, particular as it concerns the writing of an "alpha heroine" who is quite literally the "alpha" of her pack.[15] One of the handful of romance authors to be profiled in the documentary film *Love Between the Covers*, Barot has also written an invaluable brief history of LGBTQ romance publishing, "Queer Romance in Twentieth and Twenty-First Century America: Snapshots of a Revolution" (2016).

As the work of Juhasz, Betz, and Lynch et. al. indicates, scholars of lesbian romance have had no trouble integrating ideas from the study of heterosexual romance into their analyses. Few scholars of heterosexual romance have returned the favor, making Stephanie Burley's "What's a Nice Girl Like You Doing in a Book Like This? Homoerotic Reading and Popular Romance" (2003) all the more notable and significant a contribution. As she "highlights the subterranean homoeroticism in the romance industry that has gone unnoticed in recent scholarship" (127), Burley brings queer theory to bear on romance, notably Eve Kosofsky Sedgwick's notion of "homosocial desire," developed in *Between Men: English Literature and Male Homosocial Desire* (1985), and she enthusiastically deploys a "queer reading strategy" that draws out "the fluidity of sexual fantasies that circulate around erotic texts, no matter how stable they appear to be on the surface" (129). Burley engages in detail not simply with novels and previous scholarship (Radway, Modleski, Juhasz) but with author statements and interviews; her goal, she insists, is not to "*out* the legions of writers, fans, and critics who participate in this discourse, but rather to *point out* the importance of homoeroticism to the genre" (130), posing such questions as:

> how can a woman-authored industry produce erotic pleasure reading for women without becoming homoerotic? What narrative and discursive apparatuses prevent romance readers who profess a deep and abiding love of their favorite authors and fellow readers from seeing themselves as homoerotic subjects?
>
> (128)

In the "homoerotic counternarrative" Burley establishes, "romance reading is a sexual-textual practice whereby adult women attain fulfillment at their own hands and through the pens of the female authors they love and admire" (137). The reference here to the hand is, of course, masturbatory, that is, through reading the romance novel a sexual pleasure is achieved, and in this way, Burley counters those who have "resisted the idea that the books they love and sell are pornographic" (137): an intervention that goes all the way back to ideas first raised by Snitow.

Burley's article is an important theoretical intervention in the study of popular romance because it is interested in the triangulation that unfolds between a reader, a heroine, and an author, and because it seeks to apply queer theory to a notoriously heteronormative and heterosexist genre. Laura Struve has likewise more recently argued that homosociality (although she never calls it such) is a valuable rubric with which to think about the romance novel. In "Sisters of Sorts: Reading Romantic Fiction and the Bonds Among Female Readers" (2011), she argues that, "despite the genre's conservative ideology, which focuses on heterosexual courtship and marriage, romance readers make connections with other women, and they use the internet to help foster this community" (1290). Struve's argument shares much more in common with the feminist practice of consciousness raising than it does with the queer theoretical work of Sedgwick, and might be seen as a retreat from Burley's more radical rethinking of the genre; that said, Struve's emphasis on how the internet has changed the triangular relationship between authors, readers, and heroines (or texts, more broadly) offers an important new area of scholarly focus, and much more could be done on how gender and sexuality play out in these social media connections.[16]

In her dissertation, *Radicalizing Romance: Subculture, Sex, and Media at the Margins* (2008), Andrea Wood notes a problem with reading romance in terms of homosociality. "Burley's queer reading of romance," Wood explains, "remains restricted to … female readers and characters" (30). Throughout her dissertation, Wood asks important questions about the readers who are left out or set aside in Burley's schema, "seek[ing] to take up where [Burley] left off by considering readers who identify with texts that reflect LBGTQ sexualities" more broadly (30). The queer reading practice envisioned by Wood imagines desire as polymorphous, or at least more complicated than Burley imagines: for instance, Wood's chapter "Who Says Men Don't Read Romance?: The Gay 'Harlequins' of *Romentics*" focuses on men who read romance, a hitherto almost taboo topic in popular romance scholarship, as well as a chapter on straight women (or "'straight' women," as she calls them) who read queer texts such as boy-love manga (*yaoi*) as part of a "global counterpublic." Wood also moves intersectionally to look at queerness, trauma, and Black sexual politics in the work of Zane, the groundbreaking African American author of erotica and erotic romance. In short, Wood imagines both the reading of popular romance and romance itself as queer categories, never as stable or as monolithic as one might imagine from the catchphrase that romance is "by women, for women, and about women."

In their edited collection, *New Approaches to Popular Romance Fiction* (2012), Frantz and Selinger included a number of essays that sought to think queerly about the popular romance novel. Kathleen Therrien's essay, "Straight to the Edges: Gay and Lesbian Characters and Cultural Conflict in Popular Romance Fiction" considers the ways in which "gay and lesbian characters serve as markers of what ideological territory will—or emphatically will *not*—be contested, shifted, or conceded" (165). In this way, Therrien notes that gay and lesbian characters have had a historical role in romance novels long before the rise of LGBTQ romance novels, but that their role served ideological purposes, often policing gender and sex norms, in a way to reinforce the heterosexuality of the protagonists. Likewise, Frantz's essay in the collection sought to expand the scope of sexuality beyond what kink theorist Ivo Dominguez describes, in *Beneath the Skins: The New Spirit and Politics of the Kink Community* (1994), as the "myth of monosexuality" which envisions sexuality as a single "continuum with heterosexual and homosexual as its poles" (48). Drawing on Dominguez's contrasting model of "polysexuality," which sees sexual identity as "a multi-dimensional, inter-woven combination of orientations" (49), Frantz argues that in the BDSM erotic romances of Joey Hill, "BDSM does not refer merely to sexual activities and practices; for some, BDSM goes much deeper than what they *do*. For them, BDSM is their primary sexual identity: it becomes who they *are*" (48). To demonstrate this, Frantz carefully and closely reads Joey W. Hill's *Holding the Cards*, a novel which subverts a variety of genre conventions equating femininity with submission (the heroine of *Holding the Cards* is a sexual dominant) and masculinity with dominance (the hero in Hills work is often both an "alpha male" and a sexual submissive). In so doing, Frantz claims, "Hill interrogates and rewrites the romance genre's construction of ideal masculinity and, indeed, the romance genre itself" (58). Frantz's essay suggests that the visibility of E.L. James's *Fifty Shades of Grey* has, perhaps, occluded how radically other romance authors and novels were using BDSM to investigate the genre before that more conservative text appeared, and also that scholarship on kink and popular culture that has appeared since Dominguez's 1994 volume (e.g., Ariane Cruz's *The Color of Kink: Black Women, BDSM, and Pornography*; Catherine Scott's *Thinking Kink: The Collision of BDSM, Feminism, and Popular Culture*; or *BDSM in American Science Fiction and Fantasy* by Lewis Call) might be a valuable resource for future work on intersections of power, sexuality, gender, and race in popular romance.

Although Frantz's essay is not often cited as a source, subsequent romance scholarship has followed her lead in expanding the vision of sexuality beyond a "monosexual" model. There has been a growing, though limited, interest in bisexuality and the popular romance novel, as in Ann Herendeen's essay, "The Upper-Class Bisexual Top as Romantic Hero: (Pre) Dominant in the Social Structure and in the Bedroom," which braids together sexuality and class in relation to Herendeen's own novels, notably, *Phyllida and the Brotherhood of Philander* (2008) and *Pride/Prejudice* (2010), a queer or "slashed" retelling of Austen's *Pride and Prejudice.* A later chapter by Herendeen, "Having it Both Ways; or, Writing from the Third Perspective: The Revolutionary M/M/F Ménage Romance Novel" (405–19), further demonstrates her interest in challenging ideas of heterosexuality and monogamy as central to the romance genre. Beyond this, we have also seen a small, but growing, body of scholarship on so-called "ménage" romances: an early subset of what has become the subgenre of polyamorous romance. Carole Veldman-Genz's essay, "The More the Merrier? Transformations of the Love Triangle Across the Romance," focuses on the triangle, a figure of desire of interest to a range of critics from René Girard to Eve Kosofsky Sedgwick, and she notes her interest in "both the critically acclaimed male/female/male triad and the previously ignored female/male/female triangle" (111). In reading the previously ignored triangle, Veldman-Genz "highlight[s] the feminocentric potential these structures displace in a genre centred upon female desire, subjectivity, and women's authority/authorship" (111).

Many questions can be asked about the relationship between these texts and the social realities regarding sexual ménage or threesomes and the emerging social reality of polyamorous relationships, especially in times such as ours, wherein we see a loosening of gendered norms (Scoats, Joseph, and Anderson 2018), as well as an interest in non-monogamies (Frank 2013; Schippers 2016) and the impossibility of monogamy (Anderson 2012; Perel 2017). To date, very little has been done on these topics, with both real-world social arrangements and their representations in popular romance evolving faster than romance scholarship. The same is true of popular romance novels and transgender studies. Thanks to independent publishers, a growing body of novels exists that represent transgender folks—some by cis-gendered authors, some by trans writers—but although excellent critical writing on these books has appeared on line (e.g., Xan West's essay "On Internalizing the Cis Gaze When Thinking About Sex and Relationships," which discusses Austin Chant's romance *Peter Darling*), these books remain invisible in peer-reviewed romance scholarship: a significant gap. Little has been done to explore the relationships between queer romance and what Lisa Duggan calls "homonormativity," which is "a politics that does not contest heteronormative assumptions and institution, but upholds and sustains them, while promising the possibility of a demobilized gay constituency and a privatized, depoliticized gay culture anchored in domesticity and consumption" (50). In short, as Andrea Wood and I wrote as the editors of a special issue of the *Journal of Popular Romance Studies* devoted to "Queering Popular Romance" (2016), "although there is burgeoning interest in LGBTQIA romance on the part of both LGBTQIA and straight authors, queer romance fiction remains peripheral to most academic accounts of the genre."

Heroic masculinities

Popular romance scholarship has largely focused on women, femininity, and heterosexuality, and when it does focus on men, this has largely been in terms of the discourses of power and patriarchy. Rarely was the performance of masculinity a concern. As such, one of the most interesting areas of development in recent years has been the study of men and masculinities in popular romance, not just at the level of characters, but also at the level of the roles men play in the industry, from readers to acquisition editors and publishers. Admittedly, much remains to be written, and a worthy site of analysis would be larger scale studies of how men read romances and what kinds of romances they read. Masculinities come into play not just in the heterosexual and heteronormative romances to which we have grown accustomed, but also, and importantly, in queerer manifestations of the genre. In this section, then, I address a growing body of scholarship on the critical study of men and masculinities and popular romance studies.

Much of the research on men and masculinities in popular romance has been at a textual level. Writing in 2002, Sarah S. G. Frantz writes that "the inclusion of the hero's perspective in narrative is the biggest change that romance has undergone in the last fifteen years" (18),[17] and it is perhaps the case that the novels considered by Snitow, Modleski, Radway, and others, were not presenting the complex and complicated hero that Frantz traces to the late 1980s and early 1990s. In any case, scholars are now asking more intricate and nuanced readings of the hero, his masculinity, and his maleness, while not surrendering a critical reading of these masculinities, particularly the matter of orthodox or hegemonic masculinity, a traditional, white, cisgendered, masculine corporeality, recalling here Erving Goffman's oft-cited description of this masculinity as

> young, married, white, urban, northern, heterosexual Protestant father of college education, fully employed, of good complexion, weight and height, and a recent record in sports ... Any male who fails to qualify in any of these ways is likely to view himself—during moments at least—as unworthy, incomplete, inferior.
>
> (128)

Contemporary scholars are thus not merely recuperating or re-centering men, but rather drawing on the growing body of scholarship in masculinity studies to explore the complexity of these characters.

Nowhere, perhaps, is this task more thoroughly considered than the edited collection, *Women Constructing Men: Female Novelists and Their Male Characters* (2010), which develops the study of how women write about men. While *Women Constructing Men* is largely focused on the literary rather than the popular, it contains one groundbreaking piece on popular romance, Frantz's "I've tried my entire life to be a good man: Suzanne Brockmann's Sam Starrett, Ideal Romance Hero," and the methods and approaches on display throughout the volume provide a language for thinking through female-authored masculinities. In her essay, Frantz shows how Brockmann is able to "construct, deconstruct, and reconstruct Sam's masculinity" over the course of six books (229). Frantz argues that Brockman is able to do this,

> in two powerful ways: by testing out four romance hero archetypes—the rapist hero, the rake, the unforgettable former lover, and the superhero—discarding each one as inadequate to the construction of a truly romance-worthy hero deserving of a happy ending; and by presenting two themes as particularly constitutive of masculinity: Sam's use of nicknames, both for himself and for Alyssa, and Sam's relationships with tears—again, both Alyssa's tears and his own.
>
> (229)

It is worth noting that for Frantz, tears in popular romance novels do quite a lot of work, especially around masculinity. For Frantz, in the romance novel, "boys do cry" (2009): quite a departure from the depictions of romance heroes in earlier scholarship, and an invitation for the discussion of popular romance novels to include a broader definition of masculinity.

One notable beneficiary of this call for different discussions about masculinity has been Jayashree Kamblé. In *Making Meaning in Popular Romance Fiction: An Epistemology* (2014), each chapter—on capitalism, war, heterosexuality, and white Protestantism—is mediated through a focus on masculinity. Drawing on Fredric Jameson's notion of "the political unconscious" rather than feminist and gender theories, Kamblé affords observations on characters in relation to the historical-political contexts in which the novels are written. Thus, for example, Kamblé argues that the military hero in late twentieth- and early twenty-first-century American romance is an "adaptation of the romance hero" which shows that "the genre is cognizant of the particular economic and military nexus" of this period: an approach that sharply contrasts with and usefully complements Frantz's discussion of military heroes in Brockmann (61). Likewise, Kamblé considers how the gay rights struggles affected the popular romance novel, suggesting that we might read the hypermasculinity of the 1970s as a reaction against gay liberation. Kamblé's intervention is an important one because it speaks explicitly to the cultural framework and context in which a text is written. That is, one cannot, nor should one, read these novels ahistorically or transhistorically; instead, one ought to remember, as Jameson would have it, to "always historicize!" (9).[18]

Veronica Kitchen has explored military masculinity and popular romance in her article, "Veterans and Military Masculinity in Popular Romance fiction." Kitchen argues that the popular romance novel "reinforces images of the solider as a resilient hero with a resilient intimate partner that are part of a larger social project implicating the family of soldiers in their recovery" (2). The recovery Kitchen is considering is post-traumatic stress disorder, a concern also considered by Kamblé, both in the *Making Meaning* monograph and in her earlier essay, "Patriotism, Passion, and PTSD: The Critique of War in Popular Romance Fiction" (2012). However, for Kamblé the hero is damaged by the state's organized violence, who must be healed by love that pulls him out of a militarized masculinity. In both Kitchen and Kamblé, then, we find the common trope of the hero who must be healed or cured so as to be able to love fully. Nonetheless, for Kitchen, these novels participate in the military industrial complex, and thus, she braids together popular romance studies, critical military studies, and critical studies of men and masculinities. In this way, Kitchen, like Kamblé, expands the scope of analysis to look at the sociological and cultural roles these novels play and how they respond to those contexts.

In my own work, "the romance novel depends on and is committed to an ideology of masculinity that needs to be engaged with and critique by scholars of critical masculinities" (2016 "Purity" 25). In my work, I have asked scholars of men and masculinities to take the popular romance seriously—in a sense, shifting the critical direction. If popular romance has much to say about masculinities, then surely masculinities has much to say about popular romance. In particular, I am interested in exploring Eva Illouz's question, "why is traditional masculinity pleasurable in fantasy?" (58), a question she poses in *Hard-Core Romance: Fifty Shades of Grey, Best-Sellers, and Society*. For me, as for others, "the hero is a representation of hegemonic masculinity," which is a kind of masculinity that has been called into question by a range of scholars including feminist theorists and scholars of men and masculinities. I am returning to the questions that motivated some of the early scholarship on the popular romance novel, for instance, the "spectacular masculinity" of Janice Radway (128) and the even older notion (in Snitow and Modleski) that the hero is an enigma to be understood. He is a bastion of hegemonic masculinity, which might be understood in common parlance as a kind of "toxic masculinity," and yet, within the popular romance novel, it is this very kind of masculinity that is often—though not always—on display. (The enigma, in short, is no longer *what kind of man he is* or *why is he behaving this way* but *why is such a version of masculinity still so pleasurable to readers?*)

Even as I am interested in Illouz's question, I am also interested in less traditional masculinities, for instance, the figure of the virginal hero. In my article, "Theorising Male Virginity in Popular Romance Novels" (2011) I sought to open the discussion of male virginity and provided a structuralist or archetypal reading of these heroes. My interest at the time was in thinking about how male virginity might challenge the structure of romance. This article considers a handful of novels that all introduced readers to a virginal hero and introduced a series of types of virgins, which I call archetypes, that appear within the genre: the sick virgin, the student virgin, the genius virgin, and the virgin-as-commodity. Today, these categories might be expanded, especially since this article did not consider male/male romance novels.

Future studies of masculinity and popular romance will want to explore the growing interest in the "fluidity" of masculinity. If society continues to see a decrease in homophobia as Mark McCormack has argued (2012), and we see a proliferation of masculinities (Anderson; Bridges; Bridges and Pascoe; Heasley; Hill) and shifting paradigms about acceptable behavior amongst men, for example, from spooning, cuddling, and kissing, (Anderson, Adams, and Rivers; Anderson and McCormack) to "the relaxing of the straight male anus," (Branfman, Stiritz, and Anderson 2018) then, one would hope, the popular romance genre would reflect these shifts. Where some of these shifting masculinities have been witnessed are in the space of male/male romance novels, which have remained surprisingly un(der)studied, given their market presence and growth since the mid-2000s. (The *Globe and Mail*, a national newspaper in Canada, has noted that "man-on-man fiction ... has taken a significant bite out of one of publishing's biggest markets".) M/m romance does not by any means eschew spectacular or hegemonic masculinity, but it is also a site of a far more diverse array of gender representations, "from the campy queen, to the alpha male, to the butch bottom, to the gay-for-you hero" (Allan 68).

One study that pays particular attention to these shifting masculinities is Marlon B. Ross's "'What's Love But a Second Hand Emotion?': Man-on-Man Passion in the Contemporary Black Gay Romance Novel" (2013) which braids together sexuality and race in important ways. In his article, he challenges the "homonormal formula of gay love as identical to and equal with white middle-class heterosexual procreation" (676), and shows,

> *why* the homonormalizing hegemony needs to exclude black men from romance and *how* this racial exclusion produces further linguistic and ideological confusion into the project of imagining black man-on-man passion as both realistically grounded and socially resonant as black indigenous fantasy.
>
> (676–7)

Ross's article builds on intersectional approaches to consider the complicated questions found in Black queer studies, especially when those questions involve men.[19] While Ross admits that these novels do "not explicitly challenge the romance formulae upon which both the heterosexual and more recently homonormative genre is anchored," we must, at the same time recognize that

> by putting new wine in old bottles, however, these black gay romancers create room for black men in love with other men, and Harris and Hardy do so while making the white heternorm peripheral to the exploration of black man-on-man passion.
>
> (Ross 683)

Ross's article is an important intervention in the study of popular romance formula precisely because it considers race, sex, and gender, and reminds readers of the importance of an intersectional approach to the study of the genre.

The rising popularity of male/male popular romance novels has sparked interest in the readers of these books. Kacey Whalen's MA thesis, "A Consumption of Gay Men: Navigating the Shifting Boundaries of M/M Romantic Readership," focuses at length on the texts and readers of K.J. Charles, one of the most acclaimed authors of M/M romance. Whalen's thesis explores why women might want to read and/or write male/male romance novels, looking at reasons that readers themselves describe. These include "acceptance," "the novels help to guide activism," "the novels provide a better understanding of various and differing experiences," "two men are more appealing," the relationships are "more equal," "love is love," an "exploration of sexuality," and a desire to avoid problematic female representation (12–30). Of course, as Whalen notes, there are issues and problems to be accounted for as well, noting that

> perhaps the largest qualm opponents of women engaging with m/m romance novel have is the very gender of the participants themselves. Much of the contention around the genre comes from women writing about gay men for profit—without having their lived experiences—with an audience comprised mainly of other women.
>
> (30)

This is an important critique of the m/m romance novel, particularly as there is a kind of cultural appropriation; however, such a critique often does not take into account the intersectional politics of the authors and/or readers. That is, many of the authors of m/m romance are themselves diverse: queer men and women, genderqueer, agender, and transgender. But, importantly, as Sarah Frantz has noted, "M/m is still growing as a genre ... It's had and continues to have growing pains, but it's maturing quickly" (in Bhattacharjee (22); a point echoed by Whalen (82)). And while the genre is maturing, so too must the criticism of the genre. Indeed, there is much to be written on male/male romance novels as cultural artifacts and as objects for consumption, as well as the common themes that appeared in critiques of the genre, for instance, straight women consuming and writing fictions about gay men. But, for instance, how are critics to account for the homonormative impulses and desires of the genre? How can a radical potential be imagined in what remains a relatively conservative genre that celebrates marriage and being, in the words of Andrew Sullivan, "virtually normal"? (1995). The male/male popular romance is a rich area of research that will certainly provide much to critics working with queer theory, psychoanalysis, critical studies of men and masculinities, and sexualities studies.

Conclusion and future directions

In an endnote buried in her book, *Happily Ever After: The Romance Story in Popular Culture*, Catherine Roach presents a series of questions, all of which, I think speak to the future of the study of gender and sexuality in popular romance novels. Roach writes:

> So what about the male reader, the lesbian reader, the queer reader, the asexual reader? What are the meanings, the pleasures, and the alienations of the romance reading experience for them? More generally, how does diversity in gender and sexuality change people's relationships to the wider romance story as it operates in culture? How does this diversity queer the romance story? Although today's popular romance is not read exclusively by heterosexual women, such is the main target audience. As the genre continues to develop and change the rise of more LGBTQ (lesbian, gay, bisexual, transgender, queer) books and publishing lines, it will be fascinating to think more about these larger questions and broader demographics.
>
> (199, n. 8)

While Roach is speaking here about readers, it would seem to me that these same questions could and should be asked of authors and publishers, most of whom are themselves readers of romance. Like Roach, I am fascinated by what these shifts in culture might mean for the popular romance novel. There are so many aspects of gender and sexuality that have yet to be accounted for, for instance, how does asexuality affect the romance novel, especially when it seems so predicated on sexuality? How might trans⋆ romance novels affect the genre—for instance, how will trans⋆ characters challenge what remain its gender norms? How will these trans⋆ identities be represented by cisgender authors? How are other archetypes of the popular romance novel affected by a growing popular interest in gender and sexuality more broadly, for instance, how are the representations of virgins and virginity loss changing in romance? Many of these topics are starting to be addressed in conference papers, and many have been discussed on author and reader websites, but as I write this, few have been explored in peer-reviewed scholarly publications.

One unresolvable conundrum, or at least one that has ongoing permanence, is the relationship between pornography and popular romance. Future work should continue to think about this relationship because both pornography and popular romance have much to say not only about gender and sexuality, but also how gender and sexuality inform and help us understand ideas like love and desire. Certainly, we have witnessed some interest in popular romance and pornography, such as isolated chapters in Susan Ostrov Weisser's *The Glass Slipper* and Catherine Roach's *Happily Ever After*, but it seems that much remains to be written. One of the most exciting works to tackle this in recent years is Lucy Neville's *Girls Who Like Boys Who Like Boys: Women and Gay Male Pornography and Erotica* (2018), which considers the reasons why women consume gay male erotic and pornographic texts ranging from films to slash, romance novels, and *yaoi* (m/m "boys-love" media, including manga, anime, video games, and so on). This study braids together textual analysis, visual analysis, critical theory, and human participatory research, and thus reminds us of the interdisciplinary importance of the study of popular romance.

Finally, in recent years, we have seen a growing interest in the ways nationality and nationalism can affect and influence the romance novel: a topic that lends itself to analysis along gender lines. María del Mar Pérez-Gil's "Representations of Nation and Spanish Masculinity in Popular Romance Novels: The Alpha Male as 'Other'" considers how discourses of gender and nationality inform one another in the treatment of Spain and Spanish men; a similar concern is the focus of Amira Jarmakani's *An Imperialist Love Story: Desert Romances and the War on Terror*, which studies "desert romances" not only in light of a global-political context (the post-9/11 historical moment) but in terms of how romance novelists construct and represent Arab and/or Muslim masculinities. Building on Jarmakani's monograph and on related studies of Orientalism, gender, and romance by Burge and Teo and Teo, Kecia Ali's essay "Troubleshooting Post-9/11 America: Religion, Racism, and Stereotypes in Suzanne Brockmann's *Into the Night* and *Gone Too Far*" explores the interplay between racial, religious, national, and gendered identity in the heroes and heroines of these texts: a useful model for scholars interested in applying general claims about the genre (or particular subgenres, such as desert or military romance) to the analysis of particular novels and authorial oeuvres.

The task of studying popular romance fiction can seem daunting because the archive is so deep and diverse and the possibilities so many. That said, the range of disciplines and contexts in which popular romance can be discussed has greatly expanded in the past decade, and scholarship focused on gender and sexuality in the genre has begun to appear in perhaps surprising places: for example, the *Journal of Men's Studies* has now published a few essays on the popular romance novel (Allan; Pérez-Gil 2019), and *Critical Military Studies* has also published an article on veterans and military masculinity in the genre (Kitchen 2018). These are, therefore, exciting times to study popular romance. The attributes that can make the genre daunting to study also ensure that it will remain a fruitful area of inquiry for many years to come.

Notes

1 I thank Sophie Been for her assistance with this chapter. The phrase "Harlequin Formula" appears in a range of articles on romance (Carroll; Darbyshire; Holmes; Kipnis; Mulhern; Taylor) as does the phrase "Harlequin Romance Formula" (Dolan; Roy).
2 For critiques of this idea see Ruti.
3 See Illouz.
4 Although Roach discusses the romance/pornography nexus throughout her book, her most explicit treatments of the topic can be found in the chapter "Good Girls Do" (78–103). More on Roach's thought and related scholarship can be found in Chapter 19 (which she co-authored) of this Research Companion.
5 Kinsale's argument has been given greater philosophical (Heideggerian) elaboration in Deborah Lutz's monograph *The Dangerous Lover: Gothic Villains, Byronism, and the Nineteenth-Century Seduction Narrative* (2006).
6 Scholarship on modern popular Gothic romance antedates and overlaps with these pieces by Snitow and Modleski (who has a separate chapter on the Gothic in *Loving With a Vengeance*), and it often addresses issues of gender and sexuality. This scholarship and its legacy are explored in detail in Chapter 4 of this Research Companion.
7 Raewyn Connell, for instance, had not yet published *Masculinities* and had only begun to develop an account of something akin to what we now call "hegemonic masculinity."
8 "The longing for reunion for the mother overrides taboos on homosexuality," Radway explains, and this in turn sometimes provokes romance authors to other and abject lesbian

characters, in order "to demonstrate otherwise, to assert, in effect, that mother has nothing to do with lesbianism!" (154).

9 Radway would later describe these novels as documenting an "anxiety about gender construction" that is "widespread in the culture" ("Romance and the Work of Fantasy" 409). For an extended discussion of the hero's heterosexual masculinity in the 1970s–80s as an anxious or defensive reaction to alternative masculinities at the time, including the rise of gay rights, see Kamblé (87–130).

10 In addition to Illouz's monograph *Hard-Core Romance: Fifty Shades of Grey, Best-Sellers, and Society*, discussed below, I would point readers to Claire Trevenen's "Fifty Shades of 'Mommy Porn': A Post-GFC Renegotiation of Paternal Law" (2014).

11 For more on Australian romances, including from a gender/sexuality perspective, see Bellanta (2014) and the scholarship reviewed in Chapter 3 of this Research Guide; for more on African American romance, see Chapter 10.

12 Kamblé, too, sees the genre's insistence on heterosexuality as betraying a fundamental anxiety, with attention to cross-dressing as a motif. See in particular her chapters on "Heterosexuality: Negotiating Normative Romance Novel Desire" and "White Protestantism: Race and Religious Ethos in Romance Novels," both in *Making Meaning in Popular Romance Fiction*.

13 For accounts of lesbian pulp romance, on its own and in dialogue with more recent romance fiction, see Lynch, Sternglantz, and Barot (2012), Matelski (2016), and Gunn and Harker (2013). For curated samples of these texts, see: Bronski (2013); Slide (2013); and Forrest (2005).

14 The shorthand "F/F" is used to indicate that the protagonists of a text are both women; this category overlaps with lesbian romance, but may also include novels where either one or both of the women is bisexual or pansexual, rather than lesbian.

15 Lynch is also an established lesbian romance author, under the name Nell Stark. The relationship between "Queering the Romantic Heroine" and Stark's novels has yet to be explored.

16 For some first steps along these lines, see Greenfeld-Benovitz, "The Interactive Romance Community: The Case of 'Covers Gone Wild.'"

17 It is, perhaps, worth noting that the genre did not exclusively offer the heroine's perspective before the turn that Frantz describes. E.M. Hull's *The Sheik*, for example, spends a good deal of time in Sheik Ahmed's point of view.

18 Kamblé's insistence on a rigorously historicist approach to popular romance aligns her with the arguments of Mary Bly in "On Popular Romance, J. R. Ward, and the Limits of Genre Study." For more on Bly and historicist readings of romance, see Chapter 13 of this Research Companion.

19 For a larger consideration of Black queer studies, see: Ferguson's *Aberrations in Black: A Queer of Color Critique* (2003); Johnson and Henderson's edited collection *Black Queer Studies: A Critical Anthology* (2005); Johnson's edited collection *No Tea, No Shade: New Writings in Black Queer Studies* (2016).

Works cited

Ali, Kecia. "Troubleshooting Post-9/11 America: Religion, Racism, and Stereotypes in Suzanne Brockmann's Into the Night and Gone Too Far." *Journal of Popular Romance Studies*, vol. 6, no. 2, 2017, n.p.

Allan, Jonathan A. "The Purity of His Maleness: Masculinity in Popular Romance Novels." *Journal of Popular Romance Studies*, vol. 42, no. 1, 2016a, pp. 24–41.

Allan, Jonathan A. *Reading from Behind: A Cultural Analysis of the Anus*. University of Regina Press, 2016b.

Anderson, Eric. *The Monogamy Gap: Men, Love, and the Reality of Cheating*. Oxford University Press, 2012.

———. *21st Century Jocks: Sporting Men and Contemporary Heterosexuality*. Palgrave MacMillan, 2014.

Anderson, Eric, Adi Adams and Ian Rivers. "'I Kiss Them because I Love Them': The Emergence of Heterosexual Men Kissing in British Institutes of Education." *Archives of Sexual Behavior*, vol. 41, no. 2, 2012, pp. 421–430.

Anderson, Eric and Mark McCormack. "Cuddling and Spooning: Heteromasculinity and Homosocial Tactility among Student-athletes." *Men and Masculinities*, vol. 18, no. 2, 2015, pp. 214–230.

Barot, Len. "Queer Romance in Twentieth- and Twenty-First-Century America: Snapshots of a Revolution." *Romance Fiction and American Culture: Love as the Practice of Freedom?*, edited by William A. Gleason, and Eric Murphy Selinger, Ashgate, 2016, pp. 389–404.

Bellanta, Melissa. "A Masculine Romance: The Sentimental Bloke and Australian Culture in the War- and Early Interwar Years." *Journal of Popular Romance Studies*, vol. 4, no. 2, 2014, n.p.

Belsey, Catherine. "Carol Thurston," The Romance Revolution: Erotic Novels for Women and the Quest for a New Sexual Identity "(Book Review)." *The Modern Language Review*, vol. 85, no. 4, 1990, pp. 906–907.

———. "Rev. Of *the Romance Revolution: Erotic Novels for Women and the Quest for a New Sexual Identity* by Carol Thurston." *Modern Language Review*, vol. 85, no. 4, 1990, p. 907.

———. *Desire: Love stories in Western culture*. Oxford: Blackwell, 1994.

———. "Popular Fiction and the Feminine Masquerade." *European Journal of English Studies*, vol. 2, no. 3, 1998, pp. 343–358.

Betz, Phyllis M. *Lesbian Romance Novels: A History and Critical Analysis*. McFarland, 2009.

Bhattacharjee, Mala. "It's Raining Men: Tackling the Torrents of Male/Male Romantic Fiction Flooding the Market." *RT Book Reviews*, Sep. 2012, pp. 22–26.

Branfman, Jonathan, Susan Stiritz and Eric Anderson. "Relaxing the Straight Male Anus: Decreasing Homohysteria around Anal Eroticism." *Sexualities*, vol. 21, no. 1–2, 2018, pp. 109–127.

Bridges, Tristan. "A Very 'Gay' Straight? Hybrid Masculinities, Sexual Aesthetics, and the Changing Relationship between Masculinity and Homophobia." *Gender & Society*, vol. 28, no. 1, 2014, pp. 58–82.

Bridges, Tristan and C.J. Pascoe. "Hybrid Masculinities: New Directions in the Sociology of Men and Masculinities." *Sociology Compass*, vol. 8, no. 3, 2014, pp. 246–258.

Bronski, Michael, ed. *Pulp Friction: Uncovering the Golden Age of Gay Male Pulps*. St. Martin's Griffin, 2013.

Burge, Amy. *Representing Difference in the Medieval and Modern Orientalist Romance*. Houndmills, Basingstoke, Hampshire: Palgrave MacMillan, 2016.

Burley, Stephanie. "What's a Nice Girl like You Doing in a Book like This?" Homoerotic Reading and Popular Romance." *Doubled Plots: Romance and History*, edited by Susan Strehle, and Mary Paniccia Carden, U of Mississippi, 2003, pp. 127–146.

Carroll, Noël. "The Paradox of Junk Fiction." *Philosophy and Literature*, vol. 18, no. 2, 1994, pp. 225–241.

Cohn, Jan. *Romance and the Erotics of Property: Mass-Market Fiction for Women*. Duke University Press, 1988.

Darbyshire, Peter. "The Politics of Love: Harlequin Romances and the Christian Right." *Journal of Popular Culture*, vol. 35, no. 4, 2002, pp. 75–87.

Dixon, jay. *The Romance Fiction of Mills & Boon, 1909-1990s*. University College London Press, 1999.

Dolan, Jill. "The Dynamics of Desire: Sexuality and Gender in Pornography and Performance." *Theatre Journal*, vol. 39, no. 2, 1987, pp. 156–174.

Dominguez, Ivo. *Beneath the Skins: The New Spirit and Politics of the Kink Community*. Daedalus, 1994.

Duggan, Lisa. *The Twilight of Equality: Neoliberalism, Cultural Politics, and the Attack of Democracy*. Beacon Press, 2003.

Ferguson, Roderick A. *Aberrations in Black: A Queer of Color Critique*. University of Minnesota Press, 2003.

Fletcher, Lisa. *Historical Romance Fiction: Heterosexuality and Performativity*. Ashgate, 2008.

Forrest, Katherine, ed. *Lesbian Pulp Fiction: The Sexually Intrepid World of Lesbian Paperback Novels 1950-1965*. Cleis Press, 2005.

Frank, Katherine. *Playing Well in Groups: A Journey Through the World of Group Sex*. Rowman & Littlefield, 2013.

Frantz, Sarah S. G. "'Expressing' Herself: The Romance Novel and the Feminine Will to Power." *Scorned Literature: Essays on the History and Criticism of Popular Mass-Produced Fiction in America*, edited by Lydia Cushman, and Deidre Johnson, Greenwood Press, 2002, pp. 17–36.

———. "Darcy's Vampiric Descendants: Austen's Perfect Romance Hero and J. R. Ward's Black Dagger Brotherhood." *Persuasions Online*, vol. 30, 2009, http://jasna.org/persuasions/on-line/vol30no1/frantz.html.

———. "'I've Tried My Entire Life to Be a Good Man': Suzanne Brockmann's Sam Starrett, Ideal Romance Hero." *Women Constructing Men: Female Novelists and Their Male Characters, 1750–2000*, edited by Sarah S. G. Frantz, and Katharina Rennhak, Lexington Books, 2010, pp. 227–247.

———. "'How We Love *Is* Our Soul': Joey W. Hill's BDSM Romance Holding the Cards." *New Approaches to Popular Romance Fiction*, edited by Sarah S. G. Frantz, and Eric Murphy Selinger, McFarland, 2012, pp. 47–59.

Frantz, Sarah S. G. and Katharina Rennhak. "Female Novelists and Their Male Characters, 1750–2000: An Introduction." *Women Constructing Men: Female Novelists and Their Male Characters, 1750-2000*, edited by Sarah S. G. Frantz, and Katharina Rennhak, Lexington Books, 2010, pp. 1–10.

Goffman, Erving. *Stigma: Notes on the Management of Spoiled Identity*. Simon & Schuster, 1963.

Goris, An. "Matricide in Romance Scholarship? Response to Pamela Regis' Keynote Address at the Second Annual Conference of the International Association for the Study of Popular Romance." *Journal of Popular Romance Studies*, vol. 2, no. 1, 2011, http://jprstudies.org/2011/10/"matricide-in-romance-scholarship-response-to-pamela-regis'-keynote-address-at-the-second-annual-conference-of-the-international-association-for-the-study-of-popular-romance"/.

Gunn, Drewey Wayne and Jaime Harker. *1960s Gay Pulp Fiction: The Misplaced Heritage*. University of Massachusetts Press, 2013.

Heasley, Robert. "Queer Masculinities of Straight Men: A Typology." *Men and Masculinities*, vol. 7, no. 3, 2005, pp. 310–320.

Herendeen, Ann. *Pride/Prejudice*. HarperCollins, 2010.

———. "The Upper-Class Bisexual Top as Romantic Hero: (Pre)dominant in the Social Structure and in the Bedroom." *Journal of Popular Romance Studies*, vol. 3, no. 1, 2012, http://jprstudies.org/2012/10/the-upper-class-bisexual-top-as-romantic-hero-predominant-in-the-social-structure-and-in-the-bedroom-by-ann-herendeen/.

———. "Having It Both Ways; Or, Writing from the Third Perspective: The Revolutionary M/M/F Ménage Romance Novel." *Romance Fiction and American Culture: Love as the Practice of Freedom?*, edited by William A. Gleason, and Eric Murphy Selinger, Ashgate, 2016, pp. 405–419.

Hermes, Joke. "Sexuality in Lesbian Romance Fiction." *Feminist Review*, vol. 42, no. 1, 1992, pp. 49–66.

———. "Entertainment or Enlightenment - Sexuality in Lesbian Romance Novels." *Argument*, vol. 34, no. 3, pp. 389–402.

Hill, Darryl B. "'Feminine' Heterosexual Men: Subverting Heteropatriarchal Sexual Scripts?" *Journal of Men's Studies*, vol. 14, no. 2, 2007, pp. 145–159.

Holmes, Diana. *Romance and Readership in Twentieth-Century France: Love Stories*. Oxford University Press, 2006.

Iannacci, Ellio. "What Women Want: Gay Male Romance Novels," *The Globe and Mail*, 11 Feb., 2011, n.p.

Illouz, Eva. *Hard-Core Romance: Fifty Shades of Grey, Best-Sellers, and Society*. University of Chicago Press, 2016.

Iser, Wolfgang. *The Implied Reader: Patterns of Communication in Prose Fiction from Bunyan to Beckett*. Baltimore: Johns Hopkins UP, 1974.

Jameson, Fredric. *The Political Unconscious: Narrative as a Socially Symbolic Act*. Cornell University Press, 1981.

Janice, Radway and Janice Radway. "Romance and the Work of Fantasy: Struggles over Feminine Sexuality and Subjectivity at Century's End." *Viewing, Reading, Listening: Audiences and Cultural Reception*, edited by Jon Cruz, and Justin Lewis, Westview Press, 1994, pp. 213–231.

Jarmakani, Amira. *An Imperialist Love Story: Desert Romances and the War on Terror*. New York University Press, 2015.

Johnson, E. Patrick and Mae G. Henderson, eds. *Black Queer Studies: A Critical Anthology*. Duke University Press, 2005.

Juhasz, Suzanne. "Lesbian Romance Fiction and the Plotting of Desire: Narrative Theory, Lesbian Identity, and Reading Practice." *Tulsa Studies in Women's Literature*, vol. 17, no. 1, 1998, pp. 65–82.

Kamblé, Jayashree. *Making Meaning in Popular Romance Fiction: An Epistemology*. Palgrave MacMillan, 2014.

Kipnis, Laura. "Feminism: The Political Conscience of Postmodernism." *Social Text*, vol. 21, 1989, pp. 149–166.

Kitchen, Veronica. "Veterans and Military Masculinity in Popular Romance Fiction." *Critical Military Studies*, vol. 4, no. 1, 2018, pp. 34–51.

Lutz, Deborah. *The Dangerous Lover: Gothic Villains, Byronism, and the Nineteenth-Century Seduction Narrative*. The Ohio State University Press, 2006.

Lynch, Katherine E., Ruth E. Sternglantz and Len Barot. "Queering the Romantic Heroine: Where Her Power Lies." *Journal of Popular Romance Studies*, vol. 3, no. 1, 2012, http://jprstudies.org/wp-content/uploads/2012/10/JPRS3.1_QueeringHeroine.pdf.

Matelski, Elizabeth. "'I'm Not the Only Lesbian Who Wears a Skirt': Lesbian Romance Fiction and Identity in Post-World War II America." *Romance Fiction and American Culture: Love as the Practice of Freedom?*, edited by William A. Gleason, and Eric Murphy Selinger, Ashgate, 2016, pp. 87–104.

McAlister, Jodi. "'You and I are Human, and There Is Something between Us': Untamed and Queering the Heterosexual Historical Romance." *Journal of Popular Romance Studies*, vol. 5, no. 2, 2016, http://jprstudies.org/wp-content/uploads/2016/07/YAIAH.07.2016.pdf.

McCormack, Mark. *The Declining Significance of Homophobia: How Teenage Boys are Redefining Masculinity and Heterosexuality*. Oxford University Press, 2012.

Miles, Angela. "Confessions of a Harlequin Reader: Romance and the Myth of Male Mothers." *The Hysterical Male: New Feminist Theory*, edited by Arthur Kroker, and Marilousie Kroker, New World Perspectives, 1991, pp. 93–131.

Modleski, Tania. "My Life as a Romance Reader." *Paradoxa*, vol. 3, no. 1–2, 1997, pp. 15–28.

———. "My Life as a Romance Writer." *Old Wives Tales: Feminist Re-Visions and Other Fictions*, I.B. Tauris, 1998, pp. 66–79.

———. *Loving with a Vengeance: Mass-Produced Fantasies for Women*. Routledge, 2008.

Moore, Kate and Eric Murphy Selinger. "The Heroine as Reader, the Reader as Heroine: Jennifer Crusie's *Welcome to Temptation*." *Journal of Popular Romance Studies*, vol. 2 no. 2, 2012, n.p.

Mulhern, Chieko Irie. "Japanese Harlequin Romances as Transcultural Woman's Fiction." *The Journal of Asian Studies*, vol. 48, no. 1, 1989, pp. 50–70.

Mussell, Kay. "Where's the Love Gone? Transformations in Romance Fiction and Scholarship." *Paradoxa*, vol. 3, no. 1–2, 1997, pp. 3–14.

Neville, Lucy. *Girls Who Like Boys Who Like Boys: Women and Gay Male Pornography and Erotica*. Palgrave MacMillan, 2018.

Patrick, Johnson, E., editor. *No Tea, No Shade: New Writings in Black Queer Studies*. Duke University Press, 2016.

Perel, Ester. *The State of Affairs: Rethinking Infidelity*. Harper, 2017.

Pérez-Gil, M. D. M. "Representations of Nation and Spanish Masculinity in Popular Romance Novels: The Alpha Male as 'Other.'" *The Journal of Men's Studies*, vol. 27, no. 2, 2019, pp. 169–182.

Radway, Janice. *Reading the Romance: Women, Patriarchy, and Popular Literature*. Chapel Hill: University of North Carolina Press, 1984.

Regis, Pamela. "What Do Critics Owe the Romance?" *Journal of Popular Romance Studies*, vol. 2, no. 1, 2011, http://jprstudies.org/wp-content/uploads/2011/10/JPRS2.1_Regis_Keynote.pdf.

Roach, Catherine M. *Happily Ever After: The Romance Story in Popular Culture*. University of Indiana Press, 2016.

Ross, Marlon B. "'What's Love but a Second Hand Emotion?': Man-on-Man Passion in the Contemporary Black Gay Romance Novel." *Callaloo*, vol. 36, no. 3, 2013, pp. 669–687.

Roy, Srijanee. "Indian Chick Lit: Desiring or Deriding the 'Other'?" *Gendering the Narrative: Indian English Fiction and Gender Discourse*, edited by Nibedita Mukherjee, Cambridge Scholars Publishing, 2015, pp. 43–52.

Ruti, Mari. *The Case for Falling in Love*. Source Books, 2011a.

———. *The Summons of Love*. Columbia University Press, 2011b.

———. *Penis Envy & Other Bad Feelings: The Emotional Costs of Every Day Life*. Columbia University Press, 2018.

Schippers, Mimi. *Beyond Monogamy: Polyamory and the Future of Polyqueer Sexualities*. New York University Press, 2016.

Scoats, Ryan, Lauren J. Joseph and Eric Anderson. "'I Don't Mind Watching Him Cum': Heterosexual Men, Threesomes, and the Erosion of the One-time Rule of Homosexuality." *Sexualities*, vol. 21, no. 1–2, 2018, pp. 30–48.

Sedgwick, Eve Kosofsky. *Between Men: English Literature and Male Homosocial Desire*. Columbia University Press, 1985.

Selinger, Eric Murphy. "Re-Reading the Romance." *Contemporary Literature*, vol. 48 no. 2, Summer, 2007, pp. 307–324.

Selinger, Eric Murphy and Sarah S. G. Frantz. "Introduction: New Approaches to Popular Romance Fiction." *New Approaches to Popular Romance Fiction*, edited by Sarah S. G. Frantz, and Eric Murphy Selinger, McFarland, 2012, pp. 1–19.

Slide, Anthony. *Lost Gay Novels: A Reference Guide to Fifty Works from the First Half of the Twentieth Century*. Routledge, 2013.

Snitow, Ann Barr. "Mass Market Romance: Pornography for Women Is Different." *Radical History Review*, vol. 20, no. 20, 1979, pp. 141–161.

Struve, Laura. "Sisters of Sorts: Reading Romantic Fiction and the Bonds Among Female Readers." *The Journal of Popular Culture*, vol. 44, no. 6, 2011, pp. 1289–1306.

Sullivan, Andrew. *Virtually Normal: An Argument about Homosexuality*. Vintage Books, 1995.

Taylor, Jessica. "Romance and the Female Gaze Obscuring Gendered Violence in the Twilight Saga." *Feminist Media Studies*, vol. 14, no. 3, 2014, pp. 388–402.

Teo, Hsu-Ming. *Desert Passions: Orientalism and Romance Novels*. University of Texas Press, 2012.

———. "Orientalism, Freedom, and Feminism in Popular Romance Culture." *Romance Fiction and American Culture: Love as the Practice of Freedom?*, edited by William A. Gleason, and Eric Murphy Selinger, Ashgate, 2016, pp. 181–203.

Therrien, Kathleen. "Straight to the Edges: Gay and Lesbian Characters and Cultural Conflict in Popular Romance Fiction." *New Approaches to Popular Romance Fiction*, edited by Sarah S. G. Frantz, and Eric Murphy Selinger, McFarland, 2012, pp. 164–177.

Thurston, Carol. *The Romance Revolution: Erotic Novels for Women and the Quest for a New Sexual Identity*. University of Illinois Press, 1987.

Trevenen, Claire. "Fifty Shades of 'Mommy Porn': A Post-GFC Renegotiation of Paternal Law." *Journal of Popular Romance Studies*, vol. 4, no. 1, 2014, n.p.

Veldman-Genz, Carole. "The More the Merrier? Transformations of the Love Triangle Across the Romance." *New Approaches to Popular Romance Fiction*, edited by Sarah S. G. Frantz, and Eric Murphy Selinger, McFarland, 2012, pp. 108–120.

Weisser, Susan Ostrov. "Is Female to Romance as Male Is to Porn." *The Glass Slipper: Women and Love Stories*, Rutgers University Press, 2013, pp. 171–180.

West, Xan. "On Internalizing the Cis Gaze When Thinking about Sex and Relationships." *Kink Praxis*. 29 March, 2017, https://xanwest.wordpress.com/2017/03/29/on-internalizing-the-cis-gaze-when-thinking-about-sex-and-relationships/.

Whelan, Kacey. "A Consumption of Gay Men: Navigating the Shifting Boundaries of M/M Romantic Readership," Dissertation, DePaul University, 2017.

Wood, Andrea. *Radicalizing Romance: Subculture, Sex, and Media at the Margins*. Dissertation, University of Florida, 2008.

Wood, Andrea and Jonathan A. Allan. "Introduction. Queering the Popular Romance." *Journal of Popular Romance Studies*, vol. 5, no. 1, 2016, http://jprstudies.org/2016/07/special-issue-queering-popular-romance-editors-introductionby-andrea-wood-and-jonathan-a-allan/.

21 Love and romance novels

Hsu-Ming Teo

Romantic love is not a specific, precise emotion; it is a bundle of ideas, values, and feelings, and a historically changeable set of cultural practices. The historian William Reddy, who specializes in the history of emotions and investigates cultural texts in conjunction with current psychological and neuroscientific scholarship, argues that there is no universal understanding of "sex" or "love," or the relationship between the two. While all human societies share the experience of sexual desire, affection, and what Reddy calls a "longing for association" (6), the meanings of sex and love are culturally constituted and do not exist independently of historically-specific societies. As sociologist Steven Seidman observes, "love has no essential or unitary identity. Not only does its meaning change over time, but within a given society at a fixed time there will be variations in its meaning" (4). For instance, factors such as "gender, class, education, or social status shape cultural meanings and practices" of love (4). Thus "what has been called by one name—romantic love—was actually a variety of emotional states within different historical situations" (Lystra 28).

That romantic love is socially and culturally constituted, and historically contingent, has important implications for romantic fiction. As understandings of love transform over time, these changing meanings are reflected in how romance novels represent falling in love, being in love, what love means, and what love is supposed to do to and for lovers. In turn, the discourses of love represented in romance novels feed back into and influence how particular societies recognize and understand the operation of romantic love in popular culture. This chapter explores how love is represented in romance novels. It begins with an outline of the ways in which ideas about romantic love have developed and changed over the course of the nineteenth to the twenty-first centuries, and it then considers the extent to which these changing ideas about love have been reflected in romance novels during this period. The chapter concludes with a discussion of the extant scholarship—mostly generated by feminist academics in the wake of second-wave feminism—about how we should understand portrayals of love in romance fiction, and what implications these meanings have for society and for romance novels themselves.

Love in the Western world

The one fundamental idea about romantic love in European-derived cultures throughout the last millennium is that love—especially "true love"—is different from, and superior to, lust or sexual desire even though it incorporates desire; love transcends the physical appetites of the body. As William Reddy observes:

> In a common Western way of feeling, romantic love is paired with sexual desire. The lover feels both at once, yet the two feelings are in tension with each other. Desire is an appetite, self-regarding, pleasure seeking. Love is other-directed and entails placing the good of the beloved above one's own.
>
> (1)

This dualism between love and desire, between the attitudes of the mind/soul/spirit as opposed to the appetites of the body, is peculiar to Western society. It developed during the eleventh and twelfth centuries when the troubadours employed at various southern French courts conceptualized true love as a sacred force that could transcend sexual desire and elevate the lover to a sacred, pure plane of love that was spiritual in its effect. Scholars are divided over how this particular notion of love originated, variously attributing it to an autochthonous development in the Occitan region (Rougemont); claiming that it had Hispano-Arabic roots in Andalusia and spread to southern France (Menocal); or, most recently, arguing that this ideology of romantic love—called *fin'amors*—developed in response to the sexually repressive dictates emerging from the Catholic Gregorian reforms that began in the middle of the eleventh century. The Church held that the body, as a base, separate entity from the soul or spirit, was inherently sinful, and therefore sexual desire was impure, polluting the spirit and imperiling the immortal soul. In response to such sexually repressive dictates, troubadours and the aristocratic elite they served developed an alternative, sacred vision of love that mastered and purified sexual desire (Reddy chapters 1 and 2).[1]

Whatever the origins of this concept of romantic love, it was unique to Western Europe. In his comparative study of non-European writings during the same period from Japan and South Asia, Reddy argues that there is no similar distinction between the desires and appetites of the body, and that of the spirit or soul, because human sexual activity was regarded as inherently spiritual in such cultures. Lynn Pan, in her exploration of the philosophical and literary roots of love in Chinese writings, agrees that romantic love is unique to Western culture because Chinese culture did not envisage a mind/body or spirit/body split and therefore could not conceive of a sublime, spiritualized love that transcended bodily sexual desire.

This point is significant because the idea that true love is a transcendent force distinct from lust continues to dominate romance novels today. The one story that the popular romance tells over and over again is how romantic protagonists (especially the hero) learn to love, rather than merely desire, each other:

> True love motivates the lover to master self-regarding desire. Loving self-restraint, because it subordinates desire to concern for the other's well-being, in turn renders desire potentially innocent. When the beloved returns one's love, and when neither of the two lovers' well-being is threatened by sexual embrace, then love and desire may both be fulfilled without harm. The opposition between love and desire is thus a productive one.
>
> (Reddy 1)

It produces, among other things, the happy ending to modern romance novels. Since the Middle Ages, other fundamental ideas have gradually accreted around the Western concept of true love: it is monogamous, lasting, individually focused, and individuating. The object of love is not interchangeable with others, and love confers distinction upon the lover and the beloved, making them unique and special. Beyond these enduring core qualities, however, other clusters of ideas and values around love have changed over time.

Various ideas about romantic love have circulated across European cultures since the twelfth century, finding expression in, for instance, Renaissance poetry and Shakespearean comedies. However, despite the existence of romantic love as a literary ideal, it was not until the late eighteenth and early nineteenth centuries that marriage for love rather than for interest (for example, strategic alliances, class status, or economic reasons) began to be contracted on a wider scale in Europe (Giddens 39) and the newly formed United States of America (Rothman 31, Stone 19). The nineteenth century saw the spread of marriage for love and, unsurprisingly, the rise of courtship stories and advice literature that began to articulate new ideas about romantic love in Western societies. Prior to the eighteenth century, love was understood as a set of actions and behaviors such as cooperation, mutual assistance, and self-restraint. It was demonstrated by social rituals and observable behavior. By the nineteenth century, however, love was increasingly understood in terms of self-fulfillment through the "capacity for sharing feeling and intimacy" (Gillis 88).

Once love was redefined primarily as feeling, once its value inhered in individual self-fulfillment, the issue of how to recognize such feelings, and what these feelings entailed, became a problem for courting couples. In Britain, for example, when love and marriage became entangled, love became something of a puzzle because the stakes for true love were so high. If contracting a marriage no longer depended on parental arrangement but on love, then it was important to recognize and understand when one was truly in love, and loved in return. People in the late nineteenth and early twentieth centuries sought advice about how to recognize emotional authenticity, how to determine if what they were feeling was really love, what part passion played in love, and whether sexual desire was really love (Langhamer chapter 2). Increasingly throughout the twentieth century, the British would come to redefine love as "modern mutuality" and equal partnership—rather than "Victorian complementarity"—in gender roles (Collins 5). Love became dependent on equality in relationships, demonstrated by mutual decision-making, active companionship, and shared passion (Collins 5).

The most sustained studies of how ideas about romantic love have changed over the last few centuries have focused on American society (e.g., Bailey; Illouz; Lystra; Rothman; Seidman; Shumway; Weisser). In the United States during the eighteenth and early nineteenth centuries, the feeling of love was vaguely defined: "it must be more compelling than friendship, more lasting than passion, more serious than romance" (Rothman 36). Indeed, "romantic feelings"—intense attraction, sexual desire, passion, a longing to be with the beloved, and other excessive emotions—were initially viewed as a dangerous counterfeit for love because they were wild, unstable, self-indulgent, and impermanent (Rothman 39). By the mid-nineteenth century, however, "romantic feelings" had become an integral part of "falling in love." These intense feelings remained ill-defined because Americans during that period tended to spiritualize love, regarding it as "essentially a mystery, at its essence beyond analysis" (Lystra 6). Because love was believed to be an uncontrollable, unfathomable force, lovers experienced some confusion in recognizing love or understanding love. They were perhaps more clear-sighted with what they wanted from marriage: "mutuality, commonality, and sympathy between man and woman—precisely those qualities most likely to bridge the widening gap between home and world" (Rothman 107). One of the most significant practices of romantic love during nineteenth-century courtship was thus the full disclosure of the private "self" during courtship. Only through complete candor, openness, and honesty could courting Americans understand the uniqueness of each other's individual self, "merge" these selves through a shared intensity of emotion, achieve reciprocal understanding (Lystra 8–9), and perhaps guarantee that there would be no surprises after marriage that might disappoint their spouse and make them fall out of love.

The emphasis on self-disclosure and its association with the practice of courtship meant that "intimacy" in its modern sense first came to be associated with romantic love during this period. "Intimacy" is a historically unstable and elusive concept. The term defines a quality of "closeness" and interpersonal interaction that, over the centuries, has meant physical proximity, familiarity, and sexual and other forms of bodily contact (Jamieson "Intimacy as a Concept"). From the nineteenth century onwards, "intimacy" was used to describe a shared emotional closeness, reciprocity, and intellectual understanding and compatibility producing feelings of happiness. That romantic love should engender expectations of intimacy and happiness was a novel concept. If we look at earlier romantic literature such as medieval romances, the lover yearns for the beloved, but does not expect love to be fulfilled in marriage, let alone expect love to lead to intimacy in the sense of close proximity, sexual relations, or companionship. Love is not about the fulfillment of pleasure but is instead often associated with pain: love has to be proved through devoted service which often entails quests, suffering, sacrifice, and even humiliation. In the Middle Ages, there was little expectation that romantic love would be requited. To love without expectation of reciprocity, Susan Ostrov Weisser observes, is what distinguishes the premodern ideal of love from the modern expectation that romantic love is "*constituted by the equality of loving feeling and commitment*" (Weisser 6, italics in original text).

Lystra argues that during the nineteenth century, the entangling of romantic love with the practice of intimacy initially served to ameliorate the social, economic, and political conditions of gender inequality by helping men to identify fully with the desires and emotions of the women they courted. Because men in love were supposed to please and serve their loved one, women tested their suitors emotionally to determine their level of commitment as well as their true character. These tests consisted of a series of emotional crises brought on by women attempting to gauge the extent of men's self-disclosure and, crucially, disclosing their own deepest self-doubts, fears, and flaws to their suitors, criticizing themselves to ascertain the answer to the all-important question: "Will you love me even with all my faults and shortcomings?" Suitors who passed the test answered by "praise, reinforcement of esteem, refocusing on the strengths of the beloved rather than weaknesses" (Lystra 38). Women in turn were also tested by the emotional uncertainties and sufferings of courtship: Was what they felt really love? Was their love requited? How were they to recognize love? Would courtship end in marriage? Could love last? Could it provide true companionship and mutuality? How were they to read moments of silence and distance? For both men and women, then, pain and anxiety were understood as an integral part of love for they "gave a sharper definition to the joys of love" and intensified the emotions that had come to be associated with love (Lystra 51). This process of testing and reassurance, emotional crises of doubt and fear followed by praise that strengthens self-esteem and emphasizes the uniqueness and worthiness of the beloved, has characterized the plots of many Harlequin Mills and Boon novels of the twentieth century.

By the early twentieth century, the meanings and social practices associated with romantic love changed as parental influence waned, as women gained more liberty outside the domestic sphere, especially after they began to develop a measure of economic autonomy. While older understandings of love prevailed throughout the century, they were joined and sometimes supplanted by a focus on love as pleasure: pleasure gained through experiences of consumption, and pleasure experienced through sexual experimentation. Some of these changes were connected to the replacement of the ritual of courtship with the practice of dating (Bailey 15; Shumway 66). Courtship took place mainly in the domestic sphere, often under parental supervision, and it revolved around talking—communication. Dating took place in the public sphere—tea rooms, restaurants, dance halls, cabarets, cinemas, drive-ins—and it revolved around consumption both before and during the date. Men and women had always sought to present themselves attractively especially during courtship, but Eva Illouz (34) argues that during the early twentieth century, this process of beautifying oneself became increasingly dependent on purchasing new commercial products (such as deodorant, mouth wash, breath fresheners) that were specifically associated with images of successful romance via their advertising campaigns. Illouz observes that this "romanticization of commodities," whereby objects associated with dating acquired a romantic aura in advertisements and movies, was accompanied by the "commodification of romance," whereby "romantic practices increasingly interlocked with and became defined as the consumption of leisure goods and leisure technologies offered by the nascent market" (26). Thus where courtship had involved the giving of love tokens such as flowers, cards, and locks of hair or other mementos of romance, dating often involved gifts that were purchased: chocolates or perfume, for example. The emphasis of dating was increasingly on the pleasures of the senses rather than the complete disclosure of the self. Indeed, Ellen Rothman argues that candor and frankness were restricted by the venues of dating that

> lent themselves to sexual experimentation but not to emotional openness. Dancing cheek to cheek or sitting side by side in a darkened nickelodeon may have invited new physical freedom, but neither encouraged the heart-to-heart talking that had occupied couples in earlier generations.
>
> (225)

Consequently, Steven Seidman argues, the meaning of sex in relation to love underwent a significant transformation during the twentieth century as love became sexualized:

> Love changed from having an essentially spiritual meaning to being conceived in a way that made it inseparable from the erotic longings and pleasures of sex. By the early decades of the twentieth century, the desires and pleasures associated with the erotic aspects of sex were imagined as a chief motivation and sustaining source of love. The Victorian language of love as a spiritual communion was either marginalized or fused with the language of sensual desire and joy.
>
> (4)

By the mid-twentieth century, sex was understood as an integral part of romantic love, and marriage advice manuals focused on how to improve sexual experiences for men and women. To some, self-disclosure was not considered important; indeed, it could be detrimental to the maintenance of romantic love. The pioneer of advice columns, Dorothy Dix (journalist Elizabeth Meriwether Gilmer) informed her readers that

> What we don't know doesn't hurt us in domestic life, and the wise do not try to find out too much ... Nothing does more to preserve the illusions that a man and woman have about each other than the things they don't know.
>
> (Rothman 226)

To others, however, the ideal marriage (and, later in the century, all romantic love relationships in general) was not only sexually satisfying, but also based on ideas of mutuality, partnership, and companionship—in a word, intimacy. David Shumway suggests that from the 1960s onwards, influenced partly by marriage and relationship therapists and post-1960s self-help books, Americans' ideas about love conjoined romance, sex, and intimacy (67). To Shumway, "intimacy" functions as a "discourse" in the same way that "romance" does: it entails a set of ideological concepts, statements, and associated social practices that accrue the aura of "truth" over time. If romantic love is something mysterious and irrational that one "falls" into, irresistibly, intimacy is a condition of, and a process within, a relationship that one can rationally analyze and use communication techniques to improve (Shumway 136). Far from romantic love being a haven from the world of work, love relationships are now something that couples "work on." Yet exactly what "intimacy" is remains unclear, thus its achievement is elusive. Romantic intimacy is about self-disclosure through talking—sharing your deepest feelings, but also assuming that the triviality of quotidian life is interesting to someone who loves you. Yet it is also about *not* having to talk since it is "an emotional situation in which nothing needs to be said because the partners know each other so well and trust so deeply" (Shumway 142). Intimacy is an absence—the absence of loneliness (Shumway 141)—which suggests it is a psychological or emotional state. But Lynn Jamieson argues that it is also a set of sustained actions that go beyond talk and shared emotions, for mutual self-disclosure is not the

> sole or necessarily the ascendant type of intimacy between couples. Love and care expressed through actions is a very different dimension of intimacy from "knowing" ... For couples who live together, the time, money and effort each devotes to their household often symbolises [sic] love and care for each other.
>
> (Jamieson "Intimacy Transformed?" 485)

Although men demonstrate intimacy through "instrumental" love—that is, doing things and being supportive (Cancian)—women still seem responsible for managing intimacy, devising strategies or manipulative tactics to create the illusion of intimacy (Jamieson "Intimacy Transformed?" 485), and receiving plenty of advice from women's magazines as to how to do so (Weisser 68).

By the twenty-first century the United States, at least, was steeped in a contradictory culture of romantic love and intimacy, fueled by a century of mass-market entertainment wherein the promise of the American Dream could be fulfilled by falling in love (Roach). Romantic love is a story that gives meaning, coherence, and purpose to people's lives:

> According to this story, despite the risks, love is what gives value and depth to life. Our purpose is to bond with a well-suited mate worthy of our love and to love and be loved by this mate within a circle of family and friends. Here, life is a high-stakes quest for the Holy Grail of One True Love. This search is driven by yearning and desire for the paradise of this romantic happily-ever-after. We chase romance, we structure our lives around it, we fashion much of our art and culture from it. The romance story is not only a narrative but becomes also, more disturbingly, an imperative.
>
> (Roach 4)

In a secular, capitalist society that uses sexualized individuation to sell products while reducing individuals to interchangeable commodities, romantic love has become a secular religion in which the "the redemptive or resurrection power of love" heals all wounds, conquers all, functions "as a positive force for the good in people's lives," and makes the world a better place (Roach 23).

How do we recognize this love, though? Weisser argues that contemporary popular culture reinforces the message that "true love" is the love relationship that lasts. If it doesn't last because it is no longer thrilling or fulfilling, then it wasn't "real love" to begin with, and the search begins again for the one true love. Meanwhile, in order to cap divorce rates and to stop couples from getting off the "marriage-go-round" (Cherlin), the discourse of intimacy is offered as the next ameliorative stage in romantic love, following the intense emotional high of romantic passion, because intimacy can be worked upon and developed. Yet Shumway argues that the promise of intimacy may be as elusive and evanescent as romance:

> the degree of promised closeness may be as extreme as the degree of rapture promised by romance. The intimate partner is not merely a companion but a soul mate. Anything less seems to be grounds for therapy or for searching elsewhere. In this way, intimacy may become just as productive of dissatisfaction as romance has been.
>
> (Shumway 156)

Within contemporary romantic love relationships, intimacy is made to bear the weight of existential meaning, religious purpose, and a variety of human desires—themes that are explored in Eric Murphy Selinger and Laura Vivanco's following chapter (Chapter 22) on "Love and/as religion."

The late twentieth and twenty-first century thus consolidates several historical traditions into a modern concept of romantic love that is characterized by the following fundamental ideas: love incorporates sexual desire and passion but it exceeds or transcends physical desire; it is altruistic toward the beloved; because deep intimacy is an integral part of true love, it functions best in relationships between equals where there is the potential for mutuality, partnership and companionship; it must be freely chosen; it is monogamous and lasting; and it confers distinction upon lovers, making them unique, special and profoundly individual in each other's eyes. To what extent are these ideals and developments in the conception of love evident in romantic fiction over the last two centuries?

Love in romance novels[2]

Before I discuss love in the romance novel, it is important to consider the ways in which love is *not* represented. The romance genre is overwhelmingly heteronormative and this focus on love between men and women is inherently restrictive. Additionally, love in mainstream romance novels is very limited in terms of who is worthy of falling in love and being loved in return. For the better part of the last two centuries, non-white people were excluded, relegated to the roles of villains, seductive "other" women, or helpful hands serving and facilitating white love. While the "Latin lover" was introduced in the 1920s, together with the pseudo-Arab sheikh who is actually a European in disguise, stories of interracial love have been rare until the end of the twentieth century. Mainstream heroines these days continue to be mostly Caucasian, while Black love is generally segregated within its own publishing lines: the Kimani/ Arabesque line (2005 to 2018) produced by romance publishing behemoth Harlequin, or publishing houses such as Kensington/Dafina. Asians hardly feature in romance novels as the main romantic protagonists (see Teo "Cultural Authenticity" for a discussion of East Asian romance novels).

Moreover, until the last decade of the twentieth century, the overweight were barred from stories about love. Even today, although "plus size heroines" are becoming more popular to the extent that there are websites compiling such books (e.g., Goodreads.com has "Imperfect Heroine/Hot Hero" and "Plus-Size Heroine in Romance" lists, the All About Romance website has a "Plus-Sized Heroines" list and the Heroes and Heartbreakers blog has constructed a "Top 10 Phattest Plus-Size Heroines" list), overweight heroes are still rare (Brown). The same applies to heroes and heroines with atypical bodies: they only start appearing toward the end of the twentieth century but are still comparatively uncommon (see the list "Disabilities in Romance" in the All About Romance website, which also includes mental disabilities such as depression or PTSD). Women with a sexual history seldom feature as romantic heroines even though this is almost a mandatory requirement for romantic heroes before they meet the heroine. The elderly rarely appear, while the welfare-dependent, uneducated, and abject poor seldom feature as romantic protagonists. Only recently have non-heterosexual romance novels started being published, although the LGBTQIA market is a rapidly growing one, especially with the onset of digital publishing. Indeed, digital publishing has revolutionized how love is portrayed in romance novels because it has created niche markets that cater to a much greater diversity of people with different race and ethnic backgrounds, physical appearances, and sexualities. As long as the publication of romance novels was dominated in the mid-twentieth century by Harlequin Mills and Boon, editors chose conservative manuscripts that would appeal to the widest readership; those stories that would not offend important markets with depictions of adulterous love, for example, or interracial relationships (McAleer 122–3).

The fantasy of romantic love in mainstream romance novels, then, is confined to mostly white, middle- or upper-class, heterosexual, physically attractive, and economically successful characters who are rarely older than 40. Love stories focus primarily on young, white, affluent, successful individuals who are exceptional in one area of their life. But within these limitations, there are certain features of romantic love that remain constant in romantic fiction. First is the concept of "true love": the idea that there is a "right" partner who is the soulmate of the hero or heroine, and with whom love will be at its most passionate, affectionate, transcendent, and joyful. Later, after the sexualization of the romance novel, this idea of exclusivity extends to the notion that sex can only reach the greatest heights of ecstatic fulfillment or be at its most orgasmic with the right partner (McAlister). Love is also characterized by generosity, compassion, kindness, and altruism, but also suffering, sacrifice, pain, and grief. (The difference is that modern romances end optimistically, whereas mid-nineteenth to early twentieth-century love stories do not necessarily end with the couple living "happily ever after.") Love in romance novels is often elusive: it is difficult for protagonists to find, recognize, or discern love in others. It produces chaotic and turbulent emotions, is easily misunderstood, creates uncertainty, and makes the lover intensely vulnerable. The experience of emotional disorder can only be resolved with the confession of love. "I love you" is the magical phrase that begins to heal all wounds and right all wrongs, eventually enabling the resolution of the plot (see Cohn 32; Belsey; Fletcher; Goris). Beyond these characteristics, however, there have been significant changes in the way romance novels have portrayed love over the last two centuries. These changes largely affect moral character, attitudes toward romantic feelings, sexual desire and behavior, and the heroine's autonomy, especially as indicated through occupational or professional fulfillment, and changing practices of consumption. What follows is a necessarily generalized account of some of the ways ideas about love have changed over time.

Romance scholars such as Ramsdell and Regis (16 and 63) contend that the modern romance novel developed from Samuel Richardson's *Pamela*, Jane Austen's novels, and Charlotte Brontë's *Jane Eyre*. These canonical texts established the romance novel's focus on the heroine's emotions and experiences, emphasizing courtship and the developing love relationship between hero and heroine, exploring the obstacles to the fulfillment of love that need to be overcome, and depicting the changes in character and circumstance that allow the lovers to be united in an optimistic ending that allows the reader to imagine this love relationship continuing into the future. Richardson's *Pamela* has little to say about love. Mr. B's rapacious lust for the teenage maidservant Pamela is converted to a type of love—altruism, putting her interests and welfare before his own sexual desires—because of her "virtue": her resistance to his attempted seduction and rape without the promise of marriage. But we don't know why she falls in love with him when he releases her from his imprisonment to return to her parents. As Regis points out, returning home is a "step backwards" economically and socially (68) whereas returning to B offers "financial security, protection from some of the perils of pregnancy, legitimacy, and a large step up in status" (71). *Pamela* ends as a novel about courtship, but whether it is a novel about love—where affect wins over interest—is questionable.

Austen's novels are thus the first to explore love from a woman's perspective, trying to balance the older, traditional model of marriage for interest with the new bourgeois ideal of marriage for love.[3] Many readers are familiar with the trajectory of love in *Pride and Prejudice* (1813): moved by his altruism toward her family, Elizabeth Bennett overcomes both her injured pride at being initially slighted by Mr. Darcy and her subsequent prejudice against him. Mr. Darcy's growing attraction to Elizabeth, springing from her lively mind and manners, leads him to fall in love with her despite his initial disdain at her lower social status and her family's public display of impropriety. Eventually, love transforms his attitude toward her family from long-suffering forbearance to genuine acceptance and generosity. But love is perhaps most thoroughly explored in Austen's last novel, *Persuasion* (1817), during the conversation between Anne Elliot and Captain Harville where both debate whether men love more strongly than women. Here, love is characterized not only as depth of feeling, but also as sacrifice, endurance, loyalty, and constancy—of loving when all hope of requited love is gone. This is a reference to the medieval and Petrarchan tradition of the male lover who loves passionately, loyally, and hopelessly. Indeed, Captain Harville appeals to the canon of poetry and prose that proves men's faithfulness in the face of women's inconstancy, but Anne argues that extant literature cannot provide any proof of women's love since "Men have had every advantage of us in telling their own story . . . the pen has been in their hands" (219). Austen's revolutionary move, then, just like all other romance novelists after her, is to give voice to women's views about love, courtship, marriage, and gender relations.

Yet Austen's portrayal of love is not always what we might expect from a romance today. Toward the end of *Emma* (1816), George Knightley declares his feelings for the novel's eponymous heroine by telling her: "I have blamed you, and lectured you, and you have borne it as no other woman in England would have borne it" (417). We know that we are in a different regime of romantic love when a woman's acquiescence to her stern, would-be lover's scolding provides proof of character and, hence, worthiness of love. Modern readers recognize the romantic attraction to personality and physical appearance, and the yearning to be with the beloved that characterize love in Austen's novels. And yet, Austen makes it clear that the feelings of love—romantic feelings—are an inadequate foundation for marriage. Relationships that are formed purely on the basis of sexual desire and romantic feelings or sensibilities—Marianne Dashwood and John Willoughby in *Sense and Sensibility* (1811), Lydia Bennett and Wickham in *Pride and Prejudice* (1813), Maria Bertram and Henry Crawford in *Mansfield Park* (1814) do not last or end happily. Romantic feelings must be accompanied by qualities such as education, refinement, gentility, rational self-control, and values such as honor, altruism, generosity, and even long-suffering patience for, as Stephen Kern (chapter 1) argues, pre-twentieth-century heroines spend much of their early lives waiting for love. These qualities and values must be shared by the romantic couple. While the values may be universal, Austen associates the desirable qualities with the upper-middle classes, and class boundaries are clearly demarcated in her novels.

In addition to love, the hero must possess sufficient wealth to be able to support a family. Money is important, although it is not a sufficient basis for marriage. At the end of *Sense and Sensibility*, Elinor Dashwood and Edward Ferrars are able to marry only because Colonel Brandon gives Edward the living of Delaford parsonage, thus providing him with a clergyman's income. In *Emma*, when Mr. Knightley talks about the advantages Frank Churchill is able to bestow upon Jane Fairfax, he comments: "A man would always wish to give a woman a better home than the one he takes her from" (416). And, of course, Lizzie Bennett mischievously claims to have fallen for Mr. Darcy when she first set eyes on the grounds of Pemberley. Austen is surprisingly open and pragmatic about the degree of affluence needed to sustain the love-match. By contrast, the issue of a sustainable income for marriage is rarely ever mentioned in contemporary romances even though romantic love in these novels is predicated upon capitalism and consumption (Kamblé chapter 1). Another point of difference is also that in Austen's novels, family and close friends of the lovers must accept their union, and if social ties have been broken in the course of courtship, these must be restored—however tentatively—by the novel's end. This is not necessary in contemporary romances, especially of the mid-twentieth-century Harlequin Mills & Boon variety featuring Cinderella plots where orphaned heroines are cruelly treated by their relations. In these novels, the hero rescues the heroine (or vice versa) and gives her a family, thus replacing rather than restoring her relationship with her existing family.

In all these aspects of Austen's novels, we see an ideal of love that maps on to the developing notions of romantic love and the ideal of the love-match that characterized the nineteenth century: the ambivalent value for romantic feelings combined with a lingering mistrust of them; the emphasis on good character; and the disclosure of the self during the long passages of conversation between the couple following the confession of love, when they dissect the courtship and reveal how, when and why they fell in love—a scenario that is also found in many contemporary romance novels. Take, for instance, Linda Howard's romantic comedy/suspense, *Mr. Perfect* (2003). After the romantic protagonists first have sex, the hero's response is a disgruntled "Shit!" as he realizes he has fallen in love with her. He then lists all the things that make him love her: profanity, rudeness, aggression, eccentricity, and off-beat sense of humor in addition to her sexual attractiveness (chapter 21). Howard's novel, with its "potty-mouthed" hero and heroine who openly desire each other and whose courtship is very sexual, could not be more different to the restrained manners and submerged sexuality of Austen's novels, yet both authors agree that a confession of love cannot be complete without intimacy, and intimacy is achieved by sharing the private self and analyzing their relationship.

Intimacy is also highly prized in Charlotte Brontë's *Jane Eyre*: Mr. Rochester begins to fall in love with plain Jane because he is able to talk to her freely and intimately, and he in turn encourages her honesty and directness of speech when they are alone. Their love is fostered by their deep understanding of each other, their intellectual compatibility, and their great esteem for each other. Yet the model of romantic love presented in this model is otherwise very different from Austen's. Brontë despised Austen's depiction of love, claiming "[t]he passions are perfectly unknown to her" (Weisser 36). The Augustan use of reason to temper emotional excess or sensibility, the wariness of romantic feelings and the higher valuation of affection based on esteem for character, the concern for social propriety and respectability—all seemed a bloodless, heartless, lifeless type of love to a novelist influenced by the Romantic movement's emphasis on primal emotion and the extreme experience of passion and the sublime. In *Jane Eyre*, "romantic love entails intense feeling, uncontrollable longing even in the face of almost certain rejection, and . . . strong erotic desire in women as well as in men" (Weisser 40–1). In this sense, *Jane Eyre* may be a stronger influence on modern romance novels than Austen's fiction. While Austen's heroines may still form the basis of recognizable types today, apart from Mr. Darcy, it is doubtful if any of Austen's other heroes would provoke wild and passionate love from a romance heroine today. Mr. Rochester, however, in full sway of erotic passion and tempestuous feeling, sexually potent and predatory, moody, and menacing, careless of class and conventions, is still imprinted on the Alpha hero today. Susan Ostrov Weisser argues that Charlotte Brontë

> has influenced our contemporary ideas of romantic love so that we now expect uninhibited feeling, intense passion, and the drama of strong emotion to define

> romance, integrated with pragmatic compatibility, psychological intimacy, and marriage.
>
> (49)

Post-Brontë, the romantic fiction of the nineteenth century that Rachel Anderson surveys, written by bestselling novelists such as Charlotte M. Yonge and Rhoda Broughton, feature love relationships characterized by a roller-coaster ride of extreme emotions. There is much psychological and emotional suffering, trembling, rapture, ecstasy, and a sense of love as a sublime, transcendent force that saves, redeems, and purifies hero and heroine alike. Unlike Austen's novels and *Jane Eyre*, many of the mid- to late nineteenth-century three-volume romantic fiction ended tragically with death parting the romantic protagonists due to a belief that "traditionally, the truest, purest romantic love is a fatal love" (Anderson 26). This tradition is still evident in contemporary love stories written by Nicholas Sparks, Robert James Waller's *The Bridges of Madison County* (1993), or Nicholas Evans' *The Horse Whisperer* (1995), where the romantic protagonists are parted by death or other circumstances at the end.

The opening of Charles Mudie's Select Library in 1842 and the establishment of W.H. Smith railway bookstall created a publishing boom and whetted appetites for love stories that provoked much censure from clergymen and critics. In response, Victorian novelists injected their romantic fiction with a strong element of spirituality, ensuring that however emotionally overwrought the language might be, and whatever outlandish twists of plot might occur, heroines were chaste, spiritual, and given to prayer. Naturally, the good were rewarded while villains were punished. The overt Christianization, spiritualization, and sacralization of love in romantic fiction chimed with the nineteenth-century view of love as sublime and mysterious, and the search for spiritual communion as well as intimacy with a spouse discussed above (see Lystra 242–57). Despite the secularization of romance in the twentieth century, such a view of love, with its vague appeal to God and to the spiritual, continues in the United States through the genre of Christian inspirational fiction, a genre that Lynn S. Neal (2006) has traced back to the publication of Grace Livingston Hill's *The Finding of Jasper Holt* in 1915 (31). It is also reflected in the novels of the popular and prolific British historical romance writer Barbara Cartland whose novel *The Poor Governess* (1982), for instance, ends with the proclamation that hero and heroine had found "the love that all men and women had sought down the ages ... Then there was only the light of God to inspire, guide and protect them, all through their lives together" (2013 Kindle ed., location 2346–52).

Nineteenth-century romantic protagonists ultimately fall in love with each other because, beyond any romantic feelings they might have, they admire each other's moral character and principles. The hero is either worthy of the heroine, or he makes himself so. Thus does the nineteenth-century heroine—constrained economically, socially, and by rigid gender roles—ensure that she attains economic justice, psychological and emotional support, and a happy marriage. A love that is based especially on the hero's sterling character continues to feature in the lengthy romance novels of the early twentieth century. In Gertrude Page's *Love in the Wilderness: The Story of Another African Farm* (1907) and *The Rhodesian* (1912), or Australian novelist Rosa Praed's *Lady Bridget in the Never-Never Land* (1915), heroes are honorable, honest, self-sacrificial, physically and mentally strong, entrepreneurial in spirit, and dedicated to nation-building and the cause of the British Empire. As jay Dixon (51) suggests, these qualities are represented by the adjective "white" during this period (see Chapter 23 in this volume, and also Teo "The Romance of White Nations" and *Desert Passions* for an extended discussion of whiteness in romance novels). White heroes and white love of the early twentieth century are safe for heroines; they have little to fear from their future husbands.

All this changed after the publication of E.M. Hull's blockbuster novel *The Sheik* (1919) and the eponymous film starring Rudolph Valentino, where the villainous hero—the cold and brutal Sheik Ahmed Ben Hassan—abducts Lady Diana Mayo, rapes her, and makes her fall in love with him despite his deplorable character. During a historical period that saw the growing sexualization of love, and an increasing emphasis placed on appearance, spectacle and consumption, virtuous character counted for little. Extreme emotions, wild passion, good looks, sexual attractiveness and the visually stunning furnishings and fashions of the 1921 film formed the romantic basis of love. Believing the sheik to be Arab (which, of course, he is not since he is revealed at the novel's end to be the son of a Spanish woman and an English peer), Diana abandons herself to a

> love of such complete surrender that she had never conceived. Her heart was given for all time to the fierce desert man who was so different from all other men whom she had met, a lawless savage who had taken her to satisfy a passing fancy and who had treated her with merciless cruelty. He was a brute, but she loved him, loved him for his very brutality and superb animal strength. And he was an Arab! A man of different race and colour, a native ... A year ago, a few weeks even, she would have shuddered with repulsion at the bare idea, the thought that a native could even touch her had been revolting, but all that was swept away and was nothing in the face of the love that filled her heart so completely. She did not care if he was an Arab, she did not care what he was, he was the man she loved.
>
> (133–4)

Pamela Regis argues that "*The Sheik* is the ur-twentieth-century popular romance novel" (123) because it cut out the rambling subplots of the Victorian three-volume romantic novels to focus solely and wholly on the developing relationship between its romantic protagonists, and because it focalizes the plot almost entirely through the heroine (120). But *The Sheik* is significant for another reason. It marks the point in the development of romance novels where love no longer needs to be based on Austen's criteria of upstanding moral character, emotions under the sway of reason, propriety and respectability, and social, educational, intellectual, and psychological compatibility; the point where Charlotte Brontë's Rochester—morally flawed, emotionally unrestrained, compelling in his passion and redeemed by love at the end—becomes the model for twentieth-century Alpha heroes. In Hull's novel, Diana Mayo falls in love with the sheik despite his abusive, depraved character, and despite the differences (so she believes) in their standing in every area of life. Love here does not need to be rational or moral, even though it does redeem and transform the Sheik somewhat at the end of the novel. Love is mysterious, irresistible, overwhelmingly passionate and erotic. It begins wholly as the province of the feelings rather than the mind or morals. This paradigm of love would come to dominate many Harlequin

Mills and Boon romance novels from the late 1960s to the 1990s, but in the first half of the twentieth century, it remained marginal among romance authors despite its popularity with readers.

Hull's notion of love was resisted by many of her contemporaries, notably her fellow desert-romance novelist, Kathlyn Rhodes, who insisted that love had to be more than passion and desire. In her popular 1909 novel *The Desert Dreamers*, Rhodes created two heroines who fall in love with the same man, one after the other: Emer and her cousin Diana. Emer is a New Woman who equates passion with love, believes that love purifies sexual desire—an idea that harks back to the medieval notion of *fin'amors*—and has an affair with the hero without marrying him. She argues that

> many women are afraid ... to love openly and passionately, having a pathetic idea that passion and immorality are synonymous. Yet we women as well as men are charged with passion, let the prudes and the ignorant deny it as they will. For we are none the less pure because the kisses of the men we love thrill us through and through, because we lie in their arms as sentient, sensitive beings rather than passive automata, sexless dolls.
>
> (34)

Before the hero can marry her, Emer falls off a horse and dies in the desert, suitably punished by Rhodes. At that moment, the hero realizes that

> he and Emer had proved unworthy of their own high ideals of love and morality. Their love, though it could never have been more unselfish, more absolute, might have been a finer, greater thing if they had been strong enough to deny themselves the gratification of their passion until they were lawfully wedded in the sight of God.
>
> (219)

Even after the publication of *The Sheik*, Rhodes continued to insist in novels such as *Desert Lovers* (1922) that passion was not love because love involved more than the sensations of the body. In this novel, the Englishman Kendall declares his love for the heroine in a moment of drunkenness: "I'm mad for love of you—you little witch with your golden hair and your big eyes ... life's nothing, less than nothing, to me unless I get you!" (38). He wants her "adorable body," which is as important as her "little white soul." Naturally, his fate is to die before the novel's end—thus punishing him for his lasciviousness and leaving the heroine free to be courted by the real, gentlemanly hero.

This rigid moral code and the insistence that real love would subordinate the fulfillment of sexual passion to the requirements of social propriety and marriage can be found in Harlequin Mills and Boon romances until the 1970s, and also in the chaste and "wholesome" historical novels of Barbara Cartland. In *The Wings of Love* (1962), Cartland's villain, Lord Ravenscar, attempts to force himself on the heroine, who is greatly alarmed when "his lips fastened to hers" and she "felt his passion rising within him like an evil flame" (qtd. in Greer 198). It is for the hero to teach Amanda how a man who truly loves her will treat her:

> he lifted the hem of her white muslin gown and touched his lips with it. "Amanda," he said, "that is how a man, any man, should approach you. No one—least of all Ravenscar—is worthy to do more than to kiss the hem of your gown."
>
> (qtd. in Greer 199)

In Cartland's novels, love incorporates intense passion but transcends it, elevating the beloved to the place of God. Love produces a deep yearning, but it is ultimately mystical and ineffable, represented by Cartland's overuse of ellipsis to express the inexpressible. Upon hearing the hero's confession of love, the heroine of *The Poor Governess* (1982) realizes, "I love ... you! *I love ... you*! I know I must be ... dreaming ... please ... kiss me again ... in case I wake up" (Kindle ed., location 2276).

It is instructive to compare Cartland's portrayal of love with that of her contemporary, the historical romance novelist Georgette Heyer. As critics (Bywaters 493, Regis 126) note, Heyer was greatly influenced by Austen's novels and she injected her romances with a good measure of irony and bathos. Heyer's novels retain Austen's notion of love as passion under rational and moral control, and the class-based nature of successful marriages, but they waver in their representation of love as intellectual and educational compatibility. In Heyer's earlier novels such as *The Black Moth*(1921), *The Transformation of Philip Jettan* (aka *Powder and Patch*, 1923) *The Corinthian* (1940) and *Arabella* (1949), the age gap, and the intellectual and educational distance between the worldly hero and the infantilized heroine, is considerable; what they have in common is a physical attraction, affection, and similar moral values and social status. In the majority of Heyer's postwar novels, however, the heroine is often portrayed as an intelligent, sensible, practical, "unromantic" woman who is the intellectual equal of the hero. In these novels, love is based on attraction, affection, humor, and psychological and intellectual compatibility. It is not spiritualized, sensationalized, or overwrought as in a Cartland novel, and it is not the province of extreme emotions. At its most intense—usually at the conclusion of the novel—passion can be signified by the hero's "savage" or "masterful" kiss that sometimes serves to reveal the hero's love to the heroine. In *The Grand Sophy* (1950), the hero asks Sophy to marry him, "vile and abominable girl that you are." When Sophy exclaims, "You cannot love me!" the hero "in a very rough fashion jerked her into his arms, and kissed her. 'I don't; I dislike you excessively!' he said savagely. Entranced by these lover-like words, Miss Stanton-Lacy returned his embrace with fervor" (372).

Yet Heyer also portrays older, pre-romantic notions about love as commitment to domestic life, care, consideration, and common interests, rather than wild and evanescent passion and desire. In *A Civil Contract* (1961), the handsome, aristocratic hero and the plain, bourgeois heroine undertake a marriage of convenience to restore the hero's family fortunes, despite the hero being in love with a beautiful and elegant member of the aristocracy. In the end, he comes to love deeply his plain and dowdy wife, who is capable of giving him more comfort and support than the self-centered beauty for whom he felt a fleeting desire in his youth. That the strength and stability of married love arises from being anchored in the ordinary, familiar, and domestic—rather than the romantic, passionate, and exotic—is something that Heyer increasingly emphasizes. In *Frederica* (1965), the aristocratic hero gradually realizes that he loves the eponymous heroine and her family when he is willing to shoulder the responsibility for their welfare and future. Frederica, in turn, also articulates a comfortable, companionate, and domestically-centered understanding of love, rather than one that is just based on passion and romantic feelings:

> Is it like *that*? Being in love? You see, I never was in love, so I don't know. . . . It has always seemed to me that if one falls in love with any gentleman one becomes instantly blind to his faults. But I am *not* blind to your faults, and I do *not* think that everything you do or say is right! Only—is it being—not very comfortable—and cross—and not quite *happy*, when you aren't there?
>
> "That, my darling," said his lordship, taking her ruthlessly into his arms, "is *exactly* what it is!" (378)

This emphasis on the domestic was typical of the 1950s. As jay Dixon notes, Mills and Boon novels of the same period also have a strong element of comfortable friendship underlying the love relationship (156).

By the mid-twentieth century, love as portrayed in romance novels has been secularized, and it is increasingly associated with overwhelming passion and sexual desire, but it is still mysterious.[4] Heroines often do not understand what love is. They fail to recognize or interpret their own feelings correctly, sometimes confusing fear for desire, and passion for hatred. This is particularly the case for romance novels featuring villainous heroes: the Alpha hero or "dangerous man" (Krentz) based on iterations of Mr. Rochester and Sheik Ahmed Ben Hassan. Villainous heroes had appeared in Heyer's *These Old Shades* (1926) and *Devil's Cub* (1932), but after the 1970s they come to populate Harlequin Mills and Boon romance novels set in "exotic" Mediterranean countries where "Latin lovers" tyrannize over valiant heroines: Violet Winspear's *The Tower of the Captive* (1974), for instance, Lynne Graham's *The Veranchetti Marriage* (1988) and *The Greek Tycoon's Blackmailed Mistress* (2009), Helen Bianchin's *The Stefanos Marriage* (1990) and *In the Spaniard's Bed* (2003), and Penny Jordan's *The Demetrios Virgin* (2001).The resurgence of Harlequin sheikh romances in the late twentieth century (see Teo *Desert Passions* chapter 6) also saw virginal heroines threatened by Alpha Arabs in novels such as Winspear's *The Sheik's Captive* (1979), Emma Darcy's *The Falcon's Mistress* (1988), and Miranda Lee's *Beth and the Barbarian* (1993). Following the pattern of *The Sheik*, love initially takes a masochistic, irrational turn with heroines helpless to resist their violent feelings for the seemingly sadistic, villainous heroes. Yet it is important to note that by the end of these novels, these heroes have been tamed and transformed into kind and considerate men, and their ruthlessness toward the heroine is instead harnessed to protect their wives and families.

The Dangerous Hero characterized the transformation of the historical romance from the 1970s onwards, when, after Avon Books' publication of Kathleen E. Woodiwiss's *The Flame and the Flower* (1972), single-title romance novels set in the past became increasingly sexualized with regard to descriptions of sex before marriage, and Americanized in terms of their authorship. Chapters 9, 19, and 20 in this volume discuss issues of sexuality. Suffice it to say here that although there may have been a "revolution" (Thurston) in the explicit language used to describe sexual scenarios and the growing length of these passages, love had long been sexualized in romance novels. Indeed, it could not be otherwise, with scholars (Rothman, Lystra, Seidman, Illouz) arguing that the early twentieth century saw a widespread secularization and sexualization of how love was understood. Even love in a Cartland novel was highly sexualized, although expressed in the overblown euphemisms of passion and emotional ecstasy. Germaine Greer scoffs at Cartland's heroine in *The Wings of Love* because when Amanda felt the hero "kissing the palms with reverence," she experienced "a hungry passion that made her thrill until her whole body trembled with a sudden ecstasy" (qtd. in Greer 199–200). "They have not actually kissed yet," Greer notes acerbically; "Indeed when handkissing results in orgasm it is possible that an actual kiss might bring on epilepsy" (200). By the mid-twentieth century, readers had come to understand that if the heroine feels an irresistible sexual attraction to a man, it is because she is in love with him. Her body recognizes the hero's innate good qualities even though his words and actions might initially convince her mind that he is not to be trusted. This is a distinct change from how love was portrayed in the early twentieth century, when sexual attraction—or "fascination"—was still regarded suspiciously, and the man for whom the heroine might initially feel desire was not necessarily the hero.

The Dangerous Hero of the 1970s and early 1980s is often associated with romances featuring rape or aggressive seduction, such as *The Flame and the Flower*, Rosemary Rogers's *Sweet Savage Love* (1974) or Johanna Lindsey's *Captive Bride* (1977). However, the extent to which these historical romances feature plots where the rape of the heroine transforms into love has probably been overstated.[5] Even in Woodiwiss's *The Flame and the Flower*, the heroine does not fall in love with the hero until he repents of his initial drunken rape and changes his behavior toward her, treating her with kindness and consideration, and restraining his own sexual desire for her until this desire is consensual. In Woodiwiss's other novels such as *A Rose in Winter* (1983), Laurie McBain's *Devil's Desire* (1975), or the majority of Lindsey's historical romances, rape does not feature as part of the romantic relationship, although what we would today understand as sexual harassment certainly does.

Rather than straight sexual assault that transforms into love, what these early sexualized historicals showcase is hate-sex, where heroine and hero overwhelmingly desire each other while simultaneously disliking each other because of artificially contrived misunderstandings or psychological and emotional damage from the past. Both do not recognize they are in love because they have not experienced love before (mistreated, orphaned heroines were popular in both contemporary and historical romances during this period), and the heroine, in particular, is afraid of the menacing hero as well as her own uncontrollable desire for him. Love and desire thus produce a state of fear and confusion because the heroine cannot understand why she starts falling in love with the hero, whose character and actions she misunderstands for most of the novel.

The Americanization of the romance genre from the 1980s onwards brought a change in how the romance plot was focalized. American authors increasingly showed the hero's point of view (Frenier 72), allowing the reader and the heroine to understand his thinking, motivations, and actions. The harsh Alpha hero was joined by a new, "soft-centered," kinder, more humorous, and generally more congenial hero. New Zealand romance writer Daphne Clair observes that from the 1980s onwards, "American editors ... began insisting on sensitivity, humor, understanding, and patience in the romantic man. Not content with claiming the right of equality with men, they now boldly demand that men should, dammit, be more like women—the ultimate subversion" (Clair 70). Romance writers were quick to respond. "Instead of sexual antagonism they used style, wit, emotional warmth, and sometimes explicit, tender, and sensual love scenes to hold reader interest"

(Clair 70–1). Perhaps more than any other American novelist, Nora Roberts has developed various types of "soft-centered" American heroes who ensure that when the heroines fall in love with them, intense sexual desire is balanced with growing friendship, shared interests, shared ambitions, and shared humor. This is evident in Roberts's romantic suspense novels such as *Carnal Innocence* (1991) and *Carolina Moon* (2001), which feature mild-mannered, laid-back, gentle heroes. Increasingly, what romance novels portray is not simply the extended moment of falling in love or having sex, but the development and maintenance of intimate relationships up to and after marriage. Discourses of intimacy, which, as Shumway argues, characterize the self-help book movement of the 1980s and 1990s, increasingly appear in late twentieth- and twenty-first-century romance novels. Discourses of romance and discourses of love both "promise a great deal in the name of love," Shumway observes. "Romance offers adventure, intense emotion, and the possibility of finding the perfect mate. Intimacy promises deep communication, friendship, and sharing that will last beyond the passion of new love" (27).

Jennifer Crusie's *Fast Women* (2011) exemplifies the disillusion with the discourse of romance alone, and the turn to the self-help discourse of intimacy to supplement romantic love. Indeed, in the acknowledgments page of *Fast Women*, Crusie cites the influence of Abigail Trafford's *Crazy Time* (1982), describing this self-help book as a "brilliant, compassionate study of divorce and recovery." *Fast Women* traces the unraveling of three marriages that were based on romantic love: the hero's, the heroine's, and her sister-in-law's. In the majority of romance novels, a marriage that ends in divorce is proof of the fact that it wasn't actually based on "real love," and that the spouse was not "the one." The next hero or heroine who comes along is actually the "true love." This aligns with Weisser's trenchant criticism (discussed above) of the contemporary belief that love is real love only if the relationship lasts; if it doesn't last, *ipso facto* it wasn't real love, and the search for true love begins anew. Crusie refuses to play this game in *Fast Women*. She makes it clear that these first marriages were all based on real love, but the individuals within the marriage changed over time. In the case of the two women, their first husbands could not accept how they had changed. Their growing maturity, independence, self-sufficiency, and competence had to be suppressed, and they had to keep pretending to be their former, youthful selves to keep the marriage going. Eventually, they reached a point where they could no longer do that. The heroine Nell tells her sister-in-law,

> If you can look at somebody and say, "I never loved you, you were a mistake," that's one thing. But if you look at him and say, "You were everything and I poisoned it because I wouldn't stand up for myself," that's hard.
>
> (331)

She was once truly in love with her former husband, but now she hates him because of what their marriage has done to her, even though she knows he's "not a bad guy" (379).

The problem with the discourse of romance that Crusie points to is this: romance novels assume that real love transforms the lovers until they are the right fit for each other, and the happily ever after then follows. But what if the hero and heroine continue to change and grow as individuals after marriage? The discourse of intimacy is offered as a possible solution to this dilemma: if only the hero and heroine can talk enough, reveal enough about who they are, what they hope and fear, what they want, and how they think, then maybe that might be enough to keep them "necessary to each other." In the end, both the hero and heroine in *Fast Women* decide to take a gamble on marriage again, knowing this time that marriage is "*a snare and an invitation to pain . . . It's compromise and sacrifice, and I'll be stuck forever with this man*" (417, italics in original text). The novel ends with the reader hoping that the discourse of intimacy will be sufficient to maintain this relationship and make it last, but the ending is haunted by Nell's earlier realization that "it might not be [forever] . . . nobody knew forever until the end" (278). What she is left with is determined optimism: "*That'll have to be enough,* she thought, and then she closed her eyes and loved him back" (278). There is an unstated and uneasy acknowledgment here that, as Shumway (156) observes, intimacy may prove to be just as fragile and elusive as romance in holding a love relationship together. The HEA ending thus depends on an act of faith (which confirms Selinger and Vivanco's point in Chapter 22 about the underlying religious trajectory of contemporary romance novels)—something that is further developed in Crusie's novel *Bet Me* (2004).

Crusie, more than other romance writers, sometimes takes a knowing, self-reflexive, meta-romantic approach to the genre. She began publishing in the 1990s, but by the twenty-first century, romantic love and the HEA seem to have become a problem for her. How could love guarantee the HEA if both author and reader follow the logic of plot and character development after the end of the novel? *Bet Me* (2004) is in many ways her metaphorical throwing up of her hands, giving up on trying to make the love plot work toward the HEA. This novel is the most metafictional of Crusie's romances, involving a satire of studies about romantic love, and self-consciously employing the overarching framework of the fairy-tale to ensure a post-courtship happy ending. Cynthie, the "other woman" who is a rival for the hero Cal's affections, is a psychologist whose studies have helped her to develop a four-step plan to falling in love. Using this model, Cynthie plots her moves to ensure that Cal falls in love with her. It doesn't work, because although Cal has had romantic feelings for her in the past, he has never developed "intimacy" with her. Instead, he falls in love with the overweight heroine Min because she knows him, understands him, lends him unquestioning moral support even when she criticizes him, and she can talk with him about absolutely everything under the sun. Cal does the same for Min, but she is still worried about whether they will make it as a couple at the end of the novel:

> The happily ever after . . . All the stuff we just did, the romance part, the fairy tale stuff, I know how that works, I read the stories. . . . But they don't tell you about the happily ever after. And as far as I can see, that's where it all breaks down. Fifty percent of marriages end in divorce, and yes, I know those statistics are skewed by repeat divorcers . . . but I'm worried. There aren't any happily ever after stories. That's where it ends. Where the hard part starts.
>
> (397)

Cal provides a simple solution drawn from the discourse of intimacy: "I think we just stick together. Take care of each other. Pat each other on the back when things get tight. . . . Bet you ten bucks we make it" (398). Working at the relationship, in other words, will see them through. The novel, in fact, explicitly articulates the transition from the discourse of romance into the discourse of intimacy in an exchange between Min and her best friend Bonnie, who is an advocate for fairy-tale love throughout the novel. Once Min admits that she too "wants the fairy tale," Bonnie advises her that "the only illogical thing you have to do is believe. After that you need brains" (338) to "figure out how" to work at achieving the happy ending. Yet it still takes an act of faith on Min's part to "believe" that "*This is really forever*" (italics in original text). As with *Fast Women*, underlying the resolute optimism of the romantic protagonists is an apprehensive recognition that the discourse of intimacy cannot guarantee a happy ending any more than can the discourse of romance. We as readers simply have to believe—have faith—that hero and heroine will make it, and perhaps that is why Crusie fashioned *Bet Me* as a meta-romantic fairy-tale with a fairy godmother (the godlike author) to guarantee the HEA.

Beyond interpersonal relations, a number of other things characterize successful love relationships in many modern romance novels: meaningful work, and fabulous wealth to facilitate romantic consumption. According to jay Dixon Harlequin Mills & Boon heroines have always worked for a living (7–9, 53). Be that as it may, until the 1970s most working heroines gave up their jobs or careers to become homemakers upon marriage. The assumption was that they would be fulfilled as wives and mothers. There are still homemaker heroines in contemporary romance novels today, but most writers and readers take it for granted that although love, marriage, and families constitute a happy ending for heroines, women need more: they need fulfilling careers or a meaningful purpose in life outside of the domestic sphere in order to have a satisfying future. Modern heroes recognize this and they respect and even nurture the careers and ambitions of autonomous, economically independent heroines. But if work is important, so is play.

The portrayal of romantic love is increasingly intertwined with the pleasures of material consumption. As argued above, money and property rights have always mattered in romance novels. Historical romances have always featured heroes who are socially and economically elite, and Anderson argues that the "town" romances of the 1920s and 1930s display romantic consumption in venues such as dance halls, tea rooms, restaurants, shows, and nightclubs (195–6). But now, more than ever, extravagant wealth is needed to fuel extravagant consumption. This is obviously a generalization; many contemporary novels such as Nora Roberts's *The Fall of Shane Mackade* (1996), *Blue Smoke* (2005), or *Chasing Fire* (2011), for example, or Linda Howard's aforementioned *Mr. Perfect* (2000) and her other romantic suspense novels feature working-class heroes who are not particularly wealthy. Yet Howard's *Now You See Her* (2003) and many of Roberts's other romances have at least one romantic protagonist who is extremely rich, even though this wealth has been hard-earned. Affluence allows consumption to be cast as romantic practice, as well as enabling romantic love to succeed. As Jayashree Kamblé argues, the hero's wealth

> will always ensure a future devoid of financial hardship, but more importantly, will create space for an unending courtship even after the wedding. The Harlequin Mills and Boon hero's independence from an earned wage is a marker that he is free to resume the role of suitor to his heroine at any time during the marriage without any financial risk to their life together.
>
> (Kindle location 692)

The transition from the mid-twentieth-century emphasis on love as extreme, extravagant, ungovernable emotions to a late twentieth/twenty-first-century notion of love as sexualized fantasies of extravagant consumption can be seen in the changing titles of Harlequin Mills & Boon romance novels. Since Harlequin titles are often imposed by the publisher on a manuscript, these titles are indicative of the kinds of coded fantasies of love Harlequin believes will appeal to readers at a particular time. When we look at the prolific British novelist Penny Jordan's Harlequin Mills & Boon titles from the 1980s, the emphasis is on psychological interiority and on phrases that evoke tempestuous emotions: *Escape from Desire* (1982), *Passionate Protection* (1983), *Savage Atonement* (1983), *The Inward Storm* (1984), *Force of Feeling* (1988), *Bitter Betrayal* (1989), and *Passionate Possession* (1992). The twenty-first century, however, sees a greater emphasis on the hero's economic status or profession, and his ownership of the heroine as a result of his wealth. Hence we have Jordan's *Expecting the Playboy's Heir* (2005), *The Italian Duke's Wife* (2006), *The Future King's Pregnant Mistress* (2007), *The Sheikh's Blackmailed Mistress* (2008), *The Boss's Marriage Arrangement* (2008), *Virgin for the Billionaire's Taking* (2008), *Captive at the Sicilian Billionaire's Command* (2009), *The Wealthy Greek's Contract Wife* (2009). Other Harlequin authors have followed suit: Lynne Graham's *The Heiress Bride* (2002), *Marrying the Millionaire* (2006), *The Greek Tycoon's Defiant Bride* (2008), and *The Italian Billionaire's Pregnant Bride* (2008), for example; or Lucy Monroe's *The Billionaire's Pregnant Mistress* (2003), Rebecca Winters's *The Renegade Billionaire* (2015), Sarah Anderson's *Twins for the Billionaire* (2017), and Lucy Ellis's *Redemption of a Ruthless Billionaire* (2018). As Jan Cohn argues, the key to understanding the hero in these novels is to realize that "the sexual and the economic have become fused, creating a tense and ambiguous pairing of mutually referential signs. Sexual power *means* economic power; economic power *means* sexual power" (41).

Love is supposed to offer something that cannot be bought by the market. It is not supposed to be reducible to an exchange value any more than the individuated lover should be commoditized and exchangeable with any other person. The lover and the beloved are supposed to be unique, authentic, and irreplaceable. But in the world of late consumer capitalism, when romance is expressed and sustained through material consumption, love becomes co-opted by the market, operating as a function of the market rather than transcending the market or presenting an alternative realm of values to it. According to Eva Illouz (1997), "consumption and romantic emotions have progressively merged, each shrouding the other in a mystical halo. Commodities have now penetrated the romantic bond so deeply that they have become the invisible and unacknowledged spirit reigning over romantic encounters" (11). Illouz is writing about love in late capitalism generally, but this Marxist analysis also typifies some of the critiques that have been leveled against the representation of love in romance novels over the last half-century.

Scholarship on love in romance novels

The earliest sustained critique of the representation of heterosexual love and marriage in romance novels came from the prominent second-wave feminist, Germaine Greer. In *The Female Eunuch* (1970), Greer excoriates romantic love as an ideology and practice that reconciles women to accepting an oppressive patriarchal system:

> Love, love, love—all the wretched cant of it, masking egotism, lust, masochism, fantasy under a mythology of sentimental postures, a welter of self-induced miseries and joys, blinding and masking the essential personalities in the frozen gestures of courtship, in the kissing and the dating and the desire, the compliments and the quarrels which vivify its barrenness.
>
> (Greer 190–1)

Basing her critique on Georgette Heyer's *Regency Buck* (1935), Barbara Cartland's *The Wings of Love* (1962), and a handful of other novels, Greer argues that romance novels celebrate the worst aspects of love in patriarchal society and are nothing more than "mush" or "trash" because they feature "utterly ineffectual heroine(s)" who, far from striving for liberation from patriarchal oppression, instead end up "cherishing the chains of their bondage" (Greer 176).

For Greer and other second-wave feminists, romance novels do indeed portray contemporary ideas of romantic love accurately, but love in patriarchal society is precisely the problem for women. Love disempowers women, making them vulnerable to abuse and exploitation, justifying the restricted life opportunities available to them, and diverting their energies from overthrowing this system. Love encourages women to be submissive and servile. Feminist criticism of romance novels during the 1970s and 1980s focuses on concern about "images of women" represented in romance novels, and how stories of romantic love elaborated in these novels are damaging to women in all sorts of ways: economically, physically, psychologically, emotionally, and sexually. Ann Douglas accuses romance novels of being "soft-core porn" for women, in which "women's independence is made horrifically unattractive and unrewarding, her dependence presented as synonymous with excitement" (28). Tania Modleski argues that romance novels are disguised "revenge fantasies" where the cold and brutal hero's initial ill-treatment of the long-suffering heroine is avenged when he cedes power to the heroine at the end of the novel simply because he has fallen in love with her. Modleski contends that the contradictory demands placed on the heroine and reader, particularly acceding to the plot formula that romantic love will force a resolution in marriage, produces a text that resembles the state of hysteria. Thus reading romance novels is detrimental to women's mental health and emotional well-being.

Jan Cohn adds that romance reading is a noxious practice because "romance tells over and over a story about power deeply encoded within a story about love" (3). The moment when a heroine falls in love is the "nadir of her adventure" because love "places the heroine in peril of a shameful dependency" upon the cruel hero (29). Anticipating Lisa Fletcher's argument, based on speech-act theory, about the importance of the incantation "I love you" as *the* defining speech-act of the romance, Cohn suggests that love must always be announced because

> it is, in fact, the saying that matters, the speaking of the word. No romance hero, moreover, whatever offenses might be laid to him, ever speaks the word "love" in vain. Nor, once said, can love be withdrawn; nor will it ever alter.
>
> (32)

The hero's confession, "I love you," signals to the reader that he has been tamed and redeemed by love, and the heroine's "emotional battering . . . will never occur again" (173). The outward, visible sign of this redemptive, transformative love is his sharing or conferring of property rights upon the heroine—her hard-won reward for the suffering she has undergone at his hands.

Other feminists of the period are more sympathetic to how romance novels address women's needs. Feminist critics such as Ann Barr Snitow and Janice Radway contend that romance novels help to meet women's sexual and emotional needs, helping them explore new sexualized identities by focusing on sexual relations within a context women desire: romantic love and emotional fulfillment. Snitow agrees that romance novels are indeed pornography for women, but she argues that "there is something wonderful in the heroine's insistence that sex is more exciting and more momentous when it includes deep feeling"—which is how love and sex are portrayed in romances. Moreover, Snitow is the only critic from this period to point to a significant disjunction between feminist formulae for women's liberation and women's own hopes about love and emotional connection:

> The ubiquity of the books indicates a central truth: romance is a primary category of the female imagination. The women's movement has left this fact of female consciousness largely untouched. While most serious women *novelists* treat romance with irony and cynicism, most women do not. Harlequins may well be closer to describing women's hopes for love than the work of fine women novelists. Harlequins eschew irony; they take love straight.
>
> (160)

Snitow notes that for women to turn to such stories to meet vicariously their need for love, and to imbue their life with emotional warmth and "human values," is not a slur upon them, but upon patriarchal society: "The world that can make Harlequin romances appear warm is indeed a cold, cold place" (160). Janice Radway agrees. In what is perhaps the most famous study of romance novels of the 1980s, Radway's *Reading the Romance* argues that in a patriarchal society, marriage is organized in such a way that women provide support, care, and emotional work for their husbands and children but do not receive this nurturance in return. They do this unpaid work because it is justified by love. For Radway, romance novels vicariously provide women nurturance and fulfill their unmet emotional needs, but they are not ultimately helpful because they do not provide a plan for any revolution in social organization.

These feminist scholars read a limited sample of romance novels from a particular period—the 1970s and early 1980s—and treated novels within the genre as if they were all the same, historically unchanging in their representation of love and gender relations. Rita C. Hubbard was the first scholar to acknowledge difference and development within the genre, and to consider how it had changed over time. Studying 45 romance novels published between 1950 and 1983, Hubbard concludes that

> In the 1950s, romance novel relationships were basically complementary. This behavior mode was challenged in the 1960s and 1970s novels by tentative female rebellion to male dominance. It was replaced in the early 1980s romances with

> a symmetrical relationship style when both sexes began to share traits formerly considered gender-specific.
>
> (113)

However, the one idea that remains constant throughout this 33-year period, Hubbard argues, is the notion that love sanctions and justifies the often unreasonable actions of heroes and heroines. It attributes bad behavior to the right motives, and allows each to view the other in the best possible light. Love "transforms the faults of the hero—moodiness, arrogance, and occasional cruelty—into expressions of caring. Love permits the hero to view the heroine's weakness, ignorance, and capriciousness as endearing qualities" (117).

In her analysis of the growing sexual explicitness of romance novels, Thurston agrees that romance novels from different periods, and written by different novelists, portray a wide range of ideas and mixed messages about love (106). Barbara Cartland, for instance, imagines heroines experience love as "protection, submission, and service to others." For them, love means being transported "up to the stars" sexually—after marriage, of course. For the heroes, Cartland portrays love as a means of "possession and control—over the heroine's heart, mind, soul, body, and property" (38). During the early days of the "romance revolution" in the 1970s, Thurston notes that the heroine in Rosemary Rogers' novels experienced love as a mixture of pleasure, pain, cruelty and punishment, but although readers accepted this in some historical romances, they largely rejected such a picture of love in contemporary romances (50-f1). By the mid-1980s, romances began to feature new types of heroines who were more independent and autonomous, and representations of love began to change. The new heroine experiences

> a specific kind of love, one that frees respect and the right of self-determination from gender . . . In these stories, the heroine's ability to overcome hardship is a metaphor for her struggle and eventual emergence as an individual capable of the kind of love that overcomes all problems and obstacles.
>
> (86)

Mariam Darce Frenier similarly suggests that a change in how love was represented took place with the Americanization of the contemporary romance in the 1980s. Frenier argues that the Harlequin Mills & Boon romance novels of the 1970s and early 1980s equated love with lust and portrayed love as a dark obsession—evident in titles such as Ann Cooper's *Battle with Desire* (1978), Charlotte Lamb's *Dark Dominion* (1979), Yvonne Whittal's *Bitter Enchantment* (1979), and Daphne Clair's *The Loving Trap* (1980). Bitter jealousy was a sign of true love during an age that frequently featured the British heroine's painful competition with the "other woman" for the hero's attention and love. Frenier contends that with the publication of American-centered Silhouette Books in the 1980s, heroes became "more tender" and less hostile toward women, and "American heroines were not forced to see cruelty as love" (71). Yet Frenier remains concerned about the portrayal of love in popular romances. Even in modern romances, readers learn that "jealousy and possessiveness are characteristics of true love; that true love is monogamous and usually comes once in a lifetime; that such love means two become one instead of remaining separate people emotionally; and that separation should cause withdrawal symptoms" (105). In other words, love is represented unhealthily as addiction, and heroines, no matter how modern, "remained addicted to heroes who were addicted to them" (106). Even when feminists concede changes in romance novels that empowered women, they still worry about what romance reading is doing to women.

However, where feminist critics assume that writers and readers identify with the mistreated and misunderstood heroine and thereby open themselves up to potential abuse in real life, romance novelist Laura Kinsale argues that readers more typically use the heroine as a "placeholder" in journey of love with the hero: "the reader thinks about what she would have done in the heroine's place" (32). Readers analyze the heroine's emotions, responses and reactions to the hero and compare it to how they would have responded in the same situation (32). The romantic adventure is an internal one with readers experiencing "what a courtship feels like," but this is a courtship carried within the "androgynous reader" who situates herself with both hero and heroine (39). Doing so produces intense and varied emotional experiences during the act of reading romance novels akin to feelings of the early stages of romantic love: anticipation, excitement, sexual desire and arousal, pain, and cathartic relief and exultation when the barrier to love is overcome. According to romance writers, then, love is the mediating force that reconciles hero and heroine. Love motivates change: change in agendas, life goals, character, and behavior—for the better, naturally. Furthermore, love triumphant does not draw the heroine into the hero's world; instead, love feminizes the hero and draws him into the heroine's world, where he comes to share her values (Barlow and Krentz).

Here, then, are two diametrically opposed views about love presented in the first wave of feminist scholarship on romance novels and the second wave of romance authors' response to this scholarship. Feminist critics argue that romance novels stir up in women a yearning for romantic love in real life, but this is detrimental to women because romantic love is an ideology justifying the continuance of a patriarchal social order that disempowers and disadvantages women. Their focus is on the gendered social, political, and economic effects of romantic love. Romance novelists, on the other hand, focus on the individual effects of romantic love for fictional, fantastical heroes and heroines, arguing that love ameliorates differences, reconciles conflicts, and provides hope. As romance novelist Elizabeth Lowell puts it, "only in romances is an enduring, constructive bond—love—between a man and a woman celebrated" (90).

> That is the key. That is what makes romances unique and uniquely powerful in their appeal. Other styles of fiction deal at length with hate, murder, greed, lust, treachery, brutality, pettiness, vicious sexuality, violence, and unspeakable human degradation. If love appears in these novels it is in a minor role, a comet burning across the dark night of the soul leaving greater darkness in its wake. In romance novels, and in romance novels alone, love between a man and a woman is affirmed as an immensely powerful *constructive* force in human life.
>
> (90)

The current third wave of romance scholarship moves away from the question of whether portrayals of love in romance novels are good or bad for women, to ask instead how love is represented, how it functions in individual novels, and how these representations develop over time and across different cultures. In her survey of 80 years of Mills and Boon novels, jay Dixon concludes that the emphasis on love in romance novels changes over time. In the early twentieth century, love is still conceptualized as religious salvation or redemption (168). By the mid-century, love is based on mutual friendship that grows over time but it is also, in direct contrast, a sudden force that overwhelms. By the century's end, irresistible sexual attraction is an inescapable part of the experience of love. The romance, however, is always about love as the *raison d'être* of life; it socializes the hero into the world of the heroine, and it brings both on a journey of growth into adulthood, through which men and women become equal (33–47, 173). Above all, love in a Mills and Boon novel is "symbolized by the word 'home'—a place of caring, of emotional connectivity, of safety, of peace" (177).

Like Dixon's argument, Catherine Roach's analysis of love in romance novels is overwhelmingly positive. Roach suggests that romance novels are important because they provide foundational scripts that socialize Americans, teaching them how women and men should relate:

> Find your one true love—Your One and Only—and live happily ever after. To the ancient and perennial question of how to define and live the good life, how to achieve happiness and fulfillment, American pop culture's resounding answer is through the narrative of romance, sex, and love.
>
> (3)

Even though Roach cautions that there are other ways of thinking about loving relationships and other ways of being happy other than the romantic couple, *Happily Ever After: The Romance Story in Popular Culture* is ultimately a paean to the healing, redeeming, transformative, liberating, sex-positive and pleasurable effects of love as represented in romance novels and as practiced in real life. Love is the "ultimate concern of human life" (11). It is a "positive force for good" (22), bringing out the best in people: "love tempers pride, harsh judgment, and the violent outbursts of a reflexive defensiveness. Love grants the inner peace and self-confidence for the lover to become a stronger and wiser person. It leads to compassion, mercy, understanding, and kindness" (169). The romance novel ultimately entails hope because it "stakes its claim on the belief that the world is a good place and that despite all of life's injustice and suffering, both love and love stories make the world a better place" (23).

Other studies of love in third-wave scholarship on romance novels have bypassed the more common focus on dominant paradigms of white British and American romances to investigate lesser-known and more marginal bodies of romance fiction. Some of the most significant insights into love in African-American romance novels can be found in William Gleason and Eric Murphy Selinger's edited collection, *Romance Fiction and American Culture: Love as the Practice of Freedom?* (2016). Three chapters in this volume focus on Black American romance novelists. Julie Moody-Freeman and Conseula Francis both agree that one of the key problems Black romance novelists face is how to represent Black women's love and sexuality in white mainstream culture where a host of racist stereotypes about sexually transgressive Black women circulate. White stereotypes are not the only problem. Francis argues that the belief in Black culture that professional "Black women are unlovable" because they "have sacrificed relationship happiness to their ambitions" amounts to blaming bourgeois Black women for their difficulty in finding Black men as marriage partners, either because these men are unsuitable or unavailable (178). Moody-Freeman and Francis argue that where some Black women writers have employed the "politics of respectability" to counter such representations, populating their writings with Black women who foreground their morality, intellect, and middle-class virtues at the expense of suppressing their sexuality and shielding their bodies (Moody-Freeman 117; Francis 179), romance novelists such as Brenda Jackson and Zane restore the erotic in Black love, albeit in very different ways. Jackson embeds sexual desire and practice within a patriarchal Christian tradition where Black men take responsibility for emotional and sexual love, marriage, and family, insisting that Black men can indeed be the plausible and trustworthy heroes of Black romantic love (Moody-Freeman 117–33). Francis, on the other hand, focuses on the way Zane reframes sex as liberating, rather than oppressive, for Black heroines, who also find romantic love emotionally fulfilling (169–79). Francis argues that contemporary Black romance is revolutionary: it "doesn't throw out 'respectability'; it does, however, question the assumption that respectability is the end-all and be-all of black female existence, and that it precludes a wide range of sexual desires, activities, and satisfactions" (180).

The third chapter on Black romance in *Romance Fiction and American Culture* focuses on Beverly Jenkins' historical romances. Rita Dandridge argues that in Jenkins' novels, love among Black Americans is shown to be complex and multifaceted. It is not restricted to romantic love. Indeed, novels such as Jenkins' *Night Song* (1994) and *Through the Storm* (1998) begin with the heroine's display of love: a selfless agape love for humanity that in Black American history is associated with "those individuals who have sacrificed their lives in racially uplifting efforts in order to elevate the downtrodden and dispossessed persons in the race" (152). The love story Jenkins tells in these novels is not simply about courtship and romantic love; it is about how erotic love, represented by the hero's desire for the heroine, becomes fused with, and balances, the heroine's agape love for others, displayed in her community work. Eros intersects and clashes with agape when hero and heroine meet, and the hero sexually desires the heroine but obstructs her in her uplifting efforts, creating instability in their relationship with each other as well as those around them. However, the plot moves toward a resolution when hero and heroine incorporate both eros and agape within a relationship based on mutuality and friendship, and care for others demonstrated in the heroine's uplifting work.

The extant scholarship on love in romance novels provides many insights into what role love plays in maintaining and transforming gender and power relations; whether it is oppressive or liberating; how changing ideas about love as discourses of romance, sex, and intimacy become entangled at the end of the twentieth century; how novelists—as opposed to critics—treat the function of love within the romance plot; and how love in Black romance novels can break out of the stifling "politics of respectability" in dynamic and revolutionary ways, transforming respectability to include sexual and emotional pleasure and satisfaction. These insights are important and significant. Yet it remains the case that aside from Roach's monograph and Dandridge's chapter, none of these works are focused specifically on love in romance novels; their arguments about love are often incidental to broader arguments about other subjects. To date, the most sustained studies focusing specifically on love in romance novels have probably been produced by me (Teo "We Have to Learn to Love Imperially," "The Romance Novel," and "The Romance Novel in the Anglo-Cultural Tradition") and my co-authored work with Jodi McAlister on love in Australian romance novels. In my research into late nineteenth- and early twentieth-century Australian romance fiction ("We Have to Learn to Love Imperially"), I argue that historical conditions and literary traditions create a culture of pessimism as far as love was concerned in the nineteenth century. Women novelists did not believe love was sufficient to ensure a happy marital life for women because they set their stories in the

Australian bush or frontier, where the hardships that were experienced by women —the difficulties of pioneering farmsteads, environmental disasters, rampant alcoholism among men, and a culture of misogyny that saw the frequent abandonment of wives and children—were too well-known in colonial society. By the early twentieth century, however, Australia had become an independent nation and romance novelists rushed to join in the nationalistic project of literary nation-building, developing specifically Australian ideal types of heroes and heroines who could make love relationships succeed against the odds. The sturdy, independent Australian heroine whose character was honed by hard work and an intangible but spiritual connection to the land is able to succeed in forging a love relationship of companionship and mutuality with the hero as his "mate" because she is no stranger to work. The land itself mystically blesses and nurtures romantic love—an idea that continues well into romance novels written in the late twentieth and twenty-first centuries, as Jodi McAlister and I argue ("Love in Australian Romance Novels"): "the Australian bush plays an integral role in amplifying the emotional lives of Australians, and for producing successful Australian love relationships. Lovers find themselves and each other through encountering the Australian bush" (202), and the land—as the "third point in the Australian love triangle"—teaches heroes and heroines how to love (204).

My work has focused on the following research questions: how is love represented in heterosexual romance novels? How do ideas and representations of love change over time, and across different societies? What social, political, cultural, and historical conditions make love likely to succeed? What conditions create difficulties for novelists in plotting a plausible happy resolution to the love story? What is the function of love in these novels: what is love supposed to do, or to what broader purposes is love harnessed? How do we read discourses of love, sexuality, and intimacy intersectionally across and against the grain of, for example, class, race, ethnicity, or histories that are not conducive to romantic love? My ongoing research into how love structures the romance plots of historical novels, and how history militates against the straightforward functioning of the romance plot, are tentative steps in this last direction.

Clearly, there is still so much we need to understand about the representation, role, and operation of love in romance novels. We need more studies that focus on traditions of love in different regional, national, and historical societies, and diverse sexual cultures; on how representations of love in different subgenres of romance—historical, inspirational, LGBTQIA, for instance—shed light on key issues of our own time; on what assumptions different authors hold about romantic love, how they treat it in their oeuvre and whether, like Crusie, their handling of love changes over time; and how the proliferation of niche subgenres and digital publishing is affecting the types of love and range of lovers that now crowd into popular romance fiction.

Notes

1 See Eric M. Selinger and Laura Vivanco's chapter "Romance and/as religion" in this volume for a more detailed discussion of Reddy's thesis and how it relates to romance novels.
2 Some parts of this section have appeared in Teo "The Romance Novel."
3 For a more in-depth discussion of love in Austen's novels see Polhemus and Weisser.
4 This secularization, however, is a superficial phenomenon relating specifically to the effacement of overt aspects of Christianity in modern romance novels. As Selinger and Vivanco's chapter

shows, love in romance novels remains pervasively and persistently religious. Catherine Roach, too, argues that romance novels continue to promulgate a "religion of love" (22–3).

5 See Sarah Frantz Lyons and Eric Murphy Selinger's discussion of the crucial differences between *The Flame and the Flower* and *Sweet Savage Love* in their 2016 chapter, "Strange Stirrings, Strange Yearnings: *The Flame and the Flower, Sweet Savage Love*, and the Lost Diversities of Blockbuster Historical Romance."

Works cited

Anderson, Rachel. *The Purple Heart Throbs: The Subliterature of Love*. London: Hodder & Stoughton, 1974.

Austen, Jane. *Emma*. 1816. Penguin, 1966.

Bailey. *Beth. From Front Porch to Back Seat: Courtship in Twentieth-Century America*. Johns Hopkins University Press, 1988.

Barlow, Linda and Jayne Ann Krentz. "Beneath the Surface: The Hidden Codes of Romance." *Dangerous Men and Adventurous Women: Romance Writers on the Appeal of the Romance*, edited by Jayne Ann Krentz, University of Pennsylvania Press, 1992, 15–30.

Belsey, Catherine. "Postmodern Love: Questioning the Metaphysics of Desire." *New Literary History*, vol. 5, no. 3, 1994, 683–705.

Brown, Sonya C. "Does This Book Make Me Look Fat?" *Journal of Popular Romance Studies*, vol. 1, no. 2, 2011. http://jprstudies.org/2011/03/does-this-book-make-me-look-fat/.

Bywaters, Barbara. "Decentering the Romance: Jane Austen, Georgette Heyer, and Popular Romance Fiction." *Georgette Heyer: A Critical Retrospective*, edited by Mary Fahnestock-Thomas, Prinnyworld Press, 2001, 493–508.

Cancian, Francesca M. "The Feminization of Love." *Signs*, vol. 11, no. 4, 1986, 692–709.

Cherlin, Andrew J. *The Marriage-Go-Round: The State of Marriage and the Family in America Today*. Vintage, 2010.

Cohn, Jan. *Romance and the Erotics of Property: Mass-Market Fiction for Women*. Duke University Press, 1988.

Collins, Marcus. *Modern Love: An Intimate History of Men and Women in Twentieth-Century Britain*. Atlantic Books, 2003.

Crusie, Jennifer. *Fast Women*. St. Martin's, 2001.

Crusie, Jennifer. *Bet Me*. St. Martins, 2004.

Dandrige, Rita B. "Love Prevailed despite What American History Said: Agape and Eros in Beverly Jenkins's Night Song and through the Storm." *Romance Fiction and American Culture: Love as the Practice of Freedom?* edited by William A. Gleason, and Eric Murphy Selinger, Ashgate, 2016, 151–166.

"Disabilities in Romance." All About Romance, www.likesbooks.com/disability.html. Accessed August 31, 2015.

Dixon, jay. *The Romance Fiction of Mills & Boon, 1909–1990s*. University College London Press, 1999.

Douglas, Ann. "Soft-Porn Culture." *The New Republic*, vol. 11, August 1980, 25–29.

Fletcher, Lisa. *Historical Romance Fiction: Heterosexuality and Performativity*. Ashgate, 2008.

Francis, Conseula. "Flipping the Script: Romancing Zane's Urban Erotica." *Romance Fiction and American Culture: Love as the Practice of Freedom?* edited by William A. Gleason, and Eric Murphy Selinger, Ashgate, 2016, 167–180.

Frenier, Mariam Darce. *Good-bye Heathcliff: Changing Heroes, Heroines, Roles, and Values in Women's Category Romances*. Greenwood, 1988.

Giddens, Anthony. *The Transformation of Intimacy: Sexuality, Love and Eroticism in Modern Society*. Stanford University Press, 1992.

Gillis, John R. "From Ritual to Romance: Toward an Alternative History of Love." *Emotion and Social Change: Toward a New Psycho-History*, Edited by Carol Z. Stearns, and Peter N. Stearns, Holmes and Meier, 1988, 87–122.

Gleason, William A. and Eric Murphy Selinger. *Romance Fiction and American Culture: Love as the Practice of Freedom?* Ashgate, 2016.

Goris, An. "Mind, Body, Love: Nora Roberts and the Evolution of Popular Romance Studies." *Journal of Popular Romance Studies*, vol. 3, no. 1, 2012. http://jprstudies.org/2012/10/mind-body-love-nora-roberts-and-the-evolution-of-popular-romance-studies-by-an-goris/.

Greer, Germaine. *The Female Eunuch (1970)*. HarperCollins, 1993.

Howard, Linda. *Mr. Perfect*. Pocket Books, 2003.

Hubbard, Rita C. "Relationship Styles in Popular Romance Novels, 1950–1983." *Communication Quarterly*, vol. 33, no. 2, 1985, 113–125.

Hull, E.M. *The Sheik*. 1919. New York: Buccaneer Books, 1921.

Illouz, Eva. *Consuming the Romantic Utopia: Love and the Cultural Contradictions of Capitalism*. University of California Press, 1997.

"Imperfect Heroine/Hot Hero Contemporary Non Paranormal Romance." Goodreads.com, www.goodreads.com/list/show/41973.Imperfect_Heroine_Hot_Hero_Contemporary_Non_Paranormal_Romance. Accessed August 31, 2015.

Jamieson, Lynn. "Intimacy Transformed? A Critical Look at the 'Pure Relationship.'" *Sociology*, vol. 33, no. 3, 1999, 477–494.

Jamieson, Lynn. "Intimacy as a Concept: Explaining Social Change in the Context of Globalisation or Another Form of Ethnocentricism?" *Sociological Research Online*, vol. 16, no. 4, 2011. www.socresonline.org.uk/16/4/15.html.

Kern, Stephen. *The Culture of Love: Victorians to Moderns*. Harvard University Press, 1992.

Kinsale, Laura. "The Androgynous Reader: Point of View in the Romance." *Dangerous Men and Adventurous Women: Romance Writers on the Appeal of the Romance*, edited by Jayne Ann Krentz, University of Pennsylvania Press, 1992, 31–44.

Krentz, Jayne Ann, editor. *Dangerous Men and Adventurous Women: Romance Writers on the Appeal of the Romance*. University of Pennsylvania Press, 1992.

Langhamer, Claire. *The English in Love: The Intimate Story of An Emotional Revolution*. Oxford: Oxford University Press, 2013.

Lyons, Sarah Frantz and Eric Murphy Selinger. "Strange Stirrings, Strange Yearnings: The Flame and the Flower, Sweet Savage Love, and the Lost Diversities of Blockbuster Historical Romance." *Romance Fiction and American Culture: Love as the Practice of Freedom?* edited by William A. Gleason, and Eric Murphy Selinger, Ashgate, 2016, 89–110.

Lystra, Karen. *Searching the Heart: Women, Men and Romantic Love in Nineteenth-Century America*. Oxford University Press, 1989.

McAlister, Jodi and Hsu-Ming, Teo. "Love in Australian Romance Novels." *The Popular Culture of Romantic Love in Australia*, edited by Hsu-Ming Teo, Australian Scholarly Publishing, 2017, 194–222.

McAlister, Jodi Ann. "Romancing the Virgin: Female Virginity Loss and Love in Popular Literatures in the West." Ph.D. dissertation, Macquarie University, 2015.

Menocal, Maria Rosa. *The Arabic Role in Medieval Literary History: A Forgotten Heritage*. University of Pennsylvania Press, 1987.

Modleski, Tania. *Loving with a Vengeance: Mass-produced Fantasies for Women*. Archon, 1982.

Moody-Freeman, Julie E. "Scripting Black Love in the 1990s: Pleasure, Respectability, and Responsibility in an Era of HIV/AIDS." *Romance Fiction and American Culture: Love as the Practice of Freedom?*, Edited by William A. Gleason, and Eric Murphy Selinger, Ashgate, 2016, 111–127.

Neal, Lynn S. *Romancing God: Evangelical Women and Inspirational Fiction*. University of North Carolina Press, 2006.

Pan, Lynn. *When True Love Came to China*. Hong Kong University Press, 2015.

"Plus-size Heroine in Romance." Goodreads.com, www.goodreads.com/topic/show/976525-plus-size-heroine-in-romance. Accessed August 31, 2015.

"Plus-Sized Heroines." All About Romance, www.likesbooks.com/curvy.html. Accessed August 31, 2015.

Polhemus, Robert. *Erotic Faith: Being in Love from Jane Austen to D.H. Lawrence*. University of Chicago Press, 1990.

Radway, Janice. *Reading the Romance: Women, Patriarchy, and Popular Literature*. University of North Carolina Press, 1984.

Ramsdell, Kristin. *Romance Fiction: A Guide to the Genre*. Libraries Unlimited, 1999.

Reddy, William M. *The Making of Romantic Love: Longing and Sexuality in Europe, South Asia and Japan, 900-1200 CE*. University of Chicago Press, 2012.

Rhodes, Kathlyn. *The Desert Dreamers*. Hutchinson, 1909.

Rhodes, Kathlyn. *Desert Lovers*. Hutchinson, 1922.

Roach, Catherine M. *Happily Ever After: The Romance Story in Popular Culture*. Indiana University Press, 2016.

Rothman, Ellen K. *Hands and Hearts: A History of Courtship in America*. Harvard University Press, 1987.

Rougemont, Denis de. *Love in the Western World* (1956). Translated by Montgomery Belgion, Princeton University Press, 1983.

Seidman, Steven. *Romantic Longings: Love in America, 1830-1980*. Routledge, 1991.

Shumway, David R. *Modern Love: Romance, Intimacy, and the Marriage Crisis*. New York University Press, 2003.

Snitow, Anne Barr. "Mass Market Romance: Pornography for Women Is Different." *Radical History Review*, vol. 20, 1979, 141–161.

Stone, Lawrence. "Passionate Attachments in the West in Historical Perspective." *Passionate Attachments: Thinking about Love*, edited by William Gaylin, and Ethel Person, Free Press, 1988, 15–26.

Teo, Hsu-Ming. "The Romance of White Nations: Imperialism, Popular Culture and National Histories." *After the Imperial Turn: Thinking With and Through the Nation*, edited by Antoinette Burton, Duke University Press, 2003, 279–292.

Teo, Hsu-Ming. *Desert Passions: Orientalism and Romance Novels*. University of Texas Press, 2012.

Teo, Hsu-Ming. "'We Have to Learn to Love Imperially': Love in Late Colonial and Federation Australian Romance Novels." *Journal of Popular Romance Studies*, vol. 4, no. 2, 2014. http://jprstudies.org/2014/10/we-have-to-learn-to-love-imperially-love-in-late-colonial-and-federation-australian-romance-novelsby-hsu-ming-teo/.

Teo, Hsu-Ming. "The Romance Novel." *Gender: Love*, edited by Jennifer C. Nash, Macmillan, 2016, 255–270.

Teo, Hsu-Ming. "The Romance Genre in the Anglo-Cultural Tradition." *Oxford Research Encyclopedia of Literature*. Oxford Unviersity Press, 2018. DOI: 10.1093/acrefore/9780190201098.013.415. http://literature.oxfordre.com/view/10.1093/acrefore/9780190201098.001.0001/acrefore-9780190201098-e–415

Teo, Hsu-Ming. "Cultural Authenticity, the Oppressive Family, and East Asian Romance Novels." *Journal of Popular Romance Studies*, vol. 9, 2020. https://www.jprstudies.org/2020/03/cultural-authenticity-the-family-and-east-asian-american-romance-novels/.

Thurston, Carol. *The Romantic Revolution: Erotic Novels for Women and the Quest for a New Sexual Identity*. University of Illinois Press, 1987.

"Top 10 Phattest Plus-Size Heroines." Heroes and Heartbreakers, www.heroesandheartbreakers.com/blogs/2011/08/plus-size-heroines. Accessed August 31, 2015.

Weisser, Susan Ostrov. *The Glass Slipper: Women and Love Stories*. Rutgers University Press, 2013.

22 Romance and/as religion

Eric Murphy Selinger and Laura Vivanco

> "Romance is the heart of life. Without it, the world would be a very small, sad place to live."[1]

Karl Marx famously stated that the "wretchedness of religion" was "at once an expression of and a protest against real wretchedness. Religion is the sigh of the oppressed creature, the heart of a heartless world and the soul of soulless conditions. It is the opium of the people" (131). Romance, too, has been described by skeptics as offering an addictive promise of escape from real-world troubles even as the genre offers quiet support for the political status quo. David Margolies, for instance, argues in "Mills & Boon: Guilt Without Sex" that "As in Marx's description of religion as an opiate and the heart of a heartless world, the romance offers escape from an oppressive reality, or justifies it as a vale of tears that women pass through to salvation" (12) and Bridget Fowler, in *The Alienated Reader: Women and Romance in the Twentieth Century*, draws on the same description, noting a "strong resemblance" between religion and romance, in that just as the former is "the plane on which the masses express their true material and social needs," the latter is "also the 'heart of a heartless world'" (174–5). As Teresa L. Ebert explains in an essay for *Textual Practice*, such parallels are based on the sense that religion and romance both "explain the material by the immaterial and substitute a change of heart in the subject for the material transformation of objective conditions" (10). Like other forms of popular culture, Ebert writes, romance resembles religion in that they both "re-orient the subject but leave intact the objective social conditions in which she lives. They do this by supplanting social justice and economic equality with love, intimacy, and caring" (10).

This is, to be sure, only one of several possible accounts of either religion or romance. Scholars of religion and social justice movements in the United States have often discussed the central role of churches in fostering civic and political engagement, arguing that far from supplanting social justice work or dulling like an opiate, religion has been "an important domain for contesting market and state institutions" and a spur to "public and civic action" (Hondagneu-Sotelo 5). Likewise, although research is needed in order to determine the extent to which romance reading has the same practical effects, it is clear that, at the very least, romance novels and novelists have raised public awareness of a range of social, political, environmental, and health issues.[2] They have, moreover, frequently dealt with them in ways which do not imply that all injustices and traumas can be solved by true love alone—even as they treat true love in ways which imply a complex set of debts to, and reinterpretations of, religious discourse.[3] To understand the relationships between religion and popular romance thus demands an expansive, rather than reductive, set of approaches. This chapter surveys how romance scholars have discussed how religion, especially Christianity, can be read as a romance; how Christianity and other religions have shaped the history of, and been represented in, the romance genre; and how the vision of love promulgated by the romance genre, even in ostensibly secular texts, can often be read as a religious or divine phenomenon: something *unconditional, omnipotent,* and *eternal.*

Religion as romance

Although critics skeptical of the promises and effects of religion have tended to point out its parallels with romance in order to condemn the latter, there have been more positive assessments of the similarities between the central narratives of romance and Christianity, a religious tradition which "is easily read as a love story" (Roach 171). In *Happily Ever After: The Romance Story in Popular Culture,* Catherine Roach deploys a "two-directional religious analysis" (172) to explore parallels between the underlying narrative of Christianity and what she sees as a singular "romance story" that pervades not only romance fiction, but all forms of popular media and culture. This "story" is, to be precise, an imperative —"Find your one true love and live happily ever after" (2)—and Roach argues that this great romantic commission maps neatly onto "the ideal relationship between the believer and the One True Love of Christ the Son or the Christian Father God, and then the believer's reward of life everlasting" (171). Roach sets aside the "chicken-and-egg" question of whether a belief in the healing "resurrection power" of love (172) comes to the romance story from Christianity, or whether this faith in love predates Christianity and has been baptized, so to speak, by later theology. Instead, she makes synchronic, non-denominational claims such as "stories of the Christian God and romance intertwine easily because both entail belief in the divine power of love" (23) and

> the love of a good woman, or good man, or God, or Son of God, has the power to heal all wounds. . .to forgive all sins stretching back to the stain of original sin, to resurrect a dead man, to save a lost soul, to integrate false persona and true self, to make a real man—or real woman—out of you.
>
> (172)

Claims such as these align theological and secular, psychological discourses without addressing potential conflicts or tensions between them. Roach writes, that is to say, from a *functionalist* perspective rather than a theological one, leaving space for future research that disaggregates both the religious and romance sides of her analysis.

Roach is not the first romance reader, author, or scholar to perceive that "the mythic narrative of Christianity follows the pattern of the romance narrative" (Roach 171). In a memorable passage from Lynn S. Neal's *Romancing God: Evangelical Women and Inspirational Fiction,* Christian romance author Robin Jones Gunn makes a similar claim to explain the congruence between her evangelical faith and her chosen genre. "When I was young, as a teenager, I read a love story that changed my life," Gunn recalls telling a skeptical radio interviewer.

> "In the first few chapters everything falls apart and you think they're never going to get back together again. And then, about three quarters of the way through, he does everything he can to prove his love to her and she still won't come to him and be his bride. But then in the last chapter he comes riding in on a white horse and he takes her away to be with him forever." And the interviewer said, "Hmmpf, how could that change your life? It sounds like a formula romance novel." I said, "Really? I was talking about the Bible—white horse and everything."
>
> (183)

Like Roach, Neal comes to popular romance scholarship from the discipline of religious studies, but where Roach takes on "the romance story" and her own experiences as an "aca-fan" of the genre (including her efforts to write and publish romance novels of her own, under the name Catherine LaRoche), *Romancing God* is a more narrowly focused ethnographic study of American evangelical women readers—mostly white, some African American—and their engagement with the subgenre of Christian popular romance fiction. Chapter 18 of this volume deals in depth with this subgenre; after offering a useful history of its publication in the United States, Neal turns to an in-depth exploration of "the ways readers *used* evangelical romance" as part of their "devotional lives," a use that "both configures and reflects their daily practice of religion" (10–11, emphasis added).

As Neal points out, there is substantial Biblical support for considering God to be "the ultimate lover" (159), from the love lyrics of the Song of Songs to the injunction in the first epistle of John (4:7–8) to "love one another: for love is of God: and every one that loveth is born of God, and knoweth God . . . for God is love." Such passages are central to the understanding of Christianity which is shared by Neal's interview subjects, and the novels they read—which "narrate the power of God's love, not the force of his judgment"—help them to "realize and remember a romancing God" (159). Readers use the sentimental "religio-romantic" (39) framework supplied by fiction to interpret God's work in history and in their individual lives, and they study scripture through the interpretive lens that romance provides. Neal quotes several interview subjects, for example, who testify to the impact of reading Francine Rivers's *Redeeming Love*, a novel which transforms the brief, schematic Biblical treatment of the prophet Hosea and his wife Gomer into a sweeping romance between Michael Hosea and Angel (née Sarah) during the nineteenth-century California gold rush. "You know the story [of Hosea]," one tells her, "but it doesn't really hit you as loud in the Bible as it does in the book" (164). For such readers, Neal explains, "fictional devotion transforms hearing into knowing, doubt into certainty, and a vague sense of God into a clear daily reality" (166).

This romantic account of Christianity has had both theological and aesthetic critics, not least within American evangelical culture itself, but Neal is scrupulously nonjudgmental. "Understanding this religio-aesthetic world, which lauds the very concepts that many disdain—mediocrity, predictability, utility, and sentimentality—forces us to re-examine our own scholarly imaginations," she notes (195), and *Romancing God* offers a measured, reflective example of how this re-examination might proceed, not only in future work on the evangelical genre world she studies, but on readers and texts from other religious traditions. Does a comparable reading of religion as romance happen, for example, among the authors and readers of Islamic romance, which is increasingly published around the globe in both mainstream and web-based (e.g., Wattpad) publishing contexts?[4] Do Jewish romance authors and readers read scripture, post-scriptural source texts, or Jewish customs and observance through a romantic lens? Can something similar be seen in texts that draw on non-Abrahamic traditions—for example, in Buddhist or Hindu romances—and how might these differ, either in terms of the texts or their reception? These are questions that further research should address.

Although Neal briefly mentions historical precedents for contemporary evangelical culture's model of a romantic God, neither she nor Roach discuss when or how this romantic vision of Christianity evolved, and neither explores the history of romantic love in terms of its incorporation of Christian language and ideals. Such topics have, however, been treated at length by others, and two turning points seem of particular note for the study of romance fiction from a religious perspective: the emergence of "*fin' amor*, or, literally, 'refined love'" (May 119) in Western European writing of the twelfth and thirteenth centuries; and the exaltation of marriage by the Protestant Reformation. (For an extended discussion of romantic love in popular romance, see Chapter 21 in this volume.)

Religion and romance: a shared history

In *Love: A History*, British philosopher Simon May writes that in the poems and prose that describe *fin 'amor* we find a "revolutionary thought: a single human being might be worthy of the sort of love that was formerly reserved for God" (129). As Rosemary Radford Reuther explains, although

> Christian ascetics since Origen had labored to distinguish the spiritual love of God from sexual passion ... from the twelfth century, the two had begun to flow into each other. Poets of secular love had adopted elements of religious language, while contemplative writers, such as Richard of St. Victor, recognized that sexual passion and spiritual love passion, though morally opposite, were psychologically similar.
>
> (180)

The roots of Roach's "two-directional religious analysis" (172) in which the love of God and the love of a good fellow human are not only functionally indistinguishable, but also often share the same discourse, may thus lie in the *fin 'amor* revolution—as, perhaps, does the romance genre's faith that love "tempers pride, harsh judgment, and the violent outbursts of a reflexive defensiveness," instilling in their place such qualities as "compassion, mercy, understanding, and kindness" (Roach 169). In the *fin 'amor* tradition, after all, to love another person properly is to transform the self through the cultivation of "'courtly' dispositions of service and courtesy, patience and proportion" and thus join, whatever one's social class, "the nobility of the heart" (May 128).

To cultural historian William M. Reddy, the crucial revolution of *fin 'amor* (or, as he spells it, *fin'amors*) lies less in its focus on a human beloved than in its attitude toward sex. "Certain twelfth-century aristocrats and their imitators insisted that sexual partnerships became a source of moral improvement and transcendent joy if they were founded on 'true love' (*fin'amors*)," he writes in *The Making of Romantic Love: Longing and Sexuality in Europe, South Asia, and Japan, 900–1200 CE*. Although scholars differ on the sources of this transformation, Reddy observes that there is "general agreement that the twelfth century's positive vision of sexual partnerships was something entirely new in Western literature and that such positive visions have been constantly with us ever since" (41). Rather than trace this vision to Muslim or pagan sources, as others have done,[5] Reddy attributes it to an aristocratic revolt against Gregorian church reformers who "systematized in an extreme form the doctrine that sexual appetite was an outgrowth of original sin" (87) and thus brought what had previously been a marginal ascetic strain in Christian thought into central institutional prominence. Against this account of all sexual impulses as tainted by sin, even within marriage (43), champions of *fin'amors* riposted with the claim that true love was "[s]o holy … that any sexual enjoyment that furthered love's aims" was thereby rendered "good and innocent" (44). For Reddy, this new "love doctrine" thus begins as a form of "covert religious dissent" (44), blossoms into a "full-fledged shadow religion with a morality and a ritual all its own" (167), and lingers on in the "typical Western configuration of 'romantic love,'" in which true love not only stands "in sharp contrast to sexual desire" considered as mere lust or appetite, but also offers the key to "mastering and purifying desire" into something sacred and worthy of praise (45).[6]

Although Reddy devotes only a few pages to the afterlife of *fin'amor* in modern romantic love culture—he discusses its echoes in films from the 1990s and early 2000s (380–6), and makes a brief but provocative argument for reading *fin'amor* as an instance of what Eve Kosofsky Sedgwick calls "queer performativity" (387)—the links between this turn in religious history and the development of popular romance fiction have been discussed at greater length by Joseph Crawford. In *Twilight of the Gothic: Vampire Fiction and the Rise of the Paranormal Romance, 1991–2012*, Crawford notes that the "appearance of the aristocratic cultural ideal of *fin' amor*, 'fine' or 'courtly' love, which postulated the then almost unheard-of idea that, under the right conditions, love between men and women could potentially be a morally or spiritually ennobling force," was not simply concurrent with the "rise" of the heroic romance as a literary genre in twelfth-century France," but a crucial factor contributing to the popularity of this genre—which, in turn, became identified with the love ideal it espoused. ("[S]o thorough" did the identification of this new code of courtship with this new form of writing eventually become," Crawford explains, "that, when we wish to refer to intense and ennobling love-relationships today, we no longer speak of *fin' amor*: we refer, instead, to 'romantic love'" (12).) The opening chapter of Crawford's study, dryly titled "The First 800 Years," tracks the emergence, dismantling, and return of fiction in which "'romantic love' went alongside 'romantic heroism' and 'romantic enchantment'": a combination so enduringly popular that

> when we consider the modern literature of supernatural-themed romance fiction, our first question should not be how stories of love and the supernatural came to coexist within the same genre; rather, we should investigate how it came to pass that, after five centuries of unity, they ever came to be separated.
>
> (12–13)

We must be careful not to overstate the similarities between these early "romances" and the modern romance novel. Although both may insist on love as "a morally or spiritually ennobling force" (Crawford 11), the former offered no guarantee that its lover-protagonists would end up alive and together, while in modern romance novels the Happily Ever After (HEA) or at least Happy For Now (HFN) ending "is inherent from the very beginning of the story, as part of its narrative structure" (Roach 173). This generic emphasis on successful courtship points to the second turning point in the history of romantic love and religion: the Protestant Reformation.

As Stephanie Coontz observes in *Marriage, a History: How Love Conquered Marriage*, "many scholars trace the celebration of married love and companionship to the Protestant Reformation in the sixteenth century" (123), and although it may be argued that the Reformation merely "accelerated" a "trend toward idealizing marriage" (Coontz 132), it is clear that the relative value of marriage and celibacy played an important role in religious debates of the time:

> Protestants bitterly opposed the papacy's policies and pronouncements on marriage ... Catholics were wrong, they said, to call marriage a necessary evil or a second-best existence to celibacy. Rather, marriage was "a glorious estate." ... Faced with these attacks, the Catholic Church stiffened its position on the spiritual superiority of celibacy. In 1563 the Council of Trent declared: "If anyone says that the married state excels the state of virginity or celibacy, and that it is better and happier to be united in matrimony than to remain in virginity or celibacy, let him be anathema."
>
> (Coontz 132–4)

Although "these differences meant less in practice than in theory" (Coontz 134), the Catholic Church continues to uphold the ideal of priestly celibacy and it is still possible to find traces of Reformation-era debates over the relative statuses of celibacy and marriage in twenty-first-century popular romance fiction. Nettie, the heroine of Piper Huguley's *A Treasure of Gold*, is initially convinced that she will never marry because she is "someone who has been set apart from others ... If I were in the Catholic faith, I would probably be someone who would join a convent" (97). In response Jay, her hero, asks "Do you really believe that is what God wants of you? He wants you to live and to share in his gifts. One of his greatest gifts is the love between a man and a woman" (98). Given that it concludes with Nettie and Jay's wedding, the novel would appear to endorse the opinion that marital love is a greater gift than celibate religious life, a denouement that may lend support to Jayashree Kamblé's assertion that the "structures of feeling and being" in the romance novel are "ineluctably grounded" in a "Protestant ethos" (Kamblé 131).[7] (Some counter-examples to Kamblé's argument will be discussed below.)

Among Protestants, as Ian Watt explains, "the assimilation of the values of romantic love to marriage ... occurred particularly early in England, and was closely connected with the Puritan movement" (155). Puritans considered "sensuous delight in the body of one's spouse ... an essential element of the comfort which marriage must provide" (Leites 388) and over time their "conception of marriage and sexual relations generally became the accepted code of Anglo-Saxon society" (Watt 137). The author Samuel Richardson "played an important part in establishing this new code" (Watt 137): a significant fact for the history of the romance novel since Richardson's *Pamela* (1740) is often discussed as a progenitor not only of the novel in English, but specifically of the romance novel.[8] In this context, it is worth noting that Richardson "regarded himself as a moralist first, committed to the social as well as spiritual reformation of his readers," writing a novel rather than a conduct manual in order to "steal in" doctrines of Christianity "under the fashionable guise of an amusement" (Houlihan Flynn ix–x). Jane Austen, who has been described as "the mother of the romance novel" (Tyler 240), also "stole in" such doctrines and did so with such skill that Richard Whately, who would later be appointed Anglican Archbishop of Dublin, "extolled Austen's novels in the *Quarterly Review* (1821) for rendering moral lessons and Christian principles more instructive by unobtrusively conveying them through lifelike characters and everyday settings rather than by making them 'too palpably prominent'" (Liebenow 121).

Pamela and Austen's novels would nowadays be shelved as "literature" rather than as "popular romance" but across the nineteenth century Christianity was an important element of popular fiction as well. As Rachel Anderson notes in her pre-history of modern popular romance, *The Purple Heart Throbs: The Sub-Literature of Love*, "God was still very much in evidence in all forms of popular fiction in the 1850s" (20) and she quotes an 1897 *Publisher's Circular* declaring that "Of all forms of fiction, the semi-religious is the most popular" (141). Although in "the later years of the century the great tide of religious fervour was beginning to ebb" (22), it never entirely receded, Anderson observes; for example, Florence Barclay's deeply religious romance novel *The Rosary* (1909) "was said to have been read and wept over by every housemaid in the British Isles" (121).

Although Anderson's history recounts a gradual de-Christianization of popular romantic literature, this does not equate to a secularization. Periodic flare-ups of an "erotico-spiritual religious revivalism" (151) punctuate her narrative, so that even during a decade like the 1930s in which "the majority of romantic novelists ... showed little interest in God" this shift did not remove religion from romantic fiction. Rather, religion in romance "shook off even the pretence of Christianity and appeared in its true light as a religion of erotic love," in which "[t]he state of *being in love* became for the romantic heroine what the state of grace is to the Christian" (205). Anderson does not take this "religion of love" particularly seriously: she pokes fun at "heroines' vaguely Christian feelings" and the way that "[i]n" times of elation or distress, romantic characters still resorted to prayer, though to whom or to what they prayed is usually left unspecified" (207). Yet even these comments allow us to view with some skepticism claims by scholars about the lack of religiosity in later romance —as when Batsleer et al, for example, sharply contrast Barclay's *The Rosary* with modern works in terms of the earlier novel's deployment of religious ideas and discourse.[9] Indeed, if religiosity is muted in the majority of romance novels published since the 1940s, this may have less to do with the tenor of the times than with the exigencies of mass-market publication, as when Alan Boon, of the romance publisher Mills & Boon, declared that "As a minor line of policy, we have sought to avoid 'red-rag' controversial problems—two of which traditionally are politics and religion" (McAleer 190).

In Anderson's account, then, religion in romance persists, but in a watered-down form, declining from doctrinal specificity to an uncontroversial, vaguely upbeat form of romantic uplift. "There are today [in the early 1970s] still some novelists who admit freely to specific Christian beliefs which they try to incorporate into their novels," she concludes, but "the majority of today's romantic novelists are far less specific about the motivating ideals behind their work," so that "[t]heir ideals tend to be undefined spiritual qualities" (275). Yet the strand of romance writing which explicitly interweaves romantic love with substantive and quite specific theological material continues, and not only in the evangelical Christian "inspirational" romance subgenre discussed in Chapter 18. The work of Alex Beecroft, an "asexual, queer positive" Christian romance author who writes romances featuring pairs of male protagonists, offers a case in point. As Eric Murphy Selinger has argued, Beecroft's breakout novel *False Colors* deploys carefully-chosen scriptural echoes and Christian tropes in defense of embodied same-sex love, including precisely the Biblical quotes and arguments that were raised at the 2007 Church of England synod, a year before the novel's publication, to push for the inclusion of queer Christians in church life ("Redeeming M/M Love"). Beecroft has also described receiving "an amazing couple of emails" from a man who had used another novel, *Captain's Surrender*, "to reassure his friend, who was coming to the realization that he was gay, that this didn't mean he was also damned. My writing saved a man from despair and from losing his faith" (Beecroft, "Alex Beecroft"). Such pastoral work by popular romance authors is not uncommon; indeed, Vivanco argues that "modern popular romances are novels whose authors have assumed pastoral roles, offering hope to their readers through works which propagate faith in the goodness and durability of love" (*Faith, Love, Hope*, "Introduction," n.p.). More work needs to be done to identify and analyze modern romance novels containing strong religious elements which are published by presses or imprints which are not dedicated solely to publishing religious fiction—and, in addition, to novels whose religious elements are not those derived from Protestant Christianity.

Studies of Anglo-American popular romance fiction tend to emphasize the genre's Protestant foundations, but other forms of Christianity have also found a home in the genre. Scholars of post-Civil War Spanish literature have explored its *novelas rosas*, romance novels in which the heroines tended to share "key attributes with the docile, passive feminine model nurtured by the Catholic Church" (O'Byrne 44) under the Franco regime. Diana Holmes' *Romance and Readership in Twentieth-Century France* offers an extended discussion of "Marie Petitjean de la Rosière (1875–1946) ... [who] published her first romantic novels in the early 1900s" and whose "brother Frédéric (1876–1949) acted as her business manager, adviser, and general collaborator," joining with her as co-author under the *nom-de-plume* "Delly" (49). "In the 1930s and 1940s," Holmes writes, "Delly was already a brand name, the guarantee of a page-turning, pleasurable read that was nonetheless entirely in line with Catholic, conservative values ... Delly novels express the values of the conservative, Catholic French Right" (49–50). To date there has been little research into English-language Catholic romance authors, but one novel by Meriol Trevor, better-known for her work in other genres (including a biography of Cardinal Newman) is discussed in Janice Radway's influential *Reading the Romance: Women, Patriarchy, and Popular Literature*, and Lynn S. Neal's *Romancing God: Evangelical Women and Inspirational Fiction* includes quotations from an interview with another Catholic author, Peggy Stoks, who sees her fiction as an opportunity "to explain the Catholic faith to my Protestant brothers and sisters" (111). The blockbuster popularity of Stephanie Meyer's *Twilight* series has been the occasion for a good deal of scholarship on the relationship between these novels and Meyer's faith community, the Church of Jesus Christ of Latter-Day Saints. Margaret Toscano offers a nuanced account of Stephanie Meyer's "subtly subversive" engagement with Mormon faith and practice in *Twilight* (21), situating her work at the crossroads between "19th-century Mormon culture with its emphasis on heterodox theology and 21st-century Mormon culture with its struggle to conform to conservative American politics and orthodox Christian values" (22). Much more could be done with the ways that other branches of Christianity appear in popular romance, since Quaker characters, Amish characters, and Russian Orthodox icons have all made notable appearances in the genre.[10]

In addition to romances which express, more or less explicitly, a range of types of Christianity there are those which are built around other faiths. In the 1850s and 1860s, for example, the German-Jewish reading public could find stories in which "falling in love with a future mate typically went hand in hand with falling in love with Judaism itself" (Hess 119) in the pages of the *Jüdisches Volksblatt.* Works of popular romantic fiction were also written in Ladino (the language of Sephardi Jews, which is very similar to medieval Castilian/Spanish) and published in Istanbul between 1930 and 1933; the Sentro Sefaradi de Estambol is currently republishing 16 of these, making them available for future study (Gerson Şarhon). Turning to Islam, in twenty-first-century Indonesia, "popular literary tastes have ... shifted to Islamic novels. This began with the resounding success of the novel *Ayat ayat cinta* ("Verses of Love") by Habiburrahman El-Shirazy" (Rani "Islam, Romance" 60) in which "[t]he love conflicts of the protagonists have as their moral anchor an Islamic moral scheme" (Rani "Islam, Romance" 71). The Indonesian Islamic romances were "well received in Malaysia, and can be said to have catalysed the emergence of similar novels" there (Rani "The Conflict of Love and Islam" 418). Muslim romantic fiction is also flourishing in Nigeria (Whitsitt). English-language Jewish and Muslim romances also exist, but not in great numbers and they have yet to receive sustained critical attention; one notable exception is Layla Abdullah-Poulos's essay "The Stable Muslim Love Triangle—Triangular Desire in Black Muslim Romance Fiction," a groundbreaking study of how this emerging textual corpus combines "Islamic, African American, and American notions of love, courtship, and sexual dialogue" (2).

Non-Abrahamic belief systems also make an appearance in romance fiction, and these are a fertile ground for future scholarship. For example, the *Heart Sutra* is quoted and repeatedly referenced in Sherry Thomas's *My Beautiful Enemy*, and Eric Murphy Selinger has argued that Buddhism plays as central a role in that novel as the Bible does in Francine Rivers's *Redeeming Love*; however, the imprint of Buddhism on the work of other Buddhist-identified romance authors (e.g., Jeannie Lin) has yet to be investigated.[11] Allusions to Brahma, Vishnu, Shiva, and Krishna make similarly brief but significant appearances in the Indian-born American author Sonali Dev's *A Bollywood Affair*, as does one to Ganesha in Sandhya Menon's *When Dimple Met Rishi*, and whether these gestures reward theological reading or are exclusively points of cultural reference needs to be addressed. Nora Roberts, a hugely popular late twentieth- and early twenty-first-century author, includes explicitly spiritual elements in some, though not all, of her works, and as Christina Valeo points out, when she "turns to magic, she often uses Pagan belief systems like Wicca" (237). Much more might be done with the role of Wicca in Roberts's work and in books by the erotic romance author Joey Hill, who credits an embrace of "the Wiccan faith" in her 20s as a signal moment in her development as an author.[12]

Romance as religion

Alongside texts which suggest that romantic love can lead to, or develop alongside, spiritual growth in one particular religious tradition—and, conversely, those which suggest that a particular tradition provides the appropriate discourse, imagery, or conceptual framework to understand the protagonists' love—it has also been suggested that in many romance novels love itself functions as a religion. "Although they may no longer believe in God, readers do still believe in love," Anderson writes (262), and these readers are not alone. As levels of religious belief have declined in the West, philosopher Simon May explains, human romantic love has been

> widely tasked with achieving what once only divine love was thought capable of: to be our ultimate source of meaning and happiness, and of power over suffering and disappointment. Not as the rarest of exceptions but as a possibility open to practically all who have faith in it, with the consequence that romantic love "is now the West's undeclared religion—and perhaps its only generally accepted religion."
>
> (1)[13]

The "romance narrative," Roach elaborates, "is mythic or religious: it often functions as a foundational or idealized story about the meaning and purpose of life. According to this story, it is love that gives value and depth to life" (Roach, "Getting" n.p.). Indeed, "[a]s popular romance scholar Eric Selinger puts it, love or marriage can come to function as that which we 'believe in,' as 'a source of meaning and purpose and value. . .as a priority that determines other actions and beliefs'" (Roach *Happily* 169).

Selinger's source for this claim—which Roach draws on as well—is Robert M. Polhemus's *Erotic Faith*, a study of love in literary fiction from Jane Austen to D. H. Lawrence and (in the coda) Samuel Beckett which has recently proved influential in the study of popular romance. Polhemus defines "erotic faith" as "an emotional conviction, ultimately religious in nature, that meaning, value, hope, and even transcendence can be found through love—erotically focused love, the kind of love we mean when we say that people are in love" (1); across the nineteenth century, he argues, "[n]ovels were to erotic faith what Bibles, churches, and chapels were to Christianity" (4), promulgating "the grand matrimonial ideal of a union that would be erotic, romantic, nuptial, moral, and spiritual too" (22). This new ideal has its roots in older Protestant claims about the value of marriage, but only in the early nineteenth century do historians find that "human affections were beginning to be placed above religious ones," so much so in fact, that "the personhood of the loved one, by the 1830s, had become a powerful rival to God as the individual's central symbol of ultimate significance" (Lystra 241–2).

The term used by Victorians to discuss this emerging rivalry between the human beloved and God was "idolatry." "For Victorian Protestants," Kathleen Vejvoda explains,

> this term meant more than simply the worship of graven images: it became the privileged term for denoting any devotion to a person, thing, or idea that hinders or supplants one's relation to God. It is this more inclusive meaning that especially fascinated the Victorians, and which, in the form of human idolatry, became the focus of so many marriage-plot novels in the period.
>
> (241)

Evidence of this period concern can be found in Charlotte Brontë's *Jane Eyre* (1847), where Jane acknowledges that for a time her love for Mr. Rochester was dangerously, sinfully excessive:

> My future husband was becoming to me my whole world; and, more than the world: almost my hope of heaven. He stood between me and every thought of religion, as an eclipse intervenes between man and the broad sun. I could not, in those days, see God for his creature: of whom I had made an idol.
>
> (277)

Subsequent events force her to acknowledge the primacy of God over the demands of the human beloved: a resolution of the rivalry that *Jane Eyre* shares with twentieth- and twenty-first-century inspirational romance novels such as Francine Rivers's influential *Redeeming Love*, in which both hero and heroine "must learn to keep their earthly love in proportion to their relationships with God" (Gordis 333), since only after the "relative place of God and earthly spouse" (Gordis 336) has been established can the novel's marriage plot be resolved.

A different resolution to the potential conflict between religion and romantic love can be found in the work of the immensely prolific Barbara Cartland, who "began incorporating a spiritual dimension in her fiction" (Rix paragraph 3) in the 1930s and who depicted romantic love as a conduit to the divine. Although her "novels promoted conservative Christian values" (Rix paragraph 24), they also

> promoted what she referred to as a "religion of love," a concept she explained as a theo-philosophical concept in her many non-fictional books. The myth that Cartland cultivated in her novels was that we are saved from our material-physical prison by love ... A key notion in Cartland's romantic universe is the idea of the "Life Force" ... which upholds the human spirit and brings men and women to a realization of their inner selves. The "Life Force" infuses romantic love with divinity and brings the individual into unity with a higher principle.
>
> (Rix paragraph 2–3)

Decoupled from "conservative Christian values," a Cartland-like "religion of love" continues to be found in a wide range of popular romance novels, notably in the way that depictions of physical attraction and bodily affection are infused with the language of spirituality. A "focus on the ineffable" typifies the genre, Jayashree Kamblé argues, pointing out

> its foundational notion of soul mates and of spiritual unions (often certified when couples experience simultaneous orgasms), and ... the primary importance it gives to the verbal expression of love in sanctifying a marriage of bodies as well as of the spirits "in" them.
>
> (150)

Kamblé sees this insistence on the verbal and the spiritual as evidence that the genre prioritizes "the spirit over the body," and she notes that "romance readers frequently argue that sexual descriptions in novels are only important and acceptable if they reinforce an extra-physical bond" (150–1). Characters in romance novels sometimes espouse what sound like similar views. In Roseanne Williams' *Love Conquers All* (1991), Ty and Rianna feel that, because of familial opposition, their relationship can only be a temporary one but, after they have intercourse for the first time,

> "I've never felt the oneness I feel," he said. "Not until now with you."
> "Me too. Until now I thought it was a myth."
> "Staggers the mind, doesn't it?"
> She nodded. "And the body."
> "And the heart. . . . And the soul . . . What we have here is more than a fleeting thing . . . What we have here is . . ."
> "Don't say it, Ty," Rianna warned him softly.
> "We already said it without words," he murmured . . . "We can't take it back. We're falling" (177).

Without that feeling of "oneness" that brings mind, body, heart, and soul into alignment, this passage suggests, the lovers' connection could only be, at best, a "fleeting thing." Now that such a union and alignment have been accomplished, however, their bond is something out of "a myth": that is, it marks an irruption into the merely human realm of something transcendent and, for the moment, too sacred and too powerful to name ("Don't say it, Ty"). What they "have here" is not simply human love, then, but a love divine: the kind that is another name for God in Christian tradition ("God is Love" 1 John 4:8; 1 John 4:16), and the kind that can appropriately serve as a guarantor or ground for being. An exchange in Madeleine Ker's *Danger Zone* (1985) makes this theological connection clear. "You're my whole life . . . I'd have nothing without you. Be nothing," she tells the hero. "That's what love is," he replies (184).

Love divine

On a structural level, it might well be said that the romance genre itself would "be nothing" without the exaltation of romantic love which gives meaning and purpose to its plots. Simon May has argued that in Western culture romantic love has been given characteristics "properly reserved for divine love, such as the unconditional and the eternal" (4) and credited with the power to redeem "life's losses and sufferings" (2). Even when they are not made explicit, these are precisely the kinds of claims about the power and durability of romantic love which are embedded in the deep structures of the genre. John Cawelti's early description of romance as a genre founded on the "moral fantasy" of "love triumphant and permanent, overcoming all obstacles and difficulties" speaks to this structural role of love divine (41–2), and we can hear it in the theological discourse embedded in the Romance Writers of America definition of the genre. "In a romance," the organization declares, "the lovers who risk and struggle for each other and their relationship are rewarded with emotional justice and unconditional love" (Romance Writers of America). Sidestepping the question of precisely who or what will reward the lovers—karma? Christ? the conventions of the genre?—this definition insists that the universe of any romance novel will be a providential one, and its deployment of the phrase "unconditional love" as part of the lovers' reward for their "risk and struggle" signals that a divine or religious type of love is now seen as definitional of the genre, at least in its North American context.[14]

Although there are many qualities that might be attributed to romantic love as a religious (or divine) phenomenon, then, three seem particularly common in romance novels and in the scholarship on them: romantic love is said to be *unconditional*, *omnipotent*, and *eternal*.

Unconditional

In *The Glass Slipper: Women and Love Stories*, Susan Ostrov Weisser notes the enduring popularity (not least in popular romance novels) of the idea that romantic love should be "entirely unselfish, about caring and *caritas* for the individual" (174). Weisser's immediate pivot from "caring" to "*caritas*"—the Latin word used to translate the Greek *agape*, and not etymologically related to "caring"—signals her sense of the religious roots of this love ideal, which she understands to be "based on the Christian ethos that the spirit is higher than the flesh, that 'real' love of any kind is measured by the degree of concern for the other, not intensity of passion" (Weisser 175). May, too, traces the idea that "genuine love" is "unconditional, enduring and selfless" (236), summarizing the (in his mind flawed) logic of the ideal this way:

> (i) God is, by definition, absolutely sovereign. Nothing beyond God can therefore condition his acts of love . . .
> (ii) All genuine human love depends on, and is to imitate, God . . . Therefore:
> (iii) All genuine human love must be unconditional.
>
> (236)

Although neither Weisser nor May subscribes to this love ideal—May because it is "fundamentally untrue to the nature of human love" which, "like everything human, is conditioned" (237); Weisser because it masks a pernicious set of gendered power dynamics (see 174–5, 120)—their analyses speak to the way that depictions of love as unconditional inscribe religious values into both explicitly Christian and ostensibly secular popular romance texts.

For the evangelical romance readers studied by Neal, God "romances humanity through his presence, guidance, and most especially his unconditional love" (166), with human love and marriage offering a local instance and reflection of "the greater unconditional love of God for humanity" (167). Novels such as Francine Rivers' *Redeeming Love* show what this love can look like in action, not only in terms of the unconditional love of God for the book's traumatized and self-loathing heroine, but in the way that this divine love is bodied forth on the human level by the novel's hero, Michael, who loves and forgives his wife no matter her past or present transgressions (165). Yet what Michael displays and explains as an *imitatio dei* differs more in idiom than in kind from the vision of "what love was all about" that is articulated by the heroine of Jane Arbor's secular Mills & Boon novel *Golden Apple Island* (1967):

> You disapproved, even were shocked by some traits in your woman . . . in your man. You saw their faults, suspected their weaknesses, quarrelled with their difference from you. But loving them, you forgave them everything; they had only to need you and you would run [to them].
>
> (92)

Although Arbor does not quote or allude to scripture to prove that love forgives everything, as an evangelical novelist might (see, for example Proverbs 10:12 or 1 Corinthians 13:7, although translations differ), her description of what it looks and feels like to love unconditionally resonates with the descriptions offered by Neal's readers of how God loves them, reassured by Christian romance fiction that "God would not forsake [them] no matter what, that 'no matter where I go, no matter what happens, he is going to be there'" (166).

In secular romance novels, unconditional love may be offered as something that characters must learn to "believe in" in order to achieve their happy ending, both in the secular sense of a belief that it exists, or *can* exist, and in the theological sense of a creed to which they subscribe. In Jennifer Crusie's *Anyone But You* (1996), for example, the novel's hero, Alex, its heroine, Nina, and Nina's best friend, Charity, are all convinced that being loved depends on meeting some set of conditions: attractiveness, youth, social status, career, and the like. Charity writes a bitterly satirical book about her dating life, and when a local book group reads it in manuscript, the group's leader, the happily dating 75-year-old Norma, critiques the way that the manuscript's protagonist kept

> making conditions for herself. If she lost ten pounds, the relationship would work. If she wore the right clothes, the relationship would work. She never believed any of the men could love her for herself, no matter what she looked like or what she said. . . . She didn't believe in unconditional love.
>
> (116)

The scales having fallen from her eyes, Charity brings Norma's lesson to Nina. "[Y]ou don't believe Alex could love you because your body is forty years old and your face has some wrinkles," she tells her friend. "Norma hit it right. You don't believe in unconditional love" (119). Charity continues to repeat this message—literally using the same words, "you don't believe in unconditional love" (174)—until the novel's final chapter, when Nina finally accepts the critique, internalizes the lesson, and admits to herself (speaking to her dog, Fred) that "Alex loves me unconditionally . . . I know that. There is no doubt in my mind. It's just my ego in the way" (178).

In Crusie's novel, "unconditional love" is treated as a secular, psychological term, not a matter of theology. The first character said to bestow "unconditional love" on anyone is Fred, Nina's dog (19), not God the Father or Christ, and Norma, who brings up the term at that pivotal book group meeting, is a model of feminine muscularity, elegance, and upbeat sexual agency, not a Michael Hosea-like figure of faith. In this secularity, Crusie perhaps takes her cue from Erich Fromm, whose *The Art of Loving* she has recommended to aspiring romance novelists ("Emotionally Speaking"). Fromm briefly equates unconditional love with God's grace, particularly as this is understood in Protestant thought (62), but he mostly takes a psychological approach to the ideal, describing it as "one of the deepest longings . . . of every human being," not least because it assuages concerns that other kinds of love might raise. "[T]o be loved because of one's merit, because one deserves it, always leaves doubt," Fromm writes:

> maybe I did not please the person whom I want to love me, maybe this, or that —there is always a fear that love could disappear. Furthermore, "deserved" love

> easily leaves a bitter feeling that one is not loved for oneself, that one is loved *only* because one pleases, that one is, in the last analysis, not loved at all but used.
> (Fromm 41–2)

These are precisely the worries about conditional love that Crusie's characters must overcome. Yet even as she sticks to Fromm's more secular analysis, Crusie tips her hat to the deeper religious history of unconditional love by having the character named Charity—as in "faith, hope, and charity," from the Latin *caritas*—be the character to take up and preach Norma's gospel. (As May notes, Christian traditions are sometimes "preserved and even intensified by our secular age" (236).)

Research remains to be done on "unconditional love" in popular romance fiction. Does unconditionality work as a defining quality for love in purely secular romance contexts, or does it always bring with it a trace of religious reference and discourse? Has the feminist critique of unconditional love been incorporated into popular romance? If so, how is it addressed? Do romance novels ever extol the value of *conditional* love, which in Fromm is co-equal with unconditional love, since both are necessary elements in a "mature" version of the emotion?[15] And although "unconditional love" is part of the RWA definition of the genre, is this a transnational ideal, or more specifically an American one?

Omnipotent

The very structure of popular romance, in which obstacles are always overcome, tends to represent love as omnipotent, or almost so. The nature of the "barrier can be external ... internal ... or both" (Regis 32) but in many cases it takes the form of a protagonist's seemingly unshakable conviction that they are unworthy of love. As Polhemus has noted, however, "Men and women in the hold of erotic faith feel that love can redeem personal life and offer a reason for being" (1) and such protagonists therefore eventually recognize that they can indeed by redeemed by love.

In *Anyone But You*, redemption comes when characters come to believe that they can be (and are) loved unconditionally, regardless of their age, appearance, or economic status. They are saved, we might say, not by works but by faith, albeit faith *in love*; that said, there is little in the plot that emphasizes the grandeur or extremity of love's saving power. To see love's omnipotence in action, it helps to consider the most extreme form of the redemption plot, in which the power of love is demonstrated via the redemption of the seemingly unredeemable: "the demon lover ... the subject who lives imprisoned in the blighted landscape of his own mind, who is doomed only to repetition and a desire for death until his possible redemption by the utterly unique moment of love" (Lutz, ix). As Deborah Lutz explains in her loosely-Heideggerian study *The Dangerous Lover: Gothic Villains, Byronism, and the Nineteenth-Century Seduction Narrative*, the one who loves such a figure partakes of love's omnipotence, in that she

> can grasp the power of impossibility; she can make the world possible by being, herself, the plenitude, the immanent meaning of existence for him. The hero's belief in his brilliance, his superior, misanthropic position above all others and their run-of-the-mill lives, is so very believable to the heroine that to change this decimation to plenitude becomes her reason for being.
> (5)

Rather than debunk or critique the appeal of this love plot, for example on feminist grounds, Lutz offers a critical idiom sympathetic to its larger-than-life, even mythic stakes: meaning and nihilism; hope and despair; being and nothingness.

In most romances the "demon lover" is not, literally, a demon, but it is common to find him "described as a devil, a demon, a tiger, a hawk, a pirate, a bandit, a potentate, a hunter, a warrior. He is definitely *not* the boy next door" (Barlow and Krentz 19). As romance authors Linda Barlow and Jayne Ann Krentz have observed,

> The concept of being forced to marry the devil ... resonates with centuries of history, myth, and legend. Both reader and writer understand the allusions. ... Both reader and writer also have a vast acquaintance with the devil-heroes who appear in romance novels, since there is a time-honored tradition of heroines sent on quests to encounter and transform these masculine creatures of darkness.
>
> (18–19)

The most vivid instances of this plot will perhaps be found in paranormal romances and romantic retellings of myth, since here we can find demons, "devil-heroes," and assorted lords of the dead represented quite literally. Yet even when the "devil-hero" is specified as such merely by association or allusion, the mythic contours of the plot will often be apparent. In Laura Kinsale's *Flowers from the Storm*, Eric Murphy Selinger has thus argued, the author repeatedly associates the novel's hero, the Duke of Jervaulx, with Milton's Satan, not least by having heroine Maddy muse that he "chose to reign in Hell, *like Satan in the poem*" (Kinsale 391, Selinger's emphasis). As the novel ends, Maddy revisits and mulls over this connection, calling the Duke "a star that I could only look up and wonder at" and concluding that she is "glad thou fell, and I can hold thee in my hands" (526). Selinger teases out the implications:

> The religious myth implied is as remarkable as it is heretical. In Kinsale's revision of *Paradise Lost*, Satan and Eve, not Adam and Eve, become the original romantic couple. Jerveaulx/Lucifer's "fall" into the hell of Blythedale is a *felix culpa*, since only in his fallen state can he tempt and seduce Maddy/Eve, thereby saving her from meekness and solitude. The "fall" of Maddy/Eve becomes a sensual incarnation, since only when her spirit is fully and erotically embodied can she save Jerveaulx/Satan, her tempter.
>
> ("How to Read" 40)

In this novel, then, the omnipotent power of love lifts up the fallen, redeems the captive, transvalues terms like "wickedness" and "falling," and levels hierarchies, including the one that distinguishes popular from literary texts.

In a brief, lyrical essay on the "demon lover" as a romance hero, author Anne Stuart discusses two aspects of this fantasy's appeal. One is a fantasy of female power, since the heroine of such a novel takes a hero "capable of killing, of destroying everything" and "lead[s] him into light" (86) thereby proving herself to be "very brave, very sure, very worthy" (87). Behind this, however, lies a fantasy about the power of love itself. "The bond between heroine and hero is more than romantic, more than social," Stuart insists. "It is a spiritual, intellectual, sexual bond of the soul, one that doesn't end with till death do us part. It is a bond that surpasses death and honor and the laws of man and nature" (86). The fact that this bond surpasses *honor* as well as death and nature hints at some of the research questions that have yet to be addressed when it comes to love's omnipotence. How do romance authors and readers negotiate the tension between the "moral fantasy" of "love triumphant" in romance (Cawelti 41) and other moral questions or duties, such as whether there are some crimes or dishonorable acts that place a protagonist outside the reach of love's salvation?[16] What might Anna G. Jónasdóttir's and other feminist analyses of "love power" reveal about the practical and purely human acts through which Omnipotent Love is made manifest in romance narratives, and about who is charged with performing them, book by book?[17] And how might the representation of love as omnipotent in popular romance respond to the loss of faith in romantic love described by Allan Bloom, Vivian Gornik, and others as a signal feature of modern literature and culture?[18] (Does the presentation of love as omnipotent speak to a continuing faith, or to an anxiety being assuaged? The answer may well vary from author to author, text to text, and context to context.)

Eternal

To conclude her encomium to Omnipotent Love, Anne Stuart observes that the kind of love she is describing is one in which "eternity comes into play, changing a simple meeting of minds and bodies into something that transcends time and space" (87). The omnipotence of love here shades into another, related, equally theological quality: the ideal of Love Eternal.

Lynne Pearce argues that it is because "what we think of today as specifically *romantic love*" draws on the model of spiritual love (*agape*) that, "despite the persuasiveness of the psychoanalytic models, Western culture still clings to the notion that 'true love' is both durable and non-repeatable: it is, by definition, an emotion that *stands the test of time*". Romance novels use a variety of strategies to mark the love between their protagonists as "true" in this time-defying sense. The betrothals, weddings, and children that often appear at the end of a novel with a traditional "happily ever after" (HEA) ending are institutional and familial structures that represent futurity, and even those novels which offer instead no more than "a casual understanding that the romantic partners will stay together and give the relationship a try (the 'HFN' or 'Happy for Now')" (Selinger and Gleason 7) often supply symbolic substitutes for these more formal structures, as when the hero of Victoria Dahl's *Start Me Up* asks the heroine "will you let me move temporarily into your town and take you out to dinner a few times a month so you don't forget me this winter," only to hear back from her, "Aren't you going to get down on one knee [as in a wedding proposal] while you ask that?" (366). Futurity, that is to say, takes many forms, but the happy ending of a romance novel seems always to involve the protagonists remaining together and in love.

As with love's omnipotence, love's eternal quality can be most vividly displayed in paranormal romance, in which many protagonists have extended lifespans. Anne Stuart, whose essay on the demon lover was quoted a moment ago, has even written one paranormal romance, *Dark Journey* (1995) in which the hero is Death itself. By embracing him (both literally and metaphorically) the heroine chooses "The endless night that held nothing but him" (107) and as "he kissed her. Forever was just beginning" (108). As Isabel Santaulària has argued, however, even a paranormal romance ending featuring a vampire hero "capable of turning the proverbial 'eternal love' into a real possibility" can "problematise the eternal togetherness at the core of romance fiction's resolutions" (119, 124). In her essay "The Fallacy of Eternal Love," Santaulària analyzes the ending of Linda Lael Miller's *Forever and the Night*, in which the vampire regains his humanity before marrying his human heroine. Although she can no longer remember him in his previous state and is clearly happy in her marriage and very much in love with her new husband, she does recall what she believes is a dream of a vampire. To Santaulària this would appear to symbolize the fact that, "even when partners decide to cling together for life, they soon enough become aware of a mismatch between the romantic ideal and the actual person in the everyday once the initial fascination begins to wear off" (125). The promise of *eternal* love, then, remains attached to the fictive or dream world—the world of romance—even within the larger boundaries of this particular romance novel, which suggests a metafictional critique of the genre's promise elsewhere.

In *Revolutions of the Heart: Gender, Power and the Delusions of Love*, Wendy Langford gives what we might read as an extended version of this critique. "One striking feature of romantic love," she writes, is that

> while it appears as a coherent "life narrative," perhaps especially for women, this coherence is at once everywhere disrupted by a hiatus. This intervenes, for example, in the form of a popularly assumed distinction between the "falling in love" stage and some later stage of love. One is never quite sure how the latter arises from the former, except that "you have to work at it." The dislocation is present too in romantic fiction, which almost invariably leaves the heroine poised at the "threshold" of her new life. This convention in turn reflects the "happily ever after" closure of fairy-tales. Meanwhile, established love relationships are generally considered quite apart from romance.
>
> (64)

Langford's assessment of the conclusion of romances is broadly correct, but there are also some romances which depict the rekindling of a failed or failing relationship. Perhaps these may be read as indications of popular romance's conviction that the emotions of the "falling in love" stage never entirely disappear and that even when the initial, transfiguring light of love within a relationship appears to have been extinguished, it may in fact remain as a banked fire. As romance reader and reviewer Sarah Wendell argues,

> while many romances are the depiction of falling in love once and for all, treating your personal romance as a repeated courtship keeps that relationship happy and healthy.
>
> Is the never-ending courtship present in romance novels? Well, it's not exactly present in a single novel—but it is present in the entire genre, one happy courtship after another.
>
> (182)

What Langford describes in temporal terms as a "hiatus" might thus also be conceived of as a lacuna or slippage between what David Shumway describes as the discourse of *romance* (which leads up to the closure of the happy ending, with the promise of eternity) and the discourse of *intimacy* (which purports to describe the dynamics of existing relationships, happy or not). The practice that Wendell describes of "treating your personal romance as a repeated courtship" would thus seem to be a mechanism whereby the "intimacy" model tries to incorporate recurrent moments of or sojourns through "romance."[19]

Romance novels have long featured epilogues as a way to represent protagonists enjoying the "happily ever after" of their love stories. More recently, An Goris has observed, a new compositional structure has emerged. In "character-based romance series," readers are given the opportunity to read about "a group of recurring characters (siblings, colleagues, friends, inhabitants of a small town, etc.)," and although each novel "in the series features the complete romance narrative of one member of the group" the reader will be able to catch glimpses of former protagonists enjoying their "happily ever after" even as the current protagonists work toward their own.[20] But these novels do not always represent a simple recurrence or extension of romantic happiness. Rather, Goris explains, "in narratively actualizing —i.e. depicting—the post-HEA, the serialized romance novel broaches a new aspect of the romance narrative and creates, as it were, a new narrative space": one in which the genre's longstanding focus on questions of how romantic love develops can widen to include questions of "how romantic love is sustained," and at what costs.

Goris focuses in depth on two authors who work in serial forms, Nora Roberts and J. R. Ward, but the questions she raises about the post-HEA are applicable to the many other romance novelists who now write in series, and they suggest that the more-than-human "love eternal" that has long defined the genre now exists alongside, or in contrapuntal tension with, an interest in love as a time-bound, quotidian practice.

Conclusion

Book after book, popular romance reaffirms its belief in love's power to create lasting happiness. Each novel is an affirmation which does not lose but rather gains power with repetition, and reading popular romance fiction through a religious lens enables one to look at the enduring issue of repetition in the genre—repeated plots and character types; the repeated act of romance reading—in new ways. Künne thus suggests that "reading romances can be considered as taking part in the reenactment of the mythical commemoration of the ritual of the Sacred Marriage" (265); on a more quotidian level, one might think of repetition in popular romance as being akin to that to be found in the compiled stories of the lives of saints, founders and early followers of a religious sect which are read by believers to maintain and strengthen their own faith.[21] This latter interpretation, which explains both the similarities between romances and the generally exceptional nature of their protagonists, also explains the apparent inconsistency identified by Susan Ostrov Weisser:

> while our egalitarian idea of romantic love implies that everyone deserves and can get love, love stories present a different picture: the ones who are lovable and are loved ... are also represented as a privileged class, to be imitated or at least envied.
>
> (11)

If love is a modern religion then it is perhaps only to be expected that its stories will depict the most exceptional love stories: many belief systems claim to provide the key to everlasting life and happiness to all but, nonetheless, hold up certain particularly holy individuals as examples to be admired and, where possible, imitated.

Some devoted adherents of the belief-system encoded in romance fiction bear witness to it in para-texts and other non-fiction pieces of writing. Tara Taylor Quinn, an author with Harlequin romance, has blogged about the day she

> had an opportunity to have a one on one, private conversation with one of Harlequin's highest executives. We were talking about the higher purpose of our books. The ultimate task we face, and the reason we do what we do—to offer a message of hope to the world.
>
> On a surface level, Harlequin books are pure entertainment. But to so many, they are so much more . . . In a world where so much feels hopeless, they are pure hope.
>
> No matter what the genre, from clean to racy, from fanciful to hard hitting suspense, these books all have one thing in common. Every single one of them ends in an uplifting way. Because in the end, love is real. And it IS the strongest, most enduring entity of all.
>
> ("Tuesday Talk Time")

An author biography for Bobbi Smith, meanwhile, states that she

> is a firm believer in the power of love. Love, she feels, does indeed make the world go round. It is the perfection of human nature and our true reason for being . . . Love gives us the strength to keep on going against the most insurmountable odds. Love alone provides the nourishment for the soul . . . Love is pure, selfless, and everlasting. Love is timeless, transcending all barriers, touching our hearts even across vast distances and untold years. Love does indeed conquer all. To be loved is to live happily ever after, and that is Bobbi Smith's wish for you.
>
> (376)

Smith's encomium to love brings to mind St Paul's statements in 1 Corinthians 13 about the ways in which love "always protects, always trusts, always hopes, always perseveres. Love never fails . . . And now these three remain: faith, hope, and love. But the greatest of these is love." Smith is far from the only author whose statements about love recall a religious creed, in which the believer lists the articles of their faith. Jennifer Crusie once explained that she wrote romance fiction because "I truly do still believe in the existence of unconditional love, I still believe that it's what holds humanity together, and I absolutely believe it's the best of all possible things to write about" ("Why I Know" 226). Similarly, Susan Elizabeth Phillips avers that "although I'm not conventionally religious now, I very much believe in redemption. I believe that love is the most powerful force. All that sappy stuff, I believe with all of my heart" (Selinger "An Interview" 9).

Do *all* romances, then, express a quasi-religious belief in romantic love? The generalization may be misleading. Even if there is something providential about the structure of the romance novel, with all things conspiring, eventually, to bring about the

HEA, love is only one of many values espoused by the genre, and not all novels or novelists give the demands of romantic love a higher priority than the demands of other goods, such as honor or duty to country. In contrast to Anne Stuart, who has extolled a love that "surpasses death and honor and the laws of man and nature" (86), Jo Beverley observes that "beliefs about heroism, about honor, shape my characters' dilemmas," and that love, even "true love," does not get the last word.

> If . . . I believed that the search for true love overrides all other values, then Deirdre in *Deirdre and Don Juan* would not have had a problem. As soon as she realized she was in love with Lord Everdon, she would have kissed goodbye to the man she had promised to marry. However, she and Howard Dunstable had exchanged promises and her given word was more important to her than self-gratification.
>
> (33)

Perhaps what one can say with certainty about all romances is that they provide a space in which authors and readers can explore religious and philosophical questions about morality, life's meaning and purpose, and the nature of love. More scholarship is needed to address in detail the substance of these explorations, the compositional means with which they are undertaken (plots, allusions, iconography, post-HEA scenes, etc.), and the relationships between the explorations of such questions in romance and those to be found in other forms of fiction and popular culture.

Notes

1 Romance author Judi McCoy quoted in *Romance Today: An A-to-Z Guide to Contemporary American Romance Writers* (Charles and Mosley 266).
2 See, for example, Crusie Smith ("Romancing Reality"); Jensen makes a comparable argument in *Love's $weet Return: The Harlequin Story* (64).
3 For a discussion of how romance fiction depicts social issues and practical responses to them, see Vivanco, *For Love and Money* (54–60). For an extended discussion of modern popular romance novels from a religious perspective, see Vivanco's online work-in-progress, *Faith, Love, Hope and Popular Romance Fiction*.
4 For more on the emergence of Muslim romance fiction in online platforms, see Parnell.
5 For a useful overview of this history, see Lazar; a recent in-depth discussion of possible Muslim influence can be found in Menocal.
6 For an extended treatment of how nineteenth- and twentieth-century Catholic and Protestant theologians and public figures brought this re-evaluation of heterosexual sexuality into mainline Christian thought, see Gardella.
7 We have elided here Kamblé's assertion that this is specifically a "*white* Protestant ethos" (131) not least because both Huguley and her characters are African American, which may complicate Kamblé's claim. Kamblé's chapter on "Race and Religious Ethos in Romance Novels" focuses on a particular construction of the relationship between (racialized) body and spirit in white-authored texts, drawn in large part from Richard Dyer's *White: Essays on Race and Culture*; although she discusses South Asian romance author Nalini Singh in this chapter, she does not take up African American romance fiction—nor, indeed, texts by white authors whose representations of body and spirit might not fit Dyer's conceptual model, from John Donne to Alex Beecroft.
8 Pamela Regis argues that Richardson "brings the courtship plot, which is to say the romance novel, into more than prominence. He makes it famous" (63).
9 "The novel is shaped by a religious dualism between soul and body, transcended by the effects of prayer and by the supernatural power of religious-erotic music," they explain, and "[i]t is

this religiosity, with its unequivocal representation of divine intervention in the love affair, which distances *The Rosary* most clearly from contemporary romance" (Batsleer et al. 90).

10 Quaker characters (who may or may not be accurately portrayed) feature prominently in Laura Kinsale's *Flowers from the Storm* and in *False Colors* by Alex Beecroft. A Russian Orthodox icon is of central importance in *Lord of Scoundrels* by Loretta Chase. So-called "Amish romances"—that is, romances with ostensibly Amish characters—have received extended scholarly treatment by Weaver-Zercher.

11 For Selinger on Thomas, see "Use Heart in Your Search"; for Lin as someone who grew up Buddhist, see Lin, "On Core Themes" and "Jeannie Lin Tells Us."

12 The subject of Wicca comes up in several interviews with Joey Hill, often as part of the context for her work in the erotic romance subgenre: e.g., in answer to the question "What brought about the incorporation of more explicit erotic elements, and why are they integral to your work?" Hill notes that one crucial step was when she "embraced the Wiccan faith in my mid-twenties," in part because she "loved the idea of sex being used to raise spiritual energy in the Great Rite" ("An Interview"). On a related note, in "Medieval Magic and Witchcraft in the Popular Romance Novel," Carol Ann Breslin observes that the heroines of many romances set in the Middle Ages, "Through their magic, their potions, and their spells . . . seek to restore, heal, and promote peace and love for their own hearths and their nations" (78) and, moreover, that although in such settings one might "expect the Church to be at the center, pursuing and condemning the practitioners of witchcraft and magic," generally "there are no interventions by Church officials" (84). While Breslin speculates that this absence perhaps reflects "the modern de-emphasis on religion and church" or could be the result of the authors' decision "to create a landscape where women of special gifts and powers can work out their destinies unencumbered by the structures of patriarchy" (84), Breslin does not go as far as to suggest that they could be expressions of faith in an alternative belief system such as Wicca.

13 It should be noted that this development is not entirely without precedent given that "medieval courtly love borrowed the sentiments and language of Christian discourse, particularly mystical discourse. Moreover, something of the humanly erotic also remained within sublimated mystical discourse, fusing the two experiences and making it more difficult to distinguish one from the other. This paved the way for romantic love, the descendent of courtly love, to contain the possibility of this deeper theological meaning and religious experience within it" (Raghu 18).

14 For arguments concerning whether "unconditional love" is a Biblically-grounded concept, see May (95–118). In popular culture, the equation of unconditional love with God's love for humankind was given memorable (and, indeed, danceable) articulation in Donna Summer's reggae-inflected 1983 hit "Unconditional Love," whose lyrics glossed "unconditional love" as the way to love "just like Ja do": a "non-reacting, everlasting" enactment of what the song calls "*agape* love."

15 Fromm's distinction between unconditional and conditional love might fruitfully be compared to the the binary of "ecstatic" and "legalistic" modes of faith (including faith in love) deployed in Vivanco's *Faith, Love, Hope*. For a definition of these terms, see "The Ecstatic and Legalistic Modes of Faith" (https://www.vivanco.me.uk/node/424); for their deployment in analyzing a particular novel, see "Ecstatic and Legalistic Literary Traditions: Rose Lerner's *In for a Penny*" (https://www.vivanco.me.uk/node/452)

16 "For a conceptual framework that addresses the competing claims of romantic love and legal, social, and moral rules, see Vivanco's discussion of "Rules and Emotion," (*Faith, Love, Hope*, https://www.vivanco.me.uk/node/448).

17 For an introduction to Jónasdóttir's work and some of its implications, see the essays gathered in *Love: A Question for Feminism in the Twenty-First Century*, edited by Jónasdóttir and Ann Ferguson.

18 See Bloom, *Love and Friendship*, and Gornick, *The End of the Novel of Love*.

19 For a comparison of romance heroines to virgin martyrs, see Wogan-Browne (95-99). For an extended discussion of Shumway, see Hsu-Ming Teo's chapter in this collection.

20 Goris, An. "Happily Ever After ... And After: Serialization and the Popular Romance Novel." *Americana: The Journal of American Popular Culture (1900–present)* 12.1 (2013). www.americanpopularculture.com/journal/articles/spring_2013/goris.htm

21 Künne, Regina. *Eternally Yours: Challenge and Response: Contemporary US American Romance Novels by Jayne Ann Krentz and Barbara Delinsky*. Berlin: Lit Verlag, 2015. Another religious parallel has been suggested by Roslynn Voaden, who sees similarities between the romance genre's "focus on a woman's brief moment on the threshold" and medieval women mystics' "unitative visions, where the visionary yearned to be united with" Christ and is "eternally positioned in that moment of consummation" (79–80).

Works cited

Abdullah-Poulos, Layla. "The Stable Muslim Love Triangle – Triangular Desire in African American Muslim Romance Fiction." *Journal of Popular Romance Studies*, vol. 7, 2018, n.p.

Anderson, Rachel. *The Purple Heart Throbs: The Sub-Literature of Love*. Hodder and Stoughton, 1974.

Arbor, Jane. *Golden Apple Island*. Mills & Boon, 1967.

Barlow, Linda and Jayne Ann Krentz. "Beneath the Surface: The Hidden Codes of Romance." *Dangerous Men and Adventurous Women: Romance Writers on the Appeal of the Romance*. Edited by Jayne Ann Krentz, University of Pennsylvania Press, 1992, pp. 15–29.

Batsleer, Janet, Tony Davies, Rebecca O'Rourke and Chris Weedon. *Rewriting English: Cultural Politics of Gender and Class*. Methuen, 1985.

Beecroft, Alex. "Alex Beecroft – WRITER". *Arts Illustrated: Celebrating the Arts*. April 28, 2015. www.artsillustrated.com/alex-beecroft-writer.

Beverley, Jo. *An Honorable Profession: The Romance Writer and Her Characters*. North American Romance Writers. Edited by Kay Mussell, and Tuñón. Johanna, Scarecrow, 1999, 32–36.

Bloom, Allan. *Love and Friendship*. Simon and Schuster, 1993.

Breslin, Carol Ann. "Medieval Magic and Witchcraft in the Popular Romance Novel." *Romantic Conventions*. Edited by Anne K. Kaler, and Rosemary Johnson-Kurek, Bowling Green University Press, 1999, pp. 75–85.

Brontë, Charlotte. *Jane Eyre*. Ed. Margaret Smith, Oxford University Press, 1980, 277.

Cawelti, John. *Adventure, Mystery, and Romance: Formula Stories as Art and Popular Culture*. University of Chicago Press, 1976.

Charles, John and Shelley Mosely, eds. *Romance Today: An A-to-Z Guide to Contemporary American Romance Writers*. Greenwood, 2007, 266.

Coontz, Stephanie. 2005. *Marriage, a History: How Love Conquered Marriage*. Penguin, 2006.

Crawford, Joseph. *The Twilight of the Gothic? Vampire Fiction and the Rise of the Paranormal Romance, 1991-2012*. University of Wales Press, 2014.

Crusie, Jennifer. *Anyone But You*. Harlequin, 1996.

Crusie Smith, Jennifer. "Romancing Reality: The Power of Romance Fiction to Reinforce and Re-Vision the Real." *Paradoxa*, vol. 3, no. 1–2, 1997, pp. 81–93.

———. "Why I Know I'll Continue to Write Romance until They Pry My Cold Dead Fingers from around My Keyboard." *North American Romance Writers*. Edited by Kay Mussell, and Tuñón. Johanna, Scarecrow, 1999, pp. 225–226.

Dahl, Victoria. *Start Me Up*. HQN, 2009.

Ebert, Teresa L. "Hegel's 'Picture-thinking' as the Interpretive Logic of the Popular." *Textual Practice*, vol. 28, no. 1, 2014, pp. 9–33.

Fowler, Bridget. *The Alienated Reader: Women and Romantic Literature in the Twentieth Century*. Harvester Wheatsheaf, 1991.

Fromm, Erich. *The Art of Loving*. Harper & Collins, 1956. Harper Perennial Modern Classics, 2006.

Gardella, Peter. *Innocent Ecstasy: How Christianity Gave America an Ethic of Sexual Pleasure*. Oxford University Press, 1985.

Gerson Şarhon, Karen. "Haberes Buenos Ke Tengamos Siempre." *Şalom Gazetesi* 27 Haziran 2016. www.salom.com.tr/haber-99748-haberes_buenos_ke_tengamos_siempre.html

Gordis, Lisa M. "'Jesus Loves Your Girl More than You Do': Marriage as Triangle in Evangelical Romance and Puritan Narratives." *Romance Fiction and American Culture: Love as the Practice of Freedom?*, edited by William A. Gleason, and Eric Murphy Selinger, Ashgate, 2016, pp. 323–346.

Goris, An. "Happily Ever after... And After: Serialization and the Popular Romance Novel." *Americana: The Journal of American Popular Culture (1900-present)*, vol. 12, no. 1, 2013. www.americanpopularculture.com/journal/articles/spring_2013/goris.htm.

Gornick, Vivian. *The End of the Novel of Love*. Beacon Press, 1997.

Hess, Jonathan M. *Middlebrow Literature and the Making of German-Jewish Identity*. Stanford University Press, 2010.

Hill, Joey Hill. "An Interview with Joey W. Hill." https://emmanuelledemaupassant.com/2016/09/01/an-interview-with-joey-w-hill

Holmes, Diana. *Romance and Readership in Twentieth-Century France: Love Stories*. Oxford University Press, 2006.

Holy Bible, New International Version http://biblehub.com/1_corinthians/13.htm.

Hondagneu-Sotelo, Pierrette. "Religion and a Standpoint Theory of Immigrant Social Justice." *Religion and Social Justice for Immigrants*, edited by Pierrette Hondagneu-Sotelo, Rutgers University Press, 2007, pp. 3–15.

Houlihan Flynn, Carol. *Samuel Richardson: A Man of Letters*. Princeton University Press, 1982.

Huguley, Piper. *Treasure of Gold*. Samhain, 2015.

Jensen, Margaret Ann. *Love's $weet Return: The Harlequin Story*. Women's Educational Press, 1984.

Jónasdóttir, Anna G. and Ann Ferguson, editors. *Love: A Question for Feminism in the Twenty-First Century*. Routledge, 2013.

Kamblé, Jayashree. *Making Meaning in Popular Romance Fiction: An Epistemology*. Palgrave Macmillan, 2014.

Ker, Madeleine. *Danger Zone*. Mills & Boon, 1985.

Künne, Regina. *Eternally Yours: Challenge and Response: Contemporary US American Romance Novels by Jayne Ann Krentz and Barbara Delinsky*. Lit Verlag, 2015.

Langford, Wendy. *Revolutions of the Heart: Gender, Power and the Delusions of Love*. Routledge, 1999.

Lazar, Moshe. "Fin'amor." *A Handbook of the Troubadours*. Edited by F. R. P. Akehurst, and Judith M. Davis, University of California Press, 1995, pp. 61–100.

Leites, Edmund. "The Duty to Desire: Love, Friendship, and Sexuality in Some Puritan Theories of Marriage." *Journal of Social History*, vol. 15, no. 3, 1982, pp. 383–408.

Liebenow, Franklin E. Jr. "Review of *Jane Austen and Religion: Salvation and Society in Georgian England* by Michael Griffin." *Religion & Literature*, vol. 38, no. 2, 2006, pp. 121–123.

Lin, Jeannie. "Jeannie Lin Tells Us: How My Worst Seller Became a Bestseller and What It Means to Write 'Different.'" *RT Book Reviews*. March 3, 2014. www.rtbookreviews.com/rt-daily-blog/jeannie-lin-tells-us-how-my-worst-seller-became-bestseller-and-what-it-means-write-%E2%80%9Cdi

——— "On Core Themes, Genre Writing, Romance." www.jeannielin.com/on-core-themes-genre-writing-romance

Lutz, Deborah. *The Dangerous Lover: Gothic Villains, Byronism, and the Nineteenth-Century Seduction Narrative*. Ohio State University Press, 2006.

Lystra, Karen. *Searching the Heart: Women, Men and Romantic Love in Nineteenth-Century America*. Oxford University Press, 1989.

Margolies, David. "Mills & Boon: Guilt Without Sex." *Red Letters*, vol. 14, 1982-83, 5–13.

Marx, Karl. "A Contribution to the Critique of Hegel's *Philosophy of Right*: Introduction." Trans. Annette Jolin and Joseph O'Malley. *Critique of Hegel's "Philosophy of Right,"* edited by Joseph O'Malley, Cambridge University Press, 1982, pp. 129–142.

May, Simon. *Love: A History*. Yale University Press, 2011.

McAleer, Joseph. *Passion's Fortune: The Story of Mills & Boon*. Oxford University Press, 1999.
Menocal, Maria. *Shards of Love: Exile and the Origins of Lyric*. Duke University Press, 1994.
Neal, Lynn S. *Romancing God: Evangelical Women and Inspirational Fiction*. University of North Carolina Press, 2006.
O'Byrne, Patricia. "Popular Fiction in Postwar Spain: The Soothing, Subversive *Novela Rosa*." *Journal of Romance Studies*, vol. 8, no. 2, 2008, pp. 37–57.
Parnell, Claire. "Reading and Writing Muslim Romance Online." [abstract]. http://iaspr.org/wp-content/uploads/2018/06/IASPR-2018-CONFERENCE-PROGRAM.pdf
Pearce, Lynne. "Romance and Repetition: Testing the Limits of Love." *Journal of Popular Romance Studies*, vol. 2, no. 1, 2011, n.p http://jprstudies.org/2011/10/%e2%80%9cromance-and-repetition-testing-the-limits-of-love%e2%80%9d-by-lynne-pearce.
Polhemus, Robert M. *Erotic Faith: Being In Love From Jane Austen to D. H. Lawrence*. University of Chicago Press, 1990.
Radway, Janice A. *Reading the Romance: Women, Patriarchy, and Popular Literature*. 1984. University of North Carolina Press, 1991.
Raghu, Jyoti. "True Love's Kiss and Happily Ever After: The Religion of Love in American Film." *Journal of Popular Romance Studies*, vol. 5, no. 1, 2015, n.p. http://jprstudies.org/2015/08/true-loves-kiss-and-happily-ever-after-the-religion-of-love-in-american-filmby-jyoti-raghu.
Rani, Mohd. Zariat Abdul. "Islam, Romance and Popular Taste in Indonesia." *Indonesia and the Malay World*, vol. 40, no. 116, 2012, pp. 59–73.
———. "The Conflict of Love and Islam: The Main Ingredients in the Popular Islamic Novels of Malaysia." *South East Asia Research*, vol. 22, no. 3, 2014, pp. 417–433.
Regis, Pamela. *A Natural History of the Romance Novel*. University of Pennsylvania Press, 2003.
Rix, Robert W. "'Love in the Clouds': Barbara Cartland's Religious Romances." *The Journal of Religion and Popular Culture*, vol. 21, no. 2, 2009. web.archive.org/web/20091119103047/www.usask.ca/relst/jrpc/art21%282%29-LoveClouds.html.
———. "Getting a Good Man to Love: Popular Romance Fiction and the Problem of Patriarchy." *Journal of Popular Romance Studies*, vol. 1, no. 1, 2010, n.p. http://jprstudies.org/2010/08/getting-a-good-man-to-love-popular-romance-fiction-and-the-problem-of-patri archy-by-catherine-roach/.
Roach, Catherine M. *Happily Ever After: The Romance Story in Popular Culture*. Indiana University Press, 2016.
Romance Writers of America, "About the Romance Genre." Accessed May 7, 2016. www.rwa.org/Romance.
Ruether, Radford. *Rosemary. Goddesses and the Divine Feminine: A Western Religious History*. University of California Press, 2006.
Santaulària, Isabel. "The Fallacy of Eternal Love: Romance, Vampires and the Deconstruction of Love in Linda Lael Miller's *Forever and the Night* and *for All Eternity*." *The Aesthetics of Ageing: Critical Approaches to Literary Representations of the Ageing Process*, edited by Maria O'Neill and Carmen Zamorano Llena, Universitat de Lleida, 2002, pp. 111–126.
Selinger, Eric Murphy. "How to Read a Romance Novel (And Fall in Love with Popular Romance)." *New Approaches to Popular Romance Fiction: Critical Essays*, edited by Sarah S. G. Frantz and Eric Murphy Selinger, McFarland, 2012, pp. 33–46.
———. "Redeeming (M/M) Love: Christian Romance and Erotic Faith in Alex Beecroft's *False Colors* and Alexis Hall's *Glitterland*." Presentation at the Popular Culture Association/American Culture Association's national conference, New Orleans, March 2015.
——— and William A. Gleason. "An Interview with Susan Elizabeth Phillips." *Journal of Popular Romance Studies*, vol. 5, no. 1, 2015, n.p. http://jprstudies.org/2015/08/an-interview-with-susan-elizabeth-phillipsby-eric-murphy-selinger.
———. "Introduction: Love as the Practice of Freedom?" *Romance Fiction and American Culture: Love as the Practice of Freedom?* Edited by William A. Gleason, and Eric Murphy Selinger, Ashgate, 2016a, pp. 1–21.

———. "'Use Heart in Your Search': Erotic Faith, the Heart Sutra, and the Allusive Art of My Beautiful Enemy." Presentation at the Sixth International Conference on Popular Romance Studies, Salt Lake City, Utah, 2016b.

Smith, Bobbi. *Timeless Love*. Avon, 1993.

Stuart, Anne. "Legends of Seductive Elegance." *Dangerous Men and Adventurous Women: Romance Writers on the Appeal of the Romance*. Edited by Jayne Ann Krentz, University of Pennsylvania Press, 1992, pp. 85–88.

———. *Dark Journey*. 1995. Reprinted in *Strangers in the Night*. Silhouette, 1997, 7–109.

Summer, Donna. "Unconditional Love." *She Works Hard for the Money*. Mercury, 1983.

Taylor Quinn, Tara. "Tuesday Talk-Time – At the Heart of Harlequin." The Pink Heart Society, March 22, 2016, https://web.archive.org/web/20160809092827/http://pinkheartsociety.blogspot.com/2016/03/tuesday-talk-time-at-heart-of-harlequin.html.

Toscano, Margaret. "Mormon Morality and Immortality in Stephenie Meyer's Twilight Series." *Bitten by Twilight: Youth Culture, Media, and the Vampire Franchise*, edited by Melissa Click, Jennifer Stevens Aubrey, and Elizabeth Behm-Morawitz, Peter Lang, 2010, pp. 21–36.

Tyler, Natalie. "Jennifer Crusie on Jane Austen as the Mother of the Modern Romance Novel." *The Friendly Jane Austen: A Well-Mannered Introduction to a Lady of Sense & Sensibility*. Viking, 1999, pp. 240–242.

Valeo, Christina A. "The Power of Three: Nora Roberts and Serial Magic." *New Approaches to Popular Romance Fiction: Critical Essays*, edited by Sarah S. G. Frantz, and Eric Murphy Selinger, North Carolina: McFarland, 2012, pp. 229–239.

Vejvoda, Kathleen. "Idolatry in *Jane Eyre*." *Victorian Literature and Culture*, vol. 31, no. 1, 2003, pp. 241–261.

Vivanco, Laura. *Faith, Love, Hope and Popular Romance Fiction*. https://www.vivanco.me.uk/node/428, n.p.

———. *For Love and Money: The Literary Art of the Harlequin Mills & Boon Romance*. Humanities-Ebooks, 2011.

Voaden, Rosalynn. "The Language of Love: Medieval Erotic Vision and Modern Romance Fiction." *Romance Revisited*, edited by Lynne Pearce, and Jackie Stacey, New York University Press, 1995, pp. 78–88.

Watt, Ian. *The Rise of the Novel: Studies in Defoe, Richardson and Fielding*. 1957. Pimlico, 2000.

Weaver-Zercher, Valerie. *Thrill of the Chaste: The Allure of Amish Romance Novels*. Johns Hopkins University Press, 2013.

Weisser, Susan Ostrov. *The Glass Slipper: Women and Love Stories*. New Brunswick: Rutgers University Press, 2013.

Wendell, Sarah. *Everything I Know About Love I Learned From Romance Novels*. Naperville, Illinois: Sourcebooks Casablanca, 2011.

Whitsitt, Novian. "Islamic-Hausa Feminism Meets Northern Nigerian Romance: The Cautious Rebellion of Bilkisu Funtuwa." *African Studies Review*, vol. 46, no. 1, 2003, pp. 137–153.

Williams, Roseanne. *Love Conquers All*. 1991. Mills & Boon, 1992.

Wogan-Browne, Jocelyn. *Saints' Lives and Women's Literary Culture, 1150–1300: Virginity and its Authorizations*. Oxford: Oxford University Press, 2001.

23 Race, ethnicity, and whiteness

Erin S. Young

> [A] novel's impact on the culture at large depends not on its escape from the formulaic and derivative, but on its tapping into a storehouse of commonly held assumptions, reproducing what is already there in a typical and familiar form. The text that becomes exceptional in the sense of reaching an exceptionally large audience does so not because of its departure from the ordinary and conventional, but through its embrace of what is most widely shared.
>
> —Jane Tompkins, *Sensational Designs: The Cultural Work of American Fiction, 1790–1860* (xvi, 1986)

I begin this chapter's discussion with the above passage for a couple of reasons. First, although Tompkins is not referring specifically to popular romance novels,[1] her claims are absolutely applicable to the kind of "cultural work" that romance novels do: authors of the genre engage with their readers' shared values and assumptions about romantic love, courtship, and intimacy by addressing them in what some—but not all—might consider to be formulaic narrative structures. In today's publishing market, if a novel is considered "exceptional" for reaching an "exceptionally large audience," there's a good possibility that this novel is a popular romance novel. According to Romance Writers of America, romance novels comprise 34 percent of the U.S. fiction market, and in 2013, the estimated total sales value of romances was $1.08 billion ("Romance Statistics"). Furthermore, many romance novelists have critically discussed a kind of social contract that exists between authors and readers. One pertinent example is the use of what Linda Barlow and Jayne Ann Krentz, in their essay, "Beneath the Surface: The Hidden Codes of Romance," refer to as coded language: "In a sense, romance writers are writing in a code clearly understood by readers but opaque to others" (15). In short, romance writers and readers share a particular set of assumptions and expectations about the novels—and about romantic love—that enable the effective utilization of coded language, images, and descriptions: "[The fictional world of romance] is an active, dynamic realm of conflict and resolution, evil and goodness, *darkness and light*, heroes and heroines, and it is a familiar world in which the roads are well-traveled and the rules are clear" (Barlow and Krentz 15–16, emphasis mine). A significant number of the authors' examples deal with the contrasts of "darkness" and "light." Heroines are light, and heroes are dark; the authors note that by the romance novel's conclusion, "[The heroine] has succeeded in shining light into the darkness surrounding the hero" (Barlow and Krentz 20). Barlow and Krentz argue that readers understand such tensions—hero/heroine, darkness/light—as part of "a time-honored tradition" of storytelling that goes back to ancient mythology.

But—and here, I get to my second and more important point—whose mythology? Barlow and Krentz's examples are entirely Western, ranging "from ancient Greece to Celtic Britain to the American West" (16). And more importantly, whose shared assumptions? Tompkins analyzed works of American fiction produced from 1790–1860, a period in which the readers, writers, and publishers of said fiction were predominantly white. According to a 2016 infographic released by Nielsen, 81 percent of popular romance readers were also identified as white ("Romance Readers by the Numbers"). Whiteness, along with other racial categories, is constructed through cultural narratives like fiction, perhaps especially popular fiction, and perhaps popular romance fiction even more so. The symbolic language and imagery are cornerstones of the genre, but they are also, as many scholars have noted, heavily racialized. Further, popular romance fiction is particularly sparse in its representation of non-white characters in general, and of non-stereotypical representations specifically. Popular romance, in sum, has a race problem. As this chapter will demonstrate, many authors, scholars, and fan communities are making major strides in combating the problem. However, much more work is needed from scholars (both academic and para-academic)[2] to address the genre's racial gaps and to explore the more inclusive romance fiction that began to proliferate in the twenty-first century, as well as to denaturalize the constructed cultural narrative of whiteness. Although historically white, popular romance novels have gained significant diversity in authorship, readership, content, and publishing over the last few decades. Romance scholars will find many opportunities for intervention here; the notable changes in race, ethnicity, and whiteness that are occurring in the genre need unpacking, and as the discussion of relevant ethnic scholarship below suggests, emergent literature and its corresponding scholarship are often mutually constitutive.

Many of the scholars who have published on race/ethnicity in the popular romance novel are well-versed in the post-Civil Rights era ethnic literary movements that gained prominence both inside and outside of the academy. Potential scholars will also find a great deal of utility in this literature, criticism, and theory. African American literary scholarship has focused on cultural recovery and revision, particular literary movements (e.g., the Harlem Renaissance), as well as black literary responses to white racism (Rivkin and Ryan 960). Toni Morrison, whose *Playing in the Dark: Whiteness and the Literary Imagination* (1992) serves as the primary theoretical lens for Stephanie Burley's seminal analysis of whiteness in romance fiction discussed later in this chapter, is also a Nobel- and Pulitzer-winning author of African American fiction and poetry. Not unlike popular romance writers who have made scholarly contributions to the field, many of the foundational authors in U.S. ethnic literary traditions have also functioned as some of their most prominent literary critics. As a romance academic who has published on representations of Asian/Asian American characters and places in the genre, I owe much of my critical perspective to Asian American(ist) scholars like Elaine H. Kim, Lisa Lowe, Frank Chin, and Yen Le Espiritu, not to mention the postcolonial theorist, Edward Said. Scholars interested in Latinx/Chicanx romances (or romances featuring such characters) will likely find post-structuralist concepts of territoriality and hybridity useful, as well as the concept of "border theory" developed by Chicanx theorists like Gloria Anzaldúa. Native American literary critics, such as Paula Gunn Allen and Gerald Vizenor, should be essential reading for romance scholars interested in Native American-authored novels, in addition to representations of Native peoples and nations in the genre at large. It is also imperative for scholars to read and think critically about how whiteness operates in popular romance. Several of the authors discussed in this chapter explore how historical constructions of whiteness have informed—and continue to inform—romance structures, characters, and settings, but given the overwhelming whiteness of the genre, much more work is needed in this area to further our critical understanding of how race functions in the popular romance novel. The scholarship discussed in the remainder of this chapter demonstrates how the foundational ideas of race theorists and ethnic literary critics can be effectively utilized in the analysis of race, ethnicity, and whiteness in popular romance novels.

This chapter's organization is as follows. First, I discuss two pieces of scholarship that reveal how race—particularly blackness and whiteness—get constructed in romance fiction through symbolic language: Stephanie Burley's "Shadows and Silhouettes: The Racial Politics of Category Romance" and Jayashree Kamblé's "White Protestantism: Race and Religious Ethos in Romance Novels." Their essays draw from theoretical arguments on racialized narrative structures from Toni Morrison and Richard Dyer, respectively. As Burley and Kamblé demonstrate, Morrison's and Dyer's analyses have tremendous utility for romance fiction, precisely because of its reliance on formulaic conventions and coded language. Hsu-Ming Teo's "The Romance of White Nations: Imperialism, Popular Culture, and National Histories," situates these racial constructs within the context of imperialism, arguing that popular romance contributed to the production of racial difference in support of colonial agendas. This discussion will be followed by an inquiry into white supremacy and privilege, as they are explored in my article, "Escaping the 'Time Bind': Negotiations of Love and Work in Jayne Ann Krentz's 'Corporate Romances,'" and Danielle N. Borgia's "*Twilight:* The Glamorization of Abuse, Codependency, and White Privilege." From here, I review critical readings of characters of color and interracial romance in Andrew F. MacDonald's "The Romance Genre: Welcome to Club Cherokee" and my essay, "Saving China: The Transformative Power of Whiteness in Elizabeth Lowell's *Jade Island* and Katherine Stone's *Pearl Moon.*" I then explore black/white interracial romances in Guy Mark Foster's "How Dare a Black Woman Make Love to a White Man! Black Women Romance Novelists and the Taboo of Interracial Desire" and Kim Gallon's "'How Much Can You Read about Interracial Love and Sex without Getting Sore?' Readers' Debate over Interracial Relationships in the *Baltimore Afro-American.*" This chapter concludes with an examination of an online discussion that demonstrates the critical work (both self-critical and literary/cultural critical) that is being accomplished outside of academia, yet within the romance community, or at the border between them.

Making whiteness strange[3]

One of the earliest pieces of romance scholarship to address race explicitly is Stephanie Burley's "Shadows & Silhouettes: The Racial Politics of Category Romance" (2000). Burley states, "My aim is to ... examine how racially encoded language, trope, and ideology function in 'white' category romance" (324). The foci of her analysis are the Silhouette *Desire* category romances *Men of the Black Watch* by B. J. James. Burley's essay notes that the white heroines of the series are "consistently represented as lighter and whiter than their [male] counterparts," while "all of the heroes, none of whom could be described as Black or African American, are associated with various notions of 'darkness'" (Burley 324). Burley, however, is largely interested in how symbolic blackness operates in these novels, and her analysis is informed by Toni Morrison's theorization of the "Africanist presence" in *Playing in the Dark:*

> [Africanism] is a dark and abiding presence, there for the literary imagination as both a visible and an invisible mediating force. Even, and especially, when American texts are not "about" Africanist presences or characters or narrative or idiom, the shadow hovers in implication, in sign, in line of demarcation.
>
> (Morrison 46–7)

Morrison argues that this Africanist presence is an integral feature of American literature. Freedom and individuality have been dominant themes in the literature since the American canon was in its earliest stages of formation, and "nothing highlighted freedom—if it did not in fact create it—like slavery" (Morrison 38). In short, the Africanist presence has long functioned as an effective backdrop or foil that throws tales of (white) American heroism and individualism into sharp relief. Burley's analysis of B.J. James' category romances demonstrates how such narrative strategies may be utilized in popular romance fiction.

At the crux of Burley's argument is the claim that "while heroes like men of the *Black Watch* are temporarily linked to blackness, much cultural work is done to ensure that they are recuperable within the white-centered romance narrative" (332). The heroes are shrouded in enough dark imagery to be coded with "danger, mystery, sensuality, and otherness" (328), but they also "are constantly saving the innocent white heroines from 'dark threats,'" creating a "dynamic [that] reinforces the hero's titillating, but temporary, association with black otherness" (332). By the novels' end, after all internal and external threats are vanquished, the heroines have "succeeded in shining light into the darkness surrounding the hero[es]," thereby exemplifying Barlow and Krentz's formulation of how lightness and darkness operate in romance fiction (20). Burley's argument, however, moves such symbolism from the abstract to the racialized particular. Morrison notes that the Africanist presence "becomes the means of thinking about body, mind, chaos, kindness, and love [and] provide[s] the occasion for exercises in the absence of restraint [and] the presence of restraint" (47). B.J. James' *Black Watch* heroes struggle with and eventually overcome their inner "darkness" in order to be suitable mates for their white heroines. Thus, romance novels that employ such symbolic tactics are effectively, to borrow Morrison's phrasing, "romancing the shadow" and "playing in the dark." The elements of "blackness" that must be ultimately rejected in order for "whiteness" to prosper—sexuality, desire, danger—serve as provisional playgrounds for the protagonists. The reproduction of whiteness is ensured through the temporary foray into blackness, but blackness is strictly controlled so as not to pose a threat to the continuation of whiteness. Morrison's theories are arguably underutilized in the analysis of popular romance fiction, considering how provocatively they overlap with the genre: romance has long been lauded for its celebration of freedom by both authors and academics alike,[4] and this freedom is characteristically thrown into sharp relief against a background of explicitly racialized otherness or symbolic darkness constructed through the requisite coded language.

I would argue that Burley's article remains relevant today, since such coded language is still commonplace in many popular romance novels, yet it is not until 14 years later that Jayashree Kamblé's "White Protestantism: Race and Religious Ethos in Romance Novels," the fourth chapter of her book, *Making Meaning in Popular Romance Fiction: An Epistemology*, pushes this critical examination further. Just as symbolic blackness takes on particular forms and meanings in literature, so does symbolic whiteness. Kamblé challenges the assumed universality of mass-market romance fiction by identifying the elements in characterization and narrative structure that are, in actuality, specifically Western and white: "the genre relies on structures of feeling and being that are ineluctably grounded in a white Protestant ethos, and may be promulgating them as the norm (at least for romantic behavior) to its worldwide audience" (131). Kamblé supports her argument with close readings of Lisa Kleypas' *Seduce Me at Sunrise*, a rewriting of Emily Bronte's *Wuthering Heights*, and Nalini Singh's corpus of paranormal romances. *White: Essays on Race and Culture*, by prominent film scholar, Richard Dyer, plays a key role in Kamblé's theoretical framework for the analysis of how Western cultural assumptions about whiteness permeate the protagonists' characterization: "whiteness lies on one end of a spectrum representing beauty, the eternal soul, sexual control, and economic striving, and darkness on the other, suggesting ugliness, a corrupt body, sexual dissolution, and lethargy" (Kamblé 132). Whiteness, like blackness, is of both the mind and the body, but only in whiteness can the spirit transcend the body through "enterprise": "It is a polyvalent yet exclusionary Christian ideology that rests on the notion of a 'spirit' divorced from the body, yet tied to it due to the imperative of reproducing and protecting the selfsame ideological identity" (Kamblé 133). In short, white enterprise means having the "energy, will, ambition, the ability to think and see things through" such as "discovery, science, business wealth creation, the building of nations, the organization of labour (carried out by racially less humans)" (Dyer 31 qtd. in Kamblé 133). However, whiteness is inextricably linked to the body through the necessity of physical reproduction. Here lies a great tension, or contradiction, in how whiteness gets constructed, which Dyer calls "the conundrum of sexuality for whites": "To ensure the survival of the race, they have to have sex—but having sex, and sexual desire, are not very white: the means of reproducing whiteness are not themselves pure white" (Dyer 26). Dyer's analysis here not only provides us with a useful framework for thinking about how race and sexuality intersect in meaningful ways; it also helps us unpack one of the central narrative characteristics of the vast majority of popular romance novels: the white hero's struggle to control his sexual desires.

Kamblé argues that Kleypas' *Seduce Me at Sunrise* provides an exemplary model of "a man's struggle against the temptation of sexual desire and a woman's to reconcile reproduction and chastity" (134). The novel's heroine, Winnifred "Win" Hathaway, is described through the hero's eyes as "an otherworldly creature as pale as moonlight, her hair silver-blond, her features formed with tender gravity" (qtd. in Kamblé 135). She epitomizes "the Caucasian gentlewoman, as the acme of whiteness, [who] represents a colorlessness that can translate into an absence of defining properties, and thus run[s] the risk of insubstantiality and death" (134). This construct of the white woman is situated firmly at the whitest end of the white-dark spectrum, but the construct of the white man resides in much murkier territory. The novel's hero, Kev Merripen, is a Roma orphan fostered by Win's family. While physically darker than his heroine, Kev exhibits a struggle for control of his sexuality that marks him as white in spirit: "sexual control is the way for men to enact whiteness, to set themselves apart from the darker Other within and outside oneself" (Kamblé 135). Kev performs a key element of what Dyer calls "the story of whiteness":

> Dark desires are part of the story of whiteness, but as what the whiteness of whiteness has to struggle against. Thus it is that the whiteness of white men resides in the tragic quality of their giving way to darkness and the heroism of their channeling or resisting it.
>
> (Dyer 28)

Dyer's "story of whiteness" aligns nicely here with Morrison's claim that the "Africanist presence" creates opportunity to exhibit the absence or the presence of restraint (Morrison 47). It is important to note that, as Kev demonstrates, this "white" narrative arc of male sexual control is not exclusive to white men (although it is arguably far more accessible to some racial and ethnic identities than others). In other words, it is essential to understand that particular narrative structures exemplify "white poetics," but these structures do not necessarily align neatly with characters' racial identities, despite the fact that they often do (Kamblé 132). Further, this distinction between racialized narrative arcs and the racial identities of characters is integral to understanding Toni Morrison's notion of "playing in the dark": "There is no romance[5] free of what Herman Melville called 'the power of blackness,' especially not in a country in which there was a resident population, already black, upon which the imagination could play" (Morrison 37).

While Morrison is keenly interested in how blackness has been constructed in U.S. literature, Hsu-Ming Teo's "The Romance of White Nations: Imperialism, Popular Culture, and National Histories" (2003) looks beyond the boundaries of the nation-state in her analysis of post-imperial popular romances, noting that "the global reach of the romance industry has disseminated these texts in ways that not only inhibited what they could say about race and racism, but also created a transnational community of white readers" (Teo 280). Many of the manuscripts in this review focus deeply on textual analysis, but Teo's chapter draws from her training as a historian to situate the evolution of popular romance within the context of imperialism: "Empire romances were written predominantly by Anglo-Saxon women for other white readers—European, American, or colonial—and from very early on their romantic fantasies were inflected, even produced, by race" (Teo 283). Like Kamblé, Teo acknowledges that a white–dark spectrum of racialization inflects how heroes and heroines have been characterized in romance fiction, with white women "naturalized as the heroines of romance" (284), and in the twentieth century, "a sleight of hand that substituted dark-hued white men and brown heroes for darkness, while the historical legacies of colonialism and slavery have worked to keep black people at the margins of romance or to exclude them completely" (289). While much romance scholarship engages with national legacies in popular romance literature (British and American being the most common), Teo urges us to consider the ways in which popular romance and its formulaic conventions have functioned to reinforce colonial and imperialist projects: "The female romance novel must end in domesticity and the creation of stable white families. In this way, women's romances played a vital role in the fantasy of community, nation, and empire building" (Teo 285). Teo's chapter should be of particular interest and importance to new scholars in the field, because it establishes that the genre has been explicitly racialized from its very inception, particularly in its construction of whiteness.

Burley's and Kamblé's contributions demonstrate the efficacy of analyzing popular romance literature through the lens of a particular theorist, which is not an uncommon approach for race scholarship in the genre. It's worth noting, however, that overreliance on a particular theorist or theory may constitute a missed opportunity; in putting these two pieces in conversation with one another, I was repeatedly struck by how effective it would have been for Morrison and Dyer (or any grouping of scholars that examine both "whiteness" and "blackness") to be integrated into a single theoretical framework, in either or both articles, to produce a more complex analysis of how "whiteness" and "blackness" are constructed to be mutually informative. Part of the problem, I suspect, is that romance scholarship on race/ethnicity has been sparse enough to make difficult the recognition of a clear, academic trajectory. This is a problem that can only truly be rectified with a richer body of scholarship, and along with it, a greater shared understanding of the theoretical models that align well with the genre.

White supremacy and white privilege

Whiteness affords a wide array of privileges in popular romance fiction. The option of "playing in the dark," as described above, is one example of such privileges, but there are many more that warrant examination. The essays discussed in this section explore some of the dominant expressions of white privilege and supremacy that are apparent in the genre, but much more critical work is needed to thoroughly investigate the ways in which they inform the courtship rituals and romantic settings that are often constructed as universal in romance novels.

My article, "Escaping the 'Time Bind': Negotiations of Love and Work in Jayne Ann Krentz's 'Corporate Romances'" (2010), analyzes how race and class privilege intersect to carve out time and space for the urban protagonists to develop romantic relationships despite their intense professional obligations. More importantly, I argue, the protagonists' whiteness correlates directly with corporate nepotism; distinctions between work and family life are elided when one's employees are literal family members. The novels' premise—heroines inheriting businesses from family patriarchs—is far more available to white protagonists than their non-white counterparts, whose ancestors would have been stifled by myriad legal exclusions throughout U.S. history.

The central conflict in Krentz's corporate romances is the negotiation of work and home life. The heroes and heroines are depicted as being good at work and bad at love. The romantic couples are initially thrown together in a reluctant professional partnership, and a secondary mystery plot (missing person, unsolved murder, etc.) provides the impetus for the development of a more intimate relationship between them. For example, in Krentz's *Flash* (1998), Olivia Chantry inherits 49 percent of Glow, Inc. from her deceased Uncle Rollie, only to discover that Rollie had a silent partner, Jasper Sloan, who owns the other 51 percent of the company. Their relationship is initially confrontational, but they begin to work together when one of Olivia's relatives (and employees) goes missing. As they investigate the mystery surrounding this disappearance, their professional relationship blossoms into a romantic one. What becomes painfully clear, however, is that their race and class privilege play a significant role in their ability to pursue courtship and intimacy. As Eva Illouz argues in

Consuming the Romantic Utopia: Love and the Cultural Contradictions of Capitalism (1997), "romance is a good unequally distributed in our social structure; love provides personal freedom only to those who already have a measure of objective freedom in the workplace" (qtd. in Young 103). Olivia and Jasper both evidence such personal freedom through workplace freedom, in several different ways: they are not bogged down by daily domestic chores, they adjust their schedules to spend time together, and they exhibit a great deal of control over their private environments—they may live in Seattle, but their homes and consumption practices demonstrate that they possess the wealth to bring exotic locales and foods to their own doorsteps (Young 105).

These privileges have a direct impact on the success of the protagonists' personal and professional relationships. In *Flash*, Jasper and Olivia assume the roles of patriarch and matriarch at Glow, Inc. These roles are both figurative and literal, as the majority of the employees are members of the Chantry family. The partnership is egalitarian, as one would expect in a contemporary romance novel, but the nepotism that ensured this hierarchical structure is never addressed nor questioned. In the novel's final chapter, a relative/employee inquires if Glow, Inc. will remain a family-run corporation. A few passages later, Olivia and Jasper announce that they plan to have children, thereby implying that the inheritance model will continue into the next generation and beyond. Their proclamation functions as a guarantee that whiteness will be reproduced, but also that the privilege and power of whiteness will remain exclusive.

It should be clear that I read the inheritance model as a signifier of whiteness, along with the freedom the protagonists experience in terms of finances, labor, and time. However, future scholarship in this area would ideally investigate my claims further—do race and socioeconomic class become too easily conflated here? Further, what kinds of markers would make whiteness more visible in such texts? It's also worth noting that there are romance writers of color creating what I would call "corporate romances," but with protagonists who are not white. For example, an African American family-run corporation is at the center of Brenda Jackson's Steele series. Does corporate ownership, and the inheritance model, function similarly in non-white romances? More research is needed here to fully develop this line of inquiry.

The tropes of white privilege discussed above are prevalent in the popular romance genre, but they are typically rendered invisible in the narratives. A possible exception to this rule is the paranormal romance subgenre. As Danielle N. Borgia states in "*Twilight:* The Glamorization of Abuse, Codependency, and White Privilege" (2014), "[The] persistence of whiteness as a predominant factor in U.S. identity is not acceptable in other forms of discourse; yet the Gothic trope of the vampire enables this reactionary value to re-enter the mainstream" (Borgia 166). Borgia argues that the supremacy and privilege of whiteness are made quite literal in Stephenie Meyer's *Twilight Saga* through her particular construction of the vampire. Before I delve further into her analysis, it's worth noting here that paranormal romances provide enormous potential for the deconstruction of racial hierarchies and heteronormative structures. In her previously discussed chapter, Jayashree Kamblé notes that the "paranormal is the genre's turn toward the carnivalesque (with its connotations of challenging the socially regulated everyday world) ... paranormal romances introduce a version of ethnic diversity within the otherwise racially unmarked mainstream of romance fiction through the carnival narrative" (149). My engagement with the paranormal, in this chapter, will be limited to Danielle N. Borgia's explicit examination of race in the *Twilight* series, for a couple of reasons: 1) as with desert and African American romance, this anthology includes a chapter dedicated to the paranormal romance, and 2) quite often, paranormal explorations of race operate metaphorically. This is not to suggest that metaphoric investigations of very real racial politics are unimportant, but I am also wary of the paranormal's ability to construct a comfortable distance between us (readers, writers, and critics alike) and the ways in which race functions to empower and disempower real people, structures, and institutions. As romance author Beverly Jenkins has famously noted, "you can relate to shapeshifters, you can relate to vampires, you can relate to werewolves, but you can't relate to a story written by and about black Americans? I got a problem with that" (NPR Interview). For all of these reasons, this chapter's discussion is limited to those works that focus specifically on the themes articulated in this section: white privilege and white supremacy.

Borgia's essay, like my analysis of Krentz's corporate romances, explores intersections of race and class privilege. In Meyer's *Twilight* series, the supremacy of whiteness is first made explicit in the allure of the vampires' white skin: "Bella's excessive praise for the beauty of the pale, white skin of the vampires in *Twilight* expresses a thinly veiled homage to whiteness as a physical, cultural, and social superiority" (Borgia 165). Borgia argues that the beauty of whiteness in these novels is epitomized in Meyer's famous deviation from narrative norms in the vampire's relationship with sunlight. Meyer's vampires sparkle rather than burn when exposed to the sun; theirs is an otherworldly whiteness that is to be coveted: "[Bella] objectifies Edward in terms that emphasize the purity of his white skin" (165). Borgia also notes that Meyer constructs a direct correlation between the Cullens' whiteness and their superiority, both in their physical bodies and in their home environment: "Bella stands in awe of the beautiful, white house, noting that its 'walls, high-beamed ceilings, the wooden floors, and the thick carpets were all various shades of white'" (166). Borgia reads Bella's obsession with becoming a vampire as an obsession with gaining access to white privilege and the status it affords. She also notes that the novels are set in the predominantly white town of Forks, Washington. Their only substantive engagement with characters of color is the Quileute tribe of the nearby LaPush reservation. The Quileutes are werewolves who serve as foils that emphasize the superiority of vampires: "These characters are portrayed as largely controlled by their bestial nature ... their instincts, rather than their rational thoughts and conscious emotions, control them" (167). While the Cullens are depicted as cerebral, civilized "vegetarians" who have learned to master their inner monsters, the Native American werewolves struggle to control their beasts. A key example of this is the werewolves' practice of imprinting on their soulmates, which removes choice from romantic relationships. Borgia argues that imprinting is a "lesser kind of love": "Edward clearly asserts the hierarchy of rational choice over involuntary passion when he tells Bella that the imprinting of Sam and Emily 'is very nearly as strong as the way I feel about you'" (169). The example of Sam and Emily supports Edward's claim; Emily's face bears the scars of an attack from Sam, because he failed to control his wolf. Their relationship is depicted as loving, but the strength of this love is undermined by the horrific abuse that Emily suffered at Sam's hands. In contrast, Edward exhibits an extreme control over his own physical interactions with Bella, to ensure that he never hurts her. Borgia's piece is less theoretically inclined than the previous works discussed, but its close reading of Meyer's vampires as emblems of whiteness makes a meaningful contribution to the field. In my view, Meyer's choice to align these diametrically opposed monster identities with racial categories echoes Dyer's discussion of the white-dark spectrum. White vampires transcend their bodies, and Native American werewolves fall victim to their animal natures. Meyer's indulgence in such stereotyping of non-white bodies is egregious, but far from unique in the popular romance genre, as the following section on characters of color and interracial romance will illustrate.

Interracial romance and characters of color

Historically, the genre has been predominantly white in terms of authorship and character representation, but some interracial pairings have emerged as somewhat commonplace in particular subgenres of romance. The Arab hero/white heroine combination is a staple of the "desert romance" subgenre (see Chapter 11), and many readers will be familiar with the Native American hero/white heroine pairing in historical captivity romances. While not constituting its own recognized subgenre, the romance novel that features a white hero and East Asian heroine is not unusual. Interracial romances featuring Black/white protagonists[6] have long had a strong readership in the romance community, although they were often relegated to smaller presses, like Genesis Press' Indigo Love Spectrum, before online publication became more commonplace. As the genre continues to evolve, and certainly as authors of color working in the genre continue to gain prominence, the characters in romance novels become more representative of the heterogeneity in the U.S. and Europe, as well as the rest of the globe. Scholarship addressing interracial romance and characters of color, while currently minimal, will surely grow in response. The remainder of this chapter addresses said scholarship.

In "The Romance Genre: Welcome to Club Cherokee," a chapter from *Shape-Shifting: Images of Native Americans in Recent Popular Fiction* (2000), Andrew F. MacDonald discusses the early American captivity narratives that inform the popular romance genre's engagement with Native Americans, as well as the themes and tropes that are prevalent in these novels. MacDonald argues that the figure of the Native American serves as an access point for a wide range of fantasies:

> Americans, in general have a sense of ownership of the Indian that doesn't exist with other wild, free, and exotic bands … for Americans, playing Indian is both a literal activity and an overarching metaphorical construct, an imaginative safety valve that finesses the strictures of a limiting mainstream identity.
>
> (134)

In historical Native American romances, which constitute the bulk of the subgenre, the interracial relationships between Native Americans and white settlers function as a critique of the regressive gender politics that dominated eighteenth- and nineteenth-century America. MacDonald notes that these novels are typically set in either the eighteenth-century colonial period or the nineteenth-century frontier era, neither of which commits authors to acknowledge the genocide of Native Americans, and thereby facilitates an unmitigated focus on cross-cultural differences in constructions of gender and sexuality. In the case of white heroines,

> The novels celebrate the thrill and danger of being stolen away by a "savage" male but also the power of love to tame the brute … Once she has tamed him through love, the woman is freed both from her personal captivity and from the

> social restraints of her own culture, which limited female roles and blocked self-fulfillment.
>
> (130)

MacDonald also claims that white women readers become sutured to the Native American women in the hero's community,

> who represent all that American and Canadian women might wish for themselves: independence, competence, physical courage, survival skills as well as artistic skills, a wild freedom and lack of restraint that enable unfettered choices about sexual relationships and lifestyle, exotic beauty and desirability, and caring lovers who choose them over family, race, and culture.
>
> (135)

It's worth noting here that the Native American romance subgenre affords white women authors and readers the opportunity to challenge the role of white women described in Dyer's "story of whiteness," and it should come as no surprise that this challenge is effected by yet another example of "playing in the dark"; the fantasy of being the Native American woman, or of becoming romantically involved with a Native American man, defies the idealized construction of the white woman as pure to the point of disembodiment. In these novels, white women are freed from the restraints of white society: "Puritanical white sex for procreation is set off against Indian sex for pleasure and mutual satisfaction, a gift of love" (MacDonald 141). Robin Harders' essay, "Borderlands of Desire: Captivity, Romance, and the Revolutionary Power of Love," in *New Approaches to Popular Fiction: Critical Essays* (2012), affirms MacDonald's claims:

> The implications for romance are provocative and substantial: the more traditional social values the genre consistently celebrates—monogamous, heterosexual love, marriage, domesticity, the nuclear family—do not have to be mere performances of Euro-American patriarchal supremacy, but can be subversive, even revolutionary, in their contemplation of a new social reality.
>
> (Harders location 2632–5)

It may seem obvious to state that "Euro-American patriarchal supremacy" has been devastating to Native Americans as well—from the genocide of nations to the violence of forced assimilation—yet, existing scholarship reflects a primary focus on white women and the myriad socio-political restrictions they faced.

On the surface, the subgenre seems to offer a positive representation of Native Americans and their cultures, but the novels are clearly drawing from the same set of assumptions—articulated in Dyer's white-dark spectrum and its correlations with physicality—as Meyer's more obviously problematic depiction of Quileute werewolves. MacDonald concludes that the subgenre largely "fails to confront genuine cultural differences," but Native American authors, like Cherokee Mardi Oakley Medawar[7], have the potential to take the genre "in new directions more attuned to the realities of their culture ... and rise above the limitations of convention to create individuals becoming aware that cultural differences can divide in ways far less predictable than mere gender differences" (154, 155). MacDonald's analysis suggests that racial and cultural differences are often invoked for the primary purpose of freeing whites from restrictive boundaries. The following discussion of interracial Asian and white romances demonstrates that such differences may also be invoked to emphasize the superiority of Western (white) culture and values to the point of justifying their global dominance.

In "Saving China: The Transformative Power of Whiteness in Elizabeth Lowell's *Jade Island* and Katherine Stone's *Pearl Moon*" (2016), I argue that the inclusion of Asian heroines alters the genre's narrative goal of the conventional gendered victory—typically afforded to white heroines—to racial and national victories for the white, Western heroes. The gendered victory I speak of here has been referenced by many romance scholars; it is perhaps most eloquently described by Jayne Ann Krentz in her introduction to *Dangerous Men and Adventurous Women* (1992): "In the romance novel ... the woman always wins. With courage, intelligence, and gentleness she brings the most dangerous creature on earth, the human male, to his knees" (8). In other words, despite the hero's significantly greater social, political, and economic power, the heroine succeeds in converting him to her worldview; in effect, she transforms and domesticates him. However, the Asian heroines in *Jade Island* and *Pearl Moon*, Liane and Maylene, are denied this conventional gendered victory. Rather, *they* are transformed by their white heroes. Both are biracial (Asian and white) heroines who identify more strongly with the Chinese side of their heritage, but they have also been traumatized and abused by their Chinese family members and the culture they represent: "In both novels, the Chinese family and community functions as a regressive past in which individual desires and feelings are painfully oppressed, and defined roles are marked by an extreme enforcement of gender inequality" (Young 206). Like the heroes of Kamblé's and Burley's essays, Liane and Maylene struggle with darkness, but the root of that darkness is made explicitly racial and cultural, rather than sexual. Caught at the intersection between competing corporate interests, these heroines ultimately reject the constructions of regressive Chinese culture that they initially represent, and choose instead to embrace the individualistic and liberating Western cultures that their heroes introduce them to: "These novels reveal that the typically unmarked hero of popular romance is both white and Western. More important, perhaps, they illuminate particular racial and national anxieties that emerge out of a global economy" (206). Such anxieties are alleviated as the heroes gain corporate and economic footholds in Chinese territory.

It should come as no surprise that many of the Chinese characters in these novels are depicted in stereotypical fashion. Chinese men, in particular, are devoted to tradition and unrepentant in their sexism, while Chinese women are typically repressed and unexpressive. In *Pearl Moon*, Maylene channels the Tin Man stereotype in a Hong Kong that Stone constructs as analogous to the land of Oz; she is first depicted as the Tin Man with her "badly rusted" and "forgotten emotion" (218). Once the two halves of her identity are reconciled, she is recast as Dorothy, who has found "where she belongs" after undergoing the emotional transformation that her hero has facilitated. The most egregious character, however, is Lee Chin Tang in *Jade Island*. Once romantically involved with Liane, Lee abandoned her for a family member with higher status. Obsessed with upward mobility, conniving, and described as "an incredibly good-looking leech" with "feline, almost feminine beauty," Lee is reminiscent of both a "dragon lady" and a "Fu Manchu," two Asian stereotypes that have been pervasive in the U.S. since the nineteenth century. Scholars interested in furthering research on Asian stereotyping in popular romance will find Yen Le Espiritu's *Asian American Women and Men: Labor, Laws, and Love* (2007) particularly useful for the political and economic context it provides in understanding how these stereotypes came into popularity in the United States. Another useful resource is *Asian American Dreams* (2000), by Asian American activist and journalist, Helen Zia, which is a core text in most Asian American Studies programs. Zia's interviews, situated within the larger historical trajectories of Asian immigration and exclusion in the U.S., explore how Asian American individuals have been affected by cultural biases, discrimination, and stereotyping.

Negative cultural portrayals and stereotypical characters are problems that plague many romance novels featuring characters of color, but the essays discussed in this section by Guy Mark Foster and Kim Gallon explore the complicated relationship that black readers have with interracial romance fiction, due to the historical trauma that black communities have suffered under white supremacy. Their pieces reveal that while popular romance fiction is often perceived as apolitical and ahistorical, black readers have demonstrated a painful awareness of the political and historical contexts that affect their access to, and desire of, interracial relationships with white people. Foster argues that, for black women readers, romantic desire for white men cannot be easily divorced from the historical legacy of abuse and dehumanization that black women have experienced at the hands of white men and the institutions they control. In Gallon's essay, readers of the *Baltimore Afro-American*, a prominent African American newspaper in the 1930s, found through a discussion of letters "a voice to proclaim their desire for representations of love, romance, and sex between blacks and whites where little opportunity existed for this articulation in other arenas of public life" (Gallon 112).

Foster's analysis, "How Dare a Black Woman Make Love to a White Man! Black Women Romance Novelists and the Taboo of Interracial Desire," is framed by the black feminist theoretical works of bell hooks and Patricia Hill Collins, both of whom should be required reading for any scholar interested in exploring intersections of race and gender in the popular romance novel. hooks and Collins acknowledge that black women's choices in love have been limited by the social pressure to regard white men as unacceptable romantic or sexual partners. In *Black Feminist Thought: Knowledge, Consciousness, and the Politics of Empowerment* (1990), Collins observes that "freedom for black women has meant freedom *from* white men, not the freedom to choose white men as lovers and friends" (Collins qtd. in Foster 110, emphasis in original). Foster argues, "black women who chose to read romances often had to engage in Herculean feats of imagination just to find pleasure in them," such as imagining themselves as white readers, imagining the hero and heroine are black, or imagining that the protagonists have no race at all (Foster 106). However, Foster also argues that the formulaic conventions of the romance novel afford particular opportunities for freedom in contemplating interracial desire: "the genre offers contemporary writers a ready-made literary form upon which to engage the pain and degradation that such relationships have historically caused for black women outside the text" (115). For Foster, popular romance is particularly useful for these purposes because of its typical reliance on the HEA (happily ever after); whatever anxiety and fear is produced through the novel's conflict is ultimately resolved by its conclusion, making the genre something of a safe space in which to explore the historical context that informs this interracial pairing (Foster 105). Just as the genre has potential to provide a cathartic and liberating experience for black women readers, Foster goes on to suggest that black women writers of these interracial romances are creating agency for themselves "in choosing to author non-pathologized portrayals of mutually consenting romantic and sexual bonds between black women and white men" (111).

The letter writers of Kim Gallon's "'How Much Can You Read about Interracial Love and Sex without Getting Sore?': Readers' Debate over Interracial Relationships in the *Baltimore Afro-American*" (2013) also demonstrate a keen awareness of the political/historical context surrounding the interracial love stories of their time, as well as reader agency in choosing how to interpret interracial desire. Gallon analyzes a reader debate that occurred through letters in the *Baltimore Afro-American* from April–July 1934, a debate that centered on the newspaper's coverage of interracial romance news stories and its publication of interracial romance fiction. Gallon's main argument is that "the *Afro-American* and its readers created deeper meanings about interracial romantic fiction by linking it with ideological and political issues such as race pride, civil rights, and the role of the newspaper itself" (105). Her analysis of these letters reveals a range of responses from readers. While some felt the material was inappropriate for the newspaper, "many readers who supported the publication of the stories viewed the *Afro-American* as operating as a challenge to white gatekeepers who conspired to keep information about interracial relationships a secret" (Gallon 109). Others felt "that interracial romantic fiction would further black progress for civil rights" (110). For some letter writers, the discussion created a space to explore the very real social conditions that prohibited interracial romance, providing "an opportunity to highlight a longstanding system of brutality against African Americans" (111). Ultimately, Gallon's study explores the complex ways in which black readers have contemplated and contextualized interracial love and desire, and how—as Foster's piece echoes—despite the pitfalls of interracial romance, it is ripe with opportunity to address lived realities and celebrate the freedom of choosing whom to love.

Race/ethnicity in the romance community

It is essential for emerging scholars in the field to be aware of popular romance criticism occurring in spaces outside of academia, particularly in online romance communities. Online spaces like "Smart Bitches, Trashy Books," which is frequented by readers, authors, and scholars alike, afford significant opportunities for reflection on race and ethnicity in popular romance, as this particular discussion demonstrates. It has already been noted that when romance novels depict characters of color, particularly when the authors are not members of the groups they're depicting, it is not unusual for the characters to be crafted in a stereotypical manner. This is, perhaps, especially true when the characters of color are supporting characters who serve only one or two key functions in the novel, and are thus shallowly rendered. In *Jade Island*, for example, Lee Chin Tang serves as a foil to Kyle; he highlights Kyle's white American strength, size, and heroism. In her book review of Mary Balogh's *Someone to Love* on Smart Bitches, Trashy Books, Carrie S. takes Balogh to task for such a character, the nameless "Chinese gentleman":

> He has no personality other than being an elderly Chinese master of "Oriental" arts who makes cryptic yet deep and wise comments. He doesn't even have

> a name. He has no role than to further Avery's emotional journey. It's embarrassing. It's mercifully brief, but intensely cringe worthy
>
> (Carrie S.)

This critique launched a vibrant discussion of the character, and ethnic stereotypes in the romance genre in general, in the review's comments section.

Many commenters also expressed disappointment with Balogh's "Chinese gentleman." Some proclaimed they wouldn't read the book: "I would normally by [sic] this book because I love Balogh. I won't now and I'm happy to have a this [sic] forum in which to say why" (Peggy). Others expected more of Balogh: "I'm happy that Balogh is still writing, but I do feel that someone of her skill and experience should be able to do better than to use an ethnic caricature" (Hazel). Some commenters, of course, found the critique to be unnecessarily harsh, noting that such a minor character may not warrant fleshing out, or like Fredda Bloggs, arguing that popular romance doesn't need to be political: "I read romance for fluff ... I want pretty frocks, and tea drinking and some witty conversations. If I wanted gritty social commentary I would be reading another genre." As Carrie S.'s response to Fredda Bloggs indicates, the assumption that fully developed characters of color equals "gritty social commentary" is erroneous: "The idea that people of color could not possibly have happy romances with each other in periods other than our own is bizarre." She then suggests that Ms. Bloggs familiarize herself with the works of Beverly Jenkins and Courtney Milan.

Another defense came in the form of "historical accuracy," which led to a fascinating experiment by one of the commenters. Madge, who is not surprised by Carrie S.'s review (but clearly disappointed with it), "figured ... there would be gnashing of teeth because there were only white people in a Regency." Fredda Bloggs notes that "White regency is historically accurate when you look at the upper classes. It still pretty much is accurate as regards the upper classes." The suggestion that a character such as the "Chinese gentleman" could not have a plausible back story that would lead him to Balogh's hero was challenged by Allie, who said, "It would have taken a 3-second google search and an extra three words to give the character a name, and 5 minutes to come up with some sort of back story to flesh the character out more." Rebecca decided to do exactly that by scanning a Wikipedia timeline of Chinese history. She shares her research in the discussion and creates a plausible back story for the character, as well as a name: "let's imagine that Avery's mentor was a boy from a Chinese family, born around 1720, and baptized Joao by a Portuguese missionary priest." Rebecca proves, in a very short amount of time, that "historical accuracy" is not a convincing defense in this case (and probably most cases), and she makes visible the presence of Chinese people in Regency England for everyone participating in the discussion.

One of the most significant moments in the conversation occurs when Balogh herself interjects to defend her character's portrayal:

> The Chinese gentleman was in a physical and spiritual place far beyond anything the hero knew. He was seen as a man far SUPERIOR to the duke, a man of deep wisdom. Is that stereotypical? I know Indian, Native American, American, Canadian (etc. etc.) people whom I revere for the same reason. And racist? Is it racist to imagine that a Chinese gentleman living in Regency England might

> know things about body, mind, and spirit that the typical Englishman might not have known? In what way do I treat this gentleman in a racist way?

Here, Balogh offers a new defense: the positive representation. Unlike the scheming Lee Chin Tang of *Jade Island*, her "Chinese gentleman" is superior to the hero, both physically and spiritually. For Balogh, such a positive representation cannot be racist. SB Sarah (presumably Sarah Wendell), informs Balogh that her character "is essentially a 'Magical Asian,' a relative to the equally damaging trope of the 'Magical Negro,'" and she provides a useful definition of the latter term, which is further elucidated by Carrie S.:

> The Chinese gentleman has one job—Provide the Rich White guy With Cryptic Wisdom. It's no wonder that he doesn't have a name—he's not a person. He's a device. And as is so often the case, what makes this device a racist one in [sic] the pattern of using ethnic minorities as devices to further the white character's journey.

The most striking response comes from another popular romance author, Courtney Milan, who explains how, as an Asian American, she has been affected by stereotypes. She also provides the following explanation of why Balogh's choice was problematic:

> I think the first knee-jerk reaction of white people portraying people of color in fiction is this: "I don't want to be racist, so I'm going to make sure that this person is as wonderful as possible." The end result is that they create a character who has no goals, motivations, or conflicts, and since the portrayal is supposed to be positive, that means the author can't show them operating in opposition to your protagonist, so they exist in the story solely to help the (white) protagonist.

Milan's heartfelt response, from the perspective of an Asian American romance author, acknowledges Balogh's good intentions while also holding her accountable. And with due credit, Balogh re-enters the discussion toward the end and acknowledges what she's learned from it: "This has been very educational, and I thank you all for the comments and explanations. I am being sincere here! . . . I will do better in the future at least on this specific issue."

I have chosen to conclude with the optimistic example above, because it demonstrates that there is hope in addressing the problems with race, ethnicity, and whiteness in the popular romance novel that the publications discussed in this chapter have revealled. Clearly, many readers, authors, and scholars alike are holding romance novels to higher standards in their treatment of race. Further, online spaces like "Smart Bitches, Trashy Books," create opportunities for having difficult but necessary discussions about how the genre can do better. We need more diverse novels—with characters of color existing throughout history and around the globe, with protagonists whose racial identities are fully developed and not made symbolic. But as scholars, we must think more critically about how the genre has been and continues to be racialized, as well as the unique opportunities the genre affords in addressing and healing racial trauma.

Notes

1 It's also worth noting that Tompkins' *Sensational Designs* has long been acknowledged as a significant progenitor to the first-wave of popular romance criticism for recognizing that formulaic features in fiction perform "cultural work," and thus serve an important function in a nation's literature.
2 Lois Beckett's 2019 article from *The Guardian*, "Fifty Shades of White: The Long Fight Against Racism in Romance Novels," is an excellent example of para-academic reporting on popular romance: www.theguardian.com/books/2019/apr/04/fifty-shades-of-white-romance-novels-racism-ritas-rwa.
3 Dyer 4.
4 See *Romance Fiction and American Culture: Love as the Practice of Freedom?* (eds. Gleason and Selinger 2016).
5 Morrison's use of "romance" here refers to the American sentimental romance, rather than the popular romance novel specifically.
6 In internet parlance, these are typically coded as Black Woman White Man (BWWM) or Black Man White Woman (BMWW).
7 Medawar, to be clear, is not a popular romance novelist, but rather a mystery author who integrates strong romantic plots in her novels. Native American authors of romance fiction include Kari Lynn Dell, V.S. Nelson, Pamela Sanderson (Karuk), and Evangeline Parsons Yazzie (Navajo).

Works cited

Barlow, Linda and Jayne Ann Krentz. "Beneath the Surface: The Hidden Codes of Romance." *Dangerous Men and Adventurous Women: Romance Writers on the Appeal of the Romance*, edited by Jayne Ann Krentz, U of Pennsylvania Press, 1992, pp. 15–30.

Borgia, Danielle N. "*Twilight*: The Glamorization of Abuse, Codependency, and White Privilege." *The Journal of Popular Culture*, vol. 47, no. 1, 2014, pp. 153–173.

Burley, Stephanie. "Shadows and Silhouettes: The Racial Politics of Category Romance." *Paradoxa: Studies in World Literary Genres*, vol. 5, no. 13–14, 2000, pp. 324–343.

Carrie, S. Rev. Of *Someone to Love*, by Mary Balogh. *Smart Bitches Trashy Books.* 3 November 2016. Web. Accessed 18 April. 2017.

Dyer, Richard. *White: Essays on Race and Culture.* Routledge, 1997.

Foster, Guy Mark. "How Dare a Black Woman Make Love to a White Man! Black Women Romance Novelists and the Taboo of Interracial Desire." *Empowerment versus Oppression: Twenty First Century Views of Popular Romance Novels*, edited by Sally Goade, Cambridge Scholars Publishing, 2007, pp. 103–128.

Gallon, Kim. "How Much Can You Read about Interracial Love and Sex without Getting Sore: Readers' Debate over Interracial Relationships in the *Baltimore Afro-American*." *Journalism History*, vol. 39, no. 2, 2013, pp. 104–114.

Harders, Robin. "Borderlands of Desire: Captivity, Romance, and the Revolutionary Power of Love." *New Approaches to Popular Romance Fiction: Critical Essays*, edited by Sarah S. G. Frantz, and Eric Murphy Selinger, McFarland & Company,, 2012, pp. 133–135.

Kamblé, Jayashree. "White Protestantism: Race and Religious Ethos in Romance Novels." *Making Meaning in Popular Romance Fiction: An Epistemology*, Palgrave MacMillan, 2014, pp. 131–156. ProQuest ebrary.

MacDonald, Andrew F. "The Romance Genre: Welcome to Club Cherokee." *Shape-Shifting: Images of Native Americans in Recent Popular Fiction*, Greenwood Press, 2000, pp. 113–155.

Mayer, Petra. "Beverly Jenkins Wraps Bitter History In Sweet Romance." *NPR*, 8 Aug. 2015, www.npr.org/2015/07/29/427416512/beverly-jenkins-wraps-bitter-history-in-sweet-romance.

Morrison, Toni. *Playing in the Dark: Whiteness and the Literary Imagination.* New York: Vintage, 1993.

Rivkin, Julie and Michael Ryan, edited by. "Introduction: Situating Race." *Literary Theory: An Anthology*. 2nd ed. Oxford, UK: Blackwell, 2004, pp. 959–963.

"Romance Readers by the Numbers." *Nielsen*. 26 May 2016. Web. Accessed 18 April 2017.

"Romance Statistics." *Romance Writers of America*. Web. Accessed 18 April 2017.

Teo, Hsu-Ming. "The Romance of White Nations: Imperialism, Popular Culture, and National Histories." *After the Imperial Turn: Thinking with and through the Nation*, edited by Antoinette Burton, Duke University Press, 2003, pp. 279–292.

Tompkins, Jane. *Sensational Designs: The Cultural Work of American Fiction, 1790–1860*. Oxford University Press, 1986.

Young, Erin S. "Escaping the 'Time Bind': Negotiations of Love and Work in Jayne Ann Krentz's 'Corporate Romances.'." *The Journal of American Culture*, vol. 33, no. 2, 2010, pp. 92–106.

——— "Saving China: The Transformative Power of Whiteness in Elizabeth Lowell's *Jade Island* and Katherine Stone's *Pearl Moon*." *Romance Fiction and American Culture: Love as the Practice of Freedom?* edited by William Gleason, and Eric Murphy Selinger, Routledge, 2015, pp. 205–221.

24 In response to Harlequin

Global legacy, local agency

Kathrina Mohd Daud

Romance fiction is dominated by the Anglophone market, but both outside and in response to this market, local and national traditions exist, resisting the sameness that might well be imposed by transnational publishing corporations such as Hachette, Macmillan, Penguin Random House, Simon and Schuster, and HarperCollins—the parent company of Harlequin Enterprises. Scholars since the turn of the century have been increasingly attentive to how romance novels, especially category romances, translate into non-English cultures, including the Indian, Japanese, Malaysian, and Nigerian contexts, but also how these contexts have their own traditions outside of the dominant Anglophone sphere. This chapter will trace the influence and presence of the Harlequin Mills & Boon novels in the global context to consider their impact on indigenous literary ecosystems.

Introduction

> Today, anthropologists and evolutionary psychologists generally assume that passionate love and sexual desire are cultural universals. Cross-cultural researchers and historians point out that culture can have a profound impact on people's perceptions, experiences, and feelings about love, and about what is permissible and appropriate in their expression of romantic and passionate feelings.
>
> (Hatfield)

Love, Madonna sang in 1981, makes the world go around. How exactly it makes the world go round, on the other hand, remains the subject of much interest and study. How do different cultures express romantic feelings? What concerns about kinship, authority, governance, and tradition mediate the expression and experience of these feelings? How have local practices, understandings and experiences of romantic love been affected by colonialism, globalization and the subsequent flows and migrations of culture? How in turn do local practices contribute to global narratives about romantic love, if there is such a thing?

This chapter will approach these questions by considering the global phenomenon of Harlequin romances, and how local literature has responded to the ubiquity and dominance of the Harlequin model, using the case studies of India, Japan, Malaysia, and Nigeria. In looking at the scholarship on Harlequin in the world, it became clear that the Harlequin publishing house, and the Mills & Boon line which has become synonymous with its name, dominates both the romance market, and the scholarship that has mushroomed around local forms of popular romance globally.[1] The Harlequin Mills & Boon romance is associated with a specifically Western cultural form of romance and romantic ideology; subsequently, much of the research that has been done on local forms of popular romance has considered how the Harlequin model has been received, adapted and translated, and responded to in the local context. The production of local romance is often discursively positioned, then, in relation to Western production and narratives of romance.

Primarily by necessity, much of the preliminary scholarship on local forms of popular fiction has been linguistic, sociological, anthropological, ethnographic, or historical in nature. Additionally, this scholarship has attended to broad general overviews of popular fiction, highlighting the "heritage of generalization" which Selinger and Frantz point out as the practice in popular romance scholarship, which "rarely attend[s] in any detail to individual novelists, let alone individual novels" (6). There is a rich tradition of single-country studies of popular romance, but few comparative studies. This chapter works between both of these constraints: in offering the beginnings of a critical overview of global forms and scholarship of popular romance, it has not been able to consider individual texts; and although four countries are considered, their contexts are so different that it would take a different kind of study to examine them in any significant comparative fashion.

This chapter will first offer a brief introduction to the history of Harlequin romances and their prevalence in the global market. It will then review the localizing practices of Harlequin as mapped out by various scholars, before looking more specifically at how the local literary ecosystems in India, Japan, Malaysia and Nigeria have reacted and responded to the popularity of the Harlequin romance.[2] The chapter will close with a few reflections on directions for future studies, and offer a brief comparative analysis of the four countries considered.

Harlequin: a brief history

The story of Harlequin's dominance in the romance publishing industry has been ably documented by scholars over the last few decades (Rabine; Grescoe; Dixon; Darbyshire; Tapper; see also Chapter 16 in this volume). Romance is a worldwide billion-dollar industry, increasing annually, and which comprises 13 percent of all adult fiction sold in North America. Tapper points out that the continued popularity of romance must be understood "within the same profoundly unstable commercial climate in which numerous other book sectors have faltered" (250), attributing this success in large part to romance publishing's consistent "progressive" approach to the publishing business, including "diversification of content, cultivation of reader feedback, early adoption of ebook technology and consistently strong branding" (251).

Within romance publishing, Harlequin Mills & Boon (HMB) is the "800-pound gorilla of the category" (*Publishers Weekly*, Tapper 251), and has been lauded for its "aggressive, forward-thinking" and innovative business practices in the industry (Tapper 251). HMB is the world's largest producer of mass-market romance, and has been since the 1980s. Founded in 1948 in Canada, Harlequin published its first Mills & Boon romance in 1957 (Grescoe 52). At the time, Mills & Boon was a separate British publisher, which had been founded in 1908 in the U.K. by Gerald Mills and Charles Boon. Harlequin acquired Mills & Boon in 1975 to secure a supply of serial romances that would enable it to expand its market, particularly in North America.

Since then, Harlequin has continued to grow. It was acquired by HarperCollins in 2014, and with ownership of both the Silhouette and Mills & Boon imprints, it continues to be the most well-known publisher of romance in the world, despite increasing competition after the Penguin Random House merger in 2013.

The Harlequin text that is most familiar to readers, and which is most often referenced by the scholars and participants in the studies covered in this chapter is what is known as the Mills & Boon category romance novel, "a short (50,000–55,000 words) paperback novel published monthly in a paratextual easily recognisable series or imprint of thematically similar stories" (Goris 59). The HMB category romance has a history of commissioning books and launching whole lines to appeal to various demographics, including the Love Inspired imprint in 2000, aimed at capturing the Christian market, and the Harlequin Kimani line in 2006, to appeal to the underrepresented African American readership. HMB has also announced that its imprint Carina Press, will be launching a "trope-driven LGBTQ+ contemporary romance line, Carina Adores" in 2020 ("About Harlequin").

Tapper notes that HMB is not alone in the romance publishing industry in its willingness to "diversify its offerings, along with a stalwart refusal to flinch away from social, cultural and demographic change" (251), nor is it alone in soliciting and capitalizing on reader feedback and interaction to guide its strategies, particularly through nurturing a far-reaching web-based community and becoming early adopters of ebook and app technology (256). However, Tapper argues that HMB was one of the first drivers of innovation which has allowed it to "carve out a niche within the digital sphere that has been critical to its continuing success" (257). In its material production, distribution, and its willingness to embrace and reflect socio-cultural change in its narratives, HMB has been able to grow from strength to strength and continue to dominate the romance publishing industry.

Harlequin's localizing practices

Harlequin's global presence and successful penetration into local markets has been the subject of a range of scholarship. Based in Toronto, Harlequin publishes "more than 110 titles a month, in both print and digital formats, in as many as 150+ international markets and more than 30 languages, on six continents," with 95 percent of their sales coming from outside of Canada ("About Harlequin"). Until its acquisition by HarperCollins in 2014, HMB had principal offices in 17 countries, including New York, London, Paris, Mumbai, Rio de Janeiro, and Istanbul, covering North and South America, Europe, and Asia. In older promotional literature, Harlequin noted licensing agreements with businesses in another 12 countries, including in the Australasia region. Currently the promotional literature from HMB notes only three offices, in Toronto, New York and London, with no information on active licensing agreements.

From the beginning, the majority of HMB sales have come from outside Canada, and Harlequin's corporate page takes pride in HMB's historically international reach:

> After the fall of the Berlin Wall in 1989, Harlequin employees gave away more than 720,000 books at border checkpoints across the Eastern Bloc. Just two years later, Harlequin had sold seven million romance novels in Hungary alone and

> reached $10 million in sales in the Czech Republic in 1992. By 1995, it had released 550,000 copies of its titles in Mandarin Chinese, paving the way for the opening of offices across the world, from Tokyo to Mumbai.

Although HMB's promotional literature starts after the fall of the Berlin wall, Grescoe, Darbyshire, Goris, McWilliam, and Tapper have mapped HMB's earliest overseas subsidiaries from 1974 in Australia, swiftly followed by Holland in 1975, West Germany in 1976, France in 1978, and Scandinavia, Greece, Mexico, Venezuela and Japan by the end of the 1970s. These overseas ventures evolved fluidly from joint ventures between Harlequin and local publishers (in which Harlequin licensed book rights to local publishers to be released under their own imprints) (Grescoe 106), to the opening of Harlequin offices overseas, which experimented with producing local lines (with variable success), and translating and distributing existing titles. Historically, apart from these experiments, local production has not formed a large part of HMB's strategies overseas; it has focused instead on "literally translating works into the local language and conceptual system" (McWilliam 142).

An Goris attributes Harlequin's success in overseas markets to three factors: "strict narrative conventions, (materially) easily recognizable books and well developed, local marketing and distribution networks" (Goris 59). Scholars have generally paid particular attention to two facets of this success: 1) HMB books' ideological value as a Western product with narratives which embody capitalist idealism (Darbyshire 6) and 2) HMB's strategies and practices in localizing their products to appeal to local demographics.

Even before Harlequin's first European office was established in Holland in 1975, Paul Grescoe notes that Harlequins had already begun to appear in other languages (106). However, both Grescoe (109) and Darbyshire (3) point out that one of Harlequin's first attempts to localize their product, in the case of Germany in 1976, was rejected by German readers. Thinking that German readers might reject the Britishness of the HMB books at the time, the HMB joint venture in Germany had experimented with Germanizing the contents and authors of the books. It turned out, however, that Harlequin's popularity in Germany, and later on in Austria and Switzerland, were directly attributable to their "foreignness" (Grescoe 9), with readers "rejecting romances that weren't American or English" (Darbyshire 3). Darbyshire situates this phenomenon, and later on Harlequin's popularity in Eastern Europe, within a more "general continental demand for American cultural products" (4) during the period linked to a growing antipathy for the old communist order in Europe. Harlequin books appealed because of their embodiment of capitalist values, including lavish and conspicuous consumption (5). Both Grescoe and Darbyshire note that the "standard Harlequin narrative" (6) at the time, usually involved a union between rich and handsome heroes and heroines from middle- to lower-class backgrounds, depicting a successful union as having some material aspect to it. In fact, Darbyshire argues that overseas interest in Harlequin books has less to do with the specificities of American/British culture than it has to do with the fantasy of capitalist success and "American-style capitalism" (8). Darbyshire points out Harlequin's declining success in the increasingly affluent Japan as partial evidence for this argument. This observation on Harlequin's appeal is echoed by scholars on Harlequin in other contexts, including Parameswaran's work on Harlequin's reception in India, in which she asserts that a large part of the appeal of HMB to Indian readers is its window into (white)

American and European consumer culture (840). The question then becomes, how has the appeal of this specific capitalist fantasy figured into Harlequin's localizing strategies?

Scholars have looked closely at the question of what gets adapted to local markets in Harlequin books, and how. Grescoe has outlined a practical history of Harlequin's continued translation and adaptation practices overseas, after Harlequin's early failed attempt to localize the books in Germany, which has included hiring local teams of skilled translators, as well as the commissioning of local writers to produce HMB books (although this has been largely limited). In "Romance the World Over," An Goris further breaks down Harlequin's localizing process into "a three-stage procedure encompassing selection, production and finally marketing and distribution" (60). It is during the production stage that "the most drastic and extensive localizing intervention" (60) has occurred, of which translation might be a part. Goris' study looks both at the translation of the text, as well as the adaptation of its paratextual elements, including cover blurbs, introductory pages, titles, series names and cover art, to appeal to local markets.

Goris concludes in her study that the foreignness and exoticism of American/British values (62) is an important part of Harlequin's appeal in local markets around the world. In fact, the HMB English-language novels which are the source texts for local translations are written by "a nationally and culturally diverse group of (mostly) female authors, with the majority being American, followed by Britons and Australians" (67). She argues, however, that Harlequin's translation practices are such that they homogenize and neutralize many of the textual elements which are present in the original English-language texts and which distinguish between American, British, and Australian culture and values. Part of this homogenization, which erases much of the diversity within the texts, is a perpetuation of an idealized global capitalism within the novels, which is argued by Darbyshire to be the fundamental appeal of romances.

This neutralization of culture, which is often enacted through deletion of potentially unfamiliar references rather than through explanation, is partly why translated HMB texts tend to be much shorter than their English-language originals. Beyond this neutralization, scholars have noted that further adaptation or translation has to be enacted to conform, appeal to, or appease local sensibilities, particularly around issues of gender and sexuality (Grescoe 111; Goris 60; Tapper 252). For example, the level of explicit sexuality is reduced in romances published in Asia, the Middle East, and some parts of Europe, including France; this is reflected both in textual deletions and paratextual changes ("tamer covers" Tapper 252). Single-country studies, or single text studies, such as those conducted on Harlequin or other popular romance in Japan (Mulhern), Turkey (Schell), India (Uparkar), and Italy (Bianchi and D'Arcangelo) amongst others, have been able to look in more depth at the specificities of translation and adaptation and the insights these can offer into a range of cultural practices and norms.

As noted earlier, translating existing English-language texts has formed the larger part of HMB overseas strategies—the extent to which HMB texts have been produced locally has been minimal. In Italy, Harlequin is published by Italian media giant Mondadori, which mainly commissions the translation into Italian of Harlequin novels written by American, British, and Australian authors. Only 1 percent of the texts published by Mondadori are actually written by Italian authors (Bianchi and D'Arcangelo 248). In France, only 10 percent of the books are "commissioned French originals"

(Grescoe 111). In Turkey, all HMB publications are translations of existing English-language texts. McWilliam also notes that although Australian authors have written successfully for HMB for years, it is only since 2006 that HMB has commissioned Australian authors from within the country, rather than commissioning them through HMB's North American or British editorial offices (143). McWilliam marked this movement as a shift away from "a branch office operation which distributes products created elsewhere, and towards a creative branch which distributes products it has created" (143). Similarly, in India, which is considered one of the biggest markets for HMB romance novels outside the United States, United Kingdom, and Canada (Uparkar 321) HMB only launched the production of local romances in 2008. This inattention to local production may have something to do with what Goris argues is "the importance of the foreign and the exotic in the appeal of [Harlequin] romance novels to their (target) audiences around the world." Goris contends that this appeal is the reason why "since the global expansion of Harlequin's publishing activities, local romance novels have consistently failed to attract audiences in, e.g., the Netherlands, France, Austria, Switzerland and Germany" (62). This failure may be partly the reason why Harlequin has not historically prioritized local production of its novels.

While local romances may have failed in the countries Goris lists, they have flourished outside of Europe. An example is that of the francophone Adoras series which was established by publishing house Nouvelles Éditions Africaines (NEI) in Cote d'Ivoire in 1998 (Moudileno, 120). NEI was founded in response to marketing research that African readers were satisfying their desire for love stories through Western imports like "the Barbara Cartland books or the famous Harlequin series" (121). NEI became known as the "African Harlequin" (122), a locally produced series based on the Harlequin model but "specifically tailored to an African public" (121). The Adoras series was not just successful commercially, it is one of the few indigenous productions of popular romance which has established an international presence and readership. While the books are "primarily distributed in West Africa—Cote d'Ivoire, Togo, and Senegal" (121), they have also been circulated and sold in the rest of the francophone world, including France, Cameroon, and Chad. Consequently, NEI and the Adoras series have been endorsed at the national level by the Minister of Culture of Cote d'Ivoire who praised NEI for promoting literacy, and producing "work in the national interest" (Moudileno 121).

This brief example highlights the economic and cultural incentives for local publishers to launch "homegrown" (Moudileno 121; Mulhern 51) versions of the romance novel featuring local heroes and heroines, who are situated in familiar cultural and geographical spaces and practices. In the case of NEI above, the critical and national acclaim afforded the publisher and its works, offers to scholars a new line of inquiry. The Adoras series, and its elevation to "national" work is significant for several reasons. Firstly, as a francophone medium, the popularity of the Adoras series raises questions about production of literature in the "former colonizer's language" (122). Previously, writers from the African francophone canon had aspired to be read by the mass majority, and had been ignored—this had been attributed to illiteracy or an aversion to French as a colonial leftover. The popularity of the Adoras series suggested that these reasons were inaccurate; or at least that the postcolonial literary landscapes of Cote d'Ivoire, Togo and Senegal needed to be re-examined. The question of the language of local literature, or national literature in previously colonized nations around the world is almost always a fraught one, tied up as it is with anxieties over a postcolonial, fragmented identity. That the Adoras series was lauded for its national value despite its being in the language of former colonizer, offers another perspective on postcolonial identity and literary production.

Second, because they were created in direct response to Harlequin's popularity, Moudileno examined the narrative and thematic structure of the Adoras texts, to consider how they reflected and represented local realities. Moudileno concluded that as "Africanized" versions of Harlequin novels, the Adoras novels create at the paradigmatic level a problematic and fictive Africa to enable the protagonists to make the same narrative journey toward happy endings that their Western counterparts make. In other words, replicating the successful narrative structures of Harlequin novels required local authors to create in turn an Africa, and a culture(s) which could accommodate these journeys. This creates deeper questions about the extent to which the romantic love which Harlequin has successfully exported across the world, can truly be localized, or whether it is only a new form of cultural imperialism.

Both of these anxieties are rooted in the questions and anxieties of postcolonial identity. To examine these anxieties further, in the next section, I will look briefly at local responses to Harlequin and production of romance in Japan, India, Malaysia, and Nigeria.

Local responses to Harlequin

It is notable that Grescoe's well-known 1996 study of Harlequin ends on a speculative note about the company's future in China. In 1995, Harlequin had managed to convince the Chinese authorities to allow the dissemination and publication of a test run of 20 Harlequin titles that had been translated into Mandarin (550,000), and ten English-language titles (200,000 copies) (Grescoe 296). As with other overseas ventures by Harlequin, the novels were edited to "accommodate local sensibilities" (296), including customized cover art. Accessing China's 1.2 billion consumers (at the time) had long been a Harlequin goal, and at the time of Grescoe's study, it was unclear whether "Harlequinizing" China would be possible past the initial test run.

Grescoe ends his book-length study on Harlequin with a few reflections on the cultural impact the Harlequin juggernaut has had on local literary production.

> True, many North Americans and Europeans read translations of stories from other cultures and learn from them or are entertained by them—without losing their own sense of self and place. But for consumers who live in a have-not nation and have only meager disposable incomes or limited access to books, the inexpensive, widely distributed Harlequins might substitute for their own literature of any kind. Unfortunately the Chinese today seem not to be telling their own important stories ... So it seems that Western romantic fiction is becoming part of what Jianying Zha in *China Pop* calls the nation's current need for "Culture Lite."
>
> (300)

The problem with Grescoe's reflection on consumers in "have-not" nations is that it brushes over the complicated relationship that many formerly colonized nations have with America and Britain (whose representation is strongest in the distributed Harlequins). While consumption of Harlequins in China may primarily be a matter of material convenience and financial access, with the effect of shaping aspirational culture, as Grescoe seems to be suggesting, the aspirational status of the worldview they offer is also part of the legacy of colonialism in countries such as Malaysia and India.

Ultimately Grescoe concludes that

> call it Western arrogance or cultural chauvinism (as many will), but of all the things North Americans could be sending a country where personal freedoms are curtailed, where the standard of living is low, and where travel to the rest of the world is not an easy possibility, perhaps sending the Chinese our romantic stories set in faraway, exotic lands and always delivering on the promise of a happy ending is not such a bad thing, after all.
>
> (301)

Still, Grescoe expresses unease over the potential power Harlequins' dominance had to affect or influence local narratives of love.

How have local producers of romance, well aware of the problematic underpinnings of these romantic, imported novels, responded? I turn now to some brief case studies of local production in Japan, India, Malaysia, and Nigeria.

Japan

Despite initial resistance by Japanese publishers to Harlequin when first approached in the late 1970s, two years of market research convinced Harlequin to go ahead, even though they had to open their own office instead of partnering with a Japanese publisher (Grescoe 116). In 1979, when Harlequin hit the shelves in Japan, they had a turnover of 1.2 million books within the first half-year. By 1998, Shibamoto Smith reports, "Harlequin Tokyo employed four hundred English-to-Japanese translators and was advertising production levels of 16,000,000 volumes annually" (97).

In response to Harlequin's popularity, the Sanrio Company, which originally imported the Silhouette series, initiated Japan's first romance line, "original New Romances to be written by Japanese women" (Mulhern 51), soliciting manuscripts through an annual contest for the Sanrio Romance Award in 1982. The Sanrio New Romance, written by Japanese women, in the model of "fans-turned-authors" (52) with (mostly) Japanese protagonists, was written without the "tipsheet stipulating acceptable form and content" (52) characteristic of Harlequin and Silhouette at the time. But as Shibamoto Smith notes, Sanrio (and Oto Shobo, which launched the Crystal Romance series in 1996) did incorporate the happy ending, a narrative criteria set by Harlequin. (Grescoe relates an anecdote in which the editor in chief of Harlequin, after being informed that Japanese readers were used to unhappy endings, "idly suggested that perhaps Harlequins in Japan should have unhappy endings" (298), although this particular adaptation has never occurred.) This narrative criteria of the happy ending instead redefined romance for a generation of Japanese readers, who until then had been used to tragic romance or *hiren* "blighted love" (98); younger Japanese readers, affected by the Harlequinized newer discourses of love circulating, prefer the happy ending (Shibamoto Smith 98).

Shibamoto Smith contends that the Harlequinization of the Japanese romance fiction market is not limited to thematic or narrative devices, but the creation of a whole new genre unknown to Japanese literature. Previously categorized simply in "current release" or "women's fiction," romance has now been elevated to its own separate and highly visible category in Japanese bookstores (98). Indeed, Mulhern explains that the domestically produced Sanrio Romance represented an important transcultural moment, in which Japanese women writers turned the imported romance genre into a medium of their own, sharing certain literary and cultural paradigms with Western romance, but unmistakably Japanese in its physical and personal environments (67).

This observation is echoed and developed by Shibamoto Smith, who argues that despite the influence of Harlequin, domestically produced romance fiction has a clear and distinctive Japanese identity absent from translated Harlequins. In a comparative literary analysis of Harlequin and Japanese category romances, Shibamoto Smith traces this distinctive identity out using the tropes of the hero and heroine's physical descriptions, as well as their interactional styles (100), which she argues, are in contrast to those of the translated Harlequins, in which the hero and heroine speak Japanese, but "inhabit 'western' social fields and react in ways that—whatever their suitability in those social fields—are not the ways that Japanese true lovers speak, behave and come to their own 'happy ending'" (99). These significant differences suggest that although they constituted a response to and variant of the popular Harlequin model, domestically produced romances in Japan were able to carve out a local identity within the genre. Harlequin's arrival in Japan was significant in creating a space and moment for the romance genre, but within it, Japanese writers were able to acquire, appropriate and adapt the medium for the development of a distinctive narrative identity.

India

Mills & Boon arrived in India even before Harlequin acquired its first M&B title. They were brought in by British women—teachers, governesses and the wives of British colonial administrators and military personnel (Parameswaran 835).

This led to small quantities of Mills & Boon titles being exported by British publishing firms to India in the two decades before India achieved independence. After independence, Indian bookstores began to distribute the novels, and today India is one of the biggest markets for HMB novels outside of the U.S., U.K., and Canada (Uparkar 321). Despite this long history, however, it was only in 2008 that HMB launched a local romance line of *desi* or indigenous romance by local Indian writers.

Prior to this, however, Rupa & Co. had launched a line of Indian romances in 1994 to compete with the imported Mills & Boons. These romances, "set in India with Indian characters" (Parameswaran 840) were penned by Indian women "claiming credibility as writers in the promotional literature because they had read 'scores and scores of Mills & Boons'" (840) (echoing the Sanrio New Romance model). The line was a "resounding failure," partly because, as Parameswaran goes on to explore in her ethnographic study of female Indian readers of HMB, the appeal of Western Mills & Boons is precisely their foreignness, and their place as a window into a particular white material culture.

Indeed, the editor of the Rupa & Co. romances, Aditya Mukherji, attributed their failure to the fact that "these girls only ... want to read about foreigners" (Parameswaran 840). Parameswaran's interviewees affirm this, specifying further the particular kind of foreigner (white, European): "We would not be able to think of Chinese or African men dating, giving a woman flowers, or driving Ferraris and drinking champagne" (839). It became apparent that the Indian readers of HMB romances were not aware of or interested in multicultural romance novels—Parameswaran's study thoroughly unpicks the threads of race, class, material consumption, sexuality and nationalism in her interviewees' responses to conclude that Indian readers of HMB are drawn to a global and cosmopolitan consumer culture embodied in the aspirational romances and white/European heroes. In the case of India, the appeal of HMB's owes as much to colonial legacy as it does to a transnational capitalist fantasy.

At the same time, however, Parameswaran shows that the rejection of "Indian Mills & Boons" or Indian romance, is specific to the medium of the popular Harlequin paperback. As one respondent explained, "When we want to enjoy good Indian romance we watch Indian movies. A lot of films are trash, but I love good Indian films ... I think Indian romance is best on film not in books" (840). Another respondent agrees, saying "Indian romance is different. It's slow and grand. It needs to be in a movie or on TV. It needs music and color!" (840).

Parameswaran uses this example to reject the common cultural fear in India and in many postcolonial nations, that consumption and love of Western narratives compromises local and national identity. Parameswaran argues that the romance novel consumer in India may have transnational fantasies, but that their pleasure in Indian romances, and their preference for them in a different medium to Harlequin paperbacks, demonstrate that their "inner realms of imagination and desire" are not "interpellated only by Western popular culture" (840). The HMB novel offers a very particular pleasure and fantasy rooted in their Western settings and ideologies that is suited to the paperback medium; Indian romances are perceived to require a different medium, particularly the new media of TV and film. In addition, in a study deciphering the linguistic machinations of the more recent *desi* HMB, which are written in English but incorporate Hindi, Uparkar notes that localized HMB variants are problematic inasmuch as they export an Orientalized, Other-ed India for the consumption of Western readers while providing a source of cultural nostalgia for Indian readers. This inability so far to incorporate Indian stories into the HMB narrative structure satisfactorily, coupled with the failure of Rupa & Co. to capture a readership for their local romances, and in contrast with the general satisfaction with the Western settings of "traditional" HMB texts, bears further study. It may be that HMB is seen as a specifically Western cultural product, and that hybridization such as Rupa & Co.'s to assimilate local Indian romance is neither necessary nor desired by the consumer. The failure of Rupa & Co. to capture a readership and the stated preference for the cinematic medium to represent local romance by Parameswaran's interviewees indicate that for now, there is general satisfaction with the HMB texts as they are, without the incorporation of Indian stories.

To conclude this section on India, it is worth noting that despite the ready availability of HMB novels in India, Puri and Parameswaran highlight that readers often encounter accusations of consuming "corrupt" "perverted" (Puri 440–1) literature that glorifies a Western promiscuity and immorality and which threatens the cultural norms regarding respectable female behavior and sexuality. Both Puri and Parameswaran note that this common perception of romance novels has affected modes and discourses of reading the texts, as well as reader perceptions of their own selves. A particular postcolonial consideration is the fact that, in India, the Mills & Boon romances have never been translated at all, but read in English. Parameswaran and Puri note that both the English language and the thematic content of the novels are important in readers' self-identifications as cosmopolitan global consumers. In this particular context, the international nature of the HMB text, indicated through the untranslated use of English, raises the cultural capital of the texts and its readers, introducing an aspect of class to considerations of HMB as a material product.

Malaysia

Thus far, I have covered some indigenous publishing houses which sought to produce local romances in direct or indirect response to the popularity of Harlequin Mills & Boon. I want to turn some attention now to indigenous popular romance production which does not explicitly position itself within this discourse.

English-language scholarship on popular romance in the Malaysian context is scattered and draws heavily on Malay-language sources—including conference proceedings, paper presentations, and newspaper articles. I was not able to find English-language scholarship on the impact of HMB in Malaysia. The presence of HMB novels, however, is confirmed by a throwaway comment in a paper on reading habits and literacy in the higher education classroom in Malaysia: The novel-reading habits of the sample learners were "confined to Mills and Boon, Sydney Sheldon, Danielle Steel and even Enid Blyton" (2007).

Studies conducted by Ruzy Suliza and Sahizah and Mohd Zariat confirm the strong tradition of Malay-language popular romance from the 1920s to the mid-2000s, which were dominated by "nuances of sex and erotica" (Zariat 419). These studies also note the shift from these erotically flavored romances to Islamic romances in the late 2000s, citing the influence of nearby Malay-speaking, Muslim-majority Indonesia, which saw a similar shift from erotic novels to popular Islamic novels following the blockbuster popularity of Habiburrahman El-Shirazy's *Ayat ayat Cinta* ("Verses of Love") in 2004 (60). Zariat contends that the most popular Islamic Indonesian novels were "also well received in Malaysia and can be said to have catalyzed the emergence of similar novels" (418) Similarly, Malaysian readers had become weary of sexual themes and "a surfeit of erotic novels on the market" (Zariat 422). Mohd Zariat does not document the origins of Malaysian popular romance, but Ruzy Saliza and Sahizah observe that there was a sudden increased production of Malaysian romance fiction (70) to the level of "thousands on a monthly basis" (70) due to the popularity of British and American chick-lit, in particular *Bridget Jones' Diary* in 1996. Local cultural production is framed here as a response to global and in particular Western literary trends. However, Ruzy Saliza et al. note that this is an observation, and no study has been carried out to confirm the correlation between increased local production of romance and the appearance of Western chick-lit. Additionally, Ruzy Suliza and Shahiza also offer as an alternative explanation for this increased production that "Malaysian readers who are not proficient in English and not able to read chick-lit novels which are best sellers in many Malaysian bookstores turn to Malay romance as a substitute" (70).

Despite the scarcity of Anglophone scholarship on Malaysian popular romance, however, the fear of imported culture and subsequently an American/Western cultural imperialism and loss of local culture, which has already been damaged by the colonial legacy, is alluded to in several studies of popular romance in the other postcolonial contexts, (Marsden 91; Ruzy Suliza and Shahizah 70; Whitsitt 139) and can be kept in mind when considering the Malaysian context. These studies note that this fear is particularly sharp in societies experiencing high degrees of social and political transformation, as is the case in Malaysia. In particular, "Western notions of romantic behaviour" (Whitsitt 140) are viewed harshly as basically promiscuous and immoral (140; Parameswaran 847), and antithetical to local, cultural, and religious values, and as such, a sinister vehicle for moral and social decay. These views, a clear postcolonial legacy, influence the production and endorsement of local Malaysian literature.

For example, in contrast to the national endorsement of NEI's Adoras line in Cote d'Ivoire, the Malaysian Institute of Language and Literature's decision to begin publishing "popular" texts (romance in particular), was criticized as a betrayal of fundamental literary and national principles. Given its responsibilities as the body that determines the National Laureate and the South East Asian (SEA) Write Award, Mohd Affandi Hassan bitterly claims that the decision will "diminish literariness and deaden the mind of its audience, [proliferate] works that are of little value, and [privilege] the trivialities of life" (70). Ruzy Suliza and Shahizah summarize the criticisms as a fear that "popular discourse will lull readers into worldly gratification which is against Islamic principles" (70). On the other hand, Mohd Zariat points out, the "extraordinary" popularity of Islamic romance reflects the increasingly religious priorities of the youth demographic which consumes them, and who are eager to discover "their imagined and desired selves for the first time on the big cinema screen [and in romance novels] free from the standard portrayals of explicit sex scenes" (Heryanto) that were the hallmark of previous Malay popular romance.

Both studies position the Malay production of popular romance in a more diverse context beyond Western romance and HMB, drawing on multiple sources of influence. It is the national policy which amplifies anxieties about Western cultural influence, although the place of the Western romance novel in these anxieties has not been delineated with any detail in any study. Future studies of Malaysian popular romance may want to consider in more detail the possibility of East Asian influence on these texts, including the impact of Korean and Japanese serial romantic dramas, which are one of the major cultural products within the region. The relative chastity, family orientedness, and duty narratives of these dramas make them, culturally, a more palatable fit for the various audiences in the region, particularly in Southeast Asia, and thus just as likely a source of influence as Western popular romance.

Nigeria

Nigeria achieved independence from British rule in 1960. The spread of Western education, the English language and Christianity, hallmarks of the British Empire, had by then left an indelible mark of all aspects of Nigerian life, including creative production. English is the official language of Nigeria, although Hausa is the most widely spoken. Some of the most well-known postcolonial Nigerian writers, including Chinua Achebe, known as the father of Nigerian literature, the Pulitzer Prize winner Wole Soyinka, and more recently the MacArthur Fellowship recipient Chimamanda Ngozi Adichie, write in English, the only pan-Nigerian language. This choice in Nigeria, as elsewhere in the postcolonial world, has been the subject of much ideological contention. To what extent can the language of the colonizer accurately represent the identities and stories of the previously colonized? To what extent has the development of postcolonial national identity required a new language? These questions and others have dogged the development and languages of literature in postcolonial nations. While novels and other works which have achieved critical acclaim or representative status in a nation find themselves particularly fraught by these questions of chosen language, popular fiction has been relatively freer of these concerns and can choose the language most likely to appeal to the widest segment of their expected readership.

According to Wendy Griswold and Misty Bastian, Harlequin novels began appearing in Nigeria in 1979, and "while Nigerians continued to provide a market for the romances written by Western authors, they began writing their own romances in the late 1970s" (329). In Griswold and Bastian's examination of these Anglophone Nigerian-published and written romance novels, they conclude that the widespread emergence of Nigerian-produced romance modeled on Harlequins was at least partially the direct result of a hegemonic "influence of an imported, or imposed, Western formula" which coincided with "an increased demand for popular fiction" (345) created by a significant rise in literacy after the 1970s. Griswold and Bastian's examination of Nigerian-produced romance notes several key differences from the Western Harlequin model, however, including the evolution of a "sequential" narrative pattern (in which the hero is not introduced at the outset of the novel, but instead very late in the plot, after the heroine has cycled through a number of relationships), "feckless, faithless and incompetent" heroes, as compared to the "strong, successful, arrogant but fundamentally loving" heroes of the Western model (340), and the occasional tragic ending.

Griswold and Bastian also point out that romance stories had existed in the form of market pamphlet literature since at least the 1950s, appearing in various cities around Nigeria. Whitsitt notes that in the present day, this market literature constitutes a "burgeoning corpus of contemporary Hausa popular literature," and while it can be found in various cities including Onitsha, Kano, Zariya, Kaduna, Katsina and Sokoto, the "majority of the books are written and sold in Kano" and thus "the literature's English moniker is Kano market literature" (119).

Early in 2016, the Kano market literature version of the popular romance genre, known as *Littattafan Soyayya* (books of love) in Nigeria, received Western media attention, with many media outlets, including the CNN, *New York Times*, and NBC framing both the production and the consumption of these popular romances as a subversive form of Islamic feminism. Whitsitt argues that while these soyayya novels possess "aesthetic, thematic and social similarities" with Onitsha literature, which was written "predominantly in English" but which "catered to the tastes of the more or less literate, Westernized Nigerians" (138), they are more properly placed in the context of indigenous African written literature, primarily because of the language (soyayya novels are written in the Hausa language). While their production is not explicitly placed in the context of response to Western romances, Whitsitt posits that the cultural concerns and critiques generated around soyayya books, which are those of "cultural contamination" (139), are a response to the increasing influence of both Western and non-Western (primarily Indian film) culture in Hausaland in recent years.

Kano market literature has more resemblance to pulp fiction, in terms of materiality, sheer volume, and use of indigenous language, than it does to popular fiction. As Whitsitt notes, Kano market literature is written in Hausa and set in the conservative Muslim environment of Hausa society (137), and its popularity can be attributed to its ability to use the narrative structure and mode of popular romance to interrogate and articulate the tensions of "social and cultural ruptures in an era when traditional values must negotiate the onslaught of modern life" (139). While the earlier, Westernized,

Onitsha chapbooks sought to integrate and normalize Western norms, the sympathies of Kano soyayya novels lie with the Islamic sensibilities of its readers. Indeed, Whitsitt notes that many of the writers of soyayya literature consider themselves "cultural navigators aiding the confused in an era of social transformation," guided themselves by a "sense of civic and religious duty" (141). Hausa women writers are proudly feminist, and their feminism is deeply entrenched in Islamic jurisprudence and theology, refuting the concerns of soyayya critics, who accuse the novels of inculcating "Western notions of romantic behaviour" (140), here codified as immoral and promiscuous behavior, a perspective echoed by local critics of romance in previously colonized countries in Asia, the Middle East and Africa. Whitsitt notes that the primary concerns of soyayya literature revolve around improving access and advocating for female education and the abatement of *purdah* (female seclusion) restrictions, while also condemning forced marriage and discouraging polygamy, drawing on "close reading[s] of Islamic injunctions" pertaining to the rights and responsibilities of women in order to "undermine certain cultural norms that have proven inimical to female rights, such as forced marriage" (134).

Ultimately, soyayya literature is one of the few forms of local popular romance which seems to bear little to no direct linkage with Western forms of popular romance, including the Harlequin line, even as they are seen as "riddled with so-called Western notions of love" (Whitsitt 120). Instead, it emerged as a response to local socio-cultural transformation, and shifting gender relations, particularly in terms of polygamy, marriages of coercion, and the education of females (Whitsitt 139). Notably, Whitsitt posits that Indian films may have had the strongest influence on soyayya literature. So while there is some cultural anxiety over the "Westernized" values of soyayya literature, Whitsitt shows that this anxiety is unfounded (and generally stems from authorities who admit to not having read any soyayya literature) (141). Overall, soyayya literature seems to be a vehicle for negotiating the maintenance of local cultural and religious values in light of the inevitable reach of globalization and Westernization.

Conclusion

Bodil Folke Frederiksen posits that research concerned with popular culture has "moved away from intrinsic analyses of the form and content of cultural products, to the complex interplay between production and processes of reception on a global and regional scale" (209). That has in large part been the case in this chapter, as much of the scholarship has situated the study of local popular romance in the context of response and discourse of Harlequin's reach, but it is to be hoped that as the empirical groundwork continues to be laid out, scholarly concerns can now begin interrogating individual texts in more detail, particularly seminal ones. This is of course a mammoth task, particularly when considering the (lack of) accessibility to the diverse languages of indigenous romances, and the question of production and medium.

The dominant anxiety over the popularity of Harlequin romances in postcolonial nations was that of cultural imperialism. Conversely, readers themselves offered a mixed response to this anxiety. In India, readers consumed Harlequin romances for their very foreignness. Reader expectations for Indian romances remained different from their expectations for Western romances, however, while in Japan, there was a more fluid relationship between the Western romance and a Japanese context. For example, there was a clear influence on the Japanese romantic hero and the happy ending; but local production was able to sketch out a distinctive Japanese identity. In West Africa, the Adoras series found mass appeal as the "African Harlequin," drawing clearly on Mills & Boon as a literary antecedent, whereas soyayya literature in Nigeria and popular Malay romance in Malaysia did not have palpable ties to Harlequin. Nevertheless, all forms of local romance are enmeshed in the discourse of the influence of Western romance and morality on local cultural and religious sensitivities.

In tracing the movement of Harlequin into these four case-study contexts, this chapter has shown that local forms of romance, embedded as they are in specific and particular historical, material, and cultural frameworks and literary ecosystems, have resisted the homogenizing tendencies of HMB as a cultural imperative. These are not the only parts of the world where such resistance can be documented, and scholarship is needed on other local forms and traditions of popular romance, with the understanding that each will demand appropriately contextualized theoretical frameworks and approaches: frameworks and approaches that may be quite different than those that have been used on their global counterparts.

Notes

1 See Chapter 1 and Chapter 16 in this volume for more on the history of Mills & Boon and Harlequin.

2 I have chosen these four countries because of the richness and range of scholarship available, but they are not the only places where local popular romance traditions (including chick-lit) have drawn scholarly attention. More limited or preliminary work has been done on popular romance fiction in France (Holmes; see also Capelle), Sweden (Ehriander), Italy (Balducci), Portugal and Spain (Bazenga, Pérez-Gil, González-Cruz, Vera-Carzola), The Caribbean (Soto-Crespo), Guam (Rodríguez), Hong Kong (Lee), China (Feng), Uganda (Spencer), and South Africa (Spencer; Vitackova; Frenkel; Gupta and Frenkel). In 2019 the Romance Writers of America awarded research funding to two Australian scholars, Jodi McAllister, and Claire Parnell, to document and analyze the "genre world" of #RomanceClass, a transnational community of Filipino authors, publishers, and readers of English-language Filipino romance founded by author Mina Esguerra.

Works cited

Abdul Rani, Mohd. Zariat. "Islam, Romance and Popular Taste in Indonesia: A Textual Analysis of Ayat Ayat Cinta by Habiburrahman El-Shirazy and Syahadat Cinta by Taufiqurrahman Al-Azizy." *Indonesia and the Malay World*, vol. 40, no. 116, 2012, pp. 59–73.

———. "The Conflict of Love and Islam: The Main Ingredients in the Popular Islamic Novels of Malaysia." *Southeast Asia Research*, vol. 22, no. 3, 2014, pp. 417–433.

"About Harlequin." *Harlequin*, Harlequin Enterprises Limited, www.harlequin.com/shop/pages/about-harlequin.html. Accessed Sept. 17, 2019.

Balducci, Federica. "When Chick Lit Meets Romanzo Rosa: Intertextual Narratives in Stefania Bertola's Romantic Fiction." *Journal of Popular Romance Studies*, vol. 2, no. 1, 2011.

Bazenga, Aline. "Language Awareness in Four Romances Set on the Island of Madeira." *Love, Language, Place, and Identity in Popular Culture: Romancing the Other*, edited by María Ramos-García, and Laura Vivanco, Lexington, 2020, pp. 69–82.

Bianchi, Diana and Adele D'Arcangelo. "Translating History or Romance? Historical Romantic Fiction and Its Translation in a Globalised Market." *Linguistics and Literature Studies*, vol. 3, no. 5, 2015, pp. 248–253.

Capelle, Annick. "Harlequin Romances in Western Europe: The Cultural Interactions of Romantic Literature." *European Readings of American Popular Culture*, edited by John Dean, and Jean-Paul Gabilliet, Greenwood Press, 1996, pp. 91–100.

Darbyshire, Peter. "Romancing the World: Harlequin Romances, the Capitalist Dream, and the Conquest of Europe and Asia." *Studies in Popular Culture*, vol. 23, no. 1, Oct. 2000, pp. 1–10.

———. "The Politics of Love: Harlequin Romances and the Christian Right." *The Journal of Popular Culture*, vol. 35, no. 4, Spring 2002, pp. 75–87.

Ehriander, Helene. "Chick Lit in Historical Settings by Frida Skybäck." *Journal of Popular Romance Studies*, vol. 5, no. 1, 2015.

El-Shirazy, Habiburrahman. *Ayat ayat Cinta ("Verses of Love")*. Republika-Basmala, 2004.

Feng, Jin. *Romancing the Internet: Producing and Consuming Chinese Web Romance*. Brill, 2013.

Frederiksen, Bodil Folke. "Popular Culture, Gender Relations and the Democratization of Everyday Life in Kenya." *Journal of Southern African Studies*, vol. 26, no. 2, June 2002, pp. 209–222.

Frenkel, Ronit. "Pleasure as Genre: Popular Fiction, South African Chick-lit and Nthikeng Mohlele's *Pleasure*." *Feminist Theory*, vol. 20, no. 2, 2019, pp. 171–184.

González-Cruz, María. "Isabel. "Othering and Language: Bilingual Romances in the Canary Islands."." *Love, Language, Place, and Identity in Popular Culture: Romancing the Other*, edited by María Ramos-García, and Laura Vivanco, Lexington, 2020, pp. 53–68.

Goris, An. "Romance the World Over." *Global Cultures*, edited by Frank A. Salamone, Cambridge Scholars, 2009, pp. 59–72.

Greenfield, Jeremy. "Three Reasons News Corp Bought Harlequin, World's Biggest Romance Book Publisher." Forbes, May 2, 2014. www.forbes.com/sites/jeremygreenfield/2014/05/02/news-corp-buys-harlequin-worlds-biggest-romance-book-publisher-three-reasons/#42ecd0ea2bd0.

Grescoe, Paul. *The Merchants of Venus: Inside Harlequin and the Empire of Romance*. Raincoast Books, 1996.

Gupta, Pamila and Ronit Frenkel. "Chick-lit in a Time of African Cosmopolitanism." *Feminist Theory*, vol. 20, no. 2, 2019, pp. 123–132.

Hashim, Ruzy Saliza and Shahizah Ismail Hamdan. "Facets of Women in Malay Romance Fiction." *Kunapipi*, vol. 32, no. 1, 2010, pp. 67–79.

Hatfield, E., & Rapson, R. L. "Passionate love and sexual desire: Cross-cultural and historical perspectives". *Stability and change in relationships*, edited by A. Vangelisti, H. T. Reis, & M.A. Fitzpatrick, Cambridge, England: Cambridge University Press, 2002, 306–324.

Heryanto, Ariel. "Upgraded Piety and Pleasure: The New Middle Class and Islam in Indonesian Popular Culture." *Islam and popular culture in Indonesia and Malaysia*, edited by Andrew N. Weintraub, Routledge, 2011, pp. 76–98.

Holmes, Diana. *Romance and Readership in Twentieth-Century France: Love Stories*. Oxford University Press, 2006.

Lee, Amy. "Forming a Local Identity: Romance Novels in Hong Kong." *Empowerment Versus Oppression: Twenty First Century Views of Popular Romance Novels*, edited by Sally Goade, Cambridge Scholars Publishing, 2007, pp. 174–197.

Marsden, Magnus. "Love and Elopement in Northern Pakistan." *The Journal of the Royal Anthropological Institute*, vol. 13, no. 1, Mar 2007, pp. 91–108.

McWilliam, Kelly. "Romance in Foreign Accents: Harlequin-Mills & Boon in Australia." *Continuum*, vol. 23, no. 2, 2009, pp. 137–145.

Moudileno, Lydie. "The Troubling Popularity of West African Romance Novels." *Research in African Literatures*, vol. 39, no. 4, 2008, pp. 120–132.

Mulhern, Chieko Irie. "Japanese Harlequin Romances as Transcultural Women's Fiction." *The Journal of Asian Studies*, vol. 48, no. 1, Feb 1989, pp. 50–70.

Nambiar, M. K. Radha. "Enhancing Academic Literacy among Tertiary Learners: A Malaysian Experience." *3L Journal of Language Teaching, Linguistics and Literature*, vol. 13, 2007, pp. 77–94.

Parameswaran, Radhika. "Western Romance Fiction as English Language Media in Postcolonial India." *Journal of Communication*, vol. 49, no. 3, Sept 1999, pp. 84–105.

——— "Reading Fictions of Romance: Gender, Sexuality, and Nationalism in Postcolonial India." *Journal of Communication*, vol. 52, no. 4, Dec. 2002, pp. 832–851.

Pérez-Gil, María del Mar. "Britannia's Daughters: Popular Romance Fiction and the Ideology of National Superiority (1950s-1970s)." *Love, Language, Place, and Identity in Popular Culture: Romancing the Other*, edited by María Ramos-García, and Laura Vivanco, Lexington, 2020, pp. 13–24.

Puri, Jyoti. "Reading Romance Novels in Postcolonial India." *Gender and Society*, vol. 11, no. 4, Aug. 1997, pp. 434–452.

Rodríguez, Carolina Fernández. "Chamorro WWII Romances: Combating Erasure with Tales of Survival and Vitality." *Journal of Popular Romance Studies*, vol. 8, 2019, n.p.

Schell, Heather "The Silk Road of Adaptation: Transformations across Disciplines and Cultures." *Bringing the Mid-West to the Middle East: An Analysis of a Harlequin Romance in English and Turkish*, edited by Laurence Raw, Newcastle-Upon-Tyne: Cambridge Scholars Publishing, 2013, pp. 160–171.

Shibamoto Smith, Janet S. "Translating True Love: Japanese Romance Fiction, Harlequin-Style." *Gender, Sex and Translation: The Manipulation of Identities*, edited by Jose Santaemilia, St. Jerome Publishing, 2005, pp. 97–116.

Smith, Bardwell L. *Narratives of Sorrow and Dignity: Japanese Women, Pregnancy Loss and Modern Rituals of Grieving*. Oxford University Press, 2013.

Soto-Crespo, Ramón E. "Archipelagoes of Romance: Decapitalized Otherness in Caribbean Trash Fiction." *Love, Language, Place, and Identity in Popular Culture: Romancing the Other*, edited by María Ramos-García, and Laura Vivanco, Lexington, 2020, pp. 83–94.

Spencer, Lynda Gichanda. "In Defence of Chick-lit': Refashioning Feminine Subjectivities in Ugandan and South African Contemporary Women's Writing." *Feminist Theory*, vol. 20, no. 2, 2019.

Tapper, Olivia. "Romance and Innovation in Twenty-First Century Publishing." *Publishing Research Quarterly*, vol. 30, no. 2, 2014, pp. 249–259.

Uparkar, Shilpa. "Desi Love Stories: Harlequin Mills & Boon's Indian Enterprise." *Australasian Journal of Popular Culture*, vol. 3, no. 3, 2014, pp. 321–333.

Vera-Cazorla, María Jesús. "'And They Drive on the Wrong Side of the Road': The Anglocentric Vision of the Canary Islands in Mills & Boon Romance Novels (1955–1987)." *Love, Language, Place, and Identity in Popular Culture: Romancing the Other*, edited by María Ramos-García, and Laura Vivanco, Lexington, 2020, pp. 25–40.

Vincent, Kerry. "Anglophone Fiction in Swaziland: A Preliminary Study." *Research in African Literatures*, vol. 43, no. 2, Summer 2012, pp. 173–185.

Vitackova, Martina. "Representation of Racial and Sexual 'Others' in Afrikaans Popular Romantic Fiction by Sophia Kapp." *Tydskrif Vir Letterkunde*, vol. 55, no. 1, 2018, pp. 122–133.

Whitsitt, Novian. "Islamic-Hausa Feminism and Kano Market Literature: Qur'anic Reinterpretation in the Novels of Balaraba Yakubu." *Research in African Literatures*, vol. 3, no. 2, 2002, pp. 119–136.

———. "Islamic-Hausa Feminism Meets Northern Nigerian Romance: The Cautious Rebellion of Bilkisu Funtuwa." *African Studies Review*, vol. 46, no. 1, 2003, pp. 137–153.

Index

For Product Safety Concerns and Information please contact our EU representative GPSR@taylorandfrancis.com
Taylor & Francis Verlag GmbH, Kaufingerstraße 24, 80331 München, Germany

www.ingramcontent.com/pod-product-compliance
Lightning Source LLC
Chambersburg PA
CBHW081921130726
47908CB00018B/2658
9780367543204